TUMP

TUMP

J. Baptiste

Book design by Sarah E. Holroyd (http://sleepingcatbooks.com)

First published 2012
This edition published 2016

ISBN-13: 978-0-9945574-0-7
ISBN-10: 0-9945574-0-X

For my children,
with love

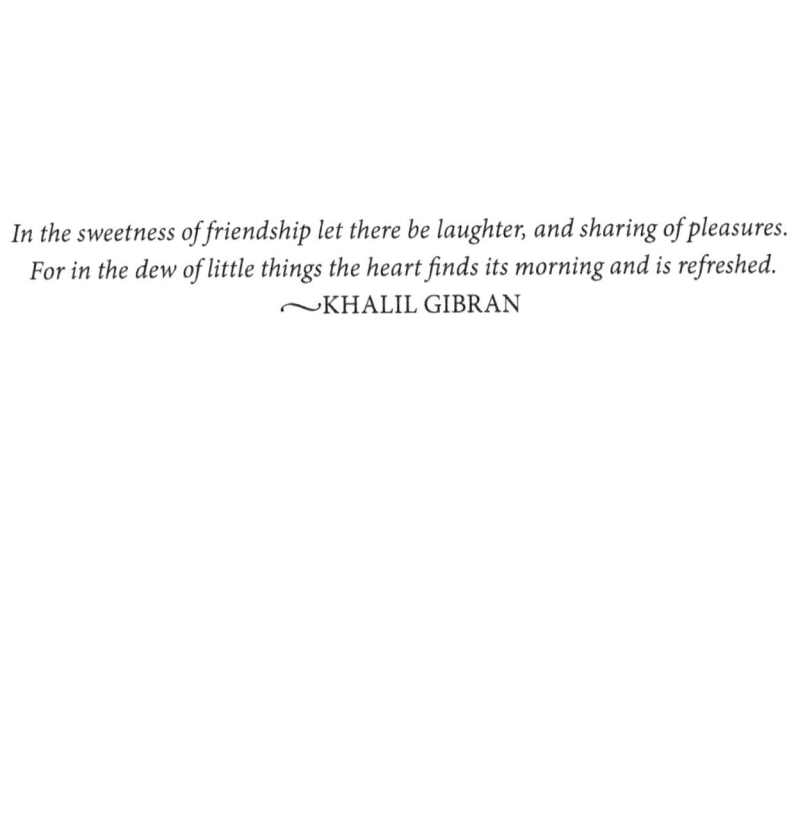

In the sweetness of friendship let there be laughter, and sharing of pleasures.
For in the dew of little things the heart finds its morning and is refreshed.
~KHALIL GIBRAN

CONTENTS

Prologue xv

Part One
Slipping Away 1

White Winter's Song 3

Good Neighbours 8

True Love Ways 14

Slipping Away 21

Mmeerah! 32

Awful Unravelling 39

Queen of Greens 55

Roof Of The World 69

Weed's Yard 79

Fox! 85

Missy-Belle 95

Seeing Double 102

Pebble Practice 111

Return To Brickfield 118

Folly—Enough! 129

Sisters of The Shell 140

Storm 153

Part Two
The Travellers' Tale 161

Falling star 163

Ground Spring Warren 170

The Bard 182

Coldest Glass 194

Home 203

Door of Little Appreciation 212

Clever Fixer Stops By 223

Fixer 232

Keepers of the Seed 242

Visitation 251

Wood Pail 261

Planting Out 272

Dark Leaves 283

Busy Paws. 290

Leaping the Ditch 298

Forest Queen. 306

Reluctant Bard 313

Far-Seeing-Eye 319

Part Three
Blue House South Facing 333

Zechariah The Great 335

Tump is Warning Given 347

Precious Scratchings 355

Peace by Moonlight. 367

New Friends 381

Simple Rudy 390

Creek Side. 399

Hargolin. 406

Heat 414

Farewell 426

Penance 432

Deeky Boy. 442

Bernard. 450

Great Grandfather Provides. 463

Forest 474

Fine Strapping Lads! 485

Borderland 496

Francis 507

Lilith Awake!. 514

Gazuzzlement Means Gone 528

Revelation. 537

Pick-up. 549

Most Beautiful Warren 557

Arise! 570

For Lilith. 583

Acknowledgements. 593

About the author. 595

ILLUSTRATIONS

Radiola 2

Grammy 54

Beach 162

Epic 181

Hill 193

Fixer 241

Cloud 282

Move! 354

Scratching 366

Tree 398

Bernard 462

Mutant 484

Beast 548

Seed 582

PROLOGUE

Gather 'round children and I will tell you a tale of strange realms, of far-flung impossible worlds, of miraculous beginning, of the best of times and times ill, of Folk of Fur, of Tall Ones and mystery without end.

There was a day in the Most High Place, where time is not as we know it, when Great Grandfather went down to the stream to write. He would settle upon the soft grass, take out a blank scroll and pen a few words to record His ideas. The skies were clear, the sun warm, and the sound of the creek, a merry babbling. It was all so pleasant that soon, before writing even one word, Great Grandfather dozed off...

He dreamed a dream of Himself, and in the dream he stood in a beautiful garden. It was a wondrous place, full of light and life, where good nourishing produce of every type and variety flourished. There were fruit trees and vines of berry and grape. And, as well, there were strange, exotic varieties of growing things. There were trees of "description", and, trees of "knowledge" and "life".

Great Grandfather's attention lit upon a row of cabbages, and in pausing to study them, He noted that all was not perfect as should be.

Addressing the plants, He declared, 'You fellows are not doing as well as the rest, are you? You'd best grow, or I'll be seeing to you with my hoe, and you know what that means.' Taking a packet of new seeds from His waistcoat pocket, He opened it, He said, 'I will plant these in your place.'

Then, Great Grandfather sneezed. It was a truly almighty, kazooning sneeze, which gusting forth, blew a large number of seeds away from His paw. Seeds flew all about to settle then, scattered about His feet.

Great Grandfather carefully swept them together and scooped them up. He returned them to the packet for later planting, but still all was not as should be. The packet seemed ever so slightly lighter. A seed was missing. One seed scattered along with the others by His breath was lost and, must be found.

Hunkering down and then searching about, Great Grandfather noticed a small dark hole, an opening in the garden bed, and, peering into it, He called, 'Hello down there! I have a favour to ask!' It was not long then, before a head emerged, and a disgruntled creature demanded, 'What is it? I was trying to sleep for goodness' sake! What do you want?'

Pointing, Great Grandfather said, 'A seed is lost. It's gone down into your place, and I want you to fetch it for me.'

Assuming an amiable tone the creature told Great Grandfather, 'Oh, sure, my liege! Just as soon as I'm rested—if I find it—you'll have it back. How's that sound, Old Sport?'

Receiving such easy response, Great Grandfather was not deceived.

The sly one slipped from the light, going deep down into a system of voids and, before long, the seed was discovered resting in a lonely place at farthest end of long dark narrowness.

Desiring to keep the treasure, but imagining the true owner's displeasure and the inevitable, ensuing confrontation, feelings of trepidation were accepted as reason enough for taking deceitful action.

Seed in mouth (for, the creature has no paw) it went lower—as far down as it could, to darkest, bottom-most place. Down there was a narrow crack or fissure, in the fabric of void, and what next it did with the seed was most spiteful.

The creature shoved it—shoved as hard as it could—so the unfortunate thing squeezed through the crack and then went falling into an altogether other realm! The seed had been through a lot and fortune should have smiled upon it, but after falling for a long, long way, it lobbed in a most unlovely place, a wet place of sour rank odour, of unpleasant sound … its luck nowise improved.'

Part One
Slipping Away

Radiola

WHITE WINTER'S SONG

Sweet blessed night—night of bright starlight with a full moon looking down. Most everyone was topside, whilst in the meeting place below, Sherbrook, his poor heart racing fit to bust, romanced Mavis Whitepaws. From the old Radiola came the sound of *White Winter's Song*, and apart from that smooth melody and those seductive lyrics, he wondered what more any beau needed in wooing his heart's desire. But then, of a sudden, a great caterwauling wrenched them from reverie. All of *White Winter's* was drowned out!

'Emergency! Emergency! Ground-quake! Ground-quake!' Charlie Noy-Breen shouted at the top of his lungs. He came heltering down from the warren's main entranceway and in an instant of incredulity Sherbrook was mighty suspicious. Did ne'er-do-well, Charlie Noy-Breen have designs on Mavis Whitepaws? Was this dramatic interruption a cunning ploy, Charlie's tricky way of messing with his wooing the youngest and prettiest of the Whitepaws gals?

Then, a roaring wave of rumbling and shaking of everything all about, and great clods of dirt began pouring down from above! Seeing Mavis Whitepaws cowering at a far end of the meeting place, Sherbrook knew love's true course was swept aside.

Close on Charlie's heels were others, heltering into the burrow and tumbling, wild fur flying against both Charlie and him! Pandemonium reigned! And, in the midst of such shemozzle, Sherbrook realized that the old Radiola was done for!

Then, Uncle Bucky arrived, nursing a paw, holding it close like it hurt something bad.

One in the milling throng was unruffled. Simple Rudy was as calm as calm could be. Wearing an odd, distracted expression, Simple seemed not at all affected by the ground-quaking end to everything, and in Sherbrook, realization dawned. Rudy, though simple was blessed. Immediate circumstance however, allowed no time in which to ponder such revelation—the end of the world was imminent! An enormous clod of dark topsoil lobbed, thudding, a mere whisker away! Taking charge, he shouted over the hubbub, commanding, 'Let's move it! Go deep everyone! Go deep!' Into the mêlée he cried, 'Get a wriggle on, Mavis, my dear! Get your hindquarters down to Level C!' There was no real way of knowing if she heard, but the crush of pressing bodies moving to Warren Central's lower reach gave hope.

At the confining chamber of lowest Level C, bodies pressed to crushing discord and Sherbrook exclaimed, 'The Tall One never churns at night so what *is* it?' And having addressed no one in particular, he was not surprised when none deigned answer. He tried again, 'All of you were out there—Mavis Whitepaws and I were inside, so didn't see anything— just the roof of the meeting place falling in on us! What *is* it?' There was a long silence and after several moments had passed, Sherbrook cleared his throat in preparation for a third attempt.

A helpful soul pre-empted, 'Oh, don't go on and on. Just shut up, Sherbrook.'

Sherbrook did not immediately respond. But, those dismissive words were bothersome and they stayed with him. No longer able to let the matter rest, he enquired, 'Shut up ... was it?'

'No.'

'Was.'

'No. You're mistaken.'

'I'm not.'

Someone interjected, 'She did not tell you to shut up. No. It was, "*Hush* up."' Whomever had spoken, found the exchange equally exasperating, but for a reason different than his. They were close allies. Must be. There was nothing wrong with his auditory sense, but now was not the time for further comment.

'Has anyone seen Uncle Bucky?' a small, querulous voice enquired. It was a youngster and, Sherbrook was not certain, but believed it was Skip the Seer.

The troubled voice, conveying great concern, came again and still went unanswered, "Where is Uncle Bucky?' Then, quiet weeping was heard.

Fear locked down the inclination to communicate, but hearing the youngster's selfless enquiring as to an oldster's whereabouts, Sherbrook was inspired to ask. 'Have any of you seen Mavis Whitepaws?' So fearful were they that none were inclined to provide the slightest comfort, and Sherbrook knew better than press his luck.

Most often unoccupied and dry, the stale atmosphere in Level C was now damp and infused with the odour of anxious fear. It was crowded, and fertile ground for unpleasant behaviour. Most refrained from making verbal protest but surreptitious delivering of digs and pokes was soon common practice. Of these, Sherbrook received his share, and knew the culprit must be Grammy Graymark.

Penchant for radish and in particular, those of the white variety, was her undoing. A strong telltale odour emanated from off to one side, and knowing that of those present, she most favoured that particular vegetable, her identity was not concealed. Sherbrook, granting age due deference, had determined at the outset to refrain from retaliating, but if he was recipient of further sly jab, he was not sure that he could restrain himself. Whilst gentle, Folk of Fur were not always patient and forbearing, not as they liked to believe. They were sociable by nature but the close proximity of so many kin, tested both courage and fortitude. A shared sense of dread remained monumental despite a long time passing, yet, still from above, came dull rumbling.

Sherbrook caught himself deciding between fates. He might prefer being devoured by the monster traversing back and forth overhead, to being buried alive in a familiar environment. Knowing was problematic, but if granted real choice, the latter was the sadder, because Warren Central was home, and home meant safety. He must still his imagination and think on it no more. There was much dark irony in knowing that if not for Uncle Bucky, then Warren Central would never have included Level C. If not for him, they'd already have suffered an horrific fate. When scrambling last in line and making for deeper territory, Sherbrook had seen an enormous quantity of soil cave in on Bucky; and so, with lame paw and goodness knows what else ailing him, Uncle Bucky had no chance at all. For now, Sherbrook would not speak of it.

'We'll have to draw straws...'

'What?' After so much quiet, hearing a voice was shocking.

'That's what we should do. Draw straws and send out a scouting party.'

'A *party*, you say?'

'That's right.'

An ignoramus responded, 'Considering the prospects, that's an insensitive choice of words.'

Another dullard asked, 'Where will we get straws?'

Sherbrook could take no more. He exclaimed, 'All right! I'll go!' And demonstrating minimum decorum, he shoved Grammy Graymark aside. He would go as a party of one, or so he thought. Then, Simple Rudy spoke up, and that voice was unmistakable, 'Can I come too, *please?*'

'Sure you can, Simple,' he said, 'You can follow me to gazuzzlement; if that's what you want.' And giving the others fair warning, 'We'll have no complaining, when Rudy and I are excavating. I hope that's understood? When we shower dirt over you, cover your faces with your paws.'

'Hop over here, Rudy,' he instructed. 'Watch out for Grammy Graymark as you go by, she's a delicate old bag of bones and she won't enjoy being poked, will you, Grammy?'

'Cheeky young whippersnapper!' Grammy spat.

'He's brave, though, my Sherbrook!' declared a voice coming to his defence. That voice came from a distant part of the burrow and, of course, belonged to none other than his own sweet Mavis. He'd heard nothing from her until now, and heart melting, he returned the call, 'Fret not, Mavis Whitepaws! We're going to get you out of here!' He could just not describe the affection he felt for that gal!

Bucky shook himself off. His mind was racing. He thought, Kin—what were they worth? They'd gone heltering to the safety of Level C, down into the far most reaches of Warren Central—just *leaving* him here! For one insane instant, he imagined clawing his way back to the surface world to beg for mercy. But then, the old Radiola lay half buried near the centre of the ruined chamber. He would hide beneath its sturdy bulk!

He was injured, but dug at frantic pace, and then scrambled deep down. The old Radiola's valves were broken and shattered—they would glow no more—poor sacred things! He had discovered the old Radiola long ago, lying abandoned in the field outside the warren, and after Clever Fixer got it going for him, it became his most treasured possession. Clever was a miracle working, total genius and had wired the Radiola *unwired*, he said, after the way of Tall One Terrence Thiery. He just plugged her into the ground and away she went.

But this was no time for pondering the past! The churner's powerful roaring had faded—now its loudness resumed, and the monster was headed his way—great eyes ablaze, piercing darkness as it churned all in its path!

'Obscenity!' Bucky protested, shivering. But then, over the sound of his mind's fervent rambling, and, untamed roaring from above, came the sound of a familiar voice. Yelling fit to bust, 'Uncle Bucky! Move it! Get yourself down here!' And someone was shoving at his hindquarters!

GOOD NEIGHBOURS

'Give him a kick, Rudy!' It was a most dire moment and Rudy was demonstrating respect for Uncle Bucky! Sherbrook shouted again, 'Get him *moving* before we're gazuzzled!'

There was no time for niceties. Scrambling from the mouth of the new escape route, Sherbrook noted, one of Bucky's ears protruded from beneath the Radiola. Bucky had not made much of a job of hiding himself.

Gesturing Rudy away, Sherbrook did not hesitate, but sank his teeth into the gnarled tip of that vulnerable ear. Bucky let out a most horrible, outraged shriek and he moved! He almost bowled Sherbrook over, in heltering for the safety of Level C! Making his own dash for safety, Sherbrook glanced back and saw the old Radiola sliced right down its middle! Just sliced in two, by the kazooning thing! The ear-splitting noise of it was excruciating!

Once down in level C, Uncle Bucky declared. 'It churns at *night*. It's huge! I've never seen its like!' He paused, then, 'Avarice is involved, of that I'm certain, and that's nothing more than a fancy name for greed! So, despite our showing admirable restraint in gathering penance from the planting place, it's my guess, the Tall One's doe has stooped to exaggeration and informed on us.

'She's not dissuaded the husband from calling in his vile new instrument of destruction. They've gone out of their way in misconstruing the taking of victuals and wrought vengeance.' He said, 'Those victuals are of a quality appealing to those enjoying epicurean taste, and whilst many of you have a penchant for them, they do not go any way toward representing our staple diet, but you'd think we'd stripped the planting place bare!

'I must ask—it's rhetorical of course—why we troubled in the first place, to make good neighbours of ourselves. You'd think, wouldn't you, we'd tunnelled in mindless, selfish fashion, undermining *their* dwelling!'

All Bucky said was true, and there were quiet murmurs of agreement, but whilst Bucky spoke, the half-listening Sherbrook strategized. A matter required attention.

Then none spoke, and seeing opportunity, Sherbrook said, 'I must compliment you Rudy, on the marvellous job you did in getting Uncle Bucky moving. There were moments up there when I was sure the three of us were goners. Complete goners! If you'd not given him encouragement, we'd have been...'

'Thank you, sir.' It was one of Rudy's eccentric habits to address all and sundry as sir. He was a very polite and respectful individual. Sherbrook did not at all mind being called sir, but it cracked him up when Rudy addressed those of female persuasion that way.

Sherbrook waited for word from Uncle Bucky. Bucky though, was silent. Until now, Bucky had been an alert and astute individual, and would not have missed the suggestion that Rudy was responsible for savaging his ear when they were topside.

Sherbrook was figuring what next to say, when, Rudy spoke up, sounding apologetic and consoling, 'I'm very sorry for biting you, Uncle Bucky. I didn't mean to hurt you, sir. I wanted to save you from the churner!'

Simple Rudy had taken the blame! Sherbrook was flabbergasted! He was reminded that way back apiece, he'd decided Simple Rudy was blessed, but as to precise form such blessing took, he was not certain. But he saw now, Rudy possessed a kind of easy-going, natural cunning. This was a form of warped genius, and, what Rudy next said double flabbergasted Sherbrook. Displaying extraordinary audacity, he said, 'I will make it up to you, sir. I swear it! I will be your sidekick forever. I will find out where Clever Fixer is, and have him fix the old Radiola for you!'

'Oh, tosh and nonsense, Simple, dear boy!' Uncle Bucky exclaimed, 'You saved my life back there! And I declare right here and now, I will never forget your bravery and kindness. You just went ahead and did as I would, were the situation reversed.'

Sherbrook could take no more. But then, by the grace of Great Grandfather, another voice was heard. It was the orphan, Skip the Seer, protesting, '*I'm* Uncle Bucky's side kick, Simple Rudy—not *you!*'

'Oh bless his little heart!' one of the does exclaimed. She meant well, but young Skip interpreted her expressing sentiment as patronizing, 'Go soak yourself! I'm not a *baby* and I don't have a little heart!' Hearing such disrespect from one so young, Grammy Graymark rushed to defend a friend. 'There will be none but the most weedy of carrots for you, come supper-time, young Skip!'

Thinking better than join the fray, Sherbrook wondered, regardless of quality, where did she expect carrots to come from? Dawn was not far off, yet they were still trapped—what, for deeks' sake, was she thinking! Did she have any notion of the potential for upset in her mentioning victuals at such time?

'We were all of us young once,' declared Uncle Bucky, employing a soothing tone intended to reconcile differences, but having the opposite effect, because she who was treated to rudeness, had murmured apprecia-tive thanks to Grammy, who in turn, stated for all to hear, 'You're wel-come dear. Young ones should know their place.' This was in complete disregard of Uncle Bucky's recent exampling of need for forbearance in the face of dire circumstance. At any moment Sherbrook expected to hear complaints from youngsters who'd missed out on their supper; but heard instead, Piedmont the Bard:

'Oh the pity...
Warren bruk by mystery madness
Wish power above might disentangle
All from odd and thorny wrangle
All from dread and fearsome plight.'

The offering was a little negative, but the bard was well intentioned. By throwing his talent into the mix, Piedmont hoped to provide distrac-tion. As to the possibility of success in the endeavour, Sherbrook trusted that the grim little piece did not make for affect opposite to that desired.

Silence. Silence always followed a recital by Piedmont and although Sherbrook never mentioned it, never queried the point by asking Piedmont himself, he had on occasion wondered if those silences denoted a sort of post-versifying, mesmerized attentiveness, or whether most in attendance were uncertain as to Piedmont's being quite finished with his task.

Despite it not being, in his opinion, verse of Piedmont's usual fine calibre, several moments of quiet persisted, before Uncle Bucky queried,

'Bruk? I did catch that, didn't I, Piedmont? "Warren, bruk"—there in your second line?' And before the bard could respond, 'Is it correct use of language, old boy? Is it even an actual *word*? Or, will you be claiming poetic license again?'

'Language evolves.' Piedmont returned.

'As all things must,' someone else chipped in.

'Unless of course, they go the other way.'

'Oh, and which way is that?'

'Well ... not sideways.'

Everything, Sherbrook realized, had become far and away too déjà-vu-ish. He was, himself, feeling "bruk". Not addressing anyone in particular he enquired, 'What say, we get ourselves out of here?'

Then, 'It was sheer, unadulterated sloth!' Bucky complained. 'Sloth is to blame for there being no escape route provided down here. I recall arguing the common-sense point of going the extra distance in including a normal escape route. However, in face of self-indulgent opposition, I caved in. I caved in to sloth...'

He sounded as tired and sleepy as Sherbrook felt. There was a monotonous, droning, hypnotic quality to Bucky's voice, which didn't help matters at all. 'I recall,' Bucky reiterated, 'the day when all good common-sense was undermined by sloth.' That word, repeated the way Bucky managed it, was beginning to take on a life all its own. Sloth was everything which should be taken as wrong. In a dark, upside down way, it was being made to stand tall—awesome in magnitude—as compared to any other type of wrongdoing. And then another exhausted voice offered a fellow oldster support. 'Young bucks these days are not a patch on those of generations past.'

Feeling like mush, but summoning the necessary energy, Sherbrook commanded, 'All right! Let's get digging before we smother down here! Those of generation past caring, can sleep forever if they like, but the rest of you—let's get to it!' In the following instant, a small voice enquired, 'And *then* will there be carrots?'

'Yay! Carrots!' called another, even younger sounding than the first.

'There will be carrots, but not for awhile yet.'

'Sherbrook's a kadoodler isn't he?'

'Yes, he is!'

'We've always known it.'
And this time no one came to his defence.

***

Summoning words with which to describe the depth of emotion experienced, when, at last they were safe enough, was impossible. Feeling held for those loyal, hard working companions accompanying him in emerging from all remaining of their beloved Warren Central, would remain unexpressed; save to say, they were at one and the same time, relieved to be in the outdoors again, and yet, demoralized by the sight of furrowed land which lay in place of anything recognizable as home territory. Where once had spread the wide, grand beauty of familiar grassland, now were cruel, deep clotted scars awaiting the sun which would dry the exposed, churned surface and turn it to dust.

They stood for a while, and were as quiet as stones. Expression of grief, after all, was useless. Sherbrook decided that attempting to lighten the mood by employing even gentlest levity would be inappropriate.

It was Charlie Noy-Breen who first spoke.

'If I had the means, I'd see them gazuzzled!' was all he said. He did not sound convincing, in fact he sounded quite pathetic, but the rest were in agreement with the sentiment expressed. Slight murmurs were uttered in acknowledgement of the fact he'd spoken. Encouraged, Charlie added, 'We will overcome the churning!'

Sherbrook turned to see young Skip. He was assisting his old mentor, Bucky, by leading him by the uninjured of his forepaws. Out there, under the first insipid glimmer of dawn light, Uncle Bucky looked older and more wearied than fairer times would allow. Skip the Seer seemed undaunted by the sight of so much devastation. His, having inner view of the world, provided him uncanny ease. 'Fear not, friends,' he announced, 'We shall rise again, and our new home is a wondrous sight to behold. We're ever rid of the menace! Happiness returns!' Coming from one so young, his words were heartening. Charlie Noy-Breen responded, 'You see—it's the way of it! We *will* destroy the churner!'

'But we must wait,' Skip said, mindful that he'd not said that the churner would be destroyed, but allowing Charlie his version, 'because, first there is the problem of homelessness and then far off, away into the future, everything is altered and changed forever more.'

The future was a funny thing, unless you were "touched" like Skip the Seer. The future was as elusive as all get out, no matter what your plans, no matter how predictable outcomes seemed. A body never got the jump on the future. The past, on the other paw, was with them always. The past never truly passed away and might be the best or very worst of companions.

True Love Ways

'What do you mean?' Bucky asked, 'Changed forever more? How?'

'I don't understand the "how" of it,' Skip said, 'I know I don't "see" all of it. Many details are missing from my vision. For instance, folk are not always together as we would like, and I don't know why that is. When I see it, it saddens me, but up ahead there is much to-ing and fro-ing. I do know that we become a true force—a force for good. Everything of those far off times is wondrous!'

'Sounds like a bunch of kadoodle to me—a whole bunch of little boy's imaginative kadoodle!' declared Grammy Graymark, exiting the narrow confine of the burrow. Coming into the first weak rays given off by the day's wintry sun, she made for an uninspiring sight; she looked as mean as she sounded. Her impressive grey mark, which, Sherbrook had always considered an unattractive feature, stood out like a bruised paw, but to hear her tell of it, that grey mark was a veritable beacon in darkness, as alluring a thing as ever a thing was; that was, she claimed, as her late husband, Ronald Shortflag saw it.

Recalling Grammy's oft' vaunted account of Ronald's and her relationship, Sherbrook knew that according to Grammy, whose given name was Lillian, the relationship was a classic case of love at first sight, but Sherbrook had always entertained serious doubt as to the veracity of Grammy's claim. He could not recall Ronald ever seeming as happy with her as Grammy would have others believe. His opinion held that she imagined a tale of kadoodle proportion in order to ensure her standing with other does. She had many gullible friends. As matters were, she succeeded in securing the attention she so craved.

She was not at all fond of young Skip, ever since her cameo, a gift from Ronald, went missing, which occurred some considerable time ago. Ronald had found the cameo near the Tall One's planting place, and thinking it perfect as a token of love and esteem, had brought it home to her.

Hearing her latest attack, the ever patient Bucky, paw resting upon young Skip's shoulder, told her, 'Fine, Grammy, but it will do for now. The boy is gifted, and although you're entitled to an opinion, your timing in voicing scepticism leaves a lot to be desired.'

Sherbrook noted with pleasure, his admiration for Uncle Bucky was undiminished. Bucky made it seem a kindness he deigned respond at all to such vitriol. Grammy was subdued. She would not add further upset to the delicate and demoralizing situation.

Then, Sherbrook was mistaken, because speaking again, Grammy accused, 'Oh, he's gifted all right! Apart from a talent for incorrigible kadoodling, he has light-paws!'

Ever certain that Skip was to blame for the missing cameo, she'd as good as branded him thief, and opportunity was never missed in her reminding others of her suspicion.

When at last Mavis Whitepaws showed up, she seemed a stranger to Sherbrook. She was of course, as gorgeous as ever, and he would always see her that way. If Ronald Shortflag looked down from the Great Warren in the sky, a reluctant Sherbrook admitted the possibility of Ronald still seeing his Lillian, as gorgeous too. True love never died, or incorrigible romantics claimed as much.

The night of nights had in a general sense, lasted longer than eternity. Then, though, there was time spent when incidents dealt with had involved rushing adrenalin-altered perception, and those times rushed by in compressed fashion. Everything had, it seemed, occurred in a flash. Despite just one night's passing, Sherbrook was in for a rude surprise. He would see Mavis as if through different eyes.

Several youngsters were playing with clods. Large missiles were being hefted. They were not tossed at each other, not yet, but soon someone was bound to be hurt. From where he stood, Sherbrook was not able to discern words spoken, but he saw Mavis remonstrating with them. Not taking admonishment well, several of them argued back. He would go over and offer support, but the nearer he approached, the more distant she seemed, and reaching her, Sherbrook's smile soon faded.

'Good morning,' she said, which was apt—it being morning and all— but her cool manner was unexpected. Turning from him, she looked back across the field in the direction of the Tall Ones' dwelling place.

Contending with mystery of feminine wiles, Sherbrook wondered how far she intended taking this off-putting treatment and with genuine concern, enquired, 'Are you all right, Mavis?'

'Perfectly, thank you,' she replied. It was a short response with nothing of warmth about it and still, she averted her gaze.

He stated the obvious, 'Well now, it's been quite a night hasn't it?'

There was a nervous movement of her shoulders; not quite a shrug, but something of that, and in lack-lustre manner, she said, 'Yes indeed it has,' adding then, 'You're not wrong.'

Not wrong? He moved to touch her, and she all but flinched in avoiding his advance. He would say no more, make no further enquiry, for, every instinct informed, she no longer was his. Not knowing the identity of the interloper or to what point their trysting had progressed; he was beside himself with uncertainty. He trusted his internal devastation did not show.

There was no real sign of any rival, but whoever he was, would not declare himself, not so soon after Sherbrook's courageous effort during the darkest dilemma. The gollystomper would not want to be seen to offend established expectation, because all were familiar with the fact of his and Mavis Whitepaw's involvement. They were as good as promised to each other. If Mavis Whitepaws had caved into temptation, revealing a hitherto concealed flaw of character, then she and whoever it was, must consider themselves worthy of each other. In other words, he would sob his poor heart out at a later time. Sherbrook next caught himself wondering if such mistaken behaviour, a mere moment of weakness on her part, might be forgiven, and the answer came back, a resounding, no! She knew nothing of true love ways! Gall rising, so he feared he might choke on it, he told her, 'You'll take care and look after yourself now, won't you, Mavis?' He prayed that Great Grandfather might see to arranging appropriate, poisonous reward for the dishonourable one who backstabbed and gollystomped him.

They did not so much as touch paws in parting, and there was a sad instant of realization; no awful detail would be forgotten. Memory would rise unbidden to mind, fuelling melancholy's flame throughout the remainder of his days. He would reminisce, and recalling happiest moments would make for on-going sorrow, for he was sentimental to a fault. It was just his way.

In turning his back on Mavis Whitepaws, he noticed a small boy; witness to all. The boy wore an amused expression. Sherbrook ordered, 'Drop the clod young'un! What goes around comes around!' The clod fell to the ground at the boy's feet and, that small act of respectful obedience provided Sherbrook small consolation.

'Gather 'round folk. Everyone—attention, please!'

By now, Uncle Bucky had the rest of them assembled and gathered in an untidy semicircle before him; they were all ears. 'Good folk...' Bucky began, 'As I see the situation, we are left very little choice. And so we must take ourselves away yonder, from the home field and over the stream, to the trees up there, by the old forest.' Bucky reminisced, 'Those trees are an ancient group. They were just as enormous when I was young.' He waved a paw in vague fashion, 'Once up on the slope we can begin establishing ourselves. I'm not claiming it will be easy, but if all work well, then I'm sure we'll make a go of it.'

'But it's so far from the Tall Ones' garden!' Grammy Graymark protested.

An exasperated crony exclaimed, 'White radishes are not all there is to life, Grammy dear. We have nothing in the world! Give Bucky a chance. At least hear him out.' Hearing dissension from the rank of those counted as allies, Grammy was resistant. Sucking a deep breath drawn through the gap between too prominent teeth, a wet, whistling, hiss resulted.

'What if the creek floods?' she demanded. 'What then? If that creek breaches its banks—we will not be able to cross back over! Where then, will we be?'

Someone quipped, 'Stuck on the far side?' Humour survived, but concealed sniggers issuing from the assembly did not sit well with Grammy.

Bitterness showed. 'I've a mind to go my own way and leave you for the cruel and useless creatures you are!'

Sniffing in disdain she raised her nose in the air. If she put her snout any farther aloft then her neck might snap. Whilst not at all fond of Grammy Graymark, Sherbrook was grateful that none thought to offer assistance in packing her things, but then she had nothing of practical use to take with her; not least cherished memento survived. All would make the departure from the field on the flat lands and head for the slopes with nothing but present company.

Ever patient, Bucky enquired, 'If I may continue?' He seemed not the least piqued by anything transpiring. 'The remains of several fallen trees up there on the lowest part of the hillside should provide ample protection while excavation proceeds. There will be adequate shelter for the youngsters during the warmest part of days. There will be long green grass aplenty on the creek flats in times to come—although, it is true, there has not been much other than dry grass there of late. As for those victuals most favoured, gathered from the Tall Ones' planting place, at this side of the stream… I have never once seen the creek in flood. Those who insist upon inclusion of delicacies in their diet, will in future, have a little farther to go in acquiring, such.' He added, 'For my part, I have little predilection for luxuries.'

'Not foodstuffs,' Grammy retorted, 'But I recall something going by the name of the old Radiola!' That said, she gyrated, shimmying hips, as might any sassy young doe. So inappropriate was the sight that an embarrassed Sherbrook looked away.

Cut to the quick by her mentioning the Radiola, Bucky was unable to contain himself. He stooped to retaliate in kind. In measured tone, he said, 'Grammy Graymark—old friend? Please do everyone a favour? While crossing over there—just slip.' Unaccustomed to hearing him speak that way, all fell silent, and they looked down as if making a close study of their feet. Uncle Bucky was not least perturbed. He announced, 'All right, let's have no further ado. We shall set off.' And soon the field was behind them.

Crossing the creek flats, going through long grass, Skip the Seer had stayed close with Uncle Bucky. Sherbrook noticed the boy shivering. The sun was warming the day and so he asked, 'Are you cold, Skip? Is that it?'

Skip called back, 'No. I have a very strong sense of foreboding, and I'm not sure why.'

Thought, concerning the unenviable talents of the seer, were interrupted by Simple Rudy, who, coming alongside Sherbrook, complained, 'Sherbrook, I'm lonely. May I hold your paw?'

Sherbrook, smiling, told him, 'If you want, you may do so forever, Simple.'

He would wish they had done just that. Rudy and he were together for a while, but then he had allowed himself to be distracted by Peace

Darkling. Later, he would ask, 'May Great Grandfather grant true wisdom underlie even the smallest of deeds.'

When crossing the field, Uncle Bucky had instructed, 'Keep together now.' He did not want children slipping away, or those elderly, stumbling and falling on rough, churned ground. His job was to see that progress was accomplished without mishap occurring; but good was not served by worrying over problems before they presented themselves; soon enough they'd be there at the stream.

Sherbrook was helpful in volunteering to scout terrain at both sides of the creek; upstream and down. He went off with Simple Rudy in tow, but found no place was problem-free. The final decision would be Bucky's, and with such scant choice, Sherbrook was glad it was so.

The creek did not appear too deep, not from the grassy bank where Bucky stood surveying it. He again called, 'Gather around folk!' And when he had their attention, announced, 'Folk, serendipity favours us, because *this* spot—right here—is the best place to cross. Despite the water being quite deep, it presents the least challenge. I've learned that upstream, just before the place where the banks become steep, the stream is very fast flowing. Downstream, where it widens, it's a lot deeper than we might hope. Because there are no hopping stones down there to make the going possible, I know that by going in calm fashion, we will succeed in crossing from this point.'

There were murmurs of apprehension. Many were not as confident in the plan as Bucky hoped, and dissenting, troubled voices were heard, but to his great relief, complaining was not heard from Grammy Graymark.

'What of me? I have Ruth, Ruby, Rachel and Beck to get across! How can I get over there with my babies? Bob will have Ruben and Michael to watch. I don't think we can do it!' There were other problems and criticism. Some were vociferous in making complaint. Recalling the young mother's name as Jennie, but because he was not one hundred per cent certain of it, Bucky chose rather, to address the husband. 'Now, Bob, put your good wife at ease. Help will be given in getting the young ones across.' Hearing those words, several folk stepped forward, offering assistance.

Another insisted she had not slightest doubt she would fall in and drown. 'Because of my gammy leg! It gives me such gyp! Even getting across the field was a *frightful* ordeal!'

Bucky offered, 'You have my sympathy, Nan. I do understand.' He said, 'If young bucks were to volunteer their services, then I'm sure we can have you over there without much difficulty. One can go ahead of you and another can assist in steadying you from behind.'

There were small sounds of mirth. A close friend of Nan's commented, 'Ooh! She'll adore that! Won't you Nan?'

In fair order, all problems were addressed and solutions found. The bank at this side was fine, but the opposite was a little steep for his liking. They did not want the obstacle of a steep incline slowing their progress. Charlie Noy-Breen had expressed eagerness to help. He could assist others, and so, Bucky agreed, 'Good fellow, Charlie, get yourself over there. I'm sure you'll make a fine job of it.'

Mavis Whitepaws had pushed forward. 'I can go too. I can give assistance to those needing it.' She was a responsible individual, and so she and Charlie were assigned the task. Charlie would not prove so accident-prone with her at his side. Those of Charlie's sort did not, of course, intend clumsiness.

Slipping Away

Impatient with listening to Sherbrook and Peace Darling chatting, Simple Rudy wandered over to Uncle Bucky and Skip.

He asked, 'Uncle, can I hold your paw when we cross? Sherbrook is busy.' Before Bucky had time to respond, young Skip interrupted, 'No, Simple, Uncle is keeping *me* company! You can flibberty hop back there and complain to Sherbrook.'

'What do you mean, Skip? Uncle Bucky says, "Complaining is not a good thing."'

Bucky interrupted, 'Boys! No more of this! I can do without your bickery scratching!'

'Very well, Uncle, let Simple Rudy have his way, and everything will be just fine!'

'You're infuriating, Skip!' Bucky exclaimed, and then, 'Look, I have two paws, don't I? Why don't you each hold one?'

Skip refused, saying, 'No, I'll look after myself. I'm not helpless like Simple Rudy. Just let him take over everything! Is that what you want Uncle?' And turning away, he exclaimed, *'Good-bye!'*

Seeing him go, Simple Rudy took firm grasp of Bucky's paw. He offered consolation, assuring, 'It's all right, Uncle. Old Skip will come back later. When he's calmed down, he'll be well-behaved.'

To which, Bucky replied, 'I do hope so, Rudy, because you're both good boys.' He would not call after Skip; not this time. He reminded himself that he always treated the boys with fairness. He knew pangs of regret for having spoken so tersely, first with Grammy Graymark, and now with the boys. He must tend to Skip's feelings just as soon as there was time, but for now, other matters demanded attention.

The crossing was all but accomplished. There was a moment of levity, supplied by Piedmont the Bard who, standing poised on a stone midstream, treated them to brief verse:

'At point moot, good Piedmont makes a stand
'Gainst stream untamed—in sight of land!
Measured thus, with staff in hand
Is safe or sink, brook doth plan?'

Piedmont was a good friend, but obsessive to a fault. Bucky thought, when practicalities were seen to, he would take the bard aside and have a quiet word with him, let him know he was appreciated, but tell him to go a bit easier on himself. A short time ago he'd given the same advice to Grammy Graymark, 'Steady on now, Grammy, don't feel the need to push yourself. There's no need to rush.'

Unpleasantness was behind them. The past was where that sort of thing belonged. Grammy had responded, 'I take those words as kindness, Bucky.' And so, generosity inherent to her nature was revealed in her mentioning that quality, with regard to him. Bucky was sincere in noting that Grammy, too, experienced a successful crossing.

Now was his and Rudy's time, and with, 'Come along, youngster. Let's see if we can do as well as the rest of them,' he took a firm hold of Rudy's paw. They stepped out onto the first hopping-stone. And all was fine. But then a most astonishing thing occurred. There was a peculiar shimmering of atmosphere. The brightest, white light shone as if from nowhere, and so dazzling was it, that, Bucky was blinded!

Simple Rudy vanished! And, Uncle Bucky fell!

Simple had disappeared before their eyes! And although many of those having already crossed, now made their way farther up the hillside, several, including Charlie Noy-Breen and Mavis Whitepaws, were witness to the disaster.

Bucky fell backwards, his head cracked hard against a stone and his body flopped into the water to then be carried off downstream!

Those watching from the bank were horrified and stunned to helpless silence. Then, with initial shock passed—they shouted, *'Help! Help! Emergency! Come quick!'*

He'd gone ahead up the hillside in company of Peace Darkling. Skip was hiding in long grass beside the path. Sighting the boy, Sherbrook called, but to no avail; it was not unusual of late, seeing him so unhappy.

Sherbrook called, 'Buck up there, Skip!' but to little effect. The boy shrugged, looking just as sad. They'd not gone much farther, when desperate cries of 'Help! Come quick!' reached them. 'I must get down there!' Sherbrook exclaimed, and he took off, heltering back to the creek.

He stood helpless upon the bank, watching the remains of a dear friend carried into the wide, deep pond; carried along by the inexorable, slow moving current. He had searched to the far distance in every direction, for evidence of a Tall One's presence, and had admitted to there being not the least sign of them having involvement.

Much muttering began as alternate explanation was sought for the strange event. Many possible causes were propounded but no answer was found.

As, Mavis Whitepaws told it, 'Rudy began to glow! White light shone, and before our very eyes he vanished to *nothing!* When that light faded— *he was gone! Bucky slipped and fell!'* She told Sherbrook, 'There was something else too ... a strange odour.'

'An odour?'

'Yes, the scent of something sweet! *So sweet!* I've never before scented anything like it.'

Sherbrook directed her a curious look. The entire affair was mysterious. Mavis brushed at her dress, smoothing it.

He should not have gone on ahead. He should have stayed creek-side, but then, what might he have done? If ever there was a responsible and cautious individual, then that individual was Uncle Bucky. None might have guessed he would meet such an end.

Many were gathered at the bank.

Sherbrook said, 'It's not good, youngsters being here. This is not for their eyes. The mothers should take them back up the slope. The young bucks can help me get Uncle out from there.' Then, seeing young Skip standing alone, mournful and forlorn, he said, 'Mavis, take young Skip and keep him with you.'

Every attempt to retrieve Bucky from the creek proved useless.

Moving atop the bank, they followed the body's morbid progress as it floated downstream until, arriving at a place of deepest water, it moved as if pondering possibilities. Here the stream was less swift, acquiring more peaceful aspect; here was the broad pond, situated not very far from one of those places Bucky had decided unsuitable for crossing.

The body bobbed and rolled in a languid, lazy manner; it took a course that put it in danger of snagging on a large branch, which long ago had fallen into the creek. The greater part of the branch jutted up through the water from where its lowest part was embedded in mud of the creek-bed, but more than one sharp, sub-branch, protruded above the water line presenting a trap for Bucky.

Were he caught on that branch they'd have little chance of getting him out. They stood on the bank and watched as the inevitable occurred. There were cries of, 'No, don't go that way!' and, 'Oh deeks—someone *do* something! Look! He's turning towards it! Go 'round, Bucky! Go *around!*' All of which made it seem that Bucky was responsible for the direction his remains took and was intent upon getting it wrong.

Sherbrook joined the common cry, and waving paws in the air, heard himself shouting, 'Double Deeks! Bucky! Over this way—*please!*' Imploring was not just useless, but perhaps not altogether decent.

'What are you *doing?*' Sherbrook exclaimed, 'Just what do you think you are doing!'

'I'm trying to move him—get him unstuck. I thought—'

'No,' Sherbrook interjected, 'you did *not* think! Have some respect for the gazuzzled! Don't poke him!' Bill—or Phil had found a long stick in the grass and now extending it before him, he prodded the corpse. Stabbing at remains was just awful, and besides which, nothing would be gained; that stick was not thick or strong enough to have any practical effect. Sherbrook considered the matter and then relented.

'Perhaps you have something after all...' He asked, 'Who are you anyway—the name doesn't spring to mind.'

'Richard.'

'Ah,' said Sherbrook, 'I imagined it was, Bill—something with the "*ill*" sound—not the connotation, of course.'

'It's Richard.'

'Well, there must be a suitable stick around here, Richard—because your idea's not so terrible. I don't see old Bucky—grant him rest—complaining.

'If it were me floating there, *he* would try just about anything to get me out for proper burial.'

'That was my feeling too.' Richard shrugged and then pointed, saying, 'There's a better stick over yonder, but it's difficult to move.'

Sherbrook said, 'Let's take a look. We'll see if we can manage it together.'

Arriving at the spot, he knew they had no chance. He said, 'That's no stick, Richard. It's a log!' Then, stroking the fur of his chin and weighing possibilities, he decided, 'We'll give it a go, and if we can't move it, we'll get help from the others.' Going to one end of the fallen branch, he said, 'Lend a paw now.' And to their satisfaction, working one at each side of the branch, pushing and pulling and rocking it from side to side, it came loose. But then, without a word of warning, Richard let go and leapt away.

In the following instant, Sherbrook too, jumped back from the log. His leaping took him far, and landing in the tall grass he sounded—TUMP! There were just the two of them present, but sounding warning was second nature to Sherbrook.

Richard's expression was one of dread, as Brother Serpent slithered up from beneath the branch.

When Sherbrook had sounded TUMP, those farther afield had dived for cover. Now, Sherbrook waved, calling, 'It's fine—no problem!'

Richard observed, 'He's a big one isn't he?'

'A very respectable size,' Sherbrook agreed. 'He's drowsy. If the day was any warmer he'd be a lot more dangerous.' He said, 'In any case, we might just let him keep that branch.'

'I couldn't agree more,' said Richard, and, 'His eyes are terrible, aren't they?'

'Yes, they're not just dark and cold, it's the wicked determination behind them, the hungering after gazuzzlement.' Richard nodded, his attention fixed upon the great serpent's slithering progress. It was now exposed so that its long brown length was seen to equal that of the branch it coiled about. Watching the slick, forked tongue emerging from the hard mouth to taste the air, and imagining himself as lunch, Richard shivered.

Sunlight glinted from scales, and, Sherbrook observed, 'They always look so *clean* don't they?' Then, 'We *must* attend to Uncle. 'I just wish I could think of a way of getting him out from there, but I can't.

Richard said, 'We'll do whatever we can...'

'Yes,' agreed, Sherbrook, 'which is pretty much, nothing at all.'

Despite every attempt, Uncle Bucky would not be dislodged, and in considering failure, Sherbrook thought that whilst living, Bucky was a lot easier to sway. If still in the vicinity and watching them expend so much effort on his behalf, by now, even Bucky would exclaim, 'Deeks!' and perhaps employ stronger cuss words as well.

Many spent the greater part of the afternoon searching for Simple Rudy. They'd formed long lines and gone hither and fro through field and meadow. Had searched even those wild parts of the forest below the high hillside. They'd poked at bushes, peered behind trees and rocks and called as they went, but still, there was no sign of the boy. They would go on searching, going farther afield, they said, because no one ever just vanished. The boy was not lost to serpent, fox, or other predator, and so he would be found. When a searcher dared make the suggestion that Rudy might be hiding, he received a sharp cuff from a companion for his trouble. 'I didn't mean it—not the way you took it!' He exclaimed, 'I meant that being a bit simple—he could have gone to ground, because he's frightened by the grandfather of a racket we're making!'

Many possibilities were raised but none seemed plausible. Reports of the vanishing underwent scrutiny, until very few believed anything so mysterious had happened; crediting the incident with supernatural cause meant that witnesses were confused as to what they'd seen.

Sherbrook recalled that Charlie Noy-Breen was there when the vanishing occurred. Anyone of such high-strung nature ought not be deemed a reliable witness, and, Sherbrook found himself wondering whether, convinced of the supernatural having occurred, Charlie had exerted influence over others, persuading them that the strange and untoward had taken place, and, as for Mavis Whitepaws? After spending so much time in his dubious company, she might just as much as others succumb to Charlie's influence.

Then realization dawned. Instinct did not after all, fail him. Hadn't he *all along* suspected that *Charlie Noy-Breen was the gollystomper?* Surveying the immediate territory, Sherbrook could not see Charlie anywhere. He must be part of one of those groups still engaged in searching after Simple Rudy. He could not wait to get his paws on Noy-Breen!

Noticing the sudden change in Sherbrook's demeanour, Richard enquired, 'What is it?'

'Charlie Noy-Breen—*he's* the gollystomper!' This was a precipitous, gruff response. Richard paused, hesitating before venturing, 'Do you mean him and Mavis? Mavis Whitepaws?'

'The gollystomper—that's right!' Odd pleasure was derived in repeating the miserable truth of it. Without so much as glancing to Richard, Sherbrook continued, angry eyes peering away to distant horizon, all the while muttering beneath his breath and delighting in the imagined punishments, which Noy-Breen so richly deserved and would most assuredly receive.

Richard said, 'Oh, I wouldn't be too upset. They're made for each other.'

Force of rage colouring his countenance, Sherbrook demanded, 'Made for each other! What's *that* supposed to mean?'

A serious, full-blown ruckus seemed imminent, but then, Richard, maintaining a dignified poise and appearing quite unafraid, ventured, 'Well, Sherbrook, you're hero material, aren't you? And everyone knows that Charlie's an absolute disaster. As for Mavis, if she's chosen him above you, then she's just...'

'Just what?' Sherbrook enquired, feeling a little easier. Knowing that Richard believed him heroic went some way toward softening his stance. And when others close by heard the word hero, subdued murmurs of agreement were heard. Someone declared, 'Hear, hear!'

Sherbrook enquired further after Richard's opinion of the behaviour of Mavis Whitepaws.

Richard made more general response. 'The sisters are a fine lot, but when all's said and done, they're just does, aren't they?' This was taken as cause for knee-slapping merriment from others.

'*Just does,*' was repeated.

A familiar voice was heard then, announcing, 'No, no! The sisters are to us, complementary. They are as melody is to rhythm and beat.'

Piedmont the Bard had wandered down from the slope to see how things were coming along, and in making his approach, had overheard them. Halting on a slight, elevated rise meant that he was above them and he appeared somewhat taller than they were used to seeing him. 'You are impassioned Sherbrook, and that is understandable. Heroes are individuals possessed of much heart,' he said, continuing to address Sherbrook, 'Big hearted is fine. Best not allow heart free rein over head, though. Such, can encourage unhappy, if not downright appalling eventuality, but that's enough of my preaching.

'How are you dealing with the present dilemma? I see my old friend still floats. He was never one for lazing about. It's strange, seeing him prone now, lolling there for all to see.' Using a stout stick as support, Piedmont drew close, and reaching Sherbrook, declared, 'Bruk! Eh, Sherbrook?' Raising the stick, he tapped Sherbrook upon his chest. To declare Sherbrook startled would be an understatement. He was astonished and, stepping back, demanded, *'What was that for?'*

'For nothing,' answered Piedmont. Waving the stick in the general direction of Bucky, he observed, 'It's appalling seeing him diminished, so. We'll have a nice service for him. A few parting words will be spoken, and he'll drift according with Great Grandfather's will.'

'A service, now?'

'No, not now—but soon enough.' And with that said, Piedmont turned to leave.

Sherbrook, addressing the oldster's retreating back, called, 'Bard, is that it? Is that all you came to say?'

Piedmont did not pause in going. He did not trouble turning, but called back, 'It all comes out in the great eternal wash, Sherbrook! Ask Uncle Bucky—he would tell you no different!' They stood there at the creek's edge, looking from one to other. What did Piedmont mean?

'There goes the mysterious bard,' one of them commented, and he shrugged, but then, thinking better, amended, 'We should heed that one.'

'His every utterance has meaning,' another advised.

'The Great Eternal Wash?'

'He refers to Uncle being in the pond—that's all,' said Sherbrook, 'It's nothing more mysterious than that. He did say, "Ask Uncle Bucky."' All turned to stare at the pond. 'This is ridiculous,' Sherbrook said, 'There's nothing deep or meaningful to any of it.'

Someone insisted, 'There must be. He's not called the Bard for nothing. Deeks! *Look there!'*

Sherbrook spun around and was just in time to catch the last glow of dazzling white light, fading beyond the same rise the bard stood upon when first he greeted them. He shouted, 'Let's go!' And as they went, he shouted a warning, 'Keep away from that serpent's nest!' Several comrades altered their course.

Arriving atop the rise, there was not the least sign of the bard. Having determined that as true, Sherbrook imagined an unfamiliar odour permeated the air. A peculiar sweetness lingered, before dissipating to nothing.

Then, Richard halted alongside him, complaining, 'That was a fine waste of effort!'

Another recent arrival agreed, 'But—where is he? There's no way he could be out of sight so soon. Piedmont *can't* move that fast.' Taking charge, Sherbrook wasted no time issuing instructions, 'Richard—you're fast,' he said, 'helter up there to yon' excavation and see if he's there. The rest of us will get back to the pond. We'll join in searching for young Simple. When you've found the bard, come back and report to me.' Richard needed no urging. Away he went, and the others, happy to fall in with Sherbrook's suggestion, accompanied him back to the creek.

They would carry on searching until dusk. During one of their short breaks they'd regrouped and much was decided; if today's effort proved unsuccessful, then the search would resume tomorrow at first light.

They were a conscientious lot and in such company, Sherbrook enjoyed a wonderful sense of camaraderie; soon though, he would be disappointed. They'd just begun moving off in small parties, when an aged doe arrived at the scene with a message from Grammy Graymark.

'Grammy says you are to curtail the search,' she told them. 'You're to call it off, because does and children require attention.'

For a moment, Sherbrook believed his ears deceived him, but then he was not mistaken. He asked, 'Grammy Graymark? You mean she's sent you down here with instructions—for *us?*'

'That's correct, Sherbrook. Yes.'

Much uncertain murmuring and muttering ensued, and then one of the Small Paws family spoke up, declaring, 'Dilly *would* want me up there, helping out.'

And, another admitted, 'My Ruth must have a great deal to contend with.'

At which point, the messenger agreed, 'Those *are* valid concerns.' Having heard mention of the name, Ruth, mentioned, she enquired, 'You must be, Ralph?' She said, 'You're right, Ralph, because Ruth is not having an easy time of it up there—indeed, none of them are.'

Someone said, 'Grammy does have a point. Quite apart from the does, the older bucks must be finding the going difficult, and they should not have to manage the excavation alone.'

Others spoke up then, and it was not long before a consensus was reached. Grammy's request was reasonable. It was a helpful reminder of deeper obligation and fruitless searching for Simple Rudy should be abandoned. In less time than it took to say flibberty hop, that was just what most did.

With only several of them remaining, a dazed Sherbrook muttered, 'Well, I guess that's it then.' Looking about and feeling at a loose end, he saw Richard returning from the site of the new excavation. He was puffed-out, but brought news of Piedmont the Bard's presence up there on the slope.

Gulping for air, Richard explained that Piedmont had claimed to be present there, all the while. He denied having been creek-side with them. When words alleged as uttered by him, were related, the bard had informed, 'I'm afraid I've not the foggiest idea of what is meant by, "The great eternal wash."' In giving Richard a return message for Sherbrook, the bard deigned, 'When you get back to the pond you should tell him from me, that as I hear it, the line has a quite acceptable ring to it.'

'An acceptable ring?' A bemused Sherbrook shook his head. He thanked Richard for the message and enquired, 'We saw what we saw—didn't we?'

Richard replied, 'Maybe we did and maybe we didn't.' Shrugging, he said, 'But I will not be granting it too much thought.'

Sherbrook was silent for a moment, and then said, 'I'm going to accept that as wise advice.'

Later he would understand the significance of the messenger's arrival creek-side.

He would know that he should have sent her packing; his doing so, would have been a timely message to Grammy Graymark.

As unexpected as Unlce Bucky's passing was, none was prepared for what fate insisted they next take as their due.

MMEERAH!

'Yes, I know what you mean—I do. But just look at his tweed jacket! Look at the way debris has washed over there and banked up against him! He always took such pride in his personal appearance. It's too sad.'

He did not intend that she look. He'd waved a paw without thinking, and she glanced in that direction.

'Yes, but, Sherbrook, he *is* gone,' she kept reminding him.

'Not entirely,' he said, thinking, I know he's gone. I know it too well, but knowing doesn't help. He'd come down here to sit in the tall grass, to be close to Bucky for a small part of each day, had been doing it ever since the day of tragedy. Trouble was, the more often he visited, the worse he seemed to feel. It was morbid of him and he knew it. Aware of his growing obsession, Peace Darkling insisted upon interrupting his creek-side sojourns by showing up uninvited.

He didn't mind her company, but when he enquired regarding her motive in doing so, she told him, 'Oh, Sherbrook, I like your company. I thought you knew...' He had enquired more than once, and her response was always much the same. Apart from the time she told him, 'We all miss him of course, but you and he were in many ways alike... I realize that for you, knowing he's gone is most sad. You must feel cut off, not just from dear Uncle Bucky, but as well, from a part of yourself.'

All of which was pretty much, kadoodle. Peace Darkling was mistaken in assuming he measured up to an individual of Bucky's calibre. She meant well, though, because knowing that he was low, she'd attempted coaxing him from gloom.

Little by little, she had revealed more of herself, until a day came when she announced, 'Sherbrook, there's something I should tell you—something which I feel you'd find helpful. I have discovered a way of calming myself, and I believe that in these uncertain times, you could benefit from it.'

Knowing he did not need help, not from anyone, her words were cause for uneasiness. He was disappointed, because accustomed by now to their spending a good deal of time together, he did not want the complication of her "helping him", undermining an otherwise easy going relationship.

'Help is not required, thank you,' he said, 'I'm just feeling low, but I'll be fine.'

There was silence between them then. His attention was drawn to the flight of a dragonfly. There was a point in its smooth flight, when it came near the grassy bank. They heard the soft whirring of its wings as it hovered where many tiny bugs skipped across the watery surface. The afternoon was mild with just the gentlest of breezes, a breeze so slight that the pond was not disturbed, even by slightest ripple, but far away toward the horizon, in the direction of Tall One territory, the sky was darkening. He was going to comment on the likelihood of a storm developing when a peculiar sound distracted him. Sound of humming, he wondered, but then, no, that was not it. He'd never before heard the like.

'Mmeerah! Mmeerah!'

It was Peace Darkling! She'd crossed her hind legs, made her back very straight and her eyes were shut; each forepaw rested upon a knee. Something was amiss, because she sat there, cross-legged, producing an eerie droning. He asked, 'Peace, what is it? Are you all right?' Response not forthcoming, his discomfort increased. She behaved as if unwell! Then she stopped, opened her eyes and smiled. He eyed her with wariness. She told him, 'I have discovered a type of magic, Sherbrook.'

'Magic?'

'Yes, Sherbrook, that's what I said.'

'Well,' he said, 'It's a relief, knowing it's nothing more serious than that.'

She said, 'You should try it sometime.'

'Going Mmeerah?'

'Yes.'

'Why?' He would never consider making such spectacle of himself.

Peace said, 'You will never know why, Sherbrook, unless you try it for yourself.'

'No offence intended,' he said, 'but it reminds me of the sound made by the Tall One's cow.'

'No offence taken.' She said, 'And, Sherbrook, your observation shows you are astute.' Just then a bug chose to settle on the tip of her nose. She brushed it away with a paw.

'Astute? How so?'

'Because you've guessed it was she, Missy-Belle, who, in the first place taught me it.'

'I have?'

'Oh, yes indeed.'

It was flabbergasting, because he did not believe there was much resemblance at all. The sound made by Missy-Belle and the sound Peace Darkling made, possessed just vague similarity. He'd thought to tease her by mentioning the Tall One's cow.

Seeing him pleased now, she said, 'I know. Let's try it together shall we?'

And so it was, that they shared the very first of those experiences, Sherbrook referred to as, 'Making Mmeerah!'

Mmeerah affected a body in a quite wondrous way. He felt calm and easier going after its practice, than ever before. Soon he would not, he realized, get through days so well, did they not set aside time for Mmeerah. He decided Missy-Belle a most clever cow to have conceived such an idea and thought, Wasn't she, Missy-Belle, an extremely generous individual, imparting knowledge of Mmeerah to Peace Darkling? Many strange, mysterious events, taking place over a very long period would transpire before Peace would so much as dream of allowing him to learn that it was she alone, who discovered all of Mmeerah. Discovery of many sounds, sounds producing differing energies and results too, was hers.

Peace was not at all reliant upon information provided by Missy-Belle the cow, or for that matter, anyone else. When Sherbrook mentioned the Tall One's cow, alluding to her sound, Peace thought, yes—she saw what was meant. She next decided the imposing creature had about her something of a Missy-Belle quality; a suitable name for her might well be, just that. Having not the least knowledge of language of cows, though, meant that Peace did not at all know Sister Cow's name, she'd quite enough difficulty in communicating with those of her own kind.

Whilst not entirely solitary by nature, Peace Darkling knew herself well enough, as a quiet and private individual, possessing not much need for other's company. She did not regard others as unimportant, but it was true, her own company was most acceptable to her.

For as long as she remembered, much time had been spent in wondering over sounds and the effects they produced in a body. Whilst she'd not actually learned anything from Missy-Belle, she might well have, because in contemplating sounds of others, clues were gained to something she decided, most mysterious. Sounds, in certain of their myriad forms were energy altering, and further study of their unusual effects, might eventually lead to discovery of more than just a technique employed in gaining inner peace and tranquillity. Then, following much time spent in mimicking notes of bird-song and other creatures, after much puzzling, meaning was deduced. Of insects, Peace decided, bees were most wondrous, but many small voices of other creatures also fascinated. Nature's rhythms were best friends, but until now, none other than she had considered such voices worthy of close study. She had sensed that others might construe her time spent in uncommon pursuit, as peculiar, as behaviour went, and so she never discussed her world. Her discoveries had remained her secret until Sherbrook was introduced to them.

She gained pleasure now, seeing Sherbrook's smile when he noticed the soft sound caused by the dragonfly's wings vibrating against the air.

Peace had always liked Sherbrook, but over recent time fondness for him increased so that she felt it safe to risk more. She believed that if Sherbrook learned a means of achieving calm, then his recurring periods of debilitating low mood might be circumvented. They might then succeed in becoming as adjacent hopping stones—hopping stones embedded in a clear-running stream. Running against earlier hope, nothing was good now. In her estimation, New Warren Central could be described as a murky, sticky environment, a mired creek-bed. Sooner rather than later, something must be done to alleviate conditions and, in their working together she imagined them providing something of practical help. If such were possible, and she and Sherbrook taught them, then perhaps her energy-altering techniques might meet with acceptance and prove beneficial, perhaps something of transformative power might be imparted.

'I think,' said Sherbrook, 'we had best soon make a move. We had best get back to the warren. I've been watching yon' clouds and unless I'm mistaken, they're building to something serious.'

It was his first attempt at making Mmeerah, and he'd finished chanting well before she had. Giving his best effort, he'd taken each of her simple instructions, and they'd not chanted for long, when, an odd feel-

ing of trepidation arose in him. He'd wondered whether there might be
a danger of losing himself. A strange sensation, which he might describe
as, "melting away" was experienced, but now, all was proved safe enough
and he lay back, busy nibbling at a tasty long green shoot. His mood was
altered. He felt lighter than he had. Despite deeming himself somewhat
foolish at the outset, in following her lead, and despite ensuing dread of
impending loss, experienced whilst making Mmeerah, he was also aware
of beneficial after-effects gained. However, Sherbrook was grateful for
the approaching storm, its presence presented useful distraction. He did
not look forward to addressing the least curiosity regarding his sharing
involvement in her discovery.

Looking to the sky, Peace said, 'I'd love to see a *real* storm wouldn't
you?'

Storms could wreak havoc. They were not something looked forward
to, and so her question revealed another aspect of her nature. She was
far less predictable than he'd thought. Throughout the long afternoon,
humidity increased whilst the atmosphere was eerie and still, and then
the breeze stirred. Mere breeze was replaced by a stiff-gusting wind,
and it was not long before the sound of its rushing, blustering against
foliage and water, was loud. Reed-beds along the banks hummed and
sang as their masses bent wave-like, and long grasses growing on the
flats, rippled as if raked by the grooming claws of giants. The wide surface of the deep pond was set to unfamiliar shimmering and turned
to darkest slate; the colour of stone, yet, mirror for tempest sky above.
When lightning flashed, a crisscross movement of rippling lines of
white light broke the dark surface. Thunder rolled through churning
black above, and they, catching a look in each other's eyes, recognized
something of primordial, instinctive fear. Out there, riding upon the
deep pond's surface, all that remained of Uncle Bucky moved in rhythmic slow dance—restrained thus far from progressing downstream—
held back by his brown tweed jacket, ensnared by a most persistent
branch.

Rain swept in. Drops the size of cherries pelted, tearing against the
pond's surface and all else. They'd seen it coming and then it was upon
them! Heltering, they were soon back at the nearest of New Warren
Central's burrows—careening headlong into sentries stationed inside the

entranceway! On this occasion, Grammy Graymark's Keepers of the Way would question them more severely than was usual.

During the best of times, protocol dictated that before entry to New Warren Central's burrows was permitted, residents must submit to enquiry; cross-examination was carried out in chitchat manner. Information was gleaned regarding activity occurring during time spent outdoors. To a casual observer, unfamiliar with the way of things hereabouts, it might be assumed that folk were involved in pleasant tête-à-tête; at worst, they might believe harmless gossip engaged in. Grammy saw to the appointment of Keepers of the Way, and so all was as should be; the leader ever insisted hers was rule by kind persuasion.

But, knowing the magnitude of their mistake, neither Peace nor Sherbrook was at all surprised to find they were asked to accompany a sentry, and they wondered over the nature of the onerous "reminder" in store for them. Knowing they would not receive punishment—not as such, but would be set to the task of "learning a lesson", furtive, downcast glances passed between them.

Fact of the maelstrom was admitted, but for the present was set-aside.

They well knew, didn't they, to show consideration by deporting in a decorous manner when entering the warren? After all, Grammy Graymark's proclaiming: "The warren is home to the many. New Warren Central must not be seen as home for the selfish few," must surely have sunk in? All were acquainted by this time with the rule, observance of which was easy for anyone possessing common sense.

Here at New Warren Central, allowance was not made for young ones to scamper, heltering and kazooning, as might suit them. Such behaviour, permitted back in the old warren, was no longer deemed acceptable. None could kazoon in disregard of others rights. Each and every adult was expected to set an example of self-disciplined behaviour. Home was sacrosanct and it was part of a leader's responsibility to ensure that all respected the fact. Sherbrook and Peace were lucky then, because they were not taken before Lillian Graymark. After treating them to measured admonishment, it was decided by Keepers of the Way that the offence committed did not warrant the privilege of an audience. As, Leader, it was understood that Grammy was the busiest of does; she attended far more serious concerns. Instead, they were taken before a lieutenant, who, after pondering the matter, ordered them to take up whiskbrooms and sweep droppings away from outside the burrow entryways. In passing judgment, it was explained that the task allotted them represented the lightest of penalties. Passing droppings, "just any old where" within the vicinity of warren entryways, was no longer permitted, and so far as reminders went, they were recipients of considerable largesse. They'd find sweeping, not the least bit difficult. In granting a somewhat wistful smile, the lieutenant offered, 'The thing is, you see... If you were let off with mere verbal admonishment, then I'd know that I'd not demonstrated impartiality.'

In learning that leniency was applied, the fact of their being caught topside during a storm of uncommon magnitude, received fair mention. All was taken into account.

They could begin sweeping as soon as the storm was over and the ground out there was nice and dry.

Awful Unravelling

After the storm's passing, the atmosphere was freshened by brisk, fur-ruffling wind. Thinking to go forth with a friend, for the purpose of sur-veying territory for what should prove impressive environmental damage sustained during the night, a youngster, Samuel Long, was the first to discover that the body of their former leader, was gone. Lifted upon rising waters of the swollen creek, it had loosened from the point of anchor and gone travelling to wherever such powerful currents willed things to go. Learning of the discovery, Sherbrook hastened creek-side to see for him-self. However, once arrived, it was not possible to go as close to the creek's boundary as he would like. Both banks were breached and the lower flats flooded, but he saw it was true. Uncle Bucky was gone. Knowing it was so a great weight seemed to lift away from him.

* * *

The time had come for Piedmont to say a few words and offer a moment's silence in honour of the departed. He asked that those con-cerned, and not afraid of offending Grammy Graymark by attending there, meet down at the flats. Loss of Uncle Bucky would be marked by a few words.

His given name was Buckminster, which not many realized, because Bucky, having determined the name as cause of embarrassment, chose never to use it. Piedmont decided though, in referring to the departed, he should use the complete name; he felt certain of Buckminster's not now minding. He'd not composed anything of too sorrowful nature; wrenching tears from those attending was not the intention; neither would he versify or carry on in long-winded manner. Buckminster would not want that. Neither would Buckminster appreciate the pres-ence of thronging, curious onlookers. As it happened, few showed up. Just several close friends and acquaintances of the departed attended.

An exception however, was one of Grammy's lieutenants, who, positioned back from others, noted proceedings; words uttered would not go unreported.

Piedmont began by reminding those present of several fine qualities: 'Buckminster... Peerless leader, fairest mediator, most loyal compatriot and friend to all, we have not forgotten you. We gather here this fine morning to farewell you, friend, and to wish you safe journey to Great Grandfather's most wondrous, infinite realm. Good hearts, here present, know that certain peace, is just reward. We know it, as as we know that all of creation is held firm, kept safe, in Great Grandfather's almighty paws. Such indomitable spirit as yours, Bucky, is always guided home. Gazuzzlement can have no dominion.'

Peace scattered dandelions and wild red poppies upon the waters. Sherbrook wiped a tear from an eye, trusting no one saw him. He saw others did the same, and thought, so what? Young Skip stood unmoving and morose after the brief service, until, Piedmont said, 'Come along now friend, Skip, There's been too much sadness. We shall go to my burrows and I'll show you something—something I believe, Uncle Bucky would want you to see.'

'What?' Skip asked, sounding petulant.

'Oh nothing, nothing at all … not in comparison with a good life lost. Just, the scratchings—record of past events—descriptions of meaning...' Glancing to where Grammy's cohort spied from atop the rise, he said, 'If we are to remain at all worthwhile, we must keep such knowledge alive.'

* * *

In lamenting the awfulness of everything, Sherbrook complained to Piedmont, 'We've been gollystomped!'

A thoughtful Piedmont told him, 'Of course you are right, but that's not all of it. We, also, are deserving of blame. She would not have gotten away with any of it, had we nous enough to call her bluff at the start.'

At the outset, none had foreseen the danger in allowing Grammy Graymark to take control. Perhaps they'd been through too much already and were not quite of their right minds, but whatever causes were blamed, there were those who, too late, rued their lack of determination in refusing to go along with her. The gall and presumption shown in the first place, in her claiming authority, remained as moot point, seeming of little concern to the majority of those of New Warren Central. So far as most were concerned the fact of her seizing control was cause for small surprise. A minority numbering very few viewed her audacity as defying belief. All recognized Grammy Graymark as an oppressor, and so, wasn't wilful insistence expected of her? Didn't it follow that even the most extreme examples of coercive behaviour—coercion, in the first instance, accepted as nothing new from her—should be taken for granted.

Oft' heard was, 'Oh, that's just Grammy! It's just her way.' Over a very short time, matters had deteriorated to the point where individuals ran the risk of those in authority determining them as "uncooperative" or worse.

Dreamers entertained the notion of conditions altering. They claimed that at some stage, Grammy might willingly step down. Whilst admitting that she was not yet so aged as to allow accuracy in describing her as having one paw in the grave—she was "getting on". They may not have too long to wait, and doubters would see that day come. It was claimed that in her way, Grammy was wise, and it being so, she would come to realize that the initial, blithe acceptance of her authority represented nothing more than a small anomaly in the weave of fabric of their shared history. Soon enough, profuse thanks would be offered for her time spent in reorganizing them. Soon, they must grant her a stipend of appropriate nature—her favourite white radish perhaps—supplied gratis for all the days remaining to her, and they'd all move on.

Sad to say, they were unrealistic.

In the first instance, ordeal had provided opportunity, and then many small advantages were seized—seized at each and every twist and turn along the way, until, Grammy's inexorable ascension to a position of absolute authority was fait accompli. Seeming to have happened in no time at all, it was as if Grammy Graymark was guided by destiny's favouring paw, and soon, subjugation of all was accomplished fact; and never did her sort relinquish power. As for radish, she already received abundance from the Tall Ones' planting place. She enjoyed the finest white radish at every meal. Her every need was attended by a loyal retinue; they granted her every wish. Still though, dreaming was allowed.

In justifying protest, a dreamer might admit, 'Oh I know you're right! I know I'm just pretending, just imagining! I can't help it though. I wish *so much* that she'd come unstuck!' They hoped that growing so vain, Grammy would be vulnerable; something must cause her downfall! But wish as may, most reliable truth was that Grammy Graymark entertained not the least doubt concerning her holding position of leadership. The fact was she'd always been quite vain. She knew flattery when she heard it and would not allow it affect her. She'd spent a long time putting up with others deciding everything and now was her time. Her rightful place was ever at the head of the crowd, and she'd no intention of allowing herself undone. Doubt laid claim to places in other hearts and flourished, but would not take root in hers.

Impossibilities mooted, even the most intransigent dreamer reached the point of defeat, and must confess that it was they, and not she, allowing delusion engage and carry them away. Indulging imagination amounted to nothing more than a foolish bid for gratification, gained in bemoaning common fate in company of a trusted friend or two.

Blithe acceptance of dictate of those in authority, at first viewed by some as just cause for pride, began slipping away.

Qualities needed in exemplifying a helpful attitude were confused with those qualities required for intelligent co-operation. Possessing a good attitude was a wonderful thing, but such easy-going denial of compliance having anything of submission to it, was seen too late as errant foolishness.

By determined, unyielding will, absolute rule was entrenched, and if the slightest murmur of discontent was overheard and reported, then complainers were judged as unworthy of further munificence.

Many punishments were dealt, but one of the worst was banishment from the Tall Ones' planting place. Tall One territory, deemed out of bounds to an offender, meant they might no longer gather there. For one so unlucky, gathering luxury foodstuffs was out of the question until they received further notice. There were cases, though, where further notice never was forthcoming. Those deluded unfortunates could hang on forever, ignorant of the truth of their situations, waiting for word to come and not realizing that it never would.

'Did you know that the meeting place is now called the "Hall of Power"? I just bet you didn't, did you?'

'I did, yes… But, do you know that they've also named the wide burrow, leading to the Hall of Power?'

'No. How are we to refer to it?'

'Well, it's actually something of an embarrassment. Henceforth, it will be known as the Tunnel of Love.'

'Oh, tell me you're not serious!'

'I am.'

Sherbrook glanced skywards, disgust and disbelief showing in his expression, then, looking again to Piedmont, he said, 'They made Bruce Lop run on the spot for half a morning the other day.'

'Why was that?'

'I have no idea, but perhaps he smiled on the wrong side of his face at the wrong moment.'

Bruce was a decent chap, Piedmont thought. He said, 'Bruce gave me help once, collecting and pressing bark for scratchings. It was considerate of him.'

Sherbrook and Peace prolonged carrying out the sentence assigned to them for so long, that they half hoped those in authority had forgotten it, but then Sherbrook was summoned and informed that punishment would be more severe if he and Peace Darkling did not attend. He was told to fetch her, and hasten to that place near the oak where offenders engaged in production of whiskbrooms. They must inform whoever was in charge there, 'We are reporting as ordered, and, Lieutenant Lucille Cropper says that we should be issued whisks.' By mentioning that name, they would have no trouble at all in receiving prompt attention, and then could get started with sweeping.

Needless to mention, they wasted no further time in delaying.

Now they flicked droppings away from entranceways to burrows. Sherbrook's technique, Peace thought, left a lot to be desired, but she had not commented on it. Sherbrook had decided the chore wasn't quite so bad as first imagined, and said, 'These brooms are quite good fun, don't you think? If you bend them back—like this—you can flick the pellets a deeks of a long way! We could have contests with them—we could invent a new game!'

Having had enough of it, she told him, 'Yes, but Sherbrook, I'd appreciate you not sending them in *my* direction!'

Peace was mindful of Grammy Graymark's cleverness, demonstrated in her coming up with the idea of the whisk. Great ingenuity was shown, but it was unfortunate, Grammy, not limiting her activity to that sort of thing.

She insisted, 'Stop messing, *Sherbrook!*'

'Oh, come on!' he retorted, 'Where's your sense of fun? Flick a few back my way. I bet I can dodge them!'

Peace, standing her ground, stopped sweeping and observed, 'There are a disgraceful lot of droppings here, aren't there? By my standards, it's dreadful! I wonder what the sentence is for messing this way?'

Going closer, he told her, 'Shh! We mustn't be overheard.' And then, 'Why do you think he told us to sweep outside these burrows?' Seeing her shrug, he said, 'Because, as I figure it, these burrows are *his*.'

'Oh my, of course!' Peace said, doing her best to muffle her exclamation, 'He has us cleaning up after him! Well now, I've a good mind to...'

'No. You've mind, for nothing of the sort. That is, unless you'd like to spend the rest of your days working at this! And, there's another thing.... I'm of the opinion, that we're best off not making too good a job of it. If we do—they'll trap us into coming back for more of the same.' He said, 'Imagine it. They're chatting away together over supper, discussing this and that, when one of them happens to mention, "Ah yes—just by the by—whenever you need home duties attended to, you need look no farther than Peace Darkling. She did time the other day, down-slope at my place, and I must tell you, the gal is conscientious as all get-out! Put her on the end of a whisk and you'll soon enough see what I mean!'

'Oh?' Peace was bemused and doubting; she queried, 'They wouldn't, would they?'

He said, 'I'd bet my last endive on it,' and, 'I think you're wonderful and very gullible!' Peace blushed, and stifling laughter, feigned swatting him with her broom. He hopped away, grimaced, and went several more steps from her. He waited, ready for her to give chase.

She would have liked to retaliate, but said, 'No, we mustn't. They'll see us. They'll have us over there in the field near Old Warren Central. They'll have us picking greens!'

Sherbrook was serious. The Tall Ones' new crop had sprouted, but although tender young shoots showed as a fuzzy green haze blanketing the field's surface, the plants were not yet mature enough for real harvesting. Some were gathered and brought back to Grammy for sampling. Hearsay had it, that she pronounced them more than acceptable. He'd learned that before decreeing everyone henceforth regard them as a dietary staple, she'd used the word, "piquant", in describing their flavour. Hearing of it, Sherbrook told young Skip, he was thrilled for her opinion, but when it came to being told what to eat—*for deeks' sake*—he would not accept it! She could keep her greens! Skip's response to Sherbrook's outburst was to inform him, 'That's the very best thing. I've a nasty feeling about those greens, and it has nothing to do with the field—nothing to do with the old warren, nor, any of the unfortunate events, which occurred there. No—it's those greens in their own right.'

Sherbrook would heed all that Skip said. Maybe, though, Skip's opinion was coloured by his strong dislike of Grammy? 'Do you think that your disliking her might have something to do with your feeling?'

Skip responded, 'I don't, dislike her. I *detest* her!'

Faced by such vehement expression, Sherbrook tried, 'Yes, and you know—anyone can be influenced by strong feelings. It's natural.'

'If you eat those greens,' Skip told him, 'you will rue the day. You will be terribly ill, and far worse, besides!' He shouted more of the same, and then departed, leaving a stunned Sherbrook alone.

Peace watched him as she continued sweeping. He could tell she watched, although for much of the time his back was turned to her. Seeing him now so quiet, she asked, 'All right, Sherbrook. What is it?'

He said, 'Nothing. It's nothing at all but then again, maybe it is.'

'Oh?'

Response was not forthcoming, and so, 'Oh, for goodness sake Sherbrook!'

'Yes I know. It's just something Skip told me.'

'Yes? And?'

He stopped sweeping, and facing her, explained, 'Skip told me; if I ate those greens I'd meet with gazuzzlement! It was all very grim. Believe me, he wasn't kadoodling!'

For a moment she was silent, 'He's a strange one isn't he?' And, after a moment, 'Was he upset at the time?'

'No more than usual.'

Peace said, 'We should invite Skip to make Mmeerah.' She decided, 'The very next time we go to the flats, you must insist he come with us, because I'm sure he can benefit.' Giving a last, final flick of her broom, she determined, 'Yes, that's what's needed—I'm certain of it. Then, 'There's another thing I'm certain of. I've had enough of this! I've done enough cleaning-up in the name of co-operation!'

Sherbrook could not agree more.

Looking about, he asked, 'What are we expected to do with our brooms? Do we turn them in? Or, do we keep them?' His expression revealed something of reluctance. He'd grown fond of his, and did not want to give it back.

She said, 'We'll return them, of course.'

* * *

The day came when a crier was sent out from the Hall of Power. He stationed himself outside New Warren Central's principal entrance-way and from there, gained attention by sounding, TUMP! And again, TUMP! This made for fearful pandemonium! Heltering bodies flew this way and that! It was all, wild fur flying and loud-squealed, 'Deeks!' That was, until the crier, again shouting at the top of his lungs, commanded, 'No! No! No!' And he laughed fit to bust, before sobering and telling them, 'There's no danger! Just get yourselves over here. I have wonderful news!'

When they'd gathered and settled, he informed the populace that there was the shortest of time in which to make preparation for an up-coming, very special occasion.

There was to be a coronation.

Grammy would be queen.

She would be known as "Good Queen Lillian". In future they must address her as "Majesty" and none should forget to bow and curtsy if brought before her. As a sign of respect, heads should be lowered when she passed by.

After providing instruction concerning formalities, the crier paused before continuing, 'I have exciting news, and especially, for does!' A teasing tone was employed, 'You'll be beside yourselves with pleasure when I tell you... No, wait for it now...

'Can any of you guess my news? Can *you*, dear? Yes, *you dear!* You—in the pale blue frock—way up there at the back.' Waving his arms about in rather too frantic display of mock-frustration, 'Come along now! There's no call for shyness!'

Violet Brown looked down at her pretty blue dress, as if hoping it might include in the design, a pocket deep enough to hide in.

When friends standing close at either side of her, urged, 'Go on Vi! You *know* he means you! See if you can guess!' Violet raised her head and ventured, 'Has your news anything to do with Haberdasher Frederick? Because I saw him and his wife, Myfanwy, just the other morning, and they were—'

'We have a winner!' the crier interjected, 'Yes, everyone a winner!' And he saw that many of them looking to him from the crowd, wore puzzled expressions.

The gal was not caught out, and so—truth was—the crier was somewhat peeved.

Called upon to answer, young Violet had guessed that the crier's news had everything to do with the haberdasher's dropping by New Warren Central. But, were she allowed an opportunity in which to give a more complete answer, then the crier's imparting his remaining, exciting news would be spoiled. He, official Graymark Crier, did not want the crowd learning, so soon, the reason for the haberdasher's visiting. Before they could know, suspense should build. Proceedings must be drawn out. Fair was fair, though—the gal cowering there at the rear of the crowd had provided a clue to the correct answer.

Possessing cunning means, and trusting again to catch her out, the crier called, 'Your name, sweetie? What do your friends call you?' Shyness returned, and Violet was just the teensiest bit embarrassed. With the focus of so many eyes fixed upon her, her feeling of discomfiture renewed and she could not respond. Hurrying to her rescue, friends cried out on her behalf, 'Vi! Her name is Vi!'

'Now then, Vi—short for Violet! You are a clever young Miss, aren't you? Let's just see if you can tell us... Wait for it everyone...'

Making significant, breathless pause and adopting a conspiratorial expression, deporting as if beset by indecision, the crier enquired, 'Should we ask for more detail, everyone? Shall we? Can we expect a more complete answer from our Violet? Would that be too mean of us? Would it, friends? What do you say?'

'Give a better answer!' Someone yelled.

'Get on with it!'

'The gal is taking all day!'

'Ask someone else, Crier! Ask me!'

Poor gal; decided the crier. She might breakdown and perhaps flee. He almost felt sorry for her. Tears were the last thing needed, and so before it was too late, he snapped, 'That's it folks! We have a winner! Come along now Violet, receive your prize! And he took out a large carrot from the satchel he carried slung across a shoulder. When she refused to move, he tossed the carrot over the heads of the crowd, 'There, you see—a gift for sweet Violet! A gift from the beloved leader!'

The time was come for revealing his remaining news. Haberdasher Frederick had not dropped by New Warren Central without purpose. 'Great generosity—tremendous largesse, is shown! The leader has decreed that new frocks will be provided for does, and there are fine new pants for bucks! All will be attired and look their very best, for the coronation of Good Queen Lillian!'

After the announcement was made and the crier had taken himself back to the Hall of Power, an aid remained with the crowd to provide additional information. Perhaps the crier had not made it clear enough, that the wearing of new apparel should be considered as mandatory? In case of misunderstanding, it should be explained that apparel was not offered completely free of charge, but would be provided at significant, cut-rate price to anyone volunteering to work at harvesting greens.

The crop exceeded expectation by maturing at such an extreme rate, and a time of plenty was ensured.

Piedmont was recipient of an official invitation, but as far as the actual invitation went, he did not think very much of it. The "thing", as he thought it, was delivered by one of Grammy's closest friends, which he supposed was intended as a sign of favour, but it was nothing more elaborate than a small square of cloth. Upon first seeing it, he assumed it must be a remnant of discarded clothing, a portion of a garment deemed no longer good for normal use. He thought it most peculiar, his being presented anything so tawdry, and he wondered if Grammy had further lost her mind. Over recent time she'd gained much weight, and so he decided that she had outgrown the item it was snipped from.

Then, though, seeing Piedmont's blank expression, the messenger informed him that the swatch he held was taken from a length of cloth delivered by the itinerant, Haberdasher Frederick, for the up-coming, grand occasion. It was one of very few, small pieces cut from self-same length of fabric, which would be used as a train for Grammy's coronation gown. Coming from such, it was a memento of great worth! He was well advised to hang onto it, for over time, its worth would certainly increase.

The bard learned that, Haberdasher Frederick, in acting as principal supplier of merchandise required for such an important event, was privileged in that he'd been granted permission to advertise "by appointment" on his chattels.

As Grammy's servant prattled, Piedmont went about scrutinizing the invitation. He could find nothing by way of actual word or mark present; not least scratching was there. He turned the thing over in his paws, held it up close to his eyes and squinted. But, to no avail. Still he saw nothing, other than a square of rather ordinary looking cloth.

Watching him studying it, the eyes of the messenger narrowed as their owner indulged suspicious thought—or, Piedmont believed they behaved, so. Having decided enough was enough, he announced, 'I see—I do… But then I'm afraid that, I don't. Not at all.' Moving his head from side to side with uncertainty of it, he said, 'Because there's nothing here. There's no message.' He let out a great sigh, both his paws dropping to his sides, before asking, 'Look… Perhaps there's been a mistake made and you've brought me the wrong one. I don't mean to appear rude or ungrateful, but perhaps this one—the one you've presented me, is intended for someone else? Someone who doesn't read.' He enquired, 'Might that be it?'

The messenger directed him an odd, disdaining look, before explain-ing, 'There's not meant to be a message—not as such.' She gestured to the invitation he clutched. 'It's a very nice piece of cloth, that's all. It's *symbolic*. It's just to let you know that you are held in high regard.'

'Oh...' responded Piedmont, and then, '*I see!*' He knew relief at last, having grasped the gist of it. He asked, 'I assume then ... you have some-thing more to impart?'

He was informed, 'Grammy will be very pleased if you'll compose a little, light verse, in honour of the up-coming occasion. It won't need to be anything long winded, just something nice. Something sweet and to the point—in her words, "Mere trifle will suffice."' Explanation provided, the messenger backed out from the entryway of Piedmont's burrow, and then was gone.

Piedmont exclaimed, 'Piffle!' And, was compelled to versify:

'Trifle. Mere notion—trifle, say?
Brainchild of wretched she,
Majesty of greens from soil of crypt, once home.
Monarch of rank veg' from yon' greens-patch!
Allow first lady of those say we?
Yea, fair, that much we see,
All agree then, of this place, Queen?
Pray, nay!
Such, should never be!'

All was bent out of shape, natural order disregarded. Sherbrook, often the willing audience for diatribe by Piedmont and others, was by now in complete agreement with complaints made, that was, he reminded himself, with one important exception—exception, kept to himself until now, lest others think him prudish. He had not minded at all, Grammy Graymark's commanding Charlie Noy-Breen and other offenders, to henceforth go about their business, decently attired. She'd decreed that pants be worn at all times in public, and that was not such a terrible thing. He was grateful she'd taken upon herself solv-ing a problem he saw as having personal significance. He'd kept his opinion of the matter to himself, until that was, informing Piedmont of the pleasure gained in his not now being forced to see quite so *much* of others.

Piedmont snapped, 'So you'd swap freedom for a pair of pants?'

Sherbrook responded by demurring, 'Well, all right. Good point and point taken.' But then something of amendment was made. 'Seamstress Rose Briar has made extension to her burrows. The business *is* good for her.'

Piedmont was more than tired of hearing Grammy's cronies euphemistic description of change in so many areas of activity described as her providing "leadership and guidance".

'It's galling,' he complained, 'hearing her employ the good name of Buckminster, in gaining ends. It's just cause for umbrage! Why, I've heard that she claims, Buckminster favoured the decision to send out a party to ascertain the whereabouts of Haberdasher Frederick! The haberdasher, his wife, Myfanwy, and their team, were found at far remove from New Warren Central. After long searching by scouts, they were located all the way over at Gully Warren and once located, were requested to drop whatever it was they were doing and hasten back here in order to satisfy *her* desire!

'As it was told to me,' Piedmont explained, 'she claims that, Uncle, during his "reign"—her use of the word, not mine—always sent out parties to scout out this and that. And so in point of fact she was taking her cue from the way Uncle Bucky saw to the business of leadership! Not just that, but understand this—she claims that he, Uncle Bucky, *approves* her decisions! Present tense—do you see?'

'Mm? Would you explain it?'

'Yes. She believes that she's in touch with him! And now Buckminster, residing in another realm—a realm beyond gazuzzlement—imparts wise advice by supernatural means! She claims such ability! Carrying on communication with those departed is just another of her gifts! I swear, it's madness made manifest!'

Learning of Grammy's belief, Sherbrook laughed. He told Piedmont, 'The madder she becomes—the better it may turn out for the rest of us!'

'Not at all,' Piedmont said. 'No. The madder, the more dangerous is my belief!'

Sherbrook grew serious, then declared, 'The criers have disrespected, Tump.'

He was not present, but was down at the creek when news of the coronation was announced. Hearing of a crier, employing Tump as way of gaining attention, so that an announcement could be made, Sherbrook was incensed. Learning that none present thought to raise voice in protest was cause, he believed, for deepest shame. In expressing outrage now, he was still irate.

'It's outrageous behaviour—the misuse of Tump! In the event of danger they could go flibberty hopping straight to the jaws of gazuzzlement, all the while believing they're going to receive gifts of prime produce! The lieutenants and helpers toss stuff out as reward for "good" behaviour. Grammy's commandeered the lot. You can be ordered to pick, for example, carrots, as punishment for doing just about any trivial thing, but no one's allowed to eat them. They're kept in reserve. An ordinary thing, once known as a carrot, now goes by name of "Royal Beauty"!' Seeing Piedmont's involuntary wincing and accompanying look of disbelief, Sherbrook insisted, 'It's true—honest!'

'You're saying, she's glorified a carrot? She's granted it a title?'

Sherbrook nodded. The bard's expression of astonishment was taken as definite encouragement. 'Yes, and she has onions and garlic, taken from the Tall Ones' planting place, hanging from tunnel walls. If you happen to pass anywhere by the meeting place—I mean—the Hall of Power, and then look up, you'll see them there—onions, chives, garlic. They claim, having those around the place, "bad influence" is warded away! After relating the information, Sherbrook waved his paws all about baring their claws. He raised his eyes in mock-horror, showing their whites; producing an expression, meaning, "…strange creepiness is abroad."

Piedmont did not smile. 'There's just *one* negative influence hereabout,' He paused for a moment and then said, 'There's another thing I know, Sherbrook. I'm not at all able to versify as she wants.' He lowered his voice, fearful of being overheard. 'I won't do it. I just can't bring myself to it!'

The bard sounded very desperate, and so by way of helping a friend experiencing dilemma, Sherbrook offered, 'You could always lose your voice. That would work. They wouldn't know it was pretence. You could croak a lot—sound very choked up. You might even gag. That could be very convincing. And if you like, I wouldn't mind at all, doing the talking for you. I could explain it all by telling them you've come down with something gruesome. We can even think up a name for it—something horrible sounding. We'll tell them it's unfortunate, but ill-health won't allow you to sing her praises.'

'Praise *her?*' Piedmont muttered, feeling lost. Whilst Sherbrook's plan, if put to another, might be heard as representing an opportunity for hope, for Piedmont it just would not do; he could not pretend.

After thinking for a moment he responded, 'I'm grateful for your consideration and for the kind offer, Sherbrook. Please don't think I'm not. It's just that I'd not be comfortable living with myself. If I were to extricate myself from the mess by such means, I'd feel burdened and ever trouble over it.'

'But, you did say, Grammy expects, mere trifle,' countered Sherbrook. 'I figured—going about it my way—she'd get even less.'

'No.' Piedmont announced, 'All I can do is set forth with courage as ally, and inform her in forthright manner, of my refusal.'

'What? You can't do that!' Envisioning the venerable bard put to toil in sweeping droppings, the picture that sprang to mind was not without humorous aspect, but then for the most part, it was sad.

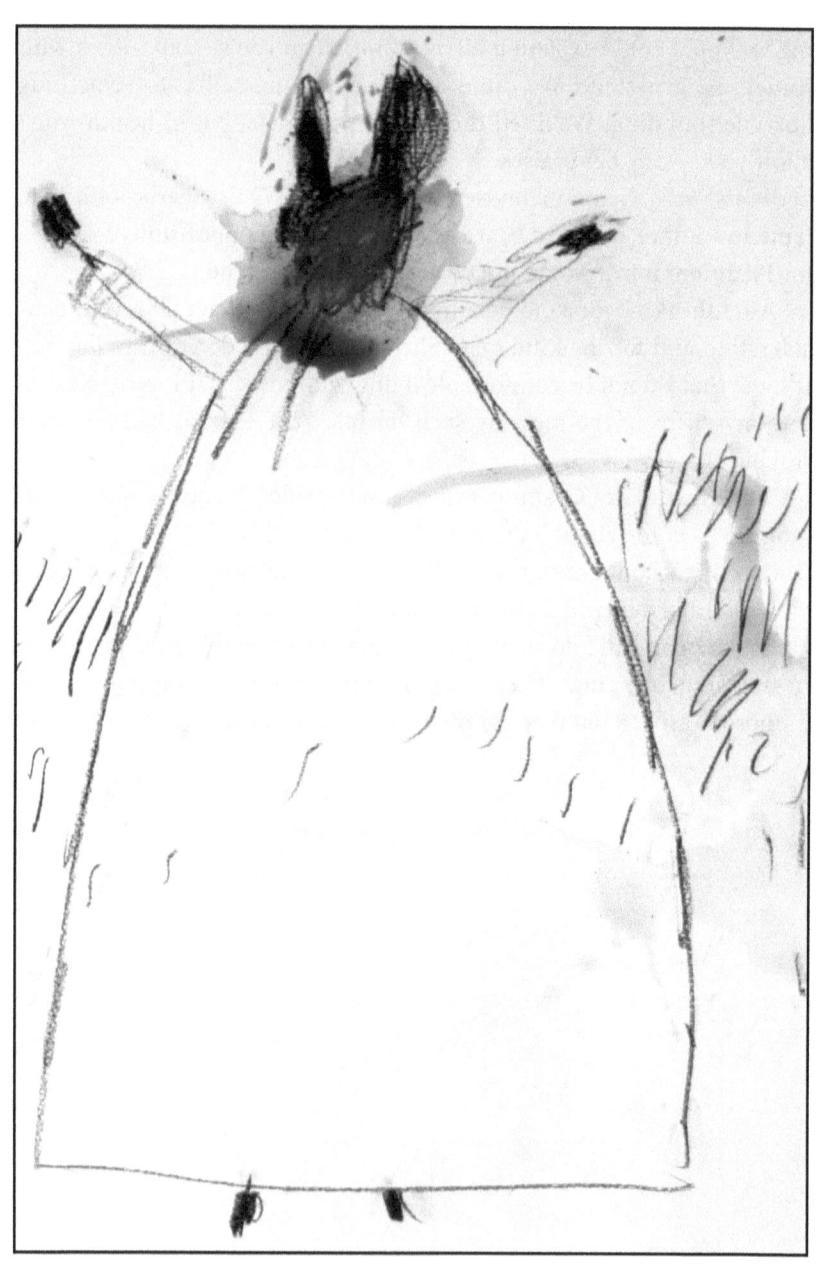

Grammy

QUEEN OF GREENS

Onlookers gathered to witness his penance, few came to deride or mock, and those who may have thought of doing so, soon enough realized they would receive short shrift from the rest. Piedmont was not set task of sweeping droppings, but was condemned to a far worse sentence.

Most came to offer words of advice, for, it could not be said that he was any good at broom making; nor was he penitent. Put to such toil, the venerable one at first sight, made for a novel spectacle, but over much time he'd given of himself in versifying, and many now saw opportunity in his predicament, to repay something they felt was owed him.

Advice took the form of instruction. Many helpful hints were proffered, such as: 'That's right, Bard—hold the straw with one paw. Get it all to the same length! And now, with your other paw, wind those lengths of long grass around and around. Make sure you have enough long lengths of grass for the last part! Quick now—weave in and out, with your grass... Yes! That's it!' And whenever Piedmont got so far—at about that point, 'Oh, deeks!' And, 'Oh no!' As, nervous and distressed, due to a natural ineptitude, he dropped everything. And so the process was begun over again from scratch. His brooms would not suit the fastidious—even those most careless would determine his product as not of much practical use.

No few of those attending Piedmont's ordeal, had themselves, at some time, served time beneath the oak. Sentries did not favour the presence of spectators, and at first instance of them gathering had ordered them to move on, but when numbers increased, they found there was little they could do to discourage the curious from showing up.

Piedmont's sentence was harsh; he was to spend as many as eight long days there. It was noted, that by not doing a thing, he was treated with more severity than those who committed a positive offence. He was always polite and respectful, never made droppings in public, and he'd never failed to wear pants.

There was nothing wrong with going there to offer the bard support, but what if a way were found to punish the rest of them for doing nothing. They joked that there was not space enough beneath the oak for so many wrongdoers, and asked, whoever would have use for so outrageous a number of whisks? Incarcerating, and setting to work such crowd as they, the great number of brooms produced would very soon form a mountain.

At first when onlookers called advice they were ordered to desist, but it was brought to the attention of those in charge that all they were doing was well in line with their sovereign's rules pertaining to good and proper behaviour. They were making themselves helpful by showing kindness and consideration to an oldster who was finding the going tough.

Someone protested, 'Just look at those old paws of his! Why! They're gammy, half crippled things! In any case, an individual of his standing and past generosity should be granted leniency! He's not had a day's real grace—not in living memory! If you ask me it's unjust! There's some hereabout, ought to be ashamed of themselves!' Having voiced open protest, the brave-hearted one dared wink to friends. Pleasure was gained in knowing opinion was shared, and then several others spoke up in support of the sentiment expressed.

'Perhaps you'd like to join him over here?' the lieutenant cautioned. 'In any case, no one's interested in your opinion. No one gives a hoot for what you think!' But, she was mistaken, because soon other voices joined in pleading; the punishment dealt old Piedmont was a crying shame and should not be allowed to continue. But continue it did, for day upon dreary day until the crowd increased in size to such extent, the recalcitrant himself recognized a crisis point was reached. It was then, Grammy Graymark, Queen of Greens, (as he named her) deigned show herself at the oak.

Regaled in finery and flanked by those of her entourage, she made for an impressive sight. As she moved forward, the crowd of lesser folk divided, making way for her. As, Piedmont saw it, they divided as a flock of starlings is rent, when a predatory hawk swoops in their midst. And then, Grammy Graymark drew herself to full height, towering over those around her. Never by any means, a diminutive individual, she'd grown larger of late and, seeing her now, Piedmont muttered, 'Obscenity...' under his breath, and let a misshapen broom he'd been toiling over, drop at his feet. 'Yes, Majesty—what is it? Here to gloat are you?' The crowd was silent. She waited before answering, and then, rather than address Piedmont, swung around so that she faced the citizenry.

She drew in a long breath, producing characteristic whistling, and then after pausing, enquired, 'Can't you trust?' To which no one replied, for none quite knew what was meant. It could be a trick question. 'Here we are,' she next said, 'enjoying another glorious day, courtesy of, Great Grandfather, and granted beneficence: fresh air, sunshine, clean babbling brook—all just, at paw. All we can hope for, to eat—including a most wondrous new crop, the like of which has never before been seen. Need I go on? Need, I? With every good thing provided in abundance, every need satisfied, what do you do? You come here to gawk at an individual who refuses to ply his trade in an honest, useful manner!'

She would not deign glance his way, but continued. 'He's shown himself undeserving of a place amongst decent folk. Do any of you know *why* he's here? Do you? Of course you don't so, I'll tell you.' She waited for a moment to pass, and then continued, 'He was asked to compose a little something in celebration of the upcoming occasion, a grand occasion, planned for the enjoyment of all, regardless of rank or standing, but when requested to compose a short verse—in point of fact, a one-liner—he refused! In his arrogance he decided we were not good enough for his over-rated talent. He's made it very plain. He no longer considers us worthy of his time. He went on—in *my* presence—threatening to leave New Warren Central! Do you hear? Yes, he thinks to desert us! And I'll warrant good greens, he's not revealed any of it! Well ... has he?'

She swung back to face Piedmont. 'And so young Piedmont, rather than allow you the luxury of martyrdom, I've decided upon kindness. It's the best thing in dealing with your type. I hereby decree, leniency granted. You may sweep droppings for the remainder of the sentence. You will make a better job of it, the lightest of tasks, than you have here! Those *things* you produce look more like rat's tails than whisks!' In making a sly aside to Piedmont, she offered words to the effect, 'Noblesse oblige eh, Piedmont?' and then went back to working the crowd. She announced, 'Now my lovelies, we're in for a very special treat—a banquette, dear hearts! *Yes, a wonderful, lavish affair!* Every fine thing is provided, including white radish rosettes, topped with fabulous, delicate garnish of greens! They're one of my absolute favourites! And on this occasion, they're for everyone! *Mm, ambrosia*—palates will be over the moon! There are sweet, wild berries for the children and, daresay some of the mothers will want to indulge? Better watch waist-lines though!'

Patting her large abdomen, in commiseration with those she imagined as sharing affliction, she chortled merrily.

And, on cue a crier called, 'Proceed this way everyone! Come one—come all, to the Hall of Power! First in, first served!' Piedmont dusted his paws one against the other, and watching others flibberty hopping for free delicacies, smiled for the first time in days.

The guard told him, 'Here you go, Piedy—give me that rubbish of yours! Here now, this is a good one. Take it—and report back here to me tomorrow. I'll show you then, where you're to sweep. Go on. You've time off! I'm doing you a favour old-timer, so wipe that smirk off your face, before I change my mind.' He wasn't about to change his mind though. He wanted to be at the banquet along with everyone else.

***

Sherbrook, Peace and Skip were not there at the oak, and so, did not see Piedmont released. They were on the flats, creek-side, making Mmeerah!

When told they wanted to involve him in something, named Mmeerah, Skip shrugged in agreement. Peace was very pleased; the boy was a lot easier to recruit than Sherbrook had been; tales involving livestock were not needed.

She was mystified though, and cast Sherbrook a questioning glance, when, Skip said, 'I've been looking forward, for a long time now, to trying this.' Sherbrook's expression revealed he was as curious as she, he'd not told Skip anything of Mmeerah before this morning. Had, Skip, Peace wondered, happened upon them, making Mmeerah. She must trust, the boy's nature did not allow he went out of his way to spy on them.

She gave simple instructions and they proceeded. 'Mmeerah!' Mmeerah carried out across calm waters of the pond, and overhead, courting swallows cavorted in magical display of flight. A spindle-legged spider walked upon water, in searching out prey, and went too far from safety, because a dark mouth, coming from beneath the surface, opened, and the spider went into it quicker than a heart's beat. A soft gusting breeze creased the pond's surface as if smoothing away blame.

'Mmeerah!' Skip chanted. 'Mmeerah!' Continuing the chant, even after the others had finished with it, Sherbrook thought he heard as well, the sound of excitement drifting down to them from up the slope. Peace, looking to Skip, smiled. Then, Skip finished Mmeerah, and exhaling, declared, 'Oh! What a calming feeling!' And, 'You're very clever, Peace, to have discovered it.'

'Why, thank you, Skip, it's sweet of you.'

'No, not sweet.' Skip said, for once not sounding the least combative, 'It's true. You are a "shining one".'

'A "shining one"?' Sherbrook asked, 'What is that?'

'You're a "shining one" as well, Sherbrook. You should *know* that.'

Peace realized, Skip's sincerity. He offered something, she thought, in return for her teaching; he was grateful for them including him. They were a small group, sharing a common interest.

Skip was very often hesitant. Having declared them "shining ones", he reverted again to shyness, seeming no different than at other times. He sat there, paws resting in his lap, offering nothing further. Moments passed and, Sherbrook, as if about to address none in particular, said, 'It's most interesting…' And then glancing to the boy, commented, 'You're a most talented individual, aren't you?'

Skip, facing Sherbrook, and sounding not shy at all, said, 'Yes.' And then, after a moment, 'And, so are you.'

'Me?' Sherbrook was curious. Skip was not known as the Seer, for nothing; it did not pay to forget with whom one spoke. Might he see something in another that others could not? But then, Sherbrook was disappointed, because, Skip told him, 'You don't shine all the time, Sherbrook—not as Peace does.'

Whatever, shining was, learning that in Skip's estimation, *his* shining was less impressive to that of Peace, Sherbrook felt deflated, until Skip added, 'Although, *when* you shine, your light is most bright.'

Peace was fascinated and enquired, 'How about you, Skip? You must shine?'

He gave her the gentlest of smiles and then laughing, said, 'Oh, me? I'm just so radiant! I have awful difficulty getting to sleep at night!'

They'd never seen him so happy. Never before this had Sherbrook heard Skip come even close to joking about himself. *This* Skip was altogether different, no longer self-deprecating, or the least difficult to get along with.

But after a moment of quietness, he said, 'Hard ones do not shine...'

Glancing away, Peace looked out across the pond and then up to cloudless sky overhead. She commented, 'It's such a glorious day.'

Sherbrook said, 'Yep, sure is a good one.'

'The best, of my life,' Skip said.

It had taken so little, Peace thought, for him to open up to them. They should have asked him to join them a lot sooner than this.

And, Skip saw light emanated from her in long, gold-white lines, radiating bands and languid moving swirls.

Sherbrook sprawled on his back in the lush grass, paws supporting his head, a long, part-chewed stalk of dry grass hung from his mouth. He nibbled at the end of it, and looked up. High overhead, a Bird of Habit scratched a familiar, white streak against the soft blue background of sky. He heard a faint rumbling as it passed into the distance. A youngster had once asked him, 'Do Birds of Habit suffer tummy-rumble?' He'd had to admit not knowing why they sounded the way they did. Birds of Habit always flew an unaltered course. They never flapped their wings, but soared. They never threatened; they were not at all as Brother Eagle. Sherbrook puzzled over Skip's talent. Some considerable time ago, Skip claimed guidance, received via a vision, and had insisted that they would move to a far better place than Old Warren Central. The prediction had not come true. Grammy's restraints and rules had assured that such happy outcome did not eventuate and the fact of life being so joyless up on the slope, mattered. Sherbrook had thought often of the possibility of moving away from New Warren Central. Perhaps he might at some later time, but what penalty would he incur, were it known that such action was planned? What punishment might be dealt?

His thoughts were interrupted, by Skip's declaring, 'It's almost time!'

'Time? Time for what?' Peace asked. Relaxing in the long, soft grass, she'd almost drifted asleep, but Skip sounded very wide-awake.

'It's almost time to rescue Piedmont the Bard and leave New Warren Central, almost time to climb the hill! And then after that, everything's fine!'

The words were rattled off at lightning speed. Peace sat up, and, for several moments Sherbrook was quietly thoughtful. He directed the boy a long and penetrating look, before determining, 'Skip, you're a *lot* better at what you do, than ever you've let on, aren't you?'

Skip told him, 'Yes, I am. I daren't open my mouth, though, because if I do, I'm accused of kadoodling or worse! Folk believe me, every kind of trouble.'

He returned Sherbrook's stare, his expression alert, and he appeared ever so mischievous. Sherbrook smiled. He exhaled the longest sigh, and what he next said, filled Peace with doubt and foreboding.

'Best get to it then, eh, Buckaroo?' He asked, 'Tell me—what do I do next? You might as well let me in on it, and then I won't be too surprised when it happens!'

Peace shivered, 'This has me very concerned,' she protested, 'Sherbrook, You're making me nervous. Why can't we just enjoy the afternoon?'

Skip said, 'Remaining here by the creek, is not what we do—not for much longer. We do as I said.' He was defensive. 'I just see it, you know, this stuff. I don't make it up. I'm not crazy!'

'I don't think you're crazy,' Peace assured. 'But, I don't have to like what I hear. I don't have to approve of what fate holds!'

Her "light" was proof of sincerity.

Sherbrook's light showed that despite any doubt, he would push forward. He wanted to believe. He wanted to trust the power of seeing. No sooner did Skip see Sherbrook's light than Sherbrook got to his feet, declaring, 'All right then. Let's go Buckaroo!'

But, immediate departure was stalled by Skip's revealing, 'Yes, but, Peace isn't coming with us.'

And hearing him, she was very relieved and wasted no time in agreeing, 'No, I don't believe I shall.'

She behaves, thought Sherbrook, as if refusing a suitor's invitation to dance. She does not realize that destiny will not be denied.

Skip told her, 'Go to the foot of the hill, Peace, and wait for us there. It's all right, because no harm befalls you. And you don't have too long to wait before we join you.'

She did not appear reassured.

Following his release, Piedmont had not gone anywhere, but remained in the vicinity of the oak. With Skip leading, they went straight there, and upon their arrival they saw that apart from the bard, no one was about. Piedmont was surprised to see them, and was most affable in greeting them, 'Hello; I thought you'd be at the banquet.' He said, 'It's where most of them are. The promise of filling the stomach is a powerful motivator, and she, Queen of Greens, relies upon it.'

Sherbrook wasted no time, but taking Piedmont by an elbow, told him, 'We will get you a good stick as soon as we can, something to help you get along, but for now, I'm lending you a paw.' He asked, 'Now—see the hill, there?'

'I do. Yes.' Piedmont scratched at his whiskers. See the hill? Of course he did! Experience of the last several days was disorienting, but had not caused him to lose his grip on sense. Sherbrook had some or other proposition for him, and, Piedmont hoped it was not anything too testing.

Then, Sherbrook asked, 'How far is it to the top? How far is that, would you reckon?'

'Well now,' said Piedmont, staring up at the hill, 'I can't say.' Going along with Sherbrook, he continued in surveying the hillside. 'No, I'm afraid you've got me there, friend Sherbrook.'

Sherbrook studied Piedmont. He asked, 'Why don't we leave right now, and find out?'

Broom making was frustrating and exhausting, but that which Sherbrook and young Skip now proposed, was impossible. Piedmont could think of a hundred reasons to disagree with expectation. He could never climb that hill, but perhaps tackling impossibility was preferable to staying hereabout. There were those times when thinking too much did not reward, and so, pushing away enormous doubt, he volunteered, 'All right then, I'm with you!' He added, 'Right behind you, will be more like it!' Even that much would present a challenge for him. Then, having just declared a willingness to accompany them, 'Oh, no! Wait—I'm forgetting!' He exclaimed, 'I can't do it! I was forgetting the scratchings! I don't know how they slipped my mind, but I can't go off and leave them. Doing so would be to my undying shame. I can't abandon them—*not to her!*'

'The scratchings won't be lost.' Skip told him, 'I promise you, you *will* have them again.'

'As you say, but how can you know? You can't be certain.' Piedmont was frantic with worry and shook his head. They might not have much time. If their departure was to remain undiscovered, they must hurry.

Sherbrook advised, 'Piedmont, trust Skip!' And, to his relief, after glancing over a shoulder to the oak, and releasing a shudder, Piedmont's mind was all but made up.

'I shall try doing that, friend Sherbrook. Yes, I shall.' Looking then, to Skip, he said, 'You're a fine boy, and I trust that in giving assurance, you're sincere, but understand that the scratchings are our most important record. They're not a complete, literal record, of course, but they do represent the history of our kind and are of inestimable worth.' Piedmont reminded himself that, Bucky always took information provided him by young Skip, with seriousness. At times, those things learned had daunted even, Bucky, and now, as custodian of scratchings, Piedmont could not deny the urge to seek extra assurance. He asked, 'Can you guarantee it? The scratchings are safe?'

'Yes.'

'Then,' determined the bard, 'Best not tarry. Yon' mountain waits!'

As they set out journeying, Sherbrook told him, 'We'll miss out on the coronation of course.'

'Yes.' Piedmont said, 'That opportunity's lost and it's upsetting, but I'll try not to dwell upon it.' He returned Sherbrook's smile.

Skip then revealed, 'She never gets to wear the crown, because, before it can happen she chokes on a stick of celery and that's the end of her.'

'You're joking!' Sherbrook exclaimed. 'You see so much?'

'Sometimes, I wish I didn't,' Skip replied. They moved up the sloping path to where Peace Darkling awaited their arrival, where the path became steeper.

'Such gift, must sometimes seem more, a curse,' Piedmont muttered. He thought, before enquiring, 'But if she soon meets gazuzzlement, our leave taking is not so imperative, is it?' They were leaving New Warren Central, but glancing up from the path, it looked a dreadful, long way to the top of the hill.

Skip said, 'Yes. But there's destiny as well. We don't turn back; we keep going, and anyway, if you stay here they will still make your life awful. They will torment you for a very long time to come.'

'How's that?' Sherbrook asked, sounding defensive on the bard's behalf.

Skip said, 'When Grammy Graymark is gone, they say that the cause of her passing, was a broken heart.' They'd almost reached the place where Peace waited.

'Ah, bruk heart...' Piedmont murmured.

Skip said, 'Yes, that's right. Their claim is that during her finest moment, you let her down. You refused to honour an old friend. Envy got the better of you.'

This was impossible to credit, and Piedmont shook his head in disbelief. It was too bizarre and nothing he wanted to hear. He protested, 'I let *her* down! Deeks!' The oldster never uttered expletive, and Sherbrook gave Skip a glance in warning. They must not upset the bard, not when he was expected to climb such a steep incline.

They went on in silence, and had progressed not much farther, when, to their dismay, out from behind a large bush, stepped Lucille Cropper!

The friends halted, rendered speechless, until Sherbrook cleared his throat, then offered, 'Why, good afternoon! Lieutenant Cropper, isn't it?' Giving his best smile, 'Yes. I remember you from just the other day!'

Studying him with narrow-eyed suspicion, Grammy's lieutenant enquired, 'Whisk duty, wasn't it?' Her smile was most condescending, and, Sherbrook noted for the first time, that one of her front teeth was chipped. Her appearance rather suffered for it. It was puzzling, he realized, because after noting the defect, avoiding focusing attention upon it was extremely difficult. He must not stare but speak! Some control of the perilous situation must be maintained, but as he opened his mouth, uncertain of what he might next say, a rustling was heard. The rustling was coming from the largest of those bushes behind the lieutenant, which meant that the lieutenant was not here alone.

Sherbrook's response to the situation was automatic, 'Oh? Affair of the heart is it?'

Lucille Cropper tensed. Judging by her expression, she would like to slap him for his impertinence!

Knowing danger, Sherbrook wondered how he might respond if threat turned to action.

Ever a pacifist, Piedmont knew his time was up. He would expire, right then and there, without further testing the course. His legs had gone to water and must soon give way under him.

Young Skip flibberty hopped, approaching the lieutenant, and, extended a paw, upon which rested a small, bright-gleaming object. Courageous in approaching the lieutenant, Skip now addressed her, offering, 'She who returns this to Grammy Graymark, will receive favour ever after. You will be esteemed above all others!'

Lieutenant Cropper, staring down, knowing what rested there, was not able to restrain herself from exclaiming, *'Why, it's the cameo!'* The legendary, Graymark keepsake! The boy was a known kadoodler, but on this occasion he spoke the truth. The item he held was of inestimable worth!

Overwhelmed with excitement—as fit to bust—she snatched it away from him!

Skip said, 'Yes. It's the cameo.' Witness to such display of greed, he asked, 'Will you be the one, to take it to her Majesty?'

Greed became avarice then, and wickedness glinted in dark, squinting eyes. The lieutenant drew herself up, and, in measured tone, she said, 'Now, just one moment you lot...'

Possessing the cameo meant elevation to the highest rank was foregone conclusion, but charging these three with theft and delivering them to Grammy. What might that mean? Prospect for further advancement seemed limitless!

They were far upslope from the warren, which meant that they were up to no good—despicable trio!

Wasn't the selfish, geriatric bard, supposed to be attending elsewhere? Broom production, wasn't it?

She'd always owned a bit of a lame-ear when it came to his stuff, and had feigned appreciation of it. He could have knocked out a few easy lines of fluff for poor Lillian, but had preferred upsetting her, by refusing. And as for, Skip the *so-called* "seer"? The boy was a thief and now she'd proof of it! There was Sherbrook. What of him? He was always a bit thick. He should know better than associate with such element as this!

They must be taken to stand before Grammy, and in short order, but then, reason gave pause. If news, of she and a "friend" spending time together in the bushes, got out … what then? After weighing potential for embarrassment against a future rich with reward, she demanded, 'Raymond, make yourself decent! We're arresting these three!' She thought, *we're going to be famous*! Nothing else mattered!

The accused ever diverted attention; a miscreant's prattle ought never receive benefit of credulity. If, in learning the worst, Tootles Cropper, her spouse, wanted to make trouble, then it would be dealt with. He was already suspicious of her and Raymond spending so much time in each other's company.

Ray would not want to be left in the shade when reward was due. His type did not hang back. He would not deny being with her. By now their presence at the banquet might be missed. She pictured Tootles down at the Hall of Power, searching amongst faces for hers; and denied a smile. Even a gollystomper, bearing treasure of the sort the Graymark cameo represented, would forever be protected; held fast to the regal bosom!

So raced Lucille Cropper's thoughts, all the while, until Skip, who'd not backed away from her, announced, 'And now you will farewell us! You will allow us to leave.'

'Oh, Raymond, did you *hear* it!' the lieutenant exclaimed, looking to Raymond, who'd come out of hiding to lend his support. She laughed, 'Can you believe your ears?' And Raymond, grin spreading across his countenance, shook his head at the idea of the boy's foolish audacity.

Skip was unfazed, 'You *will* let us pass,' he insisted, and in the moment of him speaking, a thinnest beam of white light shot from Lucille Cropper's paw! It went from hers and shot straight to his!

Again he told her, 'Let us pass, Lieutenant, because—look! Do you see now, what it is that I hold?'

There was the brooch with its bright-shining, filigreed edge, and at its centre—the graved portrait of a Tall One doe!

Lucille Cropper was agog! She examined her own paw, turning it this way and that. She knew she must hold the cameo! She'd clutched the precious thing, but now *he had it!*

Her paw was empty!

'Step aside now,' she heard him order, 'because we're leaving!' With that he tossed the brooch back to her. She heard the boy-seer, telling,

'Take the trinket back to Grammy Graymark. I give it to you, but if you think to follow us, the brooch will be gone before you reach New Warren Central, and you'll be seen by all as the worst kadoodler *ever!*'

Lucille Cropper and friend Raymond stood dumbfounded. After the trio moved off, following the course of the narrow path, they heard Skip calling back to them, 'Are you sure you have it, Lieutenant? Be sure you keep a certain grip!' They heard laughter from him, but the despicable ones were no longer in sight.

Within a short time, the three met up with Peace. She stepped out from behind a large boulder, telling them, 'I thought you'd never get here. I wondered if I was abandoned.'

Apologizing, Sherbrook explained, 'Something of a problem was encountered, but it was well taken care of.'

Later, when they were progressed into the climb, Piedmont, between short breaths, declared, 'I don't know how you did it back there, Skip. I've never before seen the like, but I'm most thankful for it.'

'By the way—just in case anyone's interested,' Skip said, 'I did not *steal* her brooch. I found it one day, where it lay in the grit at the bottom of the creek. It was glinting there and it caught my eye. I'd gone down the path to the crossing place, thinking about poor Uncle, and when I got there, I looked down—and there it was.'

'Yes, but the other thing—quite wondrous!'

'You mean, the "moving"?'

'Ah, then, that's what you call it.'

'Yes.' Skip shrugged. He said, 'Maybe I did take her brooch. I've thought about it an awful lot, and I guess I might have "moved" it to the creek in the first place, but I didn't *steal* it. Stealing a thing, and moving it are two very different things. When I was younger, I had no control over "moving" things. In fact—I still don't.' He said, 'Back there on the path, with the lieutenant, we were lucky because when I moved the cameo from her paw to mine, it was the first time I've managed "moving" anything to just where I wanted it.'

Hearing him, Peace raised her eyes skyward and gave silent thanks. Sherbrook had taken the lead and they went single file. Bringing up the rear, Peace was too far back to hear all they said, but she trusted that, Piedmont would not slip and tumble back. She wondered where they might lay their heads for the night, and thought that she might ask Skip to see ahead so that they might know.

In response to a query from Sherbrook, she heard Skip say, 'Yes, I knew it would happen, of course I did. I folded my ears so as to not hear, and I squeezed my eyes shut. I couldn't bear knowing what was to come. I couldn't prevent any of it, and so, I hid in the long grass until it was over.'

They spoke of Uncle Bucky's demise, and, Peace wished that Sherbrook would not upset the boy by further alluding to the painful event.

Finding the going tough, she called ahead, 'Can we rest?'

Piedmont cried in support, 'Hear, hear! I second the motion!'

Skip told them, 'There is a big flat stone. It's just before the very top of the hill. We stop to rest there and the view is flabbergasting!'

ROOF OF THE WORLD

'Just look at it!' Piedmont exclaimed, 'This might be Great Grandfather's view of our world.' Scanning the valley, he said, 'It's a long hop to the top, but well worth it—way across there you can see the Tall One doe!'

Raising the stick supplied by Sherbrook, when they set out, Piedmont pointed to where the farmer's wife, in the yard so distant from them, was busy hanging washing on a line.

'Even from here, you can see that line's full to overflowing,' observed Sherbrook, 'Haberdasher Frederick will be thrilled. It's decent of them, providing such abundance.'

Peace commented, 'Yes, where would we be without them? It reminds me, I've got what I'm wearing, but this old thing's not going to last long. It's threadbare. I should have thought to bring another.'

A preoccupied Skip, said, 'Way over there, where the valley narrows, that's Gully Warren.'

Sherbrook said, 'That's one long flibberty hop all right.'

Piedmont said, 'There are far more greens than I would ever have guessed. See the extent of plantings! That crop covers the valley floor!'

Directing their attention, he swept the stick in a wide-drawn arc, encompassing the vista. 'The colour of the new crop is different to that of earlier plantings. There's a blue tinge to it, and it's dark.' He continued, 'You'll have noticed the field down this way, adjacent to the one where old warren was situated, carries an earlier variety of crop, and the colour is lighter. For several long moments he was thoughtful, then said, 'I'm wondering... Did any of you, by chance, eat those greens?'

'I haven't, said Peace. 'As you say, it's dark—unnatural looking stuff. I did pick some, but thought better than eat it.'

'How about you?' Piedmont enquired, looking to Sherbrook.

Sherbrook responded, 'After vowing never to touch the stuff, I did try some. Mind you, it was just a nibble, and then I spat it out. I couldn't bring myself to go along with the idea of being *ordered* to eat it!'

Piedmont turned to Skip, who, needed no prompting, 'I would never!' he added, '*I* told Sherbrook—*don't* eat it!'

'That's right, he did,' Sherbrook admitted. 'He said I'd grow six legs and gazuzzlement would take me—something along those lines. At the time though, I confess, I thought the advice a bit panicky sounding, but in any case, I did *not* swallow. I didn't enjoy the taste.' Then, 'Why are you looking at me that way?'

Skip, shaking his head, stared at Sherbrook in disbelief. 'How,' he asked, 'could you be so *thick?*'

'I just forgot!'

'You, *forgot?*'

'Yes. It slipped my mind, but then I remembered what you told me— and I decided you might not be joking.'

'*Joking?* But I never joke—not about anything!' which was true; he didn't. Piedmont interjected, 'Deformity?'

'Oh, how dreadful!' Peace exclaimed, shuddering.

Skip asked, 'What does it mean ... deformity?'

'When a babe is born lame, with, for example, a misshapen foot, such is deformity,' Piedmont said,

'Or two heads,' Sherbrook said, pleased with the offering. But then, not so pleased, because hearing him, Peace gasped, 'Oh, Sherbrook, how *could* you?'

'Just contributing,' he said.

To none in particular, Piedmont said, 'Perhaps a more accurate, defining word would be, mutation...' He enquired of Skip, 'Envisioning the creatures, what do you "see"? Can you describe them?'

Skip said, 'Yes. They're strange and ferocious. They have four hind-legs—not just two. They have forepaws the same as ours, but theirs have much longer, sharper claws. They're strong, *much* stronger than us, and they helter like lightning! They don't wear clothes, but have bright coloured stripes—all the colours of the rainbow! They have enormous front teeth, more like fangs than teeth, and they dribble and drool a lot.'

'I think I should cover my ears and not hear any of it!' Peace exclaimed.

'What do they get up to, these monsters?' Sherbrook enquired.

'Yes,' Piedmont asked, 'Are they an insurmountable threat? Is there anything we can know in order to deal with them? Do you "see" a solution?'

'Apart from not eating greens in the first place, no, but I guess it's already too late for that. Everyone down there's crazy for the stuff!'

'Mm,' Piedmont thought hard. He said, 'There must be something.'

'There might be.' Skip said, 'I don't think they'd cause so much trouble for everyone, but for one thing. You see there's someone they take orders from. Later on, far ahead in time, he...'

He could not finish, for in that instant came a terrible kazooning from behind and above, and tearing of air, all about! Such frightening kazooning had them flattening themselves, clutching at the large stone upon which they sat.

For Skip, the smallest member of their intrepid party, it was too late!

He felt sharp, piercing talons engage with tender flesh, and knew the nightmare had begun! Brother Eagle—had him! Wanting to faint dead away—ignoring the pain of his body, where the great bird had merciless hold, and looking down, he saw the others—good friends, staring skyward—following the eagle's flight. They were helpless in seeing him carried aloft!

Terrified, and yet, seeing the terrain spread out below, Skip saw the horizon to every point was distant enough to appear as nothing more than a misty blur!

He'd not "seen" anything of Brother Eagle taking him! Gazuzzlement would be next, and second sight was not needed in recognizing the truth of it! Down there, far, far below, was New Warren Central. It appeared so small that he wondered over seeing it at all, but there it was, where the thin line of the creek dog-legged, appearing as a dark silver ribbon set into the land.

Up here, so high, the wind blew strong; it ruffled fur and chilled to bone. From nowhere then, came a great roaring which threatened to overwhelm every sense. And, a great bird—one far larger even than Brother Eagle, was hurtling towards them at terrifying, mind-numbing speed! The eagle let out a wild, desperate screeching and banked in flight! The great Bird of Habit was there—and then gone! It thundered off to disappear in misty distance, leaving in its wake, an atmosphere so turbulent that Brother Eagle, losing control and spinning from dizzying height, might plummet and crash down! As the monstrosity flashed by them, impossibility was glimpsed. A Tall One had waved to Skip, from a round-shaped opening—an opening set into the great bird's side!

Next, there came an almighty CRACK! CRACK! CRACK! The sound was like lightning splitting asunder not one tree, but at once, a forest of trees! And the sky turned dull-wintry grey. In that instant of altering a splitting occurred. Still held in cruel talons, Skip witnessed both his and Brother Eagle's "shadow-selves" soaring away! It was kadoodling madness. His eyes deceived him, because such could not be!

Brother Eagle, clutching him still, banked again, and they soared downward, losing altitude at an incredible stomach-churning rate until, regaining control, the eagle levelled out. Searching the vista stretched out below nothing was as should be. There was a grouping of rust-coloured trunks, trunks of large trees set high upon the slope above New Warren Central. There was grey mist, but no … smoke issued up from those trunks! And so they were not trees, but smoking towers! Even from such distance, these were far taller than those towers set above the roof of the Tall One's dwelling place!

Searching then for sight of the Tall Ones' home, he could not find it. No familiar field spread out below, but rather, the land was covered by water. An enormous, widespread pond reflected dull light from a grey sky. Water lay everywhere!

Brother Eagle's talons gained more secure hold in the flesh of his back and he winced, whimpering with pain. Despite the unfamiliar nature of all he saw, despite every disturbing difference, he wished *with all his heart,* that he were safe down there! And, unexpected altering occurred… It was as if the sky blinked—an instant of dark nothingness occurred. Then, bright light flashed, dazzling him, and he was rolling through tall grass! A strange sweet scent filled the air, and he tumbled like an apple, tossed down-slope, before finally coming to a halt. Then, staring skyward he saw a dark-soaring dot, and knew that Brother Eagle soared away towards dense grey cloud at the far end of a long, wintry valley.

Winded and panting, he heard himself muttering, 'Oh, deeks!' If he could speak, then his injuries might not after all, be too terrible, but further thought was beyond him.

There was the sound of a voice then, and hearing it, Skip knew he was not well at all. This was gazuzzlement—final gazuzzlement, because that familiar voice was unmistakable. Always well intentioned, Uncle Bucky had shown up to welcome him into the after-life and was asking. 'Are you okay, young feller?' The enquiry was repeated, but Skip could not respond, he had fainted clean away.

* * *

Applying a poultice of healing herbs, which was made up for her at the apothecary, by Isaac Stone, she declared his injury not so serious as first thought.

Isaac Stone was most solicitous in offering to close up shop and return home with her to take a look at the patient. She told Isaac that she did not think his doing so was necessary, at least not, as yet. If the boy's condition worsened, then she would accept his kind offer. She would, she said, ask Buckminster to go there and fetch him, but with the passing of the following three days and nights a definite improvement was observed.

Her name was Lillian, but he had always known her as Grammy Graymark.

She asked, 'Perhaps you'd like some more vegetable broth? We must build your strength. I have heaps in the cauldron. When you feel up to taking a little more, just let me know, dear, and I'll fetch it for you. I'm always close by.'

Upon first recognizing her, he'd felt as if struck by a blow. Invited to sample her "cooking", as she referred to it, he had recoiled in absolute horror. His revulsion was expressed with such vehemence, that she believed he suffered delirium, that he was half out of his mind. Making reassuring soothing sounds she tucked a rug close around his frail body. She wanted, she insisted, to provide comfort, telling him, 'There now sweet boy, you mustn't fret, because everything's fine.' Perhaps she was right and madness had him in its grip, because none of it could be happening.

He enjoyed the broth, although, in the beginning it was strange sipping warm food from the thing she called a spoon, and despite most of it dribbling down his chin, he was not able to avoid tasting it. When he did, he decided that it was nowhere near as bad as expected.

Noises were unfamiliar and strange. There was the clattering of cutlery, of pots and pans. There was the sound of something referred to as the "grate", when Buckminster went about the chore of cleaning it. There was interminable squeaking as the oddity, Buckminster sat in, rocked back and forth carrying him with it. There were too many things of which he had no idea—strange, unfamiliar odours and much else; a barrage to frail senses.

Always, she was there. 'Now youngster, take something. Please do. Just a little.' She insisted in pushing food at him. He heard, 'I've gone to so much trouble! It's seasoned with white radish and rich green parsley.' And for a good part of the time, at the foot of the soft thing, Skip lay upon—the thing referred to as a "pallet", was Uncle Bucky. Lillian received every encouragement and support. 'He's in the very best of paws my gal. You'll have him put to right in no time. Care and nourishment will have him up and about. You'll see!'

'I wish I had your confidence, Buckminster. He's still weak and frail, and I can't think what else might be done.'

'Keep on as you are, pet. Patience will have its reward.'

So attentive and kind were they, that he must recover, and in the fullness of time it was so. During convalescence his feeling toward her softened and he came to see her not so much as, Grammy Graymark, but, as kind Lillian, good companion to his old friend and mentor, Uncle Bucky, or Buckminster, as she always called him. They both shone, but still, it was a long time before Skip felt that he could trust her. His physical condition improved, but the ability to envision future events was slow to return. He saw beyond the present, but as if through a mist, and he feared never again "seeing" with true clarity. He must accept the loss, he thought, but then came more definite signs of improvement and his relief was enormous.

A day came when he delighted in telling Lillian, 'There's good news for you, and you do not have long to wait.' He was correct, because soon a messenger arrived, conveying news of an expectant niece, who, residing at some considerable distance from Brickfield, was blessed with the arrival of four bouncing babes. Receiving the news, Lillian was so thrilled that she did not think of asking after Skip's knowing of the happy event ahead of time, and so, explaining was unnecessary.

Later he asked, 'Does anyone hereabout ever call Buckminster, Bucky?'

Lillian laughed, 'No dear, I don't believe so. Is it a name you have for him?'

'Oh no, but my name's Skip, and I've often thought that, Skip has the sound of a nickname to it. It's not, though, it's my given name and is all I've ever been called. I wondered over the name, Buckminster.' He said, 'Buckminster … it's a longish name.' She was quiet for a moment and then asked, 'A "nickname", you said, didn't you? What is that dear? I can't say I've heard that one before.'

Smiling, he told her, 'Oh, it's nothing, nothing at all.'

Communication was very often frustrating due to so much being different here. Buckminster and Lillian's burrows and chambers, were lined with russet-coloured, sharp-cornered stones. They told him those stones were "bricks", and enquiring where such unusual stones came from, he was astonished to learn, 'Oh, they're not found! No, we *make* them!' He could not at first, believe them. Buckminster went on to explain, 'Clay, for bricks, is taken from the ground, from a big hole called a clay-pit, and then the clay is formed into bricks. After shaping, they're stacked in a kiln for firing. Kilns can be described as enormous ovens.' Gesturing to the kitchen stove, he elaborated, 'Ovens, such as Lillian's—yet different—a lot larger and far hotter.' He said, 'I'll take you to the yard sometime and show you the process.' He said, 'A kiln is sealed and bricks are baked or fired, at very high temperature. They are then, as you see them here.' Buckminster waved a paw indicating the walls, which curved upward and then arched over-head so they formed the ceiling of the room they were in. He said, 'Hereabout, most burrows are lined with them.'

Lillian said, 'Except, there are some who still like the smell of soil.'

'Yes,' Buckminster agreed. 'Some are sticklers for the old ways. They're entitled to choose as they see fit, but most enjoy the sense of security gained by brick-lining.'

'And it makes a place a lot easier when it comes to cleaning. It sets me on edge, thinking of all that dust and dirt!' Lillian said, 'I didn't take much convincing—did I, dear? We had the burrows made-over quite a ways back, when the kilns were first established.'

'How was the idea discovered?' Skip asked.

'Ah, well now, that was all, Weed's doing … wasn't it, Buckminster?

'He's a clever one, our Weed. You see, Weed made a doll…'

Skip had no idea what dolls were, and enquired, 'A doll?' And then rued asking, because conversation again went off at a tangent.

Lillian explained, 'Dolls are toys, dear.'

Before Skip had chance to enquire further, 'Toys are things children play with. Dolls are small figures, not always, but very often, made in a child's likeness.' Husband and wife glanced one to other, knowing that explanation seemed ever necessary.

Buckminster would relate the story of Weed.

He began, 'Weed had mud on his boots...' But then he paused before exclaiming, 'Now, don't ask about boots!' He relented, 'Oh, all right, if I must. Boots are something similar to my slippers. They're foot coverings also, but are intended for far more rugged use. In any case, Weed's boots were muddied; he'd been across the valley visiting a gal or three. Upon his return to Brickfield, he went to the town square, where, during cold times, a welcoming fire is maintained. Whilst there warming himself, he scraped at his boots and in doing so, he noted that the stuff was clay, a sticky type of dirt, as I'm sure we're all aware?' The boy must know what clay was? But then, when first seeing Lillian light the fire in the kitchen stove, they'd a hard time calming him. He'd not seen a stove before. Pushing aside thought of the distressing incident, Buckminster continued, 'Relaxing after journeying, Weed found that he'd rolled a lump of clay, 'round and 'round, in absent manner, between paws, until a ball was formed. Seeing that ball resembled a head, he then thought it might be good idea to fashion a doll. Until then, dolls were most often made of woven grass and sticks and stones, those types of materials. So, Weed made a doll of clay, but then he decided that he didn't think very much of it, and he tossed it into the fire.

'During wintry times, that fire is kept burning all night long. Brickfield Town Square is common ground ... a place shared with passers-by. Folk of Brickfield offer hospitality to the benefit of many. As example, Clever Tinker and his good wife Myfanwy—purveyors of home-wares and other useful things, often camp there, as do bands of travelling minstrels and a variety of other folk.' Buckminster said, 'By my mentioning minstrels, I'm reminded of *Brick Yard Bunny Club* and an upcoming event. The trio have honoured Folk of Brickfield, by changing their name from, *Fur-boy Ramblers* and are expected to play at the Worker's Party, which will be held at the yard. You'll soon be well enough, my boy, and we must attend! You'll enjoy yourself, I'm sure.' By now Buckminster had lost his bearings completely.

'Buckminster...'

'Yes?'

Bricks, dear?'

'Ah yes. Thank you, Lillian. Now, where was I?'

She reminded, 'Weed has thrown the doll onto the coals.'

'That's it, yes!' Impatient with himself, Buckminster drew in a breath, and following long exhalation, explained, 'Weed's doll was found on the following day, and was discovered to have turned to stone! That's the fact of it...

'After giving the matter much consideration, Weed then had the idea of brick making. There was no real kiln back then, nothing of the sort; fire-pits were used at the start. Everyone lent a paw and I helped out with digging the pits. There was a great sense of industry, and I recall those days with fondness. Many paws make light work, but again, I digress.' He scratched at his nose, then said, 'When we had the burrow made over, we felt that we'd come of age, as it were. Didn't we, Lillian?'

'Indeed yes! That day was Tump sent!'

'Praise Tump.' Buckminster said, and then recalling the high cost of lining the warren, he said, 'I worked three full seasons at the communal gardens before we finished paying it off.'

Skip thought, "Tump sent? Praise Tump?" And, reminded again that he was very far from home, attempted staying on topic by enquiring, 'How are the bricks held together?'

'Ah, well now, that's an altogether other story,' Buckminster said.

Thinking of mysterious beginnings, of mystery in general, Lillian said, 'There are those who say, Weed dreams many of his answers. They claim that Tump grants him unfair favour.'

'Yes, indeed they do,' agreed Buckminster. 'But, such notion is naught but errant foolishness. Weed is an inventive and hard working fellow, and an individual of his sort need not depend upon divine intervention for his ideas.'

So ... their name for Great Grandfather was Tump.

Lillian would not abandon the subject of mysterious cause. She said, 'There's Weed's eldest, the gal, Nancy. It's not just him alone. They claim is Tump blessed.' Before Buckminster could interject, Lillian said, 'She's blessed with the wishing trick.'

Skip queried, 'She grants wishes?'

'No. That's not it. It's nothing outlandish as that. It's a true gift, though. If, for instance, a child is having problems in understanding a lesson, then, Nancy can help. Even the most backward child, after looking into Nancy's eyes, finds a way through difficulty. If something of value is lost, such as a ring or brooch—the owner will easily recall when and where it was lost. Her mother, Mavis, jokes that her cakes rise higher, when Nancy is about the place. She claims the gal's presence is all that's required. That's the wishing trick.

WEED'S YARD

'Come along boys! Shift those barrows! Get 'em moving!'

Thus commanded an individual Skip recognized as Sherbrook. He was not Sherbrook though, but one known hereabout as Weed.

Skip did not know quite where to focus his attention. In facing conundrum, he felt an odd mixture of curiosity and nervousness.

With a cheery wave, Buckminster called across the muddy yard, 'Weed, I'm showing the boy, around—we won't be in the way!' Weed called back, 'Go right ahead, Buckminster.'

Looking to Weed, Skip determined him a little older in age than Sherbrook.

Buckminster was saying, 'I worked in construction of those kilns over yonder.' He turned then, and pointing in another direction, said, 'Over there is where clay's brought into the yard. It's later pushed into big wooden frames, which are used to mould the bricks, and then after setting out in the sun for a while, the raw bricks are barrowed to the kilns.'

Not all bricks were the same colour; there were pale ochre, dull brown and russet shades. Buckminster informed, 'The original clay-pit filled with water some time back, and was abandoned and so the clay now used, comes from a considerable distance upstream. It's barrowed all the way from there to here. It's not a job I'd enjoy!' He said, 'There's a dam upstream and water-flow is controlled by a sluice gate, a simple but effective thing, and another of Weed's bright ideas. There's ambitious talk of widening of banks and further damming. There's talk of then transporting clay down-stream to the yard, but if the proposal's acted upon, much of Brickfield town will go under water. Many will be forced to establish homes on higher ground, and of course, they'd rather stay put.' Expression serious, he said, 'It will never happen—at least, I won't see it.' Advantage of age meant that at least he and good wife Lillian would be spared such uprooting.

'For the meantime,' he said, 'bucks have families. Greens must be provided! So, needs must. It's barrows all the way.' Skip was absorbed in studying new surroundings and learning all he could, but possessing scant knowledge of almost everything Buckminster spoke of, his comprehension was minimal, and soon, talk of the unfamiliar passed through one ear and out the other.

He hoped his boredom did not show, but when Buckminster mentioned greens, Skip was alert. He asked, 'Greens?' And Buckminster, misunderstanding, protested, 'You're joshing! Aren't you? Are you claiming that you don't know what greens are?' Having traversed a narrow aisle between tall stacks of bricks, they came out onto a broad muddy area. Skip said, 'No. But what *type* of greens, do you refer to?'

'Oh, by Tump!' exclaimed Buckminster, 'How would I know what each and every buck might choose to provision his table with!'

Skip knew, explaining would be useless and apologized, 'Sorry, Buckminster. Of course I know what greens are! But, I meant...' Exasperated, he exclaimed, 'Oh, just forget it!'

Buckminster was sympathetic, 'It's just another of our misunderstandings and nothing to fuss over.' He was vague as to what next to show, but gazing about the yard, said, 'I know. Let's go across there to the office and we'll see if young Nancy's here today. You'll enjoy meeting Weed's daughter, after Lillian's talk of powers and magical ability. What do you say? Shall we do that?'

'Mm, sure,' Skip said, and wondered, 'An office?'

They went across the yard and skirting several large puddles, Buckminster commenting on the unpredictable nature of weather, said, 'It's been very changeable of late. Just when we think a dry spell is due, it comes bucketing down.'

They arrived at the office, an aboveground structure built in the form of a dome. There was a large door and next to that, a small window. Workers queued by the window and were given chits, Buckminster said, which represented payment, a record of work done at the yard and exchanged elsewhere, for other goods or services.

Earlier on, Buckminster had taken pains to explain doors. Wherever Skip hailed from must be primitive indeed, but in providing endless explanation, neither he nor Lillian derided the boy for his ignorance.

Word had spread fast in the territory, and by now everyone had heard of the strange boy who went by the name, Skip. His unusual arrival creek-side—out of nowhere—bearing injury inflicted by Brother Eagle meant he might have come from just about anywhere. His luck was remarkable, because Brother Eagle, releasing prey, was all but unheard of.

In answer to Buckminster's rap at the door, a pretty gal wearing a pink dress opened it. 'Hello, can I help you?' she said, and then recognizing him, 'Oh, Buckminster! I expected it was someone wanting to place an order. I'm filling in for Marjorie, who's off sick again. Father's so busy and he can't do everything. Mother has her paws full, looking after the others, and, I was asked to help out.'

Hearing Marjorie mentioned, Buckminster recalled a recent conversation with Lillian. After returning home from a recent trip to the apothecary, she complained, 'That, Marjorie was there again—harassing poor, Isaac Stone. She told him, his remedies are *ineffective!* The nerve of some! She's never well, but always at gazuzzlement's door! In all honesty though, I could not see too much was wrong—not, so far as her health is concerned. Weed should replace her. She's never there at the yard. Working for a living is beyond the ability of some.'

Buckminster had asked, 'What does she say ails her?'

'Oh, I don't know—some or other, awful-*itis.* But my diagnosis is bone-idle-laziness.

* * *

Nancy said, 'I've been sitting here, bored witless, no one's come by—no customer, that is.' She asked, 'You, didn't want to place an order, did you?' No, Buckminster wasn't here for that. Before he could respond, she noticed Skip, and declared, 'Hi there, stranger. You're the mystery boy who showed up down on the slope, aren't you? Come inside! Come on in and tell me all about yourself. Just wipe your feet on the mat. It's muddy out there. The rain's made a dreadful mire of the yard.'

Buckminster introduced them saying, 'He's lucky to be alive, of course. Falling from the sky isn't something a body should expect to survive! Skip's a good fellow, we've grown very fond of him.' He said, 'I hoped you might be here, Nancy, and thought of introducing the two of you.'

She exclaimed, 'Oh, yes! I'm so glad you did!' To, Skip, she said, 'I've heard about what happened—how Buckminster found you. To have the chance to talk to, the *actual you*, well—it's wonderful!'

They were comfortable in each other's company, Buckminster thought. She talked nine-to-dozen as always, and Skip seemed unable to stop grinning. He said, 'I might leave you youngsters to get to know each other. I'd like to go and see if any familiar faces are about.' He asked, 'You wouldn't happen to know, if old Cranberry Jack's still working?'

She thought for a second and said, 'Retired, I think. You'll have to ask Father about him.'

Buckminster excused himself, with, 'Yes, I'll do that. I'll be back soon. Nancy will look after you, Skip.' And so, he made off to find old friends.

With, Buckminster departed, she declared, 'I must say, you were fortunate, surviving the horror of being taken—but, having Lillian and Buckminster to care for you afterwards was *very* lucky.'

Nancy was easy-going; it was as if they were ever acquainted.

She chattered full-tilt, non-stop and he found it unnecessary to contribute much at all. Buckminster was correct earlier, about his wanting to learn all there was to know of the wishing trick, but there was no need yet, to mention it, because tomorrow, Nancy and he were to spend time together in the forest, and then he would learn all he needed to know. A vision had come flashing to mind. A vision as clear as the sound of the bell, which rang out each noon-time at the yard, so that workers knew to down tools for lunch. As he convalesced, he'd waited in expectation of its chiming, sounding throughout the valley.

Buckminster had returned to the office, and then, as they'd made to leave for home, Skip happened to have glanced out across the yard, where, standing by a tall stack of bricks he saw a young boy. The boy, stretching on tiptoes, had reached overhead and taken down a brick from the top of the stack. Half turning then, so that he faced Skip, he gave a cheery wave. The strange thing was that Skip had recognized none other than *himself!* Simple amazement preceded downright shock, because the next thing was, form shimmering, the individual had changed shape, transforming, to become a Tall One! The Tall One wore a blue suit with a white striped collar, which covered the shoulders and hung down at the back. It was tied at the front in the manner of a kerchief. With a cheeky grin, the boy turned away, and next—vanished from sight! He disappeared in the brightest flashing of light! Whereupon, Skip collapsed into a puddle of muddy water lying adjacent to where he and Buckminster stood!

Neither Nancy, nor, Buckminster had witnessed anything least extraordinary apart from Skip falling. Following his initial surprise, Buckminster bent low and lifted Skip from the mud. In wearied tone, he told Nancy, 'I'll get him home now to Lillian. Our outing's been too much for him. That's very obvious. She'll know what best to do.'

During mid-morning of the following day, Nancy came knocking at Buckminster and Lillian's door. Greeting her, Lillian exclaimed, 'It's such a treat having you visit, dear. Come in! Come in!'

'Why thank you, Lillian.'

'Here now, let me take that for you.' She took a cloth covered cane basket from Nancy, and set it upon the floor of the small foyer.

'It's a grand idea—a picnic! Your father called by earlier and told me of your plan. I assured him that, Skip is up to going out. He's fine. He needs to get out again—out in fresh air and sunshine. He should not be involved in anything too strenuous, but it would be a shame to waste such fine weather. They're in the parlour—both my boys! Come through, Nancy.' She called, 'Buckminster! Skip! Our guest is here!' She said, 'Take that chair, Nancy.' And as Nancy went to sit, 'Oh tut, I *must* have these antimacassars seen to—but I don't suppose they're too terrible! Set yourself down, dear.'

'Lillian—don't fuss, so!'

'Oh, it's all very well for you, Buckminster,' Lillian said.

'Should I put the kettle on?' Buckminster offered.

Nancy protested, 'You mustn't put yourselves to trouble on my account.' Rising to leave, she said, 'Really, we should go—shall we, Skip?' But, seeing Lillian's look of disappointment, she was patient.

As small talk, Nancy said, 'I have lemonade in my basket, and all sorts of delicious treats. I do hope you like lemonade, Skip? Mother makes the best lemonade you ever tasted!' Her light was bright. He knew nothing of the beverage, and so he responded to her question by shrugging.

Lillian enquired, 'Before you youngsters set off, I wonder, Nancy... Will you grant a small favour? I have misplaced my locket.' She explained,

'It was my most precious possession. It was a gift from Father, to my Mother. After her passing, it was given to me.' Expression forlorn, she said, 'Now, it is lost…'

Nancy was sympathetic, offering, 'Yes, of course, Lillian. You must come over here—sit close by me.'

'I'll move, said Buckminster, Here you are old gal, take my chair.'

With Lillian seated and comfortable, Nancy instructed, 'Lillian, you must not look *at* me. You will relax now. Let go and relax as if drifting. That's it. You are drifting on the softest cloud. You are not looking at me. You are looking "into" me.'

Then, after just moments, a delighted Lillian exclaimed, '*Yes—I see it!* I was outside tending the garden—toiling at the hollyhock bed and being so occupied, I did not notice when the clasp broke!' She said, 'You must all excuse me while I go and find it.' Soon, when the precious heirloom was located, there came whoops of joy from outside.

In her relating detail of the wishing trick, Lillian had said, 'The gal says nothing at all…' which was not an accurate description, thought, Skip, but he was impressed anyway, by a successful result being achieved. Lillian had no more than glanced into Nancy's eyes and then she had accurately recalled the location of her missing item.

He was eager now, to make a departure, to start down the winding path to the circular clearing in the ancient wood, where, surrounded by great ancient trees was a pleasant place to picnic. The picnic basket would be unpacked and then relaxing into each other's company and enjoying a very fine lunch, they would have Brother Fox to contend with. He saw all of it, and in the sharpest of detail.

With Nancy acting as the clearest imaginable channel for focus of his ability, their immediate safety was assured, and too, the brightest of futures would eventuate.

She was the key to so much, and if they worked together—mind-staggering phenomena must result!

Fox!

She said, 'I'm not sure, I understand. What is it that you *do?*'

He said, 'I see future events and can move things about.' He amended, 'I see things, but not always with clarity. And, I should admit—I haven't yet succeeded in developing much accuracy with the moving. I'm better with seeing future events than I am with moving stuff.' He looked down at his paws in his lap, then said, 'Apart from those times, when I'm afraid I don't see much of anything at all. I don't know why it is, but there *are* those times when, try as I might, I'm left feeling frustrated and flabbergasted. It's just the way of it.'

Nancy said, 'My gracious...' and directed him her best smile. He smiled back. She had thought him, not the least shy, but now he seemed nervous in her company. They were sitting on the picnic blanket that she'd unfolded and spread upon the grass. In the wide forest clearing, they were surrounded by magnificent giants of trees. Great branches spread wide and high overhead and patterns of soft, magical light dappled the forest floor.

After unpacking the basket and arranging the contents before her, Nancy wondered whether to offer first, the lettuce rolls or, she wondered, might he prefer to start with a little of Mother's fine cabbage slaw? She started by pouring the lemonade.

Skip was quiet since her, "My gracious..." but now he ventured, 'You think I'm kadoodling, don't you?' He sounded defensive, and she wondered whether she should feel challenged. They were here for a nice time and if anything of disagreeable nature occurred between them, then it would be due to no fault of hers. Having determined it so, she wondered whether or not Skip was too impressed back there at Buckminster and Lillian's, when seeing her little performance? Maybe he felt bound to compete with—or somehow measure up, by offering something he imagined might equal the wishing trick? If it was anything of the sort, then she must behave as ever she did, when challenged by those of competitive nature. She would dismiss the matter by adopting an easy-going, nonchalant manner, and at the same time, not demean her ability. But now, Skip asked, 'May I look into you, Nancy?'

About to pass him a cup, she instead, put it down on the blanket before her. She sighed, and then, said, 'Oh all right, if we must. I'm not at all certain of your intention, but I'll agree to try.' She gave him the softest look, and he moved closer to her.

Looking into, Nancy, he was aware of a deep and all embracing passivity. Her stillness was similar to that demonstrated by Peace Darkling, but there were important differences. The calm neutrality of Nancy was not the same as that calm experienced in practicing Mmeerah. It was peculiar, he thought, because engaging with Nancy's ability he was reminded of the way he'd felt long ago, whilst lying on the meeting house floor of Warren Central, staring into the mesmerizing valves of the old Radiola. After looking into her for just a moment, he turned from her, and asked, 'May I borrow the picnic basket?' And without waiting for her agreement, he willed it "move", so that it floated upward, away from where it had rested upon the grass, and soon it was suspended in air above them. The basket glimmered, and surrounded by a faint halo of white light, it went higher and higher. His sense of control was complete at last. Accuracy was maintained, even when he look away from her.

Nancy knew astonishment as she watched her mother's basket sailing up there amongst highest branches; she realized, she'd misjudged him.

'Oh, my...' she murmured, entranced, 'I had no idea you meant *this*.'

Preoccupied with watching the basket's meandering flight, he said, 'Oh, it's nothing, nothing at all. There are much better things we might try.'

The truth was that, something important was learned. Unlike that time he'd moved Grammy's brooch, transferring it from the Lieutenant's paw to his own, he'd not moved the basket in an instant to other location. No—this was slow moving, and he'd wondered if such were possible. Now, with the question answered, he said, 'Let's see if I can make it dance!'

Squinting and peering upward, he had the basket dance a jig. Against a backdrop of clouded-sky and leafy treetops it jiggled about then swayed back and forth. He said, 'When things move this way, it's as water flows.

A current pushes, and I feel it. Fast moving is accomplished in an instant; the sensation is nothing the same.'

'I see,' she said, but she didn't, and unable to keep from doing so, she giggled. She declared, 'Oh, you're adorable!' She leaned forward to embrace him.

'No—no!' he exclaimed. 'The basket's wobbling about. It's not going where I want it!' Hurrying on, he told her, 'And besides in just a moment or two, I'm going to have to move a fox.'

Nancy felt twice daunted.

Seeing her fearful expression, Skip said, 'Yes. He's hiding over there behind a berry bush, and believes us unaware of his presence. Don't be afraid though, as soon as he shows himself, I'm going to put him up there with the basket! We'll see him vanish and then reappear—right before our eyes. Trust me!' He shifted his attention back to the dancing basket.

She stared at him in disbelief.

Brushing away a hovering fly, he said, 'All right now. Stand up and face me. I'm going to look into you again. Yes, that's it.'

She had done as asked, but then, Nancy glanced away. 'No.' Skip told her, 'You must look to *me*—not *him*.' He said, 'Here he comes now. He knows we're on to him!'

The fox came out from behind the bush, and after slinking part way towards them, halted.

Without removing his attention from Nancy, Skip addressed the fox, 'Hello there Brother Fox. What's new?' The fox said nothing. Further lowering his voice, Skip urged, 'Nancy—the wishing trick! *Please* calm yourself.'

She was not calm, but terrified!

Skip insisted, 'Know that we're safe! Just float on a cloud as you told Lillian.'

Float on a cloud! It was ridiculous advice! She quaked so much that her knees shook! But, she squeezed her eyes shut and after ordering herself to calm, reopened them.

'That's better,' he said, smiling and, turned his attention to the foe. The fox was not young, and might not be so fast afoot as once was, but appearance could deceive.

'Listen up, kadoodler, we're not the least afraid of you,' Skip said.

Staring into uncomprehending, hideous, yellow eyes, 'You're in for a shock this time, Brother!'

He might have said more, but even as he finished speaking, the fox leapt to action!

Shrieking in horror, Nancy clutched at Skip!

No longer under direct control, the picnic basket had descended with a slow, lilting-leaf motion, until, it dropped the remaining distance, delivering the predator a glancing blow to the head, the basket bounced off and away into tangled undergrowth. Startled, the fox hesitated for just an instant—an instant was long enough! As Brother Fox sprang, and was almost upon them, Skip acted. White light flashed and the foe vanished!

Pointing to a place high amongst branches above, Skip announced, 'Yes! There he is—just where I meant him to go! Do you see?'

'I can't believe it!' Nancy exclaimed.

High overhead, perching aloft and striving for balance among thin branches, the fox voiced a woeful cry!

Then, was a far louder sound—an almighty, atmosphere rending, CRACK! It was so loud that they dropped to the forest floor, to then cower in fear. A too sweet scent filled the air.

Skip exclaimed, *'Deeks—what a kazooner!* I thought we were goners!' After getting to his feet, he said, 'It's the same sound that I heard just before Brother Eagle dropped me. The *exact* sound!' So upset was Nancy that she stamped a foot in frustration, demanding, 'Oh, *please*—what just happened? How did you *do* that?'

He was nonplussed, but then protested, *'I* didn't do it! That wasn't *me!'* He pointed to where they should expect to see Brother Fox. 'Just take a look!' Skip exclaimed, I moved him up there! But, look!'

They could crane their necks all they liked, staring overhead made no difference at all, because the fox was no longer there.

Shivering, Nancy declared, 'I don't like this at all. We're messing with something neither of us understands!'

Skip said, 'I did nothing to cause his disappearance, but someone else has. Whoever they are, has moved him...' He glanced about the forest clearing and in doing so, felt foolish. He said, 'I should mention that I had not the slightest inkling that it was to happen.'

Nancy said, 'It's far too strange.'

He said, 'Yes, but I think we should carry on with our picnic, and I have a great deal to tell you.'

* * *

When he was younger things went missing. They had moved even without his knowledge. Objects disappeared and were never seen again. Now, though, the fox had vanished, and its vanishing was not due to his doing. There was the matter of seeing himself yesterday at the brickyard. He'd witnessed a version of himself altering to become, of all things, a Tall One! So much was puzzling and disturbing.

If, Sherbrook were here, he'd tell him, 'Get a grip, Buckaroo! You can figure it!' And so, he must set to fathoming mystery.

Withholding nothing, he would tell Nancy of his world.

He spoke of many strange things, and after hearing him, Nancy declared, 'Your world sounds very peculiar to me. I don't mean to be impolite, but I can't imagine myself making do with so little or getting by without things, which here, are taken for granted. If, for example, old Isaac Stone were told of your world, a world without herbal medicines, he'd never believe such a sad truth! And, as you tell it, there's no knowledge, even of making *fire!* My goodness, I'm all but speechless!' she said. 'Even the humble brick has not been thought of!'

He said, 'I didn't expect you to decry the place.'

'Oh, I'm not. Not at all...'

'It sounds that way,' he said, feeling offended and knowing he should not have told any of it.

She replied, 'I think your friend, Peace Darkling, sounds wonderful.'

Hearing her speak well of Peace, he was mollified, and agreed, 'Yes, Peace is a shining light.'

'And—what did you say, she calls it? Mmeerah? Is that it? You must teach me it! Come on, Skip, you can show me now.' Knowing, Peace would want him to pass on the knowledge of Mmeerah, he proceeded in sharing something of his world—something she'd found not lacking.

Never before was the haunting mantra, Mmeerah, heard in Nancy's realm, and now, two small chanting voices flooded space encompassed by the great forest. Ancient trees, not so aged here as those of the forest of Skip's home realm, knowing altering of energy in true living hearts, returned something of themselves, and Nancy, a clear and perfect channel, was aware, as movement passed through stillness, of subtle yet meaningful altering. After time passed, she would remember their afternoon, not because of the fearful antics of Brother Fox, not for happiness shared in fine company and miracle working, nor tales of an impossible place, but for a very special gift passed on by a friend. If other worlds existed beyond this, then, Nancy thought, Mmeerah should resonate throughout them all.

But, Nancy did not rhapsodize; she made no comment at all. After chanting she remained still for a while, noting differences in the way surroundings were now perceived.

Skip laid back enjoying the soft comfort of the blanket upon the lush grass and stared up through the foliage to the clear sky, until, Nancy announced, 'That sweet scent, which was present after Brother Fox vanished? I know what it is! It's the smell of sweet cinnamon buns!' She said, 'First thing tomorrow morning, I shall take you to Mother Tulip's bakehouse! When her buns are taken from the oven, you'll know I'm right!'

'Buns? I'm afraid I haven't heard of those. There's something I can tell you though. I see that tomorrow morning we won't be at a place run by anyone called Mother Tulip. I see us doing something altogether different.' He paused for a moment, focusing, then exclaimed, 'Oh, deeks! *You can float on water!*'

She thought for a moment, then said, 'I have my little boat, *Missy-Belle*, if that's what you mean.' Prideful, she said, 'Father gave me her, for my last birthday. He said things were going so well at the yard, he could afford me having her. *Missy-Belle* is my treasure. Mother had reservations at first. She insisted I would tip out and drown, but Father got by her, and so, yes! I can take you out in her. We can go out tomorrow if you like.' She said, 'But, as you've already seen us doing it, I don't suppose it will be anything very special, not as you've more or less done with it.'

He said, 'No, it's not at all the way you imagine. I see things but it's not the same as doing them. Seeing is not the same as experiencing. It can be quite confusing, like double vision. Whilst I'm focused on the present moment, at the same time, I'm seeing tomorrow.' For several moments neither of them spoke. Then smiling, he said, 'Just by the way—I know of a cow named *Missy-Belle*. But then, that is not her name.'

'A cow?' Nancy asked. 'And, what, do tell, is a cow?'

He looked past her, seeming absent, then said, 'A cow is just a… Never mind!' Grinning, he said, 'It's what we shall say whenever we're tired of explaining things. We'll say, "Oh, that's another *never mind*." Not knowing the meaning of every second word is exhausting. Important things must be explained, but as for the rest, too much is confusing.'

She agreed. Considering their conversation, Nancy said, 'The worst of mysteries, are those you call Tall Ones. I cannot imagine sharing a world with giants having charge over destinies of others, by use of monstrous creatures called churners! Vile, home-wrecking things! I don't doubt a single word. To *my* mind though, it's unacceptable!' She then said, 'I'm reminded of a myth of ours. Folk sometimes remind youngsters that, if they misbehave, the Nem can get them. Nem were creatures of time long past.' She declared, 'Your Tall Ones are the Nem, but with one difference. The Nem are imagined and so were never, in true sense, real.'

'Well,' Skip said, 'There's nothing folk at home can do about it. Tall Ones are there in our world, and so we coexist.' He said, 'There are ways in which the arrangement is useful, because they provide many of the things we need.' He said, 'As example, there's my jacket, the one I'm wearing.' Touching a paw against the jacket's lapel, he said, 'This came from a Tall One's penance line, by way of Haberdasher Frederick.' He said, 'Frederick's not so much a friend; he's more of an acquaintance to all … an itinerant merchant who barters goods. He deals in clothes and fabric, bone needles and thread, things of those sorts. He works a team who take penance offerings from Tall Ones' lines.

'Tall Ones put out items of apparel for us. Things are left out, as compensation for past ill deeds. In gathering, we always ensure not too much is taken from any one line at a time. It's just not done. And, we can never know whether Tall Ones are offended before they act against us, as with their churning. They are erratic and unpredictable creatures.' He said. 'Not too much, is taken from the planting place, either. Although, the planting place is not so much about penance.'

She said, 'I like your jacket, I think it's very nice and it suits you.' He was pleased by the compliment. But then she enquired, 'Aren't there those who spin and weave? Are there those who harvest and dry rushes for papyrus? Papyrus used for disposables, such as the napkin I gave you earlier—or those who take wool from wild caesurr in the hills? What of those things?'

He picked a long thin stem of grass and stuck an end of it into his mouth. He lay back, and chewing on the stalk, recalled friend Sherbrook doing the same. He told Nancy, 'Every one of those questions can be answered by saying "never mind".' Closing his eyes, he heard her soft laughing.

* * *

The following morning, Skip awoke with a head splitting earache. He blamed the almighty kazooning sound, which was heard in the forest during the previous day. Apart from a throbbing ear and pounding head, he experienced a subtle sense of foreboding, but in puzzling over the latter and coming up with no answer, he dismissed it as nothing serious enough to worry over. Boating, as Nancy had described it, was more harmless fun than fear inspiring, and they would spend the day together doing just that. He'd seen them, safely boating on the lake and yet a feeling of trepidation persisted, and he wondered if it might be wise to alter their plans.

He had seen something of Piedmont, but the vision was faint, and knowing that Piedmont could not be counted as present here, he would grant the matter no further thought. He went to find Lillian, who often rose earlier than Buckminster, to ask if there was anything she could do to help ease his pain.

Lillian was setting the fire beneath the hob in the kitchen, but learning of his problem, she hurried to finish the task. 'Wait just a moment, my fine Buckaroo. We'll attend to it in two shakes.' Hearing her calling him Buckaroo, he knew that Sherbrook would be pleased. An expression employed by him on a regular basis was introduced and gaining acceptance in another realm.

If Lillian took it up, it would not be long and many hereabout might use it. Isaac Stone, in dispensing medicines, would tell patients, 'Take five drops of this before meals, Buckaroo, and you'll soon be right as rain!' At the brickyard, Weed would order, 'Shift those barrows, Buckaroos! Let's move 'em right now!' Weed might take to using the expression more than others because as far as this realm was concerned, he was Sherbrook. Such were Skip's thoughts, when Lillian returned from searching amongst her not inconsiderable cache of remedies.

Seeing him smile, Lillian enquired, 'Better now, is it?'

'No, it's pretty much the same,' he said, sounding a small note of defeat.

'Never mind, dear boy. I might just have found the solution! Pardon my pun. I would never make light of another's suffering. In any case, the solution…' Coming close, she instructed, 'If you'll tilt your head over to the side now, I'll pop a drop or two of this into your ear, and there should be improvement. That's right, over to one side. There … a little more.' But then, 'Oh me, oh my! That's torn it! I've dripped it onto your jacket! We're going to have to sit you down. We'll hop into the parlour.'

The tip of a white tipped ear hung down over the side of the arm-chair, brushing against the floor. Keeping his head still, as instructed, Skip asked, 'Have you ever been boating, Lillian?'

'Me? Boating? Oh, never! You won't catch me out on the lake in one of those things! I'd rather gazuzzlement of any sort than *drown!*' Sounding pleased then, for them both, she said, 'There now, those drops have gone in. Best stay as you are for a moment or two, just to be sure. There's nothing worse than earache!' She said, 'There's been great loud noise coming from the forest again. It's where you and the gal were, isn't it?' He moved his head, giving a slight nod of agreement and she asked, 'Did you see anything out of the ordinary?' He gave no response and Lillian said, 'No? I can't help but wonder whether being in the vicinity of such an almighty racket might have something to do with your ear-ache?' She said, 'There are such loud noises heard at times. They're Tump goings-on, nothing we shall ever comprehend.' Returning to the subject of boating, she said, 'You will be careful when you're way out there, in her, Missy-Galore?'

Skip smiling, corrected, 'It's Missy-*Belle*, as I recall.'

Ruffling the fur of his head she told him, 'I don't know much about this boating. Be certain though, to tell Nancy that you *must* wear one of those safety vests!'

'I will.'

She said, 'You'll see what I mean when you get down there to the lake. They all wear them. You won't forget now, will you Skip?'

Missy-Belle

Nancy's world did not lack cause for surprise. They had arranged to meet at the small pier, and arriving there and sighting *Missy-Belle* for the first time, he thought that compared to her, bricks were nothing, they no longer impressed.

Nancy's father was present. He stood on the pier, bracing against the morning's stiff breeze by leaning against a sturdy bollard. Weed Looked down to where his daughter sat in the small boat. Skip could not hear their conversation from where he stood, but Weed waved his arms about, he pointed to this and that, and so, advice was given. Nancy held a paw to her head, keeping a wide-brimmed hat from blowing away. Her hat bore a long yellow ribbon that trailed out, floating upon the breeze.

Skip had stopped in his tracks at the beginning of the wooden pier. The planks he must go across—if he was ever to get out to Nancy and her boat, were spaced far apart. Down beneath those weatherworn planks, water was seen lapping. Faced with meeting Weed for the first time he was uncertain, and now here was something else to contend with—fear of falling through huge gaps! The more he stared at them, the more chasm-like those gaps became, and he was frozen to the spot.

Noticing him, Nancy waved, calling, 'Skip! Come on!'

Weed turned and he was calling too, 'Come along lad! Don't look down. Keep your head up and get a move on!' Weed beckoned to him, and Skip did as he was told, but for the entire distance from the beginning of the pier to *Missy-Belle*, which was a lot farther than he first realized, the pads of his feet experienced an odd, nervous, tingling; it was as if they were not truly a part of him, and they would not mind letting him down.

Weed had taken time off from the yard this morning, and still wore clay-stained overalls. He would assist Nancy with *Missy-Belle*, and then after seeing them off, he would return to work at the yard. When Skip reached the end of the pier, Weed took hold of Skip's paw, saying, 'Pleased to meet you, stranger,' But then rather than release his grip, Weed took firmer hold. He lifted Skip away from the pier then set him down in the boat.

Nancy told him, 'Come sit next to me, Skip. Take care that you don't fall! Edge your way around to the other side of the tiller.' Then he was seated on a shiny-smooth, narrow wooden seat. Rocking to and fro with the motion of the small boat, was a most unfamiliar sensation.

Weed untied a rope from where it was looped over a stout bollard and tossed it into the boat, whereupon *Missy-Belle* began to move out and away from the pier.

All the while as they went, Nancy provided information, 'That's the mast. Those are sails. Wonderful aren't they! And that's the boom! The tiller is used for steering. The front is the bow, and back here's the stern.'

He asked, 'What's that, up there?'

'It's a flag', she told him, 'a type of flag called a pennant.'

Watching the flag being whipped and snapped by the crisp breeze, he'd never seen the colour red appear so bright.

'Wonderful, isn't it? All of it!' Nodding, he gripped the side of the boat. The pier and her father were left far behind and staring back over the distance covered, Weed appeared as no more than a small, blurry figure.

Nancy turned *Missy-Belle* and they tacked into the wind. She warned, 'Watch out for the boom, Skip. It swings!'

Wind filled the sail and their zigzag course carried them over the lake until they must, he thought, be sailing above Old Warren Central, or close enough to give him pangs of strange homesickness; strange, because Old Warren Central had never existed here.

Telling himself to forget the past, because reminiscing over old places and times did no good, he was aware of a dull, throbbing pain; his ear-ache was returning. Sweeping untrammelled, across the lakes surface, the breeze did not help matters, and, grimacing, he put a paw to the side of his head.

Noticing him do so, Nancy asked, 'Are you all right? What is it?'

Wincing against the wind, he muttered, 'Ear-ache.'

She said, 'There's a place farther along—not too far away. I'll beach *Missy-Belle* and we'll get out of the wind for a while. We'll have a bite to eat—not a picnic—but Mother said I should bring a few things to nibble.' She asked, 'Unless you feel that we should turn back now?'

Skip shook his head, 'No.'

Nancy said, 'We won't stay out long—at least you'll have had a taste of sailing.'

Following the shoreline, skimming along, the sleek little boat skirted past extensive beds of bull-rush and reed, and as they sailed close in to shore, several ducks, quacking and flapping wings in melodramatic panic, hurried for safe cover of a nearby reed-bed. Turning to Skip, she said, 'I'm so sorry you're not well. I meant to show you a good time.'

You are showing me a good time, Skip thought, but my ear has ideas of its own. They now passed a place where reed-beds jutted far out into the lake, and Nancy took *Missy-Belle* in a smooth, arcing course, around, then back in again closer to shore. She told him, 'This is a place where reeds are harvested—for material for scratchings and such.' Passing by the extensive beds, Skip saw a half dozen or so harvesters carrying big, flat-shaped, woven baskets. Two individuals carried these upon their heads, the baskets loaded high, as they made their way back to dry land. Seeing them walking amongst reeds, he puzzled over them not sinking. He did not envy them their occupation; but the colours they wore, bright gold-yellows, rich blues and crimson, set them apart from others of the realm.

As if knowing his thoughts, Nancy said, 'When harvesting, they wear woven things on their feet called platty-shoes. They are wide and flat, and keep them up out of the water. They clomp along over reeds and those platty-shoes bend and flatten the bed as they go. They work to either side of the path they make, and then they retrace their steps so as to preserve the beds.' A harvester waved as they went by; the others continued working, as if oblivious to their presence.

A short distance along was a small sheltered bay, where enormous willows grew, attending the lakeshore as guardians of the edge of things; their drooping presence reminding the waters, you must press landward no farther, no farther than this.

Nancy guided her small craft toward the shore. There was a slick, abrasive sound when *Missy-Belle*, making landfall, slid a short way onto the grit-surface of the beach before making an abrupt halt. Before leaving the boat, Nancy reached down under the seat and found a small cloth bag with a long strap which she slung across her shoulder, saying, 'Let's go sit under one of the big trees. We'll be sheltered up there, out of the breeze.'

Stepping from the boat, she said, 'Oh, poor Skip. Is it no better?'

He shook his head indicating no, but in doing that, felt the drumming ear threaten worse pain. He said, 'It'll go away soon I hope.' He wished Lillian was here with her drops; the medicine was not a cure-all but it had made for improvement.

'Try and eat something. Sometimes chewing can help,' said Nancy, taking a large red apple from her bag. She polished it by rubbing it against the bodice of her blue dress, then passed it to him, 'When my little brother Samuel has ear-ache, Mother gives him baby-carrots to chew on and says it helps.'

Mindful of remedies, Skip thought of Lillian and her telling him to wear a vest. He enquired, 'Are we meant to wear safety clothing for sailing? Lillian mentioned something of the sort.'

'Oh—yes! She's correct and, now you remind me, I'm very surprised Father didn't say anything! We'll wear vests for the return journey. She added, 'It's very remiss of me.' They flibberty hopped the short distance up the beach, to rest on the grass beneath the willows.

'This is a nice spot,' she said, 'Oh, look there! A butterfly! Do you see? It's flitting away above the tarrash bush!'

Skip saw the magnificent creature. Each of its wings was decorated with a dark blue circle. The butterfly returned then, to settle upon the dark foliage of the bush. There it stayed, moving its wings, and those two moving circles reminded Skip of the eyes of owls, or of the bard, he realized, because with his myopic vision, Piedmont had often peered at him that way.

It was pleasant, he decided, here under the willow with Nancy in her pretty dress and hat; and, it was so, despite any physical discomfort. Since arriving at Brickfield he had pushed away memory of many things, but he did not now push away memory of Piedmont. He asked, 'Have you ever heard the name Piedmont? Piedmont the Bard?'

'Piedmont? No. But don't you mean Pietro the Bard?'

In this world, where nothing was as straightforward as he wished, the bard must go under another, far less impressive sounding name. Skip protested, 'Pietro? What kind of name is *that?*' Before she could go further, he exclaimed, 'Deeks! Is nothing sacred?' The bard was by nature, finicky-fussy with words. To him, expression and meaning were everything. Skip imagined Piedmont would not be pleased by the idea of his alternate version engaging in the business of versifying under *any* other name. But then, he said, 'Oh, look, please don't take my outburst to heart. I'm missing my friend, Piedmont, that's all.'

Nancy's curiosity was piqued and she asked, 'You're saying that where you hail from, you, and one *calling* himself Bard, are on close terms?'

'Yes. And, we go back quite a ways. Piedmont is "*The* Bard".'

She asked, 'Then, you know this individual's work, well? Which means that you could recite something of his, for me?'

'I guess so,' Skip said, but he did not want to recite anything. 'I could, but I'm going to forego the privilege.'

'You won't recite?'

'No—I believe, I'll skip it.'

'You're going to *skip*, it?'

'Yes.'

She was not perturbed. If Skip would not recite, then, she was glad for the opportunity to do so. Hearing her new friend come close to belittling the good name of Pietro, she was more than willing to redeem the Bard's standing. Skip was in pain, but rudeness was not called for. She said, 'I know a little of the works of Pietro, *our* bard, and so, *I* shall recite for you.'

'I'm honoured,' Skip said, and settled back on the grass.

Standing straight and folding her paws at her waist, Nancy paused for a moment, before reciting:

'I am daffodil
Spun gold my name
Tump bless the meadow
Where I sing to the rain.
I am white lily
Long stamen caress
Cast long my shadow
Desire without rest.
I'm rambling Rose
Most glory is mine

All beauteous scent
Wild hearts to entwine…

Nancy declared, 'That's as much of it as I recall.' Shy of continuing, she curtsied. Skip thought her very sweet and he thanked her.

She said, 'I've wanted *The Complete Works* of Pietro for a long time now. But, because it includes verse such as, *Seduced by Loves' Eyes*, Mother won't let me have it. She says it's too "old" for me. You can imagine how it makes me feel. She doesn't realize I'm grown up—well, almost.'

Skip smiled, and getting to his feet, announced, 'And now, the amazing Skip, Buckaroo without equal—despite every suffering—will recite verse by the true bard. This,' he said, 'is from the epic, *Lament Mydor*:

'O'er Mount' and valley's windswept plain
As stone, set 'gainst hail and driving rain
Shield in paw as eagle claw, wait not in vain
Reveal sound plan for war and victory gain
Great Mydor, brethren, kin and home disdain

From place unknown, Tall Ones came
With mighty crack and lightning flame
To rend as naught this realm's name
Chief of all below and firmament
Hold firm true brave, 'gainst gazuzzlement!

'Cross pasture, cross vale Tall Ones advance
They swift pursue most deadly dance…'

Skip's voice trailed off. He paused, and cocking his head to one side, listened. Then asked, 'Do you hear it—a sort of slow, hissing, whooshing?'

After listening for just a moment, Nancy cried, 'Missy-Belle!' And they both went heltering to the beach, where, standing next to Missy-Belle, and looking out across the lake, they saw a wide wave, progressing towards them from far away.

Skip thought the wave, not too threatening. But, Nancy ordered, 'Skip! Quick! Don't stand there! Help me push *Missy-Belle* out!'

Glancing away from the shore, to look inland, Skip shouted, 'Make a dash for it! We can out-run it!' But, seeing the look she gave, he bent to helping her shove the boat back onto the lake.

'Jump aboard!' Nancy urged, 'We must have *Missy-Belle* turned into the wave!' And she soon had them sailing head on towards it.

The closer the wave came, the higher it was and Skip, hanging on for his life, thought, why, oh, why, are we doing this?

In the moment before *Missy-Belle* struck, Nancy yelled, 'You're not wrecking my boat!' Then, the prow of the tiny boat went low in the water. Skip felt his stomach sink, and a wide, grey wall towered over them! *Missy-Belle* lunged forward, rising high—higher still—carried up by the wave until her sleek bow broke through the crest!

They hovered there at the peak, until *Missy-Belle* went over—to then traverse the wake of the wave. Turning to look behind them, Nancy yelled, 'I hope the harvesters are all right!' Skip shuddered to think of their plight. He feared for them now because when he first saw it coming, he'd not determined the waves true size. Close up, it was a far more frightening thing. 'We must head farther out. The water will wash back this way!' Nancy warned.

Skip asked, 'Do you think, now, I can have one of the safety vests? *Please.*'

'Oh, yes!' she exclaimed, and they laughed at their foolishness. Then, after a moment of quiet, they laughed again with sheer relief.

Compared with the wave itself, the backwash was slight and *Missy-Belle* riding upon choppy, disturbed waters, rocked, jerking to and fro, until the last rippling eddy died and the lake surface calmed. Turning back with *Missy-Belle,* taking a wide-arcing course, they sailed to the reed-beds by the great willows to see if their help was needed.

Seeing Double

Those who earned their living harvesting reeds had dashed for the willows and managed to clamber and cling to branches as the churning mass of water roiled beneath them.

Skip and Nancy were told how, in meeting with trees, the wave had showered water up into the top-most branches, and, hearing some complain of being soaked, Skip's respect for the harvesters increased. If such was their worst complaint, then they were certainly a tough lot. But then, several harvesters, bemoaning the loss of baskets and platty-shoes, pointed out, 'It's an irreversible set back! The quota is going to be way off. By the time we replace our equipment, we won't ever make up for the time lost!'

Another reminded, 'There's the matter of cuttings already taken. That's all gone! Days of labour washed hither and yon'—most of it taken back to the lake!' Skip then wondered over their so valuing those things required in earning a living; when the miracle was, they were alive.

They left the harvesters to their problems and returned to Brickfield, to where Weed waited at the pier, fretting and worrying over their safety. Accompanying him was Nancy's mother, Mavis. With her parents, were Buckminster and Lillian, at the front of a small waiting crowd of curious, concerned onlookers.

Nancy said, 'It's a welcoming committee! That's what it is! I'm determined to see it as that.' Embarrassed by the attention, she said, 'My parents can be just *awful* when they worry! We're going to have to be calm about this and assure them everything was fine. We were never even close to harm's way.'

Seeing Lillian there with the others, Skip said, 'I'm very glad to be wearing this vest!' Within moments they were drawing alongside the mooring.

Nancy, lowering the mainsail, instructed, 'Throw the line to my father will you? Thanks, Skip.'

Weed ordered, 'Stand back now here she comes. And … here she is!' He exclaimed, 'There's a good lad!' And he caught the rope Skip had tossed to him.

With *Missy-Belle* secured to the pier, they were rushed to tell all that they'd been through. Lillian hugged him so tightly that, Skip thought she might crush him.

Then as they were led off, taking their separate ways home, Skip heard Nancy protesting, 'Mother! That's enough! Don't fuss! Leave me be. *I do not need coddling!*'

* * *

'When the wave came through it washed high upon the foreshore slopes and wiped out the greater portion of the plantings!' Lillian was upset by the prospect of future shortage. Costs would soar, she predicted. 'What they expect already, for produce such as beets and celery is an outrage— even nasty stringy-beans are expensive!' She went on to condemn the foreman and crew for mismanagement of the sluice gates situated farther upstream from Brickfield Lake. 'Those working at the communal gardens fled for their lives. They were warned by the terrible sound of it coming their way! It's a miracle that none were drowned! Our boy did not perish and I'm eternally grateful for that! It's true mercy and there's Tump to thank! I would not be able to live with myself if anything had happened to him.'

Buckminster commented, 'I would not like being in Charlie Noy-Breen's position. As, foreman up there, he's got a lot of explaining to do.'

'Explanation won't suffice.' Lillian said, 'Not after this! He'll be lucky to avoid banishment!'

This realm's version of Charlie was as accident-prone, if not more so, than his home-realm version. Skip was sorry for him, and, was no longer surprised when hearing of past acquaintances in hitherto undreamed-of relationship with their fellows. Buckminster and Lillian's relationship was the chief example of this, and by now he was so used to them, as they were here, that their earlier versions seemed not so valid. The name Grammy Graymark, along with all he knew of that individual, was now imbued with an air of unreality, and yet his memory of her tyranny remained sharp. When Lillian and Buckminster wished him goodnight, he knew that over time, memory could fade all it liked, but he would always appreciate them for themselves.

By now he had his own chamber. It was located along the main burrow from the kitchen, but the previous evening, Lillian had said, 'Sleep on the pallet in the kitchen, my boy. Rest weary bones and be warmed by the stove. It's been a big day and you've been through so much.'

'Indeed, haven't we all,' contributed Buckminster.

'Ear-ache better?' Lillian enquired.

He said, 'I think that wave frightened it out of me.'

'I don't wonder. It frightened more than that from me. Swear to Tump, I almost wet myself.'

'Lillian!'

'Yes, yes—quite right, Buckminster. Nevertheless, it's plain truth.'

Skip did not know how long he slept, before being woken by bright light flaring. Brightness was not imagined, he felt certain of that, but rubbing at his eyes and then searching in darkness, nothing was there. The last glow of embers beneath the hob meant that dawn was not far off. He was not tired and so, no matter the time, he'd slept well. Wide-awake, he eased himself up from the pallet. That bright light must have been part of an all but forgotten dream. Apart from shadowy, familiar forms, furnishings and their like, delineated by the faint glow of remaining coals, he saw no evidence of anything out of the ordinary. Lying back down, he would attempt going back to sleep.

He had just settled, when a soft-speaking voice, issuing from the far corner of the room, announced, 'Must say, you've been busy my fine Buckaroo, haven't you?'

Whereupon, Skip sat bolt upright! Querulous, he ventured, 'Who are you?' He hoped that he sounded bigger than he was, and, braver than he felt.

It was not Buckminster or Lillian, but the voice possessed a familiar quality. Peering into darkness, he made out the faint form of a stranger.

The shadow-form moved out from a corner near the fire-surround, and approached closer. Reaching the breakfast table, it paused before declaring, 'Buckaroo—there's a whole bunch of amazing things I have to show you!'

'Who *are* you?' Skip whispered.

'I don't like breaking it to you this way, my friend, but I have no choice...' the stranger said. 'I'm you, Buckaroo, that's who.'

'You're *me?*'

'Yep! Got it in one.'

Skip asked, 'Meaning that you *look* like me? You resemble me? Was it you I saw at the brickyard? I saw you stealing a brick.'

'Hush now. Let's make no hasty judgment. And we must not disturb the oldsters. Get dressed now, because we're going on a trip.' Curiosity over-riding feeling of trepidation, Skip got up from the pallet.

Reaching for his jacket, he heard, 'I'm a lot older and far wiser than you. You should trust that's true.' And then, as almost an afterthought, 'I mean you no harm.' Standing now, and with eyes better adjusted to darkness, Skip saw the stranger was both taller and broader than he. Despite those differences an uncanny resemblance was not imagined.

Neither he nor the stranger had spoken above a whisper, but now Lillian's sleepy voice drifted through the burrow from hers and Buckminster's chamber, enquiring, 'Are you all right Skip?'

He called back, 'I'm fine, Lillian.' And was grateful when silence ensued. Hoping that she had drifted back to sleep he addressed the other, 'This is all very confusing and I'm not at all certain of it, but I'm going to trust that you're not some insane kadoodler.'

'If I'm a kadoodler, then we both are.' The stranger said, and, 'Lillian's not sleeping. She's rising from her pallet and thinking of checking on you.' Wondering how the stranger might know what Lillian was doing, Skip heard, 'Hasten—and cover your eyes!' But there was no time to do so, because following an instant of sharp, piercing, brightness, the familiar surroundings were gone, and, Skip tottered on his feet in a countryside lit by bright sunshine!

Blinking, he was speechless! The one standing before him was no kadoodler, but an older version of himself, right down to his favourite blue jacket.

'To each his own—the jacket's mine,' the elder declared, 'you needn't feel proprietorial over it. Mine's a larger size.' Touching a paw to the jacket's lapel, he said, 'We've come ahead in time and that's why the sun's up, so, you can see me. Our location is far removed from Brickfield.'

Tugging at a whisker, he said, 'We're here, so that when we make the inter-realm jump, none can be upset by our mighty kazooning.' He added, 'Cover your ears and shut your eyes. I'll let you know when to reopen them. That's it. Jam those paws against 'em.' And then, CRACK! Far brighter light flashed—far brighter than before! Even with eyes squeezed tight shut, Skip was dazzled by blue-white glare!

Ignoring instruction, he lowered his paws and opened his eyes. He was confronted by terrifying, gut-churning horror! Tall Ones were everywhere! He shut his eyes, squeezed them so shut that his grimacing face hurt. From every side, from above and below, kazooning was so loud that the immensity of it must overwhelm all sense and deafen him!

'I told you, didn't I—to wait?' The elder was calm and that helped somewhat, but next, Skip felt himself lifted—picked up and held tight! The elder was saying, 'We'll open our eyes again soon, and when you see me, you won't recognize me. I'll look like one of them. Before you panic, I'm *not* a Tall One. Stop struggling!'

He would not struggle, but maintaining self-control was not easy. Voices clamoured, a great babbling multitude of them and there were sounds of footsteps, not soft padding, but staccato sharp clicking, raw shuffling and stomping.

Elder Skip said, 'We've come to this realm because there's much to learn. It is shocking and difficult and that's understood, but we are one and the same, you and I, and harm will not befall you. This is not Brickfield realm and neither has it anything to do with the old warren. From now on you must Mmeerah your way through the experience. That way's a lot easier than going to pieces over every little thing.'

He was taking that in, when a voice exclaimed, 'Oh, what a cutie! Where in the world did you get him?'

Then a second voice joined the first, 'The poor baby's sleepy! He's a *very* big boy, aren't you darling? Just the sweetest thing—I want one just like him!'

His head was stroked. His cheek was pinched, and he screwed up his face. Tall Ones did not have paws, but awful, misshapen extremities! He was unable to prevent shuddering. One of them said, 'I think he's cold—he's shivering, poor love!'

Holding him tighter and jiggling him about, elder Skip said, 'He's been a little unwell, ma'am. The vet's not a hundred per cent certain of what ails him, but he'll soon be just fine, won't you?'

Then, following the exchange, those voices were more distant. 'You'll take good care of him, won't you?' Voices further faded and despite their blending with other sounds, Skip still made out, 'They were *both* adorable!' And, he shivered in disgust.

'You should open your eyes now, Buckaroo, and take another peek, but before you do... This is a city, a great mess of a warren, which starts below ground and reaches all the way to the sky!' He warned, 'We are situated high up on something called a walkway, which is a bridge going between buildings, and from up here there's an awful lot to see. And now—don't forget—I'm not a Tall One. It just seems that I am!'

Skip opened his eyes, first one and then the other, and squinting, saw out across an enormous deep chasm or canyon, and looking down there, far below, he saw strange moving beasts of many shapes and colours, as they jostled with each other, making much noise in the process; they did not helter, but were slow moving and he heard the loud, sharp hooting of beasts protesting their positions in queues.

Elder Skip said, 'They're not beasts, Buckaroo. They're not living creatures at all; they are vehicles. There are different types; cars, buses and trucks, and most Tall Ones believe they cannot do without them. They ride in them. Away from cities, are those we call churners, but they are tractors. They are all vehicles, and they are *made* by Tall Ones. Those down there are moving at a crawl but they can move at astonishing speed, speeds you would not believe possible. There are a zillion things you must learn.'

Summoning courage to look directly at his elder, young Skip glanced up into the face of a fair-haired boy. He exclaimed, 'I'll *never* get used to any of this!' And, 'It's terrible, not understanding every second word!'

'You'll get used to it! You *do,* Buckaroo! Later, I take you to see an ocean, and you love it! You'll see what I mean. The beach is one of our favourite places! But right now, let's go check out *toys!*'

They set off, and soon the elder informed, 'Places of this sort are called food courts. They've named this one *Flavours of the World*. Next, we'll go through *Men's and Boys' Wear*, and after that I have something special to show you.' After pausing he explained, 'When we're done, we'll come all the way back through *Men's and Boys'* and we'll visit the bathroom, which is over there.' Pointing, he added, 'That will be our point of departure from the realm.' He said, 'That's the plan.'

The food court was flooded with unfamiliar aromas and the elder commented, 'I'm crazy over the smell of hot roasted nuts. That's what you caught a whiff of just now.

Then there was the noise of a tray of plates, cutlery and food, which knocked from one of many crammed tables, went crashing to the floor. Elder Skip said, 'Didn't see that coming, did you? Real kazooner, wasn't it? Mash and greens tipped everywhere. What a mess!' He said, 'You'll soon get used to the idea of Tall Ones not being so almighty perfect!'

Toting young Skip against a hip, the elder hurried through the cavernous place and they came to *Men's and Boys' Wear*. It was quieter now but this place too, was infested with Tall Ones. It was their territory and so their presence should be expected.

Elder Skip determined, 'We won't tarry going through here.' He wove a path around shoppers, but then he halted in his tracks, exclaiming, 'Deeks—look at this! This outfit is a favourite of mine. I had no idea it would come back into fashion.' A Tall One stood stock still—as if petrified with fear. The elder touched the hem of the Tall One's blue shirt. He felt the fabric, assessing the quality, then said, 'Not too terrible, but mine is the genuine article. It's from the *Edwardian* era and is called a sailor suit. Those plastic buttons do *not* belong.' He then rapped his knuckles against the Tall One's leg and a hollow sound resulted. 'In case you've not guessed,' he said, 'this individual's a kadoodling fake. The eyes are not right. In fairness, they *can* be clever and sophisticated, but for the most part, Tall Ones go about their business in misguided fashion.'

Returning the mannequin's fixed gaze, Skip asked, 'They make copies of themselves?'

'Yes. And we do too. Take, for example, me. In present form I might be considered a facsimile—a copy—but there's no real comparison. Look at me. Alongside this inept effort of theirs, I'm an absolute masterpiece, am I not? Yes. I'm perfect, down to the smallest detail. Compared to this rubbish, I'm a walking talking marvel and there's just no denying it.' He said, 'Try as they might, they can never compete with Tump.'

'Tump?'

'Yes, Tump.' He said, 'It was Piedmont who thought of naming us, but for you of course, it's not yet happened. It's quite some time away before he proposes the name. You and your friends are Tump. We, all of us, are Tump. There is an infinite number of Tump—Tump traversing both time and space—moving from realm to realm, but we won't go too much into that, not just yet.'

He was confused. If danger threatened then brave folk sounded, Tump! It was a warning given, and hearing the warning, others would know that they must flee to safety. In providing the warning an individual increased the risk of harm befalling them, because their locations were made known to an enemy, and so they were easy targets. Those who sounded Tump were held in highest esteem, and that was all that the younger Skip knew.

They passed beneath a high arch supported by large pillars. The arch was adorned with flowers forming garlands, long tendrils of leafy vine twined to the base of each pillar. Young Skip guessed that, like the staring mannequin, those flowers and vines were works of artifice. Here, soft music was the background for the sounds of many young Tall Ones, and Skip was reminded of happy times spent back at the old warren, listening to tunes from the Radiola.

Now they were hurrying down a long aisle and to either side of them were high shelves supporting an array of bright-coloured objects. 'Those are packaged items, Buckaroo.' Seeing him reaching to touch them, the elder informed, 'Those are pictures—not real things.' He took a box from a shelf and said, 'Here, take a look at this and tell me who you see there on the box?'

'Why! It's *Peace!*'

'Correct!'

With those long, sleek dark ears and large sparkling eyes, Peace Darkling was depicted standing in a field and looking up to a dark starry sky, and coming from a distant part of the field, was a churner. The elder was saying, '"*The Mighty Churner*" is a favourite of mine. Sherbrook suggested she have the Tall Ones who make such things, include warning sounds, and then Peace was okay with it. There's a churner inside the box—don't drop it!' But then—when the box hit the floor—a gruff voice and music issued from it! And he recognized the tune as a sped up version of *White Winter's Song*. The voice repeated, 'I *must* give fair warning when I churn! I *must* give fair warning when I churn!' Picking up the box and flipping it over, the elder said, 'See this hole?' He poked a finger into the hole, straight through the middle of Peace Darkling's likeness, 'I always feel disrespectful,' he admitted, 'jabbing our Mmeerah Queen.' Inside the box was a button and when he pushed it. Young Skip heard, 'There is peace in our land! Mmeerah! Mmeerah! There is peace in our land. Mmeerah!'

'What I really wanted to show you, Buckaroo, is *you*, or, *us!*' He reached to a high shelf and pulled down a larger box than the first. He said, 'Now, check this out. Listen when I squeeze "our" paw.'

They heard, 'Get down, Buckaroos! Do the good ol' Flibberty-Hop! Everybody shake it now! Come on and *shake it!*' And young Skip, having learned something of dolls from Buckminster and Lillian, but still confused by all he saw, stared as the automaton rolled its hips and stamped its feet, dancing a merry jig to a most rowdy, raucous tune. He knew now that there were not just the two of him, because peering way overhead to the top-most shelf, he saw many, many more boxes. There were so many of them that they defied counting.

PEBBLE PRACTICE

They blasted off, as the elder referred to it, from a stall in the *Men's Room,* situated at the end of a corridor, leading away from *Flavours of the World.* At their departure was a lightning flash of white-light, but no loud kazooning, as they "moved" to a place of solitude, from whence they would make an inter-realm jump. Empathizing with the occupants of stalls adjacent to the one his elder version "moved" them from, and knowing that the Tall Ones were in for a rude shock, Skip expressed reservation. He suggested that they wait until the bathroom was less crowded, but the elder insisted, 'No—we're off to the beach, and we mustn't dally!' Without preamble, he moved them!

An instant later, the elder asked, 'Not that I have to enquire, but you're flabbergasted aren't you? You cannot credit the reality of such a huge pond!'

Skip was silent. He stood for the first time on a beach before a roaring ocean, and watched as wave upon wave pounded against the pristine shoreline. Gulls hovered overhead as a brisk-blowing wind buffeted against their wings; their bright vermilion legs and beaks were set against cold-white bodies and they screeched as if vying for attention. Out from the shoreline were the forms of enormous, weathered, rock-pillars, which grew tall and then seemed to shrink in size, as a swelling mass of dark, heaving water pushed against them, then receded; the rhythmic process repeated over and again. Skip exclaimed, 'It was a day of wonder, when Great Grandfather made this place!'

Hearing that heart-felt response, the elder smiled, and gesturing, said, 'Let's go to where the cliff meets the beach and relax on the sand.' After the briefest pause, he declared, 'And because I don't want sunburn...' There was a shimmering, gentle sparkling, and his form faded until all young Skip saw, was an indistinct blur. Next—of a sudden—there he was! Sounding most emphatic, the elder declared, 'Really, you can't beat fur!'

They lay back, and so pleasant was it that, young Skip almost dozed off. Then, 'You know, you should thank me for moving the fox, back there in Brickfield realm.' And before young Skip had a chance to respond, 'You were thinking of experimenting by moving him back a little—in time, rather than leaving him in the tree. Had you done that, you might have had two of them to contend with. Brother Fox twice over. I moved him for you. I relocated him.'

He was curious and had wondered as to the possibility of moving the fox through, not just space, but time also. Reminded of it, he said, 'Well ... thank you.'

'You're welcome,' elder Skip said. 'It was nothing.'

But then, thinking of Brother Eagle, and recalling his terrifying ordeal, young Skip asked, 'If you could do it with the fox, how come, you didn't move Brother Eagle before he took me?'

Elder Skip said, 'You and he were pushed into another realm and the moment of transference was optimal.' Confusion and doubt showed in young Skip's expression. The elder said, 'It is more complicated than you can imagine.' Still, young Skip was not satisfied. The elder exclaimed, 'For *deeks' sake*—it's more complex than even I can imagine! But, according to Rudy, there was no other choice. In any case, we, Tump, agreed to introduce you, at that instant, to Brickfield realm and for good reason. Of all realms, Brickfield was chosen, because in that realm, both Buckminster and Lillian are as nice as can be. They don't come any better than they are there. We decided you should gain deeper understanding of causes and outcomes; learn more of the way of things. And so, as navigator, Simple Rudy suggested Brickfield as your destination.'

Hearing *that* name, Simple Rudy, was the last thing he'd expected. 'Simple? But...'

'Yes, Simple Rudy, the one and same, but you should understand that the Rudy we speak of is older and wiser than the Simple Rudy of your acquaintance. As navigator or way-finder, the elder Rudy has no equal. He is speeding everything up, so as to make progress easier for young Tump. That's you.' He said, 'You and your friends are our younger versions.' The day was perfection itself, and feeling the sun warming his furry body, he sighed with pleasure. After a moment he said, 'Tump is not infallible... I recollect that before Brother Eagle struck, I was overwrought. I was exhausted, but despite that I put on a brave front.' Giving a mock-shudder, he said, 'I *still* feel those talons going in!' And although the day was warm, young Skip too, was unable to help shivering, and said, 'Oh yes! It felt as if they went right through me—in one side and out the other! *Deeks, it was horrible!'*

The elder said, 'So much happened that day. I—or, I should say *we* had succeeded in moving an object with certain accuracy—a significant event so far as our ability is concerned. To her horror, the Graymark cameo was moved from Lieutenant Cropper's paw and then back to our own. Previous to that point, I admit we were a mess! After escaping with the others, climbing a veritable mountain and recalling with awful sadness the passing of Uncle Bucky, and after Sherbrook's persisting upon enquiring into our feelings, I confess it was altogether too much. We were happy to have left New Warren Central. We were set upon the greatest adventure of our young life. It's small wonder that we we failed to see anything of Brother Eagle swooping.' Moments elapsed before elder Skip said, 'In any case, after consulting the map, Simple decided upon the best measure and outcome.'

'The map?'

'Yes. The map. You'll learn of it soon enough. There's so much you must learn. We've a task ahead! As I said though, a different trail, another way, was chosen for you.' He said, 'You are my younger version and so I know you would not forgo any of that learned during your sojourning in Brickfield.' He said, 'Of course, in regard to that realm there's another matter to consider. Quite apart from Buckminster and Lillian, there's Nancy.'

'Nancy? What about her?'

'You recall looking into her?'

'Of course, yes...'

'That blank, peaceful void is a place where everything is a whole lot easier for the one looking in. Nancy is not least affected by any of it. She does nothing. If she so much as thinks of doing, then her ability has little or no effect. But in a place of such stillness results can be marvellous, even for those of most limited ability. For example, there's Lillian. When looking into Nancy, Lillian recalled the location of her long lost locket.

'In sharing space provided by Nancy's ability, energy is amplified and moves, so, for those of us possessing refined ability, results are extraordinary.

'Had you, looked into Nancy at the lake, despite your suffering earache at the time, you would have seen the wave before you heard it coming.

'Nancy's space differs from that provided by Peace Darkling. Experience of the still space of Mmeerah calms and refines energy, whilst in the still space of a channel such as Nancy, energy inspires. And in *her* practising Mmeerah, Nancy's ability too, is enhanced. Mmeerah enhances everything.'

The elder enquired, 'Do you follow?'

'Yes,' said Skip the younger. 'To move things with least effort, I need Nancy, which I'd already figured for myself.'

'You have, but there's a catch. She won't join you. Nancy won't leave Brickfield. She has her home there, her family and friends.'

'Now you've lost me.'

'You needn't fret, because it works out—*all* of it. Forget Nancy for now.' Noting young Skip's look of disappointment the elder was thoughtful, before saying, 'Who knows what's involved and how the whole mishmash works, apart from Great Grandfather, that is.

'Everything is energy. To navigate—to find our way—we'd have to be Simple Rudy. And then, being Rudy, we'd have no real idea of how we did it. We'd just do it and it would work.' He said, 'I no longer bother enquiring as to the intricacies—the whys or wherefores—of any of it. The last time I enquired, I was told, "Oh, don't bother your head, Skip. It's just different time-trails. They are young Tump. They don't have the complete bag of tricks—not yet. We flibberty hopped as best we were able, but now with our help *they* will helter!"

'It wasn't a whole lot of help, but then the important thing is the quest. We search for Great Grandfather, and one day we shall find Him.'

Hearing the elder speak of questing after Great Grandfather was not in the moment, so interesting to young Skip, as was learning of Simple Rudy, and he could no longer put off making enquiry. In response to his question, the elder exclaimed, 'Oh deeks no! I assumed it was clear. Simple did not meet with gazuzzlement in crossing the creek.' He said, 'I am more fond of him now. Although you doubt it, in time to come, you and he should get along fine.' He paused and added, 'However, you do not become me.' He smiled. 'For my part, I managed to foil the eagle's plan, but still there was much to contend with. None of it was easy. You too, were your own best friend, because after transiting between realms you freed yourself by sheer effort of will. You moved from sky to grassy slope at Brickfield settlement.' He said, 'When the Bird of Habit crossed the eagle's path, the realm of New Warren Central altered. In that instant everything was changed for you and your friends. In the instant of that great kazooning sound, a shade of yourself was carried away.'

'Yes. I saw myself and thought I'd gone kadoodling mad!' young Skip exclaimed.

'But you weren't at all. The one you saw carried away was none other than yours truly.'

Skip asked, 'What happened to you after the separation?'

'Oh, I did pretty much as you. I willed myself to move. I wasn't so fortunate though, and had an awful time finding my way back to the others.' In pondering past events, the elder assured, 'I must tell you that Tump will see you and your friends united.' He then said, 'In our time together you must learn to move objects through time—not anything so difficult as moving to other realms; that comes much later. While we're here I'm going to teach you a trick or two. You're going to have to practise, practise, and then practise, because until you master certain skills nothing will progress. Don't feel daunted because I know you succeed! Go over there and fetch a few of those pebbles. We're going to send them through time and then bring them back. Not big ones, the smaller the better at first.'

Young Skip went to where pearl-white sand met the foot of a low cliff-face. There were stones of every size and shape. He searched about, looking for those of most uncommon form and colour. Several small stones captured his attention. They were ochre coloured stones and he would learn from the Elder that their interesting shapes and markings were significant; they were the fossilized imprints of ancient mollusc; the etched forms of small creatures, which had lived at time's beginning.

Ages passed and he endured at least a zillion times, being told, 'Yes! But still, you're trying too hard! They're *pebbles* for deeks' sake! If you're angry with them, we'll be here forever!' And the often repeated, 'Envision the pebble and you, as one. You are connected, and all time, being one— means that the pebble you "move" is waiting there for you tomorrow, or yesterday, or whenever, and you can bring it back. Don't think of other moments as *away* from the present. Every time is "now". It is true that a gap exists but put *expectation* there, not space.' The elder sprawled in a favourite spot where shade was provided by a rocky over-hang. As, long-eared, elder Skip of fur, he tended more often to snap advice and instruction, and as Skip the gold-haired boy, he seemed more patient and easy going. When young Skip questioned those differences in manner, the elder accused, 'You're kadoodling—right? How can there be a differ- ence? They're—both of them—me! It's an interesting observation, but for now—back to practice! Let's have no more cunning distraction.'

One afternoon the elder announced, 'There's something I *must* attend to.' With that said, he was gone in a flash. Skip averted his eyes from daz- zling white-glare.

Occupied with moving pebbles, he sat on the sand awaiting the return of three of his favourite stones; they *would* show up at any moment. After a long time spent waiting, though, he had to admit they were lost and he'd never see them again. He'd determined that in the elder's absence, success would be his. But how much practice was required before a posi- tive result ensued?

In quick succession came five explosive flashes of brightness, all occurring at the base of the cliff. Those flashes were not caused by any- thing belonging to him. The first item to materialize was a blue and white-striped deck chair, and then another arrived. A table accompanied the second chair, a table with a round hole at its centre. Then a large box appeared and an assortment of objects including a long, fabric covered pole.

The pole hovered in space for a moment and then drove downwards, as if thrust by a powerful paw. The sharp pointed end went through the round hole in the table and then pieced the surface of the sand. Next, the fabric wound about top-most part of the pole, unfurled, blossoming, as might a flower of enormous size.

Elder Skip materialized, to announce, "It's called a beach-umbrella! I've moved a few luxury items. They're in that big box there—the cooler—

if you'd like to take a look. I've got sodas and candy. Piedmont and Peace would not approve, but they're not struggling in the heat.

Today's a lot warmer than yesterday, and I did think of moving us to a day of cooler weather, but then I had this idea. What do you say? Don't answer—not till you've tried ice cream!'

'Ouch!' Skip exclaimed. It made his teeth ache and he spat it out. Laughing, the elder said, 'Brain freeze. Let it melt in your mouth!' He poured a deep crimson liquid into paper cups. The liquid climbed the walls of the cups to froth over when it reached the top.

The elder said, 'This is cherry soda, my all time favourite.' He passed Skip a cup.

'How do you like it? Good isn't it? There's more to life than shifting stones.

A short while ago, it was, "Move this pebble. Move it from my paw and send it into tomorrow. You can do it! You're not thinking of giving up, are you? Try again!" Now it was, 'How's the cherry soda, Buckaroo?' And, 'Twinkies! Take two. There you go, I just *love* seeing you enjoy yourself!'

When the elder commanded, 'Here—catch!' Skip caught the small pebble. And then, 'Now, "move" it so that it arrives there in the bottom of the tub when you finish your ice-cream!'

Without thinking, he did as suggested, and as he finished the last spoonful of *Toffee Whip* there it was! The pebble rattled around the bottom of the container! Smiling, he held the tub for elder Skip to see, but the elder closed his eyes and leaning back in his chair, said, 'Not necessary, Buckaroo! I don't need proof. I knew all along, *we* could do it!'

RETURN TO BRICKFIELD

'How can you be certain that she won't come away with me?'

'You have a soft spot for her and knowing that's the way of it, I want to tell you that I could be wrong, but in all honesty, I can't so, let's go shall we? You'll want to bring one of those pebbles along with you, as a memento of our time spent here. Stick it in your pocket and we'll blast off for good old Brickfield!'

With a mighty, gut-wrecking roar of kazooning and an explosion of atmosphere shredding sound and light, they left the beach, and in the following instant they stood by an outcropping of ancient stones in a misty valley, situated at the opposite side of the lake from Brickfield settlement.

They were not very far removed from another small settlement, a settlement inhabited not by harvesters, but by those renowned for weaving the best platty-shoes available; platty-shoes were bartered for goods and services provided by others. The elder had brought them closer to the weavers than he'd intended, and so, without ado, he again moved them, this time to the forest outskirts of Brickfield proper.

He said, 'I could have put you back in your bed—right where I first found you—but this will do well enough. Now, when you see her, just tell Lillian that you've been out for a breath of fresh air. This is the morning of the very day you left.' Smiling, he said, 'When you're done, I'll be waiting for you in the forest clearing.' He advised, 'You might think of gifting Lillian a small token of thanks... '

'Yes, but you don't have to remind me of manners or polite behaviour.'

'Oh, I know ... it's just that I care... I *do*—and I want everything to be fine for you! Of course, I see that everything's fine, but I'm not comfortable with the thought of "us" being disappointed today.' And with that said, he turned away to go deeper into the woods.

Young Skip stood there for a moment, and he sighed. He was not at all easy with having to inform them of his intention to leave. But, he had best get on with it. And so he made off along the path, which would take him to Buckminster and Lillian's. He did not look forward, either, to receiving refusal from Nancy. He would ask her to accompany him, regardless of the elder's advice.

Taking the pebble from his jacket pocket and holding it, he examined it for a last time. It was one of the first of those stones that he'd picked up from the beach, and the very first that he'd successfully moved through time. It was a most uncommon gift, a petrified shell from a realm other than theirs. Neither Lillian nor Buckminster would know anything of its origin and he would not reveal it, he thought; he would know how special it was, and that was enough.

For many, the work of the day had not yet begun, but Lillian was an early riser, and so she would be up and the fire would be ablaze beneath the hob; he would go straight in.

As it happened, they were both present there in the kitchen. Buckminster sat before the table, examining a sheet of scratchings. Looking up as Skip entered, he said, 'Come and take a look at this my boy. It's a novel idea—the idea of an individual—goes by the name of Lucas Rutherford. He calls it, *The Daily Record*. It's a record of current events. The main item, as you might guess, concerns the terrible wave and havoc wrought. Rutherford goes into some detail, in judgmental tone, examining causes and whatnot, but then, you and young Nancy receive mention. You're mentioned in a favourable light, for returning to check on a group of harvesters. He compliments you for your civic-minded thoughtfulness, which I must say, is cause for pride.'

'Not that we need, read any fancy new scratching sheet, to know that we're proud of you,' contributed Lillian. She placed a tray of dark looking muffins on the table. 'Muffins are something I'm rather a dab-paw at, even if I do say so. This batch has turned out rather well. You must try one while they're still warm,' so saying, she passed him a plate.

Biting into the muffin, Skip decided it, rather solid fare, but he continued chewing on it, without offering comment other than a noncommittal, 'Mm.'

Buckminster gave him a glance. That look advised, 'Good boy. Opinion is shared concerning these stones, but she's put much effort into it, and we must not hurt her feelings.'

She sat down and then, after taking the first curious, exploratory nibble of a muffin, Lillian announced, 'Oh, yes. These are perfect!'

Buckminster, again glancing to Skip, chortled, saying, 'This Rutherford has a sense of humour...'

Lillian enquired, 'How's that, dear? What does he say? He *can't* make light of flooding?'

Buckminster replied, 'Oh, no, it's nothing. It's just me. I'll see humour in anything at all.'

A bemused Lillian declared, 'You are an odd one this morning dear but I'm glad you've taken the scratching-sheet, seeing as it puts a smile on your face.'

Skip, chewing, and mindful of dense objects, said, 'I have a gift for you, Lillian.' And glancing to Buckminster, 'It's small but, it's interesting, I think.'

'A gift ... you spoil us, dear. We don't expect gifts.'

He'd determined to not make too much of it, but would now give a brief explanation. He said, 'It's a stone, a curiosity I came upon, and I thought you might like it. You see, it's in the shape of something called a shell. It was once a living creature, which dwelt in an enormous lake, and in all the time of its existence it has turned from something once living, to stone. It's called a fossil'. He passed her the stone. Lillian jiggled it about in her paw and then brought it close to her face the better to examine it. She seemed unimpressed. After giving it close scrutiny, she passed it to her husband.

Buckminster studied the pebble in similar manner, before giving a slight shrug, and stating, 'My boy, I believe some kadoodler has been pulling your leg, because this stone has been worked on—been graved with a tool. I believe it's...'

Lillian interjected, 'But that said—we love it—don't we, Buckminster? It *is* unusual...' She ruffled the fur of Skip's head. Then, 'Here, Buckminster, give me the treasure, it shall have pride of place on the mantel above the hob.'

Buckminster passed it to her. She asked, 'Did you swap good carrots for it Skip or was it free, dear?' She cast Buckminster a glance. 'Swap good carrots', Skip knew, was Lillian's way of meaning, payment of any kind.

He said, 'Oh no. I found it. And because it's uncommon, I thought of you. You are, both of you—uncommon. You're the kindest people I've ever met and I'll always be grateful for all you've done for me. I thought I'd give it to you as a parting gift.'

'Parting gift? Dear boy, you did say, *parting*?' Buckminster drew himself up straight. Lillian said nothing, but raised her paws to her face, she covered her mouth, and her eyes grew large in disbelief. It was too much for her and she exclaimed, 'But where will you go, Skip? You have nowhere! What harm might befall you!'

All Buckminster asked was, 'What are your plans then, Skip?'

'I have found a way of returning to my own world,' he said.

Buckminster asked, 'World? Where is it then? You were never from hereabout. That much was clear from the moment I found you.'

Lillian leaned back in her chair, and seeing her more settled, Skip said, 'I fell from the sky onto a grassy bank here in your world, and, Buckminster, you found me. Lillian cared for me. You took a stranger into your home and you brought me back to health, but you did more than that. You gave me the greatest gift of all. Love is the word to describe the very best I'll take with me, and, I can never repay you.'

'Ah, dear boy, let's hear no talk of repayment…'

'Nor love,' declared Lillian, interrupting, a tear trickling down her cheek. 'What you describe as love, Skip, is just common decency. We've gained most by having you with us! You've brought joy to our hearts, hasn't he, Buckminster? He's been as a good son to us. She wiped away tears, imploring, 'Won't you stay?'

Buckminster said, 'Now, now. It's not for us to decide his course.'

'But, I wish It weren't so!' Buckminster, leaning across the table put a paw against hers and let it rest there.

If he did not hasten in leaving he might change his mind. Skip rose from his chair and excused himself. He went along the burrow with its russet brick lining to the front door, then, let himself out. He pulled the door shut behind him and went off to find Nancy.

No sooner was he gone than, Lillian exclaimed, 'Oh, what are we thinking! This is not right—none of it! Not right at all! We can't allow him go like this. I *must* prepare something for his journey!' She hurried to the larder to find suitable provisions, complaining, 'Now, where have I put that basket?'

Buckminster said, 'A basket's not suitable—not for a boy intent upon adventure!'

She responded, 'Rather than advise me, Buckminster, your time would be best spent in going *after* him, before he gets too far. I won't see him setting off with nothing but the jacket on his back!'

She was right, and so Buckminster would make for the outdoors. In going, he wondered at his life-long disposition to caution. For him it was far too late, he'd never know what was missed by not setting forth into the world at a young age. Then he thought, Skip intended returning home, and none but Skip might say how it was he came to Brickfield in the first place. His being there in the grass at the lakeshore could, Buckminster decided, have naught to do with actual adventuring. It was more the result of nothing other than plain, old-fashioned misfortune.

* * *

He went first to the office at the brickyard, but Nancy was not there.

'Nope. Not here, dearie. Not today. I'm Marjorie.' Her manner was curt. Towering over him in the doorway, she sniffed several times in quick succession, as if at any moment she expected to sneeze.

Thanking her, he stepped back and away.

They were well acquainted and yet he did not know the way to Nancy's home. He'd not had presence of mind, to ask the receptionist for directions, and would not further inconvenience her. Weed was not about, and so he left the yard and proceeded in making his way along the narrow dirt track, which served as Brickfield's main thoroughfare.

Without hurrying as he went, he took in the details of the surroundings and soon came to several impressive, brick-domed buildings. New Warren Central possessed nothing so grand, but these were as nothing when compared with the structures he'd seen in the realm of Tall Ones.

Set in a wall at the front of a building was a square-shaped opening, and there were displayed many items, the identities of which he could not even guess; he realized that this, was the apothecary. There were assorted urns, each bearing graved scratchings. As well, were peculiar, somewhat gruesome looking objects hanging from on high by short strings, and he was unable to imagine their true nature. Recognizing them as shrivelled, dried bodies of small, unidentifiable creatures, he shivered and uttered, '*Corpses!*' beneath his breathe.

As he stood there, the door of the small shop opened and a slight figure wearing a white apron emerged. The boy, no older than Skip, did not go off anywhere as Skip expected, but approached and enquired, 'Hello friend. You're Lillian's patient aren't you? Can I be of help? I'm Michael Stone. I saw you lingering here and wondered...'

'I am, yes. Lillian's patient, that is. I was just looking. Perhaps you can tell me what those are?' He pointed to a group of those dangling, shrivelled carcasses.

'Ornithane,' the boy said. 'It's used as an ingredient in many of my father's tonics and other remedies. It was included in your own remedy; it possesses powerful properties and you're healthy condition is testimony to its efficacy.' Smiling, he said, 'If there's nothing else, I won't keep you. I'm needed inside.' So saying, he pushed open the door and returned to work.

Turning away from the apothecary with its display of ornithane and other, less disturbing wares—including a range of short-handled brooms or brushes, Skip thought of Piedmont—Piedmont and his tatty efforts, produced beneath the oak. There was some vague similarity evident, but brooms displayed here were different in that their handles were adorned with colourful feathers. Wondering over the likelihood of those feathers once belonging to creatures, now unfortunate enough to hang by strings, he continued on his way, ambling farther along the way, and soon came to another small shop. Judging by the delicious aroma coming from the place, he knew it must be Mother Tulip's bake-house. And coming from the place at the very moment of his arriving there, was none other than Nancy's father, Weed. He spotted Weed, before the other noticed him, but then, Weed was the first to speak.

'It's the stranger!' he exclaimed, 'There you are! Here, try one of these!' He thrust a flimsy papyrus bag close to Skip's face. 'If you haven't tasted these, you haven't lived! Have the big one! There, on top!'

These were Mother Tulip's famed cinnamon buns and he would not refuse Weed's offer. Skip said, 'I've heard of these. Nancy says they're irresistible.'

'And, she's right!' exclaimed Weed, watching Skip take a first bite.

Skip rolled his eyes showing appreciation. Cinnamon buns were as good, he decided, as ice cream or any of the things Skip the elder had treated him.

Watching him, Weed exclaimed, 'Yes! Mother Tulip has another convert!' He took a bun from the bag, and then chewing, said, 'I'm guessing, but you're down this way, not for buns—but for Nancy?' And then, 'Yes, I'm correct. It's a pity there are no prizes for guessing such things.' And holding the half-eaten bun, he waved a paw in rough direction, indicating several domes situated farther along the track. 'My place is down that way. It's the one with the big red flag flying. Knowing that, you can't go wrong. You can't see it from here. It's past a bend at far end of the road. As you're headed that way, you can do something for me. You can take the rest of these—there's a good lad!' He passed the bag to Skip. 'Let Mavis know I'm going back to the yard. But, I'll be home soon for lunch. There are days when I like a hot lunch, and this is one of them.' He said, 'Now, you look out for my Nancy won't you?' And, before Skip could reply, 'But, then, it'll be the other way 'round. She'll be looking out for you!' He made to leave but turning back, said, 'I'm glad it was you and not some others I won't name, out there on the lake with my gal. Don't tarry now. Those buns will get cold.' Dusting cinnamon from his paws, Skip looked off down the sloping track.

The Weed residence must be situated close to the lakeshore, thought Skip, and he wondered if flood-damage was sustained. If Weed expected home cooking though, the home must not be affected.

He set off, looking for a flag as he went. He thought of *Missy-Belle* and her bright red pennant, and had not gone much farther, when, above the curved roof-lines of other dwellings, he saw three pointed, conical rooftops, set high upon towers. And there, flying atop tall poles was not one red pennant, but three.

Rounding a final bend he saw an enormous, rectangular flag and he puzzled over it lofting, when nothing more than a moderate breeze blew. He then made out all but invisible lines, running from a tower to the great flag's free-trailing edge. That flag would fly proud, no matter what; those lines were the means by which it was held. At the centre of the flag was an emblem, and he stood on the track, pondering it. There were the sharp-talon claws of Brother Eagle; set upon blood-red field, they were depicted in gold.

He'd no difficulty finding the main entryway. There, above wide, stone steps, was a grand arch and enormous door.

Everything about Weed was large to the extreme. As alternate version, Sherbrook, too, possessed out-going personality and so he would appreciate such magnificence as this. At one side of the door, a rope cord dangled from a small hole in the wall. He yanked on it and was pleased with himself when a loud ringing resulted.

The wave of the previous day was not powerful enough to do real damage to a dwelling as substantial as this, but strewn over wide distance, tangled heaps of uprooted foliage lay drying beneath the mid-morning sun. He saw large, split and broken pumpkins; the remains of produce washed from the communal planting place and deposited here.

When she opened the door, his astonishment was difficult to contain for she was Mavis Whitepaws! In the home realm, Sherbrook had so adored her. Here, Weed had won her favour and disaster-prone Charlie Noy-Breen played no part. This Mavis knew that Charlie was responsible for littering the territory surrounding her home and that was all. He would never, Skip thought, be accustomed to the fact of former friends and acquaintances having alternate versions.

Granting a radiant smile, she greeted him with, 'You must be, Skip?'

When he did not answer, she said, 'Come inside and we'll see what Nancy's up to.' A loud wailing came from back of the house and she called, 'Samuel, bide your time. I'll be there!' She beckoned, insisting, 'Come along. Come in. I feel I should be in five places at once!'

Once inside, and recalling his errand, he exclaimed, 'Oh, I'm to give you these. They're cinnamon buns from Weed. He told me to tell you that he expects to be home for lunch.'

'Oh, he does? Indeed! Then, perhaps he can do some small thing for me when he gets here. If I put my mind to it, I'm sure I can come up with something.' She called, 'Samuel, what are you doing?' She commented, 'Silence is ominous. Come on through, before he gets into too much mischief.'

Moving through a grand hallway she called, 'Nancy gal, your friend's here!' As an aside, she said, 'I'm always shouting to make myself heard. I'm hoarse by day's end.'

The walls here were smooth and white. Their appearance reminded of those seen in the realm of Tall Ones, and he enquired as to the material used.

'It's called plaster!' cried Nancy, dashing from a doorway and into the hall, 'I'm so glad you're here. I've wanted to show you the look-out!'

'Don't helter in the house,' her mother warned. 'Accidents can happen! How often must I warn?' She said, 'If you're going to show your friend the look-out, take care to explain the dangers.' Turning to Skip, she said, 'It's not too dangerous and I see you're sensible, but be sure not to lean out when you're up there. We don't have ways of putting boys back together again.'

'Oh, Mother, you do go on!'

'That's enough, Nancy.'

The hallway widened out in a smooth curve before opening into a great hall. At a far corner of the immense space, was a structure he would learn was a spiral staircase. Nancy made for those stairs insisting, 'Come on Skip. Let's go!'

He did not accord with her bidding, because there upon the wall opposite, was something that captured his attention. Entranced by its strangeness, he halted and stood gazing up at it. The over-sized representation bore just vague similarity to those images he was acquainted with. He'd seen Peace Darkling's likeness and much else depicted in the realm of Tall Ones, but here was significant difference. The surface of this image was not smooth but textured; it was a colourful representation of Weed, Mavis and their children. There was Nancy, at least twice as large as life, sitting at the feet of over-sized parents. She wore a yellow dress. The small boy sitting beside her, his paw resting in familial manner upon hers, must be Samuel. Skip was both enthralled and puzzled. There was certain roughness to the execution; the figures were distorted and yet truth was conveyed by emotive means. He asked, 'It is your family, I see that, but what is its purpose?'

Nancy, pausing at the foot of the staircase could not conceal her impatience, but then, growing serious, she said, 'It's a work of artifice and serves no practical purpose. It edifies though. There's more to it than the sum of the parts. As subject portrayed, you might know us better by looking into it. It conveys truth of our natures and characters. At least that's as Joshua Grey, its maker, taught me to define it. Come on! I want you to see the view from the top of the tower.'

'Then, it's versifying without words,' Skip said.

'Yes, I suppose that's a way of seeing it.'

'I find it *very* interesting, and I think he must have had a good time spreading so much coloured dirt—if that's what it is.'

'Yes, he did. He made it out on our terrace and we sat there for so long that I thought my tail would wear out. By the time he finished, there was more colour on him, than it.' She stamped up the stairway then, without giving so much as a backward glance.

A speck of unidentifiable brightness was discerned, moving against a smear of grey-green, far out across the lake; that dull green was the reed-beds they'd sailed past. There was an indistinct area of lighter green, and that was the willows. Out there, squalling wind whipped at the waters sending a fine mist through the air and small white-capped waves patterned the choppy surface. The day now, was not clear as earlier on, and so the view from their vantage point fell short of expectation.

Nancy complained, 'I've dragged you all the way up here, and now you can't see much at all.'

Not the least disappointed, he said, 'Oh no, it's wonderful. You're very lucky.' He asked, 'Have you ever slept up here?'

She shook her head.

'That's what I'd do.'

As if she did not know it, he said, 'All of Brickfield is at your feet!'

He'd turned away from the view of the lake and pointing at distant homes of the village, mentioned several of those places he recognized, saying, 'There's the home of the amazing cinnamon bun—Mother Tulip's. You can see the top of her roof and the chimney. And, over there just past that, is my home away from home, Buckminster's and Lillian's—not that I'm certain of it. No, I'm wrong about that. But, the brickyard chimneys stand out, don't they? From up here, you can see pretty much all your father does. You can spy on him, whenever you like.'

She giggled, and he said, 'Not that you'd ever want to do such a thing.' The wind gusted then, and the grand flag was set rippling to life. Skip asked, 'What is the meaning of the claw of Brother Eagle, there on the flag?'

'Father's dream,' she said. 'He dreamed of Brother Eagle.' She paused, smiling. 'You see, my father is a believer in mystery, and supports the notion of supernatural causes. He discerns strangeness in even the most mundane, everyday events. Now, please don't laugh. At his bedside, are kept leaves of papyrus and charcoal stick for making scratching, even in the dark of night. You see, he records his dreams.'

'I don't see anything odd in it.' Skip said, 'You would have to be on close terms with Piedmont the Bard to…'

'Oh! You've reminded me!' Nancy interjected, 'Go ahead now, and see if you can know what Father has planned for my birthday!'

He did know. His seeing was fine. A party of many friends gathered in the great hall downstairs. And there, included as most esteemed attraction, and reading for guests from a weighty tome, was the individual known as Pietro, a younger, more dapper version of Piedmont the Bard, and in glancing up from a page, Pietro seemed to stare straight back at Skip.

Knowing now, that she belonged here, and so, the elder was correct all along, Skip, accepted defeat. He said, 'I see Pietro the Bard has been asked to read from his *Collected Works*. I see him reading for guests at your birthday party.'

Throwing her arms around him, Nancy exclaimed, 'Oh, yes! Do tell me you *will* come, Skip! Just, *everyone* will be here!'

He could do nothing at all to alter any of it.

Journeying to realms and worlds without end should never be expected to contest with Pietro the Bard, or with, *Missy-Belle* and so much else. He said, 'I won't be here, Nancy, but thank you for inviting me.'

She, looking forlorn and pouting, declared, 'Skip, I'm speechless. What could be more important to you than my party?'

FOLLY—ENOUGH!

He had searched long for the boy and without success, but then he sighted him. Buckminster peered out now, from behind the red-berry tarrash bush. Large clumps of the bushes thrived at an outmost edge of the forest clearing and at a side of the winding path. His presence was concealed but Buckminster insisted that he was not hiding. His was not an enviable circumstance. If he were seen by others, they might assume he was involved in nefarious activity, when, the truth was, he'd halted where he had in order to regain his breath; that was what he told himself.

He'd followed the boy for quite some distance, but the youngster set a gruelling pace and had no trouble staying well ahead of him. His puffing and wheezing reminded Buckminster he was no longer as young as he'd like. Whilst coming along the way, he could have called for Skip to hear, but the way the boy took would lead him into the forest, and that was odd. Why would the boy tell them he was leaving, and then enter the forest by a dead-end route? It made no sense.

Lillian would not be pleased if he failed to return the youngster, for fussing over. By now she would have dealt with the task of provisioning him for his journey.

He raised a paw and pushed aside an obscuring, dark-leafed branch. His view was not much improved, but, Skip was seen conversing at the clearing's opposite side with another youngster. Buckminster decided better than intrude. Still holding aside the branch, he raised his other paw to his face and rubbed at first one eye, and then the other. Still, his old eyes deceived him for, together in the clearing were, two of them! Two Skips! This could not be! It was impossible!

Squinting again, and commanding his eyes to better focus, he searched for another, less discomforting truth.

But then, both boys turned to face him, and so, they were aware of his presence.

'Farewell, Uncle Bucky!' they called, 'Thank you old friend!' There was terrible flashing of brightest light and an almighty CRACK! Buckminster was knocked to the path, where he decided to stay until his ears ceased ringing. He wondered, whatever might Lillian say? She had nursed back to health, a creature of supernatural origin. She had fed it broth! Would she be fearful or consider herself blessed?

Something like superstition stirred in Buckminster, and picking himself up from the dirt he decided to say not a single word. No. What was best for his dear old gal was that she be given naught to trouble her, not so much as cause for slightest doubt.

Thinking of that pebble on the mantle at home, he reminded himself to better examine it upon his return. Young Skip was nowhere to be found in Brickfield, he would say, which was true; he was not.

He must not allow himself to be cajoled by his better-half into feeling obligated to go traipsing off, searching byways in vain search of Skip—if indeed Skip was his name—for he was no ordinary boy, but entity, the like of which no mortal should even dream of encountering. They had called him, "Bucky", which was intriguing. Long ago his mother had called him it, and mindful now of hearing again the shortened version of his name, a pleasant feeling arose in him. From time to time during his remaining days, Buckminster would find himself scratching his head and questioning the reason for their referring to him as not just, "Bucky", but, as well, "Uncle".

* * *

'Woo-hah!' Skip exclaimed, swaying on his feet. They were back at the beach, a mere instant after having departed for Brickfield.

'Flabbergasting, isn't it?' The elder said, 'Mere nanosecond has transpired, and we're back! If we had not finished our ice-cream before leaving, it would not yet have melted.' He said, 'Light was doubled at our return, and the kazooning heard upon arrival, was caused a moment earlier, by our departing.'

'But why are we back in this moment?' Skip asked. 'That was an *awful* feeling!'

'I wanted to prevent the gulls from messing with our stuff, that's all.' The elder shrugged.

Skip said, 'I'm bothered.'

'Why's that?'

'Don't you know?'

'At times, I prefer not knowing everything. I blank out much of it.'

Measuring words, Skip asked, 'You are Tump. You are a version of me. And so, who do *you* use as a channel?'

'We use Nancy.'

'Whaah?' Skip grimaced with frustration, 'How *can* that be?'

Elder Skip smiled and then, pointing to the ocean, asked, 'How many droplets make an ocean? It's not a ridiculous question. How many would you guess?' Then, presenting options, 'An infinite number? Or, do you prefer thinking of it as one, gigantic drop?'

Young Skip said, 'Please, tell me about Nancy?'

'There is an infinite number of Nancys. They're not all named Nancy. There's a Marguerite in amongst them too, because there must be. There must be several thousand Janes and a few zillion Pollyannas—not to mention a couple of Briannes, just for good measure. And there are other names, some of them well beyond pronouncing or even knowing but then, personal relationships are meaningful, aren't they?' Skip nodded agreement, and the elder continued, 'That being so, we went back to Brickfield to see if she might be persuaded to leave, but whether or not you asked it of her, she would never. She is not *your* Nancy, for the simplest of reasons. She is very happy with things as they are.'

'Well, yes,' agreed Skip, 'In any case, I did not have the heart to ask it of her.'

'Correct decision, Buckaroo! It was wise, treating the situation as you did, and you did not have to hear her refuse you. Shivering in mock-horror, he said, 'I'm glad you spared yourself *that!*'

After a moment during which neither spoke, the elder commented upon the weather, 'We must compliment, Great Grandfather on another perfect day.'

Young Skip asked, 'Do you believe you can find Him?'

'Yes, we do. Even if we're mistaken though, and we don't find Him, we're having a tremendous time trying.'

'Where, is the *right* Nancy, the Nancy, for me?'

The elder said, 'She's in your home realm; that's where. But I must tell you, she's not yet born.' That is, at the time of you leaving the realm—courtesy of Brother Eagle, she is not born.' He went on, 'She's born at a later time and it works out well, because she joins with you and your friends once everything is in place.'

He spoke of mystery, of everything being in place at some vague sounding, future time. He was confused, but, Skip would not let it show. He asked, 'Is there the slightest chance that Nancy of my home realm will refuse to join my group?'

Elder Skip sighed. He said, 'I want you to stop worrying over every detail. Allow me to demonstrate the true power of Tump.' He stood up and went a short distance across the sand. Then, without drama of either dazzling or kazooning, a magical shimmering touched the air. A sparkling of diamond-light moved swirling, whirling as slow-pooling water. Then, beside the elder on the white sandy beach was another, one whom Skip recognized.

She was not Nancy of Brickfield, not that same individual, but still, the resemblance was uncanny. Skip stared in disbelief.

She smiled, asking, 'Will you say anything?'

'Um... Yes. When next we meet, how should I ask you to come with me?'

She said, 'There's no need to concern yourself, Skip, because you don't ask me. Piedmont does.' She paused before amending, 'I should say that he doesn't ask me. He allows me to do the asking.'

'Where have you come from? I mean, you've come from another time and place, but, how?' She said, 'I've not come from another location, either in space or time. I've been with you all along as your elder.'

Turning and facing him, she told elder Skip, 'It's time now, to move things along.'

He gave a short nod of agreement and then, raising a paw high above his head, announced, 'We are Tump, divisible and yet One!'

Skip's jaw dropped so his mouth hung open. There on the beach, before him, were not two, but seven others!

Casting a critical glance, Nancy said, 'Introduction is way overdue,' and the elder, shrugged as response. Addressing young Skip then, she said, 'I shall tell you of Tump.

'From time's very beginning, the word manifest as the All. And, Piedmont best knows the power of the Word.'

The bard was impatient and after granting a nod, he wasted no time in making for the shade of an outsized boulder, which stood at the edge of a nearby rock-pool.

Nancy said, 'You are familiar with our Skip. But you have seen little of his ability and skill. The seer can move mountains and it is by his power that we traverse the currents of the All.' Smiling, she added, 'All too often without our agreement, but rather, as he sees fit.'

She had taken charge now, and elder Skip, choosing Piedmont as company, drifted off.

Peace, as beautiful as ever she was, directed him a small wave.

'Without Peace, Tump would never have been. By her teaching, our energy is raised high, that we may join with light.'

Introducing Clever Fixer, Nancy exclaimed, 'Technologist extraordinaire! The fixer is rightful inheritor, guardian of the seed. If not for his generosity, Tump would not have Great Grandfather's map.' She explained, 'Our navigator would have nothing to guide him. Fixer possesses knowledge of mystic workings and manipulation of energies.'

Skip remembered Clever from earliest days spent at old Warren Central. Most unusual in appearance, the fixer wore a dark grey, greatcoat and a peculiar three-cornered hat, sporting long, magenta, lime-green and deep purple feathers. After presenting a snappy salute, he seated himself on the sand.

Young Skip leaned back in his chair, and Nancy introduced his rival for Uncle Bucky's attention. The uncertain nature of his feelings must bear scrutiny later on.

Stepping forward, Simple Rudy raised his nose high in the air and tilted his head to one side, as if expecting trouble from hovering gulls. The mannerism was characteristic, something Simple did often, when nervous.

'Simple Rudy, savant and way finder,' said, Nancy, 'Our navigator...'

She would have said more, but, Simple Rudy interrupted proceedings by venturing close to Skip, declaring, 'Oh, you know me, Sir! I am your friend and will ever be.' He moved still closer and enquired, 'Is that chair taken or are you saving it?'

He told Rudy, 'No, I guess you can take it, Simple. I'm sure no one will mind.'

Rudy said, 'I see you have snacks, and I'm ravenous! We've all been so busy, busy, busy, haven't we?'

Nancy said, 'Friend Sherbrook puts others before himself. He is most sincere, faithful and Tump-wise! He is our sure anchor, and without him, maelstrom might carry us to peril or worse.'

'Those are generous words,' Sherbrook said, 'But, I must ask Rudy, leave something for me!'

Rudy protested, 'But I've been keeping the *best* for you!' He held aloft an all but empty pack of candy.

Sherbrook accused, 'You're a kadoodler, Rudy, because they're gone!'

Peace ordered, 'Stop, Rudy, before you make yourself ill.'

Looking to Nancy, Skip asked, 'You are not Nancy of Brickfield, that much is clear. But who are your parents? Is Mavis Whitepaws your mother? Who is your father?'

She said, 'My father is Charlie Noy-Breen. The ability to channel is passed from mother to child and not from the father. In all our searching, Tump has not discovered a Nancy born to anyone other than Mavis.' Smiling, she added, 'Which is not to say, that is always her name.' She laughed, and asked, 'I am not Nancy of Brickfield, but in my own right, I hope I'm not too much of a disappointment?'

He said, 'You could never be that.'

She replied, 'Take care, or you'll soon be as charming as your elder.'

Peace called then, to his elder, advising, 'Take young Skip back to Brickfield, and don't say you're tired of the place, because I insist upon your going.'

Nancy shared agreement with Peace. He had no say as to where they went, but if his elder complained, Skip would understand. Seeing Peace was determined, he knew they were going back whether they liked it or not.

Then, Peace explained, 'There is good reason for your returning, Skip. You must see the way life turns out for Brickfield's Nancy. You will learn of a life exemplifying Tump, at deepest level. Nancy of Brickfield is not always the indulged, spoiled child of your previous sojourns. You must gain knowledge of a life set against severe odds.'

Skip the elder was glib, complaining, 'I had planned on teaching my younger self to move living things.' He gestured overhead, 'Gulls are perfect candidates.'

Peace said, 'We will show our young charge a life moved to good outcome.'

She called, 'Piedmont and Fixer! Come now. All gather!' She ordered, 'Rudy, consult the map.'

'I have!'

With that said, writhing waveforms of translucent light, sprinkled with pinpoints of diamond brightness, moved between individual Tump, melding them. They faded from sight and when they went, young Skip heard Sherbrook, voicing exclamation over something Rudy must have said or done. 'Ah, Rudy, you break me up!' There was no longer the least sign of Sherbrook, Simple Rudy or the others. They had the beach to themselves again.

'You now know Tump is One. Now cover your ears!'

The forest clearing bore little resemblance to that he was familiar with.

'*Brickfield Town Park*,' announced, elder Skip. 'There's no accounting for taste, but I preferred it the way it was.' He said, 'You will note that electricity has been discovered and so the place can be illuminated at night.'

His attention was directed to poles, strung with wires and spaced about the area, but the park was subdued by twilight gloom; whatever electricity was, it was not working. He could not credit the fact of so much change. Upon a black-stone plinth, at the centre of a low walled, circular pond, was an imposing statue of Weed. From high vantage point, Weed was ever prepared for frowning down at passers-by. An irreverent note was supplied; his right arm and an ear were missing.

Staring up, the elder said, 'It's a pity the powers out. It would be nice to see him at his best.' He said, 'There are several spigots at the edge of this pond, and water is jetted up to wet his feet. It cascades down the surface of that black standing-stone, then back into the pond. It's quite the spectacle and makes for a fitting tribute.' He sighed and then commented, 'A point is driven home, isn't it? The shortest time ago, it was all buns and a hot lunch.' Pointing, he said, 'Graved in stone there, below our friend's feet, is acknowledgement of his benevolence and steadfast service to Brickfield.'

Encircling the pond was a wide, brick-paved promenade, which extended outwards to the broad trunks of giant trees.

'When, back in home territory, you should ask Piedmont to teach you to read. There are many versions of scratching, but when time lines run close, similar marks are often used, and meaning is comprehended.

'But now we must away, taking care how we go, because curfew is in place. We will not "move" unless menaced or cornered. If our presence is detected it can mean trouble for others. Wait just a moment, while I "see" what's ahead. Not knowing what's in store can be exciting, but with the way the realm is, there's wisdom in wanting certainty.'

A moment later, he said, 'We must wait, before crossing that second street. After that, all seems safe.' Following the dark path, the elder asked, 'How's your ability, by the way? I see your light shines bright. You should be seeing well enough. I could look and know, but will allow you privacy.'

Skip said, 'I know why we go by way of back street and alley. I see various outcomes. It's not the Brickfield of times past, is it? Not at all.'

'You're attempting to fathom the identity of those, black-garbed monsters, aren't you?'

Young Skip said, '*Watchers* aren't they? They're known as that.'

'Yes. That's as they've named themselves, but they are watchers without good reason, they do not stand watch as protectors or guardians over the welfare of others. Their aim is to ensure obedient servitude. This is a vile time in the great mix of things. Brickfield suffers occupation by invaders from far afield, by a tribe, the like of which none here knew. And, if such uninvited presence was not enough, they brought plague with them. As carriers, they were little affected by the disease, but folk of this territory were struck down in droves. You mustn't fear for your safety. The last of devastation, illness and gazuzzlement, has passed, but of itself, the invader's presence is disease. Brickfield, with its innovations and other blessings, was taken by the barbarous horde as a rich prize, but then, not much of that which they consider theirs by right of conquest, is put to good use.

'Farther ahead is a time of peace; a golden age. For now, though, watchers can be thought of as Grammy Graymark with a big stick.

The winding path brought them out to a wide, paved roadway. We'll get across here and then make the dash into yon' alleyway, the elder said, pointing to the dark mouth of a narrow way between dwellings situated across the road. Once in the alley, we must keep close to the walls as we go. Keeping his voice low, he said, 'Sometimes, even seeing is no guarantee against the untoward. Certain individuals and events are obscured or veiled.'

He provided a whispered monologue as they entered the alleyway, and young Skip, adhering to instruction by staying close to walls, had difficulty in hearing everything he said. Following along behind him, he questioned the elder's need to prattle. If he did not know better, he might decide, the elder was of doubtful nerve, but then the alternative might be as true; the elder was exhilarated and prattled because he was not able to contain his enthusiasm for the mission.

In mentioning those occasions when detailed information of future events was obscured he'd sounded as if he would not mind if such were the case tonight. Now the elder said, 'There is a whole mess of things they call trash bins further along. They're overflowing with waste. Watch out not to run into them. You would think they'd be more conscientious with cleaning away garbage after a gazuzzling epidemic's had its way.' He said, 'I don't know if you saw it, but just up here a bit, after we leave the alley, there are a recalcitrant pair who dash from one side of the street to the other. They're curfew-breakers and, they'll just make it, into the house over there.' At the end of the narrow thoroughfare they now stood facing a wide avenue. 'Just look at those two helter!' the elder said, seeing two young bucks making for safety. 'Yes, there he is. Do you see him? He's not skulking but he's not making his presence too obvious either.'

Rounding a corner farther up the street was a towering, dark-clad presence and as he progressed along the walk, he too stayed close to the walls. The elder said, 'They don't go armed for nothing so we'd best wait here before continuing. We want to proceed in the direction he's come from. Pathetic isn't it? They patrol a bone-yard. Most places here are empty. Most souls are gone, but ... hush now.'

They pressed back into a deeper shadow until the watcher had passed. A thin, tuneless whistling was heard.

The elder commented beneath his breath, 'Whistle a happy tune, eh?' Then, 'Sorry, don't laugh!' as Skip stifled the beginnings of mirth.

The elder looked up the gradual sloping road to its high end, and whilst peering down to opposite end, young Skip informed, 'He's gone now.'

'We must helter,' urged the elder and they dashed to the other side of the street. Here the alleyway, re-continued traversing between allotments, which for the most part supported Brickfield's inimitable, domed structures.

They soon arrived at the back of a larger building than others they'd passed along the way. Here the wall facing the alley was higher than at other places, and set between large brick pillars and an arch, was a solid wooden gate.

Peering close in the dark, the elder carried out a close inspection of the gate and in doing so, muttered, 'Details, details.' He admitted, 'I never saw this. It's always the little things we miss, isn't it? We can always be undone by them.' There was a very sturdy latch and he pushed against it, but to no avail.

Young Skip uttered, '*Deeks*! Maybe we won't get in without moving.' That said, he noticed something set into one of those dark-brick pillars. A peculiar looking, funnel-shaped object was positioned there at about head height. 'What's this thing?' he wondered aloud.

'Ah, I've seen this before,' the elder said, interested. 'But, it was not hereabout. It's a speaking tube. You blow into it to get the attention of someone at the other end. Tall Ones use them as a communication device on vessels called ships. I've not seen any put to use this way before. It's an ingenious piece of apparatus.' Enthusiastic now, he put his face close to an opening. He inhaled and then blew into it, but after waiting for long moments, his effort remained unrewarded. He said, 'We're going to have to "move" after all. I will not wait out here in the dark, puffing into this thing!'

Then a reed-thin whistling sounded. A hollow muffled sounding voice followed. Leaning forward, the elder cocked his head to jam an ear against the funnel opening. Apart from a blur of mumbled sound, Skip did not discern any sense of the message coming to them but, after putting mouth, rather than ear to the device, the elder hissed in exasperated fashion, 'Listen, just tell her to send someone out here to open the gate!' He added, 'Our business is important. We don't care about curfew! Tell her it's an errand of mercy!' After listening again, feigning the greatest weariness, he spoke into the funnel, 'Yes, yes. Over and out to you too.'

Moving back from the speaking tube, he told young Skip, 'That was Joseph, one of the youngsters. He's gone to get Mother Nancy. I hope...'

Very soon, a shuffling was heard from the other side of the wall, and this was followed by an ancient, ragged, all but inaudible voice enquiring, 'How may I serve you?'

And contrary to every prudent precautionary measure taken in getting them this far, the impatient elder, adopting most forthright manner, announced, 'We are not watchers by night and intend no mischief or harm. We would speak with good Mother Nancy...'

The voice replied, 'Yes, but still, it is rather late for visiting...'

Elder Skip responded, 'Folly enough! We are TUMP! Now open up!'

SISTERS OF THE SHELL

'The occupier took my father's house for barracks. It was commandeered at the very beginning.' Mother Nancy said, 'Do you recall me showing you the lookout? You were going to ask if I'd go with you, I think, but perhaps you lacked confidence. Was that it?' Skip nodded, and she said, 'I could never have acceded to going. My young life was too good to leave, but then, was it? Truth is, I've not thought of it for so long.' She smiled, and he saw the same Nancy was there still, she of forest and lake and sweet cinnamon buns. He recognized her by lantern-light, despite the effect of enfeebling age; she was grey and walked with the aid of a cane, but she was still Nancy.

'I, for one, am glad you did not go with him.'

'Yes … yes Michael,' she soothed. The decrepit oldster, Michael, had opened the gate to them. He accompanied them now, carrying a jittering lantern attached to an end of a long pole as they made their way down a long corridor flanked by balustrades, on the way to the chapel where Nancy said there was something she believed would interest young Skip.

She said, 'My old Michael is the truest companion and most loyal friend, aren't you, dear?'

'Always,' the oldster affirmed.

'It's Doctor Michael,' she explained, 'Doctor Michael Stone. You recall, Isaac Stone and the apothecary? Yes? Michael is the son of Isaac. We've long worked together. Since the outset, all through the time of plague, Michael stood firm against fear and personal interest; by his tireless effort and skill, many were spared gazuzzlement. He is my, Mydor. I have not forgotten Skip, you reciting verse of *Lament Mydor*, that day beneath the willows, "*…as stone, set 'gainst hail and driving rain.*"

'That's you, Michael, isn't it dear? Stone set, 'gainst far worse.

I have never known to whom the verse refers, but I do know a valiant heart. It's true that the time of worst travail is past but wounds are deep. Cruel joy is sifting old times. Too many friends will never again join us. Looking ahead to better times is healthy but loss is not forgotten. Perhaps the children can be free but for an oldster, it's a hard thing excising bitterness from the heart.' Coming to the corridor's end, Mother Nancy directed them to enter a large room to their right. She said, 'It's past "candles-out" but I will introduce you to our little ones before we continue on to chapel.'

Entering the room she made gentle enquiry, 'Sister Francis? There are welcome guests come visiting late. They honour us with their presence this evening. I believe they and our young ones should enjoy meeting.'

There were many youngsters present, some sitting, some recumbent. The large room was a dormitory, with pallets arranged in neat rows along the walls, and on each pallet, a youngster.

'Ah, I see good Sister Francis has been reading to you,' Nancy said smiling. 'That explains such perfect quietness. And, what is our story this evening? It must be a very good one.'

The young doe, Sister Francis, came across the room to meet them. When rising from her chair set at the room's centre, she said, her voice soft and melodious, 'Here you are, Clara, sweetheart. You must look after the scratchings until my return.' Even by flickering candlelight, Skip saw an expression of delight on the face of she, chosen from among the rest, for special duty.

'And, what is the story?' enquired Mother Nancy.

'It's from *Home Fireside Companion* Mother. Tonight's story is *Song of White Winter*.'

'Ah! The ubiquitous Pietro,' Nancy observed, and in an aside to both Skips, 'After focusing on verse, he went on to scribe several stories with children in mind. Quite marvellous, entertaining fare! For most part, the characters are a family of small creatures, abiding in a wilderness setting. The stories extol and laud virtue of home.

'You must be certain, Sister Francis, to replace *Home Fireside Companion* after each reading.' Lowering her voice so that it was no more than a whisper she asked, It's still one of those titles banned, isn't it?' She added, with helpless exasperation, 'Although, I'm sure, no one of sound mind can know why it should be so. None among *them* will have troubled to read it but then, it's the title—the word "Home", isn't it? Had Pietro thought of leaving it as *Fireside Companion*, then, authority would have passed it by.' Sister Francis said, 'On the other paw—the word *companion* is suspect. Anything having to do with friendship is frowned upon.' Mother Nancy smiled, observing, 'And, reading things that way, *fire—*side might be viewed as having a dangerous, incendiary connotation,' and each of them put paw to mouth, not wishing to laugh outright.

The elder asked, 'How do you keep the youngsters this quiet? They're so quiet, it's unnatural.' It was true, young Skip thought; there was not a peep from them.

Mother Nancy said, 'It's just their way.'

Leaving young Skip with Mother Nancy and Sister Francis, the elder went to the middle of the room, and leaning toward a frizzy-furred youngster, asked, 'What's your name, Buckaroo? I'll bet it's a good one.'

The boy told him, 'I am, Malcolm Smallflag,' and that was not all. 'My father is also Malcolm, and Mother's name is Emily. It's nice here, but one day they will come and fetch me.'

Hearing Malcolm give so much information, others began speaking up, giving their names and expressing similar sentiment. Skip told Malcolm, 'It's a fine name, but look what we've started now!' Raising his paws for silence, he said, 'If you go back to being as quiet and well behaved as before, I will show you your world as you will know it. I will promise to entertain you. '

His announcement and request were met with many small murmurs of delight.

A curious youngster questioned, 'Entertainment? What will it be? Are you going to dance a jig for us?'

Another suggested, 'He's going to sing a song. That's what I say!'

Then, speaking up, a boy told his friends, 'He said he would entertain, but that's not the important part. Our *world* is the important thing.' The elder complimented the boy for fully comprehending what he'd said. Then, they hushed, and as they were silent, elder Skip, almost whispering, so they must strain to catch what he said, told them, 'You won't know it, but with me are several friends of mine. You can't see them because they are invisible. Does anyone here not believe me? Speak up now, if you don't.' All believed, because not a single paw went up and no one spoke. He told them, 'These friends of mine you will not see, but I will speak with them and ask them to grant you a glimpse of your new world.'

Voice lowered still, but with emphasis applied, he declared, 'Tump is One! Rudy, plot our course!'

A diminutive gal sitting very close to his feet gasped, 'He called *Tump!*'

He told her, 'Hush now, sweetheart, we don't want me forgetting what I must say, do we?'

The gal shook her head. 'Uh uh,' she agreed. She put a paw over her mouth to be sure. The child was not alone in uttering exclamation, for Sister Francis was astonished also, and received reassurance from Mother Nancy, who took her paw murmuring, 'Hush now, Sister, we know they are friends. Let us open ourselves to the miracle of it.'

'Peace, initiate joining!

'Piedmont, wake up old one!

'Sherbrook, ground us!

'Nancy, stand by!

'Fixer, engage the gate!'

From a bright pin-point of white light, appearing at the ceiling above the place the elder stood, shot out myriad, crisscrossing lines until those occupying the room were contained and held enthralled, beneath a dome of thin, web-like threads of light. Then, from points where line intersected line, as water flooding into gaps, colour filled intervening spaces until a scene of undeniable reality was manifest.

Tangible, but lacking movement, all was yet frozen moment, but, even so, the quality of reality was such that a wafting breeze might be imagined caressing a cheek, or the sound of a creaking gate heard. The dormitory floor had transformed; becoming a village roadway.

From those present came expressions of wonderment and pleasure, and the elder instructed, 'Come close to me. Make a group in the centre of the room—or street.' Children gathered at the elder's feet, and he told them, 'This place is your own home territory of Brickfield.'

He said, 'To most folk here, we are less than wraith and they cannot realize our presence. The cleverest of them, though, sensing we are amongst them, will believe that they "know". Those clever folk are nonother than our future selves. In time to come, is one whom has not forgotten and recalling still, Tump visiting the orphanage this night, has kept watch for this very moment's occurring in his "present". The "present" you see now all about you, but we need not concern ourselves with him.

'This is Brickfield, after the occupation ends. I will not show you *how* the enemy is vanquished, but, all that you see about you is proof of happier times to come.'

Not understanding much of explanation, those, very young, began to fidget; they were impatient to be shown more. Elder Skip was happy to oblige. He said, 'If you will now all stand up—you can go off and explore your future home.'

And, the scene came to life. High over-head, puffs of pristine white cloud floated in a blue, summery sky. A small dust devil formed in the road and went whirling off, traversed the breadth of the dirt road and brushed against a picket fence before dissipating. From the group of children playing flibberty-hop-tag in the garden of a home, merry laughter rose to shady treetop and beyond, and was answered by nesting birds. Neighbour called to neighbour across ivy covered, dividing wall, affirming agreement regarding the day's perfection.

There was no virtual, "ring of truth" to any of it, for it was actuality and they were there.

Hearing the elder permit the orphans to go exploring, Sister Francis uttered a nervous gasp, and Mother Nancy turned to young Skip, 'They might meet with harm. Can they be lost?'

Catching up with proceedings, seeing a world he was unaccustomed to, ancient Michael cried, 'This is most wondrous!'

Addressing Mother Nancy's concern, young Skip assured, 'No one is harmed, good Mother—not as I see.'

Overhearing them the elder insisted, 'The opposite is true.'

Young Skip told Mother Nancy, 'I am your Skip, the one closest to you, but my elder is by far the wiser. If he says it is safe, then it is.'

He told Doctor Stone, 'You won't need to take that lantern with you, Doctor.' The old one muttered. He opened a small door at one side of the lantern but then, thought better than extinguish the flame; he shut the door and secured its latch. He told the lantern, 'I'll leave you burning, your service will be required later on. In the meantime, don't go out on me.'

Instructing clamouring youngsters, the elder said, 'If folk move through you, it can be unsettling and so, avoid such encounters. Do not go through walls. Respect the privacy of others. When it is time to return

I will call you and I will not want stragglers. Off you go now!' Most did just that, but two remained, and looking to him, one asked, 'Our future must hold certain keys, clues to determining moments. How are they recognized?'

Perhaps the elder had not heard. He was preoccupied and thoughtful, and then his demeanour altered and calling across the way, he enquired, 'Sister Francis—shall we?' He gave his most charming smile, and crooking an elbow, invited her to venture forth with him.

She hung back, keeping close to Mother Nancy. Nancy said, 'You never know, dear, you could enjoy yourself.' The elder smiled, and then responded to the boy, still lingering close at heel. With voice as low as a whisper, he said, 'Now, Zee, Buckaroo, you know I can't tell you that.'

'You mean, you *won't*,' Zee hissed, 'If you wanted to, you could.'

The lad reminded him of himself at that age. 'Whether I can't or won't is not the point. You'll figure it out for yourself.' She had drawn close, and he said, 'Francis, I'm delighted you can join me. She rested paw against proffered arm. He asked, 'Shall we?' And they moved from dusty roadway to proceed along the walk.

'You must forgive me, Sister,' he said, 'The sun's a-warming and I have not provided you a parasol, but omission aside, I do adore to promenade, don't you?'

Zee and friend, Bernard, chose to tag along. Whilst chatting with Francis, the elder kept an ear on the conversation of those two.

'There will be clues, Bernard.'

'Uh, huh...'

'This place is formed from everything familiar to us. There will be signs of past turning points.'

'Uh, huh...'

'So, focus, Bernard. Don't just look, but *think* about everything you see.'

'I will.'

Bernard should be complimented for being an attentive listener, thought the elder.

At opposite side of the street, his younger self was engaged in discussion with Mother Nancy. In their company was Doctor Stone. They all headed in direction of Brickfield's primary thoroughfare. In a yard farther ahead, two orphaned gals stood together amidst hollyhock plantings, admiring translucent blossoms superimposed over their own forms. Still farther distant were several pranksters who, delighting in the fact of their invisible status, engaged in repetitive leaping back and forth—in and out of two hard-toiling roads workers. The workers filled potholes and then pounded the blunt end of a crowbar against a sturdy wood plank, which they'd set against the ground.

He was successful in distracting the young sister's attention, before she noticed the orphans and their mischief, by pointing out the painted surfaces of once dull-brick, domed buildings.

She exclaimed, 'Oh, yes! It's wonderful. A rainbow has settled over everything.' Born to the realm following the invasion, all she had known was sombre, sad Brickfield. Mother Nancy and Doctor Stone, in rare, free moments, made mention in passing of earlier times.

She enjoyed hearing of the "Times of Light", as did other Sisters of the Shell, for, in the main, they were young. Information gained by hearing others reminisce was of course, not the same as experiencing those times. There were not many oldsters who survived. Many fell foul of the regime's dictate, which resulted in gazuzzlement—of not just themselves, but of family members, friends and others. Strolling arm in arm with him along Brickfield's future streets, the sister delighted in all she saw. Her inner journey of discovery, revealed a hitherto unrealized capacity for enjoyment, as her eyes welcomed each new sight.

'This is Father's business. The apothecary,' declared Doctor Stone, as they stood on the walk, before the place. Uncertainty tinged his voice. 'This must be it, but in truth, it's no longer recognizable as such.'

Seeking reassurance, he looked to his friend, Mother Nancy, who, seeing dismay in his expression, offered, 'Things change Michael. We've seen so much of it, a little more of the same is perhaps to be expected.'

He said, 'Yes, of course you're right. I can't say Father would be thrilled to see it, but those rowdy youngsters are enjoying the use of the premises. It's not such a bad thing.' Going to the entranceway, and peering inside, he said, 'They're, all of them, so fit and healthy. Although, young Celia and Rupert Streak are in there as well, and they could do with some fattening up.' He asked, 'What do you suppose it is they're playing at?'

Mother Nancy observed, 'Mm. It's not like any dance, I've seen.'

As if knowing his presence was required, the elder, still arm in arm with Sister Francis, strolled over to them. Zee and sidekick, Bernard, were in tow, sticking as mud. Skip explained, 'It's called Hargolin. It may look like a game to us, but they are not playing.'

'There's real purpose to it then—at least to them?'

'They're young, yes but any of them could cause gazuzzlement, and in the blink of an eye,' the elder said. 'They practise a most effective art of war.'

Hearing those words, Mother Nancy's interest increased. She'd heard loud cries coming from the former apothecary. She'd seen youngsters cavorting, and until now, her interest was not focused. She went closer now; the better to learn more. There was young Celia Streak and her small brother Rupert, emulating each and every stance, utterance and movement of those native to the present time. Even to untrained eye, those others possessed expert skill. Her orphans seemed as conscientious as the rest but then, Michael was right. Seen along-side those others, her poor orphans were frail. They were as thin weeds, contesting with prize-winning blooms.

Young Skip observed, 'They do not perform fast movements. If an opponent was guarded, they would not be surprised by them.'

'No, but they are practising. When employed in battle, gazuzzlement is inflicted at lightning speed. There is wizardry to it. Each breath and exhalation counts and is measured. In Hargolin, there is mystery in the movement of energy. They say that a felling blow does not so much as register upon the mind of one struck down.'

Pushing between the others, Zee exclaimed, 'I *must* know more of this!'

The elder, said, 'This could represent a turning point.'

Sounding breathless, Zee said, 'Thanks! I guess you're not *so* bad.'

'We'll wander through the old brick-yard before returning to the orphanage,' the elder said. 'Much is changed. The orphanage, by the way, now accommodates the aged. There's irony in the way things alter with time.'

He told, Zee, 'Stay here and watch. We'll meet up later.' Turning to Nancy, he said, 'Your former home, the great palace of a place, is now a venue for entertainment. That's where the dancing takes place. Would you prefer visiting there?'

She protested, 'Oh, I won't miss it. I have my own picture-book memories, though it is kind of you to think of it.'

She was beginning to relax, and did want to visit Father's place of work. It was not far to go but she thought of Michael and his knees.

As if knowing her thought, he asked, 'It's not too long a hop, is it? I'm afraid memory does not serve.'

Seeing the buildings, which once comprised the family business, she was both surprised and pleased. It was now a museum, a market place and a centre for gatherings of visitors and friends. All were catered for in most pleasant surroundings, but what most delighted her was displayed just inside the museum's large, main entrance hall. Young Skip saw it first, and both Skips directed her to look overhead, to an exhibit of special significance. Looking up, she saw, a treasure of youthful days. The skiff was suspended there above them, and she cried, 'Why! It's *Missy-Belle!*' and she reached for Sister Francis who hurried to provide her a supportive paw.

It was then that an orphan, leader of a small group of them, rushed heltering to the adults and although the children all spoke at once, he made himself heard over the babble. He announced, 'Mother! Sister! *We have seen our parents!* We've *found* them!'

Both Mother Nancy and Sister Francis were aggrieved hearing them, for, not just by knowing that this was a future time, and so, no parent of theirs could be so young and therefore recognized, but also by knowing intimate details pertaining to the circumstances of many a parent's passing, there was no doubt at all that the parents could not live. Even on this day of the miraculous abounding, the parents were in truth, not found.

Mother Nancy insisted, 'Hush now, youngsters, and hush...' When they quieted, 'Where are those you speak of? You must lead us to them and we will explain what is happening here. Can you do that? Are those you've seen nearby or far?'

'My father is across there in yon' eatery; he partakes of a strange bubbling beverage. I waved to him, but he could not see me,' complained one thickset, young buck.

'My mother is close by! She sells watermelons!' said a pretty young thing with pastel ribbons tied near her ears. 'I went close to her and *she shivered as if afraid!* Her look was *most* peculiar!'

'And, my aunt,' stammered another of them, 'I think it's she ... stands guard at the doorway to the Place of Bones!'

Uncertain glances passed between Mother Nancy, Sister Francis and the good Doctor Stone. Young Skip realized he didn't see very much of real worth. His inner vision was skewed, just blurred and indiscernible scenes were revealed. He repeated the orphan's disturbing words, 'Place of Bones...' The present reality was taking a subtle, peculiar turn. Even those things he thought he might see were mirages. He looked to the elder, 'Do you think things might be getting a little out of paw here?' He felt very uncertain. 'My feeling is strange. I sense something very unusual, an awful *branching off* in myself.' He said, 'I don't know what it can be but something's very wrong.'

Elder Skip did not respond, but after a moment, informed, 'The Place of Bones is an exhibit, a memorial to victims of repression and horror. It's sad, but it is after all a memorial to the gazuzzled, and as such it cannot be expected to be otherwise. In my opinion, the orphans cannot be harmed by seeing it and anyway it's obvious that several of them have.'

Things were awry. The elder was *not* himself! He persisted in providing, morbid, too detailed explanation. 'Those whom the orphans believe are parents, are in all likelihood themselves. However, remains of *actual* parents, just *might* be found in yon' bone exhibit. I would not hazard identifying them—not after so long   one would have to go back. The task would require the tracing of many lines.' With each word uttered by the elder, young Skip's concern grew. His elder's demeanour was cause for unnerving; a maniacal "something", shifted behind his eyes.

They'd moved away from the main thoroughfare to stand by a wall of the museum foyer where there was less likelihood of others, hopping through their invisible forms. Coming into the foyer from outside, visitors did not seem too numerous, but already, it happened that one of them was not quick enough in stepping aside, and experienced being walked through; the venerable Doctor Michael had giggled like a child when it occurred.

Facing away from the others, and facing his elder, young Skip demanded, 'Are you all right? You're *not* are you? Something's amiss. What is it? What's going on?'

Elder Skip's eyes were wild and evasive as contentious internal battling carried on. Sounding desperate he complained, 'If you must know, *they're arguing against me!* I'm having a deeks of a time trying to maintain equilibrium! Piedmont is in complete disagreement with me. He sides with Peace! And as for the fixer—he was of the opinion that it's acceptable, bringing the orphans here, but now Peace has talked him around and he no longer tolerates my helping Zee! From the outset, Sherbrook believed it my worst idea ever but he came along for the ride. The very *worst* of it, is that *Peace* threatens to shut me down! Simple Rudy does not care either way. At least I don't think he cares, but then he doesn't say much. I'm of the impression that he's not just fence sitting, but who knows, he might be indulging the sulks!' Looking to young Skip, he said, 'That's about all of it.' He asked, 'Do you get the picture? No? Well I admit it—I'm babbling—my mind helters in searching for balance! I'm confused *and* outnumbered!'

'What do you mean Peace wants to shut you down?'

'Just *that!* She can shut down the whole exercise. It's within her power to shut *me* down! She joins us in the All as One! She can end it all at any time. She..."

'Yes but what will the outcome be if her threat is carried out? Will any be harmed? The orphans or Nancy?' With each instant young Skip grew more frustrated and impatient! Elder Skip was shaky and disoriented. His beseeching, crazed eyes were large and strange in their sockets!

Through gritted teeth, the elder managed to convey, 'Nothing will happen! She'll have her way though. If Zee can't learn what I've brought him here to learn, the Brickfield we left may not improve and the future we now find ourselves occupying, will not manifest!'

'Why did they agree to set all this in motion? Why bring us here if there was not agreement?'

'There was agreement—agreement enough! But I drive the bus! *I'm* the seer! They're not! They never have any real way of knowing my intention. My light may not have been shining pure-bright and that I grant. Were they as skilled as I am then they would have seen it. They would have known, but they didn't. It was my idea to bring the boy, Zee, here without being one zillion per cent open about it. By my introducing the boy to Hargolin, and by my speaking with him earlier, Piedmont and Sherbrook deduced my intention, which I maintain is sound! *This time* we must not stand by allowing the worst to occur, whilst doing nothing!'

'I say there, are you young fellows all right?' enquired Michael Stone.

Young Skip, ignoring him, commanded the elder, 'Do it then! Do it now! Let Peace shut you down! Go ahead and allow it!'

The elder directed him a most wilful, stubborn glare but then his determination wilted.

Then, in a moment of shimmering uncertainty, bright reality faded and was lost, until...

At the orphanage, the dormitory flickered back to uncertain being. Fading and blinking occurred until blurring distorting walls, ceiling and floor reasserted sovereign substance and were triumphant in battling against another reality's drawing and shredding away. Even as startled, fearful eyes adjusted to the dimness, wave upon night-velvet shadowy wave washed back and forth through the space of the room, shifting shadows moved to an accompanying dirge of sound.

When finally, normality returned, the good doctor stooped to inspect his lantern. Pride sounded in his voice as he affirmed the lantern's usefulness, 'There we are now—you see. There's naught so good when it's dark, as a reliable lantern.'

Mother Nancy, holding paw to brow, declared, 'Skip, that was an experience I shall *never* forget! Those final moments, I do confess, were a little unnerving. Truth told, I feel a little nauseous. All in all, though, it was marvellous, wasn't it, Sister?' Despite the dim-lit surrounding, the Sister did not fail to notice her superior's penetrating glance.

Compelled to agree, Francis said, 'It was very rewarding. Thank you, Skip.'

The orphans, some making merry cacophony, others howling and weeping for not being left in rescuing arms of parents, and others, appearing numbed and exhausted by the experience, were soon quieted and convinced to thank Tump. Still there were tears though.

An orphan complained, 'There was a boy with my father, and he wasn't me.'

'He wasn't your father,' the elder said, exasperation colouring his voice. 'The one you saw as your father, was an older version of you. The child you saw will be yours.'

Mother Nancy said, 'It's all right Skip. Say no more. I'll attend to him.'

She went to the child to offer comfort, and following a whispered exchange the child was reassured and settled down upon his pallet. Mother Nancy, tucking a blanket about him, assured, 'There you are now, Alexander, I'll check on you later, but for now you look fine to me, dear.' She wished them all, 'Sleep. Dream of happiness and every good thing.'

In the small candle-lit chapel, a short time later, Nancy felt great pride as she showed them the relic, a tiny shell, fossilized evidence of eons of time passing, set against a dark cloth of rich, deepest purple, in its own ornate, carved tarrash-wood cabinet. She told them, 'It was given to us by Buckminster before he passed. He lived long after Lillian's time and spoke as if she were ever present. In parting, he would say, "I must take myself home to my good old gal." He spoke, having no doubt, regarding Lillian's remaining with him, even up to his own sad end.

'He received a brutal beating, out in the road by his home, for transgressing no law ... for no reason at all ... and so, met gazuzzlement at the paws of the unenlightened, accursed ones.' She paused to dry a tear which had fallen to cheek, then said, 'He oft' had you in mind, Skip, and was tireless in relating the tale, as he termed it, of being granted Tump blessing, in return for Lillian's fine cooking and kindness.'

'It's touching—the way you've kept it for so long. I'm honoured...' The sentence went unfinished. So distressing was the news of Buckminster's suffering cruel end that, he could not continue, but then, 'It was so simple a gift.' Thought of kind, decent Buckminster passing not once, but twice, in a cruel, undeserved manner in both realms, was cause for deepest sorrow. The elder too, was affected.

Farewells were exchanged and they parted. Alone in the chapel and mindful of her father, she recalled his so often gruff declaring, 'I do appreciate a nice home-cooked meal. I do indeed!' She wondered at the best of providers being pleased by so little.

She would check on the orphans as she always did before turning in for the night.

STORM

Lowering cloud joined with the ocean surface and the storm approached to darken the beach. The wind howled as dreadful threnody. There was an odour of damp fur. Nancy shook dampness from white-tipped ears. She requested, 'Set the shield, Clever.'

He looked into her. 'Better, my dear?'

'Thank you,' she said, and commented, 'Fixer, those feathers of yours are drenched. They're bedraggled.'

'Rain plays havoc with them,' he said.

Then the storm set more upon them.

The bard spoke; he could no longer contain himself. 'We have our ideals, Skip! If we feel *encumbered* by idealism and then, with needs-must attitude, grope our way in half-hearted observation of sound principle, we might slither down-hill to back-water, to encourage plantings of—of—*thistle!*' Piedmont, blustering, exhorted.

'Yes—with viper for companion!' Peace exclaimed.

'Tump does not war,' Sherbrook reminded them.

'No—just with each other.' Nancy observed, and did her best to hide a smile.

'Please! Let's not argue. We should be *thinking!*' Clever said, 'In the first place, I'm not at all certain there's a problem here, but bickery scratching will not get us far in solving anything!'

Simple Rudy offered, 'We could take a cutting.'

Ignoring Rudy, the elder protested, 'I'm not sorry.' Head in paws, he was unhappy, but would remain unapologetic.

'You should be!' Peace insisted.

When, Peace spoke condemning his elder, young Skip cringed. The elder shrugged.

'We could prune the line,' Simple Rudy offered. Maybe, this time someone would hear him.

'What was it you said, Simple?' Clever queried, going so close to Rudy, that the long, damp, dangling feathers of his hat drooped, sweeping against Rudy's pink nose. Rudy put paw to face and then sneezed!

'Sorry. I do apologize,' said Clever, pushing the feathers away. 'Now, what were you saying?'

'The tree is the map. The map is the tree,' Rudy told Fixer, 'Trees can be pruned.'

Fixer's eyes lit up. 'Ah-ha!' he exclaimed. 'Simple Rudy has it! It's the answer to our problem!' Slapping Rudy on the back and becoming more excited with each moment, he said, 'Yes. We will go back to the realm and do it again. We will not so much as enter into the orphan's dormitory. No, we must refuse doing that. Next time will be different.'

Peace said, 'But the line is affected by interference. Their future is altered.' She cast a sidewise glare to the elder.

'Yes,' Clever said, 'but, as Rudy has it, trees can be pruned. Great Grandfather's map is a tree, and as such, any unwanted part may be cut away from the rest!'

Sherbrook said, 'To make two paths, two futures?'

'No, one path! At least, one main line, plus, a small section of line left over after pruning. The original line will be unaltered. We will go back and excise the sojourn. We will take all of it or any part we choose. The question is—at which points, do we effect cuts?'

'If what you propose, is possible,' Peace said, 'then all of it must be taken. Remove it from beginning to end. Leave none of it. From now on, there must be complete openness. There must be no further tampering and no more weeping orphans! Tump serves good and order. Questing for Great Grandfather is our mission, and in carrying out our mission, attending to ordering events of our own line is of primary import, but even that must be seen to by subtlest passive means. And, there must be no more pilfering as we go.' She was emphatic, 'There *will* be an end to pilfering!'

'What pilfering?'

'Ice cream, chairs, the umbrella ... the cooler. Look about you Sherbrook! All of you! It's a downright disgrace!'

Elder Skip exclaimed, 'Hark, who speaks! Queen of Toys!'

'No one's going to miss that stuff,' said Fixer.

'I hope not,' said Rudy.

'Where would we be without ice-cream?' Nancy asked, of none in particular.

'Don't think of ice-cream or toys,' Piedmont said. 'Raise an edge of the shield, Fixer. It's stuffy in here. It's misting over.' A fresh briny atmosphere whipped beneath a raised edge of the translucent, dome-like energy-field, ruffling the fur of Nancy's pretty cheeks and the tips of her ears. Piedmont said, 'Perhaps, not quite so high, Fixer.' Fixer made an adjustment, lowering the shield a little.

'Time lines carry stories,' said Piedmont. ''They are tales. In composing, one must sometimes transpose.' He thought for a moment before continuing, 'There are those times, in scratching, when words may be worthy of inclusion, but for any number of reasons, they refuse to fit so, they must be removed. Oft'-times, when that removed is still good, not wanting to discard it, I will keep the segment for later inclusion in another piece, which as I understand it, is what you mean to do ... or something like it.'

'Correct,' said Clever. 'But, I'm wondering, what to cut with?'

'With, "knowing",' Rudy, told him. 'Knowing it *must* be done—it is!'

'Ah... I do confess I'm rather lost,' the fixer said. Rubbing at his head and wearing a perplexed look, he said, 'I don't know...'

Simple Rudy was shy of offering further explanation.

Peace, said, 'Mm, he means: belief in an underpinning power; power, inherent to right order, assures a beneficial outcome.'

'Oh, for deeks' sake! Why not come out and say what you mean? You mean faith. That's a Tall One concept!'

'Well, why not?' demanded, Peace, 'It's what Simple possesses.

'The tree is Great Grandfather's property. His, is the order of the All, and the tree, or map, describes that mysterious, infinite order. The savant does not arrive at point of realization via processing information through ordinary intellect, but rather, via inspiration. Simple "knows" the bond, existing between tree and owner. He trusts in the rightness of that connection. If Simple Rudy knows a thing can be done, and he acts, then, it *is* done.'

'Fine then,' said the fixer. 'What is to be done with the pruning? Energy cannot be destroyed and even if it were possible...'

'What's needed is a repository,' suggested Piedmont, giving elder Skip an accusatory look. 'A Repository of Error,' he said. 'This mistake may be followed by others and we'll need somewhere to store, as it were, scraps of scratchings.'

Returning Piedmont's gaze, elder Skip insisted, 'Nothing is wrong with any of it. There is no mistake.'

'We shall prune and graft,' said Simple Rudy, his attention taken for a moment, by a confusion of storm clouds beyond the distorting shield. 'After taking a cutting from the main line, the gap in the line is joined by grafting.'

'And the orphans can go back to *Song of White Winter*, read to conclusion by Sister Francis,' Peace said, pleased by the thought.

Sherbrook said, 'But we can't have loose ends, short, stick-like bits of lines floating about, or stored some place. No—I don't get it.'

Clever Fixer declared, 'I know. We shall make a bracelet of the cutting. We shall graft both ends of it—one t'other, and it will become a looping event. The loop is best seen as an isolated realm. Perhaps once removed from its place, it can be "hung" as it were, somewhere. It will not be attached to other lines and yet as living energy it will have a place in the tree. Rudy can find the best place to put it.'

'There are such things described in the tree. Nothing is new.'

'Pruning is already there then, Rudy?' muttered Fixer, 'I do declare it's all *most* fascinating.' Pondering possibilities he said, 'It just *might* at later time, be feasible to graft such pruning into another line...'

Peace exclaimed, 'Oh! Are you saying, you imagine Tump doing such a thing?'

Abashed, he said, 'Oh dear. Yes, Peace. I see what you mean. I was toying with notions, and that's all. We know so little. I'm interested in all of it. Even a wrong conclusion is sometimes as fascinating, or even more so, than the correct one. Searching is of primary importance to me, or the chase. That's the thing! Along the way, many things await discovery, discoveries made via both hits and misses. It's a journey through riches!'

Elder Skip said, 'No. My decision will stand. The cutting will be put to good use.' Six faces looked to him. Simple Rudy was the exception and he preferred gazing to infinity.

'When time is made to loop and play over and over, I shall move information from the Zee of that loop to Zee of earlier Brickfield. Although oblivious of ever having visited future Brickfield, Zee will learn as he sleeps. He shall dream of Tump and Hargolin. He will teach the orphans the art of war.' Addressing Peace, he said, 'As for tampering. I've heard no objecting to assisting versions of ourselves.' Pointing to Skip, he said, 'Look for deeks' sake! He's been with us throughout. It's, hypocrisy. You mind not being consulted, that's all.'

They stared, as if daring him to say more.

'You can aim as much resentment my way as you like,' he said, accepting their challenge. 'But, what's done is done. I "see" all of it. Zee and Hargolin are cause for brighter days. And not just for Brickfield realm. You have no idea of its importance in the overall scheme. Knowing what to look for, Rudy might know what I mean. But,' he said, 'fear not in any case, because it all works out.' He told Peace, 'You are right about Great Grandfather and the tree being close. We too, are His. We quest for Him but He's as close now as ever He'll be.'

Peace said, 'Skip, I'm sad for you.'

'Yes?'

'Yes, because you miss the point. It's true that Great Grandfather is ever close and too, the All is most certainly His. But still a gap must be bridged—hence, our questing. We seek to raise the vibration of energy but have a long way to go. You lower the vibration and orphans weep! We must act together, as one. Ends do not justify means. Our energy must ascend.'

'I don't think Great Grandfather smiles upon Tump, right now,' Young Skip said. 'I feel just terrible for the orphans. They'll go kadoodling crazy, experiencing déjà-vu forever.' He shivered at the thought of such fate. Sherbrook, quite despite himself, chortled. Peace glanced at him. He said, 'Imagine those bucks back there digging a ditch forever.'

Piedmont muttered, 'Stuff of nightmare...'

But Clever Fixer said, 'I wonder if those living in looping realities are aware of repetition. They may not suffer, as young Skip suggests. Perhaps for them, events are perceived as being always new, occurring always for the first time.'

Elder Skip said, 'After pruning, versions of ourselves are caught in the loop along with the others.' He offered, 'If you like, Clever, I'll accommodate your curiosity by moving you there and you can ask them about it.' He smiled. 'Is there agreement, or shall we keep young Skip here, and just forget about your younger versions? We can leave the bard back there on the top of the hill over looking Grammy Graymark's New Warren Central, along with Peace and good old Sherbrook. I wonder if they'll figure much of it out for themselves. Or, shall we get on with a little, innocent tampering?' He paused then, and they were silent. Resuming, he said, 'Very well. We shall now reveal information vital to success, and then move young Skip back to his realm of origin.'

'You needn't be quite so cocky,' Piedmont said. 'We are capable of imagining a dire outcome if they are not reunited.'

Peace condemned him with a glance.

Nancy said, 'We must set to task.' She gave Peace a smile of understanding.

Sherbrook turned to young Skip, 'Now, Buckaroo. All might be accomplished in an instant...'

Rudy interjected, 'All of it!'

'Yes, but we favour an ordered progression,' Fixer explained.

'Best be thorough,' Piedmont said.

Peeved by so much interruption, Sherbrook persevered, 'It's vital that you remember these things. First, when Clever Fixer comes by, he must be invited to stay. You need the tree and *he* has the seed. He won't mention having it. It's his little secret, but he'll reveal it when ready.

'When the tree is grown, there will be occasion of it ringing. When you hear it, you'll know what is meant and when the tree rings, it's time to bring young Nancy to the group. Now, the first time she comes, she does not stay with you. On the second occasion, she does. But, when the tree rings for the very first time, Piedmont must be sent to the forest to meet with her. Is it clear?'

'Yes,' said Skip, 'I am to insist that Clever stays. If the tree rings, Nancy must be met in the forest.'

'Correct.' Sherbrook said, 'But it's not *if* the tree rings, it's *when*. And have Piedmont invite Clever to stay. They are good friends and Fixer will accept hospitality from him.'

Nancy said, 'At the end of my first excursion, in company of Piedmont, you *must* return me to New Warren Central.'

'There is one thing more,' Sherbrook said. 'Without strict observance, nothing is begun. You must move the Radiola from the Tall Ones' dwelling place, to the edge of the field, where Uncle Bucky will find it.'

'You've practised well,' the elder said, '"Move" it through time and space as I've taught you. Have no doubt—you can do it.'

'And,' Clever Fixer said, 'one sunny afternoon I shall drop by and fix it.' Fixer was pleased with himself. 'Bucky loved that old thing—and you too, eh Rudy? Couldn't get enough of it, could you?'

'There is another matter,' Sherbrook said, 'Piedmont has something, a gift for his younger self.'

Piedmont reached deep into a pocket of his coat. Taking out a small, tubular-shaped, bright gleaming object, he said, 'Now be certain you don't drop it because it's fragile. It's a spyglass, and I'm sure to like it.' He extended the instrument to full length, and putting it up to an eye, peered into it, by way of demonstration. After sliding it back into itself, he passed it to Skip. Seeing young Skip deposit it in a pocket, Piedmont said, 'It's been wonderful meeting with you, dear boy. Our paths are certain to cross again.' And then, he thought of something else. He said, 'Tell that Piedmont not to complain so, of the pains of age. He never complains to others, but he does to himself, and doing so drives him to distraction. Assure him, his future holds not the least suffering of the sort that troubles him in his present.'

Smiling, Peace cried, 'Mmeerah!'

Sherbrook said, 'Good times, Buckaroo!'

Piedmont waved, 'Farewell, dear boy.'

Clever Fixer wished, 'Safe journey, friend!'

'We'll meet again,' Nancy assured.

'See it as fun!' the elder exclaimed.

He asked, 'Couldn't you come with me?'

'Be on your way now,' the elder said, and ordered, 'Fixer, engage the gate! Make the way!'

Simple Rudy shouted, 'Skip—you're a shooting star!'

Part Two
The Travellers' Tale

Beach

FALLING STAR

Sherbrook said, 'The best way to honour his memory is to keep going.'

'No, I can't agree to continue,' Peace said. 'Forging ahead through unknown territory without him would be foolhardy.'

'Why?'

'Well...' She paused, then said, 'He knew everything before we did. That's why. He could tell you what you were considering for supper three nights from now and then inform you, you wouldn't be having whatever it was you'd thought of. He'd name whatever it was you'd have, which would be something very different from your choice, and then he'd tell you where it was coming from and how many times you'd chew each mouthful.'

'He was not that good!'

'What? Oh you don't mean...'

'Yes, I do. He didn't see Brother Eagle. He did not see any of it coming. He missed it.'

'How can you mention it?' Peace said. 'I think that's the most insensitive, heartless thing I've heard.'

'No, it's realistic.'

As far as missing things went, Skip's not visioning Brother Eagle was about the biggest miss, anyone possessing such power could make, but then Piedmont spoke, and Sherbrook lost the chance to elaborate. 'I don't see myself trudging all the way back downhill. Not this evening. I believe we should find a safe place to spend the night and tomorrow morning we can decide what best to do. We need a good night's rest. Where to lay our heads, that's the question.'

'It's a place of slim-pickings,' Sherbrook said. 'Just look at it—there's nothing. No creek ... nothing but dusty wasteland as far as the eye can see.' He turned up his nose in disdain.

'Farther over are clumps of trees, there at the edge of the wide plain near the big stone outcropping. I see a distant patch of green,' Peace said.

'Where?' Sherbrook asked. His tone was neutral, not the least argumentative. He was diminished by the inability to assist Skip, and he was working on the possibility of further disappointment arising. 'I don't see green. Perhaps your eyes deceive you?' He peered to dull, dim distance. The sun had sunk low and was ready to vanish behind tawny barren hilltops. Shadows lengthened, making dark arms spread into a shallow vale and undulate across what appeared to Sherbrook, an uninteresting, dimming plain.

'It's flat enough terrain,' Piedmont said, 'which is good, because I don't so much mind a long hop, compared with the thought of a steep descent in darkness. Forced to retrace the way, I'd be head over flag into the waiting arms of Grammy Graymark.' He said, 'We should move on, because the day's almost gone.' He stilled an impulse to shiver; it was a day none would ever want to relive. He saw the place she meant, and said, 'Peace is right, Sherbrook. Do you see?'

He raised his staff and, pointing with it, directed Sherbrook's attention to a far-away location. Upon the slope of an unimportant looking hill was an area of shadow, an outcropping of large stones too, Piedmont decided, and those were not all that he noted. 'There is uncommon undulation to the plain.' And again using his stick as pointer, he said, 'Where those shadows stretch long, extending over the plain, a peculiar undulation stands out. It is as if someone tossed a pebble into a pond and the scene is creased by curving ripples.' He said, 'Great Grandfather includes eccentricity in his design.' He sighed, 'It's where we shall make for then, the dark shadowy place.'

'It's a long way off,' Sherbrook said, 'If you need assistance along the way, I'll lend a paw.'

'Yes,' said Peace, 'just ask.'

Apart from dry grass and the occasional tall clump of faded tussock, there were areas littered with deposits of what looked like slippery shale and, for Piedmont's sake, they were avoided. Searching in fast diminishing light, Piedmont voiced optimism, 'With a new home established, all will be well.'

The long hop was begun when Sherbrook bent to the ground and picked up a large feather, 'Well now ... look at this.'

'Throw it away. We need no reminder of the event.'

Dictated to, Sherbrook replied, 'It's a trophy, as I see it, and I'm keeping it.'

He stuck the feather atop his head as jaunty addition to appearance.

Wishing for no further upset, Piedmont said, 'Look. There's a promising-looking log. It could be hollow and if so, it will accommodate us for the night. We can rest up and continue on in the morning. I'm tired and frazzled and will be grateful if we need go no farther.'

'I'll check it out,' Sherbrook said, and went flibberty hopping away.

Peace called after him, 'If there are web spinners—shoo them!' She told Piedmont, 'I can put up with rough comfort but cannot abide *them*.'

Soon, Sherbrook called, reporting on conditions inside the log, 'It's spacious enough and it's not taken!' There was no sign of serpent or fox, which was cause for relief.

Arrived and standing before the enormous, hollow trunk, a large opening invited entry to safe haven. Communicated from farthest recess, Sherbrook's words were muffled and indistinct but then, after much shuffling was heard, he poked his head out, saying, 'It's very dry and spacious and so we ought to be quite comfortable. There were webs but they seemed old, and in any case, I've brushed them away and there's no sign of ant or centipede.

'At the far end is a crooked turn and after that is a nice place for privacy. I think that, Peace will like it.' He was going out of his way to heal any rift remaining between them.

She said, 'Thank you, that's very considerate, Sherbrook.' She too, was mindful of the need to make up.

Piedmont said, 'I'll leave my stick outside where I can find it.' Leaning the stick against a large stone, he said, 'I'm famished, but will make myself comfortable before the stomach complains. I'm not partial to dry grass, are you?' This was nothing but small talk, but then he exclaimed, 'My goodness!' In the darkening sky, where faint starlight glimmered, an outshining flash of brightness was seen, and then streaking light trailed down from the heavens. After exclaiming, Piedmont asked, 'What's to be made of it? It was no shooting star.'

Out of the hollow, Sherbrook was in time to see a fast dying, blue-white light shrink to nothing. He said, 'It's gone down near the top of the hill where we came from. There's no loud crashing—thanks be! I've had quite enough of the extraordinary.' It was yet another mystery light though, and raising his snout he tested the breeze but detected no scent of sweetness. It was nothing too out of the ordinary.

Piedmont muttered.

'Mystery lights—they bode more ill than good,' Peace said, sounding anxious. 'I must go and rest, if it's all the same. I can do without strange wishing stars.' Sherbrook stepped away, allowing access to the log.

Once inside and snug, having wrapped his long coat about himself, Piedmont, before wishing them final good night, observed, 'It's my experience, that just before dawn is when temperatures often plummet. I don't know the reason for it, but we must trust it's not cold. The log is rather exposed, but in the circumstance we're far better off than might be.'

It was unfortunate truth that Piedmont was prone to snoring and his being tired to the bone exacerbated matters. His deep, sonorous and raw sounding snoring presented serious setback to successful rest for his companions.

Solitary by nature and for the most part one who lived alone, Piedmont was unaware of the fact he snored at all. No one had ever accused him of possessing the disturbing habit. Guests, who on very rare occasions stayed overnight during visits to his burrows, had not drawn the matter to his attention. As example, Romulus Browning, the most recent guest, was around Piedmont's own age and was quite hard of hearing; and then were those who were too polite to say anything even if their slumber was disturbed. In any case a burrow was nothing the same as a hollow log.

Whereas, compact soil absorbed sound, a log was more drum-like, a chamber wherein echoes bounced about ricocheting hither and yon'. It was not long after Piedmont's wishing them a pleasant night that Peace was beside herself, and came close to screaming. Sherbrook was in closer proximity with him, and might perform a favour by smothering Piedmont as he slept.

Sherbrook had grumbled in his sleep and that brought her awake. That sound was mere introduction for far worse. The first dreadful exhalation occurred. A long, drawn out, thin whistling preceded a deceitful pause. Suspenseful silence reigned. Then, was a violent CHUDDER! CHUDDER! CHUDDER! Sherbrook muttered, and then there was nothing from him but still plenty from Piedmont. Piedmont pressed on. She wondered if Sherbrook had some clever way of dealing with the problem. She implored, 'Piedmont, show compassion!' That did no good and so she demanded, 'Let me out!'

'Mm, huh… What is it?' Sherbrook enquired. Again, CHUDDER! And, there came the sharp sound of rapping. Rat-a-tat-tat! Next, a small voice cried, 'Hello in the log! Hello everyone! It's me, Skip!'

'Sherbrook!' Peace hissed, nudging him in the ribs. 'Wake up and *you* too, Piedmont!' It could not be, Skip.

He poked his head into the opening, 'It's nippy out here. I'd like to warm up.' By now both Sherbrook and Piedmont were wide-awake.

'Hello Peace,' he said. 'Hello there Sherbrook. Hello Piedmont.' He smiled in the dark. 'It's good seeing you again after such a long time. I have an amazing amount of stuff to tell you, but I see you're tired so I'll wait until the morning.'

Peace said, 'You shall do no such thing.'

'How'd you escape?' asked Sherbrook. He wanted to pinch Skip; to be sure he was real. He ordered, 'Come on, Buckaroo, let's hear it—the full story.'

Piedmont reached and touched Skip upon the tip of his nose. 'I'm not dreaming. It's no wraith.'

While crossing the plain in darkness, he'd decided to relate all that occurred in simplest, straightforward way. 'I've been to another world,' he said, and then wondered how best to continue. They would have difficulty believing him. It was his story; he'd lived it from beginning to end and still it was hard to credit. He repeated, 'I was sent to another realm—to more than one—to places so different from this, you may find it impossible to believe.'

Sherbrook kept silent but he wondered whether Brother Eagle had dropped the boy on his head.

Peace pushed her way into Sherbrook, who, in turn, pushed against Piedmont.

Hearing the boy speak of strange worlds, she decided, 'Don't stay up telling your story, Skip. Find somewhere to sleep and we'll catch up with your news in the morning.' The boy was overwrought and kadoodling, but who could blame him.

She said, 'I will sleep near the opening. Excuse me please,' and without waiting for permission she scrambled over them.

She would rather a fox devour her than be driven mad by the bard.

'Sleeping out there is not safe,' Sherbrook advised.

'Peace will be all right,' Skip told him, 'And, it's less noisy there.'

'Less noisy?'

Skip said nothing.

After making himself comfortable, Sherbrook closed his eyes and then hoped against hope that Skip was proved right. They may yet find a grand place as predicted, somewhere to call home.

* * *

The sun was up and he was wide-awake. He asked, 'Where did you get that feather, Sherbrook?'

'Oh, it's nothing, but I was saving it for you.' He removed the feather from his fur and passed it to Skip, 'It's a trophy, a reminder of the great escape. I knew you'd like it.' He glanced to Peace, and she returned his smile.

'Thank you, Sherbrook... I don't have gifts for everyone. However, I *do* have something for Piedmont. For Piedmont, from himself! And, as well,' he said, recalling instruction given him by elder Piedmont, 'There's a message to pass on, but it's of somewhat personal nature.' Leaning in to whisper close by Piedmont's ear, he passed on the message regarding the old one's complaining over his health.

Receiving the message, Piedmont was somewhat embarrassed. Maintaining calm, in measured tone he said, 'I do try my best not to carry on. But yes, it's good sound advice.' He said, 'Thank you for passing it on to me.' Experience involving unspeakable horror meant that common respect was forsaken. Besides critical advice, a gift was mentioned, and Piedmont was wary, but would humour the poor, demented boy. 'From, myself! Well, I don't know how that can be, but it does sound acceptable.'

As far as gifts went, he was not able to recall the last occasion anyone gifted him anything apart from donations of sticks to aid him in getting about and so, wishing this might be more important than those, but knowing it was not so, he eyed Skip, his expression both curious and apprehensive. Skip reached deep into a side pocket of his blue jacket.

Catching sight of a most unusual object, shining and glittering in the first light of day, the bard was unable to prevent himself from reaching for it.

'It's delicate…' Skip advised, releasing the gift to its new, and already proud owner.

Piedmont held it, murmuring, 'Mm. never before have I seen the like. It's a *most* beautiful thing. I see that—indeed I do. Thank you, Skip. I don't know its use or purpose, but I can't thank you enough.' There were sounds of appreciation from Sherbrook and Peace.

'When you pull at the ends,' Skip told him, 'it becomes long and you look into it.'

Piedmont aimed the glass at the distant hills and exclaimed, 'Why, it's remarkable! I could not imagine it possible! I see great detail—such clarity! It's as if I am not *here* at all but am over *there!*' He continued scanning the far horizon, shifting the glass from side to side, in wide sweeps and then in lowering the instrument, he was very serious.

Perplexed by the puzzle presented, and looking to Skip, he said, 'As you tell it my boy, I, Piedmont, have gifted the wonder to myself? Then I believe we should make ourselves as comfortable as possible, and, Skip, you must do your best to provide us thorough explanation. We have not yet eaten and we're poorly rested, but before continuing on the way we should hunker down and hear you out.'

GROUND SPRING WARREN

He began at the beginning and ended at the end, leaving nothing out. During his relating of events, Sherbrook's persistent interrupting made for tough going, until both Piedmont and Peace demanded he keep his questions for later; they would never learn all Skip would tell, if Sherbrook did not shut-up. But he could not be still, and every so often fired questions, such as, 'Why would they call me Weed! It's a deeks-awful name. I can't believe my parents, in any so called realm, would be so cruel!'

Peace told him, 'Shh!' but then, at one point in Skip's tale telling, she could not help but make interruption, commenting, 'After all is said and done, you and the Whitepaws gal wed! How about *that?*'

When Skip spoke of the realm of Tall Ones, Sherbrook was hushed by Piedmont. Before Sherbrook half-opened his mouth, Piedmont insisted, 'You must relate all you recall of *their* realm, Skip.' As best he could, Skip did just that but he admitted, due to the strangeness of so much experienced, giving a sensible account was all but beyond him. He preferred telling of his newfound friend, Nancy, and describing *Missy-Belle*, the thing called a boat, but then explaining that was not simple either.

Piedmont glanced to Peace and then to Sherbrook, commenting, 'Folk of Fur float about upon water?' He knew that it could not be so. Reminding himself of the wonder held in his pocket, he reconsidered his judgment, though credulity was stretched to breaking.

In speaking of Tall Ones, and visiting their realm, mention of elder Skip's transforming to become a Tall One was best left unmentioned. But, he slipped up by mentioning having glimpsed his elder, at the brickyard as a Tall One child. All was lost, because Sherbrook broke into uproarious, thigh slapping laughter. Embarrassed for Skip, Peace lowered her gaze. He was deluded, after all, and she did not like facing him, lest he realize her opinion.

Piedmont said nothing at all, but grew thoughtful. After remaining silent for a time, he said, 'Included in material passed down to us from

generations long past, there *is* information pertaining to such strangeness as this. But, when mention occurs, Tall Ones are attributed with
performing wonders. I have never come across mention of Folk of Fur
possessing such miraculous ability.'

He said, 'Really though, we mustn't laugh at the boy, or shy from hearing him out. Such ability *is* mentioned. There's record of such and none of
it is recorded as kadoodle, but rather, as fact.' He asked, 'How is it, Skip,
that Folk of Fur perform wonders such as you describe?'

'Their wonder working is due to a combination of abilities,' Skip
explained. 'It begins with Mmeerah.' So saying, he saw Peace light up
from inside. 'In Mmeerah, our energy is raised high and joins.' He said,
'There's Sherbrook of later time, and he grounds us in journeying in the
All. And, there's the elder Bard.' He said, 'If you want to believe, you
can. If not, then don't. It already "is".' Rising, and squeezing past the others, he exited the hollow log. Once outside, he said, 'I will meet with you
later this afternoon. Over yonder where the grass is green. You know the
place.' And then he could not help but add, 'You really should believe me.'
There was a dazzling white, lightning flash, and he was gone!

She had no knowledge of cinnamon buns, but Peace exclaimed. 'Oh,
what a *pretty* fragrance!'

***

Skip would meet with warren elders, or a leader, but first, Bunty must be
rescued.

Bunty was small of stature and gentle by nature. Innate goodness did
not hold sway, though, in determining outcomes and bad experience was
too often his.

This morning was no different to many others; he was in deep water,
up to his furry chin in the stuff! As ever, he wondered over others gaining pleasure by tormenting him so. This was not the first time they had
dunked him, and so they should be bored with seeing him struggling to
climb out. The pool was not deep enough to drown him and with practice, he was becoming adept at negotiating the ordeal.

The small pond was situated on the hillside, between the embracing
trunks of two oaks. A thin-trickling surface stream, the origin of which

was a more substantial underground watercourse, fed it. To those residing hereabout, the tall oaks were guardians of their water supply.

Four bullies stood shaking with laughter at the sight of Bunty's predicament, then, hearing the sound of approaching footfalls, they readied themselves to flee. One of them warned, 'Do *not* say anything to anyone! You hear? Or, next time we'll dunk you head-first!' By the time Skip strolled into view, they were gone.

Arriving from the direction of a low-lying ridge, and coming to the place of humiliation, he went close by the pond and, reaching down, scooped the tiny boy up from the water. Carrying him, Skip continued the way downhill until they came to the warren, known as Ground Spring.

Judged by outward appearance, the warren must be small. New Warren Central was a vast metropolis, whilst Ground Spring was no more than an insignificant, isolated outpost.

But, home was home, and wherever it happened to be, that was most important; thus ran Skip's thought, as he came to an opening that served as a main entranceway.

Bunty did not fear the newcomer, and following his surprise at finding himself in saving arms, his gratitude was boundless. He said, 'I'm ever so glad that you came by when you did. We don't often get visitors!' Shivering, he offered, 'If *you* need help—ask me anything. When it comes to Ground Spring, there's nothing that I don't know.'

Skip observed, 'Folk aren't out and about. Where are they, do you suppose?'

'They're down in the meeting place,' Bunty said, 'Down there, voting for a new leader, because old Millthorpe went missing. He hasn't been heard of for so long, that someone must take his place. Some say he's been taken but others say gazuzzlement beckoned and he chose to leave home, for the final time. Many say that he was too solitary by nature, and should not have been our leader in the first place. Whatever the truth, he was not leader for long.'

The diminutive boy shivered again, and Skip said, 'Now, Bunty, you flibberty hop home and dry yourself. I'll wait here to speak with someone in charge.'

'How do you know my name?' Bunty asked, 'I haven't told you it.'

Skip shrugged, 'Maybe I saw you in trouble and your name flashed to mind. And I was right.'

'Then, you're some kind of genius.'

'And you must be too, to grant me such accurate description.' Bunty laughed. Hopping into the opening of the burrow, he halted, to announce, 'I think we're going to be good friends.'

'Correct, again,' Skip agreed. Then, the sound of footfalls faded as Bunty went deeper into the warren.

He'd not long to wait before, two gangling bucks emerged, and because they were identical twins, distinguishing between them was impossible. They went naked and so individuality could not be defined by personal preference in attire, but when they spoke, differences in both voice and personality were there. Skip would think of them as, Mori and Chuckler—Chuckler, for his chuckling so much, and the other, Mori, for presenting such moribund demeanour. With the passing of time, he would learn it made no difference to Chuckler—regardless of the subject under discussion, he would chortle. If a serious matter was discussed, he was capable of offering sound, considered opinion, but never before venting contagious chortling. Their given names were Dempster and Dimster. Skip decided that their parents might have done far better. Special consideration was reserved for Dimster, who put up with wearing such a second-rate name. He needed no other reason for being moribund.

'I'm Skip, of New Warren Central,' he said, 'I'm waiting to speak with someone in charge. I have a favour to ask.'

Chuckler mimicked, 'I'm from New Warren Central!' And, 'Oh me, oh my! Dimmie, we have a big-town-boy on our paws! Did you hear him, brother? A *favour to ask?*'

Before Skip could say more, Dimster responded, 'A favour, yes. I *did* catch mention of a favour, and brother, I believe we should give the boy the opportunity to be heard.'

The other conceded, 'Yes, yes, agreed, agreed!' Abandoning further hint of mocking tone, he was then serious, 'Dear boy, you've come a long, long way and do wish to be heard. Daresay, the favour you seek does not amount to much, but whatever it is, we won't be interested. I do apologize and trust that you won't be *too* disappointed.' Then both were silent.

Their downcast faces gave the impression that further communication was unnecessary.

Several moments later, Dimster offered, 'You should understand that my good brother can be a little difficult to deal with.' Expression forlorn, he seemed apologetic, and in the moment, Skip did not know how best respond. Then, several new voices were heard and out from the warren entranceway three faces emerged. While Skip knew some relief, Dempster was again becoming excited.

Chortling, he announced, 'Why, it's Robert! And look, here are Crenshaw and Sal! Oh, Sal! Crenshaw! *Everyone!* We have a visitor!' As if none present had seen a stranger before this, Dempster, paw stabbing at air, said, 'He comes from over the mountain, and from everywhere else as well! He's a tad boastful, but never mind! He is a visitor and it's been far too long since anyone's dropped by! He'll just have to do, won't he Crenshaw?'

Crenshaw, a tawny-furred, muscular individual, spoke, and with measured tone, addressed the twins. He said, 'Thank you twins; now that I'm here I will speak with our visitor. Your welcoming him is appreciated, but for now you may both go off to play.'

The twins bowed low, and then went paw in paw, leaving the small group behind. Dempster was heard questioning, 'But Dimmie, *what* do they expect us to play?'

'Welcome, stranger. I am Crenshaw. As Dempster said, we are not often visited, and so curiosity will have the better of all. I am Leader, and will see that you are accommodated for your stopover. We welcome travellers to our territory,' Crenshaw said. 'We enjoy hearing news of other places and our home is yours for the duration of your stay.' He said, 'Sal, you must arrange quarters for him.' But then, 'Forgive my over-sight, stranger. I've not so much as enquired after your name?' By now others were exiting from burrows making the group even larger.

Early this morning, before parting from the others, he'd seen much of what would come, but realized he'd not seen all of it. He'd seen Bunty and so knew of his watery dilemma but, seeing was far from complete; too much important detail was missing. Along with unaccountable omission, there was inclusion of information having no apparent relevance. He'd seen himself meeting with the individuals, Robert, and the doe, Sal, but there'd been nothing at all of Crenshaw; nothing of anyone resembling him. And then, he'd seen another, a bent-backed individual of very advanced age, whom he guessed, was Millthorpe; the oldster mentioned by Bunty, as holding the position of Warren Leader, before the election of Crenshaw. There was simultaneous visioning of both past and future. Then, driving the point home, an image of Lillian's stew had sprung to mind.

Glancing out across the plain, he caught sight of the others. Piedmont, Peace and Sherbrook would soon be here.

Crenshaw was unstinting in granting temporary hospitality, but if they were to take up permanent residence here, then Skip must secure agreement. Seeing the large number of those still gathering, he was compelled to ask, 'If you don't mind my enquiring, Leader Crenshaw, how is it that there are so many of you?' He said, 'Ground Spring does not give any impression of being large—not from above ground, and yet accommodations must be extensive. I puzzle over your number.'

'Our burrows are ancient,' Crenshaw said. 'They go deeper and extend farther than those of other warrens.' He explained, 'By all accounts it's true, although the claim is not made from any personal experience. I've never ventured far afield and information supplied by visitors is all I have to go on. As to our number, we are isolated here and isolation favours increase. There's not a lot to do, other than work hard and make families to support.' As an afterthought, he said, 'But for the spring, there would be no settlement at all.'

Skip thought, Uncle Bucky and Buckminster of Brickfield would appreciate these plain-living folk of wilderness. He said, 'I'm grateful for your hospitality, Leader Crenshaw. I've journeyed far, but I am not alone. Look yonder and you will see my friends approach.' After directing attention to the three, he explained, 'We are wayfarers, and we desire no further wandering. I ask that you allow us to stay in your territory. We are honest folk, seeking favour. We would be accepted by you as good neighbours.'

Crenshaw grew thoughtful. Much muttering was heard from those gathered, both for and against granting favour. Skip had hoped to secure agreement before the others arrived. Looking again to the plain, he said, 'See there, my oldster companion, Piedmont, approaches. He will be very grateful for a warm and comfortable place to stay over. He spent last night in a too well ventilated, breezy log.' He directed the leader something of a beseeching smile.

Hearing the name Piedmont mentioned, many Ground Spring folk began quiet questioning amongst themselves. One, less timorous than the rest, came forward to ask, 'Is your friend, the bard?' He said, 'It would be too much to hope, but his name, as I heard it, is Piedmont?'

'Why, yes, he *is* the bard—the Bard of the Epics.'

Change was noticeable. Expression of delight increased and then, some departed the throng to meet with the strangers. Many flibberty hopped and some even heltered to meet up with one so esteemed. The bard's name, carried far and wide by itinerants, was well known hereabout. Over time, in return for hospitality granted, many a grateful itinerant had offered renditions of the great one's work.

By the time the friends reached Ground Spring Warren, Piedmont was the focus of a worshipful, jostling crowd, and seeing him so, Skip feared for the bard's safety; despite assistance from Peace and Sherbrook, he might be knocked down. Piedmont was not one to approve of fuss of any kind, but he looked to be enjoying the attention, which was all the more surprising, because having hobbled this far he must be all but worn-out.

Noting the bard's patience in dealing with folk, Leader Crenshaw commented, 'You travel in good company.'

Most had gone to join in welcoming Piedmont. Crenshaw's friend, Robert, had gone, but now returned to the small group. Sherbrook and Peace, knowing he could now cope, left the bard to his adoring fans. Sherbrook, noting Crenshaw's dignified bearing, identified him as leader. Stepping close and raising both paws in greeting, he announced, 'Hello there, Sir! I'm, Sherbrook, and my friend is Peace Darkling.'

Skip introduced Leader Crenshaw. Then, smiling, Crenshaw declared, 'It's such an honour having the bard here at Ground Spring; we must ask if he will consider giving a recital. We must wait of course, until he's rested.' That said, he called to Robert, 'Ask them to make space for Piedmont. Allow him through. The Bard is weary to wretchedness from journeying!' To Sal, he said, 'Sister, sustenance must be provided and our guests must be given the best available quarters.'

'Should I arrange accommodation close to your own quarters, brother? Will you be moving to the larger burrows of Millthorpe?'

'I will stay where I am, Sal. Being voted Leader doesn't mean I'll abandon my burrows.' Crenshaw thought for a moment before deciding, 'Our guests can take Millthorpe's quarters, but Sal ... have those who attended the former leader, ensure the place is in order.'

Piedmont joined them then, and hearing the name, Crenshaw, he questioned, 'Crenshaw? You did say *Crenshaw?*' Gazing skyward, he sighed in appreciation. He said, 'You know, Crenshaw is a fine name.' And seeing others were curious, he continued, 'Yes. It's by no means common, not these days, but then of course, other old names have met with similar fate. Many of them are no longer heard at all.' He said, 'Although, Leader, I'm sure you're acquainted with the fact—I cannot prevent myself from reminding that Crenshaw is one of those names which is passed to us from *earliest* time.' To all gathered, he said, 'Crenshaw was the true and loyal warrior companion to none other than Great Mydor—Mydor of legendary fame.'

Crenshaw, until now, was unaware of his name being identical with that borne by an individual of glorious renown and so he was flattered, not just by learning of the name's fine heritage, but also by Piedmont's considering the matter of such great importance. Piedmont next placed a paw against Crenshaw's right arm and enquired, 'You won't mind assisting an old buck into the warren, will you Crenshaw? No, I knew you'd not object.' He then informed, 'I've noted mention in scratchings that the crest of Mydor was first thought of by Crenshaw. Indeed, yes. He, Crenshaw, decided upon the use of the clenched claw of Brother Eagle as a symbol of defiance, or daresay, a symbol of victorious triumph! It's most sad that final victory eluded them—courageous warriors, one and all. Our world since that time, is not as should be.'

'Look, Dimster!' Dempster exclaimed. 'There goes a famous *someone!* This one's no show-off. He's the genuine article!' Such an outburst caused Piedmont, in passing, to cast a curious and mystified glance.

Crenshaw assured Piedmont, 'Yes. They're contrary. They don't aim to offend. They're "touched" from birth, and anything they say should not be taken to heart.'

Crenshaw was happy to assist the bard, via a long circuitous route, to large quarters, and once there, made thorough inspection of the place, ensuring that all was ordered for his visitor's comfort. Whilst seeing to Piedmont's needs, he asked, 'The youngster, Skip, mentioned you've thought of settling hereabout?' He said, 'I want you to know, Piedmont, that you and your company are most welcome.'

Bone-weary, Piedmont replied, 'It's decent of you, Crenshaw, giving an old buck such opportunity. For now though, good leader, this old body must recuperate. We will speak later of details. For now, I would ask another favour.'

'Just ask,' deigned Crenshaw.

'I wonder if the good folk might enjoy something of light entertainment? Nothing too grand, mind you, but … my versifying? Think on it, will you? You can let me know whether the idea is acceptable.'

After all, Crenshaw had not to request favour of the bard; the bard had made the offer. The leader could not wait to inform sister Sal and friend Robert. The opportunity for performance was so well timed that, Great Grandfather could not have planned things better. Crenshaw could not have arranged a finer, celebratory event to mark his election to leadership.

After parting with Piedmont, and traversing the long burrow, which would take him to Robert's quarters, he was mindful of his mother's naming him Crenshaw. Mother had not mentioned having knowledge of the name's history. He now wondered, why, of all names, she'd decided upon it. She was no longer with them, for she had met with gazuzzlement long ago. He would ask sister Sal. Perhaps she knew something of the reasoning behind the decision.

Peace, Sherbrook and Skip were well provided for, or so they at first believed. Two friendly does, Tara and Aunt Laue, ushered them into a large chamber, which was situated in close proximity to Piedmont's quarters. The chamber was unusual in that during its excavation, large flat slabs of stone were encountered and these now served as walls, which were configured so that a disturbing echo was produced whenever an occupant spoke in anything louder than a whisper. The echoing effect was not the only thing they were unfamiliar with, for at the far corner of the chamber, at the foot of the largest of those stones which formed "facing" for the room, was another, flat-lying stone—a stone of large proportion, having a smooth, hollowed-out centre portion to it. Sherbrook questioned the others, as to the intended use or purpose of the stone. And, after considering the problem presented, Skip ventured, 'I believe— it's a rough guess, you understand—it's what's called a "toilet".'

'Which is?' asked Sherbrook.

'A toilet is a receptacle for droppings,' Skip told him.

Whereupon, Peace declared, 'Oh, how disgusting!' The word, "disgusting", replete with exclamation, was repeated as it echoed back and forth in the unusual stonewalled chamber. Skip went on to inform, 'It's nothing too terrible. The Tall Ones have them. I've seen them. Theirs are not crude things of this sort. Theirs have things called "buttons", which are nothing the same as jacket buttons, but things you push. When they're pushed, water gushes forth as a small water-fall, to flush droppings and waste into nowhere at all.' He said, 'Now, before you ask, Sherbrook. No, I don't know where it goes. It's another mystery.'

Peace said, 'I'll do my best to accept its presence in the sleeping chamber, but you will *never*, I assure you, catch me using it.'

'I think I'd venture trying it,' said Sherbrook, giving the stone an uncertain, quizzical look.

'I wouldn't mind at all,' Skip said, 'if there was a button included, but there isn't. This is a primitive effort, it's not the real thing at all.'

Changing the topic, Peace observed, 'These burrows are huge, aren't they? From topside there's no indication at all, of so much lying below.'

'Yes—they've been busy,' Sherbrook said, staring overhead to distant ceiling. 'I think it's wasted effort though, because there's something lacking. This is not what I think of as snug. A certain homeliness is missing.'

Skip said, 'Maybe I shouldn't mention it, but this place reminds me of future warrens, warrens of my vision, homes of those which Piedmont referred to as "mutant" folk.'

Hearing that subject raised, Peace said, 'If neither of you mind too much, I'm for a little shut-eye.'

'Oh yes. Feel free,' said Sherbrook, and not wanting Peace upset by mention of mutants, he cast Skip a warning glance.

In the large chamber, adjacent to theirs, Piedmont, already on his way to slumber, tossed for a final time and muttering in half-conscious fashion, declared, 'Without a word of lie, I'm beyond bruk!'

He was aware of a voice then, 'You are sleeping, Sir. Well, no matter... Upon waking you will find nibbles at your side. I shall leave them for you.' The bard muttered, and drifted deeper.

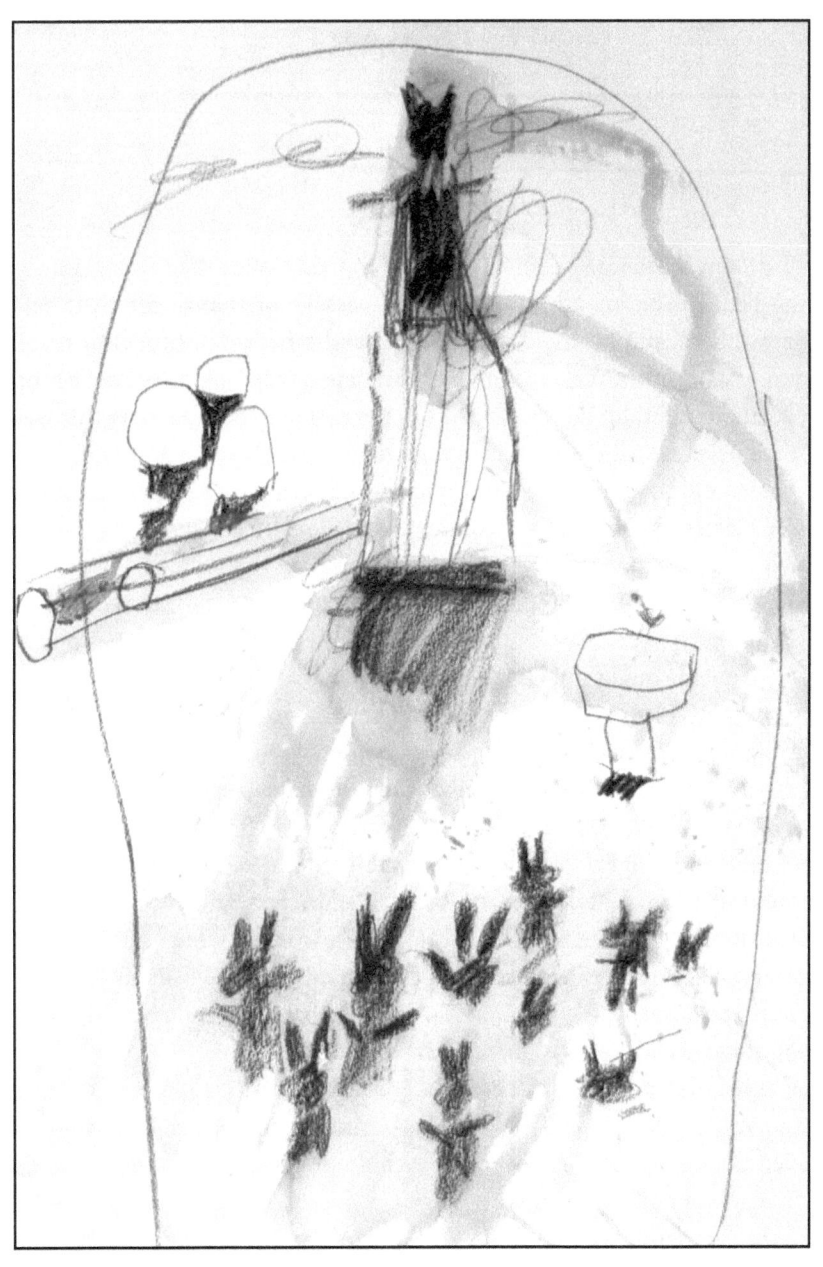

Epic

THE BARD

Piedmont stood tall, behind a large flat-topped stone outcropping, intoning beneath his breath. He offered a message of thanks for their safe arrival here, and he asked that Great Grandfather grant him clear recall and assist him in not muffing his lines. He needed his wits about him, because truth told, he was nervous to the extreme. Never before this was there occasion where he must recite before such a large gathering. His gnarled old paws clenched and unclenched, gripping at the sides of the stone lectern as he awaited a comforting response from above. He trusted that deity was not too occupied in dealing with the problems of others, and then admonished himself for allowing such anxiety-induced, selfish thought. All were deserving of assistance, and Great Grandfather's omniscient nature ought not be forgotten.

By now Piedmont was rested and so had no difficulty maintaining straighter posture than was his usual wont. Where he stood, the floor was at higher elevation than that of the rest of the great chamber, and so, appearing taller than he was, to those gathering before him, he presented an impressive sight. The capacious meeting place was filling to capacity. Looking down at his audience, as they filed in, he wondered if he should leave the stage and return to it a little later. It would have been a good idea to have Sherbrook introduce him before coming on. A grander entrance would have been effective. Coming on, as he had, to stand about, appearing at loose end was recognized now as a mistake.

Towards the front of the crowd were Peace, Skip and Sherbrook. Peace and young Skip spoke with a most diminutive youngster, and from all Piedmont gathered, in conversing with them, the tiny individual made a good job of holding his own.

Earlier, Crenshaw had offered to introduce him, but Piedmont had declined. Folk knew who he was, and what was intended but then he'd expected just a small gathering of most fervent fans of the works. Upon arriving here at Ground Spring, he was, of course, flattered by the welcome received, but he'd thought that initial excitement would have worn off. Now facing a veritable multitude, he would like to leave the platform, but doing so at this late point would be a serious mistake, and might even impress others as something of coy manoeuvring; he must act though, before nerve failed him.

At the front of the crowd, Crenshaw was in company of Sal and friend, Robert. Piedmont gestured in a manner he hoped was not too obvious, attempting to gain the leader's attention. Seeing him do so, there were several in the crowd, who, believing his surreptitious gesturing intended for them, raised paws and waved back to him. The bard's awful frustration increased. Sal, seeing him waving, realized his intention and tapped Crenshaw on a shoulder. Crenshaw, occupied in speaking with Robert, to Piedmont's enormous relief, shifted focus of attention in line with the sister's direction. Piedmont exhaled with grateful relief. Crenshaw made his way to the dais, whereupon Piedmont confessed, 'I would, after all, be grateful if you'd introduce me, Crenshaw. I'm afraid it's all just a little too much.'

'Nerves getting the better of you, Bard?' Crenshaw enquired. He said, 'I know what it's like. I suffered speaking before crowds before the election, but you get used to it. I told myself that rather than see them as many critical individuals, see them as one large entity, and it helped no end. I tried focusing on one place in particular, a space just above the most distant heads in the crowd. By doing so, I maintained a sense of being in control.' Wanting to avoid any further prolonging of the bard's agony, Crenshaw turned to the crowd and asked for quiet. He next made a short announcement, 'Good folk of Ground Spring, tonight we are privileged in having with us, one of high renown, one needing no introduction. In offering to recite the works, he is gracious. He is a new friend come from far afield. Old friends, I give you Piedmont—Piedmont the Bard.' Without further ado, the bard hopped forward, and began, 'I will recite first, the word-woven artefact, *Only a Day*. It is homage to those who fought so long ago—even, for us.

'*Only a Day*

Turn to the reflecting pool.

Traverse the winds of time.
Know the warrior's proud heart,
Beats still;
Close held in memory's grasp.

A first shout issues forth!
A withering blade, carried high,
Reflects the morning light.
First cries upon the air are heard.
Fading then ... fading...
Fading as dreams do depart.

Birthed by shade.
From dark and secret place came they.
Turn side-wise a grim, furless glance,
Turned to Folk on field of war;
To cause the day enslaved.
Only a day.

Fire and shield to battlefront
Press forth; willingness not feigned.
Companion and friend,
Ensnared by pressing vow,
Ensure Gazuzzlement unbound.

No more then to hop 'cross meadow's
Embracing charm.
For, strange mischief once came down
From nowhere at all.

Mutterers of lies.
Grande promises made to break.
Sting of Brother Bee and
Sister Wasp.
Barbs move in flesh.
From mystery peak and depth of pond,

A poison for the land.

Flame set to flame.
Native bud, sweet berry and the
Graveside flower.
The mocker from the battleground,
Loud hisses in his time.

Heroes left home places, and,
Circling lines graved once, graved times four,
And more,
Plans were formed.
And at close of day to dust returned.

A falcon hovers high.
Mere youngster is espied.
Ascending still, poised lofty,
Questions, swoop, or, wend?
Swaying, air-cuffed ... steadies then.
And, forsaking current ... falls!
And so it is.

The warrior-prince with brave company,
Steeped more in tears than blame;
To legend is consigned.
Mute the victory hymn,
Kept safe still.'

Piedmont knew satisfaction. His audience was spellbound, and following several moments' silence, a large sigh of appreciation moved through the great chamber. Such positive response was for Piedmont, as soothing balm; remaining anxiety evaporated as dew from stalk and leaf, when taken by the sun's first warm rays. Then came polite, dignified applause, and he saw Peace, Sherbrook and Skip's beaming smiles. A successful evening lay ahead, pleasure was shared, and Piedmont allowed himself to bask in an inner glow.

In the audience, Peace told Sherbrook, 'It's wonderful, seeing him receive due attention after all he's been through. She still carried the mental picture of Piedmont suffering the humiliation of broom making, beneath the oak.

Sherbrook knew like feeling. He said, 'If Grammy could see him now, eh?' and looked up at Piedmont, who prepared to make his next offering.

A bemused and curious Skip enquired of Bunty, 'How is it you dance about when the bard speaks? I saw you jigging.'

Bunty told him, 'I like the rhythm of his words. Hearing him recite, I feel like dancing.' He said, 'The effect is similar to the sound made by my wind-clickers, in the tomb of giants. They make me dance.'

Skip had no idea what wind clickers were, but hearing mention of a tomb of giants, he was attentive. 'What tomb?' he asked.

'Oh, it's not a tomb. But then, maybe it is. I don't know. In any case, that's my name for it. Perhaps I shouldn't have told you though, because I'm the one who found it and it's my secret. I'm the only one small enough to get to it.' He added, 'Not everything about being small is bad.'

Skip made a mental note; he would further question Bunty.

For now, before his audience grew inattentive and restless, the bard continued. He announced, 'Now, my next offering, is one for the youngsters.'

* * *

Further enquiry set Skip and Bunty on course to adventure.

They met as arranged, in the burrow outside the guest's quarters. It was the morning following the evening of the recital, and Bunty was bright, his mood buoyant, but Skip rubbed sleep from his eyes and his repeated yawning told him that they should have arranged to meet later than this. They did not though, want others learning of Bunty's discovery. And now, as they made the way deeper into Ground Spring Warren's labyrinth of burrows, they chatted in subdued fashion so as to make no disturbance or be overheard by others. Not many were out and about so early as this, and the deeper they went, the less likelihood there was of them coming upon anyone at all.

After some time, they were so deep and distant from the main complex, that Skip's curiosity got the better of him, and he asked, 'How come there are burrows here? I know Ground Spring has a large population but there's no one down here. It doesn't make sense.'

Bunty told him, 'That's right, no one lives here, and these excavations are old. Whilst, coming this far is not out-of-bounds, it's understood that none are expected to come so far. It's more or less, unspoken agreement, rather than a rigid rule. But in coming here, let's just say, we're breaking with tradition.'

Skip said, 'I won't tell, if you don't.' After a moment, he said, 'Let's push on then.'

He thought of old Warren Central, with its tunnel leading down to deepest Level C. That tunnel had saved folk in direst time but the tunnel Bunty took him through now was not at all similar. It was a lot larger in diameter and long; its course ran far deeper. There was about it an air of great antiquity. The farther they went, the more certain he was that none of any recent generation had set paw to toil here. They went still farther, with Bunty showing no sign of slackening pace, and Skip, already knowing the answer, enquired, 'Does anyone else ever come here?'

Bunty told him, 'No. Just me.'

Skip asked, 'What would happen if you lost your way? You could be hurt somehow, and no one would hear you shouting for help. You might never be found.'

Bunty said, 'It's a lot safer down here for someone of my size than it is at the surface. Down here, I don't have *stuff* to put up with.'

Bullies did not venture here.

Then, Bunty said, 'Every so often we'll stop to listen, in case we're followed. And from this point on, I always take a more winding, indirect route. It doesn't take an awful lot longer.'

Skip assured him that he did not mind.

They next passed through a long section of walled burrow, where the now familiar, flat-sided stone slabs formed huge, towering walls, which reminded him of the chamber he shared with Sherbrook and Peace, except that, judging by the echoes produced by their footfalls, the stones here went much higher than those others, before meeting with the dark-shrouded roof. They traversed a great chasm, and even Brickfield's unusual structures had not impressed this much.

Skip wondered how those excavating the tunnel had known to dig so as to form a passageway between subterranean stones, so that after labouring was complete, such magnificent walls were exposed? Inhabitants of Ground Spring could not by any stretch of the imagination, have positioned such weighty stones as these!

Now a faint light was seen. Skip heard Bunty, who went ahead of him, calling, 'We've not far to go now. We're almost there!' After further traversing between dark walls they emerged into a soft-lit, high-roofed chamber; a cavernous space, with a rough dirt floor. Skip was reminded again of Brickfield, with its domed buildings, but this space seemed formed by natural means. At far side of the chamber were five, straight-sided stones and their unusual arrangement reminded him of Lillian's breakfast table, but this, was far more substantial. He experienced an odd, unsettling sense of mystery. It could not be true, he thought, but instinct insisted, those stones were of Tall One origin.

Far overhead was a small opening to the world above and pale light shafted downwards. Staring overhead, he noted a thin crack, or fissure, had its beginning up there. The fissure's long-snaking course ran downwards, scaring the chamber's wall before meeting with the floor below. There was no present danger because that rent was caused long ago. Dust-motes and insects moved in shafting light and their movement was hypnotic. Seeing them, Skip detected an unfamiliar and faint, rhythmic sound. After listening for a moment, he asked, 'What did you say makes that sound? "Wind-clickers" was it?'

'That's right. Come on, I'll show you!' But then, doubting that Skip could come too, Bunty said, 'The opening is very small, so, put an ear close to it and you'll hear them, and you'll believe me.'

Skip told him, 'Oh, I believe you, Bunty. Don't doubt it.'

Close to the odd arrangement of stones, a narrow, smooth-sided tunnel went into the foot of the wall.

Down on his knees studying it, Skip knew it was artificial. Like the "table", this too, was the work of Tall Ones. He was wary of Bunty going anywhere near it, but then Bunty claimed he'd often done that very thing. Faced with his friend's impatience, Skip moved aside, allowing Bunty access to the way. Seeing him squeeze into the space, Skip bent low, and with one side of his face pressed against the ground, he followed Bunty's progress. Bunty's white tail disappeared from view as he passed through and beyond a gossamer-thin and membranous substance.

The strange material shimmered, producing a distorting effect. From opposite sides of the wall, they saw each other through a blue mist.

Bunty called, 'You would never fit. It would be awful if you got stuck part way through.'

Attempting to see where Bunty waited, Skip was unsuccessful and so he asked, 'How big is that place?'

'Very large.'

Skip said, 'Shut your eyes. Squeeze them tight shut, until I say to open them.'

Bunty trusted. His eyes were shut tight, but then they slipped back open, without permission.

Skip moved. Bunty was dazzled! Rubbing at his eyes, he asked, 'What *was* that? How did you *do* it?'

Skip replied, 'I'm magic. I can shrink myself smaller than a field mouse.'

A smiling Bunty accepted the explanation without question, whilst Skip, looking all about, was astonished by everything he saw.

This was a place of wonder. Arrived from dim cavern, he found himself now in a place of light, the light of a glorious spring day. High overhead was the bluest sky and a balmy breeze blew. They stood upon a grassy slope and, before them a narrow path wound the way down to where a wooden fence divided the scene. At opposite side of that fence, a row of tall silver trees bordered a colourful, wild flower strewn meadow, and the soft babbling of a meandering stream was heard.

Looking out to far distant horizon, Skip realized that the entire vista was held contained within an immense, ovoid shaped chamber. Nothing was missing; the place was a realm in its own right, and shifting his feet in soft grass, he was speechless. Glancing down he saw a ladybug alight to balance upon a thin grassy stalk.

Out across the wide meadow the tops of two structures were visible and their design was something with which he was familiar. Those were the rooftops of a cottage and a barn. The merry sound of clicking reached them, and Bunty exclaimed, 'The breeze has caught my wind-clickers! Come on—I'll show you them!' That said, he was flibberty hopping down the slope to the trees by the fence. Skip went after him, and arriving at the trees, saw Bunty jigged in time to an unusual, whirring, clicking sound.

From two, wide-spaced trees, stretched many lines of thin cord. Those cords formed an elaborate, intricate web, and attached at various points of the web were many feathers, their colours ranging from dull to most outstanding brightness. Small objects whirred with the breeze pushing against them. When the breeze stilled, spinning ceased, and they were seen as small, leaf-thin blades. As well, suspended amidst feathers and spinners, were hollow sticks of various lengths, and those sticks knocked against one another producing a percussive beat. That rhythmic sound most captivated Bunty. Watching him now, Skip decided that he would never jig about like that in the presence of one as serious as the bard, but they were alone, and so he joined his diminutive friend in dancing, until Skip thought, Bunty must be nearing the point of exhaustion, because Skip could no longer keep up.

When the breeze stilled, he asked, 'How about we go now and you can show me those giants?'

'All right, but they're a long way from here. The tomb is way over yonder, and you look as if you could do with a rest.'

'I'm fine,' protested Skip. Wondering over Bunty's naming something a tomb, he said, 'The wind-clicker dancing has me panting, that's all.'

'Then, would you say, I must be stronger and tougher than I look?' Bunty showed not least sign of tiredness.

Skip told him, 'Oh, yes. You're small, but you're mighty powerful, and there's no doubting it.'

Bunty said, 'I'm glad I invited you. It's a lot more fun, sharing with someone.'

They went beneath the fence, and then a narrow hopping trail led them to the stream, which they crossed by way of a rickety wooden bridge. Part way across the bridge they paused to look down over its edge to the water below. A multitude of water lilies bloomed there.

Dense-growing patches of reeds spread along the banks, and gazing along the winding creek's course, this was, Skip thought, the most pleasant of places. They were off again then, flibberty hopping along the trail leading to the Tall One dwelling. Arriving, and standing before the place, even brave Bunty was a little unsettled being here. And, lest he lose his nerve, Skip did not pause long, but went straight to the door of the cottage. Pushing it wide open, he called, 'Come on, Bunty. You found this place. Show me its secrets!'

In a room, that he decided must be the parlour, stood a large short-legged table, and on the table was a dirt filled, wooden pail. Standing in the pail was all that remained of a tree, and he had never seen its like. A deep purple and dappled trunk and branches, streaked with a yellow-green, shining substance, lent the tree a most unnatural appearance. Suspecting the tree was artificial; Skip went closer and reaching out, touched the tip of a brittle branch.

A twig snapped off, and a small inner voice cautioned, Avoid touching that resinous green substance. Skip brushed his paws together as if ridding them of contamination. His attention shifted to an odd shaped item, which rested adjacent with the wooden pail. Mindful of where he was, he decided he'd best not touch it. Rather than do so, he cocked his head first to one side, then the other, considering it, and concluded the shape of the device was formed for Tall One hands. At the object's centre was a shiny dark square, and at both sides of that were small buttons and knobs for fingers to push against. He recalled seeing similar devices, whilst in company of elder Skip. This device was a toy of some sort, and yet it did not appeal as those others had and he could not guess its purpose. Bunty shifted his weight from one leg to the other in impatient fashion and declared, 'I thought you wanted to see the giants?' Skip, turning to him, said, 'Just lead on my friend.'

Upon entering the kitchen he could not but realize Bunty's reason for naming the place a tomb for giants. For there, at the middle of the room, towered a large rectangular shaped box, and in the confined space, the box presented an impressive presence. It was indeed a true sarcophagus of giants. Its translucent, facing surface was misted over and light emanated from its interior. Going close to it, Skip recalled his elder describing such material as "glass".

Tall Ones stared out at him from the sarcophagus and at first sight of them, he jumped back in fright. Remaining alert and watchful in the moments following his initial shock, he realized that nothing other than a mistake made in first glimpsing them, was cause for believing they stared. A powdery, smooth coating of fine ice crystals covered the countenances of the Tall Ones, and light in the sealed chamber, reflected by ice crystals, had made the Tall Ones, at first glance, appear living. They'd stared down at him, returning his gaze.

'They are *my* giants,' Bunty said, revealing pride as explorer and discoverer.

Skip told him, 'Tall Ones are what they are, Bunty.' He said, 'But, you're right, they're giants, as well.' They should not be feared, but still he backed away.

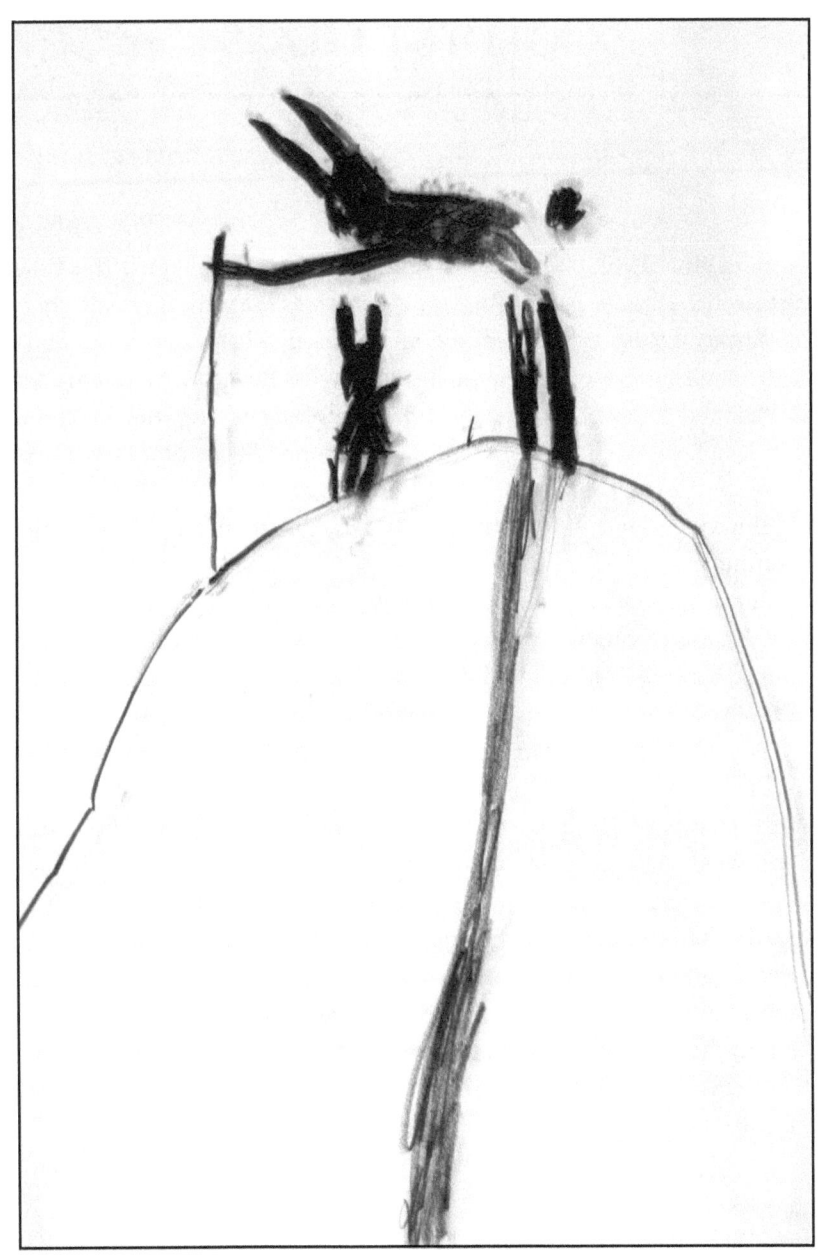

Hill

COLDEST GLASS

Steeling himself, Skip returned to stand near the sarcophagus. This time he placed a tentative paw against the glass. It was the smoothest and coldest surface he'd ever touched. He told himself, whatever you do, don't look up at those faces. In wiping his paw across the glass, he saw graved marks, and knew they resembled a form of scratching, but he could not decipher their meaning. Those marks were: *Terrence Thiery Corp. Cryogenics. Model: 307A.*

Thinking aloud, he muttered, 'Perhaps, Piedmont might know the meaning of this.'

Bunty responded, 'The bard is huge, and could never enter by the way.' He then thought further and said, 'Unless, that is, he also possesses strange ability?' When Skip did not respond, he enquired, 'Do all members of your company possess "field mouse" ability?'

'No,' Skip replied, his mood lightening, imagining Piedmont "moving" anything—least of all, himself. The thought of Sherbrook moving was even more ridiculous, but thinking then of the elders, whom he still considered the true, miraculous Tump, he realized that, Bunty's suggestion was not so off the mark, because they all *did* move. They moved together as a singular entity. Curiosity bettering resolve, he gained courage enough to look again to those faces and in doing so, heard the sound of rain falling against the roof of the cottage, and peering upward, discerning faces of a female and male, declared, 'The strangeness of it has me flabbergasted. On top of everything else, we are now treated to rain! This place is underground, isn't it?'

He enquired, 'What say you, Bunty? Is it rain I hear, or do my ears deceive me?'

'Mm. It's rained during several of my visits here. I don't mind rain.'

In studying the Tall Ones, Skip next said, 'Actually, as I see him, the great buck is the worst for wear. I'm no expert on Tall Ones and can't judge his condition, but it seems obvious that compared with the doe, he's grey and pallid. What's your impression, Bunty?' Skip thought the buck's fur-less pallor repellent, but the doe's complexion was healthy in appearance—that was, if anything so cold could be thought healthy. He did not like admitting it, but regardless of her being a Tall One, there was something there—some quality to her expression, which made her not so unattractive. As far as the creatures went, she was not so downright disgusting.

Bunty was bored with Skip's continuing interest in the giants. He'd seen them so often and was never so fascinated. He was excited by his initial discovery and their size had impressed, but he was never interested in making a study of them. 'Ho-hum.' he announced, smiling, but Skip was engrossed and failed to notice him. 'Ho-hum,' Bunty repeated.

Skip told him then, 'I know you're bored, Bunty, but what you have here is incredible.' Then, Skip sighed, and taking his attention from the Tall Ones, he turned to Bunty and asked, 'Is there anything else to marvel over?'

Bunty told him, 'Out in the other place, there is the great beast with hard skin and round paws. The eyes are as hard as the giant's tomb. If we leave now, I'll show you. There's no harm in it. It's gazuzzlement is long past and web spinners have made fine work of adorning it.'

In the short hallway leading to the back of the dwelling, an image was displayed, and recalling images claiming his attention in the past, Skip paused to study this one. The Tall One smiled … but those too short, too even, Tall One teeth were hard to get used to. Despite his awful grinning, the Tall One portrayed here in the image upon the wall, seemed intent upon conveying friendliness.

In his arms, he held a white dove and, judged by the gentle way the Tall One cradled the bird to his chest, and by Sister Dove's fearless expression in gazing to him, they must be friends. There, was indecipherable scratching: *For my perfect daughter, Lilith.*

Skip and Bunty left the house by the back door, and as the screen door swung shut behind them a sparrow flew so low-swooping, that it brushed against Skip's cheek. Startled, he exclaimed, 'Deeks! Watch out Brother!' Looking then to an area not too far distant from the cottage, he noted trees standing in rows. They must, he thought, make up an orchard, and having decided it so, he said, 'Bunty, we'll check out the monster, but first we should take a quick look at yon' trees.' Bunty's expression showed he was not pleased by the idea of them making further delay to look at boring trees, but Skip insisted, 'Come on. There might be wind-falls!'

He was correct, because lying on the grass beneath the trees were apples, pears and dingle berries. Much of the fruit was bruised and marked but it didn't matter. Lillian and Buckminster had introduced him to dingle berries and now, taking a bite of fallen fruit, he was reminded of them.

Seeing Skip smiling with obvious pleasure, Bunty needed little encouragement in joining him in sampling such fine fare, and tasting dingle for the first time, he was surprised. 'These have been rotting here for ages, and I didn't so much as *think* of trying them.' He declared, 'They're *very* acceptable!'

'Mm! Beats dry grass!' Skip said. Dripped juice discoloured the fur of his chin. He asked, 'What do you suppose *those* things are?' He pointed to a distant group of long, crossed sticks, which could be seen jutting from dusty ground in an area which for this place was unusual in that it was devoid of grass.

'Um...' Bunty hesitated, making it obvious that he'd not before this moment pondered, those sticks being where they were. Now he entertained possibilities. 'They could be part of an old fence,' he offered, and, 'They might be just about any old thing at all.'

None of which was very helpful or useful. Getting up from tree-shaded grass, and wiping his chin with the back of a paw, Skip announced, 'I'm going to take a closer look. I bet I can race you there. Let's go!' So saying, he set off, heltering to the spot, with Bunty doing his best to keep up.

Once there, Bunty complained, 'That wasn't fair! If you'd given fair warning, I could have beaten you!'

'Sure you could,' Skip, agreed, sounding rather absent, as he began studying the arrangements of sticks. There was a row of nine, tall sticks. Those long sticks, had been driven into the ground, whilst, other, shorter sticks, had been attached to them in horizontal positions. Three of those tall sticks stood bereft of their shorter, horizontal parts. Those had fallen off to lie in the dust. Set before each arrangement, the ground was mounded into low hillocks, and in that soil nothing grew. One horizontal stick carried an inscription: *One beloved of Mydor*. Not gleaning meaning of that scratching, Skip declared, 'None of this resembles any fence that I ever saw.' He'd not forewarned Bunty, before making the dash here, and seeing Bunty still peeved over the omission, he then allowed, 'You *could* be right, though. Maybe it's a fence of ancient design—a thing I'm not acquainted with.' He shrugged, then asked, 'Well, Bunty, what are we waiting for? Lead on, Buckaroo—let's go see the beast!'

On arrival at the barn, Skip had his first, close-up experience of a truck; a pick-up truck. And, as the elder had informed him, he set to informing Bunty. 'This is a vehicle and, Tall Ones ride about in them. Granted, it does appear frightening, but it's more or less harmless.'

'More or less?' Bunty enquired.

'Yes. It will not for instance, bite.'

The truck was the exact colour of the eggs of Sister Starling. During severe winds, accidents occurred. It was not uncommon for eggs to be dislodged from swaying nests, to then plummet and dash against the ground. Evidence of such unfortunate occurrences was sometimes encountered after the passing of storms and, if a starling egg suffered such fate, shards of unfathomable blue could later be found. In staring now, at the pick-up, Skip decided that it too, presented an unhappy sight. Were it not so dusty, its fine colour would show. It bore evidence of an old injury inflicted to one, large, rounded shoulder, and its flattened stones of feet, and cracked eyeglass, were naught but further sad notes, adding to the overall vision of neglect. Bunty was right, for over much time, many web spinners had toiled, and each and every one of the truck's crevices and spaces held proof of their labour. And yet, thought Skip, somehow ... in an indefinable way, the beast was magnificent still. He knew that were he, a Tall One, then he would have a strong desire to possess a thing such as this. He'd seen vehicles and been afraid of them but now, the feeling of excitement was not to be denied. He reached up, and following fumbling attempt, succeeded in opening the driver's side door.

Using the back of a paw, brisk work was made of sweeping away the cobwebs, and he peered into mysterious unknown territory. Somewhat disappointed, he noticed a big circle, attached to a substantial looking stick, which protruded out from a hidden space. At this side of the interior were several large glassy eyes, all of which had within their depths, many, finely made scratchings. There was another, stick-like thing, which extended from the centre of the floor, and at its top-most end, was something of some interest—something resembling nothing more than a deep purple, perfect plum. Lower down, just above floor level, below the important looking circle, below the shaft and eyes, were things, perhaps even more interesting than the rest. Stamping pads.

He experimented by pushing at them. He was delighted by the way they rose back to their original positions, even without his further touching them. Furniture was included; there was a wide, upholstered seat. It was something he thought Lillian would like, apart from it bearing several deep scars; evidence, he concluded, of Tall One's bickery scratching with one another.

Engrossed with the exploration of the vehicle, he'd not given a thought to Bunty's whereabouts and so was startled after calling, 'Bunty! Come here and take a look!'

Bunty, who, during most of the time taken in the inspection of the vehicle, stood immediately behind him, and hearing his name called, exclaimed, 'I'm right here—and there's no way, I'm getting in there!'

Skip told him, 'Don't *ever* do that! Don't sneak up on me that way!'

'I didn't *sneak!* I've been here all along—the whole time!'

'All right,' relented, Skip, shaking away fright, 'but, here now, I'll give you a boost. You can go first, and we'll imagine we're Tall Ones, heltering in our own truck! What'd you say?'

'I say—*no!*' Uttering those words, Bunty demonstrated most adamant refusal. 'I'm not interested in playing giants! Thank you very much all the same!' He added, 'And, there's nothing you can say, to make me change my mind.'

Skip pressed the point. Staring at Bunty, he thought for a moment and then offered, 'How about we make a deal? If you climb in and we play at being Tall Ones, then … later on, I promise to move you! Going home you won't have to get yourself all squished and dirty, squeezing through that grubby little hole in the wall.'

Bunty, looking to Skip, figured that Skip proposed *shrinking* him. "Field mouse" ability was being offered. Looking down at himself, he admitted, 'I'm already dirty.' He said, 'Dirty enough to not care about squeezing my way through the opening again.' He would not say so, because he did not want to offend, but he would prefer getting into the beast of a truck, than accept an offer of a process involving shrinkage. He was already far too small, and besides, what horror might result? His mother might never see him again, not with the naked eye. She would have to ask a favour of the Bard and borrow his instrument of magnification. He'd not himself, had the opportunity of peering through it, but had glimpsed the fine looking thing on the occasion of the bard showing it off to Leader Crenshaw.

Skip was nonplussed. How, he wondered, could anyone reject such an offer? After thinking on it, realization dawned and he said, 'I get it. You thought I was serious, when I told you I shrink. I'm right aren't I?'

'You mean to say, you don't?'

Skip, knowing he would not have his way, slammed shut the door of the pick-up. He said, 'Of course not! I disintegrate and then reassemble! Who knows? It's a mystery!' But hearing the words *"disintegrate"* and *"reassemble",* Bunty knew his decision was the right one.

There was no way he wanted anything of direct involvement with Skip's ability. Earlier in the day, seeing white light flashing and his friend materializing, to stand next to him atop the green rise, was startling. It was amazing, yes, but witnessing such a spectacle was not what had pleased him. He was pleased by the knowledge that from then on he'd have company in this, his secret place. Friend Skip had rescued him from danger as well but the truth was that Bunty was, by now, less in awe of Skip. He felt sympathetic towards him and that, for very fact of Skip's difference. Were he, Bunty, so afflicted, he would not want others to learn of it. He was sorry for Skip, because Skip did not realize that being odd was *not* a good thing. He must go out of his way in assuring his friend of loyalty. And so he offered, 'I won't ever tell others of your unusualness. I know what it's like, being thought of as different. I can keep my lip buttoned. Have no doubt on that score, but I prefer not being "moved". Thank you for the offer. I *do* know that you mean well.'

Eons ago, a long spike was driven deep into one of the barns big supporting beams, and since that time to now, from the spike, hung an object, the knowledge of which was revered by Folk of Fur. Hanging in place above the roof of the pick-up truck, the object remained unnoticed by both Skip and Bunty. The ancient shield of a warrior; the scarred, battle-worn relic, which bore as motif, worked in gold and set against rich crimson ground, the clenched eagle claw, symbol of Great Mydor.

* * *

Piedmont's performance was successful but by the following day he was morose, lacking in confidence and out of sorts. He spoke of the "final occasion of versifying", and voiced terrible dissatisfaction, more than once alluding to the relentless nature of ageing. Restless, he hopped from one end of the large chamber to other and then, after returning to his starting point, journeying was begun anew. Whilst making an energetic display of dealing with restlessness, at the same time he appeared tired despite the day having just begun. He said, 'For the *final* occasion of versifying, the recital was, I suppose, well enough received.' Sounding then even less certain, 'That is so far as I'm able to determine it.'

Seeing him downcast and sounding so forlorn, and wanting to lighten his mood, Peace set to altering the course of conversation by informing, 'These quarters of yours, Piedmont, are spacious, fine enough for one of your standing, but *our* quarters, include an item of novel interest. Yes. A repository for droppings—if you can believe it! I assure you, I'm not joking. We have a large stone, formed to unusual shape, a hollowed out affair, and as far as we're able, we've guessed *that* is its purpose.'

His interest was captured, she saw, and Piedmont asked, 'A repository for droppings? I've never heard of such. Can there be such a thing?' Curiosity piqued, he enquired, 'If it's no bother, do you think I might see it?' Smiling then, he said, 'You will recall, my dear, I was set to task in producing equipment used for the very task. Disposal of droppings! *I* possess considerable expertise in the subject.'

A short time later, standing alongside the stone, situated in the chamber shared by Peace, Sherbrook and Skip, the bard shook his head, declaring, 'No, no, no. This is a work of considerable antiquity—nothing whatsoever to do with pellet disposal.' He said, 'The whimsical notion of it being used for such purpose is not without appeal, but look, and you'll see the way it was worked at the edges—its intended use was important.' He again shook his head, muttering, 'Ceremonial perhaps? In any case, it was ages in the forming.' Sherbrook was present and suggested, 'Maybe it was used for bathing. It may not have anything to do with Folk of Fur. It might be something belonging to Tall Ones, or...'

'Yes, a pond!' Peace interjected. Then, turning to Piedmont, she said, 'You know, Sherbrook's suggestion may be correct.'

Piedmont declined agreement, protesting, 'It's not deep enough for that use unless it's a pond for tadpole or minnow.' Smiling, the bard then altered course, 'As I see the problem presented, it must be agreed that the best suggestion, winning by majority vote, is the first.'

Then, when Skip burst into the chamber, the matter was left to rest. Words tumbling from him, the youngster announced, 'I have wonderful news everyone! I've found the place where true Tump is born! It's the place of our new beginning—our perfect home!'

'That's great, Buckaroo,' Sherbrook told him. 'But Leader Crenshaw's already seen to sending out scouts on our behalf. They'll find the best places for digging.'

Peace informed, 'This morning in your absence, they offered to allow us to stay in the main warren—Ground Spring, itself. But, after discussing the proposal amongst ourselves, it was declined.'

'Yes,' said Piedmont, 'Even as early as yesterday, following our arriving here, Crenshaw's mind was made up. He told me he foresaw no problem in allowing us stay. However, we decided we'd be best off keeping to our own company,' Piedmont said. 'Best keep to ourselves, rather than run the risk of wearing out our welcome.' He said, 'None were offended by us declining such a generous offer. In fact, they were gracious—and those scouts mentioned by Sherbrook were sent forth.'

Skip snapped, 'It just won't do. No—it won't—not at all!'

Nonplussed by his outburst, the others stared.

Skip told them, 'A multitude can be sent out scouting! I don't care! The place I've found is the one we *will* have!' He added, 'You can make all the arrangements, you like but *I'm* the one who knows what's best for us!'

Going to a corner of the chamber he determined to keep all he'd learned of, to himself. He lay on the floor and thought of the sparrows he'd seen earlier. After leaving the barn and returning across the meadow and stream, to the small green hill beyond the dilapidated fence, he and Bunty had watched, dumbfounded, as a flock of sparrows flew, passing through and beyond the curved, shimmering boundary "wall" of the small realm.

According to any normal reckoning they flew beyond sky and straight into solid groundmass, which of course was impossible but then no sparrow had fallen back to ground or grass. Wherever they went, nothing had prevented their flight.

With the accompaniment of whirring and clicking rhythm of hollow sticks, he and Bunty had rested in the bucolic setting. They'd waited long, but still not one of those sparrows had returned.

HOME

From atop a hillock overlooking Ground Spring Warren, Crenshaw, in company of Piedmont and Sherbrook, said, 'Yes, I did say you could excavate in a location of your choosing, but why would you want to dig near the big split-stone, when, lower down the slope, green grass is plentiful and you are closer to the spring? I confess, the choice is cause for puzzlement.'

'The choice is young Skip's,' Piedmont responded; he'd offered the same reason several times before this. To Crenshaw's way of thinking they were mad to the point of insulting him, in choosing infertile, steep and rocky ground for a new home. Regarding madness he was correct. From this vantage point the area was seen as a dismal, foolish choice. In finding he was forced to repeat himself, Piedmont was embarrassed in having no other honest explanation for their benefactor.

Sherbrook was silent and other than attend the discussion, offered little by way of assistance. Of course he, Sherbrook, in absolute disagreement with both the choice, and too, Piedmont's allowing Skip his way, seethed and battled in not allowing true feeling to show. He'd adopted all too nonchalant an air and although present, appeared bored with the process of decision making, which Piedmont considered very unfair. Peace Darkling was coming up the slope, flibberty hopping, taking her time in getting here, and he wished to Great Grandfather that she would hasten, because she might alleviate the situation by making some or other suggestion. She might, with her not inconsiderable charm, smooth troubled waters.

Seeing her pausing along the way, Piedmont's feeling of discomfort increased. He attempted quieting himself by supposing that picking wild flowers made a lot more sense than Skip's behaviour. The boy went off this morning without a word of explanation, and then a short time later came back, giving an exact description and direction to the place he wanted them to request permission to excavate. "You must ask Leader Crenshaw," Skip said.

Of course, in requesting the use of the land insisted upon by young Skip, he was compelled by genuine appreciation for fact of his rescue from vile servitude at New Warren Central, and mysterious though it was, he admitted that despite his own lack of anything even approaching real understanding of the boy's talent, the youngster inspired belief. Thus far today, weather was no problem and that was appreciated. The day being fine meant that with final permission gained, work would proceed. Peace was not far off, and wearing a borrowed, long, russet-red dress with beadwork adornment and a long, dark, trailing sash, was in the moment at her exotic best. Fine wisps of midnight fur, softer than velvet, danced in the breeze as she approached; wild flowers were not needed to enhance sight of her. Crenshaw, not failing to recognize her beauty, performed a bow of homage and salutation, as, completing several last hops, she came to stand with them.

There was momentary quiet as none knew who should speak first, then Peace, addressing Crenshaw, explained, 'Leader Crenshaw, there's something I believe you have a right to know. The choice of site for our new home may seem inappropriate to others, and because we allow a youngster to choose for us, we open ourselves to ridicule, but, he has a certain and useful ability. He sees outcome and future events and so we trust him to know the best place, even though,' she said, sounding almost apologetic, 'as seen from here, his choice looks inhospitable.' She'd heard nothing of the previous conversation, but Piedmont thought it was as if Peace was here from the outset.

High above them, in a hollow nub of a branch, was a hive of bees and when Peace paused in making explanation, a returning bee altered course in droning flight, to inspect the blooms she'd gathered. She said, 'There are many where these are from, Brother Bee, but settle if you must,' and laughing, saw that her tolerant treatment of Brother Bee affected Leader Crenshaw.

He said, 'It's decided then, and you have my blessing. I'm no expert when it comes to the beliefs of others, but will hope that your trusting young Skip, is no mistake.' He paused, before extending further largesse, 'If there is even the *slightest* need, just ask, and assistance with excavation can be provided. There is no shortage of willing paws. That's true, I think, especially after the bard's performance. I must tell you, Piedmont;

it was for me, marvellous! I can't say I've enjoyed an evening more!' The bard did not disguise his pleasure at receiving the compliment, and for his part gave, 'I've never in all my time of versifying received such warm acceptance, and it is most gratifying. I very much enjoyed the youngsters' reaction to *Wild in the Wilderness.*'

And so, neighbourly spirit presided, and Sherbrook, glancing to Leader Crenshaw said, 'I'll get started with digging, then.' He offered, 'Allow me to offer you a helping paw, Peace.'

She told him, 'No, I'm fine Sherbrook. You'd better help the bard. He could do with a more stout stick. The one he has looks as if it might give way beneath him. We can't afford to lose him, can we now?'

Leader Crenshaw said, 'Well, good folk, there is much else to attend to, and so I'll bid you good day,' he said. 'Every success with the project, Sherbrook.'

When Crenshaw departed, Piedmont reached into his pocket and took out his spyglass. He raised it to an eye and peering through it, studied the split-rock formation and, after a moment, declared, 'A formation such as that is worthy of naming. What should we call it?' And forward thinking Sherbrook offered, *'Place of Travail* might be appropriate.'

Piedmont gave a short agreeable chuckle, but Peace said, 'It can go without naming. It's a place of new beginning. That's all we need to know.'

***

Twins, Dempster and Dimster, helped in shifting not just soil but a large quantity of rocks and rubble. They'd not been asked to help out, but worked on a voluntary basis, and Sherbrook, who enjoyed their unusual company, informed dour Dimster, 'This is no commonplace warren digging! No! *Quarrying* is what this is!'

Dempster, not Dimster, chuckled and answered for his brother, 'Yes! And that's what makes it such fun! It's different!'

Dimster advised Sherbrook, 'When the rocks are removed, you must keep them. Don't discard them or let them go rolling off down the hillside. Round ones will do that if you let them. They could prove useful at later stage.'

'That's interesting advice Dimmie, but, what might I do with a bunch of rocks? Do you have any suggestions?'

'No.'

'I don't either,' said Dempster, 'but then, you could always carry them about, or—I know!' he chortled. 'You could pass them out free to a select group of friends. And then soon, everyone would want them! You'd then be known as Sherbrook, "King of Stones"! I know you'd adore the title. Wouldn't he brother?' This made Sherbrook think of Weed, who, according to Skip, profited by offering a type of stone to others for use in warren construction, and so the idea was not so far-fetched as might be assumed. Again addressing Dimster he said, 'Know what, Dimmie? Your idea's a good one. And, someday, we might just do something of the sort, but in the meantime we'll look after them as you say, which means we're going to make a big heap of them right here, right next to the mother of all stones.'

Anything resembling true progress was impossible. This was the most difficult and slow excavation, the slowest in living memory. Ruing the fact of Piedmont's refusing to abandon faith in Skip's ability to make a sensible choice, Sherbrook looked down at his paws. They would, he knew, be wrecked and ruined tatters of things, long before he saw an end to even the first section of burrow. He would take a longer break. He wiped his paws against his chest. His striped jacket was draped across a most stubborn beast of a rock, one they had removed earlier. It was removed from an area lying in close proximity with a rough, circular opening in the ground, and before any attempt was made to budge the stone, he decided it would be wise to ascertain the nature of that hole. Then, peering into the darkness he made out nothing, other than just that, darkness. Steeling himself against the thought of Brother and Sister Serpent, he risked shoving a tentative paw down into it, but still exploration gave no answer. Standing again, and wiping at his brow, a grimy streak was made. Staring up at the mother of stones, he knew he was right in thinking of it as that. Split right down its middle, it towered high above the site. Beginning to regain his breath, he decided that having an entrance below the monster, meant that they could always find the way home. None would be lost, because the landmark was visible from far and wide. He vowed to admonish young Skip for not lending a paw with the digging; when next he caught sight of the youngster, excuse would not suffice. Skip would receive short shrift and find himself doing his share.

Piedmont was geriatric, he supposed. He decided that declaring such, did not make him guilty. The word geriatric was not an exaggeration, but an apt description of the bard. An individual of Piedmont's venerable age could not be expected to scratch about in dirt. His expertise meant involvement in an altogether other kind of scratching and, he'd be more in the way here, than anything else. Peace would not mind dirtying her paws, but the thought of her put to work, quarrying boulders ... well, he would not abide thought of it. That red dress she wore earlier, had suited her. He did not know where she was now, but she probably attended Piedmont.

Preparing to resume work, a strange sound was heard, or he believed he'd heard something. And then he was certain, for, from below ground, now came an unmistakable, far more definite kazooning!

In the great subterranean chamber an already enormous pile of soil and rock rose higher with each passing instant as, Skip moved the mountain. Bunty was there and was at once amazed and afraid. With each new delivery of soil delivered by magic means, to feed the mountain from within, Bunty covered his face with his paws and pushed back, pressing even closer against the wall. Soon, those measures provided little sense of security, and he raced for the opening of the large, high walled burrow, which led up to Ground Spring proper!

Skip had decided that in excavating the new warren, the best place to dump each new load of soil was at the central point of a heap. In carrying out the job that way, he need keep mindful of just *one* point of delivery. At the time of figuring a method, that way was seen as simpler than having to rethink coordinates; he did not favour the idea of having to raise the level of the drop-off point, but now, each time a new load of soil arrived, displacing that already present, explosive kazooning erupted, and dirt and stone shards shot about the chamber, ricocheting from walls.

From his hiding place inside the opening of the ancient tunnel, Bunty again peeped out to the great chamber. As Skip's insignificant mound grew to resemble a small mountain, the kazooning danger increased, so that by now, it seemed that thundering might shake apart the entire hill-side, and the wider territory besides!

Skip had instructed, 'Now, Bunty, you must stay here and keep an eye on things.'

In happening to glance up to the chamber's top-most point, Bunty now imagined he saw an exposed, protruding edge of the great stone move! He'd had quite enough of keeping an eye on things!

Action must be taken! Tunnelling must cease! With the awesome kazooning, all of Ground Spring was in jeopardy!

He must show initiative!

Refusing to accept a dire outcome, he leapt from his safe hiding place! Dodging hurtling missiles, he heltered to the opening of the new burrow, and then ascending the tunnel he cried, 'Skip! Stop! Stop! Desist!'

The farther he went the more his astonishment increased. Despite fear and panic he could not fail to notice the extraordinary character of his friend's work. He had imagined that a commonplace tunnel would tra-verse in steep fashion, leading away from the chamber below. He would come out topside, then, at just about any old where; but this tunnel was not the least haphazard. After negotiating a rising slope, leading out and away from the large chamber, he was surprised to find he followed the easy-going slope of a spacious and wide burrow. A burrow, tunnelled to form a wide spiralling passageway, which must end at a surface-point near the base of the great stone. Along the way were several outward-directed side burrows. He'd passed by those and kept to the primary tun-nel.

He'd not come upon Skip, not yet, but no further explosive, body-rattling kazooning sounded, and so, Bunty slowed his pace. The tunnel was not at all steep, but proved far longer than expected, and by now he panted. Realizing that Skip had achieved so much in such a short time, Bunty had difficulty accepting the truth of it.

When Skip reached an end to tunnelling, an area of ground close to the place where Sherbrook, Dimster and Dempster worked, had crumbled away. The smallest section of the out-most edge of new-formed tunnel had begun falling back in upon itself. Sherbrook, still puzzling over the cause of terrible kazooning, had detected a tell-tale sensation, as granules of soil moved against the pads of a foot. When, not just granules, but, larger chunks of soil fell away, scattering back into the new opening, he believed the disturbance meant the beginning of major subsidence. He leapt back from where he stood! He'd raised a foot, and then brought it down—sounding TUMP! The twins, fearing the ground could cave in, had jumped back and away.

From beneath them they heard 'THUD! THUD! THUD!' The frightening sound had come ever close, the sound of immense, Tumping paw!

The twins had at first gone low to ground, where they remained alert for further sound, or the slightest movement. Before fleeing downhill for Ground Spring Warren, where folk quivered and shook in every available hiding place, Dempster voiced the wildest bout of anxious chuckling!

Experiencing a sudden attachment for his project and refusing to flee, Sherbrook had dived into an insignificant hollow and made himself as small as possible. And then he'd heard, 'Sherbrook? Come out, come out, wherever you are!'

Climbing out from the hollow, to stand tall again, and dusting himself off, Sherbrook, gaining quick understanding of the situation, exclaimed, 'I thought the end was nigh!' Peering down, past Skip and into the new burrow, he could not contain his enthusiasm, 'I must say, *this* is incredible, Buckaroo! I've never before seen the like! You've burrowed a home in as long as it takes a bumblebee to belch! For deeks' sake! *How'd you do it?*'

Receiving approval, Skip confessed, 'I cheated. That's, if you must know. You see, I planned it all out and then just moved it. I went about it by moving great enormous chunks at a time!' He explained, 'In fact, the task was simplicity itself. I didn't put a paw to any of it!' He held both paws up, showing Sherbrook they were as clean as when the work was begun. He said, 'It was fun, every hop of the way!'

Sherbrook enquired, 'You do realize, what you've done, don't you?' He made a suspenseful pause. Then, 'Skip, my friend, you have *revolutionized* the excavation process! It's pure genius!' Then, a small head poked up from the opening, and Skip, who'd exited to stand alongside Sherbrook, offered Bunty a helpful paw.

Bunty declared, 'We're in for *big trouble* now!'

Sherbrook was flummoxed. Recognizing, at last, a useful purpose for friend Skip's strange ability, and being so thrilled by discovery, the twerp, having emerged topside, would spoil things by suggesting trouble!

But, then—yes! Yes!

The new process *did* possess potential for controversy! In admiring the work, such a disagreeable, troublesome aspect had eluded recognition! The fabulous process was cause of an undeniable, downright massive, give-the-game-away kazooning!

Thinking on the hop, Sherbrook instructed, 'Right then, boys! Lend a paw! Large boulders are needed!' But then, he was forgetting, wasn't he, Skip could do the job! And so, hopping away from the burrow entrance, he commanded, 'Beanie—stand back! Get yourself over here with me!'

Hearing his new friend spoken to in such curt manner and incorrectly named, Skip advised, 'He's, Bunty—*not Beanie!*'

Sherbrook was apologetic, but at the same time ever so slightly put out. He explained, 'The advice was, "Stand here with me…" *That* was the important part! But yes, Skip, point taken and no offence intended!' He said, 'Bunty, come here, if you *please?*'

When they were well back from the burrow, he told Skip, 'Buckaroo, move these boulders and fill it! Not the entire thing—just the opening!'

And then, Sherbrook and Bunty saw large stones from Sherbrook's collection vanish from the tidy heap, to reappear one upon the other, in lightning fast succession, blocking the new entryway and hiding it from view. Sherbrook smiled, impressed by the result. But then, unbidden suspicion dawned and his smile faded. What if the twerp spoke out of turn?

Getting on his knees to face Bunty, Sherbrook peered into the diminutive one's eyes and enquired, 'Now, Bunty, how'd you like to be a Buckaroo? Part of a real team?'

'Oh—*come on!*' Skip exclaimed, 'He won't tell. Will you, Bunty?'

Bunty pondered. He returned Sherbrook's searching gaze. 'Mm. I'll have to think on it…' Hearing him, Sherbrook was frustrated, sick to his stomach. But then laughing, Bunty said, 'Of course … I won't breathe a word.' And Sherbrook knew relief.

Bunty said, 'You, *Buckaroos*, sure are making a kadoodler of me!'

Skip told him, 'You were a kadoodler well before we got here, Bunty!'

Bunty laughed, but then grew serious. He said, 'There's one thing, though, something I should tell you.'

'And what's that?' Sherbrook asked.

Looking away from Sherbrook, and gazing to the great stone, he said, 'Down in the chamber, I think I saw that stone move.'

Sherbrook stared up at the split stone. He said, 'I don't believe it's going anywhere—at least, not in a hurry.' He went to where the base of the monolith met with the ground. After momentary hesitation, he gave the stone a powerful kick. When no movement resulted, he decided, 'Seems solid enough to me...' Giving a dismissive shrug, he turned to them, saying, 'Boys, time's a wasting. We must get ourselves down there to the Warren. Remember—we know nothing! Sure, we heard kazooning, but we're just as mystified as the rest of them.'

They would meet with suspicion from Crenshaw, he thought. The leader was no fool. If they were ordered to leave Ground Spring, where else might they go?

The new warren must not be revealed, which meant that he must pretend to excavate for some time to come, when in fact, the new home was complete.

He was compelled to bend the truth, and was not pleased by the fact. Besides which, there were Peace and the bard to consider. How might they react, when invited to join in subterfuge?

After descending the slope they paused before the main entryway, and Sherbrook explained, 'I'll do the talking!' He drew in a deep breath.

Following a long exhalation, he set off, heltering into the confines of Ground Spring Warren, crying, 'Brothers! Sisters! Is this the end!'

DOOR OF LITTLE APPRECIATION

They were in the chamber for the very first time, the first time that was for Peace and Piedmont. Skip had earlier shown Sherbrook the burrows and new quarters, but Sherbrook was not aware of any further surprise in store. Skip guided them down the long, spiralling, main burrow, explaining, 'Whilst at Brickfield realm, I saw a very clever idea—something they called a "spiral-stairway". In planning our new warren, I was inspired by it.'

Apart from Peace commenting, 'I'm so glad my new quarters are snug,' and, 'Thank you Skip. It's all very homely,' neither she nor Piedmont passed much comment. He could tell though, they were impressed. Along the way, Sherbrook directed attention to various details, attributes of fine workmanship, but then if either Piedmont or Peace wanted to exclaim over, or query any of it, they had very little opportunity to do so, due to Sherbrook's giving tireless, running commentary.

Sherbrook saw himself as being in charge of everything to do with works projects concerning burrows and warrens. His enthusiasm for Skip's application of talent and ability had not waned, and so, on the way down through the warren, Skip was granted little opportunity to speak. He saw Sherbrook was enjoying himself and decided there was nothing too wrong with that.

But, Sherbrook was in for the surprise of his life. They all were. And now, there was not long to wait; Skip bided his time.

There was nothing wrong with Sherbrook taking charge, but Piedmont, addressing Sherbrook, as if denying Skip's presence, asked, 'Back at the hollow log, didn't the boy make mention of the fixer stopping by at some point?' He then went on to enquire, 'Then, shouldn't there be quarters provided him? Somewhere to get him started after his arrival?'

Sherbrook explained, again, without thinking to include Skip, 'Oh yes. There's a place for Clever. It's nothing grand, but should prove adequate. He'll have enough space for those odds and ends he carries about with him.' Try as he might, to ignore those words, Skip could not help feeling somewhat hurt. He was not in outright fashion, rejected, but no one liked being taken for granted and hearing the fixer's accommodations described as "adequate", was cause for umbrage taken. Clever Fixer's quarters were fine. They were superior to those he'd prepared for himself. He had gone out of his way during the excavation to ensure everything was just so.

Bunty was not part of the present company, which was a pity Skip thought, because all credit was due him. If not for him, none would learn of the wondrous place he would reveal.

Earlier, after Skip thought to invite him along, Bunty's mother informed, 'No, he can't join you. He's a little off-colour, today.' She said, 'He's been overdoing things, what with digging warrens with you and your friends. He's just a little tyke. It's good experience for him, but he's been overdoing it.'

But, thought Skip, Bunty was not expected to dig. Over recent time, none was involved in digging. Days were spent chatting and basking in the last of summer sunshine. Time was idled away, up there by the stone, until they might declare the excavation finished. That day was not far off, Sherbrook thought. In the meantime, they were exhausted more by boredom than anything else. Skip asked Bunty's mother to pass on consoling wishes, and then had gone to meet up with the others; assuring himself that, Bunty would be fine.

They'd made a thorough inspection of their new accommodations when Peace said, 'I think it's marvellous, and I can't wait to settle in. I'm not ungrateful for hospitality, but will be a lot happier up here than down at Ground Spring.'

'I know what you mean,' Piedmont said, 'Nothing can compare with having one's own place.' He added, 'I'm impatient to start in on scratching. It's been such a long time...'

As Piedmont trailed off, considering all he might become involved with, Sherbrook announced, 'Right then, it's agreed. We'll move in! There's no point putting it off longer. We'll thank them all, and...'

Skip interrupted, 'Yes. Certainly, we must thank them. And, we can move in, but not just yet.'

'Oh? And why's that?' Sherbrook asked.

Skip said, 'There's something else you should see.'

'I thought this was all of it?'

'You've seen your quarters and you've seen the top-most part of the main burrow,' Skip told him, 'but you've not seen the rest.' Sherbrook, as the first to have been shown any of it, believed he knew it all.

'You're referring to the escape tunnel, I assume.' Sherbrook said, gesturing to where the main burrow descended, farther down from where they stood.

'No,' Skip told him, 'It's not just an escape tunnel. It's more than that. It's a *lot* more than that!' Adopting an authoritative tone, picked-up through long association with Sherbrook, Skip commanded, 'Follow me!'

After descending the long downwards-spiralling tunnel, they stood in the capacious chamber, beneath the great split-rock. Following initial amazement, over the sheer size of the place, Skip directed their attention to the mysterious opening. Then Peace was down on her knees and peering into it.

She saw a glowing light, but however hard she squinted, could detect nothing more. She asked, 'Do you suggest that, beyond this little hole—*therein*, lies further surprise?' When Skip gave no answer, the bard spoke up saying, he thought the opening so small that, even Bunty would have trouble going through it. He, Piedmont, would not bother bending low, to look into the thing. He must have slept in an unnatural position and now his back was a problem.

Sherbrook admired the enormous heap of soil and rock detritus that was "moved" during excavation of burrows, and was not interested in any distraction. He could not keep from exclaiming, 'Deeks! You are no kadoodler, my friend! *What a mountain!*'

Skip knew how Bunty must have felt in keeping secret the fact of another world existing beyond the wall.

Glancing up, Peace said, 'Sherbrook, I believe you should take a moment to see this. There's light in here, and it has about it a most unnatural quality.'

Sherbrook took her place. Peering in, he grunted, 'Yes, I see what you mean, but so what?'

Skip announced, 'I'm thinking of moving part of the wall, a small section, and then we can go beyond.'

Piedmont looked down at his feet.

Sherbrook exclaimed, 'Yes! Now why didn't I think of that?' Peace, raised her eyes to stare overhead.

Taking charge, Sherbrook ordered, 'All right, stand back everyone!' But then, having second thoughts, he hesitated, then asked, 'But, is there any likelihood of kazooning? Crenshaw's already suspicious. The slightest sound and we'll be out of Ground Spring forever!'

'There's no danger,' Skip assured. 'None at all.'

And so he prepared to move the wall. But however hard he tried, nothing happened! There was no bright flash. Nothing was "moved". Embarrassed, he said, 'That's odd...' By now, they should have passed through to the world beyond. He would try again.

But still, the wall refused to move.

Seeing him uncertain, Peace said, 'There's an unknown cause. It's nothing to do with fault or failure.' Failure was failure, and kind words did not help. Skip did not blame himself, though, and the problem must be solved.

Then Sherbrook pointed, asking, 'Skip, where does yon' tunnel lead?' He meant the tunnel, which traversed to and from Ground Spring Warren. Skip told him, 'It leads up to Ground Spring, and none apart from Bunty uses it. This great chamber and the rest of the ancient complex are his discovery.'

Sherbrook thought hard, then, 'You should fill the end of it, my friend. Block it off, and then you'll know if your ability functions. Don't be glum, Buckaroo. It's not the end of the world!'

It was all very well for Sherbrook, thought Skip, but they must gain access to the wondrous world beyond the wall. If they did not, then Sherbrook would never know what was missed. Sherbrook was saying, 'Now, as I see it, we won't want others coming here. Our new warren ends at this great chamber, and so, it represents something of an escape-way. It's our secret and it should be kept that way, by blocking the end of that tunnel over there.'

'How about Bunty?' Skip protested, 'How's he expected to get down here if we block it?'

'Easy,' Sherbrook said, 'He can use *our* tunnel. He won't mind coming down by that route.'

'But,' Peace objected, 'It's not ours to decide, as secret or private, is it? Yon', ancient tunnel belongs to Ground Spring Warren. That's true, even if folk, apart from Bunty, never use it to come here.'

'That's correct.' Piedmont agreed. It seemed to Skip that they paid scant attention to Bunty's need, but now, Sherbrook proceeded, doing his best to sound patient and fair-minded, 'If there's any objection they can always undo the work. They can move the moving, as it were. They can clear it out again! I don't see any problem. Honestly, I don't.'

Adopting a cynical, doubting expression, Peace repeated, *'Honestly...'* She said, 'Fine, but if folk of Ground Spring ever object, then the tunnel must be restored. It must be restored by us.' She said, 'They are friends, and trust must be honoured.' Turning to Piedmont, she asked, 'How say you, Bard? Does that seem fair?'

'Yes ... but first we must ascertain whether or not the boy is capable of filling it.' Staring across the wide chamber, Piedmont said, 'Look at the height of that tunnel. It towers overhead! It's not any type of excavation that I'm familiar with.' Looking about, he said, 'There's nothing usual to *any* of this.'

Skip crossed the chamber, and staring at the wall, focused.

Willing himself to calm, he aimed. Not since time spent at the beach in company of the elder, was he so focused upon "moving". Willing the rubble away from the mound in the centre of the chamber—there was a flash of white light! Soil and rock moved and the great tunnel was sealed!

And then, Skip vanished!

'Deeks! He's gone!' Sherbrook exclaimed. And in the following instant, 'What now?' for they were no longer in the cavernous chamber! Blinking, in dazzling-bright light, they stood upon a grass-covered hillock, over-looking the most beautiful world any might imagine!

Uttering a collective gasp of amazement, they heard, 'Welcome friends to a place of wonder! Welcome to friend Bunty's World of Giants! Forgive my not warning you. I just knew that, being here—you'd be glad anyway!' But then, he was not so certain.

Piedmont wobbled upon his feet and could topple over. He shivered and shook, asking, 'Is it gazuzzlement?' He searched faces for confirmation.

Sherbrook hopped to where the bard tottered, and grasping Piedmont's elbow, assured, 'It's fine, Piedmont. Keep a firm hold of your stick!'

Seeing Piedmont cared for, Peace exclaimed, 'It's astonishing—a world beneath ground! But if you think of moving me again, fair warning will be appreciated!'

In the chamber, his powers were diminished; he'd not known if moving as a group was possible. Skip was elated.

But now, fair warning must be given.

He announced, 'There are things here possessing frightening aspect.' Never before this had they been in a Tall One dwelling, and he would warn Piedmont before allowing him anywhere near the cottage kitchen.

He said, 'There are Tall Ones here. They rest entombed in ice. As you can imagine, they present a most gruesome sight.' He waved at the cottage and barn over at a far side of the meadow, and seeing their blank stares, he explained, 'We won't want anyone fainting away at the sight of them. There's more. There's a Tall One vehicle in the barn, and although we've seen those before this, we were always at a safe distance.' He said, 'But, fear not, because this one's terrorizing days are long past.'

They seemed underwhelmed, he thought, by the information provided. Sherbrook grunted, Peace smiled, and Piedmont disregarded all he said. The bard had caught sight of the clicking sticks, and went hobbling off down-slope to inspect the arrangement. Skip thought, why bother? But still, knowing a sense of responsibility, he looked ahead, searching for anything untoward. And, what he saw surprised him. They were not shocked at the sight of the sleeping Tall Ones, nor were they very daunted by inspecting the blue pick-up truck, but there was something else, something extraordinary and very unexpected.

Pondering, he looked toward the distant barn, and then went after Sherbrook, who, by now, followed the bard.

Peace, came after him, asking, 'Skip? What have you seen?'

He told her, 'Piedmont, beside himself, over the shield of Mydor.'

'What?'

'Yes. It's over there, in yon' barn.'

There was little breeze, and the clicking sticks were unmoving. He caught up with Piedmont and Sherbrook. Peace trailed in his tracks. Staring at the web suspended between trees, Sherbrook wondered over its purpose, and Skip told him, 'Wind-clickers. That's what they are. When the breeze blows they make a happy sound.' He said, 'But rather than tarry here, we should press on, because I've seen something which will be of great interest to Piedmont.'

Standing there, studying the odd arrangement of items, suspended between silver trees, Piedmont said, 'It's a most unusual, intricate web, and seeing it I'm reminded of something... For my life though, I can't think quite what.' Noting curious detail, he said, 'Those sticks, there— they're curved—curved as the leaves of some varieties of tree.' He then recalled, 'When I was a boy, we played at an interesting game. We'd find, dry, curled leaves. They had to be from the *right* tree. And by working a thin stick through the centre of a leaf, a "twirler" was made. By flibberty hopping into the wind, holding a twirler, just so, the leaf would dance and helter about! Those things kept us occupied for absolute ages. I don't recall the name of the originator of the game, but it was a nice bit of cleverness.'

Turning to Skip, he asked, 'Did I hear you say there's something of interest to me?'

Skip thought Piedmont looked his age; he appeared very old and tired.

'Yes—the shield of Mydor, his *actual* shield—it's here. Believe it or not, it's over there in yon' barn!'

'Did I hear the boy?' Piedmont asked, 'Mydor's shield has been dis-covered—*here?*' He must have misheard. He looked to Sherbrook seeking confirmation.

Sherbrook told him, 'There's no mistake, Bard.' Looking to Skip Sherbrook said, 'I hope you're not kadoodling. He'll be devastated if you are.'

Skip thought, the King of Kadoodlers casts doubt my way! He said nothing. Things were not at all turning out as expected.

They made their way by going under the rails of the fence, and in doing so, Skip saw a thin wood-plank bearing black scratched marks. He had not noticed it before this and now enquired of Piedmont, 'Do you suppose you might have some idea of the meaning of this?'

Pausing in struggling to negotiate his way past wood-railings, Piedmont glanced up, 'I can't help you, my boy. It's scratching, yes, but it's foreign to me.'

Skip wished the oldster would desist in referring to him as "my boy". They should know by this time that he was not property—no one's "boy"—other than his own.

For any comprehending meaning, the scratched board announced: *Lilith's Dream Catcher*. Beneath that was, as present company saw it, more dark mystery scrawling: *Gift from Mydor*.

Crossing the stream by the small wooden bridge, Sherbrook looked over the railing at the stream. He was delighted, telling Piedmont, 'Look, there are your minnows and tadpoles, Piedmont.'

Piedmont, pausing to observe, said, 'Ah yes, small friends,' and smiled. That positive response meant things might be looking up, Skip thought, but then, when they continued along the way, the bard's slow going was excruciating.

Arriving at the barn, Skip pointed overhead. 'You see,' he told them and, in particular, Sherbrook. 'There is the shield of Mydor.' He thought better of offering to get the treasure down for them. Waiting would do them no harm. Piedmont, seeing the high-hanging artefact, could not stop from staring goggle-eyed. He manoeuvred close in to the pick-up, showing no nervousness at all in going so close to it.

He muttered words both cautious and encouraging, 'Might it be true? There does seem to be an air of great antiquity to it.'

Sherbrook ordered, 'Come on Skip, move it! Move it down from above, before Piedmont goes mad from suspense.'

Skip sounded doubtful. 'Yes,' he said, casting glance to Piedmont. He was thoughtful, 'But I'm not certain I should...'

Impatience increasing with each moment, Peace Darkling snapped, 'Oh, come on now. Why not!' which was not a question.

Skip told them, *'If* it's the genuine article—Great Mydor's *actual* shield of war—what if I cause it damage? What then? I ask myself.'

He was surprised then, when Piedmont came to his rescue exclaiming, 'Yes. Yes, the boy makes an excellent point!' After giving the problem careful thought, he decided, 'Sherbrook must climb up there and fetch it down for me.' Scanning the rafters he offered, 'He can scale up from here, by that thing there, and then, by crawling across yon' timber, he will reach it and bring it down! That's the best way to go about it!' By, that "thing", Skip realized, Piedmont meant a ladder. Ladders, similar to the one here, were employed at Brickfield and used for stacking bricks high in kilns.

Sherbrook, peering overhead, was very unsure, but not wanting to incur the displeasure of Piedmont, he sighed and announced, 'All right then, I'll give it a try, but I can't guarantee success. That must be under-stood.'

Already, Peace was afraid for Sherbrook, but Skip decided that before speaking, he would wait until Sherbrook reached the top-most rung of the ladder.

Sherbrook's legs shook as if he did not own them, so that while he sounded confident when assuring, 'Almost there. I'll soon have it down,' those legs were in wobbly disagreement.

Skip called, 'Fear not friend Sherbrook, we're certain you can do it!' Peace went flibberty hopping by the pick-up to fetch straw from a heap situated at back of the barn. Returning with armfuls, she scattered it on the floor beneath the ladder. Seeing her do so, Skip wondered what would happen farther along in proceedings. If Sherbrook were to slip, then straw might cushion his fall, but once beyond the relative safety of the ladder, what then? Might he slip from the timber beam to then go bouncing from the roof of the starling-egg-blue pick-up? It might mean it was less far to drop, but could a truck be expected to cushion his fall? Sherbrook was by now at the top of the ladder and those legs of his were of no mind to cease shaking.

'Wait!' Skip cried, as Sherbrook reached overhead for the large beam. 'I've an idea!' All eyes turned to him. Skip proposed, 'Rather than attempt to move the treasure from up there to here—what if I moved myself? Perhaps I can unhook the shield from there and then move back down here, *with* it. How about that? What do you say?'

Sherbrook's relief was enormous. Even before the idea received approval of the rest, he'd stepped down to a lower rung. Skip thought Peace seemed a little put out, and he wondered if she were at all disap-pointed that her hill of straw would not be tested.

Piedmont made an utterance peculiar to him, an odd, questioning, 'Humph?' before granting, 'Skip, if you accomplish such deed, then you will have earned my undying gratitude.' He ordered, 'Sherbrook, come on down. We cannot have you injuring yourself!' Great relief showed in Sherbrook's expression, but he was suspicious of his physical safety being regarded so late in the piece. Before his foot found the lower rung—bright light flashed!

Bending low and taking the shield from its spike, then lifting it away, Skip tottered. Next, with more flashing brightness, he was back on the floor and passing the shield to the bard.

The bard's hungry, all devouring attention, noted details of glorious embellishment: of a clenched eagle-claw; of brightest gold; of deep, rich crimson—colour of blood; of a wonderful, carved circumference edge.

With deep reverence Piedmont turned the artefact over and then examining its reverse side he gasped. Where the powerful paw of a warrior, once held the shield by a curved band of metal, several wisps of dark fur adhered! It seemed impossible and yet even after eons had passed, here was evidence of a long ago age. There present for all to see, was a remnant of fur, of the great warrior, Mydor!

Awed, Piedmont hastened in putting the shield down, lest nerves cause him to drop it. Thinking better than to allow such a wondrous thing to touch a dirt floor, his agitation increased. He glanced toward the heap of straw arranged by Peace, and rejected it as suitable. It was straw. None knew where it might have been, and besides which, Sherbrook descended from above. Left with no other choice, the Bard went to the rear of the pick-up and laid the shield upon the lowered tailgate.

Later, in the cottage kitchen, Skip was surprised when Peace, rather than cringe, cowered in dismay at the sight of Tall Ones entombed, declared, 'Right then. This will not do—not at all!' After dashing through several chambers, she soon returned, dragging a coverlet taken from a bed.

'Give me that—that *thing* of wood, please,' she said, waving toward an item of furniture. She had no ready name for the chair; she was not the least familiar with any of that present. Not as yet, thought Skip, but judging by her behaviour, it would not be long before she'd be adjusted to seeing the place through a proprietary eye. He slid the chair close to her, and they saw her hop from it to the drain-board of the kitchen sink, whereupon she flung the coverlet over the top of the ice-tomb, hiding it from view.

Dusting her paws one against other, as if to prevent the slightest possibility of contamination and, in demonstration of satisfaction with a job well done, she announced with certain pride, 'There now. That's seen to.

We won't have to feel confronted by them. We can move about the place and make it our own.'

CLEVER FIXER STOPS BY

Days were shorter now. Trees were losing leaves and the air cooled to an autumn chill, making Skip think of old friends, Lillian and Buckminster. He admitted to thinking of Lillian's hot broth almost as much as he thought of her. Soon, temperatures would further drop and it would be not just cold, but bitterly so.

He told himself he was not depressed, not when thinking of Buckminster, Lillian, or any of those he'd met whilst sojourning else-where, or else-when, but he did experience something of lonesomeness. If he mentioned hot food, then no one hereabouts would have the foggiest idea of that referred to; not that he expected they would, but it would be nice to be understood a little better. He was spending time outdoors. He was "taking the air", which is what Piedmont called it. He claimed doing so, a good thing. Getting out and about in cooler weather was fine exercise. Weather, this cold, reminded him as well, of giants encased in ice, but in accordance with the oldster's advice, Skip drew in another deep breath. Piedmont advised, " Several deep inhalations are all that's required. It's enough to keep a body young!" To see him these days, Piedmont was no real testimony to truth of it, but Skip went ahead anyway, taking in another deep lungful of crisp morning air.

Scanning the plain from atop the high hill, he sighted someone com-ing toward Ground Spring. The distant figure was far off, slow mov-ing and headed this way. The figure was obscured from sight then, as it passed behind the trunks of a stand of dense-growing trees. Skip hopped to one side, the better to follow its progress, and from the fresh vantage point, saw that whomever it was, engaged in pushing something of con-siderable size. It was not long and the object was recognized as a barrow, a barrow similar to those used by Brickfield's brickyard workers. Soon, more detail could be made out, and the individual was recognized as wearing a dark hat with lurid appendages. Those appendages were feath-ers, Skip guessed, and knew he was right. It was Clever Fixer coming by! Despite rising excitement, he would maintain an outer calm. Stay mindful, he thought, because it's not *this* fixer you are acquainted with, but another, elder version. He stayed for further moments, watching the fixer approach Ground Spring Warren, then turned away. He did not rush, but flibberty hopped to find Sherbrook, Peace and Piedmont the Bard.

Deep below ground in Piedmont's quarters, Sherbrook was visiting. Details of a past event troubled him, and the memory of it refused to fade. There were even those times when, trying to sleep, it entered his mind to prevent him resting. Now he'd come to see Piedmont in hope of gaining answers. Dispensing with preamble, he went straight to the point, 'That time at the creek, by the deep pond, why *did* you come there and prod me with your stick?'

He may have sounded a little short, but it was too late to amend his manner. He trusted the bard had not taken offence. Piedmont grew sullen, which was not welcome, Sherbrook decided. He'd not gone to the trouble of bringing himself here, venturing against hope in search of answer, to then meet obstruction or refusal.

Sherbrook was about to clear his throat by way of showing annoyance when Piedmont looked up, saying, 'I've been asked this before. It was the youngster, Richard, who put the question to me. Yes, I'm certain of it, Richard—that was his name. At the time of interrogation, I was under the impression that the enquiry was made on your behalf.' And, Sherbrook thought, seeing Piedmont return the focus of his attention to his scratching, that it was about all he would learn, which amounted to nothing satisfactory. When, Piedmont glanced up again, he said, 'He, Richard, came rushing into me, almost tipping me flat on my face, and demanding information regarding my whereabouts! He claimed that witnesses saw me poking sticks, which was a kadoodling whopper—and I told him so! Being situated *there*, I could *not* be in two places at once!'

A question occurred to Sherbrook, and before Piedmont could go back to working, he proposed, 'What if it wasn't *you?*'

'I just finished telling you that.'

'No. I mean, perhaps it was the other you! The one who gifted you the far seeing eye? It might have been *him*.'

After pondering the possibility, the Bard allowed, 'Yes. What you say might make good sense, and could explain the confusion. The same entity and yet ... he was an altogether other "me". You may be right Sherbrook.'

Sherbrook imagined more to it and still puzzled, would not let Piedmont off. He asked, 'But why was I prodded? Why would any version of you see fit doing such a thing?'

Piedmont enquired, 'What were you doing at the time?' *He* would ask a question or two.

'Bickery scratching,' admitted Sherbrook, 'I was upset with Richard.'

'Have you ever wondered whether that other "me" may have interrupted for good reason?'

Sherbrook scratched his head, 'I was ready to do something drastic, but I can't recall what. I was in a pitiable state over losing Mavis Whitepaws. Looking back to it, it now seems ridiculous.'

'Ah, well,' Piedmont said, 'I guess we'll never know. The other me might have been motivated by nothing more than whimsy. Who can say why anyone acts as they do? If I were you, I'd pay it no mind.' He'd given up coping with sticks and no longer brought them into the warren, because curving tunnels were difficult to negotiate. Imagining having his stick beside him now, he would like to lift it and prod friend Sherbrook, just to know if Sherbrook would smile.

Then Skip burst through the entranceway announcing, 'Clever Fixer is here. He's stopping by!'

Not finding Sherbrook at home, Skip had gone farther along the main burrow looking for him. He'd run into Peace, almost knocking her down. Despite ordering himself to calm, excitement was too much and he stammered, 'I've seen Clever Fixer and everything's turning out. It's turning out just as it's meant to!' They'd gone off together then, searching for the others. Now Peace arrived, and standing behind Skip, she smiled in expectation.

With news of Clever Fixer's imminent arrival, both Piedmont and Sherbrook joined them in hastening from the warren to take up position outside on the hilltop.

They waved as Clever made his way from the flats. Several of Ground Spring's residents were also ready to greet him. Even from this far off the sound of dull squeaking was heard coming from the wheel of his barrow.

'Exciting—isn't it?' Peace Darkling exclaimed, and Sherbrook knew her delight was contagious. Piedmont picked up his stick and waved it aloft. Skip wanted to helter off down the hillside to join the small throng milling there but demonstrated self-restraint. Clever Fixer waved paws in the air in agitated fashion, doubtless instructing children to not upset his belongings by going too close to his barrow. He glanced up, taking a moment in which to call up to them and in particular to Piedmont. Sounding gruffer than Skip remembered, he called, 'Howdy there, Bard! Fancy seeing you here! I'll come up and visit soon! After I've attended to any fixing needed down here!' He called, 'It's grand seeing you!'

Piedmont returned, 'Salutations, old friend!'

Contrary to the impression given, the fixer knew all along, that they were there on the hillside.

Peace was flustered. 'We don't have anything. We've nothing to offer him in way of refreshment!'

Sherbrook assured, 'He'll be stuffed to the eyeballs long before he makes it up here to us.' He added, 'He's a popular one, isn't he?'

Skip reminded, 'No one must ask Fixer to stay, no one, that is, other than Piedmont.' He explained, 'Those were my instructions, and I'm repeating what I was told. Those instructing me were our elders.'

'Well,' Sherbrook said, 'I'm not about to twist any arms, but I'm of a mind to go down there and check out his conveyance. It looks interesting, despite its awful racket.'

'It's a wheelbarrow,' Skip told him. 'They're handy for carrying things from place to place, but best not show interest in it. It's a primitive affair and we ought to focus on what we're about. Clever Fixer is meant to come our way—the *new* way. Don't go chasing after things such as that contraption.'

Hearing him say so much, Sherbrook stared, before telling Skip, 'Thank you for that, but antiquated or what-ever, I've never before seen its like, and so I'm going to check it over for myself.'

'I could move the fixer from here to the other edge of the plain, and have him back here with us, in less time than it takes for his wheel to make a single, wonky turn,' Skip said. 'You seem intent upon denying the worth of all I've told you we're capable of.'

'There's no need to boast,' Peace advised.

'Boast? There's no boasting here,' Skip told her. 'You, none of you, appreciates what it is we're about, and I'm sick of it. To me, your attitude amounts to a type of betrayal.'

'Goodness me...' Peace said, and then was quiet.

'The things we are capable of are beyond wildest imagining,' Skip said. 'All you think of are dusty burrows and tipsy barrows. If you gave sensible thought to it, you'd know yon' contraption is, in all truth a "little brother" to such as the churner, which wrecked old Warren Central in the first place. You are the most frustrating creatures anyone could have as friends!' They could do as they pleased and he would return to the warren.

Piedmont said, 'We will have to talk sometime.'

But Skip would not heed Piedmont's bright light blazing. The bard was well intentioned but his words were dismissed with a shrug. Skip considered going to see Bunty, but changed his mind.

Piedmont wished to enquire further as to future potential and possibility. In his present mood, though, Skip was no good to anyone and least of all to himself. Bubbling excitement had turned in a moment to angry despair. It was as if, thought Piedmont, against hope and effort, they kept slipping back to go awry. He knew what Skip was upset by.

None could fail to hear Sherbrook announcing, 'All I'm concerned with is getting Clever Fixer's barrow up here to the warren. It can't be left down there with that lot. They'll upset his things.'

'Unless you intend hefting the thing on your back,' Piedmont said, 'there would seem just one other way of bringing it here. Who shall we enlist for that?'

'Skip?' Sherbrook said. And, after giving it thought, 'When no one's around to see it done.'

'That's right.' Piedmont said, resolve firming.

***

'Hop this way,' he invited. 'Come along and see the new warren. It will appeal to your curiosity. Its design forms a spiral.' He wheezed as they went, all the while providing comment concerning detail he thought must interest the fixer. He said, 'Just by the way, the scratched mark for time's passing—eons of time—is the spiral. I don't allude to mystery. There's no mystery to any of this. The warren is the warren. The mark of scratching is the mark. And then an eon, of course, is a long, long time. There's no connection. Best not see mystery where there is none.'

Now that they were inside, Piedmont knew that the fixer found the ever-curving main artery of tunnel interesting. Clever had noted the presence of much hard stone. He had seen that stones did not protrude into the burrow, but appeared as having been sheared off flat and smooth, by means unknown to him. Fixer observed, 'This place was long in the making. Excavation of this nature must have required enormous toil.'

Piedmont, with an arthritic shrug, responded in a way he trusted would give the impression of reluctance to give away trade secrets, 'Oh, yes, old friend, indeed.' He went on to mutter half beneath his breath, 'If not for rain coming down, we'd have finished in a day, and well before noon.' Hoping the comment was audible enough, he said, 'I know! You must stay here. Give the notion consideration. There's room to spare and then some. You needn't make up your mind in the moment. You never know, but without presumption on my part you understand, I'm of the opinion you might like it here.' He said, 'Anyway, here we are. This is my little place, be it ever so humble and all that.'

Whilst quarters for Peace were snug, Sherbrook's were spacious. Skip's own were small because, during excavation he'd decided he would not spend much time at home. Knowing Piedmont liked more space about him than most, personal need was considered and special requirement accommodated.

Piedmont's place was seen as spacious enough for the itinerant fixer to exclaim, 'Bard, you've done well for yourself and, it's as should be! Reward of life well lived, eh? The versifying you've done in your time. You deserve such a pleasant place as this and I'm glad you're not let down.' He added, 'It's a strange world isn't it? Oldsters, beware! That's my motto.' He asked, 'There's no fixing required here, is there? If so, give the word. My service is always available.'

Piedmont imagined the fixer's lot, and in so doing muttered to effect, 'The trail must be wearying.' He'd not seen the fixer for so long, it was difficult to recall their last meeting. Attempting to place events and make clear order of them, he asked, 'Have you tarried in the vicinity of *New*

Warren Central in recent time?' but then, 'You are aware of the fact of the old warren's suffering a sad end?' Confusion increasing, he asked, 'You do know, Buckminster passed ... by paw of fickle providence?'

Clever's startled expression told him that news of the shocking event had not until now, reached him. Clever Fixer knew naught of Graymark rule either, which meant that there was much to discuss.

Skip claimed that Graymark's rule was ended, that it was over with her passing. But then as well, Skip had vowed that the scratchings would be saved and returned, which had not happened. The boy was, without doubt, wondrous. His powerful ability was beyond anything Piedmont had ever expected to witness. As far as character was concerned, the bard believed the youngster as sincere as the day was long. Still, though, he doubted ever seeing return of the precious scratchings. Maintaining a judicious view was always problematic when questions concerning property, and especially one's own, entered an equation.

'How did Uncle Bucky pass?' Fixer asked. Shaken by the news, he was mindful of times past. For an unaccountable reason, the time spent in fixing the old Radiola, seemed to stand out from the rest. During several moments an inner voice questioned, 'What's this I'm hearing? It can't be? *New* Warren Central?'

His ever travelling from place to place meant he was often the recipient of news of another's passing. He was a good listener, but when the topic of conversation involved mortality, he tended to listen with just one ear. He sought no meaning in the passing of another, because he entertained imaginative belief regarding gazuzzlement. It was everywhere, of course. It stalked a body in merciless, remorseless manner; nothing resembling escape clause was provided. Even an imagined, alternate version of anything—supported by even the smallest grain of truth—should be seen as founded less in imagination, and might be viewed as possessing something of real reliability. Experience dictated that the first, mere morsel of a clue was all that was required in setting to solving any problem, even the most difficult. Others saw gazuzzlement as part of life itself, as unfortunate, inevitable ending to the rest. So far as he saw the matter, gazuzzlement was a problem and as such, it existed for the solving.

Learning of Uncle Bucky's passing was saddening, but now Sherbrook and Peace had joined them. Catching the tail end of Piedmont and

Clever's conversation, Sherbrook had committed something of an error in mentioning vanishing. From that point on, Fixer was alert, with both ears attending.

'I recall Simple Rudy,' Fixer said. 'I remember he was enthralled by the Radiola. I just couldn't keep him away from it. I had to insist that he allow me enough space in which to work. Once she was switched on, anyone could see he'd be impossible to tear away from it.' He enquired, 'He just up and vanished, you say? The youngster disappeared in plain view of others?'

'Vanishing? I know nothing of vanishing,' Sherbrook said, trusting that he'd not already revealed too much. Skip had told them, "Under no circumstance" was Clever Fixer to be offered anything—that was, anything that might be taken as an inducement, or even a bribe, before he saw fit to reveal the seed. Usual hospitality was allowed him, but nothing of a strange nature ought be revealed. Sherbrook was now on thin ice, as it were, for mentioning Rudy's disappearance, and he knew it. Skip was not present though, and that was reassuring. Nevertheless, Peace glanced to Piedmont, hoping he would stop Sherbrook from going any further. She then saw Skip come to the entrance of the large quarters; he waited there listening to their conversation, but had not overheard Sherbrook, she decided.

Piedmont, addressing the fixer, said, 'It's not at all late in the day, Clever, but you must be wearied from wheeling that burdensome contraption of yours. I don't doubt your day was begun at first light, then coming so far from beyond yon' plain, you must be tired. Rest awhile, old friend, and there's a permanent place for you here with us, if it suits you to accept it.' Raising a paw and covering his mouth, the bard yawned. Noticing Skip's presence, he said, 'Oh, there you are, Skip. I didn't notice you. Later on in the day, will you move the fixer's property to our guest's quarters?'

Realizing so much was expected of a small boy, the fixer gave the bard an odd look, a look decrying the fact of a youngster being ordered to do a buck's work. Rather than condone such expectation, the fixer said, 'I'll go. I can bring most of it up here later on. No one down there will touch any of it. Crenshaw's ordered them to keep away. And in mentioning him, I must say, he's somewhat of an improvement after ancient Millthorpe.'

Outside the entranceway to Ground Spring, no one was about. None showed interest in Clever Fixer's barrow with its peculiar assortment of belongings. Excitement over his arrival was past; here at Ground Spring was little need of anything approaching real fixing. The barrow was moved in a trice, to stand high on the hillside outside the new warren's opening. Skip next saw to moving every one of Clever's items from the barrow to his quarters. All items were kept ordered, as Clever Fixer had arranged them in the barrow. Confronted by the impossibility of such extraordinary valet service, curiosity would drive the fixer to mad distraction. Over nights to come he would toss and turn in trying to sleep; he'd not fathom the mystery of it.

FIXER

Doubt flooded Clever's mind, plaguing and undermining his every attempt to sleep. He went over his decision to accept the bard's generous offer to stay and settle at the unusual warren, and he could not drift off. If the correct decision was taken, shouldn't he feel more relaxed and comfortable? Should he return to the trail?

He would see how he felt about it after resting, but then, how to rest when he was so restive?

Again ... how was it possible for his odds and ends to be brought from the bottom of the hill, over such steep distance and placed in these quarters, arrayed in such neat and ordered way? No one could do it in so short a time, it was just not possible and yet, each time he reopened his eyes to look—there was the evidence—every item of his property! He would not have arranged it better, had he done it himself. Before lying down, he undressed and made a neat pile of his clothes with one exception. He never settled anywhere, without first folding his waistcoat, and then placing it beneath his head. In his doing so, two purposes were served. A pillow of sorts was provided, and as well, if thieves set upon him as he slept, they would find little chance of getting their paws on the seed. The seed, the most precious and valuable item of his inventory, was kept always in the concealed, inside pocket of said article of clothing. There was no present danger of being robbed, but old habits dictated he keep the seed close as ever—even in present circumstances; residing with decent hospitable folk.

There were those times, when, if all about was quiet enough, the seed whispered, and Clever Fixer did not like to miss an opportunity of catching whatever it wished to impart. No announcement of intention to convey secret knowledge ever preceded communication, which meant that Fixer never knew before time the precise nature of what might be learned. Over the duration of their relationship they'd become as close as any two entities could be. The seed was just that, an entity in its own right. If others were to learn of his companionship with such a thing, then they'd denounce him as kadoodling mad. And so, he would never impart knowledge of its existence and, neither would he plant it. By planting it, he would lose it forever, and if that were to happen it would be as if a vital part of him was cut away from the rest. The most dreaded possibility was that he might never hear it speak again. Its knowledge was the most secret, alien stuff. The information shared was outside anything Folk of Fur would ever believe.

He tucked the waistcoat more under his head, and listened. He lay there for a considerable time, knowing he could not settle. If the seed in seeing fit to make an utterance, spoke of matters already learned, he may be lulled into sleeping. If it spoke of Lilith or Terrence Thiery, then he would be comforted.

The seed's tough encasing husk meant it would not be damaged by his lying so close to it, but still he was unfailing in its careful treatment, ensuring he never rested the full weight of his head over it; rather than do that he positioned it adjacent with his head and close by an ear. In beginning its soft murmuring, it reminded, 'I must never be planted to ground, in soil, yes—that's a fine thing, but in a wood-pail. I must never be planted to ground...' Those words and similar, were repeated often enough to have an effect, and it was not long before Clever Fixer had his wish. Tormenting worry ceased, and he was lulled to the embrace of an altogether other place.

* * *

Before the days of travelling with the tipsy-barrow, a far more youthful Clever Fixer, chanced to contend with effects of a storm of ferocious magnitude ... no slight upheaval of nature, but a true kazooner of a thing.

Although already grown used to the itinerant life with its many ups and downs, its vagaries, disappointments and unpredictability, he told himself that due to the fact of no suitable place of shelter being available, he was in for the drenching of his young life, but tomorrow was another day and a body never knew what the new day might deliver; there were always ups and downs. He must not forget the "ups" because, whilst a "down" could always be relied upon to provide a harsh, but useful lesson, the next "up" would always eventuate.

Gathering his over-coat about him and pulling the collar higher, the better to cover his neck, he made his way to a copse of trees, hoping to gain at least minimal shelter beneath them. Darkness flooded in over the land to close out light. The atmosphere was warm and sultry, but would soon cool with the onslaught of further rain. It rained now but worse was on the way.

With large drops already pelting him, almost smarting, he did not tarry in getting himself beneath the cover of trees. Treetop foliage would, at first, give shelter, but when the real downpour came and leaves were sodden, then he would be sheltering in relentless, streaming torrent. Having no choice as to his predicament, he insisted he liked a good storm. By aiming his open mouth skyward he'd be able to drink.

For ages past, no scent of water was detected. The country he passed through was as dry as anything he'd seen before and was not inhabited by Folk of Fur. For days now he'd not seen anyone, other than a glimpse of Brother Raven, who, soaring high above, was of no mind to land. The raven did not mind so much as others, the hardship these conditions imposed, but even he did not like to touch down here. Soon it was so dark that Clever wondered at the strange sudden beauty of the short, rock-strewn dry gully, transformed to make a passage for such an incredible quantity of water.

Where he stood seemed thus far, safe enough, but with much of the gully-floor inundated by the fast flowing torrent, he found himself by the edge of a fast rising, rushing muddy stream. It was as if Great Grandfather's attention was distracted by something or other and His focus having shifted, meant that Fixer was transported willy-nilly, in an instant, to a different location; one not of his choosing. It was incumbent upon him to seek higher ground. He was drenched and could not get any wetter.

As lightning flashed and thunder roared, he ordered himself to calm. Attempting to gain an effective foot and paw-hold on the slippery clay bank near the tree beneath which he'd taken cover he was very taken-aback to witness Sister Tree struck and split asunder down her middle by a slashing blue-white bolt from a black, roiling sky.

Dim ochre clay dissolved to run between scrabbling claws. The under-taking was hopeless, and so giving up on any idea of scaling the melting bank, he looked about him searching for an alternative way out.

The kazooning noise of the tree-killer bolt was deafening, so for some time to come he was incapable of hearing further sound of thunder, torrential downpour or rushing torrent. Lapses between lightning flashes shortened and the ozone filled atmosphere assumed a peculiar power—the power to both elate and terrify at one and the same time.

Not hearing well, made for a dream-like reality and a slowing effect was perceived, this despite the natural environment's hastening to destruction. Paradox was part of the natural order. Seeing the hapless tree swept away, taken as if it were naught but frail twig, he slipped, uttering in a drawn-out, slow motion instant, 'Oh no! Deeks—what a fool I am!' He went tumbling, sloppy-sliding, himself a part of the yellow-orange tide of muckiness, downhill, into a mêlée of water, rock, branches and as well, Brother Serpent and others.

Brother Serpent had difficulty keeping his head above water; but was happy for surviving. If it were at all possible then Clever would have given a short wave in passing him by, but still was grateful that their paths did not cross any closer. He might have been viewed as an island of safety and was horrified by the thought.

With ears filling with water, he was swept along by the gully-stream for a surprisingly long distance until, arriving at a point of widening, where the terrain levelled out, he recognized the place was the same he'd traversed late afternoon of the day previous to this.

Clever noticed certain shallowness to the carrying tide and a decreasing force of current. With weary effort he picked himself up. His overcoat was heavy and slapped against his bedraggled legs. He'd not swum, but done his best to float, and effort had saved his day. Hauling off now, through shallows, moving in the direction of higher ground, he knew great relief.

He was pleased to such an extent that he almost missed seeing a dove, which, swept far off course, and then downed by turbulence, now lay in mire, not breathing.

'Poor wretched creature...' Clever declared, and made to pass on by. He knew that slammed to the ground, Sister Dove had no chance at all. Her sad plight must be witnessed over and again during the days to follow. Many winged ones must be downed, brought to a cruel end, but then he noticed something. Was there the faintest sign of life? No, he was mistaken. His first impression was correct. After taking several more, short flibberty hops, he stopped again. He could continue no farther, not without returning again to make what must be a final, last check; intuition's gnawing, should never be ignored.

In going back he would not hop, but step with care, because once disturbed, the mud sucking at his feet, would threaten having him face down in it. Backtracking accomplished, the fixer was overjoyed in realizing instinct did not let him down. In examining it on this occasion he detected a clear sign of hope, a hunger for life, present in the eye of the unfortunate mud-besmirched, and otherwise gazuzzled thing. Murky, lowering sky above, clinging mud below, Clever, carrying the dove, made cautious progress to higher ground.

When the skies cleared and all else dried out, Clever Fixer was already gone. Retracing hops of days past, he journeyed, retreating as fast as he was able, back to kinder country and fairer clime. With Sister Dove carried in a deep, grass stuffed pocket of his coat, he then made camp on a fertile slope bordering against a tame creek; a place he was familiar with, having stopped there before.

During the hop, he made infrequent pauses, but halted often enough to see to the comfort of his passenger. 'Feathered friend—Sister Dove,' he apologized, 'Please forgive my so, heltering. Your health may further deteriorate and we don't want that. We're heading for a place I'm familiar with. It's a gem of a site. Further harm won't befall you. I am the fixer, and will see you recovered!' Sister Dove's staring was too blank for his liking at first, but soon enough, she returned his gaze in what he decided was a more comprehending, and reassuring fashion. When they arrived at the favourite place, he told her, 'Here we are now, Delilah. It's a beauteous spot, very fitting for convalescence. It possesses much in way of uplifting nature.'

It did not seem right somehow to continue calling her, Sister. Formality of that type did not offer anything of kind comfort. When better recovered, her true given name might be known.

Clever gathered watercress and seeds of grasses—those things he liked—and ground them with stones. He added water into the mixture, making a fine gruel. He fed Delilah a tiny amount at a time until she showed improvement.

He found appropriate shaped leaves and used them to scoop tiny portions of water for her to drink, drop by drop, and he never stopped talking to her. If the day was fine they complimented one another for being so fortunate, and if grey skies, wind or showers were their lot, then together they complained, wishing the weather would clear again. In fact, Delilah uttered not one word, but Clever, knowing she must agree in such matters with his opinion, enjoyed imagining she voiced agreement.

They were a fine pair—good company—and harmless pretence helped Clever to keep going. By his reckoning, her well-nigh miraculous improvement was all due to careful fixing. Although knowing "healing", as a more accurate description for the result of care given, he preferred the sound of the former, and sharing his view with her, developed a fondness for rhetorical questioning, 'Who'd ever have dreamed it, eh, Delilah—me—an expert fixer of doves?'

It would not be much longer, he knew, before she would leave him. That day was one he did not look forward to with any pleasure. He would miss her, but then must resign himself to the inevitable.

As it turned out, the way of her leaving was most unexpected, and apart from bringing disappointment, he was delivered more than he could have dreamed.

Rising one morning and going to his coat, thinking that together they would greet another new day, he despaired, finding the deep pocket, apart from her bed of soft dried grass, empty. Delilah was nowhere to be seen. Calling to her several times, he realized the futility of doing so, and attempted consoling himself by humming several little fixer tunes. Composed and sung on the hop, they were a way he had of keeping himself occupied whilst traversing long tedious stretches of nothingness, which was as he described much of the country he passed through. He'd come across Delilah in such a desolate place, and so a body never quite knew what next to expect: from then on, finding the unexpected should be expected.

It was foggy down here streamside this morning, but fog was not uncommon at such a low-lying site, and he did not mind the mystery it provided. Hearing the flapping of what sounded to him as many, many wings, whilst he was doing his best in making a go of enjoying breakfast, he dropped a paw-full of nourishing juicy cress, and heltered for his hollowed out place situated beneath a long-ago fallen tree.

Abundant trees lining the bank of the stream made for a pleasant location, but dense foliage, in combination with swirling pale mist, made for dismal visibility. Peeping out from his hiding place, Clever was unable to ascertain much of goings on. All he knew was that too many Folk of Feather descended in his vicinity. At first there was the sound of multitudinous wings, and then as owners of those wings proceeded to settle, it was a little quieter. Still peering out, he discerned, perched upon every available branch, a great gathering. He experienced a feeling of edginess. He would lie low until something further happened. They were doves, because despite having settled, they would not cease making an eerie cooing. If she were here, Delilah would feel very much at home. He thought, Foolish gal—choosing to make departure sooner than necessary. But, what, for deeks' sake, did they intend? Why were they here in such number? There was a further sound of flapping wings coming his way!

Clever Fixer made himself very small, but in so doing, realized he'd made a foolish oversight. He'd not thought of donning his coat, which meant it was still lying draped across the top of the tree he hid beneath, and that meant they knew of his presence! They would not need to notice his coat, for the likelihood was they'd glimpsed him dashing here from the stream in the first place! Submitting to the reality of his situation, Clever Fixer stretched, allowed himself a small yawn of embarrassment, and then climbed out from his place of inadequate concealment, to find six doves awaited him.

They perched on a wide-stretching branch, which jutted from the trunk of his hiding-tree. He saw those first, and next noted others—twenty, thirty—he supposed they numbered at least that many—too many to count, and now more descended from surrounding trees to land on the grassy ground surrounding the place where he stood.

Soon, more joined those, and Fixer deduced that by coming in drib and drab fashion, they did not want their large number causing him concern. When the remainder finished gathering on the grass, and he was spoken to by one of those first arrivals that all the while maintained a presence upon the branch of his tree, he was both startled and surprised.

As they'd gathered, he'd ventured a short hop or two away from his place of concealment, which meant that the voice of the dove came from behind him. Noting the soothing quality of the voice, Fixer thought it as should be. Sister Dove should possess such quality, a comforting sound, unlike that of those too many voices heard earlier. This was a voice, not too much at variance with the pleasant cooing he was used to hearing from Delilah. But this was not just pleasant cooing, it was far more informative, and recognizing information might be conveyed, he could not contain himself in wishing to begin. Here was an opportunity for clear, inter-species communication. Whilst he was occupied in deciding upon the best first question, Sister Dove made a strange, surprising enquiry of her own; 'You refer to yourself as *Clever* Fixer but is it an accurate description of you?' The dove, a crisp-white, fawn-speckled creature, tempered the question by adding, 'Know that we're not here to harass or upset you.

'You've shown great kindness in going out of your way in aiding and befriending one you named Delilah. Such behaviour is lauded by our kind, but we are not here out of gratitude for that...'

Clever, forgetting his own question, showed that no offence was taken, and responded, 'My given name is Clever—always was—but you see, some time back, when pondering this life's purpose, I decided there were three things which most mattered to me. Number one was freedom, freedom to go hither and yon' wherever I pleased, and so I saw then, I must not be encumbered or foiled by notion of ownership of property or things. I would travel light. And then, whilst enjoying, for the main part, the solitary life, still, from time to time, I do enjoy the company of others. I recognize the worth of company. Those first two requirements meant, I would need to make myself useful. I needed something—a way of easing the going—something strangers might accept.' After pausing, he said, 'Strangers accepted the fixer. I'm quite a dab-paw when it comes to fixing, just about any old thing. But then, you aren't here, as you say, to thank me, which by the way is the last thing I expect.' He said, 'I did fix one of *you,* so, something must be working. Anyway, my departing this place is long over-due and so I must break camp. It's high time I hit the trail.' After all, he thought, he would not want to question Sister Dove. Compelled to give an explanation before so many strangers had, he now realized, resulted in a feeling of certain discomfiture and he would curtail spending time here. He did comment, though, 'It's interesting knowing that you communicate—apart from cooing, that is. If I mention it to anyone I'm sure I won't be believed.' With a merry chuckle Clever Fixer, went to get his coat. He thought it obvious that Delilah was here some-where, but with so many of them, and her not coming forward making herself known, he had no way of telling which of them she was. He called, 'Bye, Delilah!' adding, 'Wherever you are!' Taking hold of his coat, he made to put it on.

'You can't be leaving so soon,' the dove said, and Clever heard the rest raised cooing voices—a multitude of gentle but insistent disagreement with him setting out upon the way.

'And why is that?' Clever asked.

He was told, 'Because, we have something we must give you.'

'Oh?' he asked, showing polite interest, but not disguising the fact that he still wanted to leave. He trusted they'd allow a path for him, because he did not much like the thought of flibberty hopping, amongst them. He was bigger than they were, but their number provided authority.

Sister Dove next explained, 'We, Clever Fixer, are Keepers of the Seed. She gave a meaningful pause before continuing. 'Now, as Keepers of the Seed, we have decided that you, Fixer, are the true inheritor of such. The matter is decided or ... almost. We're almost of one mind concerning your suitability for the task.'

Hearing her, Clever Fixer sighed. He was not getting away—he saw it, and they knew it.

Watching him and seeing him change plan, they moved back away from his feet, making space enough for him to seat himself on dew-wet grass. He spread the coat at his feet, telling himself the fixer liked a good tale as much as anyone and maybe more.

Fog was lifting by now and with the first golden ray of sunlight piecing the mist, she—spokes-dove—with agitated movement, ruffled her feath-ers, puffed out her chest, and told him, 'We're very glad you've changed your mind and will stay awhile. We know you won't be disappointed.'

And, he was not, because that very morning, he learned of a most remarkable thing. As the dove started in telling the tale, he picked at the dark grey fabric of his overcoat. He'd attend to cleaning grass from the pocket later on, because doing it now, could be taken as impoliteness.

Many of the best stories began with the words: 'A long time ago, in a place far away...' This one was no different.

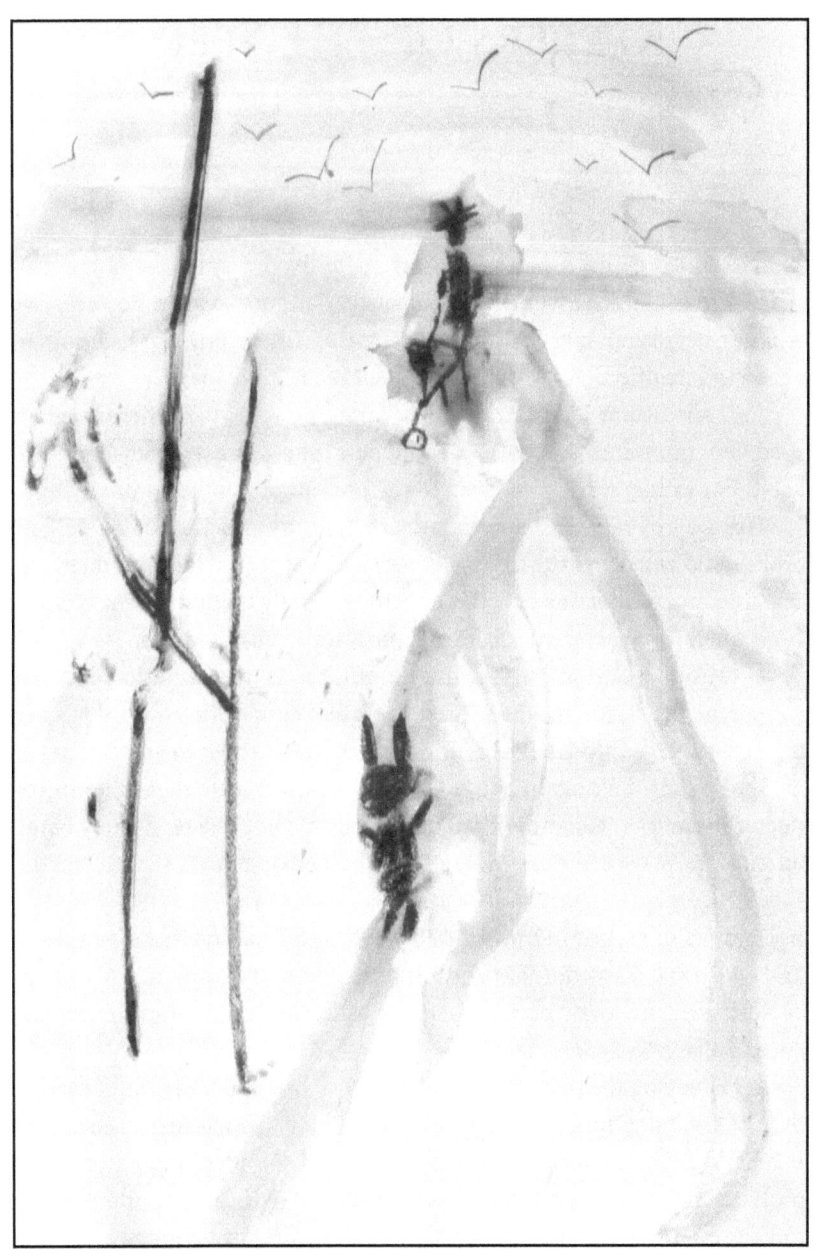

Fixer

KEEPERS OF THE SEED

'A long time ago, in a place far away there lived a Tall One, a child of sharp wit and keen, inventive intelligence. For good reason however, we will not begin our tale with him. For reason of the boy's grandmother, deserving mention.' Sister Dove set about beginning anew.

'In a far distant land, a place very foreign to our own, there lived an aged hen, or doe. In any case, a Tall One… She was extremely coarse of habit. For example she spat, even in the presence of polite company.

'Her way of repaying a slight was to vent vile, vociferous curse. She broke wind whenever the urge took her, without regard for circumstance. Sensibility of others was of little concern to her. By accounts passed down from earliest time she was deemed a most unsavoury individual.

'However, redemption lies in recognition of the fact that, as first Keeper of the Seed, she honoured the great task with admirable conscience—and granted due leniency on that count, she is deemed wise.'

The spokes-dove again paused, allowing him time to digest her introductory remarks. The individual described was not one he'd enjoy being on close terms with, thought Clever, whether or not they performed a task well.

And, as to fact of her being tall—he'd never had occasion to meet a Tall One. Imagining doing so, he must in all honesty admit to some slight curiosity, but he knew better; curiosity aside, he could forgo the experience of a face-to-face meeting.

In conveying the information, Sister Dove had expressed slightest disdain of the Tall One's deplorable personal habits, which surprised Clever Fixer. He did not think that caring for a seed sounded like an onerous, problematic chore. But then he supposed that, for an individual prone to habitual indelicate behaviour, their performing just about any simple task could be determined as something of achievement. He would not offer opinion though.

The spokes-dove was saying, 'The Tall One stared up at a giggling sky…'

'Pardon?' Fixer responded, certain he'd not heard.

Sister Dove, said, 'Much giggling was heard.' And, to further dispel confusion, 'There was a sound of merriment—*mirth*—you understand?' She said, 'Weather on the day was clement and coming from a clear blue sky, an unusual sound was heard.' Clever nodded, and she explained, 'The Tall One—mouth agape—peered up, staring overhead in an attempt to ascertain the source of such peculiar giggling. Whilst standing there looking upward, something fell plummeting from the sky and lobbed into her throat, almost choking her. Now, this "something", was a large and beautiful seed, a seed of faience blue—a thing about the size of an almond—if you've ever seen one?' Fixer shook his head, no, he was certain he was unfamiliar with the example given. 'An almond is a nut. A thing, about the size of your small to average radish.' This was not a good example and so the bird went further, 'A cherry—a grape?' The fixer nodded, satisfying the dove. Demonstrating relief, she ruffled her feathers, before exclaiming, 'The Tall One almost swallowed the thing! Luck was with her though, because, with face turning blue—matching the colour of the seed—she, gagging, coughed it up and caught it in a large work-worn hand!

'She cussed, of course, fit to embarrass anyone within earshot.

'Then, giving close inspection to the cause of her distress, she decided it an attractive piece of work. Assuming it was a gift from on high, from God, who, in a moment of generosity intended her to have it—she made it her business to honour the favour by treasuring it ever after.'

'God?' Fixer asked.

'Mm, Great Grandfather to us,' explained the dove. All she said amounted to an interesting tale, but this latest information fascinated. Knowledge of Tall Ones believing in a higher power fuelled curiosity, but what she next said was cause for uncertainty.

'With your permission, Clever Fixer, we propose a test—nothing too difficult—but a simple, straightforward test. We must know with absolute surety whether you are indeed the true inheritor.

'You understand, there can be no error? We must surrender our most precious charge, to the rightful paw?' Daunted by the prospect of undergoing a test of any sort, but sympathetic toward such a conscientious, responsible approach, the fixer again nodded and did his best to appear agreeable. Registering his nod of acknowledgement, the dove called, 'Come along now, Sybil. This is your moment! Let's get on with it shall we?' And, Clever Fixer saw amidst much ado, fluffing of feathers and melodious chorus of expectant cooing, a bird of larger build than others of the flock, strut towards him from their midst.

Others moved aside, allowing Sybil to move from the back of the crowd and she soon arrived to stand near Clever's feet.

Despite having been ordered to hasten, Sybil remained unflustered, deporting with dignified self-assurance. With the ovoid-shaped, blue seed carried in her beak, she moved nearer, skirting an edge of his coat until she stood close by his side. Lowering her head, she placed the seed upon his lap.

'And now, Clever Fixer, I ask you to pick up the seed ... Now—*don't drop it!* That's it. Hold it against your ear.' Clever Fixer complied.

He thought the blue colour of it quite wondrous, and after holding the seed to an ear, proceeded in giving the slightest shake of his paw.

His doing so met with, 'Don't rattle it about like that!' And, further, 'The treasure has been passed down through ages—by countless dove-generations! If we're to pass it to you, then we *must* see you respect it!'

'I do apologize,' Fixer demurred. He wished that he'd hastened more in preparing for departure this morning. Being spoken to by a bird was one thing, but hearing himself admonished, altogether another. But then, he was curious, and again raising the seed to an ear, whilst wondering what might next be expected of him, he was startled to hear a soft tenuous murmuring coming from the seed. It was not so much, words, but more a sonorous humming. It was, he thought, as if the seed attempted com-munication! He listened entranced. Watching him, the dove told him, 'This is the important part, Fixer ... Fixer?' Clever moved the seed so he still heard soft murmuring, but as well, was focused upon what she said.

'You must question the seed,' she instructed. 'You must ask, 'Who passes you to me? Who, above all others, is true?'

Fixer then gave the bird a look of uncertainty, a look, which said he was unwilling to go so far as make a fool of himself by making enquiry of a small member of the vegetable kingdom. He made an indecisive, 'Umm...' Embarrassed, he lowered the seed from his ear, stared at it for a moment, and then put it close to his mouth.

He did not have time to speak, before further instruction was delivered, 'It's unnecessary to speak in anything but the lowest whisper,' the dove advised, 'A raised voice is not required, nor desirable.'

He wondered if they played an elaborate game at his expense, whether, for time to come, his name would be bandied about in feathered company as dupe; brunt of mean joke. He asked, 'Are you certain that you want me to do this, because I'm not sure I have the stomach for much more of it. To tell the truth, I'm beginning to feel foolish.'

'If you receive the correct answer,' she told him, 'we will be satisfied. You may be the one, the one sought, even by the seed itself...' And so, holding the blue seed to his mouth, Clever Fixer muttered beneath his breath, those questions, 'Who passes you to me? Who, above all others, is true?'

'Put the seed to your ear again,' said the dove.

When he did so, Clever Fixer heard, not humming, but a clear, tiny voice, a voice seeming quite pleased and even thrilled, by his questioning.

Next, the same small voice declared, 'Terrence Thiery. Terrence Thiery is true! From Terrence, his child, and those present too, I am passed to you!'

The dove, seeing Clever Fixer's eyes light up, enquired, '*And...?*'

'Terrence Thiery.' Clever Fixer said. Before he said more, all about him then, was great commotion, much flapping of wings, a great deal of excited coo-cooing, strutting and milling about, and above all else he heard the spokes-dove announce, 'Friends, *this* is the day of days, for Dovedom! Clever Fixer *is* the true inheritor! At last, after eons of care giving, we, Keepers of the Seed may rejoice! The great task is done!'

Cradling the seed in a gentle paw, Clever Fixer lowered it to his lap. He wanted answers. Answers were due him, not from the beautiful and quite remarkable blue seed, but from its faithful keepers. But, he would have to wait for quiet and semblance of order to return, before having the faintest hope of being heard.

This morning he'd been surprised upon first hearing intelligible communication from a dove. But now, knowing of the existence of such a seed, a seed capable of intelligent responding went beyond his wildest imagining. He *must* learn all there was to know of Terrence Thiery.

After calling her fellows to order, the spokes-dove decided, 'And so now, flock ... our friend, Clever, must be informed of the "rule of planting", that rule which applies to the seed.' She asked, 'Are you acquainted at all, Clever, with the thing named, "wooden pail"?'

Taking the fixer's preoccupied expression as proof of ignorance, she sighed, before explaining, 'Wooden pails have another name. A "bucket" is more or less the same thing. A wooden pail is a bucket fashioned as the name describes—from wood—coming from Sister Tree. It is a vessel most often used for carrying water. Pails, Clever, are Tall One things...'

As she trailed off, wondering how a pail might be better described, Fixer knew that she made a clear explanation of a thing he already knew, and before she went to further pains in providing description of pails, he spoke up, trusting to put her at ease. 'I do know of them,' he said, 'I've seen them—along with those things known as "watering cans".'

But then, he half-wished he'd let her struggle on in her way, because she was ungracious in responding, 'Wood pail! *Wood!* The detail is vital, and cannot be over-emphasized!'

The flock delivered much serious agreement, and Fixer hoped that not too many rules were involved in looking after the blessed seed, because if there were, then despite its rarity and his wonder over it, he might soon undergo a change of heart and forego the privilege of taking on responsibility for it.

Of all creatures, he'd never minded doves. Previous to this, though, he'd no idea they were so finicky or quite so serious. He saw them now as conscientious beyond reason and sounding terse, but not caring, he asked, 'Any *more* rules? How about you give me the rest of them, and then I'll be on my way! I've got a lot of ground to cover and must get started!'

The dove told him, 'You *are* true inheritor, Clever Fixer, but you will hear me out. Yes—there are rules and the most important of them is this... The seed must *never* touch ground. It may be planted out, and yet it cannot be too often stressed—it must be planted in soil contained in a wooden pail! It must *not* be allowed to fall to the ground.' She was silent then, as were the flock, and Fixer wondered if that was all of it.

He asked, 'Is that it then?'

'Yes, Fixer, apart from love, it's about all you'll need to know.'

'Love...?'

'Care,' said the dove. 'Care—tenderness, affection and love—as *we* provided it over long ages.' Many voices then sounded agreement.

Ownership of the seed did not now, sound quite so straightforward, Clever thought. And, seeing his expression, one revealing growing suspicion, the dove confessed, 'Oh yes, Fixer … you're correct. Duty can prove onerous! It can at times be insufferable and exhausting, but then, benefit to your good self, we're sure, will be boundless.

'You see, Clever, the seed is knowledge itself. It contains within it, information—most of which is of not of slightest interest to us. We've acted in the capacity of keepers, and that's all. We've performed our duty but that's not to say the task hasn't at times proven difficult.

Difficulty is due in part to its ceaseless babbling, which on occasion has almost driven us mad. You'll learn, once it gets going, that there's no stopping it. It *never* shuts up! I don't know, but leading the solitary life you've chosen, it may be a good thing for you. It will be company—something to ward away loneliness when such besets you. We must trust that the relationship will prove pleasant enough.'

She was as sincere as ever, but Clever decided that now he wanted to know more. He was not after all in so much hurry. He asked, 'What does it speak of—when, as you say, it rambles?'

'Oh, it loves nonsense—much stuff and nonsense but then, who can say. In your role as true inheritor, you may grasp its gist, better than we.'

And that, thought Fixer, was not enlightening. He would have to do a lot of listening to the seed's ramblings and make up his own mind.

The flock was making to leave, with many at the fringes already having taken to the air, but before she left the branch she perched upon, the spokes-dove felt obliged to impart a message.

'Bronwyn asks me to convey thanks, Fixer. We doves are not so ill mannered. Bronwyn's gone back, returned to Nigel, the husband. You'll understand that he too, sends thanks. You did a marvellous job in nursing her back to health and I know by that alone, you'll make a fine job of caring for the seed! And now we must away. Who can say, but perhaps our paths may yet cross. Until then, though, Clever Fixer—happy trails!'

And so saying, she raised her wings high and swept away from her perch to go winging aloft.

As she lifted away, a rising tide of noisy white wings, lifted from grass and treetop and within moments the fixer found himself alone—alone again—apart from the seed, that was. Time would tell if he and it would get along together. If they didn't, he supposed he might give it to another, just as the flock had given it him. Better still, it could be swapped for another useful item or article. His coat for example, was rather old and tatty and did not seem to fit so well as once it had. Maybe his and Haberdasher Frederick's trails would cross and they'd attend to bartering.

Holding the curious marvel to an ear, no utterance was heard. Fixer imagined it might sleep, or perhaps it sulked, due to its being passed to his paw after spending a small eternity in the company of Folk of Feather. Countless generations of feathered carers had attended its need. Fixer decided that it was high time for change. He did not doubt that for his part anyway, fair effort would be invested in building familiarity. Then, aware of so much time passing between the time of the Tall One—she of abominable personal habit—and his "ownership" of the seed, Clever was mindful of the possibility of benefit accumulated over time. As the dove had explained it, the seed's great age meant accumulation of every sort of useful thing—of fact, of information, and knowledge.

Great knowledge could equate with great power, which was not the sort of thing to interest him. He did not view power as did others, but the power of understanding, now, that was an altogether other thing.

Clever Fixer realized he could not swap, nor barter, nor ever bargain away or lose the seed. He vowed *never* to allow such foolishness. Tucking the precious thing into a pocket of his waistcoat, he admonished, 'Phew! Fixer—you call yourself *Clever!*'

In the course of time, a great deal was learned. Clever acquired a rudimentary grasp of many disciplines, of geometry, mathematics, physics, chemistry, mechanics; he learned of frequency, of resonance, subjects and things he'd not so much as dreamed of. He was enthralled by all of it. The topic most fascinating, though, was that of Terrence Thiery.

When Terrence was spoken of he could listen for days on end and still want to know more, more of Terrence Thiery and his work and of the Tall One's home. He would learn of things, which other Folk of Fur could never credit as believable. If he believed himself solitary before acquisition of the faience blue seed, then, with times passing, he was even more so. If, rather than spend time communing with the seed, he'd the opportunity to join with the company of others, the invitation was declined. His relationship with the seed was no mere, workable partnership, but each recognized the other as kindred spirit. They'd become true-bonded friends of like-mind, and much more.

The man, Terrence Thiery, was a child of territory or country, far removed from the place he would journey to, where he would make his home; then, the backward place of his birth would hold no claim on his heart. Taking the seed with him, and not much more, he'd journey far, traversing a pond of vast proportion, to find himself in a land celebrated by Tall Ones as a place where every type of freedom was enjoyed—a place where freedom was in fact lauded. Hearing of such a place, Clever Fixer knew it as a land where dreams came true, a territory of unbound spirit and, if it were up to him, he would journey there to reside forever.

The place was called America. When Clever, thinking to journey there, as Terrence had, enquired of the seed as to the direction of America, he was told, 'No, Fixer. You don't get it! *You* cannot find the place! Terrence is not of your realm. His home is worlds away. Whilst America lies close to your territory, not so much as a whisker away, it is, at one and same time, far distant—far beyond the reach of your primitive ability.' This was injurious to Clever's feelings and seemed most contradictory.

Told that the "realm" he inhabited was not flat, but round, in fact spherical, and that it moved through an immense, airless void, he knew the information supplied was downright kadoodle. 'You possess a wonderful sense of humour,' he granted.

Catching his tone, the seed enquired, 'Do you believe that I aim to deceive? You are my friend, Clever. I would never attempt deception! Even if I thought to, I could not.'

He was then made recipient of a discourse on truth itself. The doves were an honest lot; the seed just loved to prattle.

'Lies, Fixer, are the product of a mind's belief in dull magic. There's no need for magic. Creation is infinite and rich, extending in every direction, extending inward and out, and whether believed or not, beyond even itself, there is always enough of truth to go around. Those who would lie believe in just one truth and for belief, have themselves as the truth of the lie. Truth is not "invention". It's not owned—as opinion or product of "perception"; there are not "versions" of it. No. Truth exists independent of approval. It is not "low" or "high" to be played with and it's available to all. It's always present and most wonderful to know. Truth is "light". The opposite is ingrown claws and a blanket over your head.'

There were many mutterings from the seed, many solutions provided for "fixings" and much mystery described. 'Whilst I have not been planted out, I possess within me, all that my parent knew.' The great Terrence had planted a seed, and a quite wondrous tree had resulted. 'And so, you see, Clever Fixer, it was that tree, tended by Terrence and those closest to him, which was parent to me.'

**

The young Terrence Thiery met a gal, Tess, by name, and having fallen head over flag in love, it was not long before they were wed. An inventor's lot is never easy, but Terrence worked well and with enough luck, ends were made to meet. It seemed that within the blink of an eye, the Thierys no longer numbered just two, but were three; a son was welcomed to their world. When all seemed perfect though, merciless fate favouring cruel outcome, entered in, and so it was that great unhappiness became a part of Terrence Thiery's experience. A second child, a daughter, Lilith, had come to the world, but not without dreadful cost; for during travail the mother was taken by gazuzzlement. The child, Lilith would grow to become the apple of her father's eye. The faience blue seed related this, and much more besides.

It was decided. Clever Fixer knew that he would never plant the seed. By doing so, he might never again hear it speak.

VISITATION

An eerie haunting sound was heard this morning, coming from topside. Once a body was accustomed to it, it was not too unsettling, but it *was* strange all the same. Waking later than usual, Clever lay still for a while, listening. It was odd hearing something and having no idea of what was meant by it. He'd determined the sound as made by Folk of Fur, and that no one was hurt. He decided to relax and allow himself to drift along with it. He was enjoying pondering possible meanings, but soon gave up. It was enough, he thought, knowing it was unfamiliar.

'Mmeerah!' it went. 'Mmeerah!' Over and over again it droned, nonstop and quite spookifying until it was after all too mysterious, and so he got up, donned waistcoat, jacket and trousers and went up to ascertain the reason for it.

Outside the warren entrance was an area flatter than the rest, a small plateau of sorts, and there were Peace Darkling, Piedmont, Sherbrook and the youngster, Skip.

Seeing him exit the warren, Peace Darkling beckoned. She patted an area of dry grass to one side of herself, indicating there was a place for him.

In making the gesture, she'd not paused in voicing, 'Mmeerah! Mmeerah!' Now that he was outside, the sound was a lot louder than before, but increased volume was not what impressed him.

He was intrigued because, now he was here, the air itself—the very atmosphere it seemed—underwent subtle yet definite altering, as affected by the strange hypnotic resonating.

It was as though air, leaves of treetops, grass and all else of natural surround—including him—and even the light, all aspects of the One, were effected by the entrancing sound so that the fact of underlying joy in natural joining was made more clear to him.

Sound made as a type of singing, chanted harmonic, which had all of nature, it seemed, elevated in synchronous recognition of inherent goodness and rightness of being, and Clever's spirit was lifted by it.

How could sound have such an effect? A strange and wondrous utterance indeed, he thought, and accepted the invitation to join them; he could not have prevented himself doing so. Together then, the five of them chanted, 'Mmeerah!'

He later declared, 'It's remarkable, a discovery the equal of any! I *insist* you tell me the steps you followed in achieving it.'

Defensive and quick off the mark, Peace responded, 'Fixer—I didn't *follow!* Never that! No. I took time in *observing* my world, and pondered the underlying reason for all I saw and heard.' Reconsidering those words, she told him, 'Actually though, you're right, Clever, because I did follow. I followed nature's way and then made adaptation. I followed before seeing purpose in doing so. At first, my following was reason enough. There was no hope for gain, not in any usual sense. At least, I don't think...' She trailed off.

Clever leapt in, exclaiming, 'There you are then! You did *not* think! We're always encouraged to think, aren't we? Think this and think that! Yet here *you* are, having made such discovery by letting go! You've come up with something which even one of so-called genius might spend a lifetime searching for—without making discovery at all! I think it's marvellous and I can't wait to try it again!'

He said, 'You won't practise it in future without including me, will you?' Smiling, he added, 'I won't believe you'd do that.

She said, 'Clever, you are perfect, the very individual I'd hoped you were. You do your name justice.'

He said, 'Yes I do, don't I?'

Later he went by the bard's quarters and peering in, cleared his throat, 'A-hum.' It was a sound Piedmont recognized and without troubling to look up, he said, 'Come in, Fixer. You're very welcome. I've been indulging in rather self-pitying thought. I confess to engaging in such to avoid your concluding my mood has anything to do with you.' He said, 'Come along in if you dare.'

Solicitous, Fixer offered, 'If it will help any, I'm a good listener—or have been told that's true.' The bard, not wanting to speak out at first, then muttered a single word, 'Scratchings...'

'Ah!' Fixer exclaimed, 'Then, it's your work, Bard. Got you feeling down, has it?'

'Not, as such,' Piedmont said, at last glancing up from staring at the floor.

'As such?' Clever enticed.

'It's something, Skip said.'

'Ah, then, it's the youngster?' Clever was careful; he did not want to make a problem where one did not exist. He was new to the warren and was mindful of not wanting to take sides in dispute or appear to play favourites.

'Both Skip *and* the scratchings...' Piedmont explained. 'At the time of our departing New Warren Central, I was told by him to have no concern regarding the safety of the scratchings. The epics—my works, yes—but, that's not all. As well, there are those records passed down the line to me, things of inestimable worth, entrusted to my keeping. I've come away in haste, to this place, leaving all of it. In thinking of myself, I've abandoned obligation...' Piedmont was unable to continue, and Clever saw that he was unravelling. Beginning anew, the bard was saying, 'Oh, Clever, dear friend, I experience such difficulty, such humiliation, in attempting an explanation. You can have no idea of the trial endured.'

Clever Fixer had no real idea of what was alluded to. Standing there in the bard's presence, he pondered words. Words, such as humiliation, and trial, were difficult to attach somehow, to one of the bard's high standing.

He might, he thought, be a good listener, but challenged in the present moment he could not think what might best be said to cheer Piedmont.

Coming from behind him, Clever Fixer heard a voice declaring, 'The Graymark lot back at New Warren Central had him making whisk-brooms.' Clever recognized that voice as belonging to none other than Skip.

Skip had "seen" this happening, and had to put a stop to it, because he did not want them going off at tangent. They had to stay with the present line.

This morning he saw something he'd never before seen: two timelines, each representing possible futures or different outcomes. Lines branched away from each other from the present point in time and so a choice must be made. He decided to act by preventing Piedmont further engaging in discussion of the scratchings with Clever Fixer.

Seeing such variance and outcomes was frightening and although he'd just the barest clue as to what their elders might consider as interference or tampering, he decided that guided by what amounted to not much more than intuition, he'd do something about matters. In wishing he were more self-assured, he recalled the elders' boldness in dealing with difficulty.

At the time of the elders' bickery scratching over matters of tampering, he'd just the slightest comprehension of that discussed, but he'd sympathized more with the others of them than with Skip the Elder. Now faced with a choice of outcomes, he recalled his elder regarding altering as nothing to worry too much over. The elder would be pleased with him now, he thought, but still he could not know if his choice was the correct one. Upon arrival at the entrance to the bard's quarters, when he'd spoken of Grammy Graymark and New Warren Central, Clever Fixer had swung around to face him.

'Ah, the lad in question!' Fixer exclaimed. And Skip saw that Clever stared as if hiding something. Nothing too nasty, and yet, his light showed a certain sourness in judging him. Believing he would defend Piedmont, there was present in the fixer, something of ill intent, a thing desirous of opportunity to pounce.

Skip would not allow Fixer a chance to direct anything toward him having about it the slightest element of blame.

Until now, Fixer's day to day life was that of the loner, and although no longer youthful, he lacked the subtlety of understanding in close dealing with others. His light revealed immaturity of a type with which Skip was not familiar. Fixer was not yet accustomed to life within a group, and so Skip decided he would go easy on him, because in time Clever Fixer would learn and all would be well.

Addressing Piedmont, he said, 'Bard? Cheer up! Before many moons are passed, you *will* hold the scratchings. Again—you have my word on it! Don't doubt it.'

Piedmont insisted upon remaining as downhearted as ever and was not the least reassured. Denying Clever Fixer the opportunity to speak, Skip said, 'Your waistcoat jabbers something awful, Fixer! It's fit to bust! Perhaps you'd best tend to things—those, you most understand.' Clever's light was then ashen. His heart sank low as his mind opened to mystery. He no longer entertained the notion of retaliating on behalf of a fellow oldster.

Something of fear-induced respect showed in his expression, which was not anything Skip wanted or liked. Fixer said, 'Of course, you're a group. Your business is your own. It has nothing to do with me.' Resignation showed.

Skip told him, 'Clever, you're a very welcome part of our group, but for now you'd best converse with the jabberer and not me.' He turned away to go off up the main tunnel.

Forgetting his problems for the moment, Piedmont enquired, 'In Great Grandfather's creation, what was all that about the jabberer? What did he mean by it?'

Clever Fixer replied, 'Nothing, nothing I know of. He's a strange one—the youngster—isn't he? Odd beyond reason or understanding.' He made as if to leave.

He would like to be gone, but Piedmont looked still set upon wallowing, set to wrack mind and emotion in fearful grappling with insoluble difficulty.

Fixer would employ diplomacy, 'If it were me, old friend, I'd go along with whatever the boy says. As far as *I* know of any of it, he's trustworthy enough.' And, is far too weird besides, he thought.

Piedmont offered, 'He *is* trustworthy—yes. On occasion, I've gone out of my way in defending his sincere nature and honest character. By now though, as far as the scratchings are concerned, I need something more than mere verbal reassurance.'

Impatient with himself, Piedmont said, 'Oh, I *do* trust him. But then, so much of all he says goes way over my head!'

Hearing the great bard revealing defeat, Clever Fixer was surprised. Most important to him was the boy's proven knowledge of the seed. Clever experienced the strongest compulsion to rush away to his quarters to check on the treasure, his *secret* treasure, he believed—until now!

He must ascertain truth of the matter. He must! Had the boy gained knowledge by means of sneaking about—prying through his belongings perhaps—as he slept? If Piedmont vouchsafed for the boy's honesty, then it was good enough—or was it?

Clever's thoughts raced, but doing his best to appear calm and detached, he said, 'I'm beginning to know similar feeling to yours, Piedmont, feelings of uncertainty. The youngster *is* uncommon, but for now good friend—I must away. There's a small chore needs attending to, nothing too important but I should see to it.' So saying, he backed from Piedmont's chamber.

So fast did he move in getting to the privacy of his own quarters, that arriving there, he was breathless. His waistcoat was never removed so fast; he did not just take it off, but tore it from himself. Yes! It was there still, not stolen away in darkness of night! Then, holding it close to ear, he heard 'The seer has you going—eh, Fixer? I know your heart suffers terrible quaking. Settle down now Clever Fixer, because it's rest you need, not worry and suspicion!'

Focusing on just one of those words, Clever Fixer asked, 'Seer? What the deeks are you telling me?'

Crenshaw had mentioned something to the effect of the boy being "touched". As Clever heard it, the youngster knew something of divination—was interested in that sort of thing. Others believed he possessed something of ability. But, when hearing Crenshaw mention such in passing, Clever had smiled, thinking, what superstitious kadoodle! Others would believe just about anything! Now though, the seed treated the matter with seriousness.

'The seer,' said the seed, 'sees so much, not everything, but, enough to mean others will often believe him strange and even unreliable, when the opposite is true. Harm will not befall us, Fixer, not from anything he plans. With trust, the outcome will knock your socks off.' And then, as if going off at a tangent, it asked, 'Fixer, what *is it* that you want from life?'

'From life?'

'Yes. What is it you seek? What is it you most wish for, your secret hope?'

Confused in the moment and perplexed, Clever Fixer was not serious and took a stab in the dark, 'Well, I guess, immortality wouldn't be such a bad thing,' he said, smiling 'Yes, that would suit me. I'd very much like to live forever—forever and a day.'

'Clever, as unbelievable as it will seem, with the seer for company, even something of that order may be realized.' After revealing as much, the seed, despite a contrary reputation, retreated to silence. Clever Fixer, finding he stared down at his dusty feet, wondered, 'What next?'

He'd not slept long, he thought, but he knew by the present deep, impenetrable darkness it was the middle of the night. When he lay down to rest it was still day—the late afternoon. The seed had suggested rest was needed, but he'd not realized the extent of his tiredness. He was surprised when feeling himself drifting off and away.

He'd done nothing much at all, nothing of too strenuous a nature during the day, but was invited to join in practising Mmeerah.

After that, apart from the short conversation with the bard, and distressing communication with the boy, he'd not done much of anything. He supposed that after a lifetime of exhaustive travelling, now that far less was expected of it, his body was taking its time in adjusting to a more sedentary way. It was as if it belonged not to him, but to someone else, who lent it to him for a while; just to see what he thought of it.

Having woken now, he was faced with the task of getting back to sleep. The more he tried, the more he seemed to fail.

But then he must have succeeded, because he was dreaming—must be! But deeks—wasn't it *real!* His attention was riveted and he could not look away. Standing at opposite side of the chamber, surrounded with blue-white glow, was, what seemed at first, another Clever Fixer! Then, though, ordering himself to calm, he determined a presence of arrogance—something of supercilious nonchalance, evident in both the facial expression and bearing of the other. Those tell-tale differences were proof enough in deducing that this was nothing but a kadoodling interloper!

Fixer sat up and stared back. For its part, the other persisted in directing him an unwavering, condescending stare. This was the type of confrontation most dreaded by an itinerant when camping out at night. Being set upon in darkness was an unenviable prospect and was dreaded by all wayfarers. Having avoided such a confrontation for so long, his luck was now run out; against all sane odds, confrontation occurred *after* his settling down, to go as it were, straight.

He wondered over the fuzzy, blue-white light and decided it was a trick of the light itself. A full moon shone and due to the warren's eccentric design, moonlight came to him after being reflected from the sheared-off smooth stones of the walls along the curving main tunnel. It was but a fluke effect, not evident before this, because tonight's was the first full moon since his arriving here. Such explanation was not without certain appeal. It offered far more assurance than the other, more fanciful notion that, if entertained, begged the question—what if this was indeed a visitation by a ghostly entity? Fixer shook his head. It was just not so! He did not believe in such phenomena.

And then it spoke! 'Calmed, have you?' This sent Fixer scrabbling off into a far corner, with the creature complaining, 'Oh *desist!* Don't carry on so!

'Here I am—come so far to help you out and all my trouble gets me is... Well, it's childish behaviour isn't it? It's downright disappointing carry-on.'

'Yes, Sir!' Fixer responded. 'Nice of you to think of stopping by!'

'Yes,' he heard, 'It's decent of me, but for now we must get down to business. Too much time's been wasted. If you'll be good enough to drag yourself out from the corner, I have important instruction for you.'

'Instruction?'

'Yes. Instruction concerning your diminutive charge ... the seed.' Hearing mention of the seed, Fixer was suspicious, and seeing him so, the visitor responded, insisting, 'I'm not here to take the blessed thing from you! We are Tump! Tump is no thief! Is that what you think?' Had it referred to itself in the plural? He believed so, and began searching this way and that. What low lurking monstrosity was referred to? Then, as if having read his mind, 'Tump is One! We are not here to terrify you, Fixer.' And Fixer thought he might lose his grip. He'd heard, 'Tump is *one*,' and, '*We* are not here...' He was no expert when it came to the intricacy of language; but?

Now it was telling him, 'Clever, you must show the seed. Reveal it! That's why we're here. We insist that you do so!'

Commanded thus, Fixer lost all fear. Putting paw to mouth he issued an order of his own. 'Shh!' he hissed. 'You'll wake them and then *every-one* will know of it!' Skip knew of the seed and so too did the entity in his chamber, which meant there were *two* of them. Apart from him—the rightful inheritor—two others were aware of its existence. It seemed *so* many—and both in the space of a single day! Ordered to reveal a secret pertaining to his property he was outraged. Again he hissed, keeping his voice low, 'Never! My heart's hardened against it! I can't do it—and *won't!*'

'Then you are Clever by name—,'

'Use my name against me,' Clever retorted. 'Insult me as you like, but as the true inheritor I honour a sacred trust—and you can…'

'Yes?'

'Take a flibberty hopping hike out of here! Off with you! Monstrosity! Get out!' Clutching at various items from amongst his things, he began hurling objects. No longer did he care so much if anyone else was disturbed and awakened by racket. He scored a direct hit with a piece of stale fruit taken from one of his sacks—an apple, he thought, but he could not be certain of its identity. It was hurled with true force and after striking the creature between the eyes, the item went bounding away into the dark. He continued directing barrage upon barrage of personal property.

Each time the other was struck, a dull thudding sounded, and that meant that it was solid enough—more substantial than any wraith! The more hits scored, the more it glowed shimmering, and so it was not pleased. It shouted, 'You absolute fool, Fixer!' He wished the tipsy-barrow were here, because if she were, despite the substantial weight involved, he'd not hesitate in hurling even her!

Then, the youngster was at the opening to the sleeping chamber. Looking to the apparition, the boy saw it too! Clever was pleased. It was visible to another and so he was not gone kadoodling mad.

But then the boy berated, 'After my going to so much trouble in arranging your things for you Fixer!' The boy smiled, but then he did not just smile, but grinned from ear to ear, showing he was delighted in seeing the intruder!

'Skip, assure him we mean no harm.' It sounded bone-weary tired, Fixer thought, in pleading with the youngster.

The boy had his attention, 'Clever—it's Tump! They're here to insist you do something for them.' Addressing the still glowing creature, Skip asked, 'You want him to give up the seed—right?' And smiling, 'You told me, "Don't offer him anything by way of inducement", and now, here you are visiting him?'

'This afternoon he was deciding whether or not to organize a party of Leader Crenshaw's folk. He considers it sensible, marching off to New Warren Central on behalf of Piedmont and the scratchings! He would cause much difficulty.'

'He must give up the seed, but he's the most stubborn, most obtuse individual we've ever to deal with!

'Later on, much later than this, you'll see he alters his way and to a good useful end. The self-same stubborn streak is turned to better purpose, but in the mean time—well—look at what he's done to my hat! It's *his* hat, for deeks sake!' Replacing the hat upon its head, then looking to the boy, the creature allowed, 'You must deal with him!' That said—with an accompanying mighty flash of lightning-brightness—Tump was gone!

There was no almighty kazooning, and so Skip knew they'd moved to a location in this realm. Were the sound of sky being torn asunder soon heard, then it would not be thunder at all, but Tump moving to another realm, moving inter-dimensionally, and he wished he was going with them.

Peace, Sherbrook and even, Piedmont, the deepest sleeper of all, were awakened by the hubbub, so there was more explaining to do, more getting impossible things into heads, and again, how he *wished* he too, was gone from here!

The sweet smell of cinnamon permeated Clever Fixer's chamber. It seeped out to waft along the main tunnel and riding upon air currents from topside, made drifting, downward progress, down to the enormous chamber that lay far beneath them. Clever Fixer, catching scent of it, exclaimed, 'I know what that is. It's a whiff of cinnamon!' This was something of a surprise, but then, thought Skip, Clever Fixer must know at least some small thing. Extending a paw to Clever, he said, 'Come on—out with it, Clever! Show us the seed!' As enticement, he added, 'When we've seen it, we'll help with tidying your awful mess!'

Wood Pail

In the parlour of the cottage in Bunty's realm, Clever Fixer exclaimed, 'A wooden pail!

There it is—the very thing!'

* * *

Left without a choice, he'd shown them the seed. Each and every one of them now knew of it—no thanks to prowling wickedness besetting him in the night.

When the monstrous presence left his chamber, and when he stopped shaking, he reached into his pocket and taking out the treasure, told them, 'I'm revealing it because you've been good to me, you've treated me with decency—and besides, it seems I have little choice in the matter.' Clever gave a small shrug of resignation. He was outnumbered and still felt somewhat ill-treated, not withstanding the fact of them welcoming him to their home. He thought, why should I be forced into sharing something so meaningful? The seed was not just property, but dearest friend.

Seeing it passed amongst them, he told them more than once, 'Take care! Don't drop it! It must never touch to ground! Every care is required!' As Peace Darkling examined it, exclaiming over its gorgeous colour, he insisted, 'Yes, it's a beautiful thing and it's mine!'

Despite allowing them to see it, the fact of his ownership would be understood; he was not giving it over to them. He would not feel so lost as this, were he forced to display intimate, personal articles of apparel to all and sundry. This was an uncommon ordeal, an extreme example of invasion of privacy, and he could feel no worse were sharp claws gouging at his insides. Emotional scarring would doubtless be a permanent reminder of the humiliating occasion.

The youngster, Skip, took a last turn examining the seed and then, returning it to its rightful inheritor, announced, 'It's been a dreadful night for you, Fixer. That's understood. We appreciate your sharing the treasure with us.'

Fixer thought, It's something ... at least the boy showed politeness. But he was churlish and wilful and, there was the matter of frightening otherness. He was in league with dark forces. He, Clever, would take every caution in dealing with such a one.

He replaced the seed in his pocket, its true home, and with that done felt more at ease. Looking about his chamber and detesting the interloper anew, he trusted that the offer of assistance in tidying up, would be honoured.

Apart from Piedmont, there was Sherbrook, and he thought Sherbrook a trustworthy enough individual. Peace Darkling was a most charming gal; she was inventive, genuine and welcoming. Getting right down to it, the problem was the boy. His disliking another was not pleasing, but he was a believer in the axiom, which held that first impressions were reliable. As far as weirdness went, he was no commonplace individual himself. His own unusualness, as he imagined it perceived by others, was not without sensible, albeit secret cause, his carrying about with him a most unusual and valuable item, whereas the boy was peculiar in his own right.

It seemed that no further offer of assistance should be expected. There were several long moments during which none ventured speak. The place had suffered; everywhere was strewn mess. He would attend to tidying on the morrow, but for now he announced, 'I believe it's high time the fixer hit the old sackeroo.' In making the announcement he noted an odd, furtive look passed between them, and the feeling of his not belonging here increased, but then the weird one spoke up. With none but him willing to speak, the youngster was in charge of proceedings. Allowing him to speak on their behalf seemed to Fixer, an example of awry, submissive behaviour.

'It's late and you're tired, Fixer. We're all tired, but rather than wait any longer, I think you'd best agree to allow me to "move" you. There must be more revealing—and so, with your agreement?'

Hearing moving suggested, Clever wondered if they intended providing him new quarters? Responding to his enquiring, a mute Piedmont shook his head. And, whilst the bard shook his head, Sherbrook vented an odd, small snicker, and Peace Darkling came to him. Smiling, and with consideration evident in both expression and manner, she persuaded, 'Just say *yes*, Clever...'

She rested a paw against one of his arms and told the youngster, 'Get on with it Skip. He agrees—of course he does, don't you, Fixer?'

With permission sought by one so charming, ready agreement might have been granted, but he was given no real chance to respond. He was staggered when, in the instant following her words, he discovered himself frantic and rubbing at his eyes! He would clear the effect of a dazzling lightning-flash from them! When vision cleared, he found himself standing in another place!

It was a world of magical beauty, a place of sunlight, babbling brook, chirping bird and at moment of their arrival, soft falling rain. A sun-shower occurred, making wild flowers and meadow-grass smell as fresh as a new-mown field. What impossible place was this? Where were they!

Were it not for Peace Darkling holding to his arm, he would be flat on the ground. Imploring, he said, 'Excuse me Peace, but were I to sit, it might be best.' And then looking up at the sky, his eyes further deceived him, for on high there were three starlings, which upon reaching the outermost limit of the sky ... vanished to nothingness!

He put a paw to his waistcoat and was reassured; the seed was still with him.

The boy had accomplished getting them to this place! Staring about, entertaining not the least denial of wonder of it, Clever Fixer saw no alternative other than admit the boy was *not* in league with anything of dark force. He recalled the seed's insisting that the opinionated twerp stood for the miraculous, and now, Clever Fixer had experienced that as undeniable truth.

The youngster *had* exhibited insufferable arrogance, and yet a better term than that might be an appropriate expression of self-confidence.

He had decided the boy as dictatorial, but now, who—without such power—might better lead the troupe? The answer to the question of leadership was not considered without first accounting for the fact that an oldster would be seen as best choice for the position. Oldsters were viewed as the betters of those of tender age. They were held in higher regard for reason of their possessing mature skill for the judicious use of power of authority.

In this case though, the boy would not be brooked in having his own way. He showed little respect for his elders, but then, on the other paw—weren't they lucky? Indeed they were ever so fortunate, because with him deciding things on their behalf, protection was guaranteed. Being able to move them with such ease meant that even the most geriatric should not fear meeting with the untoward.

'Bring it on, kadoodler!' Such exclamation might be their cry. 'Do your gazuzzling worst!' Potential harm-doers would soon enough know they stood no chance! This was no mere assumption, because fine proof was provided by the boy's absolute lack of fear in facing the nightmarish visitation. Even the interloper had requested the *youngster* provide aid in dealing with the matter of the seed and, in regarding that, wasn't the boy fair-minded? Yes, he was. When that difficult truth was admitted, here they all were, and he, Clever Fixer, more or less homeless vagrant, was welcomed to the company. They were now a family, or at least something of the sort.

The world he saw before him conformed to the seed's pronouncement. It was a prime example of manifestation fit to knock a body's socks off! Skip's transporting them here was nothing short of astounding! His "moving", had convinced the fixer that in deciding to reveal the seed, his choice was true. Fair exchange was accomplished, because now he could go anywhere, anytime at all, in the mere twinkling of an eye!

Waiting with the others, atop the grassy hillock, Skip saw that whilst Clever Fixer adjusted to the startling fact of instantaneous shifting through space, and to everything hereabout, his light was most unusual. Colours swirled and swam as if at odds. Long sodden-appearing tendrils fought against one another, entwining, writhing, in a disharmonious ever-altering state of disorder, which was the more disconcerting the longer he stared at it. He looked away because in studying the effect, he was nauseated. Gazing upon it again, attempting to discern meaning, and believing then, he made sense of it. He said, 'Fixer? It was no apparition you saw in your chamber. It was you. You met with your elder—a future-self. This group—our group of five, which later on will include two others—is Tump. We'll rest here nearby the wind-clickers and I'll explain some of it for you. You need to know a lot more than you do. Your light's swimming about, bickery scratching with itself as a nest of serpents.'

'My light?' Fixer queried.

'Yes, your light,' Peace told him, smiling. After further explanation, Fixer would be fine.

***

In the barn, Piedmont, showing Clever Fixer the shield of Mydor, insisted, 'It's invaluable of course. As far as rare finds go, it has no equal. And just look—over here, at the reverse side of it.' Piedmont turned the shield over with extreme care for Fixer to see. 'There now—do you see? Incredible, isn't it?' Fixer took his hat off, as if saluting such wonder, for this was legendary Mydor's shield, and right there before his eyes was actual evidence of the great one—a small remnant of fur! Piedmont voiced further expression of awe and reverence and Clever Fixer, happening to glance up to a point high upon a wall at the back of the barn, thought he saw something glinting there.

Whilst in no way detracting from the shield Piedmont took such pride in showing—up there was something which may give the lie to Mydor's shield being quite so rare as first believed. Clever's mouth gaped open in disbelief. He was at first unable to speak, but after making several unsuccessful attempts, he stammered, 'There, look! There's another one—up in the shadows! Look, do you see what I mean? Tell me—am I right?'

Sherbrook went flibberty hopping to the back of the barn with Skip in close pursuit.

Arriving at a point beneath the spot indicated by Clever, and staring up into the dimness, they saw attached to the wall, what did indeed look very much like a second shield.

Light flashed, and in a trice Skip had it down, and passing it to Sherbrook, heard Sherbrook declaring, 'I was under the impression you didn't like moving precious artefacts? That's what I thought.' He scowled.

Skip told him, 'Yes, that's right. I don't, but nothing could be as valuable as the shield of Mydor. I figured this must belong to a lesser individual. Anyway, after getting the other down, I guessed this one would be attached in the same way, and so it would be simple enough to move, from down here.' Having explained so much, he insisted, 'Go on Sherbrook— take a look at it. Have I messed it up? Is there damage? No, I don't think so—so there you are!'

The new find was passed first to Clever Fixer, who, holding it in both paws, grinned; so pleased was he. But he gave the shield not much more than short study before passing it over to Piedmont for assessment.

Piedmont announced after momentary perusal, 'After cursory inspection I believe that this find was the property of Crenshaw, or The Keeper of Rope, which makes it another extraordinary find. The keeper was second only to Great Mydor himself. Yes, Fixer, Keeper of Rope, to be sure. The symbol graved thereupon, to my way of thinking, is certain proof. It can be interpreted as nothing else.' Piedmont went on, 'I confess though, that in a lifetime's study of the records of scratchings, I've had little success in learning much of the keeper. Those stories passed down to us have not proven useful. He, and the facts pertaining to him, including anything of his actual role in affairs, is shrouded in mystery, but that notwithstanding, this shield *is* his. Who else, other than the keeper, would carry into battle a shield bearing such a symbol, a symbol of coiled rope ... I ask you?'

Sherbrook decided the keeper's shield, sombre and more serious than its companion, the bright-coloured shield of Mydor, and commented to that effect.

'Yes,' Peace agreed, 'You're right.'

The latest find reeked of gazuzzlement. With embellishment describing a black rope-noose set against silver-grey ground, there seemed to her, not much of glory or triumph to it. In no uncertain terms it pronounced, 'Warring, is my function.' She shivered, and was glad when Skip said he thought they should go across to the cottage. Clever could see the ice-tomb and its occupants, and Skip said there was something in the front room, the parlour, which should be brought to Clever's attention.

Having had more than enough of things of war, of relics more valued by others, Peace agreed, saying, 'Skip's right. We *must* show Fixer the planting place!' She saw Clever wince, but soon he must be convinced to plant the seed. If he would not, then Great Grandfather's map could not be. According to information given by the elders, the tree functioned as an essential part in their order, and it was as important as folk of the group. Skip had been told of the tree, but had not seen it. The seed *must* be planted out, and Peace could not wait to begin tending the tree.

Arrived in the cottage parlour where most everything was strange to him, Clever Fixer focused upon the one thing he recognized as familiar. He exclaimed, 'It's a wooden pail! Why—it's perfect! It's the ideal thing!' Without further ado, he made as if to tear its present, sad-looking incumbent away from the soil supporting it.

Seeing his haste, Peace ordered, 'No—don't tear it out!' She said, 'I'm sorry Fixer, but do you think it might best be attended to in gentler fashion? It might not be deceased.'

Fixer's expression said that he believed she joked. Such a dried bundle of sticks no longer lived. He asked, 'What did you have in mind?' Drawing back from the pail where it rested on the low table, he waited. He was accepted by them now and was keen to show a willingness to fit in. They'd informed him of Tump, of its meaning and their intention, but having accepted the rightness of it, he wanted to get on with planting the seed. Maybe though, he was a little too eager to get started.

Piedmont said, 'I think that we should take the pail outside. We won't scatter soil over the floor of this place.' The place was most strange. The floor covering was very soft underfoot, and those reds, those dark blues and quite fabulous colours of rich ochre, autumn russet and deep, warmest brown were all there for hopping upon.

When first seeing it, its beauty impressed Piedmont, and he had wondered at Tall Ones putting the wonderful thing to such use. He'd hesitated long enough before venturing to set dusty foot upon it, for Sherbrook, who was behind him at the time, to ask, 'Come along now Piedmont, what's the problem?'

Sherbrook, referring to the pail, offered Skip's service, saying, 'When it's moved, we'll plant the seed, but first we should find the best place to put it.' He glanced towards the open front door. Were it outdoors, the seed would benefit from sunlight and showers.

'This is *so* exciting!' Peace exclaimed, and Sherbrook thought it took little to please her.

Before the cottage was a wide area of grass, different in appearance to the grass of meadow or field. Here, grass was blue-green in colour and it grew with immaculate evenness; its soft texture was an invitation to frolic.

Unable to resist temptation, Sherbrook was down on all paws nibbling, when, Skip questioned, 'Is this artificial, do you think?'

Sherbrook, chewing, made a short, mumbled query, 'Mm?'

Skip told him, 'I believe that grass you're sampling is artificial. Tall Ones are natural kadoodlers. I've learned they prefer pretence to any thing real.' He added, 'I'd be careful, because you never know with them. You might be poisoned.'

Sherbrook was up on two legs and spitting. Flecks of green shot from his mouth. He uttered an enormous, guttural, *'Aghhh!'* He waved his paws about! Everything Skip said was true, but was too late in the telling! Tall Ones were ever cunning!

'No, its all right … I think,' Skip said. Bending low and tearing away stalks, he held them before his nose, sniffing them. He popped grass into his mouth, and chewed, savouring the flavour, which was quite entrancing to the pallet. He assured Sherbrook, 'Mm, no … my mistake. Sorry to mislead you Sherbrook. It's fine.'

Sherbrook gave Skip a sour look. Skip did not know it all, not when he could be wrong about grass.

Piedmont was out on the front porch watching them. Sherbrook called, 'How about right here in the middle of the big green area?' He stamped, showing where he meant. Before the bard could respond, he called, 'Perhaps you should try the grass here, Piedmont. It's tasty and it's *not* new greens. *I* know the difference.'

Piedmont called, 'Thank you, Sherbrook. But no thanks. By the way, I think your choice of location for the tree is ideal.' He said, 'Clever's gone to the kitchen. Peace is showing him the tomb.'

Piedmont liked the sound of the word, kitchen. He pronounced it several times over in his mind, or so he believed. But then he realized that all along he'd experimented by saying it aloud. He said it in various ways. *'Kitch…en,'* he said, and then, 'Kit...*chen.'* There was enjoyment in it, he decided.

Skip was calling, this time instructing Sherbrook, 'Stand back and I'll move it.'

Sherbrook, shouting to none other than Piedmont, ordered, 'Look the other way oldster!'

Certain then, that the bard would not be dazzled, Skip moved the pail, bringing it out from the cottage parlour. Sherbrook, bending to task, prepared to remove the mass of dried twigs from the wooden container. He commented, 'Uncommon colour isn't it? Can't say I've ever seen its like.' As he went to grasp the tree by its thin trunk, Skip stopped him, commanding, 'No, no, Sherbrook. Stand back from it!' Skip focused, taking aim. The remains of the tree then began glowing blue-white. It rose from the grass but it was stuck fast inside the pail and so the pail also ascended. When it was not very high, hovering above the grass, Skip nodded, and the tree responded by rapid shaking. Loosed from the pail then, it hovered, suspended still, as the pail dropped back to rest in an upright position upon the lawn. Seeing the roots of the tree held much clinging soil, Skip gave the tree a second shake, compelling dusty clods to loosen and fall back into the wooden vessel.

Seeing it dealt with, Sherbrook dusted his paws together as if declaring, 'There now, job well done!' as if the accomplishment was his alone. Smiling, Skip decided he was getting used to Sherbrook's way, and he didn't mind so much.

The tree hovered and Skip asked, 'Where should we put it?' After a moment of searching about, Sherbrook suggested, 'Why not move it up there to yon' smoke-tower.' That seemed to him, a fine idea. Skip thought it another example of Sherbrook's attempting to amuse himself, but then decided, Why not? He "moved" the gazuzzled mass so it perched atop the brick chimney of the cottage. It was an eccentric nest, he imagined, belonging to a bird favouring a most exotic building material. Sherbrook said, 'Now that's done with, where's the fixer?' He well knew the whereabouts of Fixer. Piedmont had informed him that Peace and Clever were occupied with inspecting those gruesome ones in the cottage kitchen. Receiving no response from Skip, Sherbrook noticed Piedmont, and putting paw to mouth, and speaking in lowered voice, said, 'Look at the oldster. He's discovered a play device!' Chortling, he said, 'Don't embarrass him, but doesn't he look a treat? It's cause for hilarity!' Skip could not agree more, seeing the aged Piedmont there on the veranda, moving back and forth for all he was worth in the rickety rocking chair.

'I'd like to try that sometime.'

Skip said, 'I'm going to get Clever Fixer.' Intent upon watching Piedmont, Sherbrook did not hear him.

The kitchen was small, but seeing an unoccupied corner of the room, Skip lit out. Moving was by now his preferred mode of getting about. He was somewhat surprised when, arriving in the kitchen, a startled Peace admonished, 'I do wish you'd stop doing that!' She asked, 'Where have you been? Where've you come from?'

Learning that he'd come from out front of the cottage, she told him, 'Well, it's very lazy of you. If you're not careful to exercise those legs of yours, then, you're going to regret it.'

'Why?'

'Because, they'll atrophy,' she said, 'Folk have legs for good reason. Without flibberty hopping, you'll soon know what I mean and you'll be sorry. Mark my words.'

Clever Fixer did not agree. If he could move, he would not hesitate to do so. Clever and Skip smiled, one to other, not minding that she saw them.

She said, 'Oh, you two... *I* don't know!' In Clever's waistcoat pocket, the seed jabbered non-stop, but none paid it mind. It prattled, 'Glorious home—home at last! Home—what joy! Oh, day of bliss!'

Earlier, when the covering was removed from the great box-like affair, the fixer was overwhelmed and could not so much as comment. He'd stared dumbfounded, up into the ice-covered faces and they'd stared back as if meeting his gaze. Awed, he had determined, 'She must be Lilith! Lilith Thiery!' Looking then to the buck, he'd exclaimed, 'He must be none other than great Terrence! Oh, deeks—I can't believe it! It's *Terrence Thiery!*' Ever willing to offer the truth of matters, the seed disagreed, saying, 'No, Clever Fixer, you are mistaken. He is Mydor, brother to Lilith.'

But so involved was he, with deciding all of it for himself, Clever had not heard. When the initial excitement passed, he'd spoken in a subdued tone, declaring, 'Poor Terrence, he seems the worse for wear. Such grey pallor is not at all indicative of good health.' His voice had trailed off, and then, after moments of thoughtful silence passed, he'd spoken again, enquiring, 'Might it be a good idea, do you think, to release him from there? Perhaps in freeing him, we might discover what ails him?'

Not believing her ears, Peace told him, 'Clever—that's the maddest thing I've heard in ages!' Wanting no more of his suggestions, she'd said, 'Leave them as they are. This was their home but henceforth they shall not intrude!'

She ordered, 'Skip? Lend a paw and please cover them!' And she went from the room. And so, acting against advice given, Skip attended to the task by employing the labour saving method. He "moved" the coverlet, thus hiding the Tall Ones from view. He then told Clever, 'We're ready out front. The pail's prepared for planting, so lead on Fixer.'

Going to the front of the cottage, Clever said, 'I'm not sure I under-stand Peace Darkling. She's distressed by a mere suggestion.'

Skip told him, 'Oh, she's all right. She can be annoying and terse but she means well and really, she's caring to a fault.'

Once outside, and passing by Piedmont, rocking back and forth, Clever laughed outright. He exclaimed, 'Ho! Bard! I declare—you've got rhythm!'

PLANTING OUT

Planting out was the most solemn of occasions for Clever Fixer. Realizing he'd never again hear the seed speak, that he was losing a dear and long-time friend, he brushed paw to cheek, wiping away a tear. He was, as individuals went, tough-minded, or so he told himself. As such, he must not break down, but still he felt he might.

He took the wondrous seed from his pocket and held it high, displaying it as if to say, 'Look, see! If any doubt my sincerity, witness my sacrifice for the group! I prepare to bury my best friend—alive!'

He would not grant voice to heartfelt sorrow, but rather announced, 'Friends, I dedicate the seed to the service of Tump! Having declared such, he bent forward and pushed the seed into soil of the wood pail.

With a quick brush of his paw, dirt was swept to cover the seed. He tamped it down, compressing it into place. Peace came forward then, carrying a small jug, and taking care not to flood it, she moistened the seed's new home.

Going into darkness, the seed had cried, 'Farewell Clever Fixer—friend! My tree *will* know you!' And then, the tiny voice was stilled.

The seed of Great Grandfather's tree—His map—now planted in the wooden pail, would lie deep hidden as if sleeping, until, moistened by rain of the realm, and too, by water from the garden tap. In accordance with the nature of Great Grandfather's will, it would soften and open, and after much effort of pushing forth, a small shoot would emerge into light. It would take much time for the shoot to become a tree, and even then, if compared with other trees, it would by no means appear enormous. It would be rather small, but despite its unremarkable size it would prove most special.

For day in and day out, the five, knowing they were Tump, sat in a circle on the softest blue-green grass surrounding the pail sounding, 'MMEERAH! MMEERAH! MMEERAH!' Joyous voices lifted to the sky where no cloud lofted, yet abundant rain fell and where as well, sun shone, though no great orb was present. Light came golden and good, as light from Great Grandfather Himself.

***

'How are you this morning, my treasure? It's a fine morning again, but then isn't it always? There's no place here for nasty weather. We should be grateful for it and of course, we are, aren't we? We are content, as appreciative, as can be.'

Each day, Peace spoke to the tree. The tree knew it was she who tended it. It understood and appreciated every kind sentiment expressed. Such was her belief; despite others having ideas of their own.

Clever Fixer called, enquiring, 'How's our friend today?' He asked, 'Imparted anything of interest or is it stubborn and mute as ever? It's a poor substitute for the seed. That's what I say!' And then he took himself off, back toward the cottage.

She had not deigned answer, but rather, addressing the tree, assured, 'We mustn't mind him, he doesn't know you—not as I do.' He'd not gotten far, and overhearing her, Clever Fixer turned as he went, telling her, 'Fret not, it's just my little joke!' This was true enough; he often passed such comment. And, just as often, Peace bolstered the tree by informing it of its worth.

To Bunty, she said, 'Now fetch me the little trowel will you? It's over there by the veranda. This soil is compacted. We must loosen it.' But then, before the ever-willing Bunty could scamper off, she said, 'Oh, look Bunty. Here's one I've not noticed before. What do you think it can be?' Not waiting for a response from him, she exclaimed, 'Why! It's the old Radiola. That's what it is!'

Bunty had never before seen its like; not so much as heard the word "Radiola", and so he'd no idea of what was meant. But now, peering at the leaf, they studied it together, and sensing the interest shown by them, the tiny leaf commenced blinking, displaying soft flashes of pale yellow light.

Putting an ear closer to the leaf, Bunty believed he heard sound emanating from it. Every leaf bore a picture, but not all images were accompanied by sound. He said, 'It's a *dancing* tune. It's very, very soft!'

Peace informed, 'It's *White Winter's Song*. Yes, that's what it is.' She said, 'I confess, I never thought I'd hear that tune again.' She listened for a moment longer, and then repeated her request, insisting, 'All right then, hop to it now Bunty, and fetch me the trowel.' She thought to add, 'You're a wonderful helper and I don't know what I'd do without you.' Pleased, he made off to do her bidding.

The foliage was dense-growing and profuse. Before this they'd not seen so many leaves upon a tree of its size. Sherbrook had good cause to comment, 'When it's matured, it will have a zillion leaves to it, a zillion at least.' He said, 'It's a harmless thing. It has no thorn.' Borne upon each tiny leaf was an image, and each of those images differed from the rest; like snowflakes, no two were the same. Sharp-detailed, the images were realistic moving pictures of every conceivable thing, and much of that depicted was beyond fathoming. Whenever an image was observed or focused upon, the tree, aware of receiving attention, of leaves coming under scrutiny, set those leaves to blinking and flashing in acknowledgement.

Sometimes when a leaf was observed flashing, other leaves at different places in the tree responded by joining in the blinking. In their giving off light it was as if communication was carried on between them, and Peace, who spent much of her time in tending the tree, knew she detected proof of sensible connection. An order was apparent in the communication between the leaves, but although deducing that much, she was unable to comprehend further meaning.

Sherbrook and Clever Fixer were in the parlour. Fixer asked, 'Just what exactly do you imagine he meant by it? Because, in responding to obvious curiosity, all I said was, "Oh, you know—we've been around and about, seeing to our business. We've been very busy tending to this that and the other." I was very vague and noncommittal.'

Clever spoke concerning his recent meeting with Leader Crenshaw. Sherbrook did not venture an opinion as to what the leader may have intended in making enquiry of the fixer, but he thought Clever made too much of the leader's apparent interest in them. Continuing, Fixer related, 'He—Crenshaw—next said, "You're quiet folk aren't you? Only on rare occasion do I see you out and about.' Fixer said, 'Being quizzed, I was given the feeling that we're suspected of something or other.' He said, 'Nefarious activity, or at the least, the untoward.'

He was silent then, as was Sherbrook. Until a rueful Fixer said, 'If I'd not put my foot to the barrow when I did, then he wouldn't have noticed me at all. He might have said nothing.'

It was ages ago, that Clever Fixer's barrow was left outside the warren entranceway. So much time had passed that by now, the barrow, once viewed as a friend, was abandoned to rust. Tipsy was become forlorn looking, and in admitting the truth of her condition, Clever did not feel too much obligation to either remorse or shame. As he saw the matter, the tipsy-barrow's usefulness was over. She had been a good thing in her day, but ease of moving had determined her as obsolete. After his going outside earlier this frosty morning, to stand there upon the hillside next to her, he'd wondered whether or not he should ask Skip to bring her into the realm of the cottage, meadow and stream, where she might serve as a reminder of days spent in wandering, and then for no good reason at all, he'd raised a foot and rested it against her side.

Days past were past; they were no more, and so deciding in favour of the least sentimental course, and already having a foot to her, Clever delivered Tipsy a slight push, the tiniest shove. He'd not meant to send her racing off downhill and he was surprised to see such slight encouragement had the effect it did. It was, he imagined, as if sensing the truth of his new feeling toward her, and determining it amounted to betrayal, she too, would show him his company was not appreciated, but scorned.

As the cantankerous barrow heltered downhill, a dreadful racket resulted. Each spin of the bounding wheel produced an agonized, ear piercing, clanging-squealing, forcing a fickle Fixer to more disown her.

Her behaviour caused him to grit his teeth. She performed a final flying leap from atop a large rounded boulder, to go hurtling through space, to land then right side up, before the main entranceway of Ground Spring Warren. And then, Leader Crenshaw, at the very instant of her halting progress, just happened to step outside to take the crisp morning air.

Of course, as Warren Leader, seeing to matters pertaining to safety was one of Crenshaw's chief responsibilities, and Crenshaw was not known to shirk. Following a brief, startling moment, he recognized the rusted barrow for what it was, and calling up the hill, admonished, 'I *say* Fixer—friend! *Do* take care!'

Clever called back, 'Sorry—accident!'

It was then Crenshaw said, 'I haven't seen you folk about for *such* a long time. You're an uncommon, quiet lot. What have you been up to?'

In off-paw manner, Clever replied, giving what he decided was an acceptable enough response, 'Oh, we've been about the place, busying ourselves with sundry matters. A bit of this and that.' Moving to the weather as safe topic, agreement was sought, by enquiring, 'A little severe this morning, isn't it, Leader? Too nippy for my liking!' And that receiving no response, Clever took as a sign of all not being as well as might be.

Informed by Fixer's dilemma, Sherbrook told him, 'I wouldn't worry over it, the leader has many things to occupy him and he won't be too concerned with us. Not seeing so much of us of late can be put down to it being so deeks-awful frigid outside—as you brought to his attention. What you said is true. We're sticking to ourselves and that's all there is to it. There's nothing wrong with respecting the privacy of others, is there?

'When the weather's warmer we'll pay them a visit, and any ruffled feelings can be smoothed.' Then an idea occurred to Sherbrook and he said, 'Or we could have Skip move Crenshaw a gift, a big bunch of prime carrots from a Tall One planting place.' He said, 'Imagine it. Think of the amazing things we can do. I don't believe we've begun to scratch even the surface, so far as possibilities are concerned.'

Then he said, 'Carrots would be a fine thing to give someone like Crenshaw. There's nothing of the sort around here. He's never even seen a carrot. He'd be beside himself!' Slapping his paws against his knees, Sherbrook laughed.

Despite his making light of things, Clever Fixer was not so sure that Sherbrook was right, not at all, because Sherbrook was not present this morning and did not see Crenshaw's seriousness.

By avoiding Ground Spring's leader for so long, they'd given cause for upset. It was a matter of the degree of offence taken, not whether or not it *was* taken. Most of their time these days was spent here in the small realm, and who, knowing of existence of such place, would blame them? Only a fool would choose staying out there, atop a bleak, craggy hilltop, or in a warren, over so extraordinary a place as this.

Any problem with Crenshaw, or other residents of Ground Spring would be solved in a most unexpected way however. Carrots, regardless of quality or rarity, as perceived by a recipient, would play no part in avoiding the difficulty. Nothing by way of escalating the difficulty would come their way, because of an idea from Clever Fixer.

He and Sherbrook lolled back, enjoying the luxurious comfort provided by the settee in the parlour. The bard most preferred the rickety rocking chair out on the veranda, and he was welcome to it. Sherbrook predicted a day would come though, when Piedmont would be let down by the rocker, because it was ancient and loose-jointed. It did not appear safe, but Piedmont was not dissuaded by the opinion of others. He loved the thing with a passion. He liked the way it moved, from cottage wall to veranda edge in small increments, with him on board, rocking back and forth. It wandered, as he saw it. He claimed it was the best thing ever for soothing frazzled nerves, not that his were fraught these days. Since coming here to such peaceful surrounds, inner calm was his, but all the same the effect the rocker produced was most surprising. It was a very satisfactory Tall One invention, the calming effect of which was exceeded only by consistent practice of Mmeerah. After each time of it carrying him to the veranda edge, they heard him dismount, as it were. Then would come rough sound as the chair was slid back to its original position, Piedmont's starting place, and then the process was begun over again. Listening to it could be annoying, but out of consideration for the oldster's feelings, they tried not to hear it.

Clever offered, 'Perhaps it might not be a bad idea were we to have young Skip fill the back door of the warren. Sherbrook, giving a curious glance, then mulling the idea over, thought, Why not? On the rare occasion of them traversing from warren to realm, they were moved by Skip. The only one not brought in by such means, was Bunty.

He said, 'Yes. It's not a bad idea at all, but then there's the small matter of Bunty.' Liking the sound of Bunty's being described as "small matter", he was unable to resist the urge to snicker. He was in fine form today; little jokes however lame, pleased him. They slipped from him without effort, one after other.

Clever, granting Bunty even less consideration, said, 'If the warren's exit, which leads into the great chamber, was filled, then none would ever succeed in finding anything to be suspicious over.

'They can go through our warren from topside, as they please, but they'll never figure where we are, or guess at what we might be doing. With the lower-most exit filled, they can assume we've gone off rambling, or some such.' It made perfect sense.

But, Sherbrook persisted, 'What of Bunty? You know how he is. He'll never permit Skip moving him. He believes it's unnatural and dangerous.'

'Humph!' muttered Clever, and crossed his feet where they rested on the low table in front of them. He was not tolerant of backward thinking. One of diminutive size ought not hold such strong opinion, not on anything, and least of all where matters affected others.

He said, 'Maybe he doesn't need to be told, not at first. Doubtless, *after* the burrow is filled and blocked, he will see the sense of it, and may *ask* to be moved.

Seeing the fixer's annoyance, which was understandable, but knowing that he knew Bunty far better, Sherbrook said, 'But he won't go for it. I know him by now, and he's a twerp—yes—but he's a very stubborn one.' He thought, There's just one other I know of, who could be described as being so stubborn, and he would not mention it, but the individual in question was Clever Fixer.

Clever suggested, 'We could always unblock the ancient, main tunnel again—the one leading down from Ground Spring.' Bunty was the only one, according to Skip, who had ever used it.

But then, speaking in unison, 'No!' That idea was thick! It failed to offer any solution, and their situation could be made worse.

Sherbrook said, 'If we're patient, there'll be no problem.'

'How so?' Fixer enquired.

'He's growing or haven't you noticed? If he gets much bigger, he'll no longer fit through the hole, and then he'll have no choice.' He said, 'Just by the by, I should not have called him a twerp. He is somewhat challenged, it's true, but he's no twerp. He's too easy to pick on and I was taking unfair advantage.'

'Don't feel too bad.' Clever told him, 'There are times when I have far worse names for him. I overheard him the other day, telling the bard, "Skip is my friend, but he's different, which must be awful for him."' Clever Fixer shook his head, declaring, 'He's young Skip's friend, and yet he's decided the boy's unnatural.' Fixer paused before continuing, 'I know his feeling—I *do*—because, I too believed Skip weird at first, but then, after experiencing moving, I was converted in a trice. We must accept the new, but Bunty believes that if a thing is new, then there must be something wrong with it. Such thinking is flawed.'

Putting away ideas of filling and blocking burrows, and Bunty too, Sherbrook commented, 'I still wonder, as to the purpose of yon', great smooth plank. The wall...'

He'd pondered over its purpose before this. They both had, but having no answer to the mystery of it, in moments of idleness, Sherbrook returned to question the thing's nature and purpose. Not knowing nagged at him, as they spent so much time in its company.

It all but covered an entire wall, the one opposite to where they sat. It was glassy-smooth—so smooth that in brushing paws over its expansive surface a body gained a curious, pleasurable sensation. Its colour was darkest grey and it lacked transparency but apart from those differences, it was of material very similar to that of the tomb in the kitchen.

Skip had been out in the barn. He'd wondered about the pickup truck, and wished his elder had given him more information regarding its like, or wished he'd thought to ask more about Tall One vehicles when he'd the chance. He'd stared at it, knowing that his feeling transcended mere curiosity. Resting in the barn it went to waste, and he'd wondered whether it made sense for an individual, such as he, to hope that one day he might drive about in it.

He would never admit to his interest in it, not to the others, but he'd spent ages sitting behind the wheel, allowing every type of imagining. Disappointed in knowing he'd never figure the working of it, he decided upon returning to the cottage.

After entering by way of the back door, he'd lingered in the small rear hallway leading through the centre of the cottage to the parlour. Sherbrook and Fixer were in there lolling about and doing nothing of much use, and Skip overheard, amongst other topics discussed, Bunty's name receive mention. Neither of them went out of their way to speak well of him.

Rather than continue on to the parlour, Skip had gone to the kitchen. So much time had passed that by now they were used to thinking of the small realm as home. Only on rare occasion did they think to visit the warren. The realm provided their every need and more, but they were bored.

Enough time had passed by now to mean Nancy was born. By now she was growing up.

Nothing of inspiration could be gained in overhearing Fixer and Sherbrook's conversation, but all was not so negative. Many positive developments had occurred. The tree thrived. Peace was right to be proud of her achievement in nurturing it. They'd practised Mmeerah together each and every day without fail, and none had complained, but rather they'd welcomed the opportunity to engage in long sessions. Energy-raising Mmeerah was fundamental to group spirit, and knowing it so, Skip wished Bunty were more of a joiner. Although Bunty was not Tump, and had no expectation of being so, Mmeerah would benefit him, but Bunty would have none of it.

He'd say, 'I don't mind helping out. I prepare very nice meals for you all. Don't I? Whilst you're all very busy, making strangeness, I see to the ordinary things. Those are the things I enjoy doing and they're of equal importance.' Maybe he was right but, whether correct or not, he was a good friend to them, and Skip knew, if Clever and Sherbrook told it more as it was, then Bunty was far from being a problem.

Peace respected and appreciated Bunty. She could not have tended the tree without assistance from him. When they partook of fine lunchtime treats, consisting of fruit and veg' taken from the rejuvenated planting place, and presented to them by Bunty; Fixer and Sherbrook had never complained; in fact they ate more than the rest of them put together.

If true "Oneness", were the goal, complaining over foibles of others must cease.

At the back of a drawer in a kitchen cupboard, Skip had, ages ago found several unopened packets of seed. He'd spent time with Lillian in her planting place, and although she'd grown flowers and not real edibles, much was learned from her. When reminiscing over his days at Brickfield, he was surprised by Bunty's showing interest in all that he'd imparted. He'd listened, and then when Skip had as good as forgotten those discussions, Bunty came to him, asking, "Come over there to yon' fruit trees, Skip, and I will show you *my* planting place!"

In showing off the small garden he had every right to be pleased with himself, for despite its insignificant size it produced fine food, and since then all had benefited.

Whilst neither Sherbrook nor Clever were by nature malicious, boredom was a poor excuse for any criticism of Bunty.

For umpteenth time, the sight of mystery cables drew Skip's attention. Those cables resembled nothing more than great veins, as they protruded out from one hanging edge of the floral bedspread, which served as a covering for the Tall Ones. They led out from a side of the tomb, to then pass through a rough-cut hole in the kitchen floor. He would never understand their purpose. He returned to thoughts of Sherbrook and the fixer. He wished they'd not go chasing through Tall One's apparel. Their habit was to rummage through the bedroom closet as if they owned it. They had no idea of how ridiculous they were, wearing those dazzling, bright coloured shirts with great blooms patterning them. None of it fitted them. They were forced to wearing belts and sashes about their waists.

They, believed they presented a bedazzling sartorial treat for the eye, but Skip thought, sensibility of others might be granted consideration. Recalling their elders provided consolation, because in time they would learn to comport themselves with more dignity.

Cloud

DARK LEAVES

At times, during stages of its growth, they believed the tree fully grown, but it continued altering, and the most curious changes were more magically subtle than those physical. Apart from moving images of every imaginable thing, borne upon leaves of multitudinous number, making for intricate detailed gallery of visual information, the tree now seemed cognizant, of those tending it.

It had grown quite lofty, making many leaf-images difficult to see from the ground. Peace, thinking that a ladder would be useful, was glad when one was provided.

'I was "led" to finding it,' she claimed. 'No sooner had I wished for a ladder than there it was! A ladder of the type affixed to the post in the barn would have been useless; I needed a smaller one.'

"Led" to the kitchen, she'd opened a cupboard door to discover the *perfect* ladder. Sensing her need, the tree had directed her to it.

From high atop the ladder, she and Bunty watered the tree, and it was quite marvellous that ribbons of light, issuing from amongst leaves, caressed their cheeks. Bunty enjoyed the comforting sensation of gentlest, feather-light caressing, which was the tree's way of offering them thanks.

Learning of the tree going out of its way to please others, Sherbrook decided he would experience it for himself, and so he climbed to very top of the ladder and waited, but nothing resulted. When tired of perching above ground, he descended to then stand beneath the tree for absolute ages, and still, not one new or unusual thing happened. He decided the tree did not like him—not to the extent it did Peace and Bunty. He would sit on the edge of the veranda and discuss the matter with Piedmont.

The bard determined the tree would doubtless reject him also; not that he was of any mind to venture surmounting the ladder to find out. As it was, he already knew it would not favour him. He thought Sherbrook was lucky, because the tree's flattering behaviour towards Peace and the youngster, Bunty, might hide something of trickiness.

'Trickiness? What do you mean?' Sherbrook asked.

'Oh nothing,' Piedmont said, before adding, 'I entertain suspicion, that's all.'

Sherbrook heard this as an evasive response.

Then the bard asked, 'There's no such thing, is there as "something for nothing"?'

'No, I don't suppose there is.' Sherbrook thought for a moment, 'You know, you're right, because it's true—there isn't.' He asked, 'But what of trickiness? What are you suggesting? I mean, it's just a tree.'

Piedmont said, 'It's not *just* anything.' He chortled, but his expression was serious.

Sherbrook protested, 'Don't misunderstand me, I know it's uncommon, but even so it's a tree, and however unusual, it can't cause harm, can it?'

This was rhetorical, but Piedmont asked, 'Can you be certain?'

'No. I guess not.' Sherbrook was a little confused. He said, 'I thought we were discussing its habit of granting reward, that's all.' Piedmont, in casting a sinister aspersion had succeeded in turning more or less light conversation upon its head. Now continuing, he said, 'It rewards those who tend it by granting a pleasurable sensation. Correct?' And when Sherbrook nodded agreement, 'What if, for sake of our discussion, it doesn't reward? What if giving anything, by way of fair and equal exchange, is not intended? What if, in assuming the tree is benevolent, we are duped? It might *take* far more than it pretends to give. What then?'

Sherbrook stared off as if to distant horizon. He stared, and then shivered, 'Brrrr!' He said, 'Piedmont, there are times when you are one scary individual! You have the fur at the back of my neck standing to attention.'

'It's just a thought,' Piedmont said, grinning.

'Yes. But it's those, "What ifs?"'

'So we'd best not ask,' Piedmont said. 'Point taken, Sherbrook. I'm bored, and that's all there is to it.' But he could not allow the matter rest. He stopped rocking to and fro to ask, 'It's not just those stroking ribbons of light, is it?' He said, 'Because Peace also claims that in certain of her actions, the tree leads or guides her. And, you may ask—so what? But to my way of thinking, it's cause for some wariness. Peace is not one to indulge imagination. She's strong-minded and sensible, and yet, of late, I do confess she has me concerned. There's the matter of her believing she was led to finding the ladder when, all along it was stored there in the cupboard. I ask you Sherbrook... Do you believe she was led to it? Did the tree, sensing she required a ladder, want Peace to have it? Has it a mind of its own? What do you think?'

'I'd say that it has a mind of its own, but it's a question of what *type* of mind. As you see it, Bard, its a kadoodler of some sort.'

'Yes, a kadoodler.' Piedmont sighed, then said, 'There have been those times when I've caught myself wondering as to the thoughts, or even ideas, it might entertain. It could be a true friend to us, or it might be a threatening presence masquerading as a passive tree. I puzzle over it and wonder how best to see it. Has it a feeling for us, one-way or other? Who can say? I can't but I don't blame myself for fearing possible harm delivered from a calculating presence. Such an entity could prove very difficult to unmask and its influence, once established, even harder to eradicate.'

'Mm.'

Piedmont advised, 'The thing called axe should be kept close to paw. It's out there in the barn, in case you're wondering.'

Unsettled, Sherbrook was becoming depressed. Thinking to change the subject, he knew, that as topics went, the bard's health would not make for an elevated discussion, but it seemed an easy alternative to further morbid chatter regarding the tree, and so he enquired, 'How's the gammy back been of late? I ask, because seeing you getting about the place, I've noticed improvement. You do not appear, if you'll pardon the observation, to hobble quite as much as you did.'

'You're right,' Piedmont said. 'And it's curious, because I *have* been a lot better off.' He said, 'I don't know if its positive result of practising Mmeerah, or if it's the tree. Perhaps, unbeknownst to me, it has seen fit to grant *me* benefit.' He laughed, 'Perhaps with mysterious means, it rewards me for being so often out here in close proximity with its presence? Whatever the cause, when compared with the tired old me, I feel like a young buck again.' Smiling, he said, 'If we're not careful, I'll soon be dancing a jig.' He said, 'It's considerate of you Sherbrook, to have noticed. You're always considerate of others and it's appreciated.'

Sherbrook said nothing, but nodded, respecting the compliment.

Piedmont informed, 'When we spent that night in the hollow log, Skip imparted a message from my elder self—from Tump that is. My elder indicated that at later time I should expect to be very fit, and now the prediction proves true.'

'What *is* she doing now?' Sherbrook asked as he looked out across the lawn. Peace was atop the ladder. She leaned, reaching out with a long stick, having cloth tied to one of its ends. Bunty held the ladder for her, but he was not strong and if Peace slipped, he would not be capable of preventing her falling.

Glancing up, Piedmont said, 'Oh she often does that. She claims it objects to having dusty leaves. As to how Peace knows of its objection is beyond me.' They watched her tending the tree and it seemed as if nothing else mattered to her.

Piedmont observed, 'She must be correct; because you can see the way it sends out ribbons of appreciation. That's what they are. Quite the convincing display of affection, isn't it? Piedmont's expression left no room for doubting the facetious nature of his observation.

Peace was more than surrounded. Ribbons of light wound about, and it was as if, embracing her, the tree was desirous of keeping her for itself. Despite the bard's suspicions, Sherbrook wondered whether they witnessed the tree's way of assuring her safety.

Skip came out from the cottage then, to join them on the veranda, and without preamble, announced, 'Soon the tree will ring, and we must make preparation for meeting Nancy. By now she is old enough, and so I need to study the map.'

Not once had they heard Skip refer to the tree as anything other than the "map". He spoke as if not recognizing it as a tree. To him it was Great Grandfather's map of the All. And now he was saying, 'I need to climb up there to see if I can read it.'

Fixer had been in the parlour and, overhearing Skip, had come out to the veranda. He said, 'You should ask Peace to tell all she knows of it. She knows the tree in intimate detail.'

Skip snapped, 'That *is* my intention,' which was too terse for Fixer's liking, and he shrugged, saying, 'It was just a suggestion.'

Peace directed his attention to several leaves, and going from one to next, she described their images. Following all she said, he missed nothing. He explained, 'I thought I'd move her from the forest clearing—bring her here by that means—but now I'm not so sure. There,' he said, pointing. 'It's Piedmont, and he's flibberty hopping with her all the way to the hill-top, to the very same location from which Brother Eagle took me. And, now look. Piedmont shows her his spyglass.' The map showed everything. It was all there—past, present and future—but he could not make sense of the connections. Lines radiated out from the leaves. They went flashing between images, from point to point. No sooner did he believe he'd caught their meaning, than altering occurred.

Myriad lines changed course, forsaking images favoured earlier, and dashed off to form connections with others, making for an ever-changing enigma.

Skip said, 'I have a sense of it making alteration *because* we study it. We're not able to both study it, and at one and the same time, *not* look at it. But as I say, I sense it's reacting somehow...'

Peace said, 'It shows stories, and depending on the actions taken by a story's participants, and the order of those actions, various outcomes result.' She said, 'But I suspect it shows far more besides.'

'Mm. Even as we watch, various outcomes keep altering, so that I can't keep up with it.'

She said, 'If Simple Rudy reads the map, then it won't be too long now and its ways will be realized. There is no real need for our attempting to fathom it.'

He thought of the elders. 'Yes. Simple reads it without puzzling over it. It's no problem for him.' He said, 'I always *knew* he must be good for something.'

She said, 'You were often at odds with each other, but you were both very young.'

'We were,' Skip conceded, 'but, let's not forget, when we bring Rudy here to us—when he's "moved"—he'll be just an instant older than when he vanished. His leaving us during the creek crossing has already occurred. It's happened, but we haven't yet caused it.' He said, 'We're responsible for it; he would not have disappeared without our moving him.'

'No matter the times I think of it, I can't accustom myself to the idea.' Peace said, 'I can't wait to have proof of it.'

He said, 'But, as to the question of Nancy. The elder Nancy told me that the bard is the one who goes to the hilltop with her. If Piedmont meets her in the clearing, there's good reason for it. And, it's shown here in the map.'

Peace was thoughtful and then said, 'In going about things as the tree shows them, it must work out.'

'But,' he said, 'the map alters, and moving her might be the best way. The thing is, though, I haven't seen any evidence of her coming to us by that means. Nothing of the sort is shown here.'

Studying altering leaf-images, he exclaimed, 'Look, there! There are Piedmont and Nancy, taking the hill path. And now—did you catch it? The bard slips when his stick breaks! And now you see, there he goes tumbling head over heels, all the way to the bottom of the steep slope.'

'Shh! We mustn't let the dear old thing overhear. We mustn't frighten him.'

Glancing to the veranda, Skip assured, 'We're far enough away for him to not hear.' He turned back to the tree and tracing a flashing, pale line with a paw, said, 'There is the cause for that disaster. If he doesn't take his tried-and-true stick with him, then he picks up any old thing from the forest floor and the stick he chooses is too frail. They've gone just part way up the hill when it snaps!'

'It's staggering,' she said.

Hearing that word from her, after seeing images of the bard tumbling, he suspected she joked. But her expression was serious and humour was not intended. Looking back to the map, he said, 'The ribbons of light give comfort. When you first told me of it, I didn't know what you meant. They hold us here, don't they?' He said, 'I wonder if, after we're through study-ing it—and, Sherbrook removes the ladder, would it lower us unharmed to the grass?'

She said, 'I wouldn't risk it.' This was cautious comment from one, who others alleged, was too enamoured with the map. Sherbrook and Piedmont were incorrect, because as devoted to it as Peace was, in nur-turing the tree, she'd lost nothing of common sense.

Looking back over a shoulder, Skip saw Sherbrook holding the ladder steady for them. He seemed as bored as ever. Skip did not know if Sherbrook cared to know anything of their observations or conclusions gleaned from the map, but in case he did, Skip motioned with a paw and, Peace saw what he meant.

With paw to mouth, he indicated that he would not speak. Looking to the place intended, Peace saw the clear image of Sherbrook standing at the edge of the deep pool. He stared out over its surface, looking toward the floating remains of Uncle Bucky, and then the tiny Sherbrook, depicted upon the leaf, swung back from seeing the pond, to argue with Richard. Peace saw they bickery scratched something awful, and push turned to shove.

Sherbrook, realizing he was pushed from behind—not by Richard, but by another—went tumbling from the grassy bank to splash into the pond. Peace, silent and staring, felt compelled to learn of what would come. She witnessed Sherbrook's desperate, vain attempt to scrabble back up onto the bank.

He was not successful, and as many diminutive figures stood back watching, she saw Sherbrook sink beneath water. He came back then to the surface to gasp and gag. She could watch no more and so looked away. But, having traced other lines as well, Skip was again pointing, directing her attention to other leaves, leaves carrying alternate images, and upon one of those she saw Piedmont coming to the top of a grassy rise—a rise, situated not very far distant from the pond. She saw, after going straight to Sherbrook, that the tiny version of Piedmont raised his stick and then used it to prod Sherbrook upon his chest. The one she witnessed doing so, was not at all their bard. He was old and yet sprightlier than their Piedmont.

Leaning very close to Skip's ear, Peace wondered, 'Perhaps these dark leaves should best remain our secret?'

And then, Sherbrook called, 'For deeks sake, Buckaroo! How long do you expect me to stand here holding this thing!' He called, 'Peace! Tell him to *finish with it!*'

Busy Paws

Skip's dream faded fast; much of it slipping away from conscious grasp as if scenes depicted feared close examination. Sunlight shone beneath the window blind, illuminating a rectangular area of the counterpane. The cottage was silent and so the others still slept, or perhaps they were already outside and had decided to allow him to sleep on. As awareness of the new day imposed itself, he reviewed generalities; those few captured parts of his dream.

Having become immortal, Tump deciphered the map; they revelled in travelling at will to explore infinite, altering reality of realms. They were undaunted by notions of paradox. When paradox was perceived as *part* of the All, then a force was exerted. But higher truth dictated that without such consideration granted, restraining influence did not fetter Tump. As an omnipotent entity, glorious freedom was enjoyed. That was until Great Grandfather made His presence known. His presence, at first unrecognized as such, was then revealed as a paw of immense size, a great expanse of furry whiteness resembling a snow covered landscape, which extended on and on forever. And then a voice was heard and the great paw moved. Skip saw long claws raised to meet with a wintry sky. Try as he might, he could not recall with anything approaching exactitude the content of the message conveyed, but even now, reassured by the sunny morning, he shivered, and felt not the least comforted. Great Grandfather's words were lost, but the residual, disturbing influence remained.

The back door of the cottage banged shut and hearing Peace call to him, he knew a feeling of relief.

She called, 'Seer … are you awake?' Her odd, addressing him as "Seer" was cause for wondering if anything was amiss. Since attending the tree's needs her manner had changed. She'd become more serious than ever and now, arriving at the doorway, she glanced into the room and announced, 'Skip, I want you to send me back.'

'Why?' he asked, surprised by the request.

'For, Piedmont's sake. For the scratchings,' she said. 'When the tree rings, then will be much to do. We'll be busy with tasks involving the Radiola and Nancy. In the meantime, retrieval of the scratchings is of great concern. As we speak, Piedmont is, believe it or not, dancing with Bunty to the sound of the wind-clickers. They're all over there. Piedmont seems more youthful than ever I've seen him, but he's worried for so long over the scratchings that I'd like to do something about it, something *nice* for him.'

'The scratchings aren't lost, they're safe,' Skip told her. 'He's dancing, you say?'

'He's beyond the meadow's edge, cavorting like someone half his age,' she said. 'I confess, when first I saw him, I felt something of embarrassment, but then I knew that as few as several days past, he was not capable of such merry behaviour and so then I was pleased for him.' She sighed, 'I saw that he was quite accomplished. You'd have to see it for yourself to appreciate it.' She paused before continuing, 'I got to thinking ... thinking of you sending me back.' She explained, 'I'm nowise afraid of Grammy, nor any of them back there, and if you'll agree to send me, I'll be happy to go. Is not the Bard disadvantaged without the records and scratchings in his possession? He's been miserable for ages and I want to do this for him. It would be wonderful seeing his mind put at ease.'

She asked, 'What do you say?'

He said, 'There must be order to all we do.'

'Yes, Skip, as you insist ... and so often, but this morning after returning from the meadow I made a close study of the tree, and there am I, depicted as plain as day in a grouping of leaves, which show me back there at New Warren Central, doing as I propose. As far as I see it, nothing untoward occurs. There's no harm done and the outcome is fine.'

'I'll come and take a look,' Skip said. He eased himself up onto an elbow, saying, 'When I received instruction from the elders there was no mention of the scratchings.'

Peace said, 'As I understand it, apart from the observance of four important matters, there's nothing preventing us from deciding things for ourselves.'

Turning to go, she said, 'I'll meet you outside then.'

He got up from the bed and then donning his jacket, heard faint murmuring of uncommon sound, the sound of wasps or swarming bees.

Sound of the front door closing was a distraction, but seeming to emanate from above, that other sound was loud.

He left the room and hurried to the front door. Once out on the veranda
he looked skyward, but saw nothing there. Out on the lawn, standing
close to the tree were both Peace, and the fixer. Fixer had returned from
across the meadow and he too looked to the cloudless sky.

Skip hopped from veranda to lawn. He realized that the strange sound
came from not one direction, but all.

Outdoors, away from the confines of the cottage, the high-pitched
droning was even more pronounced and less resembled the sound of
insects. Skip caught Clever's attention.

Clever shrugged. He screwed up his nose in inimitable fashion and
went back to staring overhead. Peace cast Skip a glance, and smiled. From
quadrants above, four different notes emanated, and then those notes
came together, uniting to produce a wondrous, all-permeating harmony.

Still on their way from dancing to the sound of clicking sticks,
Sherbrook, Bunty and Piedmont, paused at the narrow bridge and gazed
upwards. All about them in the meadow, grasses, reeds, wildflowers and
the leaves of shrub and tree moved to melodious resonance. The water
of the stream meandering beneath the bridge, upon which they stood,
shimmered with diamond light.

Chiming sounded—a sound so pure, clear and beautiful, Peace felt
she might melt from within. She might melt away as ice, compelled so by
flawless ringing. Next, more playful sounds issued from overhead. Thin-
whistling breezes conspired to combine as many woven threads, and then
joining those, were the sounds of many sticks tapped against stone. From
the far distant perimeter of the realm, small rain pattering was discerned
and as rain-sound grew louder, those sounds coming more from above went
retreating. As the rain-sound turned to that of torrential deluging it moved
in waves to chase along the perimeter of the realm. Around those waves
went and, despite their pace progressing, the sound of them then faded to
nothing. Yet not wishing to pass to silence, the sound of ringing persisted.

Lowering her gaze, Peace saw that Clever Fixer stood transfixed.
Looking then across the grassy expanse toward the cottage, she beckoned

to Skip. He did not notice her gesturing and so she called to him. He gave no sign of having heard. Calling again, she was startled when all chiming, all ringing, all sound ceased and her crying, 'Skip,' carried through stillness, was a lot louder than necessary.

Startled from reverie, Skip came flibberty hopping, covering the distance separating them, but Peace had little chance to speak, for the quiet stillness was very short lived. Again came chiming and of such volume that this time the air was split by the ground-juddering resonance. Three times came the mighty, realm-claiming chiming. Clever Fixer, knowing better than to remain standing, was quick to set himself down upon the grass.

Following Clever's lead, Peace saw Skip with mouth agape, pointing to the tree. The tree glowed crimson and orange as if it burned from deep within.

It glowed and sparked like wildfire and the sight of it was enough to cause Peace and Clever Fixer too, to hasten from close proximity with it, but Skip, shouting above the now diminishing sound of ringing, assured, 'It's all right! It's not hot! There's no heat from it!'

Clever called, 'Sure, but seeing is believing! I don't trust the look of it!'

Ever the friend of the tree, Peace now scurried from it. Her expression alert and doubting, she went farther back from it, than did Fixer. By now Piedmont, Sherbrook and Bunty, having traversed the remaining distance along the path through the meadow, arrived, but they dared not come closer. They stayed back at the edge of the meadow where it met with the lawn at the front of the cottage.

Then, as if realizing the foolishness of so much activity, and come to its senses, the tree blinked, or that is how Peace interpreted it. Experiencing a change of heart, the tree's mood altered and so, in a trice, a change occurred.

For several moments none spoke.

'Buckaroos—that was awesome!' exclaimed Sherbrook. 'I thought our luck had run out!'

'It was most unnatural!' Bunty exclaimed, and then thought to add, 'It's mad!'

Sherbrook replied, 'What isn't, around here?'

'No. It's natural,' Skip declared. 'It's not so extraordinary.' He shrugged, 'It's *new* to us—that's all. I found the experience exciting and must admit, I can't wait for more of the same!'

He heard Piedmont, who stood at considerable remove, muttering, 'Touched. That's what such comment indicates.'

Before Skip might voice objection, Clever Fixer spoke up, 'I too, confess to being impressed by the event. It's the very thing we've been expecting and for such a long time.' He said, 'As foretold by our elders, the tree informs us of the appropriate time for the child's induction into our group. Friends, the gal Nancy awaits. I will admit the tree has the most kazooning way of expressing itself, but it's what all the fuss was about! It's delivered its message and now it's up to us to attend our task.'

'Nancy must be quite a gal, to warrant such attention,' Peace said. She went close to the tree. They could not have known what ringing involved. Until the event, Peace imagined nothing more than a sound akin to unusual birdsong or the gentle murmuring of a breeze through treetops; sound she would relate to as natural. Fixer and Skip were right though, for who could guess what might be considered as natural behaviour for the tree?

She peered up into lowermost dark foliage and was startled to see numerous images there of a young gal. It seemed that each and every leaf carried its own bright shifting image of Nancy.

There was the gal, as sweet as could be, for she was little more than a babe in arms. There, she was depicted standing at an entrance of the warren. She pouted; her mother had chastised her for some or other trifle. Again, and over again, she played with her young friends upon the green sward bounding the creek in territory claimed by those of New Warren Central. Seeing all of it, Peace began questioning the wisdom of removing her from her environment and friends.

Leaves revealed the youngster romping through tall grass, whilst, unbeknownst to her, a fox peered from a place of concealment. Peace knew relief when the shifting image showed Brother Fox retreating, slinking to deeper cover, just before several young bucks met with Nancy when they emerged from the cover of a nearby thicket.

She saw Nancy encircled by enormous trees. She recited verse in the shade of the forest clearing. Seeing her there, Peace decided their assuming they'd the right to take her as misguided and wrong.

But then Skip declared, 'Peace, your light is dark. What is it?'

She told him, 'I doubt the correctness of our intention. New Warren Central is home to her. She belongs there.'

'We belonged there too, or believed we did,' Skip said, searching the leaves. Moving to another area of the tree, away from that studied by Peace, he said after a moment, 'Come around here. Take a look at this. You may change your mind.' Then, when she stood nearer him, he said, 'Follow the lines, those bright ones leading away from those happy scenes. They lead in many directions and various events occur along their courses, but they reach a point of convergence, which—as I read it—is right here.'

Following his direction, so many small differences occurred along courses taken by those lines.

He was correct. No matter which lines were followed, the outcome proved the same.

That was, apart from one exception. After traversing long paths wherein various events were depicted, all lines ended at a single point, a point where the outcome was shared. Knowing that she recognized the meaning of that shown, Skip offered, 'Good outcome is shown in the leaves over here. It's long after Piedmont leads her from the forest to the top of the hill. And so you see, Nancy *is* Tump.' He said, 'No matter your feeling, there's no other way.'

Peace could not but agree, because when Nancy was not Tump, her fate was terrible beyond anything any would wish. And when Sherbrook came to stand beneath the tree to examine leaves, and announced in no uncertain terms, 'I wouldn't wish that for anyone—not even my worst enemy!' Peace knew it was settled. They would ensure Nancy and Piedmont's meeting in the forest clearing.

Joining them, Clever Fixer looked up into the tree and commented, 'Future events can influence those preceding them... It's all *most* strange!'

'How's that?' Skip asked.

'It's shown right here.' Fixer said, 'Look, you see—everything goes awry. When this particular line is traced back to a certain point from the same dreadful outcome, to way back over here, the Radiola, moved by you, goes missing. It ends up in a bramble patch and is never found, never retrieved by Folk of Fur.

'When the course taken by the line is followed forward, Nancy meets with dreadful gazuzzlement.

'Much farther forward, and nothing is familiar to us at all. Tump forms, but fails to come into true being. It is not as we might expect.

'Most interesting, however, is the way the thin-branching line over here suggests that Nancy, heeding her mother, does that asked of her.

'As simple and small an action as that, followed all the way back across here, shows the Radiola, despite being so well concealed, is discovered. Tump forms, but very differently.

'I take it all as evidence of an event occurring in a possible future, having influence upon the past.

'To me, it's as plain as the nose on your face, or ...' he amended, 'perhaps mine.'

Peering up and seeing another depicted on the leaves of the same peculiar line discovered by Fixer, Piedmont was aghast.

Viewing evidence of his own alternate and ignominious end, he commented as if thinking aloud, 'I must say, I'm happy being a member of the group as we know it.' Tump, as depicted by the alternate line, was seen to include, quite apart from his own demise, against even most outlandish expectation, his arch nemesis Grammy Graymark.

It did not, in the moment of viewing, matter at all, that Skip had provided information regarding a far kinder, more reasonable Brickfield version of her. In the present moment, Piedmont was consumed by the most sincere doubt, in entertaining the possibility of *any* version of Grammy capable of contributing as a member of Tump.

Try though he did, a satisfactory answer to the puzzle of her being granted a wider choice of paths by circumstance, and her accepting better ways, eluded him.

Noting again an alternate outcome suffered by Nancy, Piedmont glanced away. The gal, depicted as torn and dismembered, made him ill. A mere glance and he was overcome by nausea.

Peace, shocked by the gruesome scene, moved back to make further study of other leaves, leaves showing an alternate scene. Piedmont and Nancy were seated together on the large flat stone situated atop the high hill, which provided such a fine vantage point overlooking New Warren Central.

The gal and the bard sat there in the night and, Nancy peered through the Far Seeing Eye.

The scene shown was dark, and after studying it as best she could for several moments, Peace was thoughtful, before enquiring, 'Skip? Have you ever wondered whether or not it might be possible to move light?' She said, 'I don't much enjoy the thought of us expecting the little gal to sit up there atop the hill in such awful darkness.' His expression conveyed curiosity.

The scene Peace studied then altered. The figures standing atop the hill were now bathed in light. Seeing the alteration, Skip said, 'I guess I can. There's your answer, right there.'

LEAPING THE DITCH

They'd gone to the creek to watch the game called Leaping the Ditch. The game entailed not much of what she thought of as real talent. Those participating had to be good at running and jumping and that was pretty much all there was to it. They all ran and jumped didn't they? Those were things Folk of Fur did as a matter of course. But apart from being able to run and jump, something else was required, something less common than those things, and it was essential. An individual had to be courageous, and that was something she respected, because without courage, in Leaping the Ditch, there was the possibility you might not make it across and then gazuzzlement could take you!

Away from the view of anyone farther down-stream, in the more immediate vicinity of New Warren Central, was a place where the creek doglegged, turning so that it wound back on itself before straightening its course. There was a place concealed from sight by a stand of tall river oaks and a tangle of low-growing thorny bushes, reeds and long grass. There, where the red clay banks of the creek rose higher on both sides than at any other point for a long way in either up-stream or down-stream directions, was the ditch. On one side of the creek, the high ground sloped downward and over at the other side, beyond the opposite bank, it sloped away. Brave, foolhardy boys would line up together in the small grassy clearing at the high side of the stream, and then taking turns, they would run as fast as their legs would carry them and, reaching the departure point atop the high cliff, they would leap—launching themselves through space, over the water flowing far below in the abyss—to land atop the cliff on the other side.

Each time anyone leapt the ditch, congratulatory cries would go up from those awaiting their turns, and from the gals, who would sit together in a group, at a place distant enough from that where the grass was worn thin by running feet.

Spectators did not watch from the opposite bank, but the last to leap waited there to lend a rescuing paw to the one following him across. No rule dictated they do so, but rather, it was the time-honoured way.

There were those times when an unfortunate almost failed in making the distance. They'd clutch at the cliff-top, hind-paws dangling above the terrifying depth below. Cries of helpful encouragement were then offered from every quarter. Despite the prevailing healthy spirit of contest, none of those watching wished to see worse disaster befall a fellow competitor.

Two boys first thought of the game, and they were Dennis Redsky, who was born during a dust storm, and his close friend, Livingstone. The Hoppers adopted Livingstone after his natural parents vanished one winter's night never to be seen or heard of again; search parties went out, but no trace was found. Mister and Missus Hopper said that if the others, for their part, didn't object to making a small, helpful contribution to his upkeep, they would not mind taking Livingstone in. Anything coming their way, Missus Hopper said, from the Tall Ones' planting place, would always be welcome. And so at first, being impressed by the Hoppers showing such generosity in taking in an orphan of such tender age, neighbours would drop by, giving as agreed. But that was at first, and it had not seemed long at all before occasion of dropping by occurred less often; any offering was then scant.

The Hoppers had become dependent upon donations and when gifts of assistance diminished, they found reason for bitter complaint. After taking in a foundling, they were more or less abandoned by all and sundry. They complained that they too, felt a little like orphans. Others had not helped—not to the extent promised. Witness to such complaint, young Livingstone tended to spend more and more time away from the home. His time was spent in the company of friend, Dennis.

When Dennis and Livingstone first began leaping the ditch, it was pretty much a private affair, just something they did to pass time, but before long, others had noticed them and so, they'd to wait in line—to queue in taking turns at their own game! They had even thought of naming it *Leaping the Ditch*. All of it was their idea. The name was nothing other than a simple description, but it had a good ring to it.

The area from which runners set out was not large enough to allow for more than one individual to leap at a time, and so, waiting made good sense. Forced to share, Dennis and Livingstone had accepted others joining them. But when bigger boys than they, some of them old enough to be thought of as young bucks and not youngsters at all, insisted upon joining the game, the game's originators complained, insisting that definite rules should be set in place. The interlopers would have none of it, and Dennis Redsky, Livingston, and others were made the brunt of bullying behaviour. Even most vociferous protesting was useless; push had come to shove and disaster must eventuate.

Matters had reached their worst, when wondrous intervention occurred. The diminutive Zechariah Small Paws showed up. He later said he'd been taking a solitary stroll and happened upon them at their game. He'd decided Leaping the Ditch a deeks-pathetic exercise, in which someone was bound for gazuzzling damage. He had not intended joining the queue.

Coming behind him, another boy asked, 'Will you move forward? You'll miss your turn. If you don't move, some lout will push in.'

Zechariah said, 'No, thanks. I'm a spectator. I'm working out what's wrong with this.'

The boy shrugged, 'Would you step out of the way then, because I don't want to miss my turn.'

'Oh, sure,' Zechariah said, and took himself over to one side of the small clearing to observe from that vantage point. He was not long there, when predicted outcome was realized. Having leapt as well as he was able, a small boy did not make the distance and vanished from sight as he went plummeting down into the deep chasm. Zechariah had seated himself on a patch of soft grass, but then was on his feet again and hurrying across the clearing. Squeezing between bodies, most of them much larger than his, he pushed to the very edge of the precipice to peer over.

The creek was swift-flowing at the lowest reach of the chasm and was bounded by the narrowest strip of boggy wet ground. There were many rocks, but there was a small area of low growing reeds and that was where the small boy lay. So still and unmoving was he, that gazuzzlement must have taken him.

Gawking from above, they were compelled to awed silence, and then was soft uttered, nervous murmuring. With his passing concluded … then, the boy moaned and opened his eyes. He blinked several times before returning their gaze, and next, grinned up at them. There arose an enormous sigh of relief. They saw him get to his feet, brush himself off and then do something, which, Zechariah decided, most impressive. He raised both paws high and then performed a gracious bow. Raucous cheering arose from the crowd. Along with cheers, were cries of, 'Good one, Bernie! That was your best!' and, 'Drag yourself back up here, Bernie. You can have my turn—free! They don't call you *Suicide Bernie* for nothing!' Zechariah did not lack a sense of humour. He liked a good joke, but none of this was funny at all.

The game had continued but he no longer bothered following it. He was occupied in thinking, long and hard.

Bright and early the next day, before the others arrived at the cliffs, he was there. He'd brought along a length of rope, an item that would be put to good use. He'd carried it coiled across a shoulder. By the time he arrived at the clearing by the creek, he wondered at the rope's weightiness. When he'd set out, it was not so heavy, and he'd not thought that carrying it would be enough to tire him. He hoped, Uncle Samson would not guess he'd taken it, because it had pride of place atop his list of favourite things. Samson collected things, but most of the stuff he kept was pretty useless, and not in Zechariah's opinion, worth much. If called upon to explain his action, he was sure that his uncle would not mind. If the rope ever assisted in saving a life, then that would make it *useful* and not just another item of clutter filling the trove burrow.

There was an underlying reason for Samson's so prizing the rope, and it had not much to do with the rope as such. Previous to his possessing it, it was used by Tall Ones in ensuring the enslavement of the beast known by Folk as, Titus. Terrible Titus!

Samson was fond of relating the story.

One balmy evening he was over in the Tall Ones' territory, at their planting place. He was involved in carrying out inspection of a new crop of lettuce, but after taking samples and testing them, he determined the plants too immature for real harvesting. He would return home, he decided, by going around back of the building the Tall Ones called the barn. That route would necessitate his going in close proximity with Titus; there was no danger, though, because a length of strong rope tethered the monstrosity. An end of the rope was secured to a sturdy pole, and the other was tied about its throat. By that merciless means escape was made impossible.

He was in for a surprise, because arriving at a rear corner of the building, he paused there to peer around it and lo and behold there was not the slightest sign of Titus. Curiosity was aroused and then suspicion stirred, and he took the time to triple check. It was true then, the demented unfortunate was not there.

He recalled that earlier, whilst inspecting the crop, there was a complete absence of mad howling ... there'd been none of the usual, indulgent carry-on. His next discovery was sobering indeed, for not far distant from the creature's territory there was a heaped hillock of fresh-worked soil, and realization dawned. There rested the beast.

Why, he found himself questioning, had the Tall Ones disposed of the deceased in a manner customary to Folk of Fur? Folk, seeing to such arrangement made perfect sense, the great part of their lives was spent underground, but for a surface-dwelling monster such as this, burial did not seem appropriate. How was it, Titus was considered deserving of interment? The ways of Tall Ones eluded him and he wondered if they were quite clear as to the type of creature their slave was? Perhaps uncertainty existed, but he knew they were far cleverer than that and so, that was not it.

One thing was clear enough. Beneath so much good weighty soil, Titus would prove troublesome no more.

Samson then chanced upon the rope where it was left coiled and lying in the grass. Delighted by the find, he let fly an exultant whoop of pleasure before taking it as his. It was an uncommon, fine new addition to an already burgeoning collection of treasures.

Making it back to his burrows was not made easy by having to contend with powerful odour. Miasma emanated from the rope's every fibre, and in relating details of his ordeal, Samson complained that at very many points along the way, he believed he must lie down and allow his demise— so malignant was the stench of it. He wondered how the beast had lived with himself. When it came to matters of self-grooming, the unfortunate had lacked personal pride. Reaching home territory, he knew he must find an abandoned burrow in which to store it. He could only trust that in the fullness of time, the smell would leave, or at least diminish, because as it was, there was no way he could show the thing off to friends.

Apart from the rope, Zechariah had put together a collection of small sheets of bark and a sharp stick. He'd more difficulty than expected, in stripping away bark from trees; it was not easy, obtaining sheets of uniform enough size. He liked to have things matching, and so had persevered until all was presentable. The trouble he'd put himself to would seem as no trouble at all, when he saw appreciative expressions on faces of those who played at Leaping the Ditch. They'd appreciate all he'd done, because they so very much needed organizing. He had decided to save their day.

His plans did not meet with immediate, universal acceptance, not as he'd hoped. Negotiating was pleasant enough at first, but then just three of the youngest boys were present. It was when others joined them that trouble began. Arriving with several gals, a group of older boys were soon causing grave concern, and Zechariah questioned the wisdom of ever doing favours for others. He was treated to abuse in such large measure, that he determined none worth saving.

But for innate, hitherto underutilized talent as a manipulator, he'd have received an absolute thrashing; still, he was humiliated enough without things degenerating so far. There was a point where he considered providing distraction, perhaps even forcing the enemy to sympathy by encouraging himself to vomit, but first, another course was tested. At the top of his lungs, he cried, 'Put me down kadoodler—you carry on as if your *buck-hood* is threatened!'

Those few simple words, delivered as they were, had meant freedom and much more besides. Gals, whom to that point displayed nothing of empathy, but rather nervous disdain, now laughed! They were fit to bust! And hearing so much laughter, the largest of louts, holding Zechariah aloft, enjoyed far less the way others perceived him. The torment of Zechariah was abandoned and he was dropped facedown in dirt.

The leader dusted his paws one against the other, as if ridding them of vermin and shrugging, announced, 'Come on boys—leave these *babies* to their stinking rope!'

Suicide Bernie would later describe them as, "...slinking off, like a bunch of tumpless wonders!"

Those remaining in his company had the opportunity to consider Zechariah's plans, and following much discussion, agreement was reached. During the proceedings, it came to Zechariah that later on, after enough passing of time, the game would be played in far more organized fashion, in accordance with his every dictate.

For now though, agreement provided him a satisfying inner glow, the like of which was never before his. His planning to use the rope to haul fallen parties from the chasm's depths held certain special appeal, and both Dennis and Livingston were ahead of the rest in volunteering support; they said they were relieved that good, sound common sense had succeeded in winning the day.

It was proposed that Bernard take charge of the rescue rope, which was as responsible a job as might be offered. Bernard was of course delighted by the idea. He appreciated too, the title Zechariah thought up for him and commented to the effect. From that day forth, he would be known as Keeper of Rope, and also as plain old Bernard. He should retain his first given name because, as Zechariah insisted, the name Bernard received honourable mention in the epics of the great Piedmont the Bard. Zechariah would never allow that anyone of such fine given name be referred to by anything so reminding of gazuzzlement as Suicide. Suicide was nothing pleasant and was in fact, most *un*remarkable. His standing guard over the rope would take up all of his time, which meant there would be no time left for actual leaping the ditch, but Bernard was not long in deciding he preferred devoting himself full-time to matters pertaining to his new position. From now on he was an important member of a small privileged group, a group that would often be referred to by Zechariah as "Administration".

The rope itself, regardless of any good use it might be put to, was much admired by the boys. It was around that time, they began referring to Zechariah as Zechariah the Great, which he could never hear too often.

For most part, boys played at leaping the ditch, but there was one amongst the gals who was a quite remarkable exception. Her name was Francis Darkling, and she, to the chagrin of many a boy, held records for both the longest leap, and having dared the leap, most often.

She was always present with those waiting turns. She never took time out for a break. At first it was considered by many, impossible to assess the exact number of leaps made by an individual, and so whether or not Francis was entitled to claim that record was debated.

From the time of humiliation and triumphing, Zechariah tallied scores. It did not take him long to come up with effective ways of dealing with disgruntled contestants. Soon, managing disputes was something he thought of as just part of the job. He was an expert in defending his "records", which was his name for the listings of scores. Scores were scratched by him and no other. Even before his election to the position of official score keeper, he'd gone to the trouble of allocating separate sheets of bark for participants, and during the games, those were kept always very close to paw. When a game was finished and everyone headed for home, Zechariah the Great had a secret hiding place for the records— somewhere amongst the bushes—a place no one might discover.

At first, during the earliest days, a malcontent might, in a heated moment, dare to exhibit less than complete acceptance of a decision, but then Zechariah shouted, delivering such as, 'Without me, kadoodler, there'd be no *real* contest in the first place!' He was fond of explaining, 'Listen! Here's how it is. I could make mistakes on purpose, couldn't I— with the tally? You get it now, don't you? Yes, I'm sure you know what I mean!' Coercion worked. So sincere was his contempt for those calling his judgment to account that none entertained serious doubt as to the application of that same sincerity when it came to keeping score.

FOREST QUEEN

The weather was mild and today the game went on for longer than usual. Nancy Noy-Breen, in company with friends, Emily Longpod and Sara Mazengarb, enjoyed lying in lush grass at the edge of the stream. They stared up, marvelling at the wonder of blue-sky overhead, with great billowing clouds lofting one atop the other in spectacular fashion. Such fine weather as this might be taken as proof of Great Grandfather's exceptional good humour. Lying at distant remove from the participants in the game, who always made such racket, the friends discussed for a while, attributes of a perfect cloud. They wondered whether, indeed, there could be such a thing. If ever such a cloud were to happen along, then, to Nancy's way of thinking, it would be a clean white and comprise a soft-rounded form.

'It could not be streaky,' she said. 'It would not be the least bit grey. It must not have any yellowish hue—those colours are grubby. To attain even a vague notion of perfection, it must have about it a fresh laundered look.'

'And then, such perfection melts away—right before your eyes,' Emily said.

Sara said, 'I know what you mean, but don't either of you have any love at all for *storm* clouds? I think *my* perfect cloud would roll through winter—threatening and wild. As a dark, moody entity it would bank up and up until filling the sky. Much lightning and thunder would erupt, and then before the rain came—all should be forgiven for fearing the end of their world threatened!'

'Oh, Sara,' Emily declared, 'There's no one quite so dramatic as you!'

'Truer word was never spoken,' Nancy agreed.

'Have either of you ever been up there … where the old trees, all standing stiff-to-attention, resemble grey bones?' Making enquiry, Sara lay on her back in the grass, with her eyes closed. She waved a paw in a languid manner over a shoulder, indicating the place.

'I haven't,' said Emily, and she looked up at the hillside. Of course she'd seen those trees before, a thousand times before this, but now, after Sara described them as bones, she could not help thinking of them as that. They did look like bones, and she said, 'Even from way down here, there's a creepiness to them.'

Nancy disagreed, 'I don't think of them as least creepy. To me they're just sad, sad sentinels of the past. It's all they are.'

Telling sounds made by friends were carried drifting upon the gentlest of breezes. The main crowd made up of most ardent fans, would yell encouragement and then followed drawn out, suspense filled moments of silence—silence preceding much boisterous cheering. Hearing exultant sound going up, those removed from the crowd knew that another successful leap was concluded. Hearing no worse than that, meant no terrifying cliff-hanging ordeal had occurred. Leaping the Ditch was a thrilling game—a game none but the most foolish would boast of being good at in the vicinity of an adult.

'It's boring, lying here,' Nancy declared, not meaning it. But then an idea came to her, and rising to prop herself on an elbow, she said, 'I know what we should do. We should take a stroll and see if there's anything of interest up there.'

'Where?' Emily asked.

'Oh, you're well aware of her meaning.'

'I'm not. I've not the slightest notion... Why would you accuse me? I think it's mean of you, Sara, suggesting I'd pretend.'

'Oh, come along now ... *Longpod*.'

'Yes Mazengarb?' Hearing her name used against her, this time by a friend, Emily was injured.

They're bored with doing so much of not much at all, thought Nancy. They bickery scratched over less than nothing.

Emily thought she knew Sara. Thinking better of repaying Sara in kind, she sat up and announced, 'Nancy, I think that's a very nice idea. I *would* like to go for a hippety hop stroll with you, to wherever it is you have in mind.'

'I won't be going,' said Sara.

Emily said, 'If you don't want to come, then don't. It's up to you.'

'Come along, Sara. We should all go,' objected Nancy.

'No. I don't want to.'

'Mm, I suppose it *is* growing late...' Emily said.

'And Emily,' Sara said, 'I *did* hear you telling your mother that you intended being home by now.'

'*Did* I? I don't recall promising that.'

'Yes. I was standing there and heard you say it.'

Emily fluttered her eyelashes, an involuntary, idiosyncratic mannerism, signifying to those who knew her, uncertainty and confusion. For a moment she said nothing, then, after glancing towards the forest and back again, she said, 'I guess—after all, I *should* be getting home.'

Rising to her feet, Sara granted, 'As I see it, that is the correct decision. And if you like the look of those old bones you can always visit there some other time.'

Hearing it so decided, Nancy exclaimed, 'I must say, I'm flabbergasted. One minute you're at each other's throats, and the next... I just don't know. It's *you* Sara, you always have your way!'

'That's not fair, Nancy.'

Now, Emily spoke up for Sara!

Hearing her, Nancy shrugged, deciding, 'All right, fine. I'll go by myself. You can both run home to your mothers. I guess I'll be seeing you gals around.'

And so it was, she made off alone to explore the forest.

Making her way up the hillside, she paused at one point and looking back over the way she'd come, away down there, she saw Sara and Emily; they'd not run off home at all. She wondered if they'd ever intended doing so. They'd joined up with a small group of gals so taken with leaping the ditch that they never failed to attend a meet. From where she stood it was difficult to tell whether or not the game was over for the day. She could no longer hear the sound of rowdy cheers going up, not from this distance. The place of great trees lay ahead; she'd not far to go and so she set off again, trekking her way beyond the known, into most unfamiliar territory. Going through long dry, brown and yellowed grass, she thought, I'm blazing a trail here—that's what this is. The day has been warm, and so I must take care to watch out for serpents. They are our brothers and sisters, as are all creatures, but they are not friends.

Serpents were wont to trespass upon the territory of Folk of Fur, and on occasion of them intruding into burrows, nightmarish terror preceded misery. The consequence was ever dire. She must take care and not flibberty hop right smack into one. Having cautioned herself regarding the possibility of an untoward encounter, she proceeded on her way, observing, I'm the first of Folk of Fur in endless ages to explore this place. I am intrepid in searching for answer to secrets and mysteries. I am not out here for any picnic. I am, in the truest sense, an explorer.

There was lonesomeness peculiar to this place; such lonesomeness must not be allowed to make her fearful. She arrived at the edge of a wide, circular clearing, the circumference of which was delineated by the monolithic trunks of ancient trees. Seen close up, the size of the trees was all but preposterous and earlier she'd provided them accurate description; they were indeed great sentinels. She examined the grey trunks of those closest; their skins were etched with elaborate meandering lines, which formed intricate patterns. Studying them, some deep part of her insisted that mysterious, unnatural meaning was encrypted there. If she stared at them enough the hypnotic effect induced in her might increase and so she looked away. She went to the very centre of the great circular clearing.

Standing tall then, in what she decided was the living centre of a wondrous realm, a realm guarded throughout time by an army of loyal guardians of forest all about, she knew a quiet part of her awakened to a strange awareness. Sensing the presence of authority other than theirs, the great trees might bow low in obeisance, pledging loyal servitude. This was a moment of grace, and rooted to their places, enthralled in trancelike sleep, within great trunks true hearts stirred. Stretching, she raised her paws high above her head and then lowered them. She put them together at her waist. She would improvise. After hesitating for a moment, she began:

'Since time immemorial no paw this way has passed
Neither brother, nor sister dear, no parent, friend or foe
Place of dreams, forgotten things, forgotten even woe
Grant least of seed to carrion nay, to pleasant bird or crow.
Sky above to ground beneath, no blessing is bestowed.

As dull slate is fixed without, yet pulse with inner glow,
World to darkest depth bereaved but breathing still we know.
Upon the wearied soldier's brow fair paw beseeches so,
Wills, dearest to my heart stay long and do not long to go,
Without pomp or crown or fancy dress, the Forest Queen arrives,
So those who follow true decree must now... de dah de dah...'

She was finished with it. It was forever gone, leaving none but she and giants of the forest knowing of it. Words still played in her mind, attempting to find fine places for themselves, but she would not notice them; listening to the forest she heard nothing. Not so much as the slightest twittering of birds was heard. No breeze blew. There came no unexpected crack of twig snapping, there was not the smallest sound of anything moving in grass or bush. So much silence was unnatural and she decided to set things right. She began shouting at the top of her voice, making as much noise as she could.

A young voice was shouting, '*A forest of gazuzzlement!* Oh, yes—that's what you are!'

Before she could shout again, the bard responded, declaring, 'No. It's a gazuzzled forest!' He stepped out from behind the tree. 'It's only a forest of gazuzzlement for those who see such things as I do. Now, you wouldn't like being that, would you?'

'What do you mean?' She'd spoken without hesitation and seemed not the least startled by his presence. She did not fear as another might, in finding they were not so alone.

By way of introduction he said, 'I'm Piedmont the Bard. You may have heard the name bandied about.' She was not alarmed by him appearing as he had, but now she was unsettled. Could surprise take so long to register? By continuing on as if nothing was amiss he might put her at ease. She'd asked him what he meant and so he said, 'I mean, when things at one and the same time are perceived as having many layers of meaning. And when, that seen in a given moment, is seen as being upside down, but then in the moment following, is seen as right side up, after all. Then, finally...'

'Oh, Piedmont, you are ridiculous!'

Moments of nervousness were past and he was glad. 'Am I? How is that then?'

She said, 'Your hat is on the wrong way. It's on backwards.'

'But it's a cap. It can't be on backwards.'

'That's right, Piedmont. There are some things, which are right side 'round—every which way.'

He exclaimed, 'What an astonishing, clever little gal you are.'

'No. I'm Nancy Noy-Breen.'

'Ah then, you are the daughter of Mavis; Mavis nee Whitepaws?'

'Correct.'

'And your father is Charlie, of course.'

'Charles Noy-Breen. Correct again,' she said. 'We have our very own burrows at New Warren Central. We are not situated in the outskirts, but right in the thick of things.'

'I'm pleased hearing it,' said Piedmont, 'And so, you're happy there? It sounds that way.'

'Yes, we are.'

'That's wonderful,' he said. 'Yes, indeed it is.' He seemed at a loose end for several moments, but then, after further pause, during which he took the trouble to clear his throat, 'It's been a refreshing experience conversing with one so young—one with nothing to gripe over. But I'm afraid, Nancy Noy-Breen, I must not tarry. It's been pleasant meeting with you.' So saying, he made to take his leave.

'But must you rush off?'

Turning back, he explained, 'I'm not from these parts. I make my home at considerable remove. It's way over there.' He waved a paw towards the hills, 'I live far beyond the big hill and it's been rather a long day for me. I should be getting back.' But then, 'Now that I think of it, there's been a fox sighted by my friend, Sherbrook, and sighted more than once.' He grimaced. He did not want to frighten one so young but best caution her. Better fear a fox than be devoured by it. He said, 'I don't want to interfere in your plans, but perhaps we should consider going part of the way together? We can accompany each other without either of us going too far out of our way. I intend taking the path traversing the hillside above your home.' He was the bard, a long-time hero of hers and she would not dream of refusing. They would flibberty hop together. But that was foolishness, for he was no longer the flibberty hopping type; he was, in fact, ancient. He was a great deal older in appearance than ever she imagined him, but creased and wrinkled brow and mangy looking grey fur were worn with dignity. However slow their progress might be, she was glad he'd not gone on alone. His venerable age meant that, in the event a fox came at them, they would perish. She would not think of it though, because she was going home with a living legend.

Reluctant Bard

They'd not gone far, when glancing back over the way they'd come, she said, 'It's a gloomy place … a gazuzzled forest … but I'm glad I ventured there. As I stood at the centre of the clearing, I experienced the strangest feeling.'

'Strangeness?'

'Yes. Surrounded by those great sentinels…' Having stopped in mid sentence, she hesitated, before saying, 'You would have to have been there, as me, to realize my meaning. Those trees are as gazuzzled as anything gets, but being there I could not think of them as deceased. An energy persists … an influence is exerted, and I knew its effect.'

He said, 'They are gazuzzled, and yet they are not always so.' In declaring the forest not always as she described it, she decided him somewhat confused.

Day turned to dusk and all was russet and gold. The sun hung suspended in the sky over the line of trees delineating the tops of distant hills. It remained there as if taking a long last look at the land before further descending.

Slipping along beside him, she enquired, 'Do you find enough time for work? With the attention of so many fans, you must be more than a little pressed for time. Do you enjoy that quietude necessary to the poet's day?' She would take herself off from company to sit alone at one or other of her favourite places, where she would engage in pleasant reverie. It was impossible to compose anything of worth in the midst of hubbub.

He smiled, 'I know what you mean, but I've not been involved for such a long time now, with versifying. I'm pleased by the knowledge of others seeing value in those works of mine, but I've moved on and found other things with which to occupy myself.'

'Oh,' said Nancy, hoping her disappointment would not show. 'Versifying,' he called it. And, he'd given it up.

He said, 'I find being less noticed a good thing. And there's another thing. Fun is always expected to run a poor second to those matters considered by the majority as most important. I make no apology for believing the benefits of fun underrated.'

'But weren't you having fun working?'

''I respect the craft, but I became disillusioned.' He held a long sturdy stick, which he used as a staff. He swiped at a thick tuft of mealy-grass in passing, and said, 'There's nothing complicated about it. It's simple.'

'So, one fine day you just gave up?'

'It wasn't giving up.'

'But…'

'I put one thing aside in order to have the time for others. I imagined I had no choice, other than do as others expected. I was expected to come up with verse celebrating everything from birthdays to naming days and weddings and then there was a coronation … a job I declined. There were the eulogies—I can't tell you how those got me down. I was inundated, and have no idea how I ever found the time for the epics. You see, I'd forgotten there are many things in life deserving of attention. I was both possessed and obsessed.'

'Oh, *poor* Piedmont,' she said.

'Yes. Poor Piedmont indeed,' he said. And they pressed on, up the hillside.

With time's passing, his reputation had increased, so that by the time of his and Nancy's meeting, the name was revered to the extent that many a proud parent thought of naming offspring in his honour. Of course, there were those who went ahead in doing that very thing. Others, perhaps thinking better of burdening a child by giving them so much to live up to, proceeded by naming a new-born after one or other heroic figures of more distant past. In choosing that road, they were spoiled for choice.

Nancy Noy-Breen long counted herself most fervent of his admirers and whether such was true or not, she was sincere in believing others should see her as such. Most did not read scratchings, but the works were known by heart and recited by those of her generation. The works were recited, even by distant acquaintances, their home territories lying far afield, and this was cause for pride. To residents of New Warren Central, the bard was their own, and that would ever stand.

The bard's departing New Warren Central was attributed to a falling out between him and the elderly doe, Lillian, Good Queen Lillian of Clan Graymark, or to those privileged members of her immediate family, "Grammy". He had not, it was told, gone off alone, because one or two of those loyal to him had left as well, which to Nancy's way of thinking was a fair thing, because he would not have suffered effects of solitude and loneliness. The bard had sought fresh pasture and, whilst not punished with banishment, had forfeited his rightful place in society by submitting himself to exile. Shrouded since that time by a veil of silence, anything extra, by way of detailed information pertaining to the event, was impossible to glean.

They arrived at a point on the trail where, looking down the slope, they recognized her home. New Warren Central was situated at not too great a distance below them. It was time to part company and go their separate ways, but neither wanted to hasten in leave-taking. By the last dim light of dusk, several youngsters were seen down there, where they gathered near a main entranceway.

'Look, Piedmont! There's a gal, there, wearing a dress just like mine. I do hope that awful Mona Lop hasn't had her mother run up a copy! It would be just like her!'

'You're the genuine article,' he said, 'There is just one Nancy Noy-Breen.'

Exclaiming, she said, 'Oh, now look! She's fallen flat on her face!' But then, 'Oh, I am sorry, Piedmont. You must think me terrible. I should not be pleased.'

She could be down there in no time at all, but risked, 'Piedmont, I've changed my mind.' She enquired, 'May I continue on with you?'

'What can you mean?' he asked.

'Just to the top of the hill.'

'You do know, don't you … folk are waiting for you, down there?'

Hearing nothing of definite refusal, she was encouraged, 'True,' she said, 'but the hilltop also awaits, and I want to see the stars from way up there. Let's stop talking and move on. What do you say?'

What to do? Piedmont wondered. Sounding out of sorts, he said, 'I must think on it.' He said, then, 'We must trust that by my allowing this, we don't end up in dreadful trouble with your mother. Friend Skip can see you back home. He'll be pleased to get you back there, after we've ascended to the heights, but still, I'm not at all certain of this.'

Since becoming acquainted with her, his confidence in any plan of Tump had waxed and waned. He reminded himself he was never very keen on any of it, and now, he contended with dire internal battling; his conscience insisting at one and the same time upon two opposing courses. So delightful a youngster as she should be left to get on with her life. Yet Tump and their special need for her rare ability pressed hard. This moment though, was not the actual moment of the final decision. According to the plan, she would have her life down there before being whisked away at a future time. And now she rushed him, insisting, 'Hurry up, Piedmont. *Do* make up your mind!' So insistent was she that he decided, very well then, they'd gotten this far and no real harm done, but of course his mind was not made up.

The idea of anyone of his elevated stature entertaining the thought of getting into trouble with anyone's mother, least of all hers, was absurd in the extreme and cause for merriment, but they'd been acquainted for just a short time and fearful of giving offence now, when he'd just agreed to allow her to go with him, she hugged her arms to her sides in an effort to prevent herself from giggling. Skip? She thought he must be one of those whom, long ago, went off to the high country with the bard, and she looked forward to meeting with him.

They set off, with him leading as before, whilst she followed in his steps, trekking ever upwards along the high path. The further they climbed the narrower the trail became and sometimes it was so thin, that she believed she might, with no way to save herself, put paw amiss and fall—just slip, and find herself tumbling down there, over and over through dark distance to the very bottom.

His voice drifted back to her, announcing, 'We must not dilly-dally, Nancy. We must keep up a constant pace and we won't rest before reaching the top.' She thought, Dilly-dallying—is that what he thinks we've been doing? She half expected the path would soon narrow to nothing, but after going on for what seemed a very long time, she was relieved when, again it widened. For some time now, she'd had difficulty in keeping up with him. Piedmont did not go quickly, that was not it, but when it came to possessing stamina and ability in pressing on, ever upward over distance, his dawdling pace was difficult to match. Feeling by now, quite out of breath, she wished they might pause, if just for a moment or two, but Piedmont would not stop. She believed though, she would soon give up, because she'd reached a point where she could go no farther.

Piedmont's voice floated back to her, sounding not the least exhausted. He sounded comfortable; his tone conveying the impression he was quite pleased with himself. 'We are here now—at the roof of our world!

'It's a long hop to the top,' he said. 'We've done very well. We should sit over here. Come along, take the weight off.' They sat there on a large flat stone, which seemed placed for weary travellers. Following moments during which neither of them spoke, he began slapping at his coat in a haphazard attempt to determine the contents of pockets. 'Now where is my spyglass? Where have I put it? Don't you detest it when things go missing? I confess it drives me to distraction.' Then, feeling around in one of the coat's many deep inside pockets, 'Ah ha! Here you are now. I'm so glad you're not lost!' He said, 'You'll have gathered, Nancy, I'm fond of this instrument.' He held a long, cylindrical shaped object for her to see. 'It's made of a shining material which is impressive when seen during the day. The sun is reflected by the surface in extraordinary manner, and when the spyglass is kept in pristine condition—I polish it often—you can see yourself reflected in its surface.' He said, 'I see you're wondering whether it's good for anything else.' Before she could respond, he told her, 'It is. And it's better than you might imagine. Look here. I'll show you.' Pulling at the cylinder, he stretched it out so that it was longer than before, so that now it tapered in three stages from end to end. Piedmont put the spyglass up to an eye, and holding it there, explained, 'When you look through it this way, you can see over a great distance. It has the ability to make everything appear close. There's not much of interest hereabout—not during night as dark as this—but I thought I'd show you it anyway.' He had the spyglass tilted down so that it was aimed into the dark valley. She had no real grasp of what was meant by it making things appear close up. The night had become cool, she thought, and she wore a thin frock. She now realized the foolishness of coming all the way up here with him. Earlier on, he was correct, because there *was* likelihood of being in trouble when she got home. Piedmont would not be getting into trouble though—she would. If she and his friend, Skip, heltered down the hillside track, then they'd make good time, and perhaps her mother would understand. By now, it was late indeed. If she went in by the small back entrance to their home, then she might avoid Father seeing her.

FAR-SEEING-EYE

Piedmont chuckled, saying, 'I do declare... The Tall Ones are indulging in bickery scratching!' Nancy thought, what can he mean? Does he claim that from this distance, he's able to see the Tall Ones and what they do? That was something she refused to believe. It was impossible for anyone to see so far—spyglass or no.

'Here you are, Nancy. Take it.' He told her, 'Hold it up to an eye and peer through it, as I did.' The instrument was directed towards the Tall One's home, but apart from deep night blackness she saw nothing. He said, 'You must close one eye, dear. Your left eye ... yes, that's it, you have it!' She was amazed then, because it was as if she might reach out and touch them—Tall Ones! They were delineated, silhouetted in the bright-lit square opening of their home.

She exclaimed, 'Why—it's flabbergasting! They're black beetles!'

'Beetles?' he asked. The notion of anyone seeing Tall Ones as resembling black beetles was quite beyond him.

Steadying the spyglass, attempting to keep it trained on the same place, she explained, 'Yes, beetles. When I was very young, I would capture black beetles. I pretended they were odd little folk, and they kept me company while I played. It was a favourite thing to do ... and now, looking through your spyglass, it was the first thing that came to mind. Seeing Tall Ones down there—knowing they're so very far away and yet, at the same time, so close—I was reminded of those friends of mine.' She had finished speaking when, coming from behind them, a distant voice was heard, 'There they are! I told you, Piedmont would like showing off the far-seeing-eye!'

Nancy might have been startled, but, Piedmont was quick to explain, 'Ah, at last! It's my good friend, Skip. I see he's brought Peace with him— Peace Darkling, whom you'll enjoy meeting. She is aunt to your acquaintance, Francis Darkling, who's so expert when it comes to leaping the ditch.'

Nancy lowered the spyglass. A strange sight greeted her. A boy approached, and he was not much older than she. A beautiful doe accompanied him. The bard was correct, because the newcomer bore traits shared by those of the family Darkling. Their sudden arrival was not so astonishing, but light radiated from them, making them appear otherworldly. They were Folk of Fur, but not folk as she knew them.

Drawing closer, they shone as the sun, and she heard the doe say, 'Dim the light, Skip. We don't want to dazzle Piedmont or cause the little gal more uncertainty.'

Feeling that she must defend her dignity, Nancy said, 'I'm not the least bit afraid but, folk of New Warren must think the sun rising from above the hill a most unnatural sight!'

Peace laughed, a merry sound, and by way of greeting, said, 'Hello there youngster. I am Peace and this is friend, Skip. We've waited long for this moment.'

Referred to as "little gal", and as "youngster", Nancy was not so sure of herself. The light dimmed, growing fainter until just enough brightness remained.

'That's better,' Skip said. 'I didn't mean to dazzle you, Nancy.' Coming closer, he said, 'It's wonderful seeing you.'

The bard contributed, 'Friend Skip has certain things to explain...'

Then ... the bard's and her meeting was no accident? With truth dawning, she was no longer at ease. A growing sense of betrayal was experienced and her confusion increased.

The bard had tricked her yet nothing of harm had befallen her, and she supposed that they'd gotten along well. The newcomers treated her as friend and so rather than fear them for their prearranging meeting with her, she would allow them the opportunity to redeem good will.

She said, 'You come as Folk of Fur, but I suspect you're not at all that. You're very different, and so ... what are you?'

Displaying surprising candour, Skip replied, 'We are Tump, and so are you. We are, all of us, Tump.' He added, 'But you will not be joining us so soon as this. You join with us much later on.'

Tump? It did not make sense. She heard herself asking, 'Why is that?'

He responded, 'Why is what?'

He would not cease gazing at her until, Peace Darkling said, 'She asks, *why* she does not join with us sooner than you say she will!'

Skip did not like being interrupted. He blurted, 'Nancy, we've met before this. We've met in a realm—a world other than this! But then of course, you're not the same Nancy. I mean…'

'What the deeks *do* you mean?' Nancy asked, and placed her hands confidently on her hips.

Piedmont rushed to the rescue, 'It's like this. We are a small group of individuals, set upon questing. According to all the boy claims, we are destined…'

'*Oh, mercy me!*' Peace exclaimed, and she laughed. 'What is it with you two?' She said, 'Nancy, we need your help with an important task. Without you we can't be certain of success.' She asked, 'Will you help?'

'Sure,' she said, 'As long as it's something I *can* do.' She added, 'I hope you're not kadoodling.'

'Just *one* can help us, and she is you. You are "made" for the task. Agreement is required, that's all. You must agree to allowing Skip to gaze into your eyes.' She said, 'He's not ceased staring at you, and so that's something you're already familiar with.' It was true, he'd not so much as glanced from her. Now he drew closer, and Peace said, 'He's not quite himself tonight, but he won't bite.' He gazed into her eyes for just a moment, and then Peace said, 'Good—that's it He's looked into you.' She said, 'Now, turn Nancy. Face away from him and look to the valley below.

'Look carefully and you will discern, down there amidst the gloom, the Tall Ones' home. We should see emanating from it a very bright flashing of light.'

Then, Nancy exclaimed. 'Oh, yes!' Lightning flashed! It blasted out and away from the Tall Ones' dwelling—out from that square of light, which she'd studied through the bard's far seeing eye!

'There, you see? You had no idea that you might assist in causing such dramatic event.'

She looked to each of them in turn. 'You're saying *I did that?*'

'Skip said, 'I caused the flash. I moved an item from the Tall Ones' dwelling place. Without you, I could not be certain of where it might end up. You see, Nancy, the Tall Ones' music machine, the Radiola, is now moved back through time.' He persisted, 'It is now located at a point occurring well before your birth. In fact it's twice present there, because at the point of its arrival, in what to us is the past, the Tall Ones still have it in their possession.' It was her turn to stare. She did not attempt disguising her opinion concerning his state of mind. Skip said, 'It will be discovered by an acquaintance of ours, and he is thrilled to have it.'

Piedmont asked, 'Is it at the exact location, Skip?'

'It's seen to, yes. It's precisely where we want it,' Skip said. 'I have no way of describing the powerful feeling, the sense of *extreme* accuracy, gained by looking into Nancy.'

'Then that's good enough for me,' Peace said.

To Nancy, Piedmont said, 'You must think us insane beyond belief, dear gal.' His expression was one of sympathy.

'She must,' agreed Peace and she went to embrace the gal. She said, 'You will have not much idea of any of this dear heart—not for a very long time to come. Just know that we watch over you. We are friends and we are good at keeping our word. You will see and partake in matters great and wondrous.' She hugged Nancy, telling her, 'You are Tump, and we had no better way of revealing it.'

She was not certain of anything. With Peace embracing her it was difficult to speak. She asked, 'Tump?'

'Yes, a force for good, and although you cannot yet realize it, we will *always* need you. Without you we may not amount to very much at all.'

'But how can any of it be?'

'By traversing time gal,' Peace told her, 'and for now we must send you back.' She said, 'Skip—look into her, and be sure how you go! There can be no error!'

In an instant, Nancy found herself tottering upon her feet. She swayed, dazed and lost. The air about her flooded with sweet fragrance, and she fell to the ground. The sun shone golden above a distant horizon. Consciousness slipped away and her mind flooded with a warning given somehow, by Tump. 'You must never eat New Greens!' Over and again, the warning repeated. The voice of Peace Darkling was hypnotic, insisting, 'New Greens are not for you!'

'That went well! When it comes to providing an explanation to the young, you're both wonderful examples of a clumsy approach!' Peace admonished them.

Piedmont was subdued. 'There's no longer need for the light,' he said, meaning Skip might now extinguish it. He admitted, 'Yes. I was lost in explaining our intention, but we had no difficulty in communicating as we made our way from the valley.'

Skip willed the light to dim, until all that remained was the softest glow. He would offer no explanation for his failure in communicating with Nancy. If she were anything as the Nancy he was better acquainted with, then she would take proceedings in her stride.

The old Radiola was moved from the farmhouse kitchen and back through time, and he was pleased with his accomplishment. And, far more was effected, none of which was spoken of in Nancy's presence. With Nancy now returned to New Warren Central, to a point in time during an earlier part of the present day, Skip informed both Peace and Piedmont of the rest. He explained, 'The Radiola has been moved back there to the field, where Uncle Bucky finds it, and in one and the same instant of moving it, Clever Fixer was moved. He was moved from Bunty's realm in our present time, to the day *after* the Radiola arrived in the field. He went back to old Warren Central, and adjustments and fixings were carried out without the slightest difficulty.'

In studying Skip's expression, Peace decided him not sufficiently candid.

He was saying, 'I returned Clever Fixer to the cottage in Bunty's realm...' Peace directed him a penetrating look and perhaps that was his reason for confessing, 'There is something a little strange though, which has me puzzled.'

'Puzzled?'

'Yes,' Skip said, adopting too nonchalant an air, 'There were *four* fixers back there. I saw them. They met on the path in the field, which, back then, leads to the old warren.' He said, 'At first it was worrying, realizing there were more than just one or two of them. I thought, this could present a deeks of a problem, but then I saw it all worked out, and so I decided, best not fuss over it.'

Peace asked, 'But four fixers showed up—and all at the same time?'

'Yes,' admitted Skip. Not just Peace, but Piedmont as well, appeared perturbed by the revelation.

Less certain, Skip said, 'When the elders instructed me to move the Radiola, I was not actually instructed to move the fixer back. Elder Fixer said that after the Radiola was moved *he* would then stop by Old Warren Central to fix it.' He said, 'Much of that occurring back then was confusing for me, and I now realize the likelihood of my misunderstanding those instructions. I assumed, *more* was expected of us than the elders intended.'

Piedmont appeared nervous.

Peace asked, 'He did *not* tell you to move our fixer back to old Warren Central?'

'No,' admitted, Skip.

'Dear boy,' Piedmont offered, 'you've been over conscientious.'

Peace wanted more information. She asked, 'How can you be sure that with so much moving going on, with all that toing and froing, that your seeing was accurate?'

'Because it was. It was clearer than ever,' he said. 'Nothing too outlandish has occurred, and I don't think we should be troubled. All that's happened is that four Clever Fixers met in the field. They met, and after short discussion, it was decided that the elder of them should attend the task of fixing the Radiola. And that was that. I moved our Clever Fixer back to the cottage in Bunty's realm. He was not upset or disappointed by his skills not being needed, but rather was thrilled meeting his other versions. As we speak, he's back at home in the company of Sherbrook and Bunty.'

'Who is the fourth Clever Fixer?' Peace asked, 'Where did *he* come from?'

'I have no idea,' Skip said, shrugging.

Peace said, 'Skip? For now, you must move us back to the cottage.' The remainder of their discussion was best kept for later.

* * *

Simple Rudy lay flat on the floor, on his stomach, with legs sprawled in the path of others, giving Uncle Bucky reason to advise, 'Move the extremities Rudy, if you don't want others hopping on you!' The unfortunate boy deserved fair warning. Skip was too fond of flibberty hopping close to Rudy's hindquarters in passing. Skip, Bucky decided, had no real need to pass by the old Radiola and Simple Rudy quite so often as he did. It would not be long and they would be in dispute, bickery scratching as was so often their wont, and Bucky did not enjoy having to deal with unpleasantness.

Hearing Bucky warning Simple Rudy, Skip was quick to respond, 'Yes, Simple, watch out! You're in the way! It's very selfish of you, taking every bit of space! You've left no room at all for anyone else!' Then addressing their leader, he said, 'You would think, wouldn't you Uncle Bucky, that Simple Rudy believes *he owns* the old Radiola? He thinks it's his property!'

Bucky would not deign respond. Rather, he enquired of Rudy, 'What is it you seek, my boy? Why do you stare so long at the valves?'

The youngster did not listen to actual programs, but he lay there in the meeting place, staring into the back of the Radiola, not shifting his attention from the valves' glowing presence. Bucky had enquired regarding the obsession, but his curiosity received little response, other than small grunts and murmurs. This time, he thought, would doubtless be no different from others.

But then, Simple Rudy looked up, telling him, 'It teaches me things, Uncle. That's why I like it.'

'Things?'

'Yes Sir, fascinating things.'

'Things it is then,' said Bucky, and allowed a moment's silence, before asking, 'Would those interesting things include, for example, *White Winter's Song?*' It was a popular piece hereabouts, a fine tune, and by mentioning it, Bucky was hopeful of further engaging Simple in easy conversation; for far too much of the time the youngster was uncommunicative. Bucky thought the boy not so different from the rest of them, but then Rudy responded to questioning in an unexpected fashion, disdaining interest in the song.

He told Bucky, 'No Sir, that's not it. I'm learning *real* stuff.' And he went on to say, 'I'm listening to Great Grandfather.'

Taken aback, Bucky went closer to Simple Rudy, close enough to whisper, 'My boy, I think it's just wonderful that you're on close terms with

Great Grandfather, but let's keep the matter between us, eh? We don't want to make others envious, do we?'

He said, 'Folk can be unpredictable. I'm sure you understand my meaning.' He trusted Rudy understood, because there was already more than enough bother of late, with young Skip the Seer being made the subject of cruel gossip by the Graymark doe; some exaggerated nonsense concerning her missing cameo, a keepsake, purported to possess greatest sentimental value.

Bucky could do without such foolish severity—children being suspected of dishonest behaviour. He imagined next, word would be bandied about involving a youngster claiming as truth, actual reciprocal communication with the highest being, Great Grandfather Himself, and he cringed thinking of possible outcomes. But then Bucky smiled. He reminded himself that Simple Rudy always refused involvement in even the most straightforward, mundane communication. But then, the boy confused him by telling, 'It's not Great Grandfather I'm talking with. I'm talking with a tree—His tree.'

'A tree... Hm. Well, I suppose that's all right then Rudy, although I'd still not reveal any of it—not to all and sundry—not if I were you.' Learning from trees was not seen as fuel for serious controversy. As claims went, it was not in the same league as claiming to receive information from an omniscient being. He supposed that if one went looking for it, mystery abounded, but the mysterious did not interest him; Bucky liked things kept simple and straightforward. Others, such as Piedmont, were interested in mystery and its unravelling, and they were welcome to it.

Piedmont the Bard had encouraged a small group of likeminded parties to spend time recumbent about the Radiola, attempting to make sense of the language. However, the group had soon dispersed, its members having, after all, too little patience for fathoming the meaning of Tall One lyrics. It was not too much later, that Piedmont claimed to have gained adequate comprehension of much of that heard. To be sure, the bard was tenacious by nature, and his familiarity with the "word", stood more chance of making sure sense of it than the rest of them. Piedmont, with better sense of the meaning of *White Winter's Song*, explained it to the others, and since then it had gained even greater popularity. The lyrics comprehended, folk sang along just as Tall Ones did, to the tune. The bard next sought an improved result. He wanted to record actual Tall One words in the scratchings. Achieving that, though, had proven too complex an undertaking. Examples of scratch-symbols, of Tall One language, were not come by without difficulty; the bard lacked sufficient examples of their scratching to use as reference in tackling the deciphering.

A brave-hearted buck who had once returned from scouting Tall One territory, claimed to have ventured beyond all caution, into the Tall Ones' barn—whereupon, he thought to commit to memory, the markings graved upon the body of the mighty churner. Upon returning to Warren Central, a faithful copy was made, scratched into the dusty ground outside the entranceway. So odd-structured was the language, that to this day, even most erudite Piedmont, apart from declaring those marks represented the churner's name or title, was as yet unable to meet with success in determining the precise meaning. They possessed some understanding of the spoken word, but to the bard's chagrin, the written, remained outside their comprehension.

Bucky would have a few words with the bard regarding Simple Rudy's conversations with Great Grandfather. He would learn what the bard made of it.

* * *

At the cottage in Bunty's realm, it was mid-afternoon of the day following their first meeting at the hilltop, with young Nancy.

Peace questioned Clever Fixer, 'But what was it, the fourth fixer said?' She'd deduced that the first of the four fixers who'd shown up near the old warren was the original fixer. He was the predecessor of both their Clever Fixer and Clever Fixer belonging to the elders. Trusting that was correct, she'd decided that three of the fixers present in the field near old Warren Central were accounted for. But where had the *fourth* of them come from, and who was he? And then too, there was the mystery of Clever Fixer claiming his memory of earliest time did not include the slightest recall of any meeting with other versions of himself. On the occasion of his very first journeying to old Warren Central, he'd stopped by and attended to fixing the old Radiola. He had not met with anyone along the way. He'd crossed the field uninterrupted and then reached the old warren. He met up with Uncle Bucky, who requested he take a look at something he'd discovered lying in the field—the old Radiola.

Peace again asked, 'Come along, Fixer, what *did* he say, this fourth Clever Fixer? You've said he gave a name, a name other than yours? So what was it?' Clever had had enough of the infernal cross-examination. He glanced away from Peace, to listen to something or other Skip said. In his own way, Clever was as persistent as she. By turning away from Peace, he as good as ignored her. Then he looked from Skip back to her. He exclaimed, '*Yes*—now I have it! It's *Skibeau!* That's it!'

'So, the rest of them, all three, are Clever Fixers. And then, this *Ski beau* just happened to show up out of nowhere? Just like that—giving no explanation of anything at all?'

'Yes,' Fixer said, 'But it's one word, not two.'

'What?'

'It's Skibeau,' Clever told her, 'One word. Not Ski beau as you're pronouncing it.'

'Oh.'

She wondered, had the individual named Skibeau made the original fixer oblivious to the presence of other fixers in the field? She asked, 'Did he say *where* he was from? Did he explain his purpose for being there in our territory? Did he do anything unusual? Or, when the elder fixer informed your other versions, that their assistance was not required, did this Skibeau just wander off? What *then* was his attitude, *after* the elder Fixer spoke to him? What did he do?'

'My—that's quite a list!' Clever exclaimed. 'You expect too many answers! I was there for a very short time before I was kazooned away from the location!' He glanced to Skip. His protesting was of no interest to Peace; she thought, such off-paw attitude to mystery solving, unacceptable.

'We must discuss the strangeness of the event. We'll sit outside on the veranda, and you can both recall the event. You will share the details of it with the rest of us.' Looking from Clever Fixer to Skip, she decided the matter settled.

Piedmont said, 'As I understand it, the elder was not the first of the fixers to arrive in the field. I think it obvious, taking into account the order of their arrival, that Fixer the Elder, or true Tump, was present *after* the arrival of *our* fixer. He was there *because* we had it wrong. He was there to ensure that no further complication would arise. Left to his own means, the original fixer would have managed any fixing required, without help from anyone, and the elder knew it.'

'I take that as a vote of confidence in *my* ability, Bard.' Fixer said, smiling. The bard nodded in return.

'And, the original fixer is predecessor to both our fixer, and as well, the elder fixer,' Skip said.

'Yes. We understand it. That's three of them accounted for. It's the other who presents the mystery,' Peace said. Sherbrook nodded agreement and directed a question to Clever. 'Was the other fixer, the mysterious fourth, half as good looking as you?'

'Oh, hush Sherbrook. This is serious!' Peace ordered, forestalling humorous response from Clever.

'Not as I see it,' Sherbrook said, 'From all Skip relates, arriving there and presenting as their Clever Fixer, the elders were not upset or peeved. They told our Clever that his services were not needed. They knew that Skip was aware of everything occurring, and they knew he'd proceed in moving our fixer back here to us, which was attended to. No harm was done.'

'But, who is he—the fourth of them?'

'Who indeed? We might never know...' said Piedmont.

'And that's just not good enough,' declared Peace. She noticed uncertain looks pass between the others.

Then, recalling more of the event, Clever Fixer explained, 'I do seem to recall him—Skibeau—saying he came from somewhere, or some*thing* he referred to as the thirty-ninth parallel!' Perturbed and shaking his head in dismay, Fixer admitted, 'Memory of it has just come to me. I'd forgotten it!'

Peace, after long pressing for answers, felt vindicated. She asked, 'Where or when is this thirty-ninth what's-it? Do tell? I don't suppose he offered you a map or other means of locating the place?' Getting up from where she sat at the edge of the veranda, she announced, 'I'm going to consult the tree.'

'*Wait!*' exclaimed Clever, 'There's something else—the large red berry!'

'Red berry?' Skip asked.

'Yes! And the sound of swarming bees ... a sound made by insects? I'm not certain. But I do recall something of the sort.'

'I saw nothing as you describe, Fixer,' Skip said. 'And during your sojourn my vision of the location was complete. There was no swarm. No berries.'

But Fixer went on, eyes widening as detail after detail of submerged memory returned to mind. 'No!' He exclaimed, 'I am wrong. It was no red berry, but a *vehicle!* I remember it now. He—the one calling himself Skibeau—arrived at the scene in a most strange, uncommon vehicle—a large red sphere!'

Peace exclaimed, 'We will make further study of the tree! We must practise Mmeerah and raise our energy far higher, beyond anything thus far imagined. We have much to learn! Elder Tump is one thing. They're "us" but this Skibeau is an altogether other matter. *Skibeau!'* She spat the name, declaring, 'You were entranced by him Clever! And Skip, you also were affected! We must ensure we are better prepared in future! Next, we will engage in moving the energy of Great Grandfather's tree, via the old Radiola, to Simple Rudy, and will in no wise allow ourselves undone by strangers—regardless of their masquerading in familiar guise. We'll not be distracted from our true course. We must work harder!'

* * *

Simple Rudy floated. At first, he drifted, much as a leaf might if set to float upon the waters of an all but still pond. But then all swaying motion ceased, because as quick as winking, a purposeful engagement occurred.

Accepted and embraced by a mysterious transporting force, Simple was carried up and away from his body, up, until the warren was left far behind. The warren no longer mattered; it was an all but forgotten place. Soon, with no effort of his, Simple Rudy, as if no longer extant in his own right, joined with the energy of the tree—the map—so he and it became an indivisible entity, in a place where Great Grandfather's unquestionable sovereignty permeated All.

Here, was no "Simple Rudy"—no process of naming. Here, was no yes or no. The infinite All was experienced as a place of absolute peace, in true Oneness. Events transpiring in infinite locations and encompassed by the past, present and future of linear time, could still be viewed separately, but in the context of Oneness they occurred simultaneously.

The one, known by others at Warren Central as Simple Rudy, knew the means by which time lines of realms were held separate. Realms occupying space were contained, kept in stasis by spheres. The fabric of spheres was resultant of the very unity of space and time. Energy of the spheres differed in that each resonated at its own signature frequency. Infinite in number, spheres did not interlock but sometimes moved against each other. The skins or enveloping fabric of the spherical forms was ever in flux; it was malleable, but such malleability knew limitation; making for a certain natural instability. In moving against each other, the skins of abrading spheres were sometimes breached, allowing energies free flow between them.

Inter-realm travelling, engaged in by those sojourning in linear time was not as rare as some believed.

With sufficient understanding of naturally occurring breaching of spheres, traversing between them could be accomplished by the creation of artificial ways of passage. However, in going from realm to realm, any traveller must navigate the way, and in all of eternity it seemed, there existed just one true map. Great Grandfather's map would provide Tump accurate direction, by fact of Simple Rudy's natural and unfailing ability to read it, to know it. He would read all it offered until the claim could be made that Simple Rudy *was* the map.

Part Three
Blue House South Facing

ZECHARIAH THE GREAT

'Is she all right?' Zechariah enquired. His querying received no response. He paused on the track, remaining at a short distance from them, but then thinking better than play silent witness, he went closer, repeating the question.

'I can't say!' Emily Longpod, half turning to him, exclaimed, 'She's fallen!' She was impatient, insisting, 'Come along, Sara, help me lift her!'

'No—don't do that! We should go and get her mother! I *knew* she shouldn't have gone to the forest!'

Zechariah said, 'Yes—that's by far the best thing. One of you must helter, now. Go get her Mother! She'll know what's best for her.' While Sara Mazengarb, the speedier of the two, made for the entrance of New Warren Central, Emily Longpod remained kneeling at her friend's side. Zechariah, peering from above Emily, next offered, 'She didn't fall hard. She slumped to the ground, at least that's as I saw, it wasn't a heavy fall.' And when Emily failed to hear him, he said, 'She appeared there as if out of nowhere. I was coming along the path from creek-side—and I'm not mistaken—I saw her *materialize.*'

His manner of expression carried emphasis, but emotional involve ment was not conveyed. It was as if he described a curious, yet, not outlandish occurrence and he gave no impression of real surprise. He repeated himself because Emily gave no sign of having heard him. 'No one was present on the hillside and in the following instant, there she was. She fell ... as you see.' He added then, 'It was awful.' Even in his esti-mation, he'd failed to demonstrate enough concern for Nancy Noy-Breen in her unfortunate state.

An unfamiliar odour was present; the faintest hint of unnatural sweetness, but there was no need to complicate matters by alluding to it. Instead, hunkering down so that he was close to Emily, he offered, 'It might be a good idea to hold her paws. She will know she's not alone.'

Seeing the Longpod gal taking one of Nancy's paws in hers was gratifying. Providing Emily more to occupy herself with—other than fretting—had been a good idea; she was already less upset. Her breathing seemed less that of someone giving way to panic and he wondered whether or not an unconscious individual might, at some level of awareness, register fact of receiving the touch of another.

He said, 'I'm certain that not a great deal's amiss here, Emily. Your friend will be fine in no time at all.'

For the first time, Emily Longpod deigned respond. She asked, 'Oh dear, are you *sure?*' For her at least, holding the paw of the unconscious gal had worked a treat.

He said, 'At least, Emily, she still breathes, and so we might assume she'll soon be fine.'

'Yes... Oh yes, I *know* you're right!' Emily sounded relieved. Consoled by his now more reassuring tone she even smiled. It would not be long before others came from the burrows to join them. Others must have seen Sara Mazengarb, headlong rushing to the Noy-Breen quarters, and curiosity aroused, would soon be here offering assistance.

Earlier, Zechariah had promised Bernard they'd meet at Uncle Samson's, and being a stickler for punctuality, he did not relish thought of arriving there any later than agreed. Important business required discussion and besides, he did not enjoy thought of Bernard prattling to Uncle Samson without him present. He did not like to seem uncaring; he liked Emily, and of course, Nancy Noy-Breen too, but he was not of much use here. Then he heard Emily exclaiming, 'Oh look Zech! She's opening her eyes!' And, 'What a relief! Nancy. You're such a worry!' Wondering as to the practical purpose in such circumstance, of chastising a friend, Zechariah would make immediate departure.

But then, Nancy Noy-Breen muttered and hearing her, he was torn—not so much for taking her muttering as indication of imminent recovery, but more for desiring better knowledge of those words, which were all but unintelligible. During several moments silence it became apparent that no additional, clarifying utterance was in the offing, and so he excused himself. 'There now, it's as I said. She's fine. She'll soon be her old self and so I must be off. Bernard and I have an appointment. Important, "ditch" matters require discussion.'

'Well, alright...' Emily was again uncertain, but then accepting his leaving, she told him, 'Thank you Zech, for showing such consideration.' He heard, but had turned from her and was already making his way in the twilight toward Uncle Samson's. He wondered why she troubled to thank him. He'd offered very little in the way of real help.

Reaching that point of the field, where a low swelling of ground meant that the path mounted the rise, he turned back to face the way he'd come. Many now gathered back there. Despite the difficulty of discerning individual figures, it was clear that they numbered far too many to actually assist; other than getting in the way, most would serve no purpose at all.

At a later time he would be certain to engage Nancy Noy-Breen in conversation concerning her instantaneous arrival upon the slope. He would wait until she was recovered enough from the experience. It was not in his nature to admit astonishment, but having witnessed such supernatural event he had at once recognized it as such. He would mention none of it to Bernard; the position of Keeper of Rope did not carry automatic entitlement to information.

He ought not have described what he'd seen to Emily Longpod, but in the moments following the event, words had slipped out. Descending the grassy slope now and traversing the separating distance, he saw Bernard waited for him not too far from the trove burrow. The trove burrow was situated within close proximity of others of his uncle's burrows.

Bernard possessed one remarkable quality. His loyalty was unquestioning and absolute. With more such as Bernard at his side, Zechariah the Great might achieve just about anything. Even a seeming impossibility might be tackled and accomplished. The last light from an all but vanquished sun, shone upon the grasses of the field, making the tips of myriad fronds and stalk glow golden as if precious beyond their true worth. Raising a paw, granting Bernard a perfunctory return salute, Zech, despite himself, found he was vulnerable to a rising, thrilling sensation, so that happiness and even joy rose unbidden, to enliven his spirit. Such an extraordinary wave of emotion, whilst not unpleasant, disconcerted in coming to him unexpectedly.

Bernard called, 'Keeper of Rope—present as requested, sir!' Zech, in deigning return the second of Bernard's salutes, smiled, and in the same moment experienced a disturbing effect of eddying emotion.

He must know what was meant by, *"No new greens!"* For the most part, Nancy Noy-Breen was incoherent, and yet those words: "New Greens", were clear enough and so too, was the most singular abhorrence communicated.

Bernard's expression showed he was nonplussed when the leader, having drawn nigh, so they now stood together, made an unusual enquiry, 'What do you know of greens, Bernard?'

After a slight pause, Bernard hazarded, 'They're good for us?'

'Yes. But, Bernard, I'm talking about greens of a specific type. At least,' said Zechariah, 'I believe I am.'

Following a quiet moment between them, during which he believed he better grasped the leader's meaning, the Keeper of Rope spoke up, offering, 'Ah yes, those banned greens. Yes—the poisonous stuff—the stuff grown all about by the enemy!' He next launched into providing all he knew, 'I know that their consumption by Folk of Fur is banned. The ban was put in place a generation ago, or then about, and it is believed that eating those greens is the cause of a mysterious sickness. I'm not clear concerning it, because no one ever mentions the subject. It's taboo.' He waited for something from Zechariah, but the other had remained silent and thoughtful. Bernard, believing more was expected of him, pushed on by saying, 'Apart from crossing the field between here and the Tall Ones' home, in order to make the most of penance offerings, we must have no contact with that crop.' Sounding out of breath, he finished by saying, 'Mm. That's about it. I can't add another thing.'

To which Zech responded, 'Pathetic, isn't it?'

A timorous Bernard, admitted, 'Yes, but it's all I know.' He wanted to elaborate, to explain that whilst his knowledge of those greens and the ban placed upon them was scant, he'd provided about as much information as might be gleaned from anyone hereabouts, but then, for his having gone to trouble, he received a cuff to an ear.

'Not *you*—kadoodler! It's pathetic in that no one speaks of it!' Zechariah laughed. 'Bernard, there are times when you break me up! Really, you do!'

Bernard, knowing relief, exclaimed, 'Ah, yes—the taboo!' The word, taboo, as spoken by him, sounded dark and threatening and he enjoyed pronouncing it. *'Taboo!'*

'Yes,' Zech told him, 'and the taboo must be broken.'

'What do you mean?'

'We *will* know more of those greens, Bernard. We will nag all and sundry until we're ragged—if that's what it takes. We will no longer take *no*—or silence—as an acceptable answer.' He thought, regardless of Nancy Noy-Breen and whatever her mysterious arrival on the slope might mean—regardless of the gal's delirious rambling concerning the subject of banned crops—not having the answer to the mystery of greens was not good enough, and it was high time the ridiculous taboo was disregarded. After attending to safe storage of the rope, they would go to find Uncle Samson. He, Samson, would be the first of those questioned.

As it turned out though, when they arrived at the trove chamber, Uncle Samson was already present there. He was occupied in sorting items of his extensive collection—treasure as he termed it—and so preoccupied was he, with making sense of so many jumbled items, he was oblivious to their arrival. Caught unawares, he was taken aback in realizing he was overheard carrying on a conversation with none other than himself. He did not mind so much Zech overhearing him, because the boy was used to his eccentricity, but he was made uncomfortable by Bernard's presence.

Espying the rope, which Bernard carried slung over a shoulder, he announced with more force than intended, 'I've thought of charging you hire for its use.' Seeing them nonplussed, he explained, 'It's my rope you have there. If it's important enough for you to take it without first seeking permission, then as I see it, something of a fine is in order. But I'll settle for letting you have it—at an agreed price.' Bernard was unnerved. The boy looked as though he wished to discard the rope but in resisting the urge to do so, he tightened his grip on it.

Found out, Zechariah was not the least perturbed and attempted to divert attention. 'Salutations, Uncle!' he cried, and then moved to the subject of his choosing. 'I want to hear everything you know about the greens, Uncle. I need to know why it is that we're banned from including them in our diet.' He declared, 'I don't believe for a moment, the stuff's poisonous, because the Tall Ones harvest it for their own use. There's so much of it. It covers vast fields and it's there for the taking.'

That stuff! Welcome inclusion to our diet! Samson thought, and steeling himself, pushed down an urge to shudder. Quite apart from the topic of greens, he reviewed Zechariah's manner. He was all too often distracted and even flummoxed by the boy's choice of words and turn of phrase. Just where, he wondered, was the boy coming from, in greeting him by employing such word as "Salutations"? Was he incapable of announcing, 'Hello Uncle,' as would any less peculiar individual? When compared with most others the boy was anything but commonplace. There were those times of late when his behaviour was very unsettling. Had the boy believed even for a moment that the rope missing from its proper place in the trove, went unnoticed, or that he, its rightful owner would not at some stage enquire as to its whereabouts?

Noting its definite absence earlier today had inspired him to begin reorganizing and tidying the place. Realizing the Trove was in such a state of disarray was cause for shame; such treasure deserved far better treatment, and besides which, he was now forced to admit that just about anything might go missing! With all kept in such dishevelled state he could not well enough detect the absence of items belonging to his inventory. Both boys stood waiting there in the entranceway to the large chamber. Young Bernard—"Suicide Bernie", as Samson recalled hearing others refer to him, was still distressed by his being caught out in possession of the rope and his nephew, Zechariah, was just as serious, but for reason of his own. He wanted information concerning the dread crop. They'd get nothing from him on the subject; such was Samson's determination.

Still holding the item he was in the process of moving when the two arrived, Samson knew that he must appear odd, because having found no better place yet to put it, he wore a metal bucket upon his head. The item he held was the topmost part—the detachable circular portion of the Tall Ones' waste receptacle—something he had admired and coveted long previous to commandeering it. He'd liked to have had the receptacle as well, but it had proved beyond his capability of moving due to being burdened with waste at the time: peelings of fruit and discarded, leftover veg', along with much other foul smelling discard, much beyond ordinary description. Hefting higher the thing he held, it clanged against the bucket he wore, unseating it from his head. 'Deeks! Oh, deeks!' He exclaimed, as it clattered amongst a vast array of belongings.

'It's fine, Uncle! Your high-hat is undamaged.'

'It's not the point,' Samson told him, 'there're other things of value lying all about—splendiferous things, which I will not see harmed!' And, when Zech drew close in, attempting to reassure him, Samson, wielding the troublesome object, warded him away with it. He offered apology, 'My dear boy! I am *so* sorry! Are you all right?' For Zech—to accompaniment of loud metallic clang—had gone tumbling backwards, falling amongst items viewed in the instant by Samson, as far less valuable than his nephew.

Stunned, Zechariah shook his head. He looked up from where he lay and sounding enthusiastic, announced, 'Now *that's* what I call a weapon of defence!'

'Call it what you will,' his Uncle said, 'but, in future I'll remind myself to be more careful! I must say, youngster, you're taking it well.'

'It's nothing,' Zech assured him. 'Nothing at all.' Then, getting to his feet, 'Here Uncle, let me take a better look at that thing.' Going to Samson, Zechariah took from him the large, circular object and then grasping it in both paws he turned it over the better to examine it. At one side was a protuberance, in the first place, put there perhaps for the purpose of grasping? Gripping it, Zechariah invited Bernard to come forward and attack him. He said, 'Come on now, Bernard, where's your courage? Show some fighting spirit! Come at me, giving me all you've got!'

Bernard, living up to the old appellation of "Suicide", would like to oblige, thought Samson. He looked keen enough to obey his nephew's command, but displaying reticence then, Bernard hung back. The youngster's reticence was due, Samson saw, to his presence here in such sacrosanct chamber. Samson began to feel his company was unwanted, and in his own territory. Bernard was correct, he thought, because shenanigans the like of which Zechariah encouraged must not be allowed. Zechariah knew better. They could not afford endangering the trove.

'Boys—now, boys!' he protested. 'I will grant you the use of the Weapon of Defence, as you name it, and the rope, my *precious* rope! You will have to agree to put them back when you've finished playing with them, but we cannot have aggressive goings on in here—not here! His nephew was become carried away with himself and heard little of the protest. The deal, a more than fair offering, would not be accepted.

Bernard held back, stationed still at the entrance, nervous of venturing further. He presented as a stubborn, immovable object. He would not leave without first having a word from Zechariah, who had forgotten himself!

Contrary to all he was taught, the boy jumped, flibberty hopping as a mad thing, kazooning hither and yon' about the chamber—exhorting, 'Strike! Strike the enemy down!' and, 'Gazuzzle! Gazuzzle!'

Any idea of the covering of a Tall Ones' waste receptacle proving capable of exerting such an influence as this, was beyond his understanding, but Samson did his best, crying, 'Stop! Zechariah my boy! Desist!'

He lunged towards the youngster in the hope of slowing him down, but his lunging proved wide of the mark, and Zech, perceiving he came under genuine attack, grew all the more excited and yelled, 'Come on, Keeper of Rope! Come on! Your leader must not fall!' Samson saw Bernard drop the rope and scurry to the fray. He next saw Bernard reached for something from the floor of the chamber, but in the same instant, Zechariah came at him, and Samson felt the full brunt of a blow from the "weapon of defence" as it slammed against the side of his head. The ringing of it was loud and as he staggered upon his feet, he heard his nephew's gleeful shouting, 'He's down, Bernard! Finish him, Bernard! Now *finish him off!*'

Samson did not know if the sound of those words was worse, or the sudden pain, as a terrible sharpness pieced his side. He was down, but then went farther it seemed, sinking to darkness as he lost consciousness, there on the trove chamber's floor.

Following a time of indeterminate duration, consciousness returned. He tried opening his eyes. They opened, but with greatest effort. Then he did not see much at all. Something covered his face ... a cloth? It was something of that sort. There was a sound of familiar voices. His nephew was saying, 'In the circumstance, as Keeper of Rope, your action was appropriate. You were ordered to action and you responded. I don't know what more you might expect of yourself.' Zech was calm, thought Samson, as if an ordinary accident was discussed; nothing more serious than a stubbed toe or speck of grit caught in an eye.

The other replied, 'But what if he's ... you know? What if...' Suicide could not bring himself to say it.

On the other paw, Zechariah experienced no such compunction, 'Gazuzzled, is the word you're looking for Bernard.' He then assured, 'If my uncle's met with gazuzzlement then it means that his time was due, which is all very sad of course, but nothing can be done about it and that's that. There's no point mulling it over. We must put the incident behind us, it's the sensible thing to do.'

He said, 'When interment of remains is seen to, we should rest easy. That task though, requires our urgent attention.'

Mortified, the keeper uttered, 'Remains...'

'Yes, we shall bury him here in the chamber. He's far too big and heavy for removal. He's over-weight—which to his credit did bother him.' Seeing, Bernard's quandary, Zechariah said, 'He won't have to worry about that any longer, will he?' He said, 'It's rhetorical, Bernard. No need for response.' After further considering the matter, he reiterated, 'Right here with the collection is where he most enjoyed spending time and so he'll be right at home.'

Bernard cried, 'I threw the thing, and then, down he went! It stuck him... *I didn't mean it!*'

'Get a grip, Keeper!' Zech commanded, 'I'm relying on you. So don't go to pieces. Here—help me move this stuff. There's a deeks of a lot of it, and we'd best make a start.' With Bernard hovering at close quarter, Zechariah began shifting things about, clearing space enough of the chamber floor for the excavation of a resting place.

Samson moaned, but his moaning was not loud; it was imperative that he interrupt Zechariah's plan for him. He could not allow them to bury him alive!

Then, Suicide was exclaiming, 'Oh, thanks be, *he lives!*' Samson felt the cloth covering his face pulled away; at least now he could see! With Bernard bending low to him, Samson tried to speak. His voice was dull and choked and sounded strange to him. Horrid tasting wetness rose in his throat, to fill and leak from the corners of his mouth. Tasting his own blood, whilst it threatened to drown him, was nightmarish ordeal. Attempting to communicate, he was unable to prevent his eyes drooping shut.

'He speaks!' Bernard said, 'If we helter, I'm sure we can reach help! We can save him!'

Zechariah dropped what he was doing and came closer. 'What did he *say?*' He asked, 'Did you make sense of it?'

'No,' Bernard told him, 'but he gurgled for help!' Bernard was beside himself; he said, 'I'm going! I'll be back here before you know it!'

He was at the opening to the main burrow when Zechariah thundered, 'Get yourself back here, Keeper! There's much at stake. You'll make it far worse! Do as I say!' Never before had the leader sounded so forceful. Bernard wanted nothing more than to be away from him. Samson was close to drawing his final breath—was preparing to confront the mystery of meeting with Great Grandfather, and all of it was due to foolish action of his. What punishment would be meted to the one who'd slain him? Confused beyond measure, Bernard wished he'd not been born.

Zech said, 'There's so much blood...' He prodded his uncle's cheek. Then, with one swift movement, he removed the blade from the wound. Hefting the tool, he said, 'This thing is an axe. But an axe of this small size is known as a tomahawk. Uncle was more than a collector. The things he gathered were not all that interested him; his collecting amounted to a calling. He would venture beneath the Tall Ones' dwelling place, hearkening and learning all he could. He was a most knowledgeable individual.'

Bernard shrugged, hoping that his doing so would not be taken as a rude sign of disinterest in his leader's reminiscing.

'He went so far as to attend a small study group held by the bard. Yes, the renowned Piedmont.' Zechariah informed, 'The aim was to know more of Tall Ones' language and their ways. It's difficult, crediting so rough an individual, as my uncle, with such dedication, isn't it?' Zechariah was relaxed, as if the one-sided communication was nothing other than the most pleasant discourse.

Shrugging, by way of response to questions, had proved acceptable and so the gesture was repeated. The leader's slow singsong voice affected Bernard; tiring and all but depleting his will. Suspicious of such subduing, an inner voice insisted, 'I must rush for help!' As soon as opportunity presented itself ... then ... he would go.

Then, Zechariah's droning monologue was broken off. Raising the bloodied weapon to his lips, it was granted a kiss. Revolted by the morbid deed, Bernard moved. A dark spell was broken. He snapped wide-awake and went heltering at a pace never before achieved!

In noting Bernard's departing contrary to his command, Zechariah was not very surprised. Until now, Bernard was loyal and true and reliable. Bernard was unafraid of being hurt by others, or of hurting himself, but now a significant, unenviable flaw of character was evinced. In inflicting pain on *others*, Bernard was made fearful. Pondering the fact of the matter, the leader thought it a most curious turn.

He addressed his wounded relative, 'Uncle, for what I am about to do I shall suffer remorse for the remainder of my days but time's a wasting and of necessity, matters must be hastened.' Raising the tool high overhead he averted his gaze, and hazarding a guess as to the precise location of his target, he brought the tomahawk down. The blunt edge of the tool was facing downwards so as to inflict pain, but not so much that gazuzzlement would too soon result. Estimating the degree of actual damage before delivery was difficult, but Uncle Samson continued splutter-screaming for long enough to allow Zechariah's assuming the desired effect was achieved. Uncle would transpire, nothing was more certain, but not as direct result of the most recent blow. When genuine answers to questions regarding greens were secured, then demise would be expedited.

How much time would pass before the Keeper of Rope knew his mistaken behaviour for what it was; and when would he return? In the event he brought others back with him, no matter Bernard's story, it would be disputed. He, Zechariah, might even prefer Bernard return with others, because then, as a far more persuasive witness to the unfortunate occurrence, he would offer Bernard an easy way out, and, Bernard would take it. The truth was that Bernard had picked up the tomahawk and then was careless in discarding it. It was no fault of his though, when Uncle Samson tripped and fell on the thing, thereby sustaining injury. There was so much mess in the chamber that sooner or later a mishap was inevitable. Bernard, an individual of good, but perhaps too sincere conscience, was confused. Confused, as anyone would be after such a shocking accident.

As many paws lightened the load, he would appreciate any assistance offered, in putting his relative to rest. Zechariah the Great was not much when it came to manual labour; never much the keen digger.

He would wager that Bernard would return unaccompanied. He would not be too much longer and so, Zechariah again lifted the tomahawk. As an instrument of truth finding it was an exemplary tool. It worked wonders, and this time it was raised higher, as he framed his next question. His uncle was forthcoming and provided the most fascinating information. "New" greens—or "old" greens, as far as the present generation might term them—long ago were included in the diet—were in fact relished by Folk of Fur, but their consumption produced an astonishing difference in their offspring. Not all, but many of those consuming greens, parented most unusual offspring. Those babes were not born malformed—not as Uncle, who, gurgling and sputtering between words, described them. There was nothing pathetic about such folk, decided Zech, interpreting information in his own inimitable way. They entered the world bearing fascinating alteration to their anatomy and were athletic, ferocious and quite fearless. They were bright-coloured glorious creatures! They went unrecognized as such, but in point of fact were true warriors! Learning of them, Zechariah was unable to restrain himself in seeking further and final information.

TUMP IS WARNING GIVEN

'Tump is warning given by a friend when danger threatens. Tump is no individual—not at all!

'Oh my dear—please, *do be well!*'

Nancy did not respond. Mavis Noy-Breen and father, Charlie, worried.

Three days ago, Nancy's friend, Sara, had come heltering to the Noy-Breen home, warning that Nancy had suffered an accident. Mavis dropped what she was doing and rushed from the warren to her daughter. There had been little improvement since then. Nancy suffered debilitating fever and when awakening for short periods, she was inconsolable, held in thrall of delirium, the like of which Mavis had never seen.

She was used to the child's precocious way, to her fits of fancy and whimsical notions but for the most part, the gal's feet were planted enough in reality. Her interest in the work of the bard was perhaps obsessive when compared with the interest of others, and during her illness she spoke of him. She ranted as if possessed. Mavis, not leaving the chamber for long, staying watchful at her side, hoping for sign of improvement, heard much of the old one, much stuff of sick imagining—things she did not the least like hearing.

Not until the end of the third day was a change in Nancy's condition evident. By this time, Mavis, who'd reached the point of exhaustion, felt she was in danger of going down a similar path, a path leading to madness albeit against every wise reasoning.

After three days, Nancy raised her head and asked, 'Mother? Is there anything to eat? I'm so hungry. I'm ravenous!'

Mavis put her face close to the child's, saying, 'Oh, dear heart, we have you back with us.' Going to the chamber's opening, she called, 'Charles, come quick! Come see. There's great improvement!'

Charlie Noy-Breen flibberty hopped making least possible noise. He would spend much time gathering the best produce from the Tall Ones' planting place, and in the days to come would bring her the finest carrots he could find. His daughter deserved nothing if not the very best. Not before her complete recovery would they mention Zechariah.

Over the three days following her accident, the boy, Zechariah, had come by offering commiserations. A considerate and caring nature was demonstrated. He had presented himself without fail, each day, at the entranceway of the Noy-Breen home to enquire after the state of his daughter's health, and Charlie was impressed by the attention shown her. Mavis was not so impressed, which was surprising. Learning of her outright cynicism where the boy was concerned, Charlie was compelled to defend sustaining interest. 'She'll be pleased,' he claimed. 'Just wait, Mavis, and you'll see.' Then, challenged further by his wife's doubting expression, Charlie explained, 'They are *young*, Mavis! The boy's taken with her and that's quite apart from caring for her recovery from illness. He's besotted. It's plain to see. It's not so terrible a thing. He's respectful and always polite. I can't see eye to eye with your objection.'

'Those very things you mention, are precisely what bothers me,' Mavis said.

'His qualities?' Charlie asked, smiling.

'He's delivered so many bunches of wild-flowers over the last three days, I'm tired of having our other children throw them back into the field,' was all she said.

By the following morning, Mavis decided that Nancy was well enough to receive visitors. With Mavis gone from the chamber, Sara Mazengarb protested, 'We came by earlier than this but your mother told us you were too ill to see us.'

'It's true,' Emily Longpod agreed, and glances passed between them. Sara's quick glance said she did not require validation by Emily; not in her relating the truth of matters, and Emily's said she believed Sara was too suspicious of her motive in offering support.

'We were sent packing,' Sara said.

Emily hastened to explain, 'Sent off in the nicest possible way. Your mother was concerned for you, and that was understood.'

Sara said, 'And so, Longpod and I have spent the last three days tearing at our fur, worrying over you.' On that point they were in complete agreement.

Her tone conspiratorial, Nancy said, 'Mother is overprotective. She can be rather short, at times.' She said, 'I was ill, but not from any commonplace cause.' Recognizing that mystery was hinted at, the friends huddled close, trusting that a revelation was intended. The patient was quiet before continuing, 'I was met with by strangers—entities from our future—from a future time.' She said, 'I received instruction from them.' Sara and Emily, despite those words piquing curiosity, again looked one to other and this time their glances said that agreement was shared. Friend Nancy was not yet recovered from her hitherto unheard-of sickness involving fever of mind. Knowing them, Nancy protested, 'Oh, come on now. You're my friends! Do you think I'm making it up?'

Sara replied, 'No, of course not.'

'But, you've been ill, Nancy,' Emily said. 'Indeed, we *are* friends, aren't we Sara?' Hurrying on, she enquired, 'And so who were these entities? That's as you termed them, isn't it?'

'Well, I believe that one of them was the bard.'

'The bard,' asked Sara, voice at once hushed and incredulous. 'Which bard? Who?'

'The Bard of the Epics,' Nancy said. The friends smiled and then were unable to prevent giggling. Their giggling turned to outright laughter and, confused and embarrassed, Nancy covered her face with her paws.

Seeing Nancy distressed, Emily insisted, 'Oh, Sara, do stop it!' She said, 'Nancy, we understand. You were befuddled! Your poor mind was taken by fever.'

'Yes, the mind plays tricks!' Sara said.'

'I've not been myself,' admitted Nancy, 'It was all very strange...' she paused. 'But I *know* it was true!'

'We're not saying you're making it up Noy-Breen,' Sara said. 'When health returns, then you'll know what we mean.'

They offered little choice. Nancy said, 'I suppose you may be right,' She thought, I would rather have you as friends, than not. From now on I'll not mention any of it. Pushing back feeling of deep disappointment, she knew that their friendship underwent a subtle altering; it would not continue quite as she had assumed.

Satisfied by her agreeing with their estimation of ailment, Sara, changing the course of conversation, next said, 'Of course, you can't have heard, but Zechariah the Great mourns the loss of his uncle. His, Uncle Samson, the collector of so much Tall One trash, has met with gazuzzlement.'

Emily added, 'Oh yes, and he—poor Zechariah—arranged to have his relative entombed along with items valued by him; his treasure—as Zech refers to it.'

'It made for uncommon occasion.' Sara said, 'Those attending the service were crammed into the burrow, so it was hot and difficult to breathe, and Zechariah went on and on forever in praising his relative.'

'He insisted everyone show up,' Emily said, 'out of respect.'

'Despite,' Sara said, 'Samson's being quite solitary during life and not on familiar terms with so many of those Zechariah insisted should attend.'

'He's very persuasive, isn't he?' Emily said, 'He's slight of stature, but no sooner does he open his mouth, and all and sundry stop what they're doing, to hear him.' She said, 'He's good at influencing others.'

'In any case,' Sara said, 'it was unusual enough, being present there in the trove chamber, to make the occasion bearable. You would not believe such a sheer quantity of junk was collected by just one individual, would you Em'?'

Rather than respond to Sara's question, Emily said, 'He's been here to visit you, you know.'

'Yes.' Sara said, 'Your mother asked what we think his problem is. She believes there's something not quite right with him.'

'He's been here often, and he brings you flowers.'

'Yes, but your mother has not allowed him in,' said Sara. 'Had she treated us with more consideration, then we might have provided her with detail of the great Zechariah's uncommon ways.' Nancy's curiosity was apparent but she made no comment, and Sara continued, 'There's the way he has little Bernard gather flowers for him. He doesn't at all trouble picking them himself. He sends Bernard off to the creek-side pasture to get them *for* him and then he, Zechariah, shows up at your burrows.'

'Which means,' said Emily, but was interrupted by Sara's interjecting,

'*We* have decided...'

'That he lacks sincerity,' Emily finished.

'You deserve better,' said Sara, as if it was decided.

The friends were surprised then, because Nancy declared, 'I think it's wonderful, eccentric behaviour.' Noting again, Sara and Emily's glances. She said, 'I'm amused by his unusual approach. It has a certain appeal.'

'You're joking!'

'No.'

'In any case, he's been turned away. He will not be in to see you. Your mother can't stand the sight of him.'

'Which is where another of his traits should be considered,' Emily said. Nancy and Sara waited, 'He'll persist. Someone like him is not going to accept, no, as an answer.'

Speaking in unison, both Nancy and Sara responded, 'There is no one like him!' The friends laughed, and in that small moment of merriment nothing was changed; they were as close as ever they were.

* * *

Charlie Noy-Breen took his time in flibberty hopping back from old Samson's place. Prior to his leaving the place he'd been invited by the boy, Bernard, to take with him an item of inestimable worth. Charlie was not at first sure of the item's practical use, but he trusted Bernard did not mislead. Bernard had explained that the item presented had once formed part of something Tall Ones called a tricycle, a child's conveyance. The particular item was a small "rear-wheel" from such. 'It's similar to those seen on churners and other Tall One vehicles, of course, but this is a most valuable, miniature!' Charlie knew it was valuable because, were it not so, then old Samson would not in the first place have made it part of his collection.

When it came to collecting, Samson had known what he was about. Apart from some uncertainty existing with regard to his finding a use for the item, Charlie was at first also unsure of the youngster, Bernard's, real reason in gifting it him. In crossing the field with said wheel, he decided the reason given was satisfactory enough.

A few members of the community of New Warren Central were to receive gifts from the trove. They were, albeit unknown to themselves, admired and respected for who they were by the deceased, Samson. Before meeting gazuzzlement, the oldster had informed the youngster, his nephew, Zechariah, of his intention to bequeath them special items.

Charlie's requesting information as to the identity of parties other than him, in line for receiving gifts, was met with refusal; Bernard had revealed nothing. In a very direct manner Charlie was told, 'No. None of that should concern you. You should be grateful!' Spoken to in such abrupt fashion and by one so youthful, Charlie was taken aback. To him those words had amounted to something of a dressing down, and he was inclined to deem the gift unacceptable. But then, when Bernard informed him of Samson's holding him in such high regard, Charlie had changed his mind and accepting the wheel had made sense.

By now, he found the thing interesting for its own sake. He was fascinated by the fact it possessed many impressive, shining parts, thin reeds, which radiated outwards from its centre. Charlie found that he was reminded of the sun and the way it was oft' depicted by youngsters when they scratched images of it upon dusty ground. Interest piqued, he'd learned that those many thin parts were named spokes.

Bernard had explained, 'They are related to wire, that material we see strung on those structures referred to by Tall Ones as fences. Charlie was acquainted, of course, with the material described, but feigning ignorance and seeing the youngster put to trouble in giving such a fulsome explanation, made Charlie feel better after being disrespected earlier.

Venturing little comment he'd let Bernard prattle forth, providing extensive information. Until now Charlie had entertained not the slightest interest in the language of the Tall Ones, but in making his way over the grassy field on his way home and in knowing he now owned one, he pronounced aloud the word wheel. 'It's a wheel,' he muttered, as he rolled the thing along the way. 'I have a wheel.' And so, homeward they went, with him turning it over and over upon itself, rather than lugging it across a shoulder or putting himself to so much difficulty in dragging it behind him through long, tangled grass.

'You will not bring that inside!' exclaimed Mavis.

'It was never my intention,' Charlie told her. 'I just meant you to come outside and take a look at it.'

'What is it then?' Mavis asked, expression nonplussed, as she made a cursory study of the object lying upon the bare ground just beyond the entranceway. She was curt with him, which was unfair. It was not the first time today he was spoken to with such undeserved rudeness.

Retaliating in kind, he announced, 'It's a gift from beyond the grave. It's a wheel of course!' Perhaps he was foolish in continuing, 'I should have known all along that you would have not the slightest regard for such, but it may interest you to learn that in receiving it, *I* am honoured!'

'Where has it come from?' she asked.

'I just told you,' Charlie said, puffing out his chest, 'From beyond the grave. It's bequeathed *us* by old Samson.' Seeing her look of disbelief, he repeated, 'It's a wheel! For deeks' sake, wife—a thing of great worth—a genuine *collectable!*'

'And it's bequeathed, *us?* Let's be clear now, Charlie. If I'm to understand... You claim that *I* own some share in it?'

'Yes. It's now property of the Noy-Breen family. You have it.'

'Then you must take my half back to wherever you got it,' she ordered, 'As long as I am wife to you, Charles, I want no part of it!' Turning away, she flibberty hopped into the burrow with him calling after her.

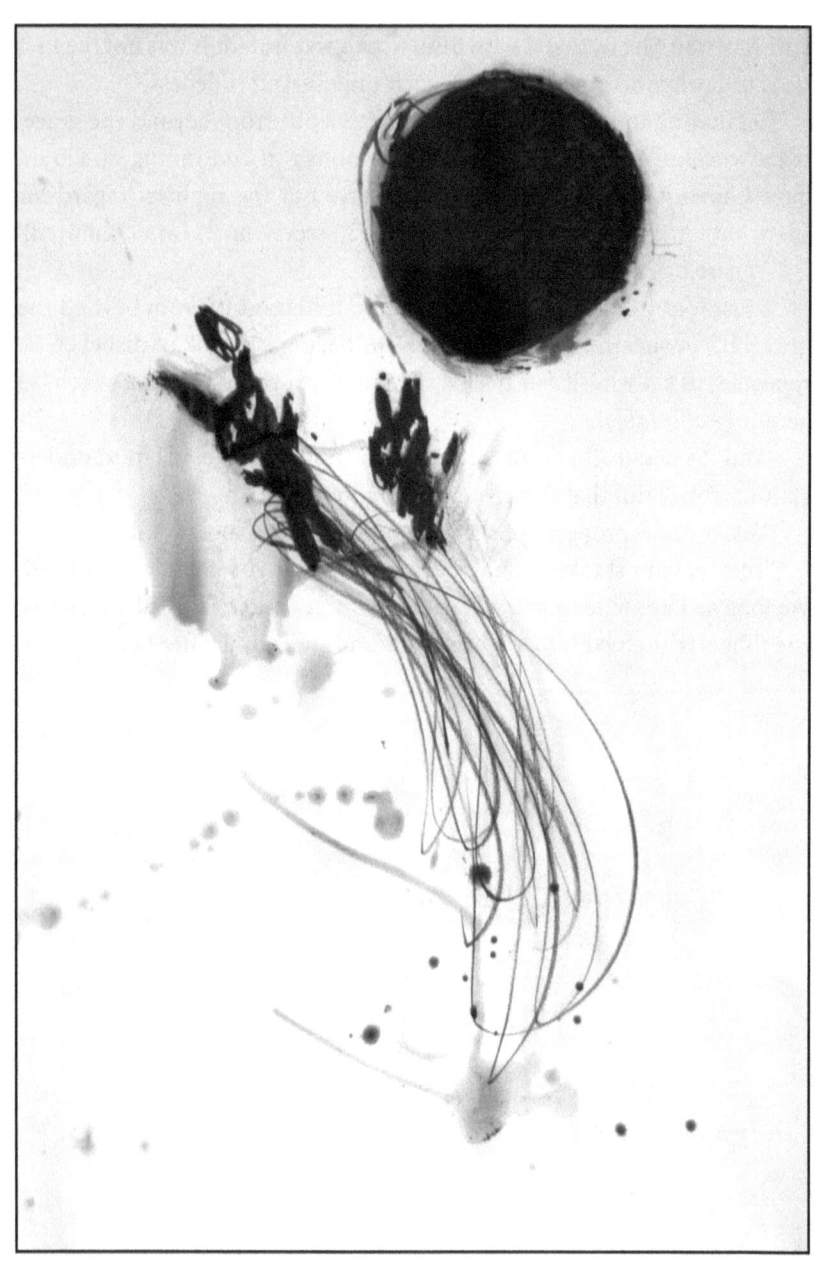

Move!

PRECIOUS SCRATCHINGS

'I will be going with you,' Peace said. 'And, Piedmont, there's no point arguing over it, because I insist.' She said, 'I will be there to see harm does not befall you. I'll watch over you.'

Piedmont did not feel any "watching over" was required, and he wondered what Peace Darkling imagined she might do in the event trouble was encountered. She would cope no better than he. In his going alone, advantage was sure, because if trouble threatened, just one of them would fall prey to it. Piedmont voiced not the least objection to her making him out as all but helpless. Previous to this, he'd done well in meeting with, and fetching, young Nancy to the hilltop, hadn't he? He would not voice disagreement with the idea of Peace accompanying him, because he did not want to risk a last moment alteration to, or even cancellation, of his plan. After such a very long time of waiting, he was to be sent back for the records, the precious scratchings, and rather than complain, he must think of her wishing to accompany him as complimentary.

Sherbrook fumed, and Clever Fixer, too, was not pleased. They wanted Skip to move them to New Warren Central, either with or without the bard! Hearing them bickering for all they were worth, over taking his place for his "own good", Piedmont could not credit it. They would go back in his stead, they said, to the time of Graymark rule—to the very afternoon of the very day during which, long ago they'd departed the place—and then they would take care of business!

Much trepidation was experienced by Piedmont when, before so much as consulting the map, Sherbrook and Fixer were ready to overlook the description of events displayed upon leaves. In selfish questing for adventure, they declared, 'The tree and its depiction of things does not matter so much...' They claimed that things shown, very often were at variance with actual events. For example, they'd not seen Skibeau. His presence during the previous sojourn was not foretold was it? No it was not, and so none of them was proficient enough in reading leaves.

Depictions of events ought not therefore, be taken with too much seriousness.

Witness to so much dissembling, Piedmont thought he might scream, but kept silent. In making a study of the tree, both young Skip and Peace Darkling, determined that if Sherbrook was allowed to venture to Graymark time, then disaster would ensue. If Clever went, then he ended in serving time beneath the oak, right there alongside Sherbrook. Beneath the oak they would endure punishment far worse than anything involving the manufacture of whiskbrooms as Piedmont suffered. In examining scenes and outcomes shown by the map, none saw anything of ill nature occurring, if Peace accompanied the bard, and so Piedmont was pleased enough in feigning complete agreement with being watched over.

When seeing that fate shared amounted to infliction of extreme degradation, Clever and Sherbrook teamed together in demanding an explanation of Skip. Most vehement of them, Sherbrook demanded, 'Why is it you do not move Clever and me back here before those kadoodling gollystompers are allowed to do that to us? That's what I'd like to know. How about it, Buckaroo? Where the deeks are *you* while this madness takes place?' Skip told him, 'How would I know? Your problem, Sherbrook, is that you expect me to know everything. You do realize, don't you, I'm *not* omniscient?'

Sherbrook, unable to drag his gaze from the tree's depictions, said, 'I must say, I don't fancy battling against Brother Serpent. Look at me there. How embarrassing! Where's my jacket? I'm *naked* for deeks sake!' He examined several other leaves, some of which showed Fixer also set to task battling the reptile, and somewhat surprised at the brave job Clever made of it, Sherbrook could not help but comment, 'I would never have guessed you so agile, Fixer, nor so fit.' He added, 'I suppose the acquisition of such physique can be attributed to all the tramping you've done, a life time's worth.'

Clever, studying leaves, responded, 'Thanks, Sherbrook, but I also am having trouble believing the Graymark doe would have us confront that thing, and without the least protection. Look, they even insist upon me going without my hat! You see there. The lieutenant is tossing it to the dirt. Indecent is what that is!'

Sherbrook told him, 'You were not there, not as the rest of us. To believe any of it, you had to have been there. At the end, Grammy was corrupt and perverse. Her every whim was indulged—every vain urge and impulse. These scenes do not surprise me. Observe, and you'll see what I mean. By the time shown here, she's degenerated to become a very nasty individual. Have you ever seen such pleasure gained at the expense of another's dire predicament? Notice the twinkle in her eye? Sickening isn't it?' Staring overhead, Clever could not other than agree, and beneath his breath he muttered condemnation. Removing his gaze from the tree, Sherbrook told Piedmont, 'You know, Bard, it's been so long, I'd half forgotten what it was like back there, back *then*. Be assured that my best wishes go with you.' Turning to Peace, he said, 'And the same applies, Peace. If anything goes awry you can just bet that the fixer and I'll be hot on your flibberty-trail! We're right behind you all the way!' He heard Clever Fixer's quiet enquiring, 'How, in name of sanity, did they manage the capture of Brother Serpent?'

'Easy,' Sherbrook said, 'See that big fellow staring out over the heads of the crowd? He's Sobriety—Sobriety Fawn. He's big, and not just big, but strong with it, and a skilled fighter. At that time, he was the best that New Warren had. Fearless Sobriety! I'd guess that Grammy had Sobriety capture Brother Serpent, rather than convince him to flee. We should feel honoured, Fixer, in knowing she thinks us tough enough to go up against such opponent.' Sherbrook recalled, 'It was ages ago when *I* met up with Brother Serpent. Some of us were in the field down by the pond, after Bucky's passing, and I was in the company of Richard, when we came upon Brother Serpent.' He said, 'He's as nasty as he looks, isn't he? When he's riled, he's *mighty fast!*'

'Oh, deeks!' Fixer exclaimed. Leaves showed the fixer struck fast in his white, furry midsection!

The serpent struck with lightning speed and for Clever Fixer it was over. When the venom took effect, he would be done and gone. But, the fixer, summoning last vestige of strength, fought on. Witnessing the way his other self rushed to aid a friend, Sherbrook cheered him on! Then Sherbrook had to look away for both his and Fixer's fates proved too similar.

'Graymark is beyond mad!' Piedmont exclaimed, expressing outrage.

'The greens cause *more* the madness!' Peace exclaimed. 'Such behaviour is the result of their consumption!' She said, 'I am not depicted here—and so I *should* accompany you Piedmont! I may not have the opportunity, but regardless of cause for all shown here, I will enjoy giving Graymark a piece of my mind and the rest of them for they *rejoice* at suffering of others!'

Skip said, 'Folk of Fur at New Warren Central should no longer concern us. Tump must become One.'

Bunty turned away from the gruesome scene. 'You special ones are sad,' he said.

'How's that?' Sherbrook asked.

Bunty told him, 'It's true—Folk of Fur *can* be cruel! But hearing you, with your outrage over what the tree shows, it's as if you believe unkindness has safe, natural limitation!' Staring at Sherbrook he said, 'Cruelty, once accepted, recognizes no bounds.'

Sherbrook protested, 'Oh, come on!' He did not appreciate such intensity from Bunty.

Forestalling further bickering, Piedmont spoke up, announcing, 'I will be honoured by your company, Peace.' In defiance of the map depicting too many horrid outcomes, he insisted, 'All must prove well, and together I'm confident that we'll make a wonderful go of it.'

'Bard?' Skip said, gaining Piedmont's attention, 'The records are voluminous. There are so many of them. My thought is that you should sit on them.'

'Sit on scratchings? I'm not sure that I understand.'

Skip explained, 'We won't want to miss anything, will we? There is far too much material involved and I want to ensure nothing's left behind. You can make a big tidy heap and then with you riding, as it were, atop the records, I will move you and the works in entirety.'

The suggestion made sense, thought Piedmont, and so he nodded agreement. But, if he were to ride scratchings, as Skip described it, then he'd be sure to place something least valuable from the collection, beneath him. Notation, representing a first, rough draft of an epic or such, would seem an appropriate choice. Skip was right, there was much back there in the chamber of records; he'd never wasted anything. It was not his wont to discard things.

Smiles passing between them, Peace Darkling again offered, 'I will watch over you.'

Taking hold of Piedmont's arm, she invited, 'Skip, will you move us?'

In the following instant, the bard was there, back where he'd long wanted to be.

Arriving at New Warren Central, at a time occurring just after Skip, Sherbrook, Peace, and he'd earlier departed, Piedmont realized that he might gaze up along the sloping path and see an earlier version of himself but decided he would not look. Knowing that his earlier self had not seen him, he would take care not to risk that happening now.

In fleeing the place, those earlier versions of them would have reached the point along the path where they contended with the Graymark lieutenant, Lucille Cropper, but Piedmont confronted another problem. There was worse than Lucille Cropper to contend with.

No matter how he searched for her, he could not see Peace Darkling anywhere. Her absence was not without irony; as desirous as she was to accompany him, she had now failed to show up!

This was no time for levity. He must think. When they first left New Warren Central, she'd gone on ahead, to await their arrival at the foot of the big hill. Scratching at his forehead, Piedmont wondered if he might find the present version of Peace waited there, along with the first. Doubting the likelihood of such an outside chance proving correct, but having no better idea of where she might be found, he set off to look for her there. Skirting around bushes and large clumps of tall growing grasses, and bending low in going by several small rocky outcroppings in following the same trail taken by the earlier Peace, extreme care was taken in assuring his presence remained undetected. Knowing that most of the New Warren Central residents were present now, at the banquet held in Grammy's Great Hall of Power, was appreciated.

Piedmont's trusting the tree in its capacity as map had increased over time, and yet some small doubt lingered. He wondered whether error should be attributed to a lack of skill in Skip's moving them, or might error rest with the tree expressing its will? Where indeed was Peace Darkling? Was her disappearance somehow arranged by the tree or was he too willing to imagine as much?

He'd tried to find her, but would hazard no further guess as to her whereabouts. He turned back upon the way. He would backtrack and see to the successful retrieval of the records, which, after all, was his purpose for returning here.

He'd not gone far when the dread voice of Lucille Cropper came to him from the path. Piedmont paused, listening. 'This will be the making of us! Her Majesty will grant us anything we wish, Raymond. You'll see!'

Preoccupied in again setting off on his way, Piedmont happened to knock a foot against a small stone. He tripped and falling, cried, 'Deeks!' And his cry was loud enough to be heard! He was astonished at how fast they reached him.

'Where are the others?' Lucille Cropper demanded. She stared down at him where he lay sprawled. Taken aback by her question, the bard expressed puzzled confusion, 'Who? Which others?' He received a kick from the gollystomper, Raymond.

Lucille Cropper searched about for sign of Sherbrook and Skip but they were nowhere to be seen. Knowing the youngster, Skip was gone, was cause for secret gratitude; the strange boy and his ways were as darkness itself. She turned back to Piedmont and after ordering him to his feet, told him, 'Bard, you are thick. You should have gone with the others, but you've lost your chance.' She told, Raymond, 'Get him moving. We're taking him back!' She clutched at the cameo as if it would again escape her. The bard was shoved, and then with Raymond escorting, Piedmont followed the lieutenant.

Arrived at the main entranceway of New Warren Central, he gazed across to that shaded area beneath the oak. Even after so much time elapsing, the place seemed imbued with threat and menace.

Days of incarceration were by no means forgotten, and a visceral shuddering coursed through him. The lieutenant was quick to offer, 'Indeed, Bard, beneath yon' oak is your rightful place. There you belong. But first you must stand before her Majesty.' She said, 'Now, Ray, he must behave...' Returning her knowing smile, Raymond was eager to provide the captive encouragement.

Realizing the intent, Piedmont hastened to explain, 'Fear not, I shall show respect! Her Majesty will be over the moon with your having me in custody!'

Lucille Cropper responded, 'She will, won't she?' And it seemed to Piedmont that they were complicit in desiring identical outcome, but the moment was gone when she snapped, 'Let's go!'

Piedmont feigned a hobbling gait; they soon might be forced to drag him. Leaving the outdoors behind, the Tunnel of Love was too soon traversed, and then sounds of merry making filled the air. There was the intermingling odour of every fine food imaginable, and something else, a gruesome odour he could not name. Never one to overindulge, the bard knew disgust upon hearing Raymond's, 'Mm! Oh yum!'

At the wide opening of the Hall of Power, the bard was sick to his stomach. He could not have imagined such excess, such gluttony. Folk behaved as if demented. Stuffing their faces—gormandizing in an orgy of consumption!

The chamber's hard-packed dirt floor pooled with vomit and Piedmont exerted conscious effort in preventing himself from gagging—stomach perilously churning, he dry-heaved. Folk engaged there in hippety-hop-splashing through the green, glistening wetness. Stench of new greens was overwhelming.

Upon moving he might have borrowed a 'kerchief from friend, Fixer, something with which to cover his mouth and nose; he must not submit to fear and disgust. Neither Raymond nor Lucille Cropper was the least upset by anything here. Their pleasure at joining the throng was undisguised. Biting down on his tongue, Piedmont's resolve firmed.

The lieutenant shouted, 'Her Majesty will not be kept waiting!' He felt a sharp jab to his side. Wincing, Piedmont raised his head high. Dragged by his arms, he was rushed forward into the mêlée! He wished that his captors would think to lift him high, as parents sometimes carried playful children; at least then his feet would be above the floor. If he looked down he knew he would lose heart.

Her Majesty, surrounded by her entourage, was situated at far remove and plunging forwards, dragged through the raucous throng, Piedmont saw Nan numbered amongst them.

She wasted no time in sidling close to Lillian Graymark, informing of his approach. Cocking her head the better to hear above sounds of debauchery, Grammy's expression became serious. Enjoying in the moment, making short work of consuming a prime example of Royal

Beauty carrot, in the next, tossing its remains to the floor, and then wiping with the back of a paw at her mouth, her expression soured. After wiping both paws on the bodice of her gown, she was prepared for meeting with him.

Noting Nan's smug expression, Piedmont knew disappointment. He'd thought they were friends, but that was long ago in a happier time. Pushing revellers aside, Lucille Cropper commanded, 'Move! Make way—flea-bait! Prisoner coming through!' And Raymond delivered loud thwacking slaps to any, too tardy. So much for caring, passive means, observed Piedmont. Things changed—and fast! An aura of unreality pervaded, and he wished he were dreaming.

In the royal presence then, he stood tall, vowing silence for the moment and gazing in forthright manner to Grammy Graymark. The look she gave him was well practised, at once haughty and challenging, and intended to wilt and shrivel. Underlings quieted, the better to follow proceedings and curious looks turned his way. His captors seemed more nervous than he. Their nervousness included much expectation, for the cameo was theirs—and the prospect of reward!

The bard was in trouble again and none would lend their support. With greens-filled bellies, they preferred his ordeal.

Many muttered now in close huddled groups amongst themselves, but those at farthest reaches of the great hall, remaining unaware of unusual entertainment in the offing, continued with stuffing themselves, whooping and hollering, so that even the faintest pretence of right-minded behaviour was abandoned.

An aged buck, part of a group of those most privileged, but whom Piedmont was unable to name, commanded, 'Silence! We will have quiet!' Coming from such quarter and delivered with such an authoritative note, the command did not require repeating. All about the hall even the most rowdy were obedient in heeding the order to silence.

As last sound of merriment melted away, the bard released a long, audible sigh. Lieutenant Cropper and Raymond spoke at once, 'Majesty we have…'

And, 'He was…'

Speaking over them, the authoritative buck snapped, 'You will wait until addressed!'

Denied the opportunity to speak, Lieutenant Cropper and Raymond were crestfallen. Her Majesty, Piedmont decided, presented a somewhat comic aspect. She was enjoying herself and beneath raised, condemning creased brow, her eyes sparkled with delight. She had not desisted in chewing upon a long stick of celery. She would not deign hear whatever it was the lieutenant would impart; Cropper could wait. Grammy chose rather to comment upon Piedmont's long sighing. 'You are tired, Bard, is that it?' In questioning him she raised an eyebrow and somehow all the while kept nibbling.

In responding, the bard gave the impression he believed her enquiry solicitous. He admitted, 'Oh, indeed yes. Weary to the bone, if you must know, Lillian.' He was quick to add, 'Weary—not in body but in spirit.' To his surprise, Piedmont then found nervousness dissipated; he did not so much dread her.

After momentary consideration, Lillian asked, '...to bone, and yet, not body? You may be losing your touch, Bard.' She took another bite of celery.

'Oh, who cares?' declared Piedmont. 'I don't.'

Bemused, Grammy scratched at her left ear. Speaking as he did in such an easy-going, off-paw manner, his responding as he had could be taken as disrespect, but Her Majesty did not seem irritated by the bard's provocative manner. Some of those present took Grammy's easy manner as indicative of boredom experienced with having the difficult bard brought to her attention again. In times to come, in relating detail of the course the meeting took, others would go so far as to describe the meeting of the sovereign and bard as a reunion of equals; there was little evidence of their being at loggerheads.

Piedmont rushing on, announced, 'The Lieutenant and her friend are most dutiful. They serve you well.' He glanced to his left, and then to the right, indicating Lucille Cropper and Raymond. 'I thought to depart New Warren Central, but it's clear now my plans are circumvented.' He added, 'Quite apart from dragging me before you, they would return your long lost keepsake.'

In the instant of his speaking, Grammy doubted her hearing, and a mixture of curiosity and confusion beset her countenance. Having the advantage, Piedmont pressed on, 'Why don't you show her Majesty what you have there, Lucille?' Lucille Cropper's moment had arrived and no further encouragement was required. Extending an open paw, she presented the keepsake.

But then, sighting such treasure, a thing of inestimable worth, something believed forever lost, Grammy was overwhelmed and with heart quickened to racing, she was compelled to cough. And she coughed again! And so, with celery lodged part way down her throat, her eyes rolled up, revealing their blood-shot whites!

A bystander cried, 'It's gone down the royal oesophagus the wrong way!'

Horrible gagging commenced, the sound of which was revolting, 'Aaarghh! Aaagghh! Gahrrf!' Unceasing spasms of retching followed as Grammy clawed at air and space before her, and then doubling over, attempted jamming a large desperate paw into the open chasm of her mouth! The other of her paws clutched at her throat! Overcoming initial shock, others then scrambled to aid her!

Mindful of the seer's long-standing prediction of Grammy's choking to gazuzzlement, Piedmont turned from the scene. They were distracted, and so *off he went*, helter skedaddling as fast as his legs would carry him! Daunted by squishy mess, slipping and sliding in most clumsy fashion, he crossed the Hall of Power! He traversed the Tunnel of Love at a mighty dashing pace! Made quite breathless, but knowing a feeling of great exhilaration, he was then out into dazzling sunlight! And next, must retrieve the precious scratchings. The dusty archive beckoned!

Arrived at the chamber he began scrabbling all about. He grabbed at everything he could lay paw to! After shoving many strayed, bundled sheets of scratchings together with the rest, so that a mountainous heap was formed, piled at the centre of the floor, he made short work of scrambling upwards. Once seated there at the peak of knowledge, perched as Brother Eagle, high upon the record of ages, he waited. He was conscientious, but if scratchings were missing, there was no longer time for concern.

In anticipating a speedy rescue, hope was not misplaced. He'd waited for just a mere moment when the chamber walls vanished! After a bright and eye-watering flashing of light was past, he looked down from his high perch, and saw smiling faces staring up at him. The precious scratchings were where they belonged, and so too was he!

Tump gathered there on the lush grass before the cottage veranda, in the realm of pleasant meadow, of merry-flowing stream beneath a cheery blue sky, in Bunty's wondrous realm.

Skip was pleased, and grinning, he looked up at the bard. Moving Piedmont was, after so much concern, accomplished and over with. He offered, 'Some ride, eh, Piedmont?'

Relieved, the bard informed, 'Oh, yes! It was quite the experience, and it's wonderful to be back.

Then staring up at him, Sherbrook enquired, 'Bard? What is it—that dreadful, stinking muck on your feet?'

Piedmont told him, 'Oh, it's nothing! I won't go into detail describing any of its cause.

'Suffice to say … a price was paid. Having paid it, I'm happy enough now.' But then, with Piedmont returned, all was not as should be.

Sherbrook, looking about, asked, 'But where is Peace? Piedmont, where is she?'

'Peace?' Piedmont said, 'Well, after so much fussing over accompanying me, she failed to show up. And when she did not arrive I wondered if…'

'Failed to arrive?' Skip interjected, 'But how?'

And so they celebrated too soon.

Scratching

Peace by Moonlight

Where, in the name of all that was good, was Piedmont? Why was he not here with her? For that matter, where was she? The present location was not New Warren Central. She had moved with Piedmont and in the following instant, found she was entangled in a thicket of bushes located creek-side. The place bore little resemblance to any of the territory with which she was acquainted.

It was night and allowing her sight to adjust, she remained still. Overhead, a full moon shone, providing enough light by which to make out her surroundings. Thin, sharp twigs clung to her clothing; she eased several of them away from her face with a paw.

The faint sound of water flowing in the nearby creek was discerned and she deduced that the stream at this point ran deep. She was about to move out from the bush, when the sound of voices reached her.

Remaining still, intent upon listening, she was not able to make out the actual words but three distinct voices were discerned. Two of them were not unusual, but the third was strange sounding and every so often its owner uttered low grunts and mutterings, which interrupted those first two voices. When the sound of weeping reached her, the likelihood of being heard was lessened and so she pushed away from entangling branches and hopped onto the open, creek-side swathe. She went across the small grassy area and paused by the trunk of a substantial tree, growing close with the bank of the creek. Peering through the foliage of low-bent branches, she made out the dim-lit forms of three Folk of Fur. She then put voices to dark shapes and, in so doing, recognized old acquaintances. There upon the shadowy creek-flats were none other than Sobriety Fawn, his wife Ruth and another, far larger individual whom she did not know. It was Ruth Fawn who cried, and the sound of her weeping tore at Peace Darkling's heart. In this place of deep, shifting shadow, drama played out. Low cloud crossed the face of a watery-pale moon.

She would know more, but would not reveal her presence. The large individual, it seemed, was the cause of Ruth Fawn's awful distress. He raised his voice, producing a loud and unintelligible utterance, and Ruth Fawn hopped nearer him. Peace was surprised when they embraced.

Sobriety spoke, 'Let him be now, Ruth. We have no choice. The boy must go. He must be sent away.' Peace puzzled over someone of such large stature being referred to as boy.

The boy stood taller, was broader, and far more substantial than was usual for folk. He was in fact the largest of their kind Peace had seen, and his abnormal size was not all, for even by the dim light, the boy possessed other disturbing attributes. His claws gleamed and were long, as moonlight reflected from them. In insisting that her eyes were mistaken, Peace was troubled by the presence of other peculiarities; despite foreboding, she must admit that the boy was mutant. This was the first of her encounters with a creature foreseen and described long ago by Skip. Skip had admonished Sherbrook for his foolhardiness in daring to sample new greens, and during their conversation had described folk such as this. Peace could not imagine the sadness involved in parenting such a one. She stepped back then, and in taking that single step, set foot upon dry and brittle grass, which was enough to alert one whom she would soon know as Chance Fawn. Chance Fawn, unfortunate son of those of old acquaintance from New Warren Central. In the moment of ruing careless action, she realized that she had arrived creek-side at a point in time far later than intended. She trusted that Piedmont was fortunate enough to have arrived at time during which the records might be collected. The bard should not have to deal with a confrontation such as her predicament now entailed. Her presence was detected, and in an instant following, he towered over her!

He presented a ferocious sight! He was bright-striped from head to toe in red, lime and soft violet. Even by pale moonlight such bizarre adornment was scarifying! The heat of his breath, as it crowded against the fur of her face, was abhorrent. Worst of all were the number of his legs! As the seer had described them, Folk of Fur were born with not four paws, but six! Skip had insisted, 'They are awesome diggers!' And now confronted by Chance Fawn, the claim was not doubted.

Hearing pleas for restraint coming from both Sobriety and Ruth Fawn provided not much assurance. Her natural urge was to quiver and shake in the youngster's presence, but with enormous effort, Peace spoke as if unafraid, offering, 'Hello dear one—I am *Tump*—my name is Peace.' She went so far as to extend a paw in greeting and was relieved when, after hesitating, the strange one, leaning in very close to her, extended a paw.

'I am Chanth!'

She smiled, avoiding pondering the possible causes of the stale odour carried upon his breath. 'Are you far from your home, Chanth?' she asked.

By then, Sobriety had joined them. He explained, 'His name is Chance. It's not Chan*th*. He has difficulty with some pronunciation.' Recognizing her, he exclaimed, 'Peace? Peace Darkling? It *is you*, isn't it? Do you and the exiles claim this territory for your own? There was much talk as to where you may have gone—much wondering and guessing as to your destination.'

Ruth arrived to stand by her husband. 'You are much missed by many of us at New Warren Central,' she said. 'Since Her Majesty passed, much has changed for us. Treatment of the bard and other unfortunates is now recognized for what it was, and is cause for disappointment.' She said, 'And now as you see, there are the new ones to contend with...'

Words trailed off. Peace moved to comfort the tearful mother, explaining, 'Ruth, the cause is new greens. You could not have known, none could.' Embracing the other, she enquired, 'All harvesting of new greens is curtailed by now, then?'

She was astonished though, when between sobs, Ruth asked, 'Greens? I'm afraid I don't understand.' Whereupon Peace, releasing Ruth and standing away from her, protested, 'Do you mean to say that none at New Warren Central have realized the fact of it?' At a loss, she asked, 'Do you not *know* by now that greens cause dire altering? Consumption of new greens is the direct cause for birth of offspring such as Chance?' She asked, 'How many are there born this way?' She was at pains to appear unflustered; there was a likelihood of panicking Chance and she must do everything to avoid that.

Sobriety Fawn then responded on his wife's behalf, revealing, 'Apart from our son, Chance, we know of just one other. She was born to another family...' Sobriety was embarrassed and could not continue.

'A gal, you say, Sobriety? What of her—this other child?'

Ruth explained, 'He would spare your feelings, Peace. The changed one—daresay, by now, embraced by merciful gazuzzlement—came to *your* family, to family Darkling.' Not wishing to know how Peace might react to such grim news, Ruth averted her gaze and looked off into surrounding darkness. Then, 'In His wisdom, Great Grandfather has seen fit to bestow upon us, changed ones. They were given to your family and ours. But now, even knowing them as our own, we have decided best return them to Him. They are an exceedingly unnatural gift.' That said, Ruth was finished with explaining.

Peace would not show her feeling but having discerned the Fawns' intention, she was aghast, shocked by learning of an unfortunate born to members of her own family, and by the desperate parents deciding upon such dark solution to the dilemma. Hoping she misunderstood, and wishing to be mistaken, she managed to sound hopeful when venturing, 'As I comprehend your meaning, you intend sending young Chance away? You would send him off to greener pasture, off farther downstream, where his difference will not be the cause of so much embarrassment for yourselves and others at New Warren Central?' She asked, 'Is that it? Do tell me I understand the intention.'

'No, that's not it,' Sobriety said, fearful of guilty shame besting him.

'Ah, then…' Peace said. Moving close to Chance she reached a paw as far as she was able, around his large girth and rested it there. She was grateful for his placid response; he voiced an ill-pronounced version of her name, 'Peash! Peash!' With the word repeated, the boy seemed delighted with his effort.

Peace decided, 'I will have none of it! Do you understand?' And, as shifting cloud subdued the moon's shining, she spoke with more force, 'You will tell me which of my family members has birthed his like. You will take this one home with you, and you must, from now on, without thought for yourselves, give warning to others of the disaster resulting from eating new greens! From now on, consumption of the crop is banned!' She paused and asked, 'Where have they taken the child—she born to my family?' Her sounding so authoritative was met with unexpected response.

'Oh no, Peace Darkling,' Ruth Fawn said, 'It's you who does not understand! You don't understand at all! Changed ones must be returned to Great Grandfather from whence they came!' Ruth no longer wept, but was now as determined as Peace. She said, 'The gal born to your sister, Harmony, and her husband, Rowdy Lewis, is no passive youngster, but one given to bouts of extreme ferocity! And our Chance, although pleasant enough as you see him now, is erratic and unpredictable! We fear for our lives and for those of others. The community ostracizes us which is understandable. Tolerance has limits. Your niece, Thorny, and our Chance are cared for and loved, but it's decided. Best they're returned to His great, loving paws!'

Peace wished, by crying, 'Skip! Save us!' Skip might hear and move both she and the creatures, Chance and Thorny, to safety. There must be a place where their kind could belong. But Skip would not hear, and she reminded herself that it was Skip, who had in the first place moved her to such a wrong location.

Help would not come, but still she could not allow harm befall the children, no matter how unnatural their form, no matter how upsetting their behaviour. She would not take into consideration the protestations of distressed parents. They were confused and it was understandable, but deity ought not in any way be made accountable for a disaster resultant of Folk of Fur hungering after the Tall One's crop. She demanded, 'Where have my relatives taken the child, Thorny?'

'They took the opposite direction,' Sobriety said. 'Whilst we came to this place, they went upstream.'

'And where are we?' Peace wanted to know. 'It's dark and I haven't at all got my bearings. I take it we're downstream at considerable remove from New Warren Central?'

But the Fawns had questions of their own. 'This is not your territory then, Peace Darkling? Is this not the place of the bard's self-imposed exile?'

'*Self*-imposed? The bard was humiliated! He was given no choice other than to leave New Warren Central along with the rest of us!' Peace went further—too far—because in raising her voice now, she demanded, 'Where were either of *you* when support was needed?'

The question was justified in the asking, but she would regret having raised her voice and employing such tone. No sooner were words uttered than Chance Fawn turned upon her. Thrown to the ground, Peace felt her body *bounce,* and then, in the following instant, she knew she was airborne and, could not credit the truth of it! Then for the second time she impacted with hard, dusty ground and knew she must accept her fate. As darkness, far darker than the dark night all about, came to her, final breath left Peace Darkling and she was taken by gazuzzlement.

But then something wondrous occurred, and perhaps it was true that gazuzzlement had not succeeded in taking her? Suspended in darkness, dazed and confused as to her fate, she was occupied in making an exploration of what she thought must be her body, and in those same moments she enquired of no one at all, 'Where am I? I believed gazuzzlement was mine.' And, from darkness came an answer.

Another version of herself, affirmed, 'Oh yes—you're correct. That was gazuzzlement. It was so sudden it was all but instantaneous. When next you see them, you will tell the others of your group that gazuzzlement was yours, that you've experienced it. You'll say, "There's not much to any of it. It was nothing, nothing at all." You will find that you're peeved by Sherbrook's demonstrating ghoulish curiosity, displaying insensitivity.' She said, 'It's quite a night that you've had, and it's not over yet.' She was still in one piece it seemed, and having discovered no evidence of dreadful injury, she was surprised. Looking up and facing her other version, she asked, 'Are you my elder? You are Tump? You have quite a nerve, haven't you, because in time before this, *you* were dealt cruel gazuzzlement by the unfortunate Chance, and now in present time, you waited, delaying an age before acting on our behalf?

'In light of your delaying, I will appreciate you telling me, just what you believe my response should be?' Seeing the other ready to speak, she recanted, 'No! Don't tell me! You expect gratitude? Is that it?' She said then, 'Just a moment—I've no sense of the least injury—and so you've taken me from the time line before the event occurred, from even before my meeting with the Fawns—before I was slammed to the ground—haven't you? And despite admitting to the fact of my gazuzzlement, there's a strong chance of your claiming next, that—I was *never* gazuzzled!' Sounding very tired, she said, 'Now don't bother replying. I'm upset with myself, that's all.'

They stood silent in the dark. In searching the dark, she realized that many things were missing, and she decided it was impossible to ascertain her whereabouts. Overhead no moon shone and lower down no tree or grass grew, dark was dense and all pervading. She would not allow omission of the familiar as a deterrent, and would stay calm. After a moment she spoke again, offering, 'All right then, we may as well get on with it. We'll move forward again, shall we—and in doing that we shall see if this time I make a better job of it? We'll see whether I can convince the Fawns and my relatives to take a more sensible course than the terrible one they're embarked upon.' She wanted to add, 'But this time, I'll be sure not to position myself in close proximity with the young monster, Chance,' but the urge to comment was denied. Her elder smiled, until Peace was compelled to ask, 'What is it?'

'Several of your assumptions are correct.' That was all that the elder said, and silence followed. Moments passed and then, diffused light was discerned, emanating from no particular place, but shining all about, its brightness increased; sublime stillness accompanied the light. Young Peace knew that Skip's power did not compare with this, for the light was growing now to become far brighter than any produced by him, and yet it was not the least dazzling to the eye. Noting such a difference, and making comparison with all she'd learned, from Skip, of Tump, Peace guessed that the version of elder Tump, accompanying her, must come from a time far distant, in a future ahead of that occupied by any version of Tump with whom her Skip was acquainted.

Next, moving occurred, and was no different from the moving she was accustomed to.

Again they were creek-side, where Peace was shaken in observing the Fawns, including the mutant child, Chance, bent low over a body and examining it for sign of life. Turning away from the corpse, she looked to her elder, for the body was all too familiar. The response was slight; the other giving the smallest of shrugs. Peace returned her attention to the Fawns, and then judging by the broken condition of the body, it should be obvious, she thought, to any but the most desperate, that they would not find any hoped for sign. And then wasn't it strange, she wondered, because the Fawns had not yet noticed their presence? It was then that the elder offered explanation. 'You are energy, Peace. You are in spirit, as some refer to the state. The Fawns do not see Tump and neither are we heard, because the frequency of our energy, of our substance, is higher than theirs. It's lighter than the frequency of tangible material of the realm. She explained, 'Our communication is carried out without words; thought passes between us and makes for less confusion. By this means, even most unfamiliar ideas are comprehended.'

She said, 'They may hear or see us if we allow them to, but, as it is, we are shielded against the possibility.'

Peace felt it was her turn to shrug, 'I don't care much for explanation. I'm far too concerned with realizing my own foolishness.' Resigned, she said, 'I'm gazuzzled, and there I am.' With a dismissive, almost disdainful gesture she pointed to the figure lying prone on the ground, but then she amended, 'I should have thought better and not trusted. I should never have believed I could deal with *him*.'

'You're too hard on yourself,' the elder said.

Peace said, '*You* did not trouble to save me.'

'But I have.'

'You have?' Peace asked, 'But not as I would wish.' For a moment she was thoughtful, then, 'Where is Great Grandfather?' She asked, 'I believed that following gazuzzlement, I might see Him. I hoped that He would show Himself.'

'Ah yes. Thus far, the Initiator proves far more elusive than we imagined. The quest, however, continues.'

'The Initiator?'

'Great Grandfather, yes—in the infinite All, All is One. He is ever the beginning and the end. He is the first cause, the infinite and eternal Initiator—the primary One.'

'Great Grandfather is *not* Folk of Fur?'

'No.'

'Not even for us?' Peace asked.

'No. But then again, yes. In any case, He does not reveal Himself—not as you wish—not to satisfy your belief or hope. He is everywhere all about and within us; and with true good heart, with eyes to see and an open mind, you can believe Him revealed.'

'Oh.'

'But in a moment it is we who must manifest, and in miraculous manner. We must create a magnificent spectacle. We shall accomplish an indelible imprinting.'

'Imprinting?'

'Indeed yes, so strong an event that it will not easily be forgotten. They will know it as truth and without so much as thinking on it. In effect, deity grants them visitation. You must not be at all afraid. Hear me now. You will play your part well. Indeed, you already have. I shall move you, or a part of you, back into your body for resurrection.'

'Resurrection?'

'Yes. And before so doing, Tump will take that which you know as your self into itself, and you will become One with us.

'Then we will enter yon' corpse, and whilst there indwelling, we will repair and heal the body so that, repaired to new, it may rise up, transformed from gazuzzlement.

'They're in for a show and are flabbergasted. None at New Warren Central will eat greens again, not at least before much time has passed. When an appetite for new greens is next indulged, a certain aspect of negative outcome is taken into account. The awful outcome is not then so disadvantageous.' She said, 'Tump finds it almost impossible, insisting upon others altering their behaviour. Wise instruction ever falls upon deaf ear. They go their own blithe ways repeating vain error.'

The elder said, 'You have seen, at first paw, what new greens can do to Folk of Fur, but you must not allow yourself tempted to interfere. This evening's measure taken is our last in preventing the consumption of those greens.'

'But...'

The elder was emphatic, 'No. Young Tump will make no alteration.' They waited whilst the Fawns proceeded with preparation for burial. The elder commented with regard to Chance's making a fine job of grave digging, 'They're tireless, they're fast and, what's more, they're neat. See the tidy way young Chance sets about the task. He does not shower soil over the place, but demonstrates meticulous care in making those many neat piles. You may rest assured knowing that your interment is well attended to.' She said, 'We shall wait for them to drop you into the hole before the performance. We'll see them cover you and allow appropriate words spoken. I do trust they speak well of us.' Smiling, she said, 'Gazuzzled, but not forgotten?'

'You're enjoying this, aren't you? You live on, and so this passing is not my end. I wish you would speak plain truth in telling of your plans.

I'd like to retain a little dignity.' But nothing was achieved or gained; remaining oblivious to criticism, the elder next exclaimed, 'There, now, finished in a trice! The grave waits, dear-heart. And now they bury you or us.' Sobriety and Ruth Fawn attended to the disposal of remains by first dragging, then shoving, the body down into the deep hole. A dull thud sounded when the corpse hit the bottom and Peace could not help but wince.

'I promise,' the elder said, 'the next experience is a pleasant one. 'You must not worry. Know that you are cared for.'

She stood with no apparent supporting firmament beneath her and a feeling of dissipation was experienced. Become lighter, she must float upward and perhaps float off altogether, all the while thinning and contracting to nothing. She was fearful, despite every assurance given.

'Mmeerah makes lightness of being,' she heard. This then was Mmeerah? Yes! But Mmeerah beyond anything dreamed.

She was no more than an idea, an idea born of a mind not hers.

She became still smaller.

Was losing her name.

'Stay mindful of *who* you are.' That was, Skip.

'You are light! Look, and you will see me beside you.'

She was Peace Darkling, and in knowing her name she thought to enquire, 'Will we raise my body? Shouldn't we attend to it?'

She heard then, 'Tump is without time. The inner place is unbound. You might sojourn here, untrammelled by time, until suns meet gazuzzling dark ends, and worlds and realms return to void.' Clever Fixer had spoken. He said, 'You are raised in body and concurrently the miracle is performed,' He added then, 'And, in truth, all else is done.'

She asked, 'Where is Piedmont?'

Shining as bright morning sun, the bard said, 'We were separated, weren't we—you and I? It was cause for much trepidation.'

'Yes. Things were awry, and through no fault of Skip's,' another said, and she was Nancy. She said, 'Before Oneness is much confusion.'

'But then,' Simple exclaimed, 'integration is wondrous!'

Piedmont said. 'In a timeless state we can know and do most things. We may travel anywhere and, as Nancy said, anywhen. There is ever more to know and yet we know a great deal of it. We alone, determine our pace.

There are those details, along our way, which we choose not to know. For example, between us is no awful secret, but we refrain from knowing all; in concealment is relief from boredom.'

'We do not like prying,' said Sherbrook. 'At least, not always...' He smiled. Until now, Peace had not noted Sherbrook's absence. Knowing her thought, he responded, 'I was off and away. We are always tidying things. I visited Brickfield realm and have just returned—come back from meeting with Weed.'

Skip explained, 'I sometimes enjoy masquerading in Tall One guise, but have tired of it of late. Sherbrook offered to stand in for me, to return to the realm of Brickfield, and after taking a brick from Weed's yard he went downstream from the settlement and further back in time, to present the brick to Weed. He enquired of Sherbrook, 'How did Weed respond?'

'I manifested as Tall One, Skip, and so he was shocked at seeing me. Then, when surprise had worn off, it was fine. Before my explanation, though, he thought a brick was the most useless thing he'd seen.

'On his return to the town square he'll go to the fireside and make a doll.'

There was something Sherbrook neglected mentioning. He said, 'Look, he gave me this....' From nowhere appeared a small round object. It floated in nothingness, inviting inspection. Sherbrook explained, 'He wanted to give something in return and I appreciated the gesture. It was all he had. It's a token, allowing admittance to the next *Brickyard Bunny Club* dance.'

'Did he think you'd like to kick your heels up?' Skip asked, smiling.

'You never know. I might.

'So the settlement of Brickfield prospers until the time of the Watchers by Night.' Sherbrook was silent. But then urged by a generous nature, he said, 'I'd like to gift the dance token to my younger self. He'll appreciate its quirkiness as much as I do.' He told Peace, 'You will find it in your possession upon your return and can give it to him.' She would pass on the small gift.

Finished with discussing sojourning with Weed, Brickfield realm and fair exchange, Sherbrook offered, 'You have not stopped wondering over the matter of our home or the lack thereof?'

Peace admitted, 'Yes, because there's nothing here.' They were friends of light, but she wondered, 'Where is the rest of it? Where was every*thing?*'

'We can show you our home,' Nancy said, 'or one of them. Our home can be any*where*; it can be any*thing* or any*when*. We can demonstrate.'

Skip said, 'Look! Watch now!' Of a sudden, light dimmed and they were situated in a snug chamber, a chamber that seemed part of a warren, an ordinary place bearing no difference to others she knew. Finding they were there, she saw light bodies growing dim so that within a very short time they were as familiar as ever they were. These were her friends, Folk of Fur, and nothing at all was remarkable or extraordinary. 'I love the old ways best,' a grinning Sherbrook told her. He said, 'I'm a push over for the smell of good digging-soil. A good old fashioned warren's just the thing.'

'And carrots,' Nancy declared. 'An ordinary carrot cannot be surpassed!'

'You see,' said Piedmont, 'when all's said and done, power is not everything. Ages ago we realized that simplest things were best not discarded as superfluous. Before knowing the truth of it, we tried many and various ways—ways you wouldn't believe!'

By now she was more at ease and young Peace wanted information—information regarding Skibeau. Skibeau and his showing up from nowhere, had bothered her very much and she hoped that now they might enlighten her as to his identity. Knowing the nature of her query before the question was put, Skip told her, 'He—Skibeau—is an "idea". He is an entity in his own right, but has his origin in the mind of Clever Fixer. In a sense, he is Clever Fixer or a part of the fixer. Skibeau is a form—a compilation of thought—thought taken on life its own. Possessing mind and will, he is energy and no less that, than we. He is a creation. He came into being or was, if you like, born, without Fixer being at all aware of the fact. But you'll understand that during the time of extensive rambling and communing with his friend, the seed, Fixer was taught. He learned much and imagined many things—most of them involving miraculous achievement. He imagined and saw himself doing many things—many of which, Skibeau is accomplished in. Skibeau is Clever Fixer's dream come true.'

'He will not cause harm,' the fixer said, 'despite delighting in confusing behaviour. I've made an extensive study of the map with Rudy assisting, and it's true, Skibeau does no harm.'

'You are certain of it?'

Clever Fixer insisted, 'He does no harm, not as we can find.'

Gesturing with a paw, Piedmont said, 'Fixer, make a window.' In the following instant a wall of the chamber became translucent. The smooth wall shimmered and dissolved, and conforming to the bard's request, a window opened, granting a clear view of the moonlit clearing where the Fawn family contended with an apparition rising from the grave. Then, hovering before them, the wraith spoke. The Fawns fell to their knees before it.

Peace asked, 'Is it me or is it my elder because if it's me, how can it be so, when I am here with you?'

Piedmont said, 'It's not the elder although she orchestrates the event. She conducts energy—your energy. It's a matter of emphasis.'

Fixer told her, 'All of us—in each and every moment, think and behave on many levels. In each individual are various layers of active mind. As individuals, there are those thoughts we are conscious of. We identify with them, believing them parts of the primary "us". The "us" recognized as "I Am". Beneath the surface of consciousness many other energies are extant and active. Skibeau is an example of creative activity of levels of mind, which despite their powerful presence, I was not aware of, not in the conscious sense. Areas, or levels, overlap and merge. They merge and sometimes, risen to surface, are emphasized, and in behaving so, are not always identified as belonging to the one recognized as primary self. That visited upon the Fawns may be taken as an example. The apparition challenging them is you—a "you", composed of parts and aspects existing at deeper level of your being than the conscious "you".

Tump would not operate using any part of you—even the deepest, most unclaimed, even disowned energies—without their full agreement and cooperation; which is all interesting isn't it, because although I tell you of it and you trust me to impart truth, you cannot *feel* it's true. You cannot *know* it.'

'Thoughts are things,' Peace commented.

'Yes!' Tump chorused. 'As, Skibeau is thought. As we are all thoughts in the mind of one named by us, Great Grandfather.'

Nancy said, 'As Skibeau is a creation of Clever Fixer; the entity—the "you" down there—is a creation of Peace the Elder. The one you see there, performing as miracle, is not yet owned by you, and yet still she is you. After the confrontation the Fawns will return with their son to New Warren Central where they will sound a warning about new greens, so that not for a very long time to come will folk consume the crop. They act according with your initial instruction to them, which, by the way, was sound advice given. The Tall Ones' crop will again be consumed by folk, but at far later time. By then there is a reason for our not preventing it.'

'It's befuddling! Peace protested.

Sherbrook nodded, sympathizing.

'Along with many other matters you are concerned for young Thorny,' Skip said, 'but you needn't fret. She's safe. It's done.' He told her, 'Soon you must leave us. You will return to the place you know as Bunty's realm. Young Tump will attend to taking Simple Rudy from your past.' He said, 'Bunty will be ever so pleased. He and Rudy are similar in age and they get along well.' He smiled. In the next instant he was serious. He snapped, 'Fixer, the gate!' And, 'You are home!'

Rocking in the chair on the cottage veranda, Bunty asked, 'Where have *you* been? We've been worrying over you!'

'Swaying upon her feet, she said, 'You will not believe the strangeness I've seen!'

NEW FRIENDS

You've been to the realm beyond life?' Piedmont asked, 'And you claim there is no gazuzzlement?'

'Yes, and no... There *is* gazuzzlement, but then too, there's continuance. Life goes on.' She thought for a moment before informing Piedmont, 'As you said at the gathering held after Uncle Bucky's passing, "Gazuzzlement has no dominion". In claiming such, you were correct.' Piedmont asked nothing more; he'd grown very thoughtful in considering the information supplied. Looking away from the bard, Peace saw Skip was as morose as ever. Catching her glance, he said, 'I sent you to the wrong place *and* the wrong time! I don't know *how* I could have made such a mistake. It's pathetic!'

Since her return, he'd insisted upon rehashing the horror; his level of confidence ebbed low. Peace had offered consolation but he was adamant in refusing to hear her. Attempting again to cheer him, she said, 'Skip, *dear* Skip, you lost me—yes! But now here I am returned and safe!' She said, 'We've all of us done as best we can. We've all blundered. We must learn from our mistakes; that's the important thing.'

'I haven't,' said Clever Fixer, looking about at no one in particular. Peace said nothing, but directed him a critical look.

'And neither have I or have I?' Sherbrook enquired. He adopted an airy manner, 'I should try much harder,' he said.

Following Sherbrook's lead, Piedmont, having had enough of pondering the fact of an afterlife, looked up. 'My record is flawless and as such, should be viewed as beyond reproach. I confess though, I look forward to committing as much error as is possible from this moment on. I have much catching up to do in regard to error and it is my intention to enjoy each and every moment of committing it.' Expression glum, he focused attention upon Skip. He asked, 'Perhaps, as you're so expert in getting things wrong, you might consider advising me as how best to go about it?'

Skip laughed. He stood up from the edge of the cottage veranda, declaring, 'Bard, you are right. I've been making myself all the more pathetic by carrying on.'

'And now,' said Peace, seizing opportunity, 'We really *must* get Simple Rudy! We will bring him forward to us! This is a wonderful day—one long awaited!'

'But, what if...' Skip began, and was overruled by a chorus of laughter.

'Come on, Buckaroo!' Sherbrook insisted, 'Let's go move an old friend! We'll gather beneath yon' tree—let's get on with it!'

'Are you ready, Skip?'

Skip nodded.

On this occasion, it was Peace, who ordered, 'Clever Fixer! Engage the gate!' Whereupon the fabric of time and space contracted and an opening formed, opening to the distant past, to the morning of the day during which Folk of Fur departed the ruins of old Warren Central and then went about crossing the creek.

Going from hopping stone to hopping stone, in traversing the stream at edge of the churned field, he was careful in heeding Uncle Bucky's instruction, 'Hold tight now! We wouldn't want to slip and fall, would we? No, my boy, we would not!' Simple Rudy adjusted his hold to better grasp Uncle's paw, and in the moment of his doing so, flashing white light dazzled—a sweet scent flooded his nostrils—he was transported to another place—a different time! He was at last (so far as those already present in the new location were concerned) brought from the far distant past to a unique realm, a realm discovered in the first place by another as young as he, to a place of wonder, to the realm of giants entombed in a cottage kitchen. At last, Simple Rudy had arrived in Bunty's realm!

Breathless, he exclaimed, 'Sirs, that was *mighty* kazooning, but where is Uncle Bucky?' Then his attention lit upon the tree and, seeing it really for the first time, Simple Rudy was distracted so that he lost interest in the oldster's whereabouts. He exclaimed, 'Why it's Great Grandfather's map! It is! Oh, I know it very well!' Turning about on the grass, and seeing Bunty for the very first time, Simple Rudy changing tack, enquired, 'What's your name?' And, 'What are *you* good at?'

After slight hesitation, Bunty replied, 'I'm Bunty.' And, after considering the second of Rudy's queries, 'Um, I would have to say dancing. That's the thing I like doing most. I'm a great dancer!'

'Will you show me?' Rudy asked.

Bunty was thrilled. He offered, 'Come with me. Come across the meadow and I'll show you my clicking sticks! You'll love it!'

They were off then, racing towards the meadow path, but reaching a far side of the lawn, Simple Rudy stopped and turned. He called, 'Skip! Do you *like* being so old?' Without waiting for a response he was off again, chasing after his new friend.

Skip did not call after him. He was not over the relief of succeeding in moving Rudy. The pace of events surprised him; the boys were immediate friends. He asked, 'Is anyone else feeling a little let down?' He'd expected more upon Rudy's arriving. More, but more of what, he could not say.

Piedmont observed, 'He's just lost Uncle Bucky. He's that to cope with. Let them play. There will be time later for seriousness.' There were murmurs of agreement with the bard's understanding of Rudy. Sherbrook smiled, telling Skip, 'Come along, you *old* Buckaroo. Let's go!' Taking hold of Skip's arm, he said, 'Let's go back to the cottage and find something to eat. I'm ravenous!'

When they were part way across the small bridge they halted. Simple Rudy leaned against the wood railing and looked down at the water's surface. Reminded of Uncle Bucky, a tear traversed his cheek to fall to the water below. Sounds of croaking frogs, of tiny chirruping birds and the background drone of humming insects filled the clean morning air. It was a fine day, a day of blue sky with just small areas of far away streaky cloud and the slightest breeze. Bunty, though, was disappointed, because his wind clickers would be still and silent.

Wiping at a cheek with the back of a paw, Simple said, 'I knew Uncle was not coming with me. The map showed it. I *wish* he was here though, because I sure do miss him!'

Bunty said, 'I've heard a lot of Uncle Bucky. Skip told me about him.' He said, 'Back there, I heard them say there's no such thing as gazuzzlement.' He looked to Rudy, hoping he was encouraged to feel a little better.

He was pleased when Rudy informed, 'I'm not going to cry, because Uncle always said that being upset does little good. He used to say, "Crying can make a body feel better, but aside from that it's not of much practical use. It doesn't solve anything."'

'I used to cry when I was bullied,' confessed Bunty, and then wished he hadn't.

'There are bullies here?' Rudy asked.

Bunty said, 'No, not here in the realm, but outside this place is Ground Spring Warren, and Ground Spring has bullies, *lots of them!*' Rudy still looked nervous and Bunty told him, 'They used to pick me up and drop me into Ground Spring pond! The pond's small, but it's way bigger than me. I could have drowned!' He said, 'The fixer and me are the only ones around these parts who know how to float, and so apart from dancing, I'm good at that too.' He added, 'Even though I detest it!'

'Is there some way you can stop them?'

'I couldn't, but Skip saved me from them, and since then they've left me alone.'

Learning of this, Simple Rudy was quiet for several moments before revealing, 'Back at the old warren, Skip always picked on me. He never threw me into the creek, but he bullied me.'

Learning of this, Bunty was surprised and shocked. He said, *'Skip? He was a bully?* I'd never have guessed it!' He said, 'I've always liked him. He's my hero—kind of.'

That considered, Rudy said, 'Well, he *is* a lot older. He might be better, by now, than he was.'

Shifting topics, Rudy ventured, 'I'm good at things too. At least there's one thing I'm good at...' Bunty was curious, and Rudy said, 'I read the map. None of them understands it but I do.'

'Yon' weird tree?' Bunty asked.

'The map, yes.' Rudy insisted, 'I read it, because I'm different.'

'Different? Being different is awful!'

'Being different is best! I love being different. Uncle Bucky told me, "Simple, my boy, be yourself—everyone else is taken! Be proud of who you are! Greatness may reside in specialness!"' Rudy explained, 'Uncle was fond of giving advice.' He told Bunty, 'After thinking on it, I decided that Uncle was right.'

Rudy did not recall ever having uttered so many words in such a short space of time, and by the time he finished he was quite out of breath. He'd decided the new boy was a good friend; if he wasn't then he, Rudy, could never in the first place have become so talkative. They left the bridge and continued along the path leading to the small, grassy area near Lilith's dream-catcher.

'We have Simple back with us. We've succeeded, but how can we ensure no further mistakes occur?'

'You might as well ask, how many peas are there in a pod?' Skip said, smiling.

'Riddling is all very well,' Peace said, 'but mystery questions involving vegetables aside, I don't see us progressing far.'

'Progressing?' Sherbrook interjected. *'Progressing?'*

Before he went further, Peace said, 'I do wish you would not interrupt!'

'Well, excuse me!' exclaimed, Sherbrook, 'I believe I deserve a say. Great progress has been made. Rudy is safe now, with us! And besides which, I thought it was agreed that Skip should not be forced to dwell on the mistake made, with you going off and becoming lost. It's behind us! We're agreed—aren't we?'

'Bickery scratching's useless,' Piedmont advised. 'Let's see if we can't get along better.'

'It's my impression,' said Clever Fixer, 'Peace questions our method.' He said, 'Recrimination was not intended. If she or any of us have anything to offer, which may improve our way of going about things, they should be heard. The more efficient we are, the better off we'll be. Anyway,' he said, 'I'm tired. I'm going to change my shirt.'

Hearing him, Sherbrook's mood lightened. He asked, 'Will you get one for me while you're about it? I'm sick of the one I'm wearing.'

'Sure.' Fixer replied, 'Any colour preference?'

'Whatever you choose will be just fine,' Sherbrook said, but then thinking better of leaving the choice to Fixer, 'Maybe something in red?' He said, 'There's a nice one in bright red, overlaid with big violet blooms. I wore it the other day. Do you know it?'

'Indeed I do,' Fixer said nodding, and he went off to the bedroom to search through the contents of the closet.

'I'm exhausted,' said the bard, 'I feel I should lie down for a while. I might go to the barn and browse through the scratchings,' Addressing no one in particular, he said, 'Reading calms me, and I like resting on the straw out there.'

Peace said, 'Clever Fixer is right, you know. I wasn't criticizing anyone, but perhaps we should rest before risking serious discussion. We're a little on edge.'

Skip said, 'I didn't mean to make light of your question.'

She said, 'I do see what you meant. It's a good question.'

'But, without answer...'

'Peas? Pods?' Sherbrook gazed to the ceiling. Impatient, he called, 'Wait, Fixer, I'm coming too!'

Alone then, with Skip, Peace said, 'Obviously, the number equals the number of peas present in any given pod, but we're not talking about pods. Problems are problems, but solutions, ever differ.' She said, 'Speaking of things in containment though, I've wondered of late, about moving our grotesques from the kitchen.'

Surprised, Skip asked, 'Do they bother you? I suppose they can be relocated, but I'm no longer disturbed by them.'

'Mm, they're covered, it's true, but they're in the way and whenever I go through the room there's no escaping their presence.'

'Where would you prefer them?' Skip enquired. 'They could be relocated to the barn. What do you think?'

'Piedmont spends a lot of his time out there.' She was thoughtful, 'And there's another thing...' Skip waited. She said, 'The tomb is "wired", as Fixer refers to it. What might happen if it's disconnected when it's moved?'

It was true, Skip thought. Substantial looking cables were connected to one side of the tomb; they snaked down through a hole in the floor. He did not at all know what might happen if those cables were disturbed. He still experienced difficulty at times, in seeing, and thought his failure was due in part to lack of self-confidence. He said, 'I should try, shouldn't I, to see if there's adverse outcome if they're moved?'

She said, 'And, while you do that, I'll go take a look at them.'

He said, 'Wait. I'll come too.'

They made their way back across the meadow to the cottage, where Rudy promised that he would show Bunty something of his skill in reading the map.

Despite the vagary of fickle weather letting them down, so many wind clickers, feathers and spinners held by so intricate a web, delighted Rudy. Bunty, seeing his new friend so involved in searching for meaning in the complex construction, decided it fair that once returned to the cottage, he'd observe with an open mind, Simple Rudy's demonstrating his special talent of communicating with the tree.

Along the way they happened upon the largest dragonfly ever, and Rudy, exclaiming over the brightness of such beautiful wings, heard, 'Their wings glow in the dark, too. I sometimes come here at nightfall to watch them.'

Simple declared, 'It's a wondrous place.' He told Bunty, 'You were brave and clever discovering it in the first place.'

Bunty could not help but puff out his chest. Wings set to whirring, the dragonfly left the railing of the bridge, and it occurred to Bunty to ask, 'There's nothing scary about talking to the tree is there? Because when Tump practise Mmeerah, peculiar things can happen.' He said, 'They don't believe themselves the least odd, but they can make me very nervous.'

Simple responded, 'In searching for Great Grandfather, they seek understanding ... the origin of light and love.'

'Um?'

'That's all there is to it,' Rudy said, 'There's nothing to feel nervous about.'

In the cottage kitchen, Peace and Skip stood studying the entombed giants. Looking up at those faces, Peace said, 'It's strange, because the thought of them is worse than confronting them. There's something about the doe, which I must admit, despite my very natural aversion, strikes something of a sympathetic chord in me. I don't mind her quite so much. Whenever I see her, I'm reminded of it; when not in her presence, it's forgotten.'

Skip, looking away from them to better study connections of cables with the lowest section of the large ice tomb. He said, 'Mm, these are important to the rest of it and I think they're best left alone. If we move the tomb, then, deeks knows what might happen. I do know,' he said, 'that you hate them being here, but relocating them by moving might prove unwise.'

'That's disappointing...'

'It can be moved...' Skip said, 'and so too, can that wire, but if I move it, I can't be certain of the result. I'm still unable to see anything much at all.'

'Perhaps we can go ahead with moving it regardless of your inability.' Peace said.

'I'm not sure.' Skip was very uncertain.

'You say you don't see much of anything, but what *do* you see?'

'I see a tangle—a confusion of events—amounting to a future of sorts, but a future which I'm sure has nothing much at all to do with us.' He said, 'A future coming about by not moving these two. I don't understand it.'

'Oh.'

'Yes. But then, Simple Rudy could perhaps better explain it.'

'He's off playing with Bunty,' she said. 'We shall see what he thinks when they get back. Things are always so complicated. It would be nice if they were more straightforward.'

That's just not the way of it though, Skip thought, but said nothing.

The front door slammed shut. Bunty and Rudy were back.

Peace called, 'Bunty, we're in the kitchen!'

Both she and Skip were dumbfounded when seeing the entombed ones for very first time. Now though, Simple Rudy exclaimed, 'Sirs! She is our friend!' Both Skip and Peace turned to face him. 'She is Lilith!' he said, pointing to the doe. 'The other is Mydor! Mydor, as you see him, has met with gazuzzlement, but Lilith is fine! On this time line—very soon—she awakes!' With effort, Peace calmed herself. She leaned against the cupboard by the sink and steadied herself. She crossed her paws at her waist and enquired, 'Lilith ... Simple? You say that her name is Lilith?'

'Yes. She and Mydor are Tall Ones from a far realm! The realm we occupy—Bunty's realm—they, long ago named the *Dove*. This realm is theirs.' Mindful of a friend's feelings, he hastened to add, 'Of course it's Bunty's too. It belongs to him also.'

Skip said, 'Piedmont will be interested to learn of there being *two* Mydors.'

'There are not two Mydors,' corrected Simple. 'There's just one. This is Mydor.'

'*This* is Mydor? This *Tall One?*' Peace stammered, incredulous. After a moment she said, 'The bard will learn nothing of it from me.'

'Nor me,' murmured Skip. The bard would be shattered. He'd spent a lifetime awed by Great Mydor and versifying on his heroic deeds. Information from Rudy might prove too much for Piedmont. Skip hoped against hope there was no truth to any of it, and that Simple had it wrong. Recalling his words, and gesturing to the ice-tomb, an incredulous Peace asked, '*She* is friend to us?'

'Oh yes.' Rudy told her, 'She teaches us many things and she learns from us.' He said, 'You, Peace, and she become the very best of friends.'

SIMPLE RUDY

'I don't know how it works,' Rudy said. 'Great Grandfather knows how.'

It was time to demonstrate his gift. Not just Bunty, but the others too, had gathered around the tree.

'This is the best way to explain what I've learned,' Rudy said. 'I will show you some of the time lines we may follow.' Rudy then hesitated, he did not want to give offence, but still must speak his mind. He said, 'There's something forgotten by you. Had you sought guidance, you may have better understood the map.'

Peace protested, 'I am fond of the tree. No one cares for it as I do, and we've asked for clarity in what it describes.'

'But Sir, you ask the tree, not Him.'

Peace implored, 'Will you desist, Rudy, in calling me, sir!'

Taken aback, he said, 'Yes. I will try.' He then persisted, 'The tree answers to Him—you should not put yourself in Great Grandfather's place by asking *it* to reveal its secrets.'

Sherbrook understood, 'Oh deeks!' he exclaimed, 'I get it! Simple's right. He is!'

'Yes!' Skip agreed.

'It's a fair point,' Piedmont said. 'More than Mmeerah is required.'

Peace smiled. She was not offended but nursed uncertain feelings.

Knowing the correctness of Rudy's advice, Clever Fixer admitted, 'I see it. I do! I must say that I'm a little embarrassed.'

'We might see ourselves as discourteous,' Piedmont said. 'We've not shown respect by asking for admittance to His territory.'

Bunty was seated on the grass near Sherbrook. Rudy gave him a sidelong glance before saying, 'Great Grandfather, it's me, Simple Rudy. Please show the wonder of your map.' Rudy waited. And he waited. For a long time they waited and still nothing happened.

Sherbrook began fidgeting in bored fashion with his claws. Fixer sat with eyes closed, thinking. At one point, Peace and Piedmont smiled one to other, before Piedmont, realizing his mind wandered, glanced away. Skip stifled a yawn.

Then, Bunty spoke, and coming upon so much silence, his words sounded louder than intended. He ventured, 'Maybe we *all* should ask?' He offered, 'I'll ask too. It might help.'

Peace agreed, 'Of course, you are right, Bunty.' She said, 'Great Grandfather please grant Simple Rudy's request.' She paused, 'Tump is your humble servant.'

With those words spoken, a gentle breeze stirred and a soft melodious chorus was heard. Carried upon currents it was a wordless sound, a sound resembling humming. It was assumed then, by those present, that in obeisance to highest authority, each and every leaf of the tree stirred in awakening and a quick delicate fluttering was heard joining with a resonant humming. The tree shimmered with gentle light. In the process of quickening it began to sway. At first it swayed from side to side so that its low-most branches swept close to the grass. The tree's side-to-side motion then altered as fiery orange glowing commenced, and the tree proceeded moving, sweeping low to the lawn in slow-swooping circular movement. At one point, branches came within such close proximity of Sherbrook that he was obliged to hasten back from it, fearing his legs might be swept away. The tree then slowed in moving, and after several moments the trunk and all but tiniest branches were stilled, so once again it was tall standing and upright in its large wood pail set upon the grass. With just small movement of leaves allowed, the tree contained the dance. Aglow, its orange colour began changing then, to melt and blend with outward-radiating rainbow-hues, which stretching and reaching aloft, painted woven patterns upon sky and cloud drifting far overhead. All the while, ceaseless fluttering of tiny leaves produced a sound reminiscent of multitudinous insects—the sound of many caught moths—their desperate wings beating a staccato rap against a window-pane.

They stared up. The bard said, 'Beautiful, isn't it?'

'It's awesome,' Sherbrook agreed.

Whilst the rest admired the display, Clever Fixer, happening to lower his gaze, noticed Rudy and what he did. Clever exclaimed, 'Look! He plucks it!'

Peace was aghast. She ordered, 'Rudy, stop it! What in deeks name do you think you're doing?'

'*Showing* you,' he said, continuing to tear leaves from the tree. 'Leaves are not just leaves.' He tossed more of them into the air overhead. Leaves did not fall to settle then upon grass but they flew upward, rising high into the sky above. Watching him plucking at the tree, Peace could not but worry over it.

Clever saw that leaves taken, were not as first thought, chosen in random fashion. Rudy claimed they were not just leaves and he was careful in selecting them. Upon each leaf taken, was portrayed a different, altering, "living" event. Glancing back to the tree, Clever saw Rudy removing more leaves and as he did so, thin lines of light ran hither and fro throughout the tree, making new connections between multitude events. Lines twisted and turned as those connections formed. A vital, purposeful activity was conveyed, and Clever was impressed. As he saw it, the tree was more "awake" now than ever it was. Returning his attention to events taking place high overhead, he was awed, seeing distant leaves fading and disappearing so that the pictures once carried by them, freed of constraining surfaces, increased in size. Moving pictures next began a dizzying, shifting upon the immensity of sky.

The bard, noting Simple muttering to himself, and reminded of *his* habitual engaging in that very thing, averted his gaze in consideration of Simple's privacy but he could not prevent hearing Rudy's observing, 'They are too big and too high up!' Hearing that, Piedmont saw the skyborne images shrink and at the same time, move lower. All the while, Rudy insisted, 'Lower! Lower!' Brought close to the ground then, three-dimensional solid figures of light moved amongst them. Skip, seeing Nancy and her friends, Emily and Sara, was astonished by such a convincing illusion of reality.

Sherbrook and Peace stood together and ducked their heads low, as row upon row of mutant folk swooped over them. Coming low to the ground, mutants brought their surroundings with them. Many excerpts of differing time lines were included from those leaves chosen by Rudy, and presented with so many snippets, from so many lines, was daunting. Shrill, screaming, mutant battalions converged upon the spot occupied by Clever Fixer and despite knowing all as illusion, he clambered to his feet in fear. He shuddered, brushing at himself as if ridding traces of contaminating influence. A garish-striped, long-clawed mutant turned back to face him. Its mighty roaring revealed enormous fangs, and confronted by the convincing presence, Fixer dodged from its path! It pursued him, lunging closer, and as Fixer stumbled back, it flickered and then melted away. To be replaced by another image, one less threatening in nature. Mavis Whitepaws heltered in the direction of the forest clearing, and, Fixer saw Charlie Noy-Breen going after her.

'Smaller,' said Simple Rudy. 'You are too big.' Obeying his command, both figures and surroundings further diminished in size.

Soon, many depictions gathered together upon an area of lawn at their feet. Now it was they who were giants. Forming a loose-knit circle, they stood surveying the muddled scene, a scene comprised of multifarious, disconnected events. Translucent, intermingled images each layered one upon another in a disconcerting tangle of movement.

Several images, it seemed, were intent upon escape and, as if empowered by a mysterious force of their own, they began separating from the main body of activity. Simple Rudy took a half step forward, raised his arms and, with paws extended at arms length, began describing imagined, diagrammatic lines in the space before him.

Despite those lines being of an imaginary nature, they began to glow bright and clear. The pattern they formed was intricate and complex. A part of the pattern, comprised of thin red lines, dipped down, lines thinning the farther they stretched. Those lines then ran at the speed of blinking until moving events were contained; no wilful event might now dash away, fleeing from the rest. Whilst further motioning with paws in the air, Simple Rudy released a short, impatient sigh. After striking out to travel in downward direction; new, incisive lines, met with and joined various separated events, arranging and connecting them to produce an order.

Observing it all, Skip said, 'This is the creation of a new line.'

'A new time line constructed with components plucked from many lines,' Fixer said.

Concerned, Peace asked, 'What of the gaps left in the original lines?'

Clever Fixer told her, 'There are no noticeable gaps in lines—not that I see.' He'd hurried away from his place in their circle to peer up at the tree. Scrutinizing it, he next said, 'Those many instances, of events taken, seem of such short duration. Already, gaps, caused in their removal, have been filled. It's as if the tree has grown missing parts back.' Examining it further, and feeling at a loss to explain all he noted there, he announced, 'Then again, perhaps it has not grown its parts back but at least compensation is made by some means beyond my present understanding. As I speak, this happens! Look and you'll see the truth of it.' Trusting him, no one moved from where they stood. The line forming at their feet was proving far too engrossing to allow attention to stray.

Entranced, Skip felt urged to enquire, 'How are you doing it, Rudy.'

Rudy responded, 'I'm not doing it.'

'But...'

'Great Grandfather does it,' Simple said. 'All time lines are His. I don't *do* any of it. We asked, and now I may show you the way of it.'

'But you've been waving your paws about...'

'Yes,' Rudy agreed. 'That's me, joining as the conductor. I could just as well be humming along and waving paws about to *White Winter's Song*. His is the power of doing.'

'How come,' Fixer asked, 'with so many leaves removed, so much information gone, there are no gaps on lines in the tree—the map?'

'I don't know,' Rudy told him, 'Time lines can exist though, even without events occurring along their paths; they are living things in their own right.' He asked, 'Does knowing that help?'

Clever Fixer paraphrased, 'Lines exist as independent entities. Nothing more is needed. No event need ever occur to justify their existing?'

'That's right.'

Perplexed, Clever Fixer said, 'I don't understand it.' Then, expression determined, he said, 'But one day, I shall.'

Two lines were formed now upon the grass at their feet. At two distinct points along routes traced by them, the lines came together, converging and intertwining, one with the other. Neither line was cluttered or jumbled, making for easy discernment of events. The location of most events depicted upon the first of the lines was New Warren Central; both it and the encompassing environs were shown. The secondary line, running for the main part parallel with the first, showed at its beginning point, Tump, in the present location and during the present time. In progressing, the lines revealed two versions of possible future activity; two points of intervention by Tump. From the second line, their line, Tump intruded into the first. Looking down at their feet they saw themselves as they now were, and traced events occurring in not too far distant, different futures.

They first looked to a future showing Nancy Whitepaws experiencing a most terrifying ordeal. There she was at their feet, portrayed in moving miniature, every detail of the scene, discernable. Distressed, she tore through a moonlit night to stand breathless and quaking, terrified of discovery. Surrounded by forest giants at the clearing in the woods, she stilled short breathing, as mutant Folk of Fur moved in, encircling the location. Then, the faintest whisper was uttered, 'Oh, Tump hear me please! Tump! If you are real... *Please do something!*'

'Oh, the poor child...' Piedmont said. Even as he spoke, blue-white lightning flashed, emanating upwards from the scene below, and then the forest clearing was quite empty. Nancy had vanished. Seeing the brightness flare, Sherbrook exclaimed, 'Yes! It's us! We save the gal!'

'It's horrible having to wait isn't it?' Skip said, 'We're forced to do nothing while she suffers.'

'No we're not,' said, Rudy.

'What do you mean?'

'There is the other point of intervention,' the fixer said. 'That's what he means.' He directed attention to a point occurring at earlier moment in the lines. There was a point other than that showing Nancy afraid and taken from the forest clearing. At the earlier time also, lines intertwined.

'Yes, now I see it,' Skip said, 'Here, where both lines plait together, well before the other, more distant entwining is shown. Back here at this point she can be taken, but then Rudy, different futures must result. Does Great Grandfather have a preference? Does it matter to Him? Which should we choose?'

'It doesn't matter to Him,' Rudy said.

'He doesn't choose?'

'No, we do.'

'But if He knows everything...'

'He is entertained by allowing us to choose, I think. If we ask, he sees our choices and can make them right, but I will look.' As Rudy spoke, new lines appeared and branching off from the points of intertwining, further lines formed to parallel those first shown. Soon, many lines were presented and so numerous did they become, that Tump retreated several steps back. It was either that or risk engulfment by moving scenes as more and more lines added themselves to those present.

Stepping still farther back, Peace exclaimed with frustration, 'This is as confusing as anything seen earlier on when *our* inexpert effort was applied in fathoming the thing!' In continuing her frantic hopping back, she called, 'Before we brought you here, Rudy!'

Feeling injured, Simple, said, 'I'm sorry, Sir...'

Piedmont stood further back than the rest of them. When the map, pushed to show more, began increasing in area, Piedmont thought of a much earlier time. He thought of Uncle Bucky's wise and far gentler way of communicating with Rudy. He called, 'Rudy, dear boy, there's another thing. I know you're doing the best you can in showing us the map and something of the way you relate to it, but, if I may make a suggestion?' He waited for a response from Rudy and then welcomed Rudy's short nod of agreement.

The bard called again, 'Rudy, you need not show us anymore. You should be content going along with Great Grandfather in your own way. We'll do our best in trusting your reading of the map—won't we, everyone? You can tell it to stop now, Rudy. There's a good boy!'

'*Yes, please!*' Peace implored.

Clever Fixer, hopping farther back, called, 'Make it quiet, Simple!'

But Skip, given up retreating from moving lines and moving events, stood amidst the swirl of activity, exclaiming, 'Simple, I'm amazed that you comprehend *any* of this!'

Rudy looked over to Skip and then to where Bunty heltered to the cottage. He called, 'Well, I do. Shown here is just the simplest version of the map. You don't need to understand any of it. I'm happy to read it on your behalf.' He added, 'It's as Piedmont says—he, Piedmont, knows what's what.'

Hearing Rudy, Skip was reminded of times long past, and more than anything else, he was pleased. He saw that Simple Rudy had closed his eyes, and that Rudy's present expression was identical to that worn by him long ago when entranced, lying upon the dirt floor, back at old Warren Central, focusing for all he was worth upon the sacred valves.

Skip was amazed anew, because Rudy's energy was joined with the energy of the map and the map was under directing energy from the All … and so, Simple Rudy was caused to rise up from where he stood. He rose high into the sky, as they stared, struck dumb by the spectacle of his ascension.

'The boy flies!' Piedmont exclaimed with delight.

'As Brother Bird!' Fixer declared, chuckling.

'He's shown us...' Peace said. There was in fact no other choice available to them, that was, other than Rudy, and she knew it. Even so, they were in good paws with Simple Rudy's knowledge of the map. This *must* be the way of it.

From the cottage veranda Bunty called, 'What if he falls?'

The map finished expanding and now began folding in upon itself, lines of encoding light bending again, making tangled puzzles.

Skip reassured, 'If he looks like falling I'll move him to the ground.' Even as Skip spoke, he saw that Rudy required no assistance from him. Simple was now lowering in a most gentle, unhurried way, like a lilting leaf to grass. At the moment his feet touched down, the bright connecting lines, each sound and the rainbow of light—all of it—finished rolling in scroll-like manner, in upon itself, and moving as if swept by the paw of a giant, returned back to the tree, where in the following instant it was as if none of it had happened.

Opening his eyes and looking down at his feet, Rudy said, 'Look, the gals are gathered; they're having fun.'

Going close to Rudy, Skip saw an excerpt, a small scene from the map, remained to play itself out on the lawn. It was a leftover—separated from all else transpired. The scene included three young gals sharing a pleasant time, creek-side, during a fine sunny afternoon. They chatted together. Then Rudy commanded, 'Scat, you gals!' And with a flash, the scene returned to its place in the tree.

Tree

CREEK SIDE

Nancy had outgrown her favourite pink dress long ago. She, Sara and Emily were on the grassy bank, occupied in weaving chains of wild flowers.

'Do you feel that we're observed?' enquired Emily.

'By whom, Longpod?' Sara asked.

'By no one in particular,' Emily said, 'It's just that if I'm being watched, then the fur at the back of my neck rises.'

'There's no one hereabout, just the children and we three, ' Sara said. 'If we were being spied upon, then whoever they were would have to have wings... There's no sign of Brother Eagle and so we're safe. There's no tree or concealing underbrush to give cover. If anyone thinks to come this way we can see him or her approach well before they reach us.' She called, 'Abernathy! Don't dare think of going close to the stream! Felicity! Leave your sister alone! You would not like it, were she to treat you that way!'

'Come over here to me,' called Nancy. 'Dandelion, *do* come here! You can have my flower necklace!' Enticed by the offer, Dandelion flibberty hopped, as fast as small legs would carry her. When she reached them, Nancy slipping the necklace over the child's head, and pushing a long, troublesome ear to one side, asked, 'Has your sister done *mean* to you?' She said, 'Never you mind, sweet heart. It's all in a day's work isn't it—putting up with brothers and sisters? But, you're all of you, best of friends really. There now, don't doubt it.' And, pulling Dandelion close to her, she hugged her favourite of Sara's children.

Sara said, 'Whitepaws, you're spoiling her again. She must learn to fend for herself.' Nancy said nothing, but looked beyond the creek to where green fields spread to distant hills in every direction other than that of New Warren Central. Spotting distant figures, she then said, 'Gatherers are returning from the planting place. They go there in increased number these days. I hope, by their taking so much, the Tall Ones are not moved to anger.'

'It's—all of it—penance offering,' Emily said. 'They have no right to be upset by us taking what's ours. They owe us—always have and always will. In any case, Zechariah's gatherers are careful. As you point out, they go in large enough groups, and they don't take too much. I know, because Francis Darkling often goes with them, and she told me so.' She said, 'They gather in discreet and measured way, not out of consideration for Tall Ones' feelings, but in consideration of crops. They are careful not to harvest too much. They know what they're doing.' She said, 'Francis was always unusual, wasn't she?' She said, 'Even from days of Leaping the Ditch, ever since very young, she preferred keeping company with boys. I recall her telling me once, when neither of us was very big, she believed gal stuff was boring. She would say, 'It isn't fair and I'm going to show them! She went on to prove her point, I suppose, by beating every record set by others.'

'They didn't stand a chance, did they,' Sara said.

'It's still true,' said Emily, 'except that now Francis defeats them with Hargolin.

'And regardless of the fact, they're all of them crazy over her.'

'No. Not all of them. They're not *all* crazy over her,' Nancy corrected.

Sara sighed then said, 'She doesn't mean *your* Zech's crazy over her.'

Urged to defend herself, Nancy made no immediate reply, but after a moment she said, 'He's not *my*, Zech. I meant most bucks. There are not *so* many of them enamoured with Francis. You exaggerate, Sara.'

Recognizing a familiar tone to Nancy's words; a familiar response to Sara's oft' repeated assumption, Emily said, 'Come on now, Sara, don't tease.'

It was Sara's turn to delay, but rather than react at all, she instead chose to call again and admonish Abernathy, 'When we get back to the warren there will be trouble, my boy. Cease tormenting the gals! Your behaviour will be reported to your father!' She then enquired, 'Is your mother well, Nancy? I know she's not been quite herself.'

'She's fine enough, I think,' said, Nancy. 'She has Ruth, who watches over her. They watch over one another and now they're both older, they are the best of friends. Ruth took care of Mother during her recent illness.' She explained, 'We all do what we can, but Ruth is her main-stay.'

'She never was fond of Zech,' Sara ventured. 'Was she?'

Emily said, 'That's an understatement.'

Nancy said, 'No. She wasn't.'

Reminiscing, Sara offered, 'I'll never forget the time she threw your father's wheel at him! It was after you're illness. Do you recall? Of course you must! One never forgets things of the sort. In any case, I was passing by on my way to the pasture, for my mother, and in going past your home, was startled and amazed by the sight of your parents. She shouted at him and poor Charlie looked fit to bust, but he said nothing at all. And, receiving nothing from him other than a rather sullen look, your dear little mother picked up the wheel and threw it at him! Holus-bolus it went, rolling along after him! The thing landed upright, then as if empowered by your mother's bewitching, it gained volition and momentum of its own and it chased him!' Laughing, she said, 'I'd never before, nor since for that matter seen anything like it. It was wonderful!'

Smiling, Nancy reminded, 'It was she of course, who overcame the difficulty of setting the wheel amongst branches of the tree above Father's resting place.'

'Oh yes!' both Sara and Emily said.

'If not for her, we would not have ladders.'

'Indeed, we would not,' acknowledged, Sara.

'Nor such strong binding twine, which in designing the ladder through necessity, is also an invention of hers,' Emily contributed. 'Folk should come up with a way of honouring such cleverness.' Continuing, she said, 'So much invention has come from does setting minds to task.'

Sara said, 'It's true, Longpod. What you say is correct. There's the ladder and unbreakable twine from Mavis Whitepaws. Then there's the peeler. Think of it, a thing so simple—a small, shaped and sharpened twig.' She thought, and then said, 'How about the whisk, then? I could not get by without mine.'

Emily said, 'Yes, I bet it's another thing first thought of by a doe. A buck would not consider such a thing as important.'

Nancy said, 'There are our clothes. We make them. Whilst it's true that cloth and some clothing come as penance offering, and much is brought to us by the company of Haberdasher Frederick and Sons, we still use thread and bone-needles in reworking cloth, don't we?' The others nodded and Nancy asked, 'I wonder who she was—that doe of far-off time—who first thought of the needle?'

'Whoever she was, she's owed much.' Emily sat close with Nancy. Deciding to lie back in the long grass, she told Dandelion, who Nancy still held, 'Let go my fur youngster. You have enough pretty fur of your own. You're quite the gal! Such blue flowers are pretty aren't they? They're a perfect match for those eyes.'

Sara returned to speaking of Zech, and the others groaned. Emulating her elders, Dandelion voiced a short humorous sound. Ever persistent, Sara complained, 'You aren't hearing me.'

'I am,' said Nancy.

'Then?'

Hoping to satisfy Sara's curiosity but at same time knowing she might never, Nancy confessed, 'He is stubborn in wanting me..'

'Which is nothing new at all,' Emily said. 'It was ever his way.'

'Yes. Since you were both very young he's seen you as right for him, but the real question has nothing whatever to do with *his* interest. The question is, will you find it in your heart to accept him.' Sara said. 'It's a saga of epic proportion.'

'I say she won't,' Emily said.

'Are you serious, Longpod?' Sara thought for a moment then said, 'Longing for such relationship should never be underestimated, Longpod. I never for a moment dreamt I'd wed and yet here I am, *Mazengarb* no more, but Sara Silvertail, with Finius for husband, and a young family. Nothing will surprise me, nothing concerning our Nancy and the great Zechariah.'

Hearing her friend speak of her and Zechariah, Nancy said, 'I do wish you would stop it. You both go on and on.' She said, 'Sara, why is it that you are capable of self-restraint where Emily's privacy is concerned, but not mine?'

Sara looked first to Emily and then to Nancy. She ignored Nancy's question, but enquired, 'My Dandelion is sweet, isn't she?'

* * *

Having crossed the field, to stand at the boundary that lay in the closest proximity to New Warren Central, Zech spoke to the group. He congratulated them on a task accomplished. Gathering and collection of penance vegetables was carried out in precise accordance with the plan; his organizational skill was respected and all was achieved without a hitch. Bernard was close to paw and carried the rope, which no longer was required as means of rescue. Leaping the Ditch had been abandoned long ago. By now, Bernard's position as Keeper of Rope, a position once envied by some, was taken for granted; his right to the title was not questioned. Their association was close, and that meant that on the rare occasion of them being apart, an order or command of Bernard's was taken with as much seriousness as those issued by the leader himself. But now, Zechariah addressed Francis Darkling; he asked, 'Were there many new lettuce left at the beds after harvesting? Were they counted?'

Francis informed, 'There are thirty nine, Leader.'

'Who made the count?'

'I did.'

'Then I'll trust it.' Zechariah told her. 'Of those learned in counting, you are the most accurate. I don't know what it can be, but not much seems to sink in. Instruction given falls on deaf-ears. Some of them, entrusted with counting, but possessing too little skill, lie, when called upon to answer! They think to deceive by picking numbers from thin air! I'm unsure as to how best address the problem but I can promise you, Francis, a solution will be found.'

'Very few have anything of natural aptitude for the task,' Francis said.

'Natural aptitude... Natural aptitude can have nothing to do with it! Whether performed by those in possession of natural aptitude or not, the count must be correct! If not, then what is it worth? It's a complete waste of time. In any case, the matter is not your problem, Francis. Tasks performed by you are always well carried out. It's not you. It's others.' He turned away to respond to something or other of Bernard's. In listening to Bernard he muttered beneath his breath, 'Aptitude ... of all the ridiculous notions.'

Catching the word, Bernard enquired, 'Aptitude?'

'Yes, Bernard, as my lieutenant, as right-paw to me, you possess some aptitude but don't ever assume that I condone your checking the count on my behalf, because in that area you lack ability. You've no more skill than the least of them. Were you to lie, believing you might get away with it, I would feel very let down.'

'I would never lie to you,' Bernard said, making fair work of hiding injured feelings.

'Then, Bernard, you should praise powers that be, that accuracy in counting is no longer expected of you.' Recent occasion was alluded to, occasion, during which Bernard was asked to make accurate count of parsnips. Laid out so they grew ten abreast in spaced rows—rows planted to extreme length—determining their true number proved quite beyond him. Despite receiving careful instruction in the art of counting, previous to his being asked to perform the task, Bernard, staring down at rows, knew in his heart of hearts that too much was expected of him. Of all numbers, one hundred always sounded to him a little too perfect and so, after more careful considering, he arrived at a decision involving the addition of number three to the number one hundred. Apart from one hundred, the number three held certain appeal; he'd no idea why, but it was so. There must be more than one hundred plus three turnips here, though? The bed under scrutiny was large enough to hold more plants than that, but in all truth, the total was beyond his ability to know. And so, his answer, arrived at by adding three to one hundred, despite being not quite so perfect as he'd prefer, would at least comprise those numbers he'd some fondness for. Something mysterious, something akin to instinct, urged, 'Go on—risk it! Nothing dared, nothing gained! In demonstrating courage, you may be correct!'

Experiencing dreadful anticipation, he drew in a deep breath and then attempting to sound confident, ventured, 'One hundred and three!'

Good did not result.

The number one hundred and three earned a severe look of disbelief and that was followed by derision amounting to outright mockery. After Zech calmed himself, quit knee slapping, laughing and every kind of kazooning carry on, he asked, 'Where did the *three* come from?'

Unnerved, Bernard admitted, 'In all honesty, I'm not sure. Why?'

'Because Bernard, the correct answer is one hundred and sixty!'

Sounding hopeful, Bernard asked, 'So I was almost right?'

'No. You were incorrect. There can be no, "almost right", not when numbers are dealt with. You may just as well have been three thousand out, in your answer. Vain attempts at squirming by the truth make no difference at all. With numbers, wrong is always wrong.'

From that day forward, as Bernard saw the matter, even nice, complete sounding numbers like one hundred, had not the least good to them. There was always certain dishonesty to business involving them; skewed at a fundamental level, their intention was not to please or gratify. Favouring *any* for inclusion in an answer was useless, because without exception they let you down. He told the leader, 'The Tall Ones should shorten the bed. They should learn to subtract.'

'Bernard,' Zech told him. 'You know that a day will come when you will thank me.'

'For what?'

'Why, for setting you straight of course, for granting you exacting honesty and not allowing you to delude yourself, for teaching and training you.'

'You mean … I owe you? Well, all right. Thanks.'

'You're very welcome, Bernard.'

HARGOLIN

The art of war was the invention of Francis Darkling, or so Francis determined others should believe. None would ever be told the truth of the matter, for, if informed of it, they might decide her of unstable mind.

In first instance the cause for discovery was nothing more extraordinary than an annoying bout of restiveness, and then fate decreed that she participate in a most remarkable event.

One warm summer's night, Francis was unable to drift to sleep and so she left her burrows. Making the short hop to the pasture where long grass edged the deep pond would not take long, and so off she went, flibberty hopping, hearing attuned to the sounds of the night, alert for the slightest hint of possible threat. Overhead, the sky was alive with flickering brightness; stars were so visible that their lights appeared needle-sharp.

Once at the pond, she noted an absence of plentiful, succulent green shoots. Creek-side grass was renowned for fine quality, but if prevailing conditions continued then the lack of rainfall would mean that remaining grass would soon be dry and brittle. The level of water in the creek was lower than usual. Zechariah was right. He'd drawn attention to the fact, but in the moment of his mentioning it, she had more or less shrugged the matter off as unimportant. Now though, the dark reflecting mass of water was much lower than usual. The bank she stood upon was higher than should be, and lacking the impetus of flow from farther upstream, the creek was very slow moving. Going close to the edge of the bank so she might glimpse her reflection set against the backdrop of starlight glinting from the pond's dark surface, Francis was mindful to not slip.

Peering down from atop the bank to the water's indigo surface, she at first saw a universe of stars and her own dark shadow shape reflected. This was all she expected to see, but then something extraordinary occurred. She saw her own shape shifting, rippling out of focus and changing to become that of another. The backdrop of reflected sky and stars faded and a bright scene appeared. Coming to view was the clear image of a young boy. This was no obscure, dark silhouette, but a sharp-defined image of a stranger. Despite reminding herself of the danger of slipping, Francis experienced such surprise that she clung in desperation to long clumps of dry grassy stalks in an effort to prevent toppling into the pond.

The impossibility of such visitation was unnerving. So real was the scene that once recovered from her initial surprise Francis thought to address the boy. She was not too shocked when he answered. He was Folk of Fur, that much was certain, but so much else was reason for confusion. He was not situated in surroundings with which she was at all familiar. His was no smoothed, dull-walled burrow but a strange, rainbow hued chamber. 'What do you mean by coming to me in the dark of night, strange boy? How is it you see fit to visit me?'

'I am Zee. Folk of this realm need help.'

'Your realm? What assistance is needed and why?' Francis asked, and then without hesitation, said, 'I will help you if I can.'

'You will?'

'Yes,' Francis told him. 'Where are you, friend? What mystery allows our meeting this way?'

'We loop,' was all he said at first.

'You loop?'

'Yes. Tump has left our realm. They've cut us off, and so we live now in time repeating over and over. To the natural inhabitants of this realm we are as ghosts and nothing more. And Tump... Taken to this realm, we were sentenced by them to never ending sojourn...' His words trailed off, but then after a moment he said, 'I fear being forever forsaken. Tedium makes madness! I'm thankful that my orphan companions do not realize our true predicament. We are held in a trap!'

Francis was confused. 'Tump?' she asked, and then, 'I take it, that you do not refer to Tump, sounded as warning?'

'No! But *Tump*—yes!' he exclaimed, 'Tump is One! And as One, Tump is power unequalled!' He rushed on, 'If not for Hargolin and the company of my *other* self coming to me during his nights, I would never have become aware of our true predicament.' He explained, 'When his physical body sleeps, my other "self" visits me. He travels away from the body there, to visit me here in my dreams. We meld, and are more then, as we were before Tump altered things. In coming from the original time-line to this realm of looping, he has learned the fundamentals of Hargolin. They were then passed to others of the original realm and they've expanded upon them until Hargolin is reinvented. Hargolin, as developed by those of the original line is not the same as Hargolin of this looping realm, but Hargolin, as practised here, was a beginning.

'Hargolin, as developed by those at the orphanage of Sisters of the Shell, is employed against Watchers of Night. They are a vile presence on the original time-line. As familiar companion to myself and partaking of his experience, I have become skilled in the art of war.' He said then, almost as if to himself, 'Of course Hargolin is as a double-edged sword.'

Francis had not the least idea of any of that imparted, and seeing her look of incomprehension, he offered, 'Apart from all else, Hargolin represents a type of awakening. Awakened more than other orphans of this realm, I know better what occurs. I know that events occurring in our looping realm must undergo altering. They *must*! By change occurring in me, other change will follow, and those changes will have further effect. Tump has decreed a time loop, but there may still be a place for the unpredictable.' He was quiet, and then he said, 'All are entranced. They live the same period of time, over and over, trapped in an unending dream. They are enthralled by illusion. For a large part of time I am as caught as the rest of them, held fast and believing each moment is new, I dream the dream, but during time spent in the company of my self, I am awakened to our true predicament. As we speak, you know me awakened, and yet for me too, a large part of time is passed as if in deep slumber.' He said, 'As you see me, I am free from servitude to looping time, free to sojourn in my true home which is Brickfield realm of my past, where, merged with my self—we battle against a fearsome foe. I war with the enemy and yet, during a large part of the time—even when awakened to reality—I have difficulty knowing if my dreams of war, of triumphs and victories, possess true substance or not. I tell myself it *is* real. It's real enough.'

Francis knew great uncertainty. She enquired, 'But what can I do? I'm here. I'm not of your strange realm. I'm ignorant of it.'

He asked, 'Do you know of Skip the Seer? Or perhaps you may have heard the name Piedmont the Bard?'

'Yes I have.' Francis said. 'I *do* know of the bard.' She saw the boy smiled; relief and pleasure showed in his expression. She explained, 'He—the bard—was long ago banished from these parts.' She added, 'His verse is still known. Many hereabouts respect his work.'

The boy then exclaimed, 'The bard is Tump! He said, 'There is Skip the Seer, who, in reaching out to touch the mind of my other self, has revealed Tump. There is the navigator, or way-finder, and then there's the fixer. There're Nancy, Sherbrook, and Peace Darkling. And together they are Tump!'

'*Darkling!*' Francis exclaimed, 'Peace Darkling? *What of her?*' Francis knew that her relative had left New Warren Central long ago, and that Folk no longer spoke of her. Peace Darkling was elder sister to Francis' mother. Both her mother and the youngest of the three sisters, Harmony, were gone from her, passed to gazuzzlement many seasons ago. Of the three, Peace Darkling was the most mysterious. Hearing of her long lost relative now, and from such mysterious source, she prompted, 'Tell me if you will, of my Aunt Peace, and those others you name.' And so it was that she learned something of Tump, from the sad and confusing boy from the looping realm.

As an image reflected upon the surface of the still pond, the boy explained, 'I am certain still, that Tump is good. Folk of Brickfield realm honour them. Tump is an entity of supernatural power. It is as lightning from sky. It brings storm to firmament and can alter reality at will. We, of the realm, looked always to Tump, to answer wishes and such. We looked to Tump, as individuals comprising the entity, for help in resolving difficulty encountered in our daily lives. And so now, realizing we endure repeated, hideous looping day, perhaps it should be deduced that something beyond even their power, went awry; I will not believe that they intended abandoning us.'

Francis prided herself on not just remarkable physical stamina and skill, but for the ability to call upon a deep well of inner strength, an ability beyond that of others, which allowed her continue where another might give in to circumstance and personal shortcoming. She was patient with others and with herself. She believed that with enough effort, invested in pursuing an outcome, success resulted, but hearing the boy describe his suffering and knowing that his companions were oblivious to his loneliness and to the true horror of their plight, she might weep.

She said, 'I comprehend so little. I would help, but doubt that I can.'

He said, 'You've heard me out, and so I know that I am believed.' He smiled. 'At the sight of me, you did not helter away, believing yourself mad. That's something.'

Returning his smile, she asked, 'But *how* is it ... our meeting like this?'

He said, 'I have no real knowledge of the why, or the how of it. Brickfield realm loops. That much I know! In puzzling over it I've thought that realms imagined as contained in an infinite number of soap bubbles may provide some clue to the way of it. Think of a great floating mass of bubbles, some of which impinge one upon another, so that during times of that occurring it may be possible for communication between inhabitants of different realms. Perhaps it's not at all the way of it, but there have been times when I've tried speaking with others. Those attempts were less successful than this. Many entities of strange, mysterious realms were afraid of me.' He said, 'Once, sensing a merging of realms, I ventured speaking into a place of peculiar mist or fog, but my calling to them was taken as cause for fear, and many small creatures skedaddled, shrieking in fright. No good came of it.'

In trying to imagine soap bubbles, Francis was at a definite disadvantage. Those of New Warren Central did not enjoy the luxury of soap; she'd not heard of it before this, but she did, of course, know what bubbles were. They formed in large floating masses upon the stream's surface, and if mischievous youngsters threw stones into the midst of them, they popped. She was troubled in attempting to relate realms with knowledge of bubbles, but refused to founder. She ventured, 'By bubbles, I wonder if you mean those water-born masses of foam—those carrying eggs of Sister Frog?'

'Frogspawn?' He said, and sounded amused. 'Yes, as an example, I suppose that will do.' Disappointment was revealed. Francis understood that the boy had deduced the fact of her realm falling far behind his own. She realized that her new friend knew she could never assist him with any problem requiring sophisticated knowledge or skill; compared with those of his realm, the inhabitants of New Warren Central were backward.

After a long silence between them, he announced, 'I know! I will teach you Hargolin! You are good company, and you look fit! I'm used to judging fitness and recognize a good candidate.' He said, 'Of course we cannot know, but the day may come when our paths will again cross, and they may cross in more actual sense. We might then spar! In any case, knowledge of Hargolin is worth owning.' He said, 'We may not have long together before our realms separate, but now I'm forgetting my manners. I haven't so much as enquired as to whether or not you're interested in passing further time in my company, or if you're curious to learn from me?' He said, 'Hargolin—the art of war, is the one thing which makes true sense to me. If you agree, I will pass knowledge of it to you.'

And so it was, that Francis Darkling set upon a course whereby Hargolin came to mean everything to her, as much as it meant to Zee. Following the first of their meetings she learned to eat, sleep and breathe Hargolin. With knowledge of its ways and skill in their employment she would become an invincible force.

His first instruction was, 'Everything is energy.'

'Uh huh.'

'There is nothing real, other than it *is* energy.' He began to move in unusual, smooth flowing, rhythmic manner.

He demonstrates a strange dance, she thought, and smiled. Guessing her thought, he halted. He said, 'No. Hargolin may resemble a dance, but appearance is where similarity ends. Dancing is dancing and it's a fine thing. Hargolin though, is the most gazuzzling of arts.'

'Gazuzzling?' she asked.

'Yes. Hargolin strikes terror into the hearts and minds of enemies, and to succeed, a devotee of Hargolin must first learn to view gazuzzle-ment without emotion. An enemy disposed of, is realized as transported to a neutral place of absolute void, not to a place of darkness. To imagine such destiny for another is hateful, but just as important … an enemy is not transported to an imaginary place of light and forgiveness. Notions of good and ill have no place in Hargolin. Feeling is eradicated and the mind does not judge. Emotion does not enter in. He said, 'Make a loop of your arms. Hold both paws before you. Take one step back from the edge of the pond. Step back towards me again—just one step... Yes, that's it. And now, if instructed to leap forward into the pond's watery depths, you *are* prepared to do so. Correct?'

'Yes,' Francis allowed. But extending her arms as instructed, she was puzzled, and disturbed by her willingness to agree with such an outrageous request. There was something about the tone employed by him—an odd, compelling quality to his voice. He next asked, 'When I ask it of you, will you turn and helter to throw yourself full force against the trunk of that tree—the tree I see standing there upon the dark slope behind you?'

'Yes,' she answered, knowing that it was true. She would do so. She asked, 'Why do I agree to carry out your suggestions?'

He said, 'Because Hargolin takes your will.' Waving a dismissive paw, he said, 'It steals the will as it takes life. Almost anything is possible. We may cause gazuzzlement and then restore life.'

'You are capable of restoring life!'

'Yes and no. A state of paralysis can be induced, or going further, hearts are made to cease beating—and all with a touch. We cause gazuzzlement and then, if quick to act, can restore an opponent to life. We are not though, capable of restoring life in every situation. Imagine you happened upon a creature deceased—let's say, a mouse dropped from a high altitude by Brother Hawk. There, lies lifeless in your path, the unfortunate mouse, and so you think to offer aid. But the mouse is forever gone. Hargolin is not healing. We are not doctors, but rather warriors.'

'Warriors possessing the capability of providing a defeated enemy something of a second chance?'

'Yes.'

'Then teach me it. You may ask anything of me. If it is within my power to give, it is yours. You shall have no need for your trancing voice. I will leap unafraid into a drowning-pond or serpent's lair.'

'Then you detected my means of ensuring agreement?'

She said, 'Yes, but if I had not in the first instant made a circle of my arms, placed my paws together and held them out before me or not taken those first small steps, back and forth in trust, then I suspect your task of gaining my acceptance would have proved more difficult.'

'For Hargolin, you are perfect!'

'When I am skilled, you may compliment me,' Francis allowed. 'For now, we must work.'

He said, 'Fall—now!'

And so she did.

Night after night she attended at the pond, knowing that soon they must part. Parting was inevitable. As great bubbles began the process of separation, realms shifted to go their ways. Set upon other courses they moved from alignment, one from other, and communication between mere folk was made difficult. When it was just possible to glimpse one another, when there was no longer anything but the smallest hope of apprehending the meaning of words passed between them, Francis heard in the stillness of night, the whispered words, 'In Hargolin deny all feeling, but Francis I can never forget you!'

He, who'd so often instilled in her the idea of mysterious void, was taken then by vast nothingness.

HEAT

Days were scorching hot and conditions were stifling even below ground level. Many of the aged and the very young were meeting with gazuzzlement. The creek no longer flowed but was a snaking ribbon of sand and stones. In places where water once ran deepest, baking mud now formed web-like scarring, beneath the relentless searing sun. With food diminishing and lack of water, more would perish. The place of burial chosen by Mavis Noy-Breen, where husband Charlie was laid to rest beneath a gnarled, solitary tree, was by now the site of too numerous fresh plots.

When Zechariah insisted she make an accurate count of new graves, Francis, uncertain as to the decency of the request and sensitive to the feelings of others, carried no scratch-bark or sharpened stick. In her tallying them, numbers were committed to memory.

Great Grandfather had turned away from them and ancient Ruth Fawn knew it. She said, 'He's been a cold stranger before this. He grants fickle care. With this heat, He's got it in for the likes of me.'

She'd spoken truer than she knew, for within three days of her speaking against Him, Ruth was called home, which was the way Mavis Whitepaws viewed her friend's passing.

'She's gone to comforting paws,' she told Nancy, 'returned to the true warren after a life too long lived. I have no right deciding such, but her lot included more of sadness than seems fair.' Standing at the graveside with Nancy and friends, Emily and Sara, Mavis offered, 'Safe journey, Ruth Fawn. You were a good friend to me.' Laying a thin bundle of dried grass gathered earlier from the field, she said, 'I'm sorry it's not more, Ruth, but you said yourself, flowers were not necessary. Now you have your "no frills" offering.' Looking away from the resting place to gaze out across broad fields lying at the opposite side of the dry creek bed, she observed, 'The Tall Ones' crop is the one green thing hereabouts, but in facing such harsh conditions, it too begins to yellow.' She paused before saying, 'Gals, you must listen with care and take these words to heart. There will be many who, seeing no alternative, will succumb to temptation. They'll take to eating yon' crop.' She said, 'The greens, new greens, as they were known during earlier time, were not declared taboo without good reason. They are poison for Folk of Fur. They cause immeasurable suffering.' She said, 'Ruth Fawn knew the truth of it. She bore a son to husband Sobriety and they named him, Chance, a true *monster* of a youngster. Sobriety Fawn's passing was long ago and no stone marks the resting place; he wanted no ceremony and wished to lie in unmarked grave. He did not wish to be remembered because of the boy.'

They were attentive to Mavis, but then Nancy was distracted, and in a hushed voice she asked, 'Why do you suppose Francis Darkling comes here? No relative or friend of hers has passed in recent time, not as I've heard.' She cautioned, 'No, Sara—don't stare. Take my word for it. She goes from grave to grave, following along rows and behaves as if counting penance veg'. Why does she do it, I wonder?'

Casting a surreptitious glance in the direction of the Darkling gal, Mavis declared, 'You're right. She tallies the number of unfortunates, on *his* behalf. Without the count he is uncertain, and so must have the precise number. The great Zechariah's obsession is control of others. He must know every detail.'

'Oh, Mother!' Nancy said. She'd heard every criticism against Zechariah before.

'"Oh, Mother?" Don't patronize me, gal. His motto is "An ear to every burrow". He's far and away too fond of knowing it all. He aims to impose more rigid and harsh rule. You'll see. The time will come when all will recognize the truth of it.' She added, 'Those ignoring obvious signs deserve no better than what they'll get.'

'Yes, but…'

'No. Allow me to finish. I know his type. Past example of such an overriding will to control was less dangerous, but the ceaseless collecting of information, the gathering of minutiae pertaining to the lives of others, is a telling flaw. In the end, information is always misused. You should mark my words. Nodding in the direction of Francis Darkling, she said, Her corpse counting over there must tell you something. If possible, his control would extend even beyond gazuzzlement!'

'For deeks' sake, Mother! He's leader. A leader must know what's going on in territory governed by him.'

'Governing? Is that what you call it?' Looking from them, Mavis addressed the grave. 'We're in for harsh times again, Ruthie. You'll be grateful not having to endure more of the same.' She looked up then, 'It sounds wrong of me, but she's better off than the rest of us. She won't have to go through things to come.'

Sara asked, 'You described their son as a monster. What did you mean by it?'

Emily, embarrassed by Sara's temerity in making the enquiry but curious too, shuffled her feet, muttering, 'Oh, Sara, she just meant...'

Emily's lame attempting to respond on her behalf was cut short by Mavis interjecting, 'We will return to my burrows and I will tell the grim tale. Hearing it will not be easy, but you shall have the truth. We cannot linger here in this sad place, with *her* present.' Glancing again in the direction of the Darkling gal, 'She will report to *him* and they may make something of us spending so long here.' Making to leave, she declared, 'She always was a bright gal—our Hargolin Queen. Pity is, she's much too close with the great leader.' She glanced to Nancy, smiling. Then, going by Charlie's place of rest, she said, 'Say something to your father in passing, Nancy gal. You never know—he may just hear you.'

Pausing on the way and seeing the ladder still leaning against the trunk of the crooked tree, where long ago she had left it, she noted two rungs were missing. Her strong twine had rotted and the rungs lay there on the ground. When she was done with putting Charlie's beloved wheel up there in the tree, she had returned home, leaving the ladder. To her surprise, others had decided it a good idea and copied it. They'd made ladders of their own, which were used to take fruit from high branches in the Tall One's orchard.

They resumed flibberty hopping, leaving Charlie's plot and Nancy asked, 'I was never certain as to why you went to so much trouble in putting the wheel in the tree. Why did you do it, Mother?'

At first she did not answer but then Mavis said, 'It was a joke.'

'A joke?'

'Yes. I put it there because he would not do without it, and he knew his playing with it annoyed me. But spite wasn't all of it, because neither

Charlie nor I were ever found wanting when it came to treating each other's opinion of the wheel, with a certain humour. You see, both Charlie and I knew the mad thing was no real gift, but was the boy Bernard's bribe. The wheel was given on behalf of the great Zechariah. It was given, my gal, in exchange for you.'

'Payment? For Nancy's favour!' Sara had fallen behind the others but she heard them. The friends had long known of Zechariah's interest in Nancy, but the idea of his offering a *wheel* in exchange for her, Sara thought outrageous.

Mavis Noy-Breen chuckled. She said, 'Oh yes, but he did not then ask for her paw—not in any honest, open way. They were young, weren't they? In any case, his unflagging attention amounted to harassment. He was relentless and my poor opinion of him hasn't changed.' She, smiling, then said, 'Samson's wheel was not offered. According to my late husband, acceptance was *insisted* upon. The Keeper of Rope, on *his* keeper's behalf, brooked no refusal. But then Charlie, of course, adored it. To him it was a marvellous plaything but then I would not let it into our home. He wanted to work on widening the entryway so that it would fit, and nagged me to see that as good sense.'

'But you refused. Oh poor Father!'

'Poor Father? No. If the wheel had been allowed into the home then it would not have been long and Zechariah would have followed. It was far better, him seeing his precious gift left lying outside in every type of weather, left, as unwanted trash.' She asked, 'Or did you want him and his little friend as guests in our home, counting carrots, cabbage leaves and what not?'

Nancy was silent.

Mavis asked, 'Would you have enjoyed that?'

'No, I suppose not.'

'You could be more definite.'

'He's not so bad, Mavis,' Emily said.

'Not so good either,' interjected Sara.

'He's just different.'

'Mm. Different—different peculiar,' Sara said.

'Here we are now,' Mavis said. She would ignore Emily's attempting to defend her daughter's indecisiveness. Come along gals, and you'll hear

Ruth's story as she told it, and then each in her own right, can determine a sensible course.' She said, 'Despite the prevailing conditions, I have two parsnips put aside for such a special occasion. You are my guests, and they'll be fair-divided.'

Mavis said, 'Charlie and I thought we'd a difficult time of raising Nancy's brothers, but knowing what others contend with can put one's own problems in a new light. You'll know what I mean when you've heard Ruth's story.' She began, 'It was a moonlit night and for Sobriety and Ruth Fawn and their young son, Chance, it was perhaps the saddest night of all. It was sad too, for Harmony and her good husband Rowdy, and their monstrous daughter. The daughter was born during a storm—a storm, which is a story in its own right. They named the daughter, poor love—Thorny. Thorny Lewis was endowed as no other—no other, either before or since. She was strong beyond belief and was wild and ferocious. Had the gal lived, then her Aunt Francis would have been challenged; Thorny would have outdone all comers, even she. I can't know for certain of course, but Hargolin may not have provided defence against an individual so endowed.' She said, 'In any case, Thorny was no more than a child when she passed. There is much sorrow in Ruth's story. It is steeped in darkness, but in darkness there is something of light, because parents *loved* their changed ones. Those afflicted were cared for and loved and it's puzzling, but they may have received more affection than normal offspring, not because they were demanding, but due to them possessing a quality of lost helplessness. Such quality played upon hearts, and drew deep from the wellspring of parental feeling. And then too, they were feared. With a single blow they could deliver gazuzzlement—even to a hapless friend. The boy, Chance, hurt Ruth, I know. And both Harmony and Rowdy Lewis nursed many bruises, scratches and other injuries. Of the two, Thorny was always the most dangerous. According to Ruth, Chance was by nature more passive, but then she was mother to the boy.

'But,' Emily asked, 'what were they like, apart from their strength, and apart from being fierce?'

'They were neither fawn nor brown or black, and could never blend with field or ground. They stood out from afar. They were bright-coloured as meadow flowers: Red, yellow, orange and even blue as sky above.

Chance wore a stripe. It ran down his back from shoulders to tail. His tail was the softest pink, as I recall.'

'And what of Thorny?'

'Similar, dear... She tended more to yellows and crimson, but their colours are not so important,' Mavis said. '*Do* take this last piece of parsnip. I'm afraid it's wasted on me. It's a little too dry. It's been kept aside for too long, but still it's an improvement on dry grass.' Sara said she would like the remaining morsel and so Mavis passed it to her. Proceeding then, from where she left off, Mavis said, 'The parents met, the four of them, and decided upon returning the children from whence they came.'

Sara's expression revealed dawning suspicion. 'What? You don't mean...' the question was left unfinished.

'Yes dear, I do. Gazuzzling a child is no one's idea of correct behaviour, but these were not just ordinary, burdensome children. We have, I fear, allowed ourselves distraction in focusing too much on their pretty colouring. I want you gals to hear me and understand. They were not normal babes, not to slightest degree. These were giants, possessing claws of such length, such sharpness, that they were capable of wreaking damage far exceeding anything inflicted by Brother Eagle. And that's by no means the worst.' She said, 'Imagine *your* feeling. What will you do my dears when *you* birth monsters, little ones possessing murderous capability, who helter not on four legs, but six?'

But for the sound of Sara munching the last teensiest morsel of parsnip, they were quiet. She had given them much to think on but after allowing a moment or two, Mavis said, 'My hope is that when hunger begins to bite, even with starvation as your lot, you will not be tempted by those greens.' She said, 'But still, all I've told so far is just the least of it.'

'It is?'

'Yes, Nancy. You will recall the time of your childhood illness?' Requiring no response, Mavis plunged ahead. 'Whilst doing my best in tending to your needs, I wondered if true madness threatened. Fever had you in its grip, and during the worst of it, I feared that you might not have long with us. You are strong willed and courageous though, and you regained yourself.' Looking to the friends and then to Nancy, she said, 'When ill, you could not help but ramble and make strange claims. You spoke of some*one*—not some*thing*, but some*one*—you named Tump. Do you recall it?'

Her spirit sank. A peculiar feeling involving mild panic ensued, and Nancy wished she were someplace else. Did she recall any of it—the childhood episode? Did Mother need ask? She must know that Tump was a most singular cause for embarrassment and sense of betrayal. For mentioning Tump, back then, present company had believed her deluded. She alone had dealt with the burdensome memory of those strange individuals.

Sounding pleased, Mavis declared, 'You will be interested to learn that they are real. Ruth met them and she told me of it, and so my gal, you were not mistaken. They exist and I have known it for some considerable time.'

'Tump? Who are they?' Emily asked.

'They are a great mystery,' Mavis said. 'They make miracles.'

Sara said, 'Nancy, it seems you're owed an apology.'

'Thank you, Sara,' Nancy said. 'But, Mother how is it that you decide me sane after hearing of Tump from your friend? Why did you not believe *me?*'

'Because you were ill and because at the time I was consumed with worry for you!'

'Forgive me, Mother, but that sounds too easy.'

'I'm sorry you feel that way dear. Isn't it best left in the past?'

Emily pleaded, 'Nancy, *do* allow your mother to finish the tale!' And so in deference to a friend, she made no more of it.

Mavis said, 'Late one night, Sobriety and Ruth took the boy Chance down the valley to a creek-side place, a place of quiet and solitude, where the dreadful deed would be attended. Rowdy Lewis and Harmony took Thorny in the opposite direction to a place upstream from the warren. None followed any real plan but knowing what must be done, they knew the youngsters must perish.' Here Mavis paused. Distracted by Sara's incessant chewing, she offered, 'If it's tough, dear, then just spit it out. I can clean it up later.'

Sara declined, telling Mavis, 'No, it's fine, but if I'm bothering you, I'll save the rest of it.' So saying, she took a piece of parsnip from her mouth and folded it away in the pocket of her apron. She sighed, and Emily looked away.

Mavis said, 'Coming upon a small clearing, Ruth and Sobriety were deciding their next step, when a sound came to them from undergrowth by the stream. They were not alone, for Peace Darkling was hiding there behind a tree. Now she and a small group of misfits, or malcontents, had departed New Warren at an earlier time. That may sound a harsh description of folk, but it's as many saw them. There was the great bard—author of the epics—and others I will not trouble to name.' Mavis said, 'With her position known, the young Chance Fawn set upon Peace Darkling, and at first she was not harmed. But when she chastised the parents, the boy struck out, and receiving a blow from the creature, the Darkling gal was gazuzzled.'

'Deeks!'

'Indeed yes.'

'What happened then?'

'They set about her interment,' said Mavis.

'I would have heltered,' confessed Emily.'

'In the circumstance, I'm sure you would not,' said Mavis. 'You would show respect. You're a good gal, always were.' Resuming, she said, 'Once interred, the gal decided that it was not yet her time, and so by miraculous means she rose from gazuzzlement to confront those who'd sent her on her way.'

'No. I don't believe it!' Sara exclaimed, 'I know poor Ruth is gone from us and that you and she were good friends, Mavis, but it can't be true.'

Nancy said, 'Sara, you were right earlier, apologizing for not finding me credible. You should keep to that course, because they are not imaginary. Peace Darkling and the bard, and Skip the Seer, are Tump.' Waving a paw, she said, 'They come from a territory beyond the high hill, and in returning me to the warren, they pushed me through time.' She said, 'I needed to be believed! I was beside myself, and small wonder. I was sent back from darkest night—to dusk of that very same day! During my time spent with them, they engaged in transporting an object, and, by wondrous means! It was something they referred to as the "old Radiola", and it was taken from the Tall Ones' dwelling place. A great bolt of lightning—an almighty flashing of light—accompanied the event! Understand that I do not boast, but they insisted that the task could not have been accomplished without my helping them.'

'They acted with assistance from you?' enquired, Mavis.

'Yes, Mother. Believe it or not, with my help.'

'How could you contribute to such magic as theirs?'

'They looked into me. That's all.'

'And what is this, looking into you?'

'I was told that if the boy, Skip, looked into me, then his ability was greatly enhanced. His deeds were then carried out with extreme accuracy.'

Mavis revealed, 'I was acquainted with Skip the Seer, and those others. I was there at the old warren, during those times spent gathered about the old Radiola. Folk loved to congregate in the meeting place, in the presence of that strange device with its sacred valves. We sang along to accompaniment of many a merry tune.'

Mavis was affected in recalling those times, and seeing her mother saddened, Nancy assured, 'It's all right Mother.' And, by way of comforting gesture, she offered a smile of understanding.

Having noted the small exchange between mother and daughter, a thoughtful, Emily, asked, 'But what of Peace Darkling?'

Sara said, 'Yes Mavis, do tell the rest of it.'

Pushing memory away, Mavis resumed, 'Ruth and Sobriety saw Peace Darkling rise from the grave. Chance too, even he of awesome strength, was afraid! The ground all about was raised up and moved. Soil heaved away from the fresh-dug grave! Stones and boulders rained down and then time stood still! The stream stopped flowing, and for all they knew, the moon stood still in its path. Then … was silence until, after some time, movement was restored. As Ruth had it, Peace Darkling raised higher, bright glowing against the night! Then, strange sound—sound of hems of many long gowns moving, touching and pressing against dry grass—was heard. And lofting above those cowering beneath, Peace Darkling commanded them, "Spare the child!" The Fawns were ordered back to New Warren Central. They were told to warn others of greens causing illness and dire change in the unborn.' Composing herself, Mavis said, 'Then, at first their warning went unheeded. The Darkling gal was correct though, and when finally the crop was declared taboo, none more such as Thorny or Chance were delivered of folk.' She then enquired, 'Have you noticed those places, small barren patches lying here and there, where nothing will grow? Well, you need not ponder, for resting in those places are those who were sustained in life by new greens. Not so much as a weed or nettle will grow in those places.'

Sara said, 'I *have* wondered over those barren patches. They lie in the direction of the forest, don't they? They form patterns.'

'That is one place,' said Mavis, 'A place chosen for being distant from the warren.'

'What of Harmony and Rowdy Lewis?' Emily asked, 'What of Thorny?'

Mavis said, 'Her parents went so far as to shove the gal into the creek, and at a deepest part. She struggled to get out. You can imagine it can't you? Much ferocious bellowing—nothing very feminine to any of it! Those great talons of hers clawed at the slippery bank, when, lo and behold, Tump arrived to berate the parents for abusive behaviour. As the Fawns were warned, so too were Harmony and husband. They returned that night, contending all the way from upstream to warren, with one bedraggled, irate gal. According to Ruth, who did not lack humour, Rowdy felt compelled to pretend clumsiness for as long as Thorny was with them. As proof of innocence he went out of his way to trip, fall, and make himself foolish; the gal knew that he had pushed her in.'

Sara vowed, 'I shan't touch those greens! I won't go near the fields again, not in any circumstance.'

'Nor me,' Emily agreed, 'but what *will* we do?'

Nancy asked, 'Do you mean, what shall we eat?'

'Dirt, if it comes to it,' Sara said. And then she asked, 'This looking into you, Nancy... What is it?'

Nancy said, 'If others look into me, then they can know themselves more than they otherwise might. They know better their abilities and dreams. Skip, of Tump, claimed his ability was magnified.' She could not miss their small smiles; they thought she exaggerated. When Sara asked if she might experiment by looking in, Nancy laughed, declaring, 'Why, Sara, I think you should be afraid. Aren't you fearful of seeing nothing at all?'

Mavis said, 'I don't doubt your sincerity gal, but I've gazed into those pretty eyes of yours on countless occasions and have seen only you.' She said, 'I've missed any strange benefit, but then I have been reminded of my loving you.'

Sara moved closer to Nancy, 'May I try?'

Emily said, 'You should look to know what we must do for our families.'

Nancy said, 'Ask whatever you will, Sara, and I will step aside.' To her mother she said, 'On those previous occasions of your looking to me, Mother, I did not step aside, but your love was returned to you.'

So saying, she stepped aside so that her friend might have a true answer.

'Oh, my!' Sara exclaimed. 'I could not have known! And yet in my heart of hearts I see that it *is* true! Although you are correct, Nancy, it *does* make me afraid!'

'What have you seen, Sara?' Emily wanted to know but Sara gave no response.

'She sees them journeying afar,' Nancy said, 'I see it too. Those she cares for are soon far from here. She and they will leave before two days have passed. Their journey is not an easy one, but Sara, when the journeying is over you *are* happy in your new home.' Sara was awed, and not just by what she'd seen. She said, 'It's a strange power you have, Nancy. All along we've been friends and yet I did not know you. Nor did I know myself. I never dreamed I might contemplate leaving New Warren. I believed it my life-long home.'

'But you have dreamed of leaving. You must have. Before now though, you were unaware of it. Nothing of mine was added to what you saw.'

'Is what I've seen predetermined?' Sara asked.

'No. In looking into me, all of that revealed surfaced from deep within *you*. If you were shown the location of something, for example something lost, then you are under no compulsion to helter to regain the item. You may choose to forget all about it. The choice is yours.'

Sara was thoughtful and so, seeing her opportunity, Emily asked, 'Nancy, let me see myself. May I?' But when Emily looked into Nancy she was presented an image of herself at home in her chamber. She had fallen asleep. She complained, 'It's marvellous isn't it? In denying hunger to come, I choose to sleep hardship away.' She said, 'It seems typical of me.' Sara was revealed an exciting future, and Emily was disappointed. She said, 'Sara gets the luck doesn't she? Why is it? For as long as I can remember it's been that way.'

For no reason other than providing a distraction, Mavis said, 'Turn yourself my way, Nancy. I will have my turn.'

'And I shall step aside.'

After a moment, Mavis muttered, 'Oh, Sherbrook...'

The name was all but whispered. Mavis' experience was not shared, for, true to her word, Nancy had stood aside. She now asked, 'Mother, what is it? What have you seen?'

Mavis said, 'Oh it's nothing. But yes, something was lost. It was so very long ago that I'd all but forgotten it.'

FAREWELL

'We are going, Finius, and shall not be returning to New Warren Central. Having to leave is sad, but forced to it, we should see it as an adventure! We can do this. I know it!'

Finius smiled. Abernathy was on his lap and Finius shifted, making them both more comfortable. Abernathy, too often saw teasing Dandelion, as entertainment, and so Finius, no true authoritarian, had insisted that Abernathy sit with him, which the boy enjoyed doing anyway. He did not immediately respond to wife Sara's insisting they take the drastic step of abandoning their home. Folk were territorial, staying put and coping in times of deteriorating circumstance. There were exceptions, but those folk were just that, exceptions. Leaving the home territory with a young family might entail confronting a worse hazard than those already contended with.

Then Finius surprised them both. He heard himself admitting, 'I've wondered about doing just that. I've worried over providing, and cannot bring myself to feed my family those greens.' Sounding weary, he said, 'There are many who don't mind consuming that crop, but folk of old were not kadoodlers. They set rules for good reason. You're right, Sara, we should take our chance,' he said. 'The question is, which direction to take?

She exclaimed, 'Finius, I *adore* you!' Hugging both him and Abernathy at once, she said, 'I will have us ready to leave by morning! We'll go with just the bare essentials, and will take the trail to the hilltop. It's steep, but we'll manage the climb. I'm so glad for your agreeing, Finius. You have no idea!'

The following morning, before the first, thin, yellow rays warmed the sky, when cold, grey light pushed stars to fading, several close friends gathered to see them on their way.

Sara fussed over the youngsters, 'Now, Dandelion, I know you're tired, still, but do try not to complain. Take Father's other paw and *do* get along with Abernathy. We're set upon an adventure. It's exciting isn't it?' She told Nancy and Emily, 'You'll look after each other, I know you will. We're not forever parted. We'll meet again.' She said, 'Smile now, Emily. Don't be downhearted. Give me your biggest hug! There, now...' She asked, 'Finius, are we ready?'

They were, and Finius told friend, Randolph, 'This is it then, Randy. If you change your mind, we'll be happy for you and yours joining us over yon' hill.'

'We may do just that,' said Randolph, 'I'll miss your company Fin'. I'll have no one to get into trouble with now!'

Grasping the paws of his children, Finius, in perhaps too commanding a voice, announced, 'Now then family, let's move out before the sun decides to bakes us in our britches!'

Abernathy and friend Randolph laughed, but Dandelion complained, 'Father, I don't wear britches! I'm a gal!'

Seeing Sara ready to set out, Finius told Dandelion, 'Britches or no, we must reach yon' heights before the sun rises too far in the sky, and if we don't want to be overcome we should not tarry here. Wish your friends final farewell and let's be off.'

Sara turned, noting for a last time faces of good friends. Perhaps they would *not* see each other again. Those left behind were, in a deep acknowledged sense, family too. As he, Abernathy and Dandelion followed after Sara, Finius, without the advantage of having looked into anyone at all, knew trepidation. The decision taken could bring worst fate to his family—a harsher fate than any owned by those, who, if aided by fortune in an effort against hardship, may survive by remaining at New Warren Central. Faithful to the truth of Sara's visioning, as she referred to it, Finius braced himself, knowing that before very long the point of no return would be reached. Even without children accompanying them, the journey would prove arduous. As it was, his small family was in for a severe testing.

Randolph called, 'Go with Great Grandfather!'

Finius heard Sara's friend, Nancy say, 'Take care in climbing the high hill, Dandelion, won't you?' They were friends, all, but from here on, they were on their own. Finius returned their waving; one last time.

They watched from the slope as the small group began the climb and when those departed could no longer be seen, Nancy and Emily went their separate ways. Nancy would return to her burrows, and Emily to hers.

'After rising before dawn,' Nancy said, 'I think I should like to rest. It seems that of late, I'm always tired.'

Emily agreed, 'I've not energy enough for plucking stalks of dry grass. Hunger is besting us.' She said, 'Look at me. I'm thinning fur and bone, and seeing you—sad to say, you're not much better off.' She said then, 'I'm glad you gave them the gourd from your mother. It was very considerate of her. At least they'll have water for the journey.'

'Muddy water,' Nancy amended. Mavis had thought to fill the shell of a gourd with water. The gourd was left over from a penance offering received during better times. Mavis had obtained water from several of those bucks digging deep holes in the creek's sandy bed. It was not much, but it was better than nothing. Small quantities of precious liquid were gained by digging down into the creek-bed at places where, previous to drought coming to the land, the waters swept against curving banks. Mavis was at first considered by those digging, as nothing more than an aged, troublesome doe. In begging for water on behalf of children who'd soon leave them, she did not mention youngsters nor anyone else departing New Warren Central, but rather explained, 'I have here a new thing, an invention of mine. I want to see if it's of practical use.' And so, one of them scooped muddy water from the sinkhole they'd dug, and filled the gourd. Seeing the hollowed shell containing water, the bucks laughed. They were as delighted by it, as Mavis. 'You're onto something old gal' one told her, 'although, I don't think there'll be too much use for it. You can always come here to drink, can't you?'

Yes, thought Mavis, that's true, but in order to do that, one must first be able bodied, as you. She said nothing but was pleased by her invention, and without wanting to make too much of it, wondered if perhaps those children setting out, might even owe their lives to what was nothing more than something thought of in a moment of idleness. She decided to tie a length of her strongest twine about the gourd's circumference. There was a slight groove already there, at what she determined represented the gourds waist. The twine, tied at such suitable point would not slip from place, and then by assuring the length of twine was long enough, the gourd would be easier to carry over a long distance; the twine should be slung across a shoulder. She went to search through her rag-tag collection of bits and pieces.

After returning to her home burrows, Nancy thought of Sara and the children and smiled with fondness. Many pleasant occasions were hers for recalling—for a large part, occasions spent creek-side. She was mindful now of small pleasantries, and of comments made by Sara's little ones. Recalling snippets of conversation was enough to make her maudlin. Having succumbed to reminiscing too much, she must go to find Emily and together they would think of distracting each other from a past shared with Sara. The past was gone, but if she flibberty hopped into Emily's burrow calling, 'Are my lashes *too* long, do you think?' then, Emily, reminded of young Violet, would know what was meant.

It was not very far to Emily's home and she was soon there. Nancy called to her friend, but then perhaps Emily still slept? Not wanting to waken her, she would not go farther along the main burrow, nor would she call out for a second time. She'd gone just several small steps inside the entranceway and receiving nothing by way of response, she retraced her steps to stand outside, not knowing quite what next she might do. The sun had risen and another scorching day threatened. Near the opening to Emily's burrows, where once grass grew in abundance, now, even dry stalks were scarce. With no slight sound of merry gurgling from nearby stream, remorseless nature was skewed against them, and she felt she would never again know anything of inner lightness or real happiness. She watched as red dust swept up from the bed of the creek to whirl spiralling aloft before the current carrying it dissipated. In the field beyond the creek many busied themselves as if there was no tomorrow. They devoured greens, and every so often the distant sound of retching reached her. When first taken into the body, greens produced sickness. At first, stomachs were unused to the plant and they revolted against it. Unheeding folk persisted, until digestive systems bowed and consumption proceeded without distressing side effect until later, Nancy thought, when it came to affecting the unborn. May Great Grandfather forgive them.

Yonder were Zechariah with Bernard and Francis Darkling; they gathered there at a tight turn in the creek. They supervised workers in digging for precious water. Her mother had not bid Sara and her family goodbye, but Nancy was entrusted to give to Sara the gift of the water filled gourd.

Nancy watched now as Zechariah bent low, his ears going from sight below the bank. Doubtless, he gave orders to those deeper down in the excavation. They would not dig without the leader seeing a better way of going about it and his organizing others was ever crucial.

'You are Nancy, aren't you—the Noy-Breen gal?' Nancy turned. The voice addressing her belonged to one whose name she was unable to place. 'It's, Fay, dear—a friend of your mother's.' The aged doe went on to explain, 'It's no wonder you don't recognize me. Just *look* at me. It's plain to see that gazuzzlement will be mercy granted.' She said, 'I'm not afraid or too set against it.' She was old, and yet not as old as Mavis. Fay had given an honest assessment of her appearance; she was not much more than a bundle of sticks. Mange had got the better of her coat, and with her travelled many flies. They droned about the tips of her ears as if undecided as to safe settling. Fay did not trouble to motion them desist, but unflinching, put up with their presence. She did not have strength enough for the small task of swatting them away. Having gained Nancy's attention, the old one looked out in direction of the wide yellowing fields and observed, 'Disgusting sound—the sound of vomiting—isn't it? One need make no such enquiry, for it most certainly is. They should not be judged, though. They know little better. They've determined the ban as superstitious rot, unproven nonsense, passed down from geriatric kadoo-dlers. To those fallen upon such hard times as these, the ban is no deter-rent. It was never explained, was it? It ought to have been, and I for one, was always of that opinion, but then, who am I? An old nobody, eh?' She said, 'Those in charge, know best!' Glancing off in a down-stream direc-tion, she said, 'That one knows every last thing! Nothing can go wrong with him as leader!' Without waiting for a response from Nancy, Fay hobbled away, chortling as if pleased with her final words. She'd not gone far, when she turned back to enquire, 'Why aren't you over there with the rest of them? It's no business of mine, but…'

'Mother explained the result of giving in to eating it.'

'Ah, yes, she would have. Of course.' Giving a curt nod, she was on her way again. Nancy watched her go. Then, because she could think of nothing better to do, she decided to return to Emily's. Emily was altogether too fond of resting. Perhaps because there was so little else to do, she would return there and take the liberty of awakening her.

The temperature was less debilitating once a body was underground, but even so the atmosphere was musty and stuffier than she would prefer. The air was unmoving and carried a stale odour. Emily's place was no different than others. Conditions were the same in her burrows. Deep enough into the depths of New Warren Central change was noticeable, but then many sought refuge from unpleasant conditions in the more deep-excavated communal burrows and chambers, which meant that space in those areas was at a premium. A price was paid whatever the choice made.

Traversing the burrow leading to Emily's chambers, Nancy detected an odd absence of sound. She paused. There was no sound at all and that was unusual, she decided. She should not expect to hear even the faint murmur of Emily's breathing, but shouldn't she expect to hear something? She was not sure as to what she meant by that. It was not only the absence of every familiar sound which piqued curiosity but the peculiar eerie quality of stillness itself. The fur at the back of her neck was all that moved, and that bristled more with each moment's passing. Not far from where she waited was a gentle curve to the burrow, and just a short way beyond that curve was the chamber where Emily slept. Light in the tunnel was dim beyond that smooth curve, dimmer than where she stood. As she started ahead, along the way, she saw an area of even darker shadow slide out from there. Her own shadow cast ahead of her, made for confusion, but still, just a short distance from where she stood was something thin—something smooth and dark glinting. In the following instant it moved again and then she was certain. There was the tail of one who drove fear into hearts! Brother Serpent had visited poor Emily as she slept!

PENANCE

Bernard protested, 'She takes her place in the field, to harass the feeders!'

'You mustn't trouble over it, Bernard,' Zechariah assured, 'She can shout warnings and make herself as foolish as she likes. She'll soon be over it, with no harm done.'

Just arrived, Francis Darkling caught the tail end of their conversation. She asked, 'Shouting over what? Her friend Emily's passing?'

'No.' Zechariah told her, 'It's the other matter. She shouts and carries on as if demented. She stands at the edge of the field, shouting, "Don't eat greens!"'

'You must have heard it, Francis? It's impossible to miss. "Your children will suffer! They'll pay the price! Eat the filthy crop at your peril!"' He explained, 'I've been busy and haven't had time to give the matter attention. There's the problem of penance offering, as you're aware. The offerings are not worth mentioning. They should be ashamed of themselves, putting out so little.' Zechariah sighed, 'There's the worrisome matter of burials. There are far too many plots to excavate, which means that the excavation of the creek-bed has slowed. And, there's the other thing—the matter of the interminable retching of one's neighbours, which does nothing to aid the spirit. The unceasing sound of it is just shocking, and so I've had not a wink of sleep.' He said, 'Busy—is not the half of it!' Returning then to the topic of Nancy Noy-Breen, he told Francis, 'She does no real harm and may cry her lungs out all the day long, but her carry-on, drives our Bernard to distraction.' Giving a sly, conspiratorial wink, he told Francis, 'She takes no notice of even his most authoritative commands. In fact she orders him, "Scat!" if you can believe it? Scat! *My* Bernard! The loyal emissary is quite beside himself. She's named him sycophant. She accuses him of demonstrating an overbearing manner, and tells him he doesn't understand. She insists, he's just wrong. At first there was comic value to it, her challenging his authority, and his bemoaning ordeal. By now though, the novelty wears thin.' Zechariah sighed, but then could not help but recall, 'There was a time you know, when I actually saw the good in her. Now though, in light of her current behaviour, I have to ask myself, whatever did I see there? Time passing can make an enormous difference can't it?' Knowing glances were passed between Francis and Bernard. Zechariah shifted his feet and he raised himself taller, the better to glower down at Bernard, for no reason at all.

With conditions deteriorating by the day, and upon every front, the cold, dispassionate side of the leader's nature was difficult to avoid. Extreme righteousness was demonstrated and a penchant for awful sarcasm indulged. Salvos of sarcasm were for most part delivered at the expense of the Keeper of Rope; his caustic excuse for wit was always evident during meetings. Francis knew that she would not like being Bernard. If the leader saw fit to deliver *her* the type of treatment, Bernard received, then she thought she would not be so capable as the keeper, of quiet enduring. Zechariah the Great was leader, and she, just as all others of the territory, was an obedient servant to his will. Offering criticism or advice would not be keeping to her place in the order of things, and so she did as ordered without voicing complaint.

They stood together by the overgrown tangle of a thorn-bearing bush, adjacent to the Tall Ones' barn. They were here to assess the situation involving penance, but as the leader had observed earlier, not much of that put out was worth taking. They were well enough concealed, but the leader talked much and spoke as if not caring if their presence was known.

Zechariah exclaimed, 'By Great Grandfather's beard! Bernard! I do declare—here she comes!' The Tall One's doe was not often seen at such close quarters, and seeing her push her way past the dwelling's protective attachment—that named door—carrying with her a large container of offerings, represented something of novelty. After she exited the structure the attachment slammed shut behind her, and of its own will. Ever fascinated by such detail, Bernard questioned, 'How *do you* imagine they've taught the door to behave as if it has a mind of its own?' Receiving no response to his querying, but not wanting to drop the matter, he went further, 'It moves back into position *every time* without them so much as touching it!'

'We know, Keeper!' Zechariah exclaimed. 'We have eyes in our heads.' He said, '*I* have eyes in my head. Do you, Francis?' Then, before she might answer, he declared, 'Yes, you do. When I peer hard enough, I see them. They're right there!' His insistent studying of her features was carried out at close range and she was made uneasy. Deciding him at best strange, and to avoid engaging his stare, she glanced away.

Bernard was not subdued, and ignoring the leader's most recent observation, he went on to enquire, 'What you said, Leader, back there a bit, has me puzzled.' Bernard stalled.

After a short moment, an impatient Zechariah asked, 'Well, what is it then?'

'Does Great Grandfather have, as you say, a beard?' The slightest note of timidity underlay his words.

By now the Tall One went about suspending offerings high on the line before her; she made a not unpleasant, contented humming sound in going about the business at hand. After watching her for another moment, Zechariah turned back to the keeper, 'It behoves me to warn you, Bernard, stay wise as you are, and best keep to simple things. It does not become an individual, as you, displaying interest in deep things.' He enquired of Francis, 'He's not the type is he, Francis, to question every small thing? To concern himself with matters that might—dread the thought—lead to philosophical debate.' And then, 'For deeks' sake, Keeper! How would I know whether the deity sports a beard!'

'But you said...'

The look he received was enough to silence Bernard.

Disdaining further involvement with the keeper and his foolish questioning, and returning to observe the Tall One, Zechariah said, 'Francis, if we are discovered and there's even the slightest sign of embarrassing, difficult behaviour from her, you will strike her with full force of Hargolin. Is that understood?'

'Strike her? A Tall One?'

'Yes,' he said. 'If I had at my disposal an army of Francis Darklings, then our kind would not at all scrape for penance. They—Tall Ones and their churners, both—would be subdued. They would be set to toil in an organized manner in the efficient raising of wholesome produce.' He said, 'In going about the territory we would no longer bow. We would no more bend the knee! In considering them, that has been my feeling of late. It was never my intention that folk be reduced to gobbling greens. I assure you, it's nothing I enjoy seeing.' After sighing long, he said, 'But needs must.'

Finished with her task, the Tall One turned to go back to her home. Zechariah said, 'Here—both of you—take a carrot or two for later on, because these are the last we'll see for a while.' Passing them out, he admonished, 'And, Bernard, this time, don't show them off. You must conceal them in your deepest dark pocket for later. There are times when I swear it's your aim in life to see me deposed as Leader! I'm joking, Bernard! If it were at all possible, you should be me, because seeing your expression, just breaks me up!'

By now the Tall One doe had returned to the dwelling. She had, after all, left the line fully laden, and that was most gratifying. In instructing them, Zechariah allowed, 'On this occasion you may take two offerings each, rather than the one. I'm surprised that she's offered so much.' Facing the limp-hanging abundance, he was generous in admitting, 'Even they, must get by in hard times, I suppose.' He determined, 'For our part, we shan't allow greed to overtake us. We must not tarry. Let's set to task before it dries. If we take it now, then who knows, but it may be possible to wring a few precious drops of moisture from it once we have it back at the warren.' Tall Ones always saw to washing as much of their vile scent from offerings as possible, and until now, taking dry items was preferred, they were less weighty and easier to carry.

Francis never sought favour, but now before moving off as ordered, she enquired, 'Leader? May I take the large indigo offering at the end of the line and have it for my own use?' She explained, 'I would make apparel suitable for Hargolin. The colour will be quite startling when my red sash is set against it.' The enquiry met doubting expression, and so Francis encouraged, 'It will provide wonderful attire for the upcoming event, and wearing it I will present a most impressive sight. As I demonstrate Hargolin—even against the backdrop of wasteland—those attending will know better times must return during the time of your leadership.'

'You flatter me Francis.'

'You are ever my leader.'

He told her, 'Taking into account your uncomplaining way, go right ahead. You may have it Francis! In the grand scheme it's naught but a trifle and you might deserve it.' Then, eyes twinkling, he could not help but involve contradiction. 'But Francis, you will owe me.' With largesse granted, Francis was pleased, but now she must disallow any notion whereby he might consider her beholden. The right to a piece of fine cloth must not be confused with any matter of duty. She would not own such obligation to anyone, not even to Zechariah the Great.

Turning back from the way Bernard had taken, and facing Zechariah, she offered, 'When the cloth is mine, I will attend to silencing the gal crying in yon' field. Her crying does not the least concern me, but by way of a fair exchange, I will trance her to good sense. I shall quiet her for you.'

'Francis, it's Bernard she troubles, not me.' Francis might, she thought, trance the leader to sensible agreement, but she would not misuse the technique of Hargolin. Instead, she chose a different tack. Never before had she spoken to him as next she did, but such a fine length of indigo material waited. It was the perfect colour, and the opportunity to possess such might never arise again. Steeling will against impatience, she offered, 'Accept my offer of fair exchange, now or leave it, Great Zechariah.' She shrugged, 'If, at a later time, I'm ordered to task, I shall refuse to employ Hargolin against such frail and distraught gal.' She said then, 'Nancy Noy-Breen has good cause to wail and berate and there are those of us who know it.' The offer was repeated, 'I will speak with her—perhaps on behalf of the keeper—whose weak whining way with her is so ineffective.'

Zechariah was taken aback by her addressing him so, but then he was amused and won over. Her derogatory description of Bernard's way helped her cause. Her contempt for such defects was cause for pleasure; pleasure gained in recognizing the opinion was shared. He was, after all, delighted with Francis, but was careful lest it show. Assuming a serious demeanour, he told her, 'Off with you then, Francis. Be on your way. Take your cloth.' And, as afterthought, 'Yes, it's a fair enough arrangement. Have a word or two in your own way with yon' howler.'

She was, he thought, the strangest of any of those under his command. Even discounting the trancing voice and the other astonishing skills at her disposal, she was always loyal and when it came to carrying out orders she was the most efficient of them all. He would have to trust she stayed loyal, because having gotten away with speaking to him as she had, what course might she pursue in wanting her way in future? One thing was certain, none would control her, for when confronting physical challenge, Francis Darkling was never the loser, and all knew it. Watching her now as she set to bundling up the length of damp, dark fabric, and seeing next, the quick way she vanished with it, going off into the adjacent field at a speed he could not credit, something else was clear to him—he too, should look his best. Francis would be back there at the warren by this time; her outshining him, would never do.

Fetching and carrying were not tasks befitting a leader's role, but with no one else about, he would attend to gathering. Hanging yonder, and moving in fiery hot, shimmering air, on the penance line, was a pair of trousers with long shoulder straps sporting bright gold-gleaming buckles. They were overalls, he thought. Then too, farther along the line was a very attractive red jacket, resplendent with a Tall One scratching. Across the back of it, scrawled in an appealing deep blue, was another of their indecipherable messages: *My Grandma loves me!* Tall Ones sometimes saw fit to convey messages—short missives graved by mysterious means upon items of penance—which, who knew, might one day be understood, but for now he would focus upon gathering the said articles.

This was a task best not rushed. In collecting penance from lines, certain requirements were met, requirements which suited not just, Folk of Fur, but Tall Ones as well. Adherence to time honoured ritual ensured that all proceeded smoothly.

For their part, Folk of Fur were not brazen. The fact of them having the upper paw, as it were, did not mean that discretion played no part. They did not flaunt their presence at lines or at planting places, but neither were they too furtive in their comings and goings; a balanced approach to dealings between parties was maintained. As recipients of penance, folk were fair-minded about the business of gathering, whilst any semblance of actual respect for those of the other side represented a ludicrous notion. So long as penance was forthcoming, Tall Ones were not expected, in any regard, to bow or scrape. Of late though, dire conditions must be taken into account. Tall Ones were neither judged nor blamed for the poor condition of the planting place. They were not responsible for the vicissitude of weather. Nevertheless, Folk of Fur were owed, and all knew it. Wisdom was not gained by too much questioning of long-standing tradition.

As the Leader of Folk, Zechariah trusted that his opposite number, the Tall One buck, would see to adequate organizing of his affairs before things too far deteriorated. Folk meeting gazuzzlement in such large number could soon be serious enough to mean his fall from position of authority. Receiving judgmental looks from resentful unfortunates, from relatives of the deceased, was become a commonplace occurrence. When out and about, he was forced to assuming an exaggerated expression and demeanour of one preoccupied with finding solutions to problems beyond solving by any but him. Obeisance of the few, including the fearsome, Francis Darkling, was all that stood between leadership and disgrace.

Flibberty hopping to stand beneath the pair of blue overalls, Zechariah noted the Tall One's shadowy form silhouetted behind the clear covering material of one of the structure's large angular eyes. He concealed himself behind the closer of the two tall poles, which held the line aloft. She'd not looked up from whatever it was she was busy with and so had not glimpsed him.

Muttering beneath his breath, he dared peep around the pole's smooth circumference. 'There she is,' he told himself, and after several moments, 'and now there she goes.' The robust doe had moved from view. Leaving the place of concealment, Zechariah went to grasp the legs of the garment. He tugged with both paws, and in a trice they were his! With overalls slung across a shoulder he went farther down the line, and next paused below the bright red jacket. Seen close up it was indeed a marvellous item. He was an expert when it came to determining size, and so knew it was perfect for him. It was not so willing to leave the line as were his new overalls, but then … it too was his!

Relieved of those garments the line rose in languid, ponderous fashion, taking the remaining penance back to higher altitude.

Adhering with best practice, now he must not tarry, but make the dash to the field. But then his attention was captured by a true rarity—a cap! They were a most uncommon offering, and he would have it! But, how best reach it? Small items did not hang low and so were difficult to grasp. He had no stick with him with which to encourage the article down.

He wished for a ladder. They were used in the collection of delicacies, but then gathering of fruit was carried out at night. Even thinking of employing one in broad daylight was tantamount to transgression.

Preoccupied with peering up at the cap, he was unaware of her sneaking approach. The enraged Tall One hollered, 'At last I have you, *thief!*'

With brow creased and eyes ablaze, Zechariah stood his ground. He returned her glowering gaze.

She exclaimed, 'It's gone *too far!* We believe in live and let live, but you vermin know no bounds!'

Wielding the biggest whisk in creation—a true-monstrous thing—she came at him! Was she ranting mad? She had exited the place by way of its front opening and then made her way to the back of the place to catch him at the line! In coming by roundabout route, she'd given no tell-tale sound.

He helter hopped, avoiding the first broad swipes of the broom! The enemy initiated actual face-to-face engagement! Brazen disregard for the rules was not understood, but he was undaunted! He would not make for cover of the field, but would soon show her he was made of tough stuff! Initiating such outrageous attack had deleterious effect and she now stood panting. In lock step with all others of late, the morning was hot, and small rivulets of moisture trickled down her forehead, cheek and fleshy neck. She was an unattractive, florid-faced opponent and not by any means was she in prime physical condition.

Clutching at offerings, the fine jacket and overalls, he did not shift the focus of his attention, but studied her for what seemed interminable moments. In demanding return of penance, the creature was deranged. Drought affected them all, and hardship extracted too heavy a toll. She still panted, but less so. She was shifty-eyed. She would soon make her move. After feigning indifference, she lunged! A fine piece of luck resulted, because in raising her giant whisk high, before bringing it down in his direction, the cap he could not reach was knocked from the line to drop at his feet. He snatched it up!

He did not then dash to escape, but bowing from the waist, addressed her, 'Your mad rule-breaking is regrettable.' After pausing and smiling in condescension, he said, 'When drought leaves the territory and you come to your senses, folk will accept extra offering by way of recompense for your unfortunate behaviour.'

He might have said more, but—was grabbed from behind! Something covered him! All turned to darkness and he heard himself screaming, '*Deeeeks!*'

The doe cried, 'Good man, William—caught at last!' Zechariah, turned topsy-turvy, found his world on its head.

Complimented by the doe, the buck was pleased with himself, announcing, 'This is the ring-leader. We'll use him to lure the rest.' From inside the imprisoning sack, Zechariah was all but overcome by the Tall One's odour.

'If I had my way,' said the doe, 'he'd be for the chop!'

'We won't do that,' said the buck. 'I'll throw a trap together and we'll see how we go.' He said, 'Mazengarb, from down at the end of the valley, bagged a crew of them last month. They took them to the sanctuary at Milltown. It was a treat for his kids, seeing so many of them close up in captivity. They look happier, he reckoned, than they do in the wild. They're treated humanely, and I'd rather not plough another warren. After the last time my feelings just about had the better of me.'

'Mm, well… ' She was uncertain, but then agreed, 'I suppose young Will' can tend it for awhile.' As William Crenshaw Senior hefted the sack aloft and made off in the direction of the barn, she called after him, 'There's something about them… I see that, Bill, but I can't abide the stealing!'

William Crenshaw called back, 'Yep—got it!' Half turning as he went, he said, 'With the drought and all—now they're getting into the main crop. They're gluttons for punishment, because it doesn't agree with them.'

If truth were told, he'd never minded them. Neither he nor Babs objected too much to the loss of a few vegetables, not as did some of the neighbours. Most of their food was store bought in any case, but he sympathized with Babs. She had good cause for detesting them. Loss of clothing, and in particular, young Will Junior's things, was more than a minor issue of contention. And, whenever their bed sheets went missing from the backyard, it was cause for outrage. Such behaviour made people know they were targets for genuine attack; it was something happening these days with increased regularity. Laundry was just not safe. Deeky-Hoppers were named for the sound they made when cornered or caught, and for their method of locomotion; they could walk but preferred hopping. Their pilfering had increased but then, there was the modifying fact of the drought taking its toll on their number, which, of course, was reason for their getting into the broad-acre crops. He'd seen them of late, over there, gormandizing even in broad daylight. Babs was right; they were out of hand.

She returned to the house and Will Crenshaw continued on his way to the barn. There at the back of the building near the workbench, was a large ball of twine hung on a nail, and he would secure the top of the sack with a length from it. Giving the bulging sack a fond slap with the flat of his free hand, he told its contents, 'Never mind, old fellow. No need for deeky-fuss. We'll have you right as rain, accommodated in no time at all.' The bulge was stilled. The hopper was playing dead. Hearing himself talking to it he decided he was glad that Babs did not hear him.

He disapproved of their ways, sure. They persisted in taking all kinds of stuff, true. As a youngster he'd thought the idea of keeping a deeky as a pet a fine idea, but back then detestation of filthy hoppers was universal. His father had been incensed by the suggestion. Will Crenshaw senior knew deep down that current thinking was enlightened; deeky-hoppers should have been provided sanctuary from the start. It was generous of the wife, allowing Will Junior might enjoy tending to the creature's requirements, when the very idea of them gave her the heebie-jeebies.

DEEKY BOY

The gal, Nancy Noy-Breen, was hysterical when shouting for help on behalf of her friend, Emily Longpod. The unfortunate Longpod was past saving. The serpent had finished its fiendish work long before help arrived. Nancy Noy-Breen's dreadful crying, "Help! Oh, help! Please, someone!" On that occasion, or her more recent noisome carrying-on over greens, was as nothing compared with the mighty hubbub produced by the Keeper of Rope when he came heltering back from the field to New Warren Central.

He'd waited in the field adjacent to the Tall Ones' home for the leader to meet up with him, and a short time ago, Francis Darkling had gone right by him without pausing in passing.

She'd acknowledged his presence though, by calling, 'I see you there, Bernard. That was all. He'd wondered, what did she mean by it: "I see you there, Bernard?" Of course she had! It was never his intention to hide from her. He was concealed from the view of Tall Ones; that was all. Perhaps her confusing statement was an example of the type of humour the leader took pleasure in. If that was it, then he was disappointed in her and saddened, because he admired her for her fine qualities. Unable to come up with any quick verbal response, he had nodded to her as she went by. She carried a large bundle, and he'd have liked assisting her in getting it back to the warren, but as efficient as she was, his help was not required.

Peering back now at the Tall Ones' dwelling, Bernard was both curious and afraid in noting that the leader approached the line. Zechariah was without company, and his daring to gather penance alone, represented uncharacteristic foolishness. In point of fact it was a rule of none other than Zechariah the Great, which decreed that none should ever go alone in Tall One territory, and the rule was a good one. There was safety in numbers. The Keeper of Rope watched as the leader moved to hide behind one of the line's trunk-like poles. Zechariah hopped out from concealment then, to make expert work of seizing a specific item from that offered as penance.

Bernard was afforded an excellent view of both front and rear of the Tall Ones' abode, and so peeking above the tops of plants, he saw the determined looking doe leave the structure by its front entryway to then move around the side of the place. She made for the backyard, and then, to his great dismay, against every sane expectation, the situation further deteriorated, because the Tall One buck exited the dwelling to follow in the footsteps of his mate. The doe carried with her an enormous whisk, and noting its size, Bernard knew her intention was every bit serious. The buck went unarmed, which was small mercy. Confronted at close quarters by one of them would be difficult enough; the leader was in for a time of it. Watching from his place amongst greens, the keeper insisted that he desired nothing more than to cover the intervening distance in heltering fashion, and to join with the leader in confronting the enemy. He could not yet, however, bring himself to do so. The leader was fleet of foot and cunning enough to extricate himself from the predicament. He could relinquish those offerings he held and then dash back to the field.

Folk were fast. They were adept in avoiding danger. Tall Ones were clumsy and slow and presented less threat than a foe such as Brother Fox. With churners as their allies they were feared, but in the present situation a satisfactory outcome seemed assured. All of that presented, held potential for a most uncommon, even, daresay, enjoyable spectacle.

But then, if questioned later, Bernard realized that he would be at singular loss to explain his not rushing forward. Anything he came up with would be viewed by all and sundry as pitiable, loathsome excuse for cowardice. And so, after rethinking his position, he must hasten his return to the warren and call for assistance. But still he remained transfixed, an immovable witness to the unbelievable sight of the leader's capture! Bernard dropped the articles of penance at his feet, and, he was off, making the mad dash for all he was worth, shouting the terrible news at the top of his lungs! He did not cease shouting, until Francis Darkling confronted him.

Screaming, terrible screaming flooded the territory all about. Occupied in remonstrating with Nancy Noy-Breen for indulging in noisome behaviour, Francis next contended with Bernard's committing an identical offence. In attempting to deal with the gal, Francis acted not only in accord with her arrangement with the leader, but in Bernard's interest as well, and so his carrying on now was anything but fair.

Previous to Bernard's rending cries, Nancy Noy-Breen had quieted, and Francis was still not recovered from an unsettling, ensuing quandary. Hearing Bernard, she was not so much annoyed by the raucous sound of him, as by his interrupting her conversation with the gal. So far as conveying anything of real information went, Bernard's carrying on was ineffective. Not one word of it could be understood.

Francis commented, 'Tiresome individual. He's never still,' and smiles were exchanged. Returning to the topic of their conversation, she enquired, 'This looking into you, as you call it—it's not something learned, but an ability you've always possessed?'

'That's right.' Nancy explained. 'It's nothing acquired. It's me, or a *part* of me.'

Earlier, Francis Darkling had made a swift, confident approach, and coming close to Nancy, had wasted no time on preamble. She had ordered, 'You will fall down gal. Fall down and stay quiet.'

It was a trancing voice, a trick of Hargolin, Francis Darkling's terrible power. And so, before Francis reached her, Nancy had thought to step aside. She was glad for having the presence of mind to think of doing so.

Francis, affecting an expert, subtle altering of voice, had issued the second of her commands, 'You will be still and silent!'

Nancy, smiling in easy-going manner, told her, 'No, Francis, I will not. I'm not the least quiet and have good reason for not agreeing with your suggestion.' She added, 'Which of course is why you are here.' If she, more or less a nobody, was apprised of the effect greens would have on the populace, then doubtless Zechariah and those most loyal to him must, at the very least, suspect dire consequences to come. Still, they allowed folk to eat the crop; it was unconscionable.

The trancing voice had not worked its magic the first or second time, but Francis was unperturbed. Employed against even a most stubborn opponent, it would have its way. She had pushed harder in attempting to take the gal's will. She had stared into Nancy's eyes, insisting, 'You are struck dumb!'

She heard, 'No, Francis. It's not me who's struck dumb but you.' Nancy had spoken the truth, for even with the power of Hargolin at her disposal, Francis Darkling was reduced to speechlessness!

Beset by anxiety, she had again tried to speak. Still, her trancing voice betrayed her! A mysterious, unknown skill was brought to bear, and she was subdued! A smiling Nancy Noy-Breen had not at all encouraged her dignity, but an explanation was offered, and in light of her inability to make even the slightest comment, Francis had little choice, other than listen.

Nancy Noy-Breen had said, 'It's Hargolin, Francis. No skill of war owned by *me* has caught you out. You are undermined by your own words. They alone have you helpless to speak. Your skilful use of a trancing voice, magnified many times over, was reflected back on you. In looking into me, you were confronted by nothing but the power of your own skill. You'll soon be back as you were, you'll be perfectly fine.' Francis Darkling had employed Hargolin against her, and mindful of the gal's temerity, Nancy could not refrain from adding, 'You will go back soon enough to being plain, *ordinary* old you.' Nancy had sighed. Her time spent warning against greens and then having to explain seeing into her was tiresome. Seeing Francis forced to silence, she'd said, 'I should take this opportunity, Francis, to thank you.' Francis dealt well with the inability to speak. She had not behaved as others might, as if angered or frustrated by her dilemma. Her expression was both curious and patient. That her voice would soon return to her, Francis had trusted, and Nancy was gratified in knowing it was so. Every so often, as Nancy spoke, Francis had raised her brow. She had smiled and gestured with her paws as a way of communicating.

Nancy said, 'After the cruel gazuzzlement of my friend, Emily, I did not thank you, Francis, for dispatching, Brother Serpent.' Francis nodded in response, accepting thanks for a task attended.

Arriving at the burrows of Emily Longpod, Francis had behaved as if the problem of a serpent warranted little thought. She had pushed her way past others, and without fuss entered the tunnel. The monster was seized by its tail and hauled out into the light. In an awesome display of skill, Francis had swung the writhing serpent in a wide circle, around and around overhead. Cries of panic and squeals of fear came from others as they hurried to move aside, providing a wide passage for Francis and her burden. She had moved away from Emily's home taking Brother Serpent with her, to a place where a great fallen log lay upon the ground. She had drawn a sharp breath; as in Hargolin, and then—brought Brother Serpent down from on high! He was brought down with such force that his clean-gleaming head was shattered to bloody pulp against the log's dull-ring-ing surface. His spine was broken in many places and despite meeting gazuzzlement the long, sinuous body had writhed in dust and dry grass, as if still living. For too long the body moved, before accepting a just end. Nancy had said, 'You deserve more, Francis, than mere thanks for your action that day. As I warn others who come here to the field, I warn you now—and from my heart—despite suspecting that you're already apprised of the truth. Don't trust those greens! If I am wrong and you do not know why I give warning, here is an explanation. Those, who think to sustain themselves by eating greens, will produce dreadful offspring. In crying warning I have taken care not to terrify young ones hereabout, but I will tell you now, that monstrous, changed new-born will come to those who feed on greens. Grotesque, oversized young ones of unnatu-ral gaudy stripe, of talon-like claw and fang!' With reflected power of Hargolin beginning to lose effect, Francis had again attempted to speak, and Nancy hastened, saying, 'Creatures with not four, but six legs and paws!' Judging by her expression, Nancy had realized that Francis might not after all be informed of consequence of consuming greens. She had been too interested in what she heard. As Nancy had finished describing dire result, Francis had discovered her voice returned.

She had demanded, 'What did you *do* to me? *How* did you do it?' She would have answers.

Knowing her truest purpose was defeated, Nancy had reiterated, 'I did nothing, Francis. As I've explained, *you* silenced yourself. I stood aside within myself. Any force exerted was yours and not mine.' She had sighed, then said, 'For now I will leave the field but I shall return tomor-row. You can depend on it. There is no wrong in my giving warning. In fact, it's sounding Tump!'

She had turned to go, but Francis was never dissuaded from an objec-tive. She had insisted, 'No! Don't leave! I *must* learn more of your mystery power! When willing you to quiet and looking to your eyes, I saw myself marching—marching in strange company over yon' hill! The vision was as clear as day! What does it mean?'

Nancy had not seen any of that envisioned by Francis. Wishing to avoid falling victim to Hargolin, she had stood aside, and so had no inkling of anything Francis Darkling had seen. She had said, 'I did not see you marching anywhere, Francis, and I assure you that I do not like you thinking of me as powerful, because mine is not power as you or anyone else might learn to own. In so saying, I do not deceive. Really, Francis, heed Tump! Eat bark from trees if you must, but don't touch those greens!' With that said, she had again made to leave.

It was then that an almighty, excruciating kazooning was heard as the Keeper of Rope emerged from that more distant part of the field where the crop, not yet disturbed by folk, grew tall. Dashing from one group of feeders to the next, throughout that part of the field lying close to the creek, and jabbering in demented fashion, Bernard pleaded, 'Oh, for deeks' sake stop stuffing yourselves and hear me!' He was Keeper of Rope and they had little choice other than hear him. News of Zechariah the Great's capture spread fast. Francis Darkling watched Nancy go. Wanting to go after the gal, she was torn for reason that when struck dumb she'd seen herself undertaking a long march—a march begun by climbing the high hill she now looked to. She had envisioned herself going in the strangest company—in company of folk of a type matching those described by Nancy Noy-Breen. It was all most strange, but now she must contend with Bernard.

***

At the barn, the Tall One wound a length of strong twine about the coarse material forming the mouth of the sack. He'd first risked a curious peek, to ascertain the creature's condition. It lay there at the bottom of the sack and was quiet enough and so all was fine. Glancing down at it, he'd imagined it might smile back at him. In the gloomy light of the barn it was difficult to tell, but it no longer played dead, and that, William Crenshaw took as a good sign. Looking up at him it had returned his gaze and behind its bright-eyed look there seemed something of decided intelligence. Fancying that he might address the creature and receive something sensible in return, Crenshaw hesitated, changed his mind, and secured the sack. Were it half as smart as it looked, the hopper would never accept confinement. It must not, by foolish action of his, gain the opportunity to escape. After double-checking that it was tied tightly enough, he hefted the sack atop the workbench at the rear of the barn.

He addressed the bundle, instructing the contents, 'There you are now, Deeky Boy. Don't wriggle about. We wouldn't want you falling from there, would we? And don't be afraid when you hear the sound of the tractor, because there's no harm to it.'

Searching through his pockets for the tractor's ignition key, he was mindful that despite them always being carried on his person, his keys seemed ever difficult to find. Locating them in a shirt pocket after short searching, he was pleased.

He would use the backhoe to make an encircling trench at the location decided upon for the new hutch.

He thought of young Will's excitement. Later, when he came in from school, he would learn they were embarked upon something of adventure. They were now in the business—father and son together—of deeky-hopper hunting. He was as thrilled at the prospect of it as he knew the boy would be.

Back in Grandfather's day before the valley was first settled, deeky-hoppers were thought of as dangerous creatures. They had caused the colony members trying times, but the same was not true now, generations later, for hoppers were not anything as they were. Their number had increased but in comparison with those presenting problems for the first colonists, they were now much diminished in physical size, strength and ferocity. The reason for their degeneration was not known and so research was long overdue, but whatever discovery was made, hoppers now posed nothing of a threat as they had.

On a shelf in the barn was a rough collection of old cans which should contain enough left over, useable paint. Crenshaw searched amongst them for a missing brush, which despite due care taken on a previous occasions, was misplaced. They might have enough paint left in those cans with which to prettify the new enclosure. Apart from dressing it up, paint would, of course, protect the timber against the elements. They might even go so far as to give the creature a name and it could be painted over the doorway. That small enjoyable task should go to Will.

Harvest time at the Crenshaw's property was not far off. At the north-ernmost end of the valley several other landholders were already bring-ing in what promised to be a good harvest. Much good could be said for the resistant seed. That was made clear over enough seasons of planting, but this latest crop, in promising high yield even despite poor conditions prevailing, was gratifying to those investing trust in it.

He decided the best place for the enclosure was between the house and the orchard, just a short distance from his half-hearted attempt at making something of a vegetable patch. The location was open, open enough for goings on to be observed from the barn, where he and the boy would spend time hiding out, waiting until the trap was sprung. They must not trouble Babs by using her kitchen or laundry as a hiding place. The trap would be sprung, of that there was no doubt. The question was, just how many hoppers would they take captive? Deeky-hoppers lived in small communities, and Crenshaw was certain that the fellow captured this morning was leader of the one situated at the far side of the creek. He'd caught glimpses of them of late, from afar. Because of heat and die-back of indigenous grasses staple to their diet, they, lacking natural cover and despite being furtive by nature, were more easily seen than in better times.

Earlier on, when speaking with Babs, he'd not thought to mention the bounty involved. Bounty had been offered for the creatures, and that could provide incentive in going to the trouble of capturing them. The new sanctuary was adjacent to the facility known as the Experimental Station, where study was carried out in many areas of research. The creatures would undergo rigorous scientific testing for the first time. Hoppers were required in sufficient number to satisfy procedure, and so, Crenshaw thought, if enough were taken, then the bounty received in payment for those delivered in good, unharmed condition, might, over time, amount to a worthwhile supplementary income. Without being too ambitious, regarding their project, he guessed that even if only a small number were caught, any payment would serve as a lesson for the boy. They could think of it as additional to his allowance, already received for small chores carried out.

BERNARD

The enemy was most cunning. In attending to detail they were not the least remiss or lacking. It was, Zechariah thought, as if their very lives depended upon conscientious behaviour and he could not help but admit grudging admiration for them. Granting unstinting attention to detail was as it happened, his way also, and this was very true when close examination of the enclosure's door and latch was carried out. Making close study of those things was an obsessively attended pastime. The latch was replete with a strange, intricate locking device. As he studied it he was reminded that there was not much else he might do. Boredom ever loomed.

Within the first few days of his captivity he had decided to view his accommodations, which Tall Ones referred to as the hutch and the run, as his own territory. In seeking to adapt to the situation every effort must be applied. If he could not do so, he might go mad. The situation was grim but rejecting all about him would amount to an intentional embarking upon inner, downhill spiralling.

There was one acceptable aspect to the situation and that was the food provided. It was of quality second to none. It was fresh, health giving produce, and to avoid gluttony, Zechariah cautioned himself, because truth was he'd already begun putting on weight. Small tell-tale signs showed, such as a slight thickening of the midriff and a plumpness of cheek and jowl, changes, which over recent days he was honest in noting. None of it was too serious as yet but must be admitted as first proof of overindulgence. But then he told himself, in going to the extreme in the consumption of several of his favourite things, such as crisp green cabbage leaves, finest carrots, broccoli and beets, small harm was done, because in all fairness, he was incarcerated, wasn't he? What else, other than indulge his appetite, could he occupy himself with? Besides, he could not countenance the thought of allowing good food to rot on the enclosure floor. Were it at all possible to do so he would share with others, but the situation dictated that he behave contrary to the impulse of a generous nature. Far from enticing anyone to come close, his every sincere effort was made in keeping folk away. Any idea of slipping leftovers to them was out of the question. Night after night friends came to stand in the field to offer reassurance and give comfort. They concealed themselves in the crop beyond the field's perimeter. By catching scents of individuals, their various locations were ascertained. Something of a game had developed, whereby he provided folk warning by making small gestures of sign language. None of it was simple, because in communicating by way of signals he must avoid the Tall Ones catching him out. Each and every night they concealed their presence across the yard in the barn, which they referred to as the hide. From there they spied upon both field and enclosure. They believed their concealment was unknown. Just who did they think they were? Folk of Fur were not thick!

Words used by his captors were at first understood as not much other than gibberish but in a very short time he'd fathomed the meaning of more than several of them. By now he knew enough so that they'd best take care when opening mouths. He would comprehend the gist of whatever might be said. But for his part, after a loud utterance of "Deeks", on the occasion of his capture, he'd voiced not one word, not so much as a single syllable of the language of folk. Apart from the expletive, they'd learned nothing from him, nothing of folk possessing a true language. With all their cunning cleverness, Tall Ones remained unaware of the truth. One thing distressed him beyond all else and that was the fact they had named him "Deeky Boy". It was outrageous, as he'd never favoured use of the expletive, although it was true, there were those occasions when it had slipped out. But now, despicable Tall Ones *named* him it! At each and every meeting the expletive was employed in addressing him! Forced to wear such an appellation, the indignity imposed was excruciating and burdensome, however he must on no account allow true feeling to show. To allow such a reaction would fulfil every cruel expectation. They'd gone so far as to make a descriptive scratching on the outside of the opening of the place, which from inside the enclosure was not at all visible. He could not see it and so they'd ensured his awareness of their intention. In doing so, the small one, son to the great buck, had not the least troubled disguising his pleasure, but was in fact gleeful.

The boy had employed a diminutive whisk and after dipping it into a container of bright coloured liquid, had made scratched marks above the door. When finished with the task, the toothsome, grinning child, informed, 'There now—there you go, Deeky Boy! That looks awesome!' And so, "Deeky Boy" was emblazoned now in brightest scarlet—there for all to see.

Zechariah was grateful Folk of Fur did not comprehend the meaning of Tall One scratchings. If they did, then the last remaining shred of personal credibility would be lost. At their first meeting the boy had introduced himself as, Will—short for William. It was not a name Zechariah was acquainted with, but as far as names went he'd decided it as not too awful sounding. Indeed, the boy, so far as *his* name was concerned, had no cause for complaint. Why then—if they believed naming a captive essential—had they not provided *him*, a decent one? Their objective in heaping derision was not at all clear to Zechariah, but as a helpless prisoner, taking umbrage was pointless; he'd no choice at all in the matter and so must put up with it. But, if freedom were ever regained, then vengeance would be his. With no real idea yet as to the precise form vengeance might take, consolation was gained from the knowledge that they were in a significant sense, *his* dupes. If fate allowed future events to turn in favour of Folk of Fur and they were taken prisoner by him, he would never dream of going so far as feeding them! Even given time of plenty, when provisioning them would amount to simplicity itself, they should expect nothing! He'd see them starve, which so far as vengeance went, would do for a start. Sustaining an enemy could not be credited as a sane policy. As strategies went, it was ludicrous. He'd asked himself many, many times, why it was that they did not in the first instance, see fit dispensing penance of such fine quality as that now freely provided? Had they done so, then the question of redress would not have arisen and his considering taking vengeful action would be unnecessary. Folk would have known them as good neighbours! Tall Ones, the strangest of all Great Grandfather's creatures, were, as he'd come to know them, perverse beyond reckoning.

They were spending another evening in the hide, and that was an important, impressive sounding name for a back corner of the barn. Naming the place, though, made watching for hoppers seem more fun than it was, and together in the hide, a strong sense of camaraderie prevailed. This evening's covert operation was underway and would reap reward, but then young Will reminded himself, they'd kept a lookout for five consecutive evenings now, peering through holes drilled in the wall of the barn to no good end. Nothing had happened. After all Father's planning and hard work, action and result were deserved. There was Deeky Boy's hutch and the enclosure, and as well, the trap. The trap was the deep, encircling trench, which was excavated around the circumference of the wire-walled enclosure. It was both wide and deep enough, Father reckoned, to prevent any hopper from escaping. In removing them from the trench they would have to be quick though, because deekies were proficient, expert diggers. They'd a long pole and net, which they planned to use for hauling the creatures out. The top of the trench was overlaid with an arrangement of wide-spaced lengths of timber, which in turn were covered by a layer of poly sheeting, supporting a thin layer of dry grass and dirt; deekies would never suspect it was there. Father dubbed the exercise *Operation: Barbara's Revenge;* in honour of Mother, who could not stand hoppers, which she always referred to as "...pesky-thieving-vermin!"

Will had as good as spent his share of the bounty they expected. He'd envisioned them driving to the Sanctuary—the back of the pickup loaded high with burlap sacks—sacks crammed full to overflowing. On the homeward journey their pockets would brim with credits. He planned on getting himself an air rifle and if he earned enough for it, a new wristwatch. He would buy an actual waterproof one this time, and not a "water-resistant", because "resistant" didn't mean much; a "resistant" could *not* be worn in the bath. Spending so long out here in the hide was fun, but by now it was, as Father said, beginning to wear a bit thin. After this long they'd expected to catch at least several deekies. He'd begun seeing hoppers as a lot smarter than he'd first thought them. Father was tiring of sitting here of an evening and for some time now made small, yet frequent, complaint. At first he'd complained about the thermos. The thermos of coffee supplied by Mother was not large enough and he hated bothering her to refill it each time it ran out, and then there was the seating arrangement. He said his behind was giving him merry hell. It was a torment sitting for so long on a rickety campstool, but the stools were the right height for peering out through the holes in the planks of the wall. So, rather than go to the trouble of making further holes, which would mean running the risk of the barn ending up looking like Swiss-cheese, they would put up with arrangements as they were. However, that being so, he, Will Crenshaw Senior, was afraid of developing something he called piles. He'd avoided going into too graphic detail, claiming that an individual unfortunate enough to develop piles, suffered a torturous time due to fact of their butt being out of whack. It was not the clearest explanation, but Will caught his father's drift. Crenshaw Senior had assumed a frightful expression and then shuddered in melodramatic fashion. Father was beginning to hate being out here.

But tonight was different. He knew it was different from those others when hearing Father ask, 'Will, pass me the net will you? We might have use for it.'

'What is it?'

'Shush now,' Will Senior advised, 'Keep your voice down. We don't want to give the game away.' After a moment he said, 'There's one of them out there, son, at the edge of the field. He's hiding behind the big strainer-post. Do you see him?'

In the dim light of dusk, Will was not able to see much, but he thought he caught a glimpse of something moving, just a quick glimpse before whatever it was, disappeared from view. He said, 'He forgot to tuck his tail in. I *think* I saw something...'

Will Senior said, 'Focus on that spot and we'll see what he does next.' He said, 'My boy, we may be in for success after all.' Without removing attention from the only hopper daring to come so close, he reached over to ruffle Will's hair. He said, 'Stay quiet. If he breaks cover and goes into the trap, he might not make much of a noise. By what I saw of him, he's not one of the big ones.'

Will Junior wasn't fazed. If they caught the smallest deeky in the world, it would be better than nothing at all. Speaking in a low whisper, he asked, 'What shall I do?'

He spoke so that his father was uncertain of his question. He said, 'Son, not *so* soft. We have to be able to hear each other.'

Will said, 'I just *meant*—you'll have the net won't you—what shall *I* do, after he falls into the trap?'

They'd been through it a hundred times, but Crenshaw said, 'Son, you'll have plenty to do after he's netted. You'll have the important job of opening the cage door so we can get him inside. I won't release him from the net until we're inside the enclosure. When you open the door you're going to have to make certain that the other one, Deeky Boy, doesn't escape. You're going to have to shoo him back so that he's away from the door.' He said, 'Of course, if he does happen to make a dash for it, Deeky Boy won't get far because he'll end up in the trap.' He stifled a chuckle, 'Don't be too excited. We'll just take it as it comes.'

Peering out, would soon be no good—by now it was almost too dark to see much of anything. Leaning towards Will, Crenshaw said, 'Tell me the combination again.'

The boy was conscientious, 'Fear not Dad. It's, *zero, zero, zero, zero!*'

Then, from the enclosure, a sound was heard.

'Quick!' Crenshaw exclaimed, 'It's the trap!' They both leaped to their feet and then rushed to the side door of the barn.

Running into darkness, Crenshaw carrying the long-handled net, called back to Will Junior, 'Use your flashlight Will! Turn it *on!*' Outpacing the boy, he saw disconcerting flickering coming from behind him, as the torchlight cut bright swathes about his legs, whilst his son, aiming the beam ahead of him as he ran, brought up the rear. The operation was going awry. In rushing from the barn, Crenshaw had neglected bringing his own flashlight. The thing was back there on the floor by his stool, but it was too late to worry about it now. After traversing between barn and enclosure, he tossed the net to the ground.

Hefting the long plank they used when crossing the trench, he called, 'Son! *Over here, boy!* Shine the light so I can see what I'm doing!' Then, with Will lending a hand, they soon had the plank in position. Crenshaw felt certain they'd caught something, and so, without first bothering to inspect for signs of anything having gone through the poly sheeting, he ordered young Will to cross the plank and unlock the enclosure door.

Grasping the net again, he told Will, 'Here! Give me the torch. Toss it back here to me!' But, Will Junior had progressed to just midpoint in making the crossing. Changing his mind, less the boy slip and fall, Crenshaw called, 'No, not yet—wait until you're all the way across!' Cursing the foolishness of leaving his flashlight behind, he decided to reconnoitre as best he could in the dark. He stood still for a moment, listening for any tell-tale sound. They played dead of course, and were good at it. From here there was no sign of a hole in the trap. The boy had reached the opposite side of the trench, and Crenshaw called, 'Throw me the torch, Will! Having caught it, he said, 'Good lad. Great throw. Thanks!'

Making his way around the outside of the trench, he was cautious not to over-step the edge. Going from the front and then around to the side, the side running adjacent with the field, he came to a place where the covering was pulled away from the edge of the pit. Something had fallen in. He bent down and pulled at the edge of the sheeting. Then, directing the torchlight downwards, curled up on the dirt floor was one of the smallest hoppers Crenshaw had ever seen. He thought, so what? It was just as Will said, "Small is fine. It's acceptable".

The creature made no attempt to move, but then it quivered. Seeing it exposed in the flashlight's beam, Crenshaw experienced a twinge of pity for it. But then, if the hopper got the idea into its head to move, it could cause no end of difficulty.

He'd not thought to divide the trench into compartments; it followed an uninterrupted route around the circumference of the wire-netting enclosure. The thing Crenshaw did *not* want now, was for the creature to go galloping the full circuit. A panicked deeky-hopper would lead them a merry chase.

Reaching down with the net he brought it in from behind the creature. He gave the long handle a decisive twist, ensnaring the hopper when netting folded about its diminutive form! And then the net was drawn from the pit to the surface. He would not succumb to temptation and examine the catch too soon.

Dreading the thought of stumbling, Crenshaw aimed the flashlight ahead of him and proceeded in making his way to where young Will waited at the gate to the enclosure. He must cross the long stretch of scaffolding-plank and get to the other side—traverse the "gang-plank", as, Will referred to it.

Conscious of progressing in a too studied fashion, placing one tentative foot after the other, Crenshaw asked, 'Will? Have you unlocked that gate yet?' He did not like sounding curt. He instructed, 'Take the flashlight from me. We don't want to lose him!'

'Can I take a look at him?'

Not disguising his impatience, Crenshaw exclaimed, 'For heavens sake! Just get the damn gate open!'

Hurt, but now in possession of the torch, Will Junior shifted the beam away from the net and aimed it toward the lock. Under the watchful eye of his father, his fingers seemed all thumbs, as he muttered aloud, 'Zero, zero, zero, zero.' The lock clicked open, and he pushed open the gate. Proceeding into the enclosure, he commanded, 'Shoo! Shoo!' Deeky Boy moved back to a far corner of the small yard. The creature stood tensing, but at the same time stared right back through bright light, studying him.

Entering the enclosure, Crenshaw leaned back; pushing against the gate, ensuring it was shut. Stooping, he put the net on the ground between himself and the boy. He said, 'Step back now, son. Give us a bit of space here.' Vigilance was crucial. 'Now, go behind me, Will. Stand over there and be sure that gate can't swing open.' Untangling the hopper from the net, he ordered, 'Shine the light here, so that I can see what I'm doing.'

In freeing the creature he could not help but note that it wore a grey shirt and jacket. He thought he recognized the shirt as belonging to his son, but did not comment. Hoppers roamed, thieving as they went. Giving the handle one final twist, the animal was freed, but then the piti-ful thing would not budge, but stayed curled up on the ground at his feet. He poked at the furry form, telling it, 'Go on buddy. Go join your friend.'

All the while, Deeky Boy stood there in silence with his back pressed up against the enclosure's wire-net wall. Crenshaw gave the latest catch another gentle prod, this time with a boot, but still it did not move. He wondered if it was injured when falling into the trench.

'He said, 'Take care as we leave, Will. We don't want them making a dash when we open the gate.' The hole in the trap could wait until the morning. In his declaring, 'We can be pleased with ourselves. We've done ourselves proud,' every word was meant. 'That's it now son.' It was way past young Will's bedtime. He said, 'Get yourself back over the pit and take care as you cross that plank.'

Then, 'Oh, damn. Sorry, old fella. I forgot! Get back over here, because it's your job to lock up.'

Whilst it was true that deeky-hoppers were bright creatures, he doubted they'd figure operating a sliding bolt. A combination lock would

definitely be beyond them. The idea of using a lock was a way of proving to young Will the seriousness of the business. The lock was old and
was found in a long disused toolbox that he'd located in a back corner
of the barn. Coming upon it, he'd thought the box contained nothing
more than junk, but then he'd happened to find the lock at the bottom,
amongst an array of things long forgotten. Brushing away dust and webs,
he examined it. It had been his grandfather's and inscribed on its surface
was: *Millthorpe Corp: Mission: Blue House.* Seeing those words, strong
feeling rose in Crenshaw, and he had second thoughts as to the wisdom
of using what amounted to an heirloom for the purpose of locking away
hoppers. Then, thinking of the boy, he had reset the combination to the
simplest number: zero, zero, zero, zero. They would use the lock, regardless of its sentimental worth.

Leaving Will to lock up, he said, 'I'll meet you back at the barn.' Beginning
to make his way back through the yard, he called, 'Don't drop that torch!'

Will shone the light at the still prone deeky. It sure was small. It played
dead but there was nothing wrong with it. They sure were cunning crit-
ters. The hopper was wearing an old shirt, which he recognized as one
of his; it had gone missing ages ago. It drove Mother crazy, she said, forever making up for loss. She would go berserk when she came down here
and spotted one of them dressed in stolen clothes. If hoppers were smart
enough to understand him, he'd advise the offender to go hide in the
hutch if it saw her headed this way.

"Weedy" sure was brave for his size. There must be hundreds of bigger ones out there in the fields and none had dared to come checking
on Deeky Boy. An individual so courageous ought to be named something with a dramatic sound to it—"Mighty Flyer", or maybe, "Warrior
Prince"—both names sounded good to him. Then, though, he was not
much of a flyer—going headlong into the trench. Tomorrow afternoon
when he was home from school, he would paint the name, "Warrior
Prince" on the plank above the enclosure's gate.

Shining the light, to take one last look at Deeky Boy before leaving,
he was surprised when, after moving two short hops from the fence, the
creature proceeded performing a jig! Grinning in unmistakable friendliness, Deeky Boy bared those dazzling-white buckteeth of his.

The dance ended with the hopper waving a paw; giving an odd, dismissive gesture. Warrior Prince had remained on the enclosure floor, but now he climbed to his feet. With several half-hearted hops accomplished, the two then stood together. The diminutive Warrior Prince leaned forward and embraced Deeky Boy. Not seeming to favour the displaying of familiarity, Deeky Boy gave an impatient shrug. Will told them, 'You guys can be friends. You'll be company for each other.' He said, 'Anyway, I've got to go now, but I'll be back tomorrow and I'll see you then.'

Lowering the light so he had a good enough view of the lock, he spun the numerals of the combination so they no longer read: zero, zero, zero, zero. Edging across the gangplank he called back, 'See you! I wish I could stay home and play with you, but I can't. At least you don't have to go to school. You don't know just how lucky you are!'

The leader had mocked the Tall One child by jigging about and baring his teeth, and next he'd offered a challenging gesture, showing he wasn't afraid of their kind. Seeing the leader behaving so, Bernard had gained courage enough to cease submissive grovelling and had climbed to his feet. Then, when the keeper, overcome by emotion and indulging momentary forgetfulness, had dared embrace the leader, the leader, not wanting to voice protest, shrugged him away.

They both were grateful in seeing the boy leave. After his departure they would wait for some considerable time before speaking. The first to speak then was Zechariah. 'Now, Keeper, whilst I do admit that it's good seeing you again, I must ask ... when can I expect something of a *real* rescue attempt?'

After a moment's silence, Bernard explained, 'Yes. I do understand. You're upset by my failure, but, I did at least try.' He repeated, 'I tried...'

He could not see much of him through such dim darkness, but, Zechariah did not the least, question Bernard's sincerity and he must make that clear. He said, 'I'm not speaking of *you*, Bernard. I am impressed with your demonstrating loyalty. I mean it—every word. But I can't help wondering what else is planned for. And by that, I mean ... what *realistic* plan is decided upon? When can I expect to be away from here?' Hearing nothing from Bernard, 'Have any of those on the outside, in the real world, come up with anything by way of a decent proposal for

freeing me?' Bernard was too silent and such tangible silence was suf-
fused with meaning. As if to himself, Zechariah said, 'There are times
when I wonder if Folk of Fur are deserving of leadership.' They weren't. It
was obvious, but someone must provide them it.

Time passed, and Zechariah was as bored as ever. Having Bernard
present did not make much difference, not when it came to the alleviation
of boredom. He'd begun imagining the possibility of questions arising,
regarding the scratched name above the gate, and thinking to dispose
of any potential for future embarrassment now, rather than find he was
confronted later on, he enquired, 'You will, I'm sure, have noticed the way
the Tall Ones respect my position, and have gone to the trouble of making the impressive scratching over yon' gate?'

Bernard, distracted by ache's emanating from every part of his body,
responded in a tired and disinterested manner, 'Um, oh yes.'

'Are you aware of the meaning of those scratchings?' the leader asked,
'Are you? Do you know, Bernard, I receive greater honour from them than
from those of my own kind?' He said, 'Cause for wonder, isn't it? Makes
you think, doesn't it? It does, me. Knowing me, as you do, Bernard, you're
aware that I am not as individuals go, the least vain or conceited but I
confess that hearing them—my *captors* mind you—explain the meaning
of those scratchings, my heart was set to racing.'

'What is the translation?' Bernard asked, curious at last, despite himself.

Without hesitation, Zechariah claimed, 'Herein resides Zechariah the
Great, Leader above all others, of Folk of Fur.'

'Well,' said the keeper, after thinking upon it. 'They've managed to fit
a lot of information on a small space.'

'They're smarter than they look,' Zechariah told him. 'They recognize a captive's true standing, but still, let's never forget that they are
the enemy...' Bending down, he picked something up from the dirt floor.
Passing it to Bernard, he said, 'Here, eat this. Give it a nibble and you'll
see that all along, they've been keeping the best for themselves.'

After taking a first bite, Bernard commented, 'Mm! Yes. This is *prime*
produce—the best broccoli I've tasted!' He added, 'Even if it's only stalks.'

'Here now.' After again stooping, Zechariah offered, 'Have a carrot,
Keeper.'

After all he'd been through this evening, Bernard was grateful for the leader's leftovers. Speaking between bites, he allowed, 'Great Grandfather provides, doesn't He? It's so true.'

To which Zechariah responded, 'I'm not sure I like the suggestion that gifts given you, originate from an alternate source. A friend's largesse ought not be so easily dismissed.'

Bernard

GREAT GRANDFATHER PROVIDES

The Tall Ones had not thought to provide a hutch of adequate size and so an uncomfortable night was endured. As far as the most basic accommodation went, the small structure was fine, but for just one, mid-sized occupant.

About half way through the night, Zechariah insisted that the keeper vacate, telling him, 'Go on—off you hop now, Keeper! Outside with you! First thing tomorrow morning, you can make a start. You have permission to excavate beneath the dwelling, which is mine by right and not because I am leader, but because I was here first.'

'First caught,' Bernard muttered beneath his breath, and did as he was told.

Bernard's time in the enclosure was not going to be time easily spent. Snuggling down close to an end of the wooden hutch, which gave shelter from the stirring breeze, he'd made himself as comfortable as circumstances permitted. Before managing to sleep, he again fretted over the ignoble way he'd gone hurtling into the ditch. By tomorrow he'd be covered in bruises, but would not complain. He thought, *some rescue attempt!* He chastised himself again for believing he'd any real chance of saving the leader. But then, he'd acted in all good conscience and as far as he saw it, had redeemed his good name. He would no longer punish himself over his earlier paralysis in the field.

When first he'd proposed undertaking the leader's rescue, Francis Darkling had all but mocked the idea, enquiring, 'You, Bernard? *You?*' Derisory titters had arisen from those present, and as things had turned out, they were of course proven correct, but it was equally true that none of *them* had stepped forward. They'd not volunteered anything at all and that included Francis. She must count herself amongst them, even she, with her extraordinary skills and ability. All in all, Bernard was pleased with himself, pleased for at least having made the attempt.

He'd ever disliked the feeling caused when a breeze ruffled his fur. Now he pressed closer against the outer wall of the hutch in attempting to avoid the annoying sensation and accompanying dishevelment. He supposed that he should feel grateful for the night having cooled somewhat, because this little breeze was the first of its kind, the very first in a long while. He told himself it was best not seeing Zechariah's taking the hutch for his own use, as anything resembling selfishness. Zechariah was, as Bernard oft' reminded himself, leader, and by dint of leadership, privilege was his. All was as should be. Anyway, he, Bernard, had always appreciated knowing the security of good, ordinary dirt beneath him; he did not entertain an inflated notion of his own importance. He supposed that now, with the two of them here, the quantity of food provided might be increased. He hoped so, because thinking back on them, those broccoli stalks were quite extraordinary fare, although it was true that following those first few nibbles, his poor empty stomach had rumbled in protest. A stomach, having gone for so long without much to satisfy it, could betray and embarrass its owner. Provided more of such fine sustenance, he would cope well enough just so long as the leader's dozing was not disturbed by anything his stomach might decide to get up to during the night. During recent time, there had been several occasions when others had complained over the way his had carried on. The leader was in fact the last of those to mention it.

He'd exclaimed, 'For deeks' sake! Keeper! Teach that stomach of yours a few manners, will you! Kazooning of churners is as nothing by comparison!' This was quite the admonishment, and not something he liked thinking of. Before drifting to sleep, the keeper decided that whilst here, he would do all he could to keep the peace between them. He would at all times exercise civility and politeness. He would do his level best.

It was mid-morning, and after sleeping in late, the leader exited his quarters. Between profound yawning and much stretching, he managed to announce, 'Bernard, I see you're up and at it. But you will come to realize that there's not a lot gained by early rising—not here. We must recognize the benefit of taking it easy, which I suggest means sleeping in for as long as possible.' He said, 'The rules here on the inside are other, than those applied out there.' He waved a paw, indicating all of the surrounding territory. 'Far and wide, Bernard, far and wide!' Whatever was intended by his repeating, 'Far and wide,' Bernard could not guess, but it was always a favourable sign, the leader referring to him by his given name, rather than by the title: Keeper.

Others might envy an individual their title; but Bernard knew better. For most of the time a title was not enhancing to one's lot. A title *was* useful in that by another's choosing to employ it in addressing one, mood and something of mood intensity, might be gauged. As example, the leader presently announced, 'They call it breakfast.' And then with extreme emphasis he repeated, 'Break-faaast!' He declared, 'Rolls off the tongue, doesn't it, Bernard?' and so his mood was pleasant enough. If "Keeper", or the more formal, "Keeper of Rope" was used, along with the mention of breakfast, then regardless of whether the leader *sounded* happy enough, he ought not be trusted as being *truly* so. Leading was never by any means a straightforward, easy task, and Zechariah the Great, through no fault of his, was sometimes overcome by dark moodiness. Brilliance of mind was not without its drawbacks.

'*Breakfaaast!*' the leader shrieked again. 'Wonderful the way I'm picking up the language isn't it, Keeper?' Chatter such as this was a product of genius at its bored best, and Bernard knew it. Having just risen, the leader was already at a loose end and so he, Bernard, had best watch out for sarcasm, belittling jokes or joshing. Best effort must be applied in conveying the impression of his taking the leader's every pronouncement with all earnestness.

Zechariah observed, 'They're tardy today. They should have come by, dropped off their offerings and left. I wonder where they've got themselves to this fine morn'?' Smiling, he confessed, 'I just adore seeing the great Tall One bow, as he comes through yon' gate. It pleases me to lean back against the wire and imagine he bows just for me; in obeisance, Bernard, which is as should be.' He said, 'You would think, wouldn't you, that with all their cleverness they'd construct an entryway suited to their height? Look at that *gate* there. Now tell me, is *that* an example of true competency?'

Commenting was the last thing expected of him and the keeper was alert enough to avoid giving agreement. Rather than agree, he gave a derisory sneer, trusting his expression would be taken as pronouncement enough.

Zechariah enquired, 'Keeper, what say you? What do you make of the accommodations?'

Rather than respond to that, Bernard flibberty hopped across the enclosure to make a close-up study of the gate. He tried pushing a paw against the inter-linked wire circles in order to ascertain the strength of the material.

The voice behind him derided, 'Don't even *think* of it, Keeper. If I could have broken through it, I would have, and well before now! The stuff,' he explained, 'is something they call wire netting, and it's as strong as—wait for it, Bernard—as strong as all *get-out!*'

Receiving little response from Bernard, just several small grunts as he persisted in pushing hard against the stubborn material, Zechariah said, 'You're a disappointment to me. There are times when I wish you were more...' He questioned, 'More ... bright perhaps? No. It's not that. Just what it is though, I'm not certain. But you are certainly lacking when it comes to relating to my humour.'

When it came to learning Tall One ways, Zechariah was quick. His natural ability in the comprehension of language and meaning was second to none. Words were not often repeated before their meanings were defined. He'd heard Tall Ones describe the enclosure as "strong as all get out". The quirky description was heard on more than one occasion. The Tall One, pleased with result of effort, was smug in declaring the trap's construction admirable and he did not mind others knowing it. Zechariah did not know why, but when the Tall One had slapped a hand against a corner post and described the work as he had, others of his kind had not laughed. They'd not seen humour in the description. Such inability in catching a good joke was something shared by Bernard, which was a bothersome fact.

Bernard asked, 'What *is* this thing?'

'Its name is Lock,' Zechariah informed. 'And its number is zero, zero, zero, zero.'

'Oh, numbers.'

'Yes indeed ... numbers. In fact, the same number repeated four times, and if anyone ever bothers to attempt freeing us, it's information were going to need. The Tall One's lock is not going to present much obstacle, because I have its number.' He explained, 'Their names of various numerals are not as ours, which means that I can't be certain as to which number is meant by zero, but it's a simple matter of trying each one in turn. It could take some time of course, but then, after wracking my brain, I have determined that their *zero*, might turn out to be the same as our naught.' He asked, 'What do you think? Does it seem a good guess?' He reiterated, 'Zero, zero, zero, zero.' He sighed, then said, 'Just do your best my friend. Do *try* to remember it. It may stand you in good stead in event of the untoward further befalling your leader.'

'I wish I could reach it!' Bernard said. But it was useless; he could not.

'Believe me,' Zechariah commiserated, 'I know how you feel; it's pointless. What's needed, is for some brave-heart to get themselves over here to rescue us.' He said, 'Francis is the best candidate, but tell me—why does she tarry? What has been discussed? You haven't said a word about any of it have you? What am I to assume?'

Bernard did not rush to respond. So *many* questions, he thought, and all of them asked in a taunting, off-paw fashion. In the manner of his asking was revealed fact of the leader not caring whether or not rescue arrived, but then, Bernard thought, the assumption was unfair. Assuming Zechariah did not care for freedom was not right. More accurate judgment would allow that the leader was desirous of rescue, but he did not much care when it came. Zechariah had been too long cooped up here and he was well fed. In the midst of drought he was far better off than most of those on the outside. He was not compelled to consume greens, as many unfortunates believed they must. Despite enduring imprisonment he'd put on weight. Bernard could not help but know there was something not quite decent in Zechariah's not attempting escape.

Earlier this morning, when the leader still slept, Bernard had made a thorough inspection of the enclosure's dirt floor, and was disappointed to discover not the slightest sign of any mark evidential of digging. The leader had not so much as scratched the surface hereabout. Bernard had not known what to think. Maybe qualities of decency or honour had nothing to do with any of it. He gave up in pushing at the gate and turned back to face Zechariah.

But then glancing past the leader and towards the sky above a distant end of the valley, he had reason to exclaim, 'Oh, deeks—look at that!'

Seeing Zechariah's nonplussed expression, he again exclaimed, 'It's a *storm*, Leader! A storm grows in yon' sky! Right there—behind you!'

Swivelling about to see what all Bernard's fuss was over, the leader was surprised to see an actual storm. It was not Bernard's imagination. Now it was his turn to exclaim. He was no longer the least complacent but excited! 'Deeks is right, Bernard! It's a true, dark monster and it's coming in fast! A storm of this magnitude could be a perfect distraction! We shall trust the good Francis Darkling realizes it, and seizes advantage!'

There was a certain, ominous stillness. No air current moved and strange silence reigned; there was something mysterious and unnatural to it. He should have noticed the change to the atmosphere, but of course he'd been focused upon the keeper's vain poking at the wire. Now though, he felt ready for anything. He was never before so happy knowing that a storm approached and they must grasp the slightest opportunity for freedom!

The sound of slamming shattered the stillness! The door of the dwelling made such a loud noise when it closed behind them, that both he and Bernard had jumped in fright. The Tall Ones were reacting to the sudden, unexpected change in the weather. The buck and doe heltered about in inimitable fashion to the barn, where she assisted him in pushing shut the structure's enormous doors. The atmosphere was no longer eerie and still, but strong flurrying winds swept in across the territory. As wind whipped, gusting at the dusty dry ground, fine sandy grit and even far larger particles whirled aloft, then drove against them where they stood.

Zechariah, his eyes streaming with tears as he wiped grit from them, cried, 'Bernard! Into the *hutch*—now! *Before we're blinded!*' But then, heltering for shelter, Bernard was blown from his feet! His small form was airborne! Through blurred vision, the leader watched his friend sail across the compound, and then, after slamming high up against the wire netting of the enclosure, he bounced back to the centre of the yard, whereupon rolling in dizzying fashion he struggled to regain his feet! Taken so off guard, and finding he flew, Bernard had no choice other than decide that dignity did not matter. He didn't care, just so long as he was not hurled up against any sharp or too unyielding object, then he *might* survive! As he flew into the netting he regretted not being carried higher. Had he gone higher, he might have been carried over the fence and out into the orchard. Fate was fickle in that it decreed he take flight without receiving the least benefit.

Reaching the hutch, the leader scurried inside. His vision was affected still, but peeking back out beyond the opening, he called, 'Don't *fight* it Bernard. It's blowing this way. *Roll with the force of it!*' Bernard heard. After curling into a tight ball he began rolling! In a trice he was delivered to the hutch! But then, once having scurried inside, they both were tremulous. Nothing was leastwise improved! The first sign of worsening came as the hutch began rocking from side to side! Aquiver, Bernard squeezed into a corner farthest from the entryway.

He hollered, '*Oh deeks!*' The small shelter began violent bucking and the floor beneath them heaved from end to end. They would be upended! A great sound of beating of multitudinous sticks flooded the air, as hail belted down from above. The wild sound of it drumming against the wooden hutch was agonizing!

As hail whistled past the opening, Zechariah yelled, 'Those stones are as boulders Bernard! There came a hollow clattering—the sound of wood beating against wood—and strange, square-shaped missiles came hurtling into the hutch! They contended with the accommodation's cavorting and at the same time, dodged sections of flying timber!

Zechariah received a solid whack to his back and howled, '*Yow! It's the end!*'

Bernard cried, 'It's the barn! These things are from the roof!' And, with those words out, as fast as it had begun, the storm began to lull.

The hutch lay upon its back, and after waiting for several moments to see whether it would again move, Zechariah decided it was fine. He announced, 'It's safe enough now, Keeper. You must climb up there and take a peek.'

Bernard was loath to move so soon. He was occupied with inspecting himself for damage; he was alive, but in nothing like acceptable condition. Now he was commanded to reconnoitre the surrounding territory. He glanced up at the opening, which was now positioned overhead. They were lucky the hutch had not ended lying facedown, because then they'd have been forced to dig a way out.

'You're going to have to give me a leg up,' Bernard said, peering at the square of sky visible beyond the opening. Looking up there was similar to looking from the floor of a failed burrow—one with the roof collapsed. The weather was quieted now, but still the sky looked ominous; inside the hutch was gloomy.

'A leg up?' the leader asked.

Bernard, having allowed his attention to drift, replied with more terseness than he otherwise would have, *'What?'* Then, before the leader had chance to react, Bernard explained, 'Yes, Leader. It's far overhead. I'm injured, and so won't be capable of reaching so high.'

That sounded sensible enough, Zechariah decided. The keeper was at last realizing his limitations and that was not a bad thing. He said, 'Oh very well, Keeper, if I must.'

Soon enough then, with effort expended by them both, the Keeper of Rope was positioned as lookout. With part of him resting outside the hutch and the remainder hanging down at the inside of the rectangular opening, he began twisting this way and that. He surveyed the scene and what greeted him was astonishing. He'd expected to see devastation, but this much destruction was difficult to credit.

'Well? What do you see?' Zechariah asked.

'I see destruction,' Bernard said.

'Yes! And?' Zechariah was fast growing impatient.

'The barn has no roof,' the keeper told him, 'It's gone, and many eyes of the Tall One dwelling are broken.'

The destruction reported exceeded expectation and Zechariah wanted to see it for himself. He said, 'Get yourself back down here, Keeper. I must take a look.'

Bernard was not amenable to the idea. No sooner had he reported interesting details of the event than the leader wanted to reverse the procedure; ordering him back down again was not at all fair-minded.

Rather than signal downright disobedience, Bernard offered, 'Oh no, I can't let you do it, Leader. Although it seems quiet—it does—I wouldn't trust it. It may not have finished running its course. Across the valley I see fierce flashes of lightning. There are several, even darker thunderheads than those we saw before the first onslaught.' He predicted, 'Unless I'm mistaken it could be of a mind to move back our way.' He said, 'But if you insist then I'm happy to get down.' He enquired, 'How's your back, where that piece of the barn walloped you?'

'Bernard! Get down!'

'If I must,' the keeper agreed, but then he was distracted and changing tack, exclaimed, 'I declare! Is that Francis I see? Unless I'm very much mistaken, she comes this way!'

In the dark, at the bottom of the hutch, the leader was furious. He ordered, 'I've changed my mind, Keeper! You will *not* get down! Now follow orders! You are to climb all the way up there. Get yourself outside. You will then reach back down here and assist me in extricating myself!'

Bernard said nothing. He would not move. Seeing Francis Darkling he was awed. It was as if he'd not seen her before this. Heltering like the wind, she wore a most attractive indigo costume with a long crimson sash trailing from the waist. She presented both an elegant and dramatic spectacle as she came dashing from the field! She leapt the boundary fence as if it were no obstacle at all, and continued on, blurring towards the enclosure! Would the great excavation slow her progress? Now that the wind had torn away its deceptive covering, it lay exposed as an open wound. It was an exceeding deep and wide obstacle and, seeing it exposed he knew the foolishness of his ever believing that he could triumph over it.

The leader continued fuming, but still Bernard did not budge. For just this once he would not rush to submit. As witness to such an incredible performance, he was mindful of Francis deserving every accolade granted. Of all folk, she was the most extraordinary individual!

Across the hail-covered yard, and beyond the barn, Tall Ones engaged in dragging away debris from their demolished home. Aided by the doe, the great buck pulled, tugging at a long length of timber, attempting to remove it from a hole in the wall. It was as if the enormous timber, thrown by an almighty paw, had succeeded in inflicting gazuzzlement upon the structure.

Coming ever closer, Francis made no sound at all, but in glancing up from assisting the buck, the Tall One doe, spotted her. She was quick to alert her mate to the fast-approaching presence, and they stood staring then, out across the hail covered yard. Despite intervening distance, Bernard was not mistaken in discerning a broad smile crossed the face of the buck and, he wondered, did the buck entertain the idea of capturing one such as Francis Darkling? The question would remain unanswered, because the Tall Ones would soon be forced to alter their opinion of Folk of Fur. Folk were nothing if not proud, and Bernard knew that skill such as Francis Darkling possessed, could not fail to impress even them.

Crossing the yard at lightning speed, she was a blur of motion! Arriving at the trap, she did not pause, but in the smoothest, wondrously fluid motion, *she leapt the ditch!*

The leap accomplished, the dark clad figure did not make an uncertain, clumsy landing but came to a sudden standstill, balanced upon the narrowest of banks! With feet placed wide apart and that perfect body poised, she drew in three sharp breaths. In the same moment, she raised high a paw...

Later, the Tall Ones would have no easy time describing what next they witnessed. They would relate the tale, but others of their kind would decide they exaggerated and some would even go so far as to accuse them of downright kadoodling. William Crenshaw would insist, "I saw it with my own eyes—swear to God—the wife was there and will vouch for it! That hopper, dressed in a bed-sheet, began to *glow!*" He could persist all he liked, but would not be believed.

Having achieved the impossible leap through space, the hopper, radiating an eerie-electric-blue-light, then, with graceful, sweeping motion, brought the paw down.

And so it was that, Francis Darkling, with the terrible, mysterious power of Hargolin, sliced through the wire of the Tall One's imprisoning fence! Her paw passed through those many wire-strands as if the material was nothing at all! She crossed the compound and went straight to the upturned hutch, where she instructed, 'Hold tight to me, Keeper, and I shall lift you down from there.' She said, 'Forgive me, Leader, but this is necessary.' And that said, she tipped the hutch, turning it right side up, and the leader toppled to a new floor.

'Francis! I've been through too much!' Zechariah protested, 'Keeper! See that she takes care!'

She said, 'We must not tarry. Quick now, Leader, climb upon my back.' Stooping low, she ordered, 'Hold to my shoulders. You too, Keeper. Hurry now, before they regain their wits!'

Hearing Bernard instructed to ride along with him, it occurred to Zechariah to question, 'Francis, are you certain that you're capable of this?' He asked, 'Do you believe that leaping so far is possible with you burdened by the *two* of us?' He gave the keeper a quick glance, the mean-ing of which, Bernard caught and then looked away.

'Leader,' she said, 'If you can be quiet, we shall soon know.'

The distance between the place where she stood and the trap's pre-cipitous edge was short, and so Francis would set out from a standing start. With passengers aboard, she ran on the spot *and took off* leaping the ditch! They were flying through space high above the deep chasm! Even with eyes squeezed tight-shut, Zechariah knew they'd made it to the other side. They had landed, and then heltered! She heltered as none ever had, and carried along at such breakneck pace, Bernard vowed that of all folk, it was Francis Darkling whom he would henceforth look up to.

In relating details of the eventful day, William Crenshaw, would claim, 'The strangest thing was the way that hail melted. It melted in the *instant* of the creature's passing. It was as if, moving at such incredible velocity, the deeky gave off actual *heat!*'

'Wow…'

'The ground was blanketed with the stuff, but when that hopper tore across the yard, hail vanished, melted to nothing in the blink of an eye! All along the way it went, hail turned to steam!' Crenshaw would scratch at his head when telling the tale. He would sound useless regret. 'Had I thought to poke through rubble, I might have found the camera. Then, though, even with photographic evidence in hand, most would claim we cleared that weird path ourselves.'

There was another thing. He could never figure why paint was taken. What possible interest could hoppers have with paint? During the day after that of the storm, the hopper had returned. Again, it had torn through the yard like a dervish, but on this occasion, went high and low, searching all over for Crenshaw knew not what, but then the creature had descended into the trench. It had come back out in one smooth leap, clutching to its breast, those cans containing remnants of paint from Will Junior's supply! No longer surprised by anything he saw, Crenshaw could not be one hundred per cent certain, but he wondered if, maybe, the hop-per had taken the brush as well.

FOREST

When the storm swept in, folk were caught by sudden onslaught and were shocked by its ferocity. When inclement weather had passed, Mavis was visited by Nancy. Both complained of burrows made damp and bemoaned the fact of them being all but unliveable.

'The musty odour is most unpleasant,' Mavis said, directing Nancy's attention to the effects of drenching. Even long after skies cleared, dank, odorous dirt floors were a problem. After the storm moved on down the valley, moisture from so much melting hail seeped even so far as the low tunnels and chambers, as if mocking efforts to make them dry. At the surface, puddles formed in every depression to remain after the storm was gone, and everywhere else was mud. Coming on the heel of drought, such an extreme change sorely tested, and Mavis was tired of coping. She explained, 'I've gathered whatever dry fragrant leaves I could from fallen branches, and spread them throughout the place, which has had some effect, but it's not enough. No matter how it's dealt with, the horrid, dank odour persists!'

'Oh, I know. It's the same everywhere. I spend as much of my time outside as I can, but then, outside is little better,' Nancy commiserated. 'Sleeping is difficult, isn't it?' Mavis heard this as a rhetorical question and so, offered no response. After several moments of silence between them, Nancy said, 'Last night I dreamed of Emily. We two, drifted upon water, a huge flood of murky brown water... We clung to a fallen log, I think it was, or a large branch anyway, and we travelled downstream. Our situation as you can imagine, was most precarious. After a while of travelling along we arrived at a place of nothing but mud. It lay everywhere all about—oozing grey mud! It stank beyond belief!' She said, 'No doubt, affected by the current conditions, my every sense inspired my sleeping mind to make and present a story. When we're awake, difficult reality is shared by many, making things seem not quite so bad.' She said, 'But, everything is not so terrible. It will not be long, and safe green shoots will show themselves, and when that happens all will be as should be. Folk will go back to true ways. There will be an end to the errant, dangerous behaviour.' She said, 'I confess to feeling foolish, making such a spectacle of myself—wailing out there in the field. I do hope my warning will prove unwarranted.' Nancy was not finished, and Mavis said nothing. 'I just want all to be well.' She asked, 'Am I *so* foolish?'

Mavis did not address the subject of new greens, nor her daughter berating those whom, faced with the prospect of starvation, had as a last resort turned to consuming the crop, rather, she said, 'You'll never guess who visited me, following the storm, but Bernard!' Seeing the information met with surprise, she said, 'Yes, the one and only, our Keeper of Rope. The poor unfortunate believes I can help him.' She explained, 'Of all of those in authority he's the one I find least objectionable. To tell the truth, I've always seen him as set upon by the rest of them. I've always believed him misused. Although, *abused* is not too strong a word to describe the treatment he receives. The great one uses him as a prop for his own shortcoming—shortcoming denied, but his, all the same.' She added, 'That's if true measure is applied.' Mavis smiled. She offered, 'Come, I'll show you what it is that our Keeper of Rope requests.' Squeezing past Nancy she said, 'It's down in my work chamber.'

'It's wonderful ... I think,' Nancy said, 'but now, you must forgive me, Mother. But, what *is* it?'

Explaining, Mavis said, "This is just the first of them. Besides this, there's another, and Bernard wants me to decorate both. They are weapons of defence and are intended for use in the practice of Hargolin.' Seeing Nancy curious and surprised, Mavis said, 'Not that I'm very interested in any of it, but I do want to help Bernard. In seeking favour he seemed so helpless. He told me he was ordered to decorate them but in his estimation he does not possess ability enough to make a success of it. He was afraid of ending in trouble.' She said, 'I assured him that my helping him would stay our little secret.'

Studying her mother's work, Nancy asked, 'Just what exactly, is depicted there? I see the clenched claw of Brother Eagle, but what does the claw hold?'

Mavis said, 'I'm glad you ask, because within the grasp of fearsome talons Brother Eagle clutches at nothing—and *that* is the point I wish to convey.' She was delighted, explaining, 'The grand thing is for the great one's use.' Responding to Nancy's questioning look, 'The weapon of defence is for the leader, the great Zechariah. You see, the emblem—the clenched claw of great Brother Eagle—holds nothing other than thin air, and that as I see it, is appropriate. Authority, as the leader's, is best seen as empty posturing.'

'Mother, it's wonderful,' Nancy granted. 'It's very creative and you've excelled yourself.' She thought that despite her mother's encryption of meaning by use of symbols, the work was well executed and the recipient, Zechariah the Great, would doubtless be thrilled with it.

Her mother now explained, 'The quite wondrous liquid I used as colouring and the tiny whisk were penance.' She said, 'Whatever else we may think of them, the Tall Ones are most ingenious.' She could not resist adding, 'But then of course I would not have minded had they done a better job of restraining the good Zechariah.' She said, 'You were right to sound the warning in yon' field, daughter, and I'm proud of you. Those pretending deafness will suffer terrible consequence. Now though, what of you my dear? What do you plan?'

'What do you mean?'

'When do you plan on leaving New Warren?'

'I won't leave you Mother. You must know that.'

'I know nothing of the sort. You must go from here. That is what I know.' Looking to one another, neither spoke.

But, Nancy could not stay silent, 'Mother I know what you mean, I do.' She said, 'It's as if I am one enormous, long sigh! It's difficult to express myself, but I stand apart from myself and look on, as a detached stranger. Whilst knowing I lack a sense of worthwhile purpose, no longer do I feel the need for purpose. This is my rightful place. This is where I belong and yet in knowing that's true, I feel I'm no more than a shadow. It makes for horrible discontent. What shall I do?'

'You must leave.'

'Leave? How can I?'

Mavis Noy-Breen said, 'Say, I set out upon a journey and all met with along the way must prove beneficial. Say, My mother wishes me happiness. Allow that when higher power than folk beckons, refusal is not brooked. Allow Tump its way.'

Her smile tinged with sadness, Mavis said, 'Along with the great storm's passing, the first of the changed ones has come amongst us.' She said, 'With that for news, you will know that your sounding warning was correct.'

'No...'

'Just this morning, to a feeder, a changed one is born. She, poor unfortunate, is the first of them. From now on, more misery will be realized. Many of their kind will be with us.' Mavis said, 'Of course, they will receive the benefit of accurate counting.' Not wanting to pronounce the name of Zechariah, she said, *'He* will know how best to solve any problems, but I suspect that organizing them out from our midst will be the last thing on his mind.' With changed ones amongst them, and with Zechariah's managing the future of folk of New Warren Central, life would be worse than grim.

'You are right, Mother.'

'I am and you must go.'

'But you must know I won't leave you.'

'I know nothing of the sort. You are not long here, and that is what I know.'

'But...'

'If Tump is as powerful as I believe it, Nancy gal, then who can say? The day may come and we will meet again.'

Hearing Tump cast in favourable light, Nancy protested, 'For me, Tump was the most unnatural, disturbing influence.'

'That's true, and I doubted you, but it was long ago.' Mavis sighed. 'My every instinct says that I now know the truth of it. We must trust. Darkness is upon us, and Tump may be a light in time to come.'

* * *

Taking little with her but a mother's blessing, Nancy departed New Warren Central for that place of encircling giants and in making for the forest clearing, trusting to leave forever the territory she knew. She did not look back.

Following after Nancy, Francis made the dash from the outlying burrows of New Warren Central to a copse of smaller trees forming part of
the fringe of the forest. To those she passed along the way, she presented
not much more than a dark, rushing blur, or so she thought.

She was disconcerted, when, after passing the decrepit Violet Wild, at
speed exceptional even for her, she heard the ancient one calling after her,
'It's pleasant now, Francis, now that such nasty weather's cleared.' Violet
was busy gathering leaves from fallen branches; those downed by the
storm, and had looked up when Francis flew by. The old one must possess
something of sixth sense, Francis decided, sharp-honed intuition at least.
All was well though, because in her dawdling along the way, Nancy Noy-
Breen had not looked to know if she was followed.

Francis soon reached a large group of trees growing at the forest edge,
and rather than take a path worn by others, she moved ahead, negotiating a way around and between clumps of underbrush. She concealed her
presence behind the most massive member of a monolithic outcropping
of dark, slick-surfaced stones. Peering beyond a tangle of rough foliage, a
clear view was granted of the forest clearing. The clearing was dark with
glistening mud, with sparse-growing clumps of sharp-fronded grasses.
Much time would pass before soft, more succulent green shoots would
emerge and spread to blanket the ground hereabout. When she entered
the wide clearing, the Noy-Breen gal trudged in miserable fashion and
then her pace slowed even more.

From her place at the base of the great stone, Francis heard the gal's
desperate cry, 'Tump! Are you real? Oh *do* be real!' Falling to her knees
in the mud, the gal was in quite a state. Francis brushed at her crimson
sash as if brushing away lint. She would reveal her presence, she thought,
but even as she thought to do so, something she could not have imagined
occurred. No leaf moved and no bird spoke. An all-subduing stillness
had descended upon the forest.

Nancy Noy-Breen's pleading, her crying out to mysterious Tump, was
answered then, but the answer had come from one of those great trees,
standing along with others to define the clearing's perimeter.

Wailing again, the gal cried, 'Not you great sentinel! I meant Tump
to hear me!' Burying her face in her paws she seemed inconsolable and,
hearing what she said next, Francis thought her most petulant. 'Great

sentinel, help me or, with all your company, fall in the storm of storms to come!'

Francis then witnessed an extraordinary process as the broad trunk of the forest giant began changing before her gaze. Shimmering blue-green light shone forth, radiating out from the trunk, and that light carried in it myriad jewel-like flecks of cold pink. Shimmering rose higher, and climbing upwards, progressed along the length of the towering trunk, the quality of light altered and the trunk assumed a strange, watery insubstantiality. As if freed of the tree's possessing it, an elegant figure stepped forth—a gal—trailing ribbons of dancing light, which it seemed wanted to draw her back into the tree's embrace. She moved with diminutive steps away from the great trunk and after halting, addressed Nancy Noy-Breen. 'I *am* Tump, Nancy dear.' She made a distracted, brushing motion with paw to cheek, and said, 'The *thick* boy—if you remember him? The boy, Skip, moved me so that I found myself sharing space with, of all things, a tree!' She waved a paw, indicating the towering presence behind her, and next, with studied lightness, remarked, 'If he can accomplish no better than this, then you *must* join us, Nancy. He's learned nothing of real accuracy. Had he not ensured I was out of phase with the frequency of the realm, before moving me, then, the outcome would have been most dire! And,' she said, 'for that, he needed *my* reminding! There might be no more Peace Darkling but almighty *ker-flumph!* There'd be not much of anything hereabout, no more New Warren Central and no more Tall Ones or their fine valley farm!

She next said, 'Your effort expended in convincing others away from new greens was admirable, despite them ignoring your warning, but then my purpose in coming here has nothing to do with that, does it?'

She said, 'Do stand up, dear! That dress has seen far better days!' And then raising her voice so it floated upon the evening air, she commanded, 'Francis Darkling come out from there! I am your aunt. I am Peace of family Darkling. Come, you must hear me.' When Francis did not move, she ordered, 'Tump commands it. Come along now!'

She told Francis, 'If you think to lay me low with the force of Hargolin, know that you will fail!'

Hearing those words from she knew not what strange entity Francis experienced a dilemma. A creature claiming itself as a long deceased relative would not be allowed to best her. She would chance pitting her skill, even against a thing of supernatural origin! She moved then with more swiftness than she had in coming to this place—much faster! She now stood at the spot where, a mere instant ago, the strange facsimile was present! Now—it was gone! It had vanished! The creature had shifted, to perch amongst the highest tree branches! Francis saw it peering down at her and its expression was mocking. The creature from deeks-knew-where believed that she could do nothing. It must learn a lesson, and so Francis raised an arm high overhead and then brought it down in swift and smooth, diagonal motion. Her arm was ablaze with blue light! Blue light sliced through the trunk of the great tree, and as the tree began tilting upon the base of its great trunk, beginning its fall to the ground, the surroundings underwent an altering.

The forest all about began folding in upon itself, and Francis discovered that her body was frozen in place! Nancy Noy-Breen was stilled too, as still and as unmoving as she. For them, time had stopped and they were prisoners.

It was as if an immense sheet of scratching was being folded away by a power beyond the comprehension of any mere mortal, as if nothing hereabout was any longer required. Francis Darkling was afraid; she could do nothing to prevent her reality from being taken.

A flickering instant later, and she was no longer anywhere near the great tree, but was again back at the edge of the wide clearing. She had been returned to stand beside the black stone monolith. And there was the great tree at a distant remove. It was not fallen, or in the least harmed, and stood as tall as ever it had.

The, by now, familiar voice called, telling her, 'Courage is a fine thing, Francis, and you possess it in good measure but if you persist in treating me as foe, then you are advised to know better the ways of your adversary. If you will not be wise, then it can be predicted that the great battle to come will have an outcome involving more of loss for Folk of Fur—far *more* of loss, than gain. Though you have no peer in practice of your art, make better determination. But for your presence in this realm, in time to come, Folk of Fur can own no place at all.'

Confusing mystery was spoken of.

Finding that she possessed freedom of movement again, Francis left her place by the stone to return to the centre of the clearing. She was careful to show not the slightest sign of fear. Reaching the centre of the clearing, she drew herself up to her full height. The creature, by supernatural means, had now come down from on high. It had returned to where it stood, when first emerged from the trunk of the tree.

Standing close now to Nancy Noy-Breen, Francis enquired of the creature, 'How is it that you have returned the great tree to completeness?'

'What tree?' The creature smiled. It was enjoying itself. Such power, Francis thought, power such as it possessed, was wasted on it. It played games with her, and she would own knowledge of its ability. She said, 'You play a wicked game with my perception of our surroundings.'

The creature offered explanation. 'Picture reality, Francis ... reality as most folk believe it. Next, imagine such reality as depicted upon a broad sheet of thinnest, moisture-softened bark and, whilst envisioning it thus, fold it in upon itself. It is folded. And now, open it again. Now, what do you see there, scratched upon the surface? Is the evidence of altering imagined? Perhaps change has occurred? Has anything rubbed off? Was alteration effected when parts of that depicted were brought to bear against other parts?' She said, 'I will not further confuse you, Francis, but you should know that such as you have seen, can be accomplished over and over again.' Smiling, it said, 'Know that despite your animosity toward me, we are well met. You are family to me, Francis, and whether or not you will believe it, you mean much to me.'

Francis responded, 'How is it that you claim me as relative? Where is my place in such family? That we are in any way related is falsehood, surely.'

Peace said, 'Francis, there is Tump above, and too, Tump below. Would that you further waken to the fact and the way of it. Whether above or below, the way of Tump is true. The time will come when you will *want* to know such truth. You have met with the youngster, Zee. Yes, the boy of the looping realm. He gave you Hargolin. He gave it, and you were not expected to count yourself beholden.' She asked, 'How is it, that after sharing such uncommon relationship with him, you have difficulty recognizing me as family?'

Francis said nothing. After several moments of silence between them, Peace Darkling said, 'Mystery abounds. There is no such thing as normality. Nothing is ever so ordinary as we like to believe it.' She shrugged, then said, 'Know better, Francis, than question *me* regarding falsehood or family.' Still, despite those words, Francis could not see the other as anything but deceiver. She snapped, '*Why* are you here?'

'Why? I'm here to take Nancy home with me.'

'Nancy?'

'Yes, Francis, for she is Tump.'

Francis said, 'The gal claims her power is *natural* and you claim the same is true of yours. Is that it?'

Following short hesitation, the creature agreed, 'Yes, my ability is natural, a result of much invested effort. Were it not so, then I should not be the least satisfied or comfortable with it.'

Francis was frustrated, her expression downcast.

Peace said, 'Francis, I know you, and know that you will recall my words. Despite my describing more of mystery than providing solution— as you see it—keep these words and do not let them slip away. They will sustain you in achieving a rightful place in the grand scheme. You are the greatest warrior of our realm. True contentment may elude you but you must entertain something of satisfaction as you go.'

Hearing admonishment, a defiant Francis asked, 'Just what creature are you? Where are you from?'

'I am a fellow traveller, Francis. Apart from that I believe I am nothing at all as you can imagine.'

When Peace Darkling and her niece, Francis, conversed, Nancy was silent, but now she asked, 'My mother is not safe, should I not stay with her?'

'You should not remain here. What can be done for your mother will be done.' Nancy's question was dismissed as if it were of little concern. Turning from Nancy and again addressing Francis, Peace said, 'Before we leave you, Francis, I must tell you that you will know the time when it comes. Do not heed the leader's wish. Do *not* war against the man, Crenshaw.' Noting a look of confusion cross Francis' countenance, Peace insisted, 'The Tall Ones, Francis. You must *not* submit to warring with them. Do not follow such course, but rather, you must cross yon' high hill and then war enough will come to those who hunger after it.' She said, 'Fear them you may, for they are indeed frightening, but in imparting the skills of Hargolin, see that you withhold nothing from the changed ones. For the task ahead they will need every skill.' Then she beckoned to the gal, Nancy Noy-Breen. She instructed, 'Come, Nancy, stand close by me.'

'Yes, but…'

Peace commanded, 'Fixer! The gate! Skip! Take us home!'

As the two vanished from sight, a fragrance flooded the air and final instruction was issued, 'Stay true now, Francis! Take care that you watch over Bernard!'

Francis was uncertain whether to credit her hearing. Final words from the creature were surely misapprehended? The creature took leave of the forest clearing in an astonishing fashion. Bright, blinding light flashed and Francis found she was alone.

Tump did not answer even the most plain, straightforward question with anything of honesty. The creature's answers were as clear as mud. To top matters off, it had issued instruction concerning the keeper.

Mutant

FINE STRAPPING LADS!

'Lads'

'Yes. Lads.'

'What does it mean?'

'It's another Tall One word, Bernard. Just one of the many I managed to pick up during my incarceration.'

Thinking back to the conversation between the Tall One father and son, Zechariah recalled hearing the word on numerous occasions. More than once, the father had complimented, 'There's a good lad, Will. Yes, excellent work!'

In speaking with the keeper, Zechariah now explained, 'It seems more pertinent than referring to them as boys or gals.' He said, 'Changed ones are nothing at all like normal boys and gals, are they? Neither are they full-grown bucks or does and so, Bernard, they are lads, fine, strapping lads. As for you and your complaining, regarding them, I will hear none of it!'

'Yes, but the enormous, orange and green one lashed out at me for offering constructive criticism of work carried out, and for no real reason! The work was substandard. I might have been injured or worse!'

'Of course you might have been, Bernard, but, fact is, you *weren't*, were you?' Zechariah insisted, 'Come along now, Keeper, put a positive face to it. Nothing less than full cooperation is required in organizing the completion of Borderland Warren. I need you up there doing your very best.' Zechariah sighed. Progress at the site lagged behind anything like satisfactory pace.

Situated farther up-slope, at a reasonable distance from New Warren Central, new burrows and chambers were to accommodate changed ones. Changed ones were not suited to living at close quarters with the rest of them, and so must be separated from normal folk. They were to be removed from their natural families and provided their own fine quarters—extensive quarters—suited to their outlandish size and at times, downright violent behaviour. Following their separation, returning to the burrows of New Warren Central would be prohibited. In any case they would have no need to return down-slope, because at Borderland, every necessity would be provided them. Once the new complex was completed and changed ones moved, they were to be supervised by the biggest and strongest individuals Zechariah could muster; keepers to changed ones would be housed along with their charges. Changed ones would be given a new and more appropriate family.

Having gone to the trouble of planning the layout of the place himself, and coming up with revolutionary new methods of construction, and putting so much thought into suitable finishing touches, such as stone-slab lining, his anticipation, experienced in desiring to see the work finished with, was ill-constrained. He'd displayed tremendous patience in the face of frustrating delay and difficulty and so could do without further incidents of changed ones losing control and causing injury to normal folk. As leader, he was ever called upon to deal with problems; and problems, since changed ones came amongst them, too often arose.

He told the keeper, 'I'm sick to the teeth of being expected to resolve situations involving foolish dispute, and I believe that for your part, you should do better.'

'But, Leader, they're *not* children! My size puts me at a decided disadvantage. I'm afraid—'

'You're afraid?' Zechariah interjected, 'Oh, come now, Keeper! We both realize they're not youngsters, not for long, are they? They mature at quite astonishing rate but then, for deeks' sake, you're an adult aren't you? As such, you must behave as one! When I'm not present, you are expected to take charge on my behalf! Again I ask myself, Bernard, where is your spine—left at home again? Does it perhaps lie neglected—mouldering upon your chamber's floor?'

'No.'

'Then, there is no excuse. You far and away too often display a need for encouragement, and I feel it's unfair. Your incessant carping over matters is inappropriate when you hold position of authority. You have *power*, my friend! Learn to use it! Up there at the site, you are my right paw. You're in charge of things!'

Sooner or later the leader would take him from the project and appoint another as overseer. Francis Darkling would, in all likelihood, be awarded the position. When the going was tough, which was all too oft' the way of it up there on the high slopes, she never minded taking on extra responsibility. Bernard was not averse to Francis helping out in situations where physical prowess played a part in resolving them, but he did like being thought in charge of things, and knowing there was imminent threat to his position, which was revealed by the dangerous note underlying the leader's most recent words, he was not at all keen on the idea of demotion, which would entail public humiliation.

Compelled to speak up for himself, Bernard trusted he sounded strong, determined and decisive. He would make himself master of good tidings! Drawing himself straight, he announced, 'I have *some* good news to impart, Leader.'

Seeing the way Bernard came to attention, Zechariah smiled, then asked, 'Good news? What is it then, this good news?'

'The great main entryway is all but completed, Leader! It is lined in precise accordance with your clever design, with magnificent facing-stones along the full length of it. Apart from the entryway, work progresses on the first of the largest chambers—'

'Clever?' Bernard's describing progress was stalled by the leader interrupting, 'My *clever* design? It's more than mere cleverness! I'll have you know the design is manifest brilliance, and when the complex is finished—in entirety—all will appreciate the fact of it!'

In learning that work at the site was so far advanced, Zechariah was reassured, but not wanting the keeper to realize anything of his pleasure, he rushed ahead, 'Bernard, when folk are confronted with Borderland, warren design will never again be seen the same! My great project is revolutionary, and all about will wish to emulate it.' Smiling then, he asked, 'Why did you not think, Bernard, to more apprise me of progress? Why did you first think of coming to complain regarding the creature attacking you? You *know* very well, that I would have been happier if informed at our meeting's outset, of progress made with work at Borderland. I would always prefer having news along such line, than hearing, for the umpteenth time, your personal drivel.'

Rather than respond in any direct way, Bernard enquired, 'Leader, how is the weapon of defence? I trust that it meets with approval.' He offered, 'The clenched claw of Brother Eagle is an appropriate symbol of might and true authority—of your leadership. I decided that nothing else could quite measure up.' He added, 'I trust that my humble effort meets with acceptance.'

'Humble effort?'

'Yes, Leader.'

Zechariah thought, Weapon of defence? Forgetfulness was not feigned; in the moment he'd not the slightest idea of that referred to, but then memory returned and he recalled allowing the keeper the task of decorating the relic. The relic was from days long passed, from days of Uncle Samson.

'Ah yes, of course!' he exclaimed. 'Keeper, I do wish you'd explain yourself. But yes—and it's quite good. It is! You have some talent and it shows.' After several moments pause, he said, 'I'm calling the thing a shield, Bernard. How do you like the sound of it? *Shield.*' He explained, 'During my time spent in yon' lock-up, before your hilarious arrival there, I heard my quarters more or less described as such. The Tall One in speaking of the hutch happened to say, "He can hunker down in it and it will shield him from the elements.". By, "he" the Tall one referred, of course, to my good self. Recalling the intended purpose of that shoddy accommodation, I decided the word, shield, as an appropriate name for the weapon you've decorated. The word has a certain appeal to it. *Our* shields will of course prove effective in protecting us from more than inclement weather.' He said, 'There is irony in appropriating bits and pieces of their language. I've named a weapon intended for employment against them with a word from their vocabulary. I do confess, I'm rather smug over it.'

Joining Zechariah in smiling, Bernard was not so much amused by the leader's habitual favouring appropriation of Tall One words, as by his referring to inclement weather. The storm, endured whilst tossed about in the Tall Ones' hutch, Bernard would never describe as inclement. Neither would he describe as shoddy, those quarters provided them; at least they'd gained adequate protection by sheltering in the tumbling thing. Much of the leader's humour was obscure and such was ever true.

Bernard knew that he was the brunt of much of it, but he was not alone in that, because over recent time it amused Zechariah to see the way the abominations laboured in the excavation of their own warren.

For Zechariah it was a source of pleasure and delight and he would comment, 'Don't you just love it, Keeper? Here they are slaving away making themselves useful members of society by toiling in the creation of their own home! They work as others never have!'

The leader may laugh over, and boast of the way the creatures worked, but nothing was as it should be, and as Bernard saw matters, the leader should be present at the excavation as often as the rest of them. The situation was confusing and so much of the confusion should not, Bernard believed, be his to deal with. Whilst it was true that the creatures were not more than youngsters, they were also powerful, and so, whilst they worked, overseeing their work was for him dangerous in the extreme. Stress was a constant companion and nerve-wracking incidents were commonplace. This morning, again, he was given cause to fear for his life. A series of events unfolded until a point was reached where, if he could have wished himself away to anywhere other than Borderland, he would have done so and never returned.

The scarifying situation had developed by his making nothing but a straightforward enquiry. 'Why is it,' he'd asked of the one in charge, 'the facing stones at this side of the tunnel are not aligned with their mates?'

'Aligned with their *mates?*' In repeating the question back to him, the large buck, was, in Bernard's opinion, rather intense. Presenting anything of serious criticism had not been Bernard's intention, but the other had taken offence and so the keeper decided that he should like to drop the matter. What did he care if the work of underlings was not perfect? Truth told, none of the goings on here was of much real interest to him, not if he gave the matter sincere consideration. But then the fellow, Red-Mark, had taken his more or less innocent querying, straight to heart.

Hoping then to clear up misunderstanding, Bernard explained, 'Yes. You see here… Here, where the facing stones align, one against the other? Do you see what I mean?'

The other directed him an odd look, the meaning of which was not fathomed, and Bernard, feeling not too discouraged, pressed on, explaining, 'Those, over there, acting as the facing to the wall at the opposite side of the tunnel, are not in agreement with these on this side. Where they're joined, the alignment shows considerable variance. There's no true match.'

Red-mark, an individual far larger than any Bernard was ever comfortable sharing close proximity with, grinned, and then Bernard, for the second time, heard his words echoed, 'The joins are not in *agreement?*'

'That is what I said, yes,' the keeper replied. He was becoming impatient with the other mimicking him. And then in continuing with explaining, he went too far, 'You'll see here, Red-Mark... As even blind buck, Freddy, would. These are not laid, as required by our leader's plan. They're something which even the thickest individual will, over time, realize as misaligned.'

During the previous night he'd not slept at all, but tossed and turned until dawn, and so he was still tired. He ever detested overseeing work at the site, and now, as ill-chosen words slipped from him, awareness dawned; trouble should be considered inevitable. Attempting to avoid difficulty, he offered, 'But then, Red-Mark—it is your name isn't it? If you're happy enough with the work, leave it as it is, and we'll see what the leader thinks of it.' He would have liked to add, 'If, at future time, the idea of coming here enters the great one's head, he will no doubt offer an opinion,' but then, he'd best not progress in that vein. There, the matter might have rested, but it did not. Red-Mark, for reason of his own, reason not recognized at first by Bernard, said, 'When he sees it, the leader will be pleased enough with our work.' Red-Mark spoke of Zechariah as if they were acquainted, as if they were on familiar terms. The leader was much revered.

Bernard smiled, telling the other, 'If *he* is pleased, Red-Mark, by anything at all, then I will visit you. I would know your secret.'

Red-Mark, not caring that others overheard, pounced upon the innocent comment, skewing everything. 'At first, you are critical of my son's work, fine enough work, for he is but young! And next you threaten to *visit* me as if I'm ignorant of your true intention! All who toil here upon the slope know the meaning of *visits* by those in authority! I have *no* secret!' Red-Mark sounded outraged but his expression revealed fear. The large buck, one of many "normals", as the leader referred to them, who toiled here in supervising changed ones, was afraid. Bernard—even as Keeper of Rope, had not been informed of any reason whereby mention of receiving a visit might result in such a sincere expression of dread. Bernard was puzzled and flabbergasted by the incident. He made a mental note and would look into the matter of folk receiving frightening home visits. It seemed very obvious to him that much went on behind his back. There were matters of which he had not been informed and he wondered how long this had been so.

Having realized that not all was as he'd believed, and having decided steps would be taken to set things right, Bernard was shocked by the changed one. Bearing a zigzagging pattern of lurid orange and green stripes and the longest talons ever, the creature, whose work in the first place, deserved honest criticism, lashed out! The creature seized Bernard about his throat and then after raising him high, held him pinned against the tunnel wall! And next, roaring into his face, it ordered, 'Leave Farder beee! Leave 'im 'lone will ya!'

With hot, rancid breath blowing against his whiskers and the fur of his cheeks, and abuse flooding his auditory sense, Bernard lost every last remnant of control and, most disgusting of all, he soiled himself. Great claws digging against veins and vitals and the recognition of imminent gazuzzlement was too much! Following release from the changed one's grip he was not able to prevent himself gagging. Dry retching had him down on his knees in the grass, and for ages after he was nothing other than a hapless wreck.

Many such incidents involving close calls, were part of everyday experience in working up the slope from New Warren Central, and, in his estimation, Bernard suffered more than reasonable expectation allowed. As Keeper of Rope, attending to duty and all that entailed took precedence over other, more personal considerations, but as he saw it, he did not deserve involvement in so frequent, stressful situations. Further rules would be put in place, and for one thing, fathers working with their sons would no longer be allowed. The practice had time and again proven a recipe for disaster. If it were permitted to continue, then days ahead would remain pregnant with potential for misunderstanding and dire outcome.

Arrived home at the day's end, Bernard went to his sleeping-chamber, whereupon he sank to his knees offering profuse thanks to Great

Grandfather for sparing him gazuzzlement. Thanks were offered for Francis Darkling's presence at the warren. Had she not been within earshot when danger ensued... Well, it did not bear thinking about. If fate ever decreed election of a new face to leadership imperative, then as far it concerned Bernard, a doe would be elected to the position, (just so long as the position of Keeper of Rope remained valid).

Francis Darkling was worthy of most elevated position.

* * *

In the dim light of dusk, across the field of upcoming battle, tight-formed ranks of opposing forces faced each other. The distance intervening between forces was not great, and the leader, looking out from where he stood upon a sloping rise, commented upon the way they were positioned. He enquired, 'Francis, why is it you allow such a narrow distance between them?'

She told him, 'They must not present disarray when confronted by a daunting number and must not resort to breaking ranks. Previous to this they've faced each other in close paw-to-paw, one on one combat and, as well, in small groups, but this exercise will sort the cowards out from the rest. If any are inclined to weaken then I will soon know it.'

'Cowards? Are there actual cowards amongst them? I wouldn't have thought so. They're all brave, courageous lads! At least that's as I see them.'

Francis said, 'They are always courageous enough in disputes with normals. They are more than proficient. Dispatching an enemy is always carried out. But, to answer your question... Yes, Leader, there are those who, in facing their own kind, would rather turn and high-tail it.' She admitted, 'They are not many, but if their number is greater than I suspect, then I shall learn of it. Those are the ones I'll be watching for.' Raising an arm aloft, Francis Darkling paused.

Before bringing the arm down, as signal to the Keeper of Rope, she informed, 'Leader, all is in readiness.' She asked, 'Shall I give the command to begin?'

'By all means,' Zechariah replied, 'Let's have the exercise underway,' but then he thought to offer, 'I must say, Francis, you've made a success of organizing them. Awaiting the spectacle, I'm not able to contain myself!'

Then, as Francis made to give the signal, she was again forced to delay by the leader interrupting, 'I know you've already given assurance, Francis, but there won't be *too* much damage done, will there? We can't have the injured lying about afterwards for long. We don't want complete decimation.' Frowning, he asked, 'As I understand it, the main purpose of the present exercise is to demonstrate basic skills and strategies?'

'Yes,' Francis allowed. Seizing the moment, she signalled by lowering the paw to her side.

On the field below, the Keeper of Rope, positioned enough away from changed one ranks, received the signal to proceed. He cried, 'Commence battle!'

Wide phalanxes of bright striped figures moved forwards towards one another. They came together in a whirl of motion, all feet and paws moving at once, and at speed! Despite the fast dimming light of dusk obscuring much detail of the activity carried out upon the valley floor, bright colourful forms engaging in destruction were visible enough from the hillside vantage point where the leader stood surveying all.

Down there much blood was spilled, much pain of injury sustained.

Zechariah the Great, interpreting all he saw in inimitable way was mindful of bright rainbows clashing in wild, beauteous dispute. And whilst witnessing the result of Francis Darkling's efficient teaching of Hargolin, her making true warriors of changed ones; his attention was distracted by an urge which, rising from within, exercised a coercive influence, and momentary recollection of Uncle Samson was his. There appeared Samson, his decrepit relative and mad collector of all and sundry. His intrusive and depressing presence, come back to haunt him. Down there upon the floor of the vale was blue fire; fire of an order he little understood and yet it was his to wield. It wrought havoc. It flashed and glowed, and brought into contact with an enemy, the awful sizzling sounded magnified. Dismemberment and cauterizing resulted in the same instant. The sound of bone sheared was discerned even from this far distant.

Sound sizzles through the gloom of day's end, observed Zechariah, and he saw trails of grey smoke or steam rising from the darkened field. The strange, writhing fire curled serpent-like, as ground-based lightning flashed over and again, continuing a magnificent hissing and crackling down there. He wondered if, in their wielding such awesome, unstoppable force, any changed one entertained a notion regarding his or her place in an alternate order. Did any seek more as their lot? If they did, then preventing them going their own way would be anything but easy; but them entertaining a notion other than that of staying alive seemed unlikely.

There was need for conservation of such valuable resource. Warriors born to purpose, they'd served well. Brought to bear against those of their kind they'd proven beyond slightest doubt, an awe-inspiring capability. Such power, in his charge, was best kept as a reward for true foes—foes deserving of cut and slash.

Voice soft, Zechariah commanded, 'Enough, Francis. The exercise is an unqualified success, and now before further punishment is dealt, it will cease.' By his grace and his alone, there was an end to pain.

Francis was heard, 'It's gratifying, Leader. Just three cowards attempted to helter from the field in the final moments.' She commented, 'Which, I admit, surprises me.' Glancing across to him and noting his dull expression, she realized the proceedings held little further interest for him.

Dispirited for no reason he would trouble defining, he offered, 'Keep the offenders safe, Francis. They shall not receive punishment. They're all of them needed, those brave-hearted and those less so inclined.' Blood chilling anguished cries filtered up from the darkened valley—beseeching cries reaching to ear as if, Zechariah decided, they went out of their ways in striving to impress.

He ordered, 'Francis, have Bernard attend to clearing the field. The fallen must be disposed of and no evidence of skirmishing will remain. Bernard must understand that the chore is to be finished before dawn. Inform the keeper that the unfortunates are to be interred upon the slope in near proximity with Borderland Warren, and not within proximity of any place used for internment of normals.' Then, scratching at his chin, he said, 'Once Bernard has attended to tidying the mess, see to it a cairn is erected, nothing elaborate, but a stacked heap of stones set close to the burial site as commemoration. Something to mark the occasion of their passing in good cause is the least we should offer.'

Over at the farmhouse, Babs prepared for bedtime and a quiet evening spent in the company of husband, William. Intent upon drawing the window-drapes, her attention was caught by something far off, at distant side of the field, and peering into the night-darkened scene, she asked, 'What in the name of Millthorpe, are they playing at over there?'

His tone dismissive, Crenshaw said, 'They'll be carrying on over having rescued Deeky Boy. Come away from the window. It's not often we have real time alone.

BORDERLAND

Separation of changed ones from parents and from normal-born siblings was not just encouraged but insisted upon. Once mutant children were ensconced at Borderland Warren, in stonewalled, purpose-built quarters, visits by family members were disallowed until such time as a child was indoctrinated to the point where an irreversible bonding with the surrogate parent, or minder, was accomplished. With enough time transpired, young ones very often no longer recognized their natural parents, and instances of them displaying suspicion towards those expecting warm signs of recognition, were common. Meetings were distressing for many a visitor greeted with cool, dismissive, off-paw treatment or, belligerent behaviour.

Before meetings with offspring were permitted, parents received advise from minders. 'There is no call for emotion or for feeling torn. Sensible acceptance is everything. It's important to keep in mind that easy-going acceptance on your part can benefit all concerned. If your behaviour is in anywise upsetting, then you're not doing them, yourself, or anyone else, any favour. We find that our changed ones *can* on occasion display certain sensitivity. If a changed one senses inappropriate feeling, they will stress and then be difficult to manage. Stay mindful that if you show the least sign of coming apart, it's my sworn duty to curtail the visit.'

Minders had the youngsters' best interest at heart and their acting in accordance with rules and regulation, deciding if a child showed disturbing sign of upset and to what extent this was true, meant their decisions were correct. They'd a job to do, and that was all. Disputing a minder's decision was neither condoned nor tolerated. A minder's word, in matters concerning those in her charge, was as good as law. As such, it was enforced by members of an elite guard, comprised of bucks, whose sole purpose was to enforce regulations aimed at ensuring moderate conduct of all parties. Arrangements made perfect sense. As the leader oft' observed, changed ones, far from presenting a liability, as some believed, were the community's most valuable asset—an asset deserving of every consideration and protection. Zechariah the Great had not left the slightest detail to vagary of chance.

Mavis Noy-Breen was sickened and disheartened, when hearing the distressing sounds of protesting children as they were taken from the care of their parents. The location of her burrows was not advantageous; the Noy-Breen home was located in one of the most populated areas of New Warren Central, which made it impossible to deny knowledge of the heart-wrenching occurrences.

Receiving a visit from Francis Darkling, Mavis was unnerved. Nothing was gained by revealing her true feeling, not in any circumstance, and when the Darkling gal called to her from outside the entranceway she knew that she was unsuccessful in concealing her surprise. She wished she were farther back in her burrow, when first she heard her name called. She would then have had time enough to better collect herself and she may have feigned sleepiness or come up with another excuse or distraction, but comfort was not gained in wishing things other than they were. Caught standing just inside the entranceway, she turned, giving a short response to what sounded more of a command, than an enquiry, 'Mavis Noy-Breen?' Just her name; but delivered in an authoritative tone.

'Yes—what?' Caught off guard, her surprise was revealed, but as well, such short response conveyed disagreeableness. Realizing the other's confident demeanour was undermined, she was not displeased and seizing the advantage, protested, 'I'm not young as I once was. Creeping up and startling me might do no good at all! You could find nothing other than gazuzzlement ensues. These old bones...' Allowing her words to trail off, Mavis then heard Francis apologize.

She said, 'Sorry. I've come here to put an idea to you.' After a moment, during which Mavis offered no response, Francis, going to the point of her visiting, said, 'I think you should consider moving from here.'

Taken aback, and tremulous, Mavis asked, 'Move? You mean move from my home? But where would I go?' Nonplussed by the suggestion and with resolve firming, she asked, 'Why would I do such a thing? I've been here at the warren for more time than I care to recall.' She said, 'We raised a family here. Charlie would turn in his grave if he learned of me agreeing to move!' What, she wondered, was Francis Darkling's purpose in suggesting she up stakes and move? Was it a suggestion, a request, or was she ordered to it? Francis Darkling was close to the leader. Her position in the hierarchy of authority was of long standing and entrenched. Being paid a visit by such as she could be seen as the same as being visited by the leader himself! Mavis was fearful; she must gain time. As if she might at any moment break into tears, she said, 'No. I can't think of it. I *won't!'*

'You will be cared for,' Francis assured. She offered, 'I will watch over you, and moving will be to your advantage. If you will consider going to a place farther down-stream—to a less noisome location...' Then, after pausing, she said, 'One of your age should not be expected to put up with such din—the unceasing and distracting hubbub of New Warren Central.' She said, 'In any case, I'll leave you now and shall return later for your decision.' After she departed, Mavis realized Francis Darkling had spoken as if her moving from her home was a foregone conclusion, and reviewing the odd meeting, she recalled Francis declaring, "One, of your age..." She wondered, did those in authority care, concerning anyone's age or what any aged individual contended with? Did they care whether or not anyone enjoyed a peaceful home environment? Mavis thought and thought, but whichever way the problem was viewed, she concluded that she was to leave New Warren Central, no matter her fondness for the old place; no matter her many memories of it, memories both good and ill. In real terms, there was naught she might do to prevent falling in line with whatever Francis Darkling planned for her.

The following morning, another visitor came calling, and in receiving him, Mavis decided she had become far too popular with those enjoying positions of power. Francis Darkling's underlying intention eluded her still, but Bernard's intention was neither mysterious nor cause for anxiety. Before arriving at the entranceway of her home, his progress was made in noisome fashion. In greeting her he smiled in a winning way. Waiting there in the entranceway, the purpose of his visit was obvious. The thoroughfare and entranceway both were capacious, but Bernard had struggled in hefting another of those weapons of defence. Seeing him now, Mavis knew he brought more work for her.

He held it up for her to see, and nervous of her voicing protest, he rushed to inform, 'Missus Noy-Breen, you would *not* believe the difficulty I've had in getting this here!' He said, 'You did an outstanding job on the first of them, and so, although I feel just terrible making the request, I wonder if you would mind too much embellishing this one?' He added, 'It's mine.' He said, 'It's not as large as the first of them, and there's nothing to hold at the back of it. You see...' he said, manoeuvring it around in order to reveal its reverse side. 'The paw-hold thingy is broken. At some stage, its been snapped right off.' He explained, 'Still, it's generous of him, letting me have it.' Mavis thought it *un*generous, and wondered over anyone gifting another such a damaged means of self-defence. She nodded, as if perhaps agreeing with Bernard's estimation of such largesse. She said, 'Bring it inside Bernard, and we'll take a look at it.' The keeper lugged it inside and then put it down on the floor of the chamber. Relieved of the burden, he stood taller. He puffed himself up in a way that suggested that as the proud possessor of such a fine thing, he could not keep from doing so.

Mavis was tactful in not going straight to mentioning the weapon's flaw. She asked, 'Exactly what manner of fine embellishment do you envision Bernard?' After a moment, during which he did not speak, but stood, paw rubbing at the downy white fur of his chin, he said, 'Um ... I believe that any decoration should be kept simple. It would be best if the result of your work was not *too* grand.'

She deduced that much of which she'd determined as true of him was not so. He was not after all, so thick. Until now she'd seen him as an easy target for disdainful treatment by others and there were those occasions when she'd decided him not very bright for putting up with it. In situations involving confrontation, situations wherein humiliating treatment must be dealt with, he lacked gumption enough to stand up for himself. It was either that or he was oblivious to offensive treatment; examples could be brought to mind proving the truth of either possibility. None of it was any of her business, but having glimpsed another, less easily categorized Bernard, Mavis found she did not despise him to the extent she did those others holding high positions. Something of a wily side to his nature was evinced.

She was ever mystified as to the origin of Bernard's title, and so now Mavis asked, 'I wonder, Bernard, what is the meaning of the title, Keeper of Rope? She explained, 'Knowing may provide me something of a clue in coming up with suitable ideas for adornment of the weapon.' She added, 'I've ever heard it as impressive sounding, but I'm afraid that I'm ignorant when it comes to the meaning.'

'Oh, it's nothing,' he said. But then, 'In the first place, the title was granted as something of a joke. As all should know by now, the leader possesses a fine sense of humour. In any case, the title of Keeper of Rope was decided by him long ago...' Bernard was pensive. He said, 'He suggested the title as a way of marking an occasion—the occasion of my falling into the ditch—during a game we all played back then.' Sighing he said, 'It seems so long ago now... It was his idea to have me stand idle, streamside, rather than make any further attempt at Leaping the Ditch because my leaping was really quite dismal. Allowed to continue, I might have sustained severe injury. It was ages before I figured and understood his intention. In any case, the good leader had me stand there upon the high bank holding the rope. The rope was taken from the renowned collection of items kept by his Uncle Samson, and I was ordered to keep it close to me at all times, keeping it ready, you see, in the event of disaster befalling others.'

Mavis said, 'As I see it, Bernard, the solution to our problem lies in your explanation. I believe that subject to your approval, the best way of showing your true worth will be to depict a coiled rope, encircling the circumference of the weapon as a noose.' In daring to utter the word noose Mavis was unsure. Touched by hearing his story, perhaps she'd now gone too far and exceeded the bounds of sensible caution? She watched as Bernard gave careful thought to her idea and then knew relief when not the smallest sign of his interpreting her suggestion negatively resulted. Still, nervousness persisted and she offered, 'Along with the question of a suitable design, Bernard, we must consider the problem of providing you with something by way of a good paw-hold for the weapon.' She insisted, 'I'll tell you what—leave it with me—I'm certain to come up with something!' And so, if not for the return of Francis Darkling, that would have been the end of it. Bernard would not have delayed in making departure.

But as it was, Francis Darkling, without so much as a by your leave, stepped in through the entranceway announcing, 'Mavis Noy-Breen, I am here as promised. You will accompany me now to the place I have prepared for you.' As if belatedly noting Bernard's presence, she said, 'Hello there, Keeper. You can come along with us if it pleases you.' Gesturing to the weapon at their feet, she said, 'Bring that thing with you, Bernard, and the paint and the whisk. If she's to work on it for you, the old one will need those things.' And without time enough in which to gather anything of real worth—any item of sentimental value; Mavis was bustled from her home. The three left New Warren Central, for, as far as Mavis was informed, a destination unknown.

Flibberty hopping between the two of them, keeping up as best she could, as they travelled far from familiar territory, she told herself, 'Mavis, you are separated from home ground; that's all. You must calm yourself. You must view proceedings as sufficient unto themselves. Imagine this as an adventure of short duration.' But then, thinking better than encourage delusion, she told herself, 'Be satisfied with not allowing fear to show.'

Having gone so far as to be out of sight of any curious enough to have noticed their departing the territory of New Warren Central, Francis again reminded Bernard, 'Keeper, still that thing, will you? Desist in banging it about!' Hearing proof of fear of discovery from one as empowered as, Francis Darkling, Mavis dared enquire, 'Where do you take me? Where are we going?'

In enquiring, she was nervous, but then she was surprised by the other's easy response, 'You will like it, I think. It's a place chosen for your safety and also for having a fine, pleasant aspect.' Francis added, as if voicing nothing more than an afterthought, 'Every detail has been attended to, old one, and so Tump can rest easy. I know now what was implied by the revelation granted.'

Hearing that name, Mavis stopped in her tracks. 'Tump?' she asked, 'What of them? What is their part in your taking me from my home?' Francis Darkling hesitated and then halted on the trail. Facing Mavis she declared, 'Your daughter is Tump, old one. It is no surprise that you know of them. Will you now claim the right, as do they, to treat me as thick?'

Mavis could not think how best respond. Francis complained of mistreatment—mistreatment, dealt by Tump—was that it? Mavis said, 'I know nothing of them, nothing of Tump, apart from that told me by my friend, Ruth.' She said, 'Before she passed, Ruth Fawn spoke of it...' She explained, 'Ruth knew very little. The thing called Tump represents great mystery! I have never been privy to anything other than the vaguest hearsay with regard to such strangeness!'

'Your daughter is Tump!'

'Is she? Can she be? Then it's the first I've heard of it! I do know that Tump thought it right, abducting her from us, her family, when she was too young to resist!'

The Keeper of Rope, as if oblivious to the others conversing, complained, 'I'm fed up with lugging this!' He said, 'I'll put it out of the way over here or, maybe I'll hide it beneath this bush.' His carrying on over places of concealment provided a distraction, so that Francis and Mavis, silent and staring each other down, read each other's sincerity. Mavis did not know much of Tump, Francis realized, and Mavis recognized that, in her own way, Francis was as distressed by Tump as she had been. An unspoken agreement was reached then, and the impulse to bickering faded. It was recognized that neither had information worth disputing. Bernard was relieved of his burden, and they resumed hopping close to the bank, continuing in the down-stream direction. During the short time of silence between them, Mavis wondered if Bernard's hiding the weapon meant he was no longer interested in her decorating it, but then he said, 'Later, I'll go back for the weapon, after we get to wherever it is we're going. I'll bring it to you Missus Noy-Breen.' His addressing her in the present circumstance, as Missus Noy-Breen was a significant reminder that his politeness had never failed to impress. As, flibberty hop they went, at considerable distance now from New Warren and the Borderland complex, Mavis thought she had feared herself taken prisoner by them—taken away to deeks knew where—but by displaying respect, Bernard granted her an increased sense of security. She would like to imagine their friendship as genuine but perhaps that was foolishness. In any case, he was a friend of a sort.

Soon they came to a pleasant clearing and, seeing the place, Mavis, demurring to a quiet, inner delight, knew that suspicion of Francis Darkling was falling away.

Bernard, resting against the trunk of a tree, declared, 'I must say this *is* a pretty place!'

'Yes it is,' agreed Francis, giving him something of an intimidating look, which seemed the more out of place considering so much pleasantness lay all about. 'Bernard,' she said then, 'you will not tell anyone of this place. Do not so much as mention it in passing. I have not gone to effort for your easy undermining.'

'Effort?'

'Yes, *effort*, Bernard,' she insisted, and then, to Mavis, 'Old one, come this way. Follow me and I will show you your new burrows.'

Hopping to a far end of the lush grassy clearing, she instructed, 'Take care how you go, because long ago an excavation was carried out here. A deep pit was dug, and we don't want you falling into it.' Halting, Mavis peered down into a large, rectangular shaped hole. Much time had passed since the excavation was carried out, and by now loose soil and detritus had spilled into the hole, eroding its sheer sides in the process. The bottom of the hole contained stagnant water and dark mud from which protruded an enormous branch. In noting the detail, Mavis, seeing no large tree stood close by, decided that the branch, after being carried along by floodwater, was then swept down into the depths where it remained. Glancing away from the pit and looking about, she saw many formations—mounds—that to her, appeared unusual and of suspect origin. She said, 'These grass covered mounds lying all about are comprised of soil which once filled the hole.' She said, 'Such mounds are not natural formations. They're formed of soil long ago expelled from the deep pit.' Mavis said, 'I have a story involving strangeness—if you are willing to hear it?'

There was no time for tale telling. Francis hastened, saying, 'Noting those ancient mounds, *I* determined them as products of the excavation. The dirt did come from the hole, yes. It's very obvious.'

But Mavis insisted, 'Mounds are scattered far and wide. There are too many of them. They're too distant from the...' Francis was not inclined to listen and so Mavis did not continue.

Francis ordered, 'Bernard, if you can drag yourself away from lazing there, you can carry out a check of the new burrow. It's up-slope from here and we must be certain it's safe.'

'Safe?' Bernard called.

'That's right. I was here yesterday seeing to everything, but I want you to look for any sign of an interloper.'

'Brother Serpent, you mean?'

'Anything ... yes. Even that, Bernard.'

'But you are far more capable than I am in dealing with danger of the sort! Why should I venture there?'

'Because, Bernard, I ask you to do so. Because you are the only buck available.'

Bernard called back, 'No!'

Expression complicit, Francis told Mavis, 'He's a disaster. As far as working in with others, he's impossible!' She said, 'Do not fear Brother or Sister Serpent. I've scouted the entire area hereabout and none make their homes in the vicinity.'

Mavis again thought the keeper's problem was not that he failed to work in with others, but that he too often complied. By now they were farther up the slope, and there it was—an entranceway to what looked a perfect place for a home. Overhead, a mid-sized tree stood providing shade from the heat of day and outside the entranceway grass grew tall. She would not have far to go when hungry. Without further ado, Francis said, 'You should go in and see what I've prepared for you.'

But then Mavis paused. What if Bernard's fearing the worst, was not groundless? Might, Brother Serpent have taken up residence here?

Seeing her reluctant to enter, Francis Darkling told her, 'If a serpent or other danger were here, I would know of their presence. It's safe. But,' she added, 'when the keeper and I return to Borderland and New Warren, we shall leave you to your own resources. I shall visit you from time to time, but it's my hope that you will fare well enough alone.'

'But—why do you do this for me?'

'Because I was witness to the creature, Tump, taking your daughter. She was taken by it from the clearing in the great forest, and although at the time, the creature gave little of real information, it did mention you and your well-being. But as well, without instruction from it, I felt urged to see to your protection.' She shrugged, and said, 'Who can say, but perhaps in acting as I do, I'm urged by mystery beyond understanding, or perhaps it's more ordinary truth at work? I may wish to procure for myself a true part in events unfolding.'

Mavis was unable to contain curiosity and asked, 'What did it look like?'

'The thing, Tump?'

'Yes.'

'As to honest appearance, I cannot say,' Francis said. 'It pretended it was a relative of mine, a relative long departed. I was unable to determine its true appearance or nature.' She said, 'My position is not so different from your own. Your daughter was taken by it and yet, still, you have no real understanding of it.'

'What's a-foot?' Bernard asked. He'd come up-slope to see why it was they had not gone underground, and was curious as to the topic under discussion.

Francis was curt, 'It's doe-chatter, Bernard, nothing for your ears. You should go up there.' She waved towards the steep rise. 'Go up to high ground, just go.'

Bernard did not budge, 'I should appreciate seeing Missus Noy-Breen's new home.' He said, 'I'm curious. Why is she moving at all? It's a nice enough spot, but why is it that you insist she moves?'

'We're old friends, Bernard. Mavis and I share a long acquaintance, and the noise and confusion of the warren is not good for an aged individual. She is better off here.'

He glanced from one to other of them. As far as he knew it, Mavis Noy-Breen and Francis were not at all long acquainted. He needed time in which to think. He asked, 'Would you like me to gather fragrant leaves for you, Missus Noy-Breen?' He observed, 'A new burrow can smell of dampness and it's not until the soil settles that odour departs.'

Francis Darkling snapped, 'Keeper, there's no need for leaf gathering. Everything is provided!'

And so knowing he would encounter nothing unexpected, Bernard left them and set off for the top of the steep rise. If anything was unusual hereabout, it was Francis Darkling and her new, caring attitude. He was irked by her overbearing manner in ordering him carry out unnecessary reconnaissance. Perhaps she was sincere in caring for Missus Noy-Breen... He reminded himself of those occasions when Francis had gone out of her way in making fine work of saving him; she'd saved his hide many a time, and that should not be overlooked. The small hill was not as small as first thought.

Arriving at the top of the rise he was in time to catch a fleeting glimpse of two figures dashing for the cover of a distant thicket. Contrary to every expectation, Francis Darkling was correct because, at the new burrows

of Mavis Noy-Breen they were observed, espied by those now making a
dash for New Warren Central and Borderland.

FRANCIS

They were in the leader's chamber at Borderland.

'Word has reached me,' Zechariah accused, 'of you, Bernard, and you too, Francis, involved in furtive behaviour with an individual, described by reliable informants as, impossibly geriatric, an ancient doe.' Zechariah paused in speaking and scratched at his chin. He was thoughtful and raised his eyes skyward before enquiring, 'What *is it* that you two are up to, at that secret down-stream location?'

Bernard shrugged, 'Well...' He hesitated, and then blurted, 'We were doing someone a good turn. Doing a good deed!'

Before he went further, Francis said, 'Bernard is right. We've done nothing to be ashamed of.' She said, 'I will not countenance our being spied upon.'

'Won't you, Francis?'

'No, Leader, I won't. And I will appreciate your revealing the names of the informants.'

'They're good scouts, Francis, and were just doing their jobs, but yes you may be correct in wanting to know them.' He said, 'It seems fair. Indeed it does.' Raising his voice, he called, 'Lads! Step lively now. Come along in!'

The sound of scuffling came to them from the long burrow outside. Bernard was not absolutely certain as to his position, but despite a feeling of trepidation he believed he'd done nothing too wrong. Yet again, the leader fussed over nothing. They'd not informed Zechariah of removing Mavis Noy-Breen from New Warren Central, but there was no actual rule in place, decreeing that their acting as they did was in any way irregular. Of that Bernard was certain. Then again, though, rules and regulations were amended from time to time and sometimes with mercurial haste and so, maybe a rule of which he was not informed, now applied. He looked to Francis and noting her expression, one of restrained anger, understood that she knew no guilt over her actions. He moved his weight from one foot to the other, wishing he'd thought to relieve himself prior to coming here. He and Francis had been ordered to attend, with indecent haste.

He glanced again to Francis Darkling, who, upon first sighting changed ones entering the chamber, had spoken with voice raised to command, 'Bow in my presence! I've learned from the leader, that the keeper and I, have been spied upon?' She was on the offensive even before the leader had a chance to open his mouth. Hearing her, the changed ones were reminded of their place in the order and they'd bowed, albeit not as low as they might. Wanting to disallow the accused any further chance of taking proceedings into her paws, Zechariah the Great had commanded, You will say nothing more Francis nor you, Keeper, until they've—'

Francis would have none of it. Outraged, she interjected, 'This is ridiculous! I will not be made subject for scrutiny! Not by these *things!*' She ordered, 'Get you, *both now,* from my presence!'

The changed ones, fur bristling and eyes downcast, hastened to obey. She was supreme mistress of Hargolin, and receiving an order or instruction from her, they were not inclined to leastwise ignore her. She had taught them everything they knew; every skill of battling and strategy of war. Zechariah was leader and as such ruled all and sundry in the territory, that was true, but it was she, Francis Darkling, who in a significant practical sense was more the leader of changed ones than he. In the moment of her commanding, "Leave now!" Zechariah was presented something of a quandary.

Zechariah's resolve firmed, and he shouted, 'Lads! Stay as you are!' He shouted, commanding those outside the chamber, 'Bring her here!' Francis appeared subdued, as flanked by guards, Mavis Noy-Breen was brought tottering into the chamber. Bernard chastised himself then for remarking that the chamber was becoming crowded. If more were ordered to enter, then there would not be air enough to go around. Unbeknownst to him, after the muttered comment was made, evidence of a smile creased his countenance. Francis, noting his smile, was quick to cast him a small, disapproving glance in warning, but then Zechariah had noticed.

He demanded, 'Why do you grin, Keeper? There's nothing amusing to any of it!'

Rather than admit to smiling, Bernard proffered, 'I'm overcome by nausea. I'm feeling quite unwell.'

'I'm very glad to hear it, Bernard.' Zechariah offered, 'In the circumstance it seems right that you should experience discomfort. Would you like to rest? Take a load off, perhaps?'

Responding to sarcasm, Bernard said, 'Oh, it's nothing terminal. Lack of air—that's what it is. There are too many of us present for the size of the chamber.' The leader directed him a curious look, before declaring, 'You may think to jolly your way out of this, Keeper, but I'll have none of your droll cleverness. Be advised—watch your lip!'

Bernard, oft' times determined as thick, in both action and deed, now received a warning for cleverness. It was a pity, he thought, that pronouncement came as an accusation.

By now, Francis had regained her equilibrium and speaking before Bernard could, she enquired, 'Mavis, are you all right? Have they treated you well enough?'

'Well enough?' Zechariah questioned, and again, '*Well enough!* The hag is in league with you, involved in deeks knows what conspiracy, and you ask after her treatment! She's up to her ears in deceit—concealing mystery!' Turning to face Francis he went close to her, shouting, 'What is this *Tump,* this *thing* you're hiding?' Tirade unceasing, so none other might gain opportunity in which to speak, he continued, 'If it does not involve devious work of Tall Ones, then what *is* it!'

Wiping droplets of spittle from her cheek, Francis Darkling sighed and then spoke most firmly, 'I do *not* appreciate your spraying me.' And for the first time, her trancing voice was brought to bear and moved against Zechariah.

'You will be calm now, Zechariah,' she said. 'Your heart does not beat without skipping. It now misses a beat. And now, another... You grow calm and as your heart beats slow, your attention is focused upon its beating.'

Returning her unwavering gaze, and looking into her eyes as she focused upon his, Zechariah responded in measured tone, 'I say now ... I do declare, I'm not quite myself ... in fact I'm quite faint.'

She said, 'Yes. Yes. And you will rest now.'

The leader's eyelids grew heavier and heavier. His feet seemed no longer to touch ground. He was lighter, that much was very certain. Lighter so that he drifted aloft, borne higher and still higher upon the softest cloud, moved by the compelling current of the gentlest of breezes. His heart's frantic beating had slowed and an exhorting voice insisted it calm still further. The voice was not recognized as belonging to anyone of his acquaintance, but then there was something of familiarity about it. It urged him to peacefulness and that seemed a fine and sensible idea. The voice was smooth and fluid. It was kindness itself, and then his mind presented him an image of sap leaking from an injured tree.

Addressing Bernard, Francis said, 'Keeper, see those guards away from here. Get them out and the changed ones, too!'

Addressing Mavis Noy-Breen, she said, 'Why don't you sit down, Missus Noy-Breen?' This was more a demand than a request. Mavis was weak in the knees. She was upset and did not need being twice told. She knew something of Hargolin and its ways as all did, but had never experienced the result of it at such close quarters. She knew both enormous relief and pleasure, seeing the great troublemaker pacified by dark means.

One of the guards, a witness to the leader's subduing, hesitated against Bernard's urging; demonstrating reluctance to leave the chamber.

Francis wasted no time, 'Leave now underling or meet gazuzzlement!' She raised a threatening paw and levelled it at him. The guard stumbled over his feet then in making a hasty retreat. Still facing Zechariah the Great, she told him, 'Zechariah, all granted you, thus far, is pleasant. But know that if your will moves contrary to mine, and you decide against our mutant legions crossing yon' high hills, then blue-fire will be your reward. Our great army soon marches, but *not* against Tall Ones. And now, Leader, I compel your mind to meet with and taste blue-fire. You will ever after dread the fire of Hargolin.' So saying she lifted a paw and passed it before his countenance. Until the moment of her doing so, the leader had worn a beatific expression, but now his expression altered to one of uncertainty. When Francis Darkling allowed her paw fall to her side, the leader dropped as a tree felled to forest floor but with some difference; Zechariah writhed in unbearable agony.

Imagined pain was not his for long, for after several moments, Francis suggested, 'Your suffering will pass now, Zechariah, and you will forget. You cannot know why, but in future you will change your plan.' From that moment forward a subtle something at the back of Zechariah's mind would not cease gnawing; something was forgotten and would not be grasped.

* * *

The army marched, Mavis Noy-Breen with it. She was at first embarrassed by her mode of transportation, but after growing accustomed to it she thought it not so demeaning. Lemrik, a changed one, a mutant of reasonably passive nature, carried her. At least they had not expected her to walk. Mavis decided that she did not too much mind being hefted as a sack of veg' and carried along, slung against Lemrik's great muscular back. She enjoyed a good talk as much as anyone, and that was not to say that she revelled in idle chatter, but during the initial part of the journey, during which the steep incline of the high hill was surmounted, Lemrik was silent. He seemed good-natured enough but only after she enquired as to his favourite foods did he begin opening up to her. He revealed a fact, which surprised her; he did not actually favour the consumption of greens. He claimed to far prefer other, more usual things, such as those ordinary, wild growing grasses found flourishing at the banks of stream and in uncultivated fields. Attempting nothing other than small talk at first, Mavis had viewed changed ones as resultant of others consuming new greens and she did not believe that a great deal could be gained by any normal, such as she, paying them too much consideration. They were not, in a valid sense, Folk of Fur. Her suffering episodes back there at New Warren Central, while enduring howled shrieks of protest as they were separated from parents, dragged at heartstrings; that was true. It was ever so upsetting hearing them, and yet there was naught *she* might do to alter any of it.

After getting to know him a little, Mavis decided that Lemrik must be different from others of his kind, but then she soon realized that not just he, but *all* changed ones were Folk of Fur—far more so indeed, than she had admitted. Conversing on the straightforward, simple topic of favourite foods, led to Lemrik revealing his enjoyment of an unusual pastime. In a deep rumbling voice, which had taken Mavis some time to get used to, he mentioned he collected grass seeds. Mavis had never before heard the like, and she asked, 'Grass seeds, Lemrik? I did hear you, didn't I?'

'Yes, I'm sure you did.'

'And you gather and *keep* them?' Mavis enquired, 'You don't eat them or anything, dear? You just set them aside, for...'

'That's right.'

'And where are they kept, Lemrik? Keeping such would not be easy. They might very easily blow away and be lost, mightn't they?'

'Yes, but I keep them safe,' he said. He then took a moment to allow her to examine a small cloth pouch he carried slung over a shoulder. He did not open it, but assured her that the contents, a wide variety of grass seeds, were held within. Noting the pouch bore fine stitching, it was evident to a trained eye—such as Mavis possessed—as the work of nimble paws, and she enquired as to its origin.

Lemrik said, 'It was made by my mother and given to me when she was still Mother.'

'When she was still Mother?' Had she heard him? She, unthinking, enquired, 'Gazuzzlement was it dear?' Then, ruing the words, she decided, Oh my! How thoughtless of me!

'She still lives,' Lemrik assured. He explained, 'We changed ones do not keep our mothers. We are "motherless sons and daughters". We belong to the leader. We are his lads, his great joy to behold.' I have not seen Mother for a very long time, not since she gave me this.' Again, pride of possession was shown in his displaying the embroidered pouch. Mavis did not in the moment know quite what to say, but then she told him, 'Well, Lemrik, I just know she ever loves you. And I would ask you to tell her from me, when next you meet, that what you have there is the finest example of stitchery I've seen! I declare it so, and when it comes to such, I'm no slouch myself. She's a talented individual and any boy should be pleased having such a mother.'

'I am,' he said, and then was quiet.

Her opinion might cheer him and so Mavis said, 'You know, Lemrik, by your recognizing seeds as worthy of collecting, you've come up with something quite original.' She said, 'I will go so far as to declare you a most innovative individual, and I think it's wonderful.'

Reaching the top of the high hill, the great army halted. The leader, in close company with Francis Darkling, the Keeper of Rope and others, surveyed the new territory spread out before them. Even Mavis, possessing eyesight not as efficient as once was, in searching the wide vista, could not but note that at far distance was a place appearing greener than the rest. There was a place where Tump might abide. The leader and those others knew it. They intended bargaining and bartering and would use her as a means of exchange. If Tump was encountered at yon' distant place, then they thought to exchange her for a secret power. Observing the great leader and his entourage, Mavis decided that none of that intended by them was very surprising. As they saw her, she was not of much worth or value; they would barter ordinary old beets for prime squash.

Seeing them so involved in important discussion, she observed, 'We are not so different, Lemrik ... we, two.'

'Those of your kind are tried and true, Mavis,' Lemrik remarked. 'And we changed ones do not belong.'

She said, 'I would not place too much trust in ideas of that sort, Lemrik. Those who come after us may see your place in the grand scheme somewhat differently. Time has a way of altering the way we are perceived.'

LILITH AWAKE!

''Pon my word!' Piedmont exclaimed, 'The monstrous thing leaks, and something dreadful! Just look at it! It wasn't leaking this morning!' Although he spoke aloud he was quite alone and addressed none other than himself.

He was going through the kitchen on his way to the small room where, of late, much time was spent going through scratchings, putting them in order and then for large part, browsing through them, which for him represented a most pleasurable pastime.

Bringing them from their previous home, out front on the veranda, was no small task, but by now, with help from Sherbrook, Fixer and Skip, transferring the last bundles of scratchings into the house was all but accomplished. Hearing of Piedmont's undertaking, Skip had offered to move them, but Piedmont, thinking better than put them at risk, declined, explaining that he preferred transporting them by paw. Skip was sympathetic of his erring toward caution and had volunteered his service in assisting with the task, regardless of them going about it in the old manner.

Going through the kitchen earlier in the day, passing by the icy tomb on his way to his library, Piedmont had not noticed anything out of the ordinary. He was preoccupied at the time and so perhaps that was reason enough for his remaining oblivious to the fact that moisture was seeping out from within the tomb's interior. Now he saw wetness covered an extensive area of floor. Being preoccupied was usual for him, and so there were times when he failed to note detail of ordinary goings on about him. Other's view of the world was somewhat different—less vague, less blurred than his—but regarding present circumstances involving so much wetness, he was sure he was not mistaken. Had the floor been inundated earlier in the day then his feet would have been wet; the dampness would not have escaped attention. No, he decided, before this, he'd not seen anything untoward. He proceeded calling again, 'Sherbrook! Fixer! Peace! *Anyone!*'

He called several times more, and when Sherbrook and Clever Fixer arrived to stand next to him, Sherbrook, agreeing with his estimation of things, exclaimed, 'Yes, Piedmont! It's melting, and right before our eyes!'

'It's making an awful mess, isn't it?' Fixer observed.

Before this, the great sarcophagus had shown small signs of seepage, but compared with this, those other occasions involved only slight melting. By now the entire floor was flooded, and in order to stay dry, they stayed back by the doorway of Piedmont's library. The tomb was covered; draped by Peace with a fine spread taken from one of the bedrooms, but as the thin ice covering the outside of the chamber melted, the covering began to move, until slipping over the smooth, slick surface, it fell to the floor. Rivulets of moisture, tracing lines upon vertical surfaces of the tomb's front and sides, conveyed an uncanny impression of life. The Tall Ones' countenances, viewed beyond such a moving surface appeared animated, and as Piedmont commented, '...perfectly grotesque.' It was, Sherbrook thought, as if the buck went out of his way in presenting them an example of his grimmest expression. And then, both Peace and Skip, with Simple Rudy flibberty hopping close behind, came into view. They would not enter the kitchen but stopped in the doorway at the rooms opposite end to that occupied by Piedmont, Fixer and Sherbrook.

'Oh deeks!' Skip exclaimed.

Peace called, 'Nancy! Come and see! The tomb thaws!'

Simple Rudy explained, 'They are not moving—not yet! Soon though, Lilith awakes!'

Bunty shivered, 'Brrrrr!'

Piedmont repeated, 'Oh, 'pon my word...' As the rate of thawing increased, more and more liquid poured from the sarcophagus.

Nancy arrived to stand close to Peace Darkling. Noticing scratching etched upon a metal plate affixed to the tomb, she pointed to it, asking, 'Piedmont, I have not seen it before—what does it mean? Is it a message?' There was: *Terrence Thiery Corp. Cryogenic: 307A.*

Calling from across the room, Piedmont told her, 'I've never deciphered it, Nancy, but I think that before much longer you may have the opportunity to ask *them!*' He waved, indicating the Tall Ones.

Sherbrook scolded, 'I wouldn't joke, Buckaroo. Look!' There, at the front of the tomb, a red light glowed. Next, an ominous pulsing began.

Piedmont did not favour Sherbrook's manner of addressing him. Without taking his attention from the blinking red light he said, 'If you don't mind too much, Sherbrook, I'd appreciate you, not referring to me as Buckaroo.

Ignoring Piedmont, Sherbrook said, 'Things are warming up.'

Peace, from the opposite doorway, observed, 'I'm noticing it too. The room is becoming ever so warm.'

Clever said, 'The device prepares to set them free.'

Simple exclaimed, 'Lilith awakes!'

Skip turned, enquiring, 'Rudy, is that *all* you can say?'

* * *

Inside the cryogenic chamber, Lilith was returning to life. Memory stirred. 'My name is Lilith,' she said, 'Lilith Thiery…'

Granting her very best smile, she offered, 'If you like, you may call me Lil—Lil, for short.' She paused, and then went on, 'I'm starting school here at Battle-Seed Elementary, because my family has moved from Wycombe Falls, which is miles and miles from here.' Looking out over their heads she explained, 'We are a small family. There are just the three of us. There's Father of course, and there's my brother, Mydor, and then there's yours truly. My brother is starting school here today—same as me—but he's a year older and so he's in a different grade. Our family name is Thiery, and although we have no mother, we're not in any way dysfunctional. In fact, we're great! I'd have to say we're great anyway, because my father's such an amazing person. Father's an inventor, which means that for us life is never *ever* boring.'

Clasping pale, thin boned hands at her waist, she grew even more serious, saying, 'Although, Mother, Teresa Thiery by name, is gone from us and is very missed, we manage to get along.' After a significant pause, she said, 'We get along without her but we know the day must come when we Thierys shall be reunited. As my father often reminds, "She's not gone, because energy cannot die and in a universe of infinite possibility, she is extant". That means that we're certain of finding her!' She asked, 'Now, are there any questions?'

A dark haired, freckle-faced boy seated close to the front of the class, grinned, enquiring, 'What kind of a weird name is My—*dor?*' His way of pronouncing the uncommon name encouraged laughter from his classmates.

Her new teacher, Miss Ravenswood, admonished, 'That's enough of that, Millthorpe. It's not our way of welcoming a new friend!' She told Lilith, 'You mustn't allow yourself to be upset dear. Millthorpe sometimes goes out of his way in forgetting himself.' Still, sniggering came from the back of the room.

It was her first day here at Battle-Seed Elementary, but, confronted by rudeness from a fellow student, she maintained poise. Hands still clasped at her waist, she stared at him, declaring, 'You, my friend, could never be the boy of *my* dreams.' And then seeing him uncertain, 'You should know that my brother, Mydor, is much bigger than you.'

Memory faded and pain found a place.

There were sinew and bone, muscle and aching teeth and mouth; all were cause of suffering, and questioning began. What *were* teeth? What were they? The word altered—became the word tooth. And then again the word teeth, returning, presented something of quandary. Tooth—teeth? Both singular and plural were involved. Drifting curiosity inspired watchfulness as many questions presented themselves, some of which received too close scrutiny.

'Why do you ask *why* I made it? I made it, that's all, Lilith. I made it for *you!*' And then the sound of merry laughter and, 'Do you like it? Of course you do!'

'You said, "Out of phase with the realm"—didn't you?'

'Are we to remain here forever? I can't bear the thought of it!'

And then suddenly she was very young. 'Not much more than a sprout,' Father said, and she sat upon his knee. 'Don't jiggle about,' he told her. 'Do try to be still. I have something wonderful to show you.' He said, 'Mydor ... bring Pedro over here to me, will you please, and we'll see just how far he can jump.'

'He can jump about—yay high!' Lilith held out a hand, index finger and thumb splayed, showing she believed that Pedro the mouse could not jump far.

Father said, 'Yes, you're correct Lilith. Even as mice go, he's no great athlete, but let's see what our small friend is capable of, if given a little help from us shall we?' Taking the mouse from Mydor, and speaking more to himself than to the children, he said, 'Sooner it was me, if I believed harm would result.'

Slipping Pedro beneath a small, gauze covered dome, an item of kitchen-ware, previously used in keeping insects from cookies or cake, Father said, 'There you are, Pedro. Good little guy!'

At a far side of the room was a workbench and directing their attention to it, Father explained, 'Now watch, because I will ask *you* to judge whether or not this *very* mouse—the same mouse you see here, and no other—has made the extraordinary jump from this bench, to the one situated at far remove!' He said, 'It would be no good thing, would it—having a cheat for a father?' And taking up a small, innocent looking device comprised of wires and electronic components, Terrence Thiery instructed, 'Hop down now, Lilith, because before we go any farther I must consult the tree.' And so the three crossed to a corner of the room where myriad tiny leaves danced with living light, and crystal brightness increased at their approach. Peering into the tree's magical foliage, Father announced, 'Ah hah, then—it's as I thought.' Shifting his spectacles, the better to see, he determined, 'According to all shown here, Pedro is one hundred per cent safe.' Without further ado, he pressed a small green button of the device he held and then after hurrying back to the workbench, exclaimed, 'Ta—rah! There you have it, you see? Our friend, Pedro, is after all, quite extraordinary! He's made the leap!' He said, 'Mydor my boy, go across to the other bench and take a look in the shoebox there. I'm certain you'll find Pedro present and none the worse for wear!'

But Pedro was *not* there!

Three days followed the disappearance of Pedro and they were the longest of days, but during the afternoon of the third day, when looking into the shoebox and expecting to see nothing, Mydor exclaimed, 'Pedro—buddy! Where've you been? We've missed you!' And so it was that Terrence Thiery confronted with fact of Pedro's delayed return, realized that they were onto something more special than first imagined. In teleporting the little guy from one side of the workspace to another, not just space, but time as well, was traversed. Then too, *where* might he, Pedro, have gone? Many questions needed answering and Terrence wished that Pedro could speak.

The grass seed picked up by the mouse was strange and unidentifiable. There it was, clinging to his fur, and upon first seeing it, intuition suggested that inter-dimensional travel might be involved. He'd come back to them, though, and for the time being, that was the important thing; it was not just the children who were grateful for his safe return.

Further calculation ensued, and then the intrepid mouse was sent forth again to traverse the winds of space and time; travelling in his wire cage the "else-when" was explored. Transporting the cage, however, would make for sad outcome and none could have predicted the sacrifice incurred. Fate ruled against the mouse returning and after much time passed, Mydor honoured brave Pedro, explorer extraordinaire, with a service, during which heartfelt words were pronounced.

Again memory shifted course, and so Lilith was taken, rushing, sliding down slope and slipping back and back to yet another beginning, back to the morning of the start of trouble—real trouble—for the Thierys. She was now seventeen years of age and the awful James Millthorpe came calling at the farm.

It was a fine crisp morning and she'd decided it a day of uncommon contentment. Bluest, cloudless sky reigned overhead and despite the surrounding field and meadow bearing little of green, and lacking definite dancing brightness, as most varieties of wildflower were yet to bloom, a pleasant enough scene, composed of hues lifted from more sombre palette was presented, a palette spread with earthing umbers and fawns.

Hearing a distant sound she went to the parlour's window, and pushing aside the net-curtain saw at farthest point along the driveway, turning in from the blacktop bordering the front of the property, the grey Plymouth owned by James Millthorpe's father. Guessing that it was James, and not his parent, traversing the long dusty distance from the main road, the earlier feeling of lightness left her. She wished that either Mydor or her father were present to greet James Millthorpe, to know his reason for visiting and then to hasten him away, but with both relatives busy in the workshop, she alone would deal with him.

Millthorpe arrived with his cousin, Jeremy Crenshaw, whom she had not met before this. More familiar companions accompanied him also. They were James Millthorpe's pets, two great mastiffs, Maximillian and

Dora. Wherever James went, so too did they. Lilith was grateful for his leaving them in the vehicle.

By now it was long ago, but the first of their mornings at Battle-Seed Elementary had been confronting enough to mean that she could not find James Millthorpe's company agreeable, and since then nothing of real friendship had formed between them. Had he arrived at the cottage door alone, then he would not have been invited in, but seeing him with company, after an exchange of perfunctory greeting, the door was allowed wide open and the two were ushered into the parlour.

Meeting Millthorpe's cousin, Jeremy Crenshaw for the first time, Lilith was distracted enough by his presence to neglect activating the alarm at the cottage doorway, which sounding a warning in the basement workshop, would apprise her relatives of the presence of guests. That small act of forgetfulness on her part was the first of a series of mistakes, which made for unforeseen, devastating outcome. Like ripples moving upon proverbial waters, complication would spread.

Lilith soon realized that nothing of interest to her was intended for discussion. James Millthorpe rushed to regale her with grandiose notions of all they intended to accomplish. Just as soon as they'd embarked upon, as he referred to it, "…the business of innovation", then most ambitious plans would meet with fruition. Such was claimed, and all without so much as the smallest of preliminary pleasantry passing between parties. An introduction was made, but in the most cursory manner. She wondered whether Jeremy might not be so boorish as his cousin, James. If the cousin was free to speak, without Millthorpe's persistent contesting his right to do so, then she might know him better. Millthorpe was unabashed, describing himself as "…a powerhouse of entrepreneurial drive and know-how!" Nothing he said would temper her longstanding opinion of him. She wished he'd shut-up. Fuelled by self-importance, a detailed description of every type of fantastic dream was paraded, and unless she wanted to run the risk of appearing to Jeremy Crenshaw, as ill mannered as was James, she must forbear hearing him out. That he, James Millthorpe, in considering her as so much bounty and aspiring to possess her, expended so much effort to impress her, did not at all occur to Lilith. She was accustomed to regard him as nothing save the most unrelenting bore.

When her father, Terrence, and brother, Mydor, transited between the laboratory and hallway the fact of extraordinary, bright light flashing from hallway to parlour could not be denied.

Unaware of the presence of strangers in the home, a startled Terrence Thiery enquired as if the untoward had not occurred, 'Now then, Lilith. Where have I put my bifocals? Have you seen them about the place?' Then, as if having just realized they were present, 'Oh hello there gentlemen! How are you and to what do we owe the pleasure?' Turning back to Lilith, he asked, 'I don't recall you mentioning we'd be entertaining guests my dear, did you?' Before she could respond he enquired, 'Is there any cake? If we have any, why not offer them some?'

Mydor, exclaimed, 'Hi there, Cren!' He declared, 'You're here to romance my pretty little sis', aren't you, Jimmy Millthorpe?' Mydor slapped him upon a shoulder and James Millthorpe flushed red.

'What *was* that?' Millthorpe demanded, referring to the Thierys' dramatic entrance.

Feigning ignorance of James' meaning, Mydor enquired, 'What? Romancing?' Grinning he protested, 'You can't hide it, Jim. The entire county knows of your feeling for her! Going close to Lilith, at the same time looking to James, he said, 'If I were you, I wouldn't bother, Jim. You're not her type.' With exaggerated politeness, he asked, 'He's not, is he, Lil? I understand your feeling, don't I?'

Lilith agreed and she smiled. She admitted, 'Yes, I'm sorry, James, but you see it's still as I said, all that time ago in grade school. How did I put it then? Oh, yes, that's right. You can *never* be the one of my dreams.' She said, 'I do wish, James, that you were forthright in declaring your intention.'

And that was when her parent announced, 'I take it then, we have no cake? Apologies are in order then, because we've nothing at all to offer guests!' He said, 'You young fellows will have to call it a day and be on your way.' Terrence Thiery went to the door and held it wide open for them.

Hurrying back to the car, James Millthorpe was heard, declaring, 'There you see, cous'—Thiery's onto something! Did you see that weird flashing light—they're onto something big!'

Turning towards the back seat, he bellowed at the hounds, 'Shut up, you two! Lie down!' and, Maximillion whimpered like a pup.

Watching from the cottage veranda, seeing the old Plymouth reach the main road, all Terrence Thiery said was, 'Well—now the cat's amongst the pigeons!'

To the astonishment of most of those who'd known him during his boyhood and youth, James Millthorpe went on to amass a fortune. When Millthorpe Corporation, through manufacture of computer software and other products, succeeded so phenomenally well, and when the names, Millthorpe and Crenshaw were household names, looked to as icons of success in the world of high-tech innovation, the Thierys had much to protect. The name *Millthorpe* was never far from Terrence Thiery's mind. When he thought of Millthorpe's unstoppable success, Mydor would declare, 'Games for kids—whoever would have dreamed it!'

Over and again, scenes presented themselves as picture cards snapped from a deck. Events were relived, some in fleeting instant, others lasting for longer than they should, until, 'What will Father think of our releasing Bessie? If he were here, what would he decide?'

'Lilith, he loved Bessie but he would send her out.' Seeing her hesitating still, not wanting to let the bird go, Mydor smiled; he insisted, 'Release her, Lilith. Let her go.'

Holding the dove close to her for a moment longer, and looking into soulful eyes, Lilith said, 'Go free, friend Bessie, taking with you the seed of the wondrous tree. Keep it always safe with you until one of true worth is met. If a true inheritor, possessing cleverness, as Father's is not encountered while you live, then pass the seed to others of your kind. We will not forget you Bessie. Go now!' She ordered, 'Mydor—open the shield!'

Bessie's white tipped wings were a blur of movement against greyness, and, released from the vehicle named for her, she was projected out to the realm beyond. Lilith and Mydor followed her flight's progress as it was depicted on the large flat-screen of the parlour wall. They saw Bessie circled high, circling over a corpse littered landscape, a scene of carnage, beneath which they were trapped in the disabled *Dove*.

And then along with so much else, the recollection of Bessie's flying free slipped from her mind's grasp. But, words—sentences—snippets of disjointed memory of much else, persisted in surfacing.

'They are not at all rabbits, are they? They're strange, huge things by comparison. Mydor, what can they be?'

And then, was a great, noisome, confusing swarm.

Swarming of words—yet, each word, separate unto self, insistent upon conveying the need for close examination—each taking a turn at playing captive to a dull-flickering eye of dawning awareness. Confronted by such a mad dance of words, and struggling towards meaningful clarity, consciousness was overwhelmed and so began the slow and inexorable slipping back to the dark abyss, and any progress made in acquiring meaning was relinquished. She could not save herself, but then saving herself did not seem to matter. She could not choose other than to allow herself carried away to sleep. Descending ever deeper, the words, "calculation" and "solution" issued from surrounding blackness. They came to her as echoes. On and on without cease they sounded. Set to endless journeying with words as companions, Lilith met, of a sudden, with a new sensation—a sensation of icy wetness and fear. And then there was a distant and unattractive, plaintive sound, not words but the sound of guttural moaning arising from a deep inner place. Such a sound compelled she deal again with dawning consciousness.

Mydor, she murmured, more than once, and in sounding her brother's name, knew her own name was Lilith. It was not now her first day in attendance at Battle-Seed Elementary, but another time. 'I am Lilith.' She repeated, 'Lilith.' And, in pronouncing her name she was, for the first time, heard by Tump.

'I believe I may just faint to gazuzzlement!' Piedmont announced. 'Its voice is found!'

Skip said, 'And so we now know her name is indeed Lilith.'

Simple Rudy was about to speak, but denying him the opportunity, Skip told him, 'I know Rudy "Lilith awakes",' Rudy smiled.

'Oh, poor creatures! It's *just awful!*' Peace exclaimed with undeniable feeling.

'Poor creatures? They're Tall Ones!' Piedmont exclaimed.

'Yes they are,' Peace said, 'but would you enjoy such ordeal?'

Sherbrook stilled his legs; they wanted to shake.

Now, all trace of frosty covering had melted away, and there inside the glass tomb, long and cold-glistening metallic arms were seen. Metallic arms which, formed as they were, bore close resemblance to the cruel appendages of Brother Mantis. Such were released to rise from hidden recesses concealed somewhere in the tomb's base, and then next a faint humming was heard. When the arms had reached as high as they would, they halted, and sharp clicking sound emanated from the tomb. And then, following an important seeming pause, long, thorn-like needles showed themselves; they protruded out from two black box-like devices, devices attached near the highest ends of those arms. As the interior of the tomb began glowing a bright radish-red, needles were seen moving. They moved to pierce the flesh of giants. Following long moments more, those needles withdrew, and then light shining within the tomb altered, changing from red to blue. Cold blue light issuing from low down near the feet of Tall Ones, next began climbing in bursting waves so that, bathed by eerie light, the occupants presented a most frightful sight, giving Skip cause to declare, 'If they become dangerous to us, I will move them!'

'It's a terrible spectacle,' Peace said, 'but, don't move them. I want to see what comes of this.'

'I too, am curious,' Fixer said in full agreement.

'Do you see what comes of this, Skip?' Rudy asked.

'No, I don't see any of it,' replied Skip. He would not let Rudy upset him.

But it was not Rudy's intention to taunt or upset, which Skip realized, after Rudy explained, 'The map depicts very many possible outcomes occurring from this point on. Lines branch off and too many futures are shown. Soon, a shift occurs. A shifting of our reality is effected, and it's effected by the tree itself.' He said, 'Flickering of all about results.' He offered, 'I think, Skip, because there are so *many* possibilities, you're not able to see with clarity.'

'The tree has decided upon a course for us?' Peace asked, surprised. 'You mean to say, Rudy, it acts of its own accord, in its own right?'

'Yes,' Rudy assured. 'That's correct.'

Piedmont said, 'I don't think I like the sound of it!'

'Everything's fine. It all works out,' Rudy assured. 'The tree is permitted to act upon its own choice; it was determined to anyway.'

He added, ' It has my agreement.'

He did not, thought Nancy, sound certain enough. She said, 'You should have consulted us.' Her objection was too late, because even as she spoke, a flickering was evident and everything all about them moved. There was a great shimmering! Shapes of objects, including the tomb, shifted and distorted, wavering in a state of flux as if memory of its original form was lost, but then, as quick as it had begun, everything stilled, to appear as fixed as ever it was. The episode was of very short duration.

Seeing it was over, Rudy said, 'There now, you see, we've branched off! And next...'

'Lilith awakes!' Skip interjected, and this time it was true.

Even as he spoke, the smooth transparent panel of the front of the tomb began moving. As it went sliding in a smooth, horizontal motion from its former position to the new, there came a loud hissing sound! Perceiving the sound as that produced by serpents, Piedmont leaped back, going farther into the library than intended.

Sherbrook and Clever Fixer, speaking as one, called, 'Take care, Piedmont!' Yet, neither removed focus of attention from the great sarcophagus!

Now it was open, and noting movement within, Nancy gasped, 'I saw the doe's arm. *It moved!*'

Peace exclaimed, 'I saw it too!'

Skip braced himself, readying to move the entire frightening mess— tomb and Tall Ones both!

Lilith, venturing a small step forward, tripped against the low wall of the sarcophagus, to fall sprawling from the tomb's embrace and land upon the flooded floor!

Eyes wide with astonishment, Clever Fixer exclaimed, 'Well! We must trust that the buck has no similar idea because if he does, then the doe's in for an awful crushing!'

Lying helpless, the doe moaned as if granting his observation credence.

Peace said, 'The buck will not be going anywhere—not as I see it.' She shivered, 'I fear gazuzzlement has had its way.' She asked, 'Nancy, go fetch a covering from one of the sleeping chambers and bring it here. We can at least see her warm.' Unsure as to the wisdom of the suggestion, Nancy did not leave, but continued staring down at the unfortunate creature.

Skip told her, 'Don't go Nancy,' and without giving prior warning of his intention to do so, he moved the Tall One doe to a sleeping chamber at the front of the cottage.

Believing matters were improved, Piedmont, after venting a long sigh, announced, 'Best gone from sight; that's if anyone wants my opinion.'

'Yes,' agreed Skip. 'And I know you won't mind, Bard, but I've moved her to the room, which until now, you and Fixer have occupied.' Thinking to allay any objection, he hastened, 'Of course, you're very welcome to take my—'

The Bard interrupted, 'You've moved the creature to *our* place? You've relocated her *there* without so much as, by your leave? I declare!'

Piedmont was beside himself. 'Such audacity!' he exclaimed.

Clever Fixer told him, 'Fret not, old friend. We can take ourselves off to yon' barn.'

'But there's a principle involved!' Piedmont protested.

'The thing is, we must recognize that accommodations are limited,' Fixer smiled. 'The creature has been moved and so we also must move. It's not fair, but it's the way it is.' He suggested, 'There is one other alternative though, Bard. We *could* share.'

'No, no. I'd never be able to sleep for fear she might...'

'Oh you two! Where's your feeling for the suffering of others? After all we've been through, anyone might believe you've learned nothing at all! The Tall One, even if she were of a mind to, is incapable of harming us! We're Tump! As such, we will see right done to others—all others,' Peace insisted, 'including those of her kind.'

'Which will lead to trouble.'

Peace said, 'Venerable Bard, when the questing is over, and we stand as one before Him, will you inform Great Grandfather of your fear and loathing for His creature? Will you admit to selfishness in resenting her return from gazuzzlement? Will you confess to disallowing she rest her head in her own sleeping chamber?'

'There's nothing deep to any of it,' Piedmont said, and he shrugged. 'I just don't like them. That's all.'

'And neither do *I*,' Clever Fixer said, doing his best to sound supportive, whilst, if truth were told, he *did* look forward to talking with the daughter of the great Terrence Thiery. During their travels, which by now seemed quite long past, the seed had often regaled him with tales of the Thierys. Nevertheless, it was as true for Clever Fixer, as it was for Piedmont; neither much fancied the idea of sharing a chamber with a Tall One. As for learning more of Terrence, Clever Fixer was prepared to bide his time.

Sherbrook announced, 'You know what? I don't like the idea much, either.' He said, 'The cottage is a little snug, and I don't believe Great Grandfather's going to be too upset if I forego the privilege of sleeping under the same roof as a Tall One. Not so long ago, they were recognized as our enemies. A lot's changed; it's very true, but still...' His words trailed off, and then he said, 'After all, Peace, she *is* a Tall One isn't she? I don't believe Great Grandfather's going to mind too much if I take myself off to the barn with the others.'

They could all do as they pleased, she thought, and rather than respond to Sherbrook, she looked to Nancy, and asked, 'Are there any carrots—nice enough ones—left in the planting place? I imagine she'll be hungry when she wakes.'

'Oh, yes, she'll be ravenous!' agreed Nancy. 'But do you think that, perhaps, a formal gift of flowers may be more appreciated at first? I can't say why I've thought of it. It's just my feeling.'

'We shall offer both,' decided Peace. Turning to Skip, she enquired, 'Where do you stand in this? What's your position?' She sounded rather terse, he thought.

He said, 'I'm the one who thought to move the Tall One to somewhere decent in the first place, or have you forgotten? I don't know what all the fuss is over. What's wrong with you all?' Catching Piedmont staring at him, his expression dour, Skip averted his gaze. He next said, 'Come along then, Bunty, let's go outside.'

Bunty was not of much help. He responded, 'Why?'

Skip said, 'We'll go see if there's any sign of rain.'

Bunty said, 'It never rains at this time of day...'

GAZUZZLEMENT MEANS GONE

'Gazuzzlement means *gone*. It's self-explanatory!' Skip protested. 'For deeks' sake, the word says it!'

Peace agreed, 'Yes, of course it does, but try telling her! Go in there presenting bouquets... Put your best effort into conveying condolence and you'll soon see there's no dealing with it! We've, all of us, had occasion to mourn the passing of others, haven't we? We've coped with bereavement? She lies there as a sack of old veg', bemoaning his passing, as if believing that so much carry on will bring him back! From the start she understood *gazuzzlement*. You should move her outside to the plot, where confronted by tangible proof of his passing, she may come to better sense!'

Hoping she did not mean it, Skip said, 'I don't think it's such a good idea. Nancy and Fixer have crafted the arrangement of wooden sticks. It stands at one end of the mound, in full accord with our knowledge of their custom. I don't see there's much more we should do.'

Peace said, 'Now, Skip... I want you to go in there and *insist* that she leave the sleeping chamber.' Fearing the Tall One might comprehend her words, she lowered her voice to explain, 'She begins to smell, which is not at all pleasant. She drags herself out to the "bathroom", as she refers to it, but then always returns to the bed. *She does not groom!*' She said, 'It's high time she ceased expecting us to wait on her.'

Skip did not respond directly. He observed, 'Curious, isn't it, that upon her awakening she was not afraid when confronting our presence? She'd not the least idea of Folk of Fur. I expected she'd show great surprise.'

'Her reaction was not one of surprise, because in time past, she was acquainted with folk.'

'I'm not so sure,' he said, and explained, 'This morning I gave Rudy firm instruction to search, focusing upon the past, but he could find no evidence there of interaction between Lilith and folk.' Skip shrugged, and then admitted, 'He's able to trace lines back to a certain point, and then, can go no farther.'

'Why not?'

'He says he doesn't understand why. It's just the way of it.'

'Even with Nancy assisting him in searching?'

'Yes, it makes no difference. As yet, they've no clue.'

'Might the tree decide matters for itself again? Perhaps it blocks their searching?'

'Simple says he can't be certain,' Skip said. 'I did ask...'

Lilith was heard calling, 'Nancy! Peace! Oh, where on earth are you?' Although the precise meaning of every word was not understood, their names and her intent were discerned.

Peace, her tone indignant, said, 'Hearing her, you will enough know that she favours Nancy above me. I was the first to defend her right to comfortable quarters after you moved her from out there on the floor but, when she calls, it's *always* Nancy she first names.'

'Are you certain of it?'

'Of course I am. I have ears don't I!'

'When you're better acquainted, you may like her more.' He added, 'Simple Rudy has always been most adamant in claiming that you and she become the best of friends.'

'So much for Simple and his claims! Friendship? I don't think so!' Sounding weary, Peace said, 'I suppose I'll just have to go and see what's required on this occasion.'

Skip directed her a look denoting sympathy, before declaring, 'I'm going to take myself off to the barn.' He knew considerable relief then, because she did not insist again that he go to see Lilith.

Peace exerted conscious effort in collecting herself, before venturing, as bidden, to the bedroom. Arriving at the bedside she stood waiting, staring into Lilith's eyes.

Peace had decided that the Tall One's eyes were attractive because of their wondrous sky-blueness. Their depths held a mysterious appeal and she was cautious not to allow herself to be too drawn by them. She asked, 'Just what is it I can do for you, unhappy one? Would you like me to accompany you to the bathroom?' She added, as matter of course, 'Perhaps you should dry your cheeks.'

But Lilith's cheeks were dry. She had not been weeping. And then for the first time, Peace saw Lilith smile. Peace decided the overall effect was not fearsome and she attempted smiling in return.

'I've decided to get up,' Lilith said. 'I've been miserable for far too long. You must think me, terrible.' Her voice was soft, and Peace heard it as melodious. Lilith seemed brighter than at any time previously. She said, 'You look pretty in my things, by the way. That T suits you. I like it. You guys have made yourselves at home, haven't you?' She said, smiling, 'It's okay by the way. I'm glad.'

She left the bed and went to stand before the dresser. Atop the dresser was an antique, wood-framed mirror, and leaning forward to see her reflection, Lilith moaned, 'Oh my—I'm a fright!' Beneath the mirror, in its supporting base was set a very small drawer. Lilith slid it open and reached inside. Feeling about, she grimaced and then said, 'Here we are. I'm glad you folk weren't inquisitive enough to find it.' Withdrawing the hand, she held a small, rectangular, shining object. Turning to Peace, she commented, 'Looks a little like a remote, doesn't it? Not that you guys would know.' She said, 'Now I'm going to find something to put on. I'm going to take a shower—a cold one! When I can look at myself without cringing, we'll chat. Have a little meet and greet. How does that sound?'

Understanding very little, Peace simply stared. The doe seemed well enough at last, which was a good thing but whilst approving of such change, Peace would keep a sharp watch out for any untoward action.

Lilith next opened several dresser drawers and in the process, commented. 'Uh huh, my jeans are here and my other stuff. Lots of these things were not your size, were they? Or they weren't bright enough for you.' She said, 'I know you guys like lots of colour.' Then she said, 'There's no belt here. One of you needed a belt, huh? Mm. Okay, I can make do.' Her robe hung on the hook behind the bedroom door and she slipped into it. Pocketing the item retrieved from the drawer, she went from the room and down the hallway with Peace following her. She did not go first to the bathroom, as Peace expected her to, but continued on to the kitchen, where, after halting before a tall cupboard she reached high overhead. She said, 'My brother Mydor's such a stickler, he always puts things in their *proper* places.' She laughed, then said, 'We should find batteries here.' After a moment of searching, she was successful, 'Yep, here we are,' she said. From atop the cupboard she took down a package. Looking about the room, she said, 'I'm not going to ask how you went about removal of the cryo-unit, not to mention, my brother.' She was thoughtful. 'Nope. I don't want to know. Not yet.'

There was sound of the back door then as it slammed shut, and Lilith said, 'That'll be Nancy I guess?' It wasn't though. It was Clever Fixer. He'd come from the barn to the cottage for no other reason than boredom, with listening to Piedmont going on and on, proposing theories relating to the incident reported by Peace, of Lilith muttering the name Mydor whilst she slept.

Piedmont's favourite theory was, 'She's had access to old documents—scratchings—it's obvious. Over much time many scratchings have gone missing. They've been lost. Some have even been stolen and she might be in possession of such records. We don't know how long she was here before our finding the place, do we?'

Fixer was exhausted with countering Piedmont and his theorizing over the mystery.

'She was here for ages, Piedmont, that's true. But she was frozen! She was in no condition to roam the countryside picking up lost property or to set forth by night to go pilfering.'

'You claim that I'm mistaken? Do you have an alternative, more realistic suggestion, Clever?'

'No, Bard. But please think about it.'

'I have, Fixer, and I don't believe that you see it. I don't!'

Rather than argue, Clever Fixer left the barn, muttering to himself as he went. Despite the presence at the cottage of the controversial Tall One he would go across there and busy himself with, he knew not what. Maybe he'd spend time on the front veranda rocking in the bard's chair, which was an enjoyable and soothing pastime. Enduring the disadvantage of self-exile he'd missed the pleasure of it of late.

Lilith pulled the loose neck of the robe to herself. She asked, 'And whom might you be, friend?' She was at first startled seeing him, but knew better than laugh outright. Still though, he did present the most extraordinary sight. She declared, 'I'm Lilith. And you—you are a great, grey buck—and one of the most eccentric looking individuals I believe I've seen. I love the hat, by the way.' Then passing close to Fixer in the confining space of the narrow hallway leading to the bathroom, she told him, 'I like it. You show tremendous flair!' She brushed the flat of a hand against a long drooping feather of the hat, and then became serious. For, there on the wall before her, was the framed photograph, the image of her father, Terrence Thiery. The photograph was given long ago. How long ago was that by now? She could not know. Holding Bessie the dove against his chest, he smiled, perhaps across intervening eons. Might they hope to see each other again? Mydor was gone...

Upon first waking she had risen from the bed, and groped her way, staggering to the bathroom out back. Going by the kitchen doorway, the grey remains of her brother were glimpsed and then she'd known he was gone. Not the slimmest hope was held. The corpse was decomposing. Alone and far from her true home, her wish was that death hasten in taking her.

In passing along the hall she had vowed not to see her father's image and resolved to remove the photograph from its place on the wall. But now she returned her father's smile.

She had brushed at the long feathers adorning the buck's hat. He was quick in backing away from her. That was several moments ago, and now he kept well away, remaining close to the back door wherefrom he eyed her with suspicion.

Wanting him to know her as harmless, she withdrew the slim device from the pocket of her bathrobe and then, holding the hand out, the palm upwards before her, the device was offered for his inspection. With her other hand she motioned, twisting it this way and that. She asked, 'Screwdriver?' This was repeated, and then deciding that doing so any further was useless, she pointed a finger at herself and informed, 'Lilith. I am Lilith.' And pointing to him, she enquired, 'And *you are?*'

His response was cause for both surprise and some amusement. 'Screwdriver,' he said.

'Why yes,' she told him, allowing her gentlest smile. 'I *will* be requiring a screwdriver. But what is your name, clever one?'

Hearing her utter his name, Fixer responded, 'Clever.' He was pleased, but could not help wondering over her accurate guessing. But then he thought she *was* after all was said and done, the daughter of Terrence

Thiery, wasn't she? The great one's daughter had recognized *him*, and that might have been expected.

He declared, 'It is something of a mystery, Lilith. But I am the one chosen as true inheritor of the seed of the wondrous tree, the map of Great Grandfather. The tree, which in the first instance was entrusted to the care of Bessie the dove... I am indeed Clever Fixer.' Extending a paw in friendship, he allowed, 'At your service.'

In revealing his relationship with the seed, he'd waved a paw in the rough indication of the tree's present location, out there on the grassy area near the front of the cottage. In offering his service, he bowed deep from the waist. Expectation ran high, but then receiving a more or less off-paw response, he realized that his words were not comprehended as well as he would like. Receiving mere, dismissive shrug, in exchange for gallantry was disappointing.

Lilith was puzzled, and more so than Clever Fixer. She wondered whether folk, now residing in the *Dove,* were descended from folk earlier met? Were these folk related to those allowed residence, albeit residence of short duration, in the *Dove* during time now long past?

Hearing the buck speak, and recognizing several of those words used by him, she could not but wonder if his knowledge of language amounted to telling proof? As yet though, none of it was easy to determine. There was another thing, a trivial point perhaps and yet cause for further puzzlement, and that was his low bowing from the waist when he introduced himself. She was made mindful of none other than Zechariah the Great. The action impressed her as similar, theatrical posturing.

Long ago, she and Mydor had arrived in a new realm, the home of creatures of fur.

Dove hovered in a clear blue sky, high above a wide sweeping terrain, sophisticated sensors and cameras were focused upon all taking place below and from far and wide afield, scenes entailing carnage were captured. The vessel's computers supplied in-depth analysis of the nightmare in progress, all of which was committed to unfailing memory.

Confronted by cruel slaughter, the Thiery's first instinct was to hasten *Dove's* departure from the location. But there was good reason for making delay. Upon the sides of the great vessel of war—warring against the creatures, later know as Folk of Fur—was recognized the logo of none other than *Millthorpe Corporation*. The Millthorpe craft engaged in annihilation of creatures indigenous to this strange new world.

Dove was no ship of war and she went unarmed. Terrence Thiery had intended her as a vessel of exploration and so designed for that purpose her presence in any location was to remain undetected. But aiming to affect an end to cruel destruction, Mydor's employing precipitous measure had resulted in the vessel ending as good as sacrificed.

When warring was over, they had done all they could to aid survivors, but they had arrived in the realm too late, and in sacrificing the vessel, had after all, achieved little good. Many of the injured were taken into the *Dove*, but just two of those rescued had survived. Too many of those warrior folk, granted sanctuary, were beyond helping. Attending to the final, unhappy task, Lilith and Mydor, bidding the survivors farewell, had transported them out from the *Dove*, and back to their devastated world they went.

Lilith recalled that with those two gone, none, save she and her brother, remained. They had remained to forever sleep, entombed in the cryo-unit, embraced and supported by its life-sustaining systems.

She wondered now, where had these folk come from, and just how many of them were here? She determined to resolve the mystery of it… For now though, she simply *must* bathe!

When Lilith shut the bathroom door behind her, Peace instructed, 'To the barn, Fixer! Off with you now! You must helter and bring the rest of them back here with you! We must gather and attempt communication with her; when she's finished preening.'

'What can she be doing?' Fixer asked, 'Whatever it is it's more than just ordinary preening. I hear the sound of flooding water.'

'She thirsts,' Peace, told him.

She trusted that Lilith would not, on this occasion, cause messy flooding. 'She grooms,' she said. 'We must ensure everyone's here when she comes out.'

Seeing him tardy, she ordered, 'Hear me, and go now Fixer. Do not stand idly by.'

'Yes Ma'am!' Fixer exclaimed. But before conforming with her command, he asked, 'Did you see her swipe at my feathers?' He commented, 'Odd gesture wasn't it?'

'She owns many fine things, Fixer. Many fine articles of apparel, and so she was, of course, full of admiration for your grand hat.'

Fixer was certain that she must be right. The screen door closed then, and he was on his way.

Arriving at the barn he found that Piedmont was not amenable with the idea of accompanying him back to the cottage.

'Peace is quite capable of bumbling her way through,' said the bard. 'The Tall One can speak with her. It is my belief however that not much use can come of any of it, because language will confound.'

Sherbrook was not averse to going, but did wish the bard were less adamant in refusing. Skip was present and he too wanted all of them over there.

Sherbrook asked, 'Why not come along with us, Piedmont? If communication is impossible it won't matter much, but if she makes herself understood, then you wouldn't want to miss hearing her, would you?'

Piedmont thought hard before replying, 'It's all this talk of Mydor. I'm distressed by it. The Tall One speaks of her brother, as, Mydor. It's cause for preoccupation and I'm afraid I dwell too much upon it. I ask myself, what of *our* Mydor, the Great Mydor of legend? All of it perturbs.'

'Well, Piedmont, in my humble opinion, ' Sherbrook said, 'you should come to the cottage with us. It could prove better than sitting out here worrying. The Tall One might provide information to clear up the confusing mess. She could make sense of everything, of stuff you have not even thought of—and in short order, besides.'

'It's no *mess!*' Piedmont protested, 'I've studied all of the available material wherein Mydor receives mention. I've studied for a lifetime, and mark my words, Sherbrook, she can't offer *me* anything by way of enlightenment.'

Going to the back of the barn, Clever Fixer called, 'Sherbrook—where is the large metal box of tools—what have you done with it?'

'Why?'

'Lilith requires a screwdriver.'

'Which is?'

'The thing you use for manicuring your claws. I believe I saw you with it, just the other day.'

'Over there upon yon' table.'

'Good. I'm glad you thought to return it to its proper place.'

REVELATION

They were gathered in the parlour, and seeing the tool put to its true, intended use, Clever Fixer was entranced. He admired the Tall One's dexterity in removing a thin panel from one of the instrument's sides. Fingers and thumb performed the task. Clutching the screwdriver and twisting it around and around, the hand made short work of the job, and although he did not like to admit it, when it came to performing delicate work, hands seemed to have advantage over paws. He could not hang back with the others, but pushed close to the Tall One, studying the way she went about it.

There was one point in the proceedings, when, addressing him, she instructed, 'Here, if you insist upon standing so close, you may hold these for me. Don't drop them, will you?'

Not understanding, he directed her a quizzical look. She said, 'Open your paw, mister. I want you to take them.' Four small, intricate-shaped items were given him. She said, 'Those are screws, clever one.'

Hearing her again addressing him by name was wonderful, but it would not do for the others to believe he entertained notions of self-importance. He trusted though, they'd not failed to catch her mentioning his name.

'Now clever one, we will replace them,' she said. And one by one the screws were replaced. Finishing the task she held the tool up, declaring, 'Thank you for finding this and bringing it to me.' She told Fixer, 'I might have spent hours searching for it.' Next, she announced, 'Friends, prepare for astonishment. In a moment we shall make sense of *everything*.'

She was quite pleased with herself, Fixer thought, and he liked the way they'd worked together.

Bunty could not be with them. He had gone outside the realm, to visit with his mother, but of course, the rest of them were present and that included stubborn Piedmont. In the end he had relented, allowing them to convince him to accompany them.

After replacing the batteries of the device, Lilith motioned for Fixer and the rest of them to sit on the sofa by the window. The sofa was large, but then she realized it would not provide space enough for so many, and looking to Sherbrook and Skip, she asked, 'Maybe, if you don't mind too much, you folk can sit here on the edge of the coffee table?' She told Piedmont, 'Why don't you sit over here, old one? You can take my brother's chair. He would not object.' Mindful at that moment of her brother being well disposed to Folk of Fur, she commented, 'Mydor held folk in great affection.'

Hearing mention of Mydor, the bard knew curiosity enough to proceed as directed in a most subdued, polite manner. Moving to the armchair he nodded to Lilith in passing. Was it he, rather than the fixer wearing a hat, he might have gone so far as to dip it, out of respect.

In questioning the reason for his change of heart, the bard realized that his previous judgment was premature in the making and was altogether too severe. He'd judged the Tall One during time of abject helplessness. If the situation were reversed and it were he, imprisoned in dread tomb of ice, and then released to topple in watery disarray, he could not hope to present anything of an appealing sight. Seeing Lilith as if anew, made all the difference to his opinion of her. She *was* a Tall One of course—always the enemy—and that ought not be forgotten, but by now Tump was powerful and wise and no longer so threatened by their species.

She was attired in apparel of the type so favoured by Clever Fixer and Sherbrook. She wore a top of the brightest yellows and blues of extravagant, wild design, in combination with a pair of dark slacks. Piedmont considered her choices enhancing to both her hair colouring and complexion. He'd often heard Nancy and Peace Darkling fussing over their choices of apparel, and so he'd not managed complete disregard of such. As for him, taking things from cottage closets for personal use, that was an altogether other matter. He'd demonstrated complete restraint. His dark grey coat with its high collar had always best suited; nothing other than it, allowed him such scholarly air.

Lilith remained standing. She jabbed a finger against a small green button set against a side of the instrument she held. Then she put the instrument down on the surface of the large coffee table, where it was within close proximity of Skip. She announced, 'Soon now, we shall better understand one another. Of course, an introduction is in order.' Making a slight bow, she said, 'I am Lilith of the realm known as Earth. And just so you understand—it's a place very far from here, and yet is at once, close by. It's a place other than your world.' But then realizing that none present had comprehended her meaning, she swore, 'Oh, deeks! The translator!'

Hearing profanity from her, they smiled. Chortling, Nancy said, 'She means no harm, and it's good to know she's nowise omniscient or perfect!' Before Lilith could bend to retrieve the device from where it lay on the table, Skip took it up and passed it to her. Taking it from him, Lilith shook it hard. Holding it to her mouth, she enunciated, 'I am *Lilith!*'

'We *know* you are!' they chorused.

And, Lilith smiled with relief, knowing that now the translator worked. She said, 'In the first place, long ago, I came here with my good brother from a realm or world other than this. We came from Earth.'

As the first to respond, Skip asked, 'Another realm? Do you know anything then, of Tump?'

Apart from the question from the small buck, naught else was forthcoming. Nothing of astonishment or wonder showed in their expressions, and registering such a complete lack of surprise, Lilith wondered whether or not they'd grasped the import of the information given. She again repeated, 'We came from another world, a world complete unto itself and far from this.' They sat there quiet and still, and so she would ask a question of her own. Looking to the youngster, she enquired, 'All right then. What *is* Tump?'

They chorused, '*We are Tump!*'

'Is it a club?' she asked. 'Or a tribal name? What?'

'Tump is One! We are One!'

She was confused, but agreed, 'Yes.' Then, after counting aloud those before her, 'But you are seven. There *are* seven of you.'

'Yes,' Peace agreed, 'that is correct.' She proceeded then with introducing herself and the others. 'I am Peace Darkling. She, who watched over and cared for you, during your recovery from the cold ordeal, and there is Piedmont, the great bard. Here is my friend, Nancy, who cared for you also.' She smiled, saying, 'The others are Sherbrook and Skip the Seer and Simple Rudy. Clever Fixer is another of us. He, you know by name. When united as one, we are Tump. Tump is One.' She said, 'Providing explanation makes for more confusion.'

After a moment's consideration she suggested, 'Perhaps we should demonstrate?'

Looking to the others she asked, 'Shall we reveal the One?'

'She's a Tall One...' Piedmont said, sounding uncertain.

'You are One?' Lilith asked, of none in particular. A line of thought was suggested, but dismissing an urge to be led by it, she shook her head.

She, of such long, pretty ears, Peace, wearing borrowed clothing with such dash and flair, considered demonstrating something, something which she'd decided was beyond verbal explanation, and now the rest of them joined with her so that they stood gathered together as a tight-knit group. They presented a sweet sight, Lilith decided. Each of them she thought, adorable in his or her way, including even, the aged buck, although it seemed that he'd decided her unworthy of complete approval. When introduction was made he was supplied an important sounding title, by Peace. The bard was as cute as a button, standing along with his companions.

Peace advised, 'You may want to cover your eyes, Lilith.'

Believing that something of a game was proposed, Lilith did as suggested. She would pretend not to peek.

She heard Peace Darkling then declare, '*Tump is One!*'

It was Lilith's turn to experience astonishment.

Since Nancy joined them, Tump was complete. Raising the frequency of energy high and achieving the state of Oneness, was accomplished in an instant, and so...

Of a sudden, before her eyes, Lilith saw the truth of it! *Tump was indeed One!*

For no longer were there seven individuals present in the parlour. White light glowed, and then as fast as it had appeared, the light grew dim and definite individuality of physical form was lost, as a strange dissipation took place. Once solid appearing figures grew faint to the eye, and yet were discernable still, as thin-drawn outlines, outlines etched in light upon the atmosphere of the room. As those translucent, ghost-figures further faded, a strange melding occurred. Individual figures imposed themselves each upon the other, creating a confusion of moving, jumbled, overlapped features. Next, each of them was made more discernable and behaved as if presenting itself for inspection, and perhaps approval. Lilith was shown a series of transparencies; each superimposed one upon the other, each making itself clear in its own moment. In the first instant, it was Peace. In the following moment, Sherbrook stood before her. And then in quick succession, all seven were present, until of a sudden they vanished. In the following instant a large shining sphere of translucent, rainbow hued, swirling light formed in the parlour. A disembodied voice announced, 'You see, Lilith… Tump is One!'

Thoughts raced. As the daughter of Terrence Thiery, she was not inclined to deny nature's capacity to embody strangeness, and yet she could not credit as actual, that which confronted her. Tremulous, she stammered, 'Oh my! Yes. You are indeed *One!* You are! But how have you achieved this?' And then recalling events, events occurring in what was now a time long past, she was fearful and she asked, 'Does this power of yours have anything to do with *Hargolin?*'

A strange, chanted sound began. 'Mmeerah!' The sound was repeated. 'Mmeerah!' The droning continued for long moments, until spoken words sounded and the chanting was subdued.

'Oh no!' exclaimed the voice, sounding as all their voices combined, yet with the voice of Nancy emphasized above others. Nancy was heard laughing. Then, 'No! Ours is another, altogether different force. The force of Tump is passive—we do not war! In warring, we would lose every quality gained.'

'Mmeerah!' Gentle harmony rang throughout the room again, until they spoke as one. 'For Tump, Oneness is as easy as breathing! We traverse both space and time, Lilith!'

Nancy asked, then, 'How is it, Lilith, that *you* know of Hargolin? Hargolin is the invention of others, others of a realm not ours.' She said, 'Francis Darkling learned of Hargolin and taught its skills of war to folk of our realm. She taught Hargolin to changed ones, the offspring of those sustained by feeding on new greens. *How*, when you have come from the tomb of ice, can you know anything of Hargolin?'

The great glowing sphere pulsed. Myriad colours wound about the surface of it, making it difficult to focus upon. The affect induced in Lilith was soporific and disorienting. She looked away from the shifting orb and towards the window of the parlour, to the meadow beyond the glass, before replying, 'I learned of Hargolin upon first arriving in your world. I learned of it first-hand and were it up to me, I would choose best to forget it.' She added, 'I learned of it from those now long deceased, from your world's earliest inhabitants.'

'From long ago?' The voice queried and then was silent, and Lilith guessed that Tump was engrossed in a discussion considered private. Then came, 'We have studied the map, searching back through time, but without success.'

Simple Rudy said, 'We find there are many recorded instances of Hargolin practiced at both New Warren Central and Brickfield realm, but in our own realm, the realm of New Warren Central, there is nothing of it before Francis Darkling chanced to learn of it.' He said, 'When Francis Darkling, peering at her reflection in still waters of the stream, communicated with one named Zee, then, knowledge of Hargolin was passed between realms.' He said, 'It is most perplexing, your knowing of it.' His words trailed off.

Skip was heard, deciding, 'We can look again for Hargolin at any time. For now though, I want to move back.' He wanted to leave the orb, to be independent again of the others.

'There is one other event shown in the map, where the art of war has involvement,' said Simple Rudy. But it has no direct relevance to Lilith and her knowledge of Hargolin.'

'What is its relevance?' Nancy asked.

'It's a future event, an event of great importance to us,' Rudy said, and then he was silent. After a moment, Skip, sounding very impatient, asked, '*What is it then, Simple?* What happens?'

'I don't like relating it,' Rudy said. 'Because, there's nothing we can do to alter any of it ... nothing at all. I've searched the map for branching lines and there are none. As far as I'm able to tell, it won't matter much, whatever we might do to alter things, the outcome is always the same.'

'Same as what?' Sherbrook sounded as frustrated as Skip had, and was impatient with Rudy's hesitancy.

'There is, much of ga—gazuzzlement,' stammered Rudy. 'At least, I believe so.'

'You believe so?'

'Oh for deeks sake Rudy!' Peace exclaimed. 'Out with it—what must we expect? Be clear. Where and when does it occur?'

'It occurs *here* but not right here,' Rudy said. 'The event is close. It's very close and it takes place topside, at Ground Spring Warren!' Sounding panicked, as if the event he described took place in the very moment of explaining it, Simple Rudy rushed ahead, 'A great army of changed ones arrives topside. They are intent upon doing battle here! They threaten good folk with gazuzzlement! Then there is nothing—nothing at all—the map is as good as blank!'

'Blank scroll..?' Piedmont muttered, and nothing more.

'As you see it, there's naught we can do about any of it—it's not pre-vented?' Skip asked.

'No.'

They were quiet, until Rudy said, 'I suppose we could try to alter the outcome, but the tree does not show us doing anything of the sort. There's nothing helpful there at all, not in the map.'

'When all turns upside-down and sours, it will be on account of the confounding tree,' Piedmont said. 'It's too much a mind its own, and I've always said so.'

Peace said, 'I can't believe we do not act to prevent so dreadful a thing happening.'

'It's Zechariah the Great,' Nancy said, 'bringing disaster with him.' She looked from one to other of them, and it was, Skip thought, as if she believed it was she, and not Zechariah, who brought harm to the helpless folk of Ground Spring Warren.

Seeing her saddened, he volunteered, 'Let's move right now! We can move to the location of the event and study the situation!' He said, 'We can go to the top of the hill and conceal our presence behind the great split-stone.' He asked, 'How's that sound?'

'No.'

'What do you mean, Simple? Why not?'

'I'm not saying...' Rudy said.

Sherbrook interrupted. 'What the boy means, is that your suggestion is fine, but it's not what we do. Great Grandfather's map shows us there topside, during an event that is terrible but it shows us present there on just *one* occasion. We do *not* hide by the great stone. Is that it, Rudy? Is that what you mean?'

'Yes.' Rudy sighed, relieved at seeing difficulty averted; he did not enjoy disagreement with Skip.

Piedmont said, 'If we are present there just once, then that's the way of it. We cannot expect to see that which is not depicted. For the time being I feel we must abandon the timeless state and further attend the Tall One.'

Clever Fixer, who was quiet all along, now offered, 'When the army of changed ones is present, we can move many times—as oft' as it suits us—their downfall and defeat are a foregone conclusion.'

Skip said, 'Anything can be changed, and at any time. Again though, I'm confounded by the tree demonstrating unwillingness by not revealing all.'

'The Tall One…' Piedmont reminded.

Knowing his feeling towards Tall Ones, Peace wondered at Piedmont showing consideration for Lilith, but then her focus of attention shifted, because at the mention of the Tall One, Sherbrook became excited.

He was most emphatic, stating, '*Yes!* I want to ask her to explain the operation of the marvel in the barn,' He said, 'I want her to explain the truck!'

Peace asked, 'Her? By *her*, whom do you mean?'

'Why, Lilith, of course,' Sherbrook said, directing Peace a look which showed he believed her worse than remiss.

'Yes.' Peace told him, 'But *she* does have a name, Sherbrook. Where are your manners?' Sherbrook exhaled as if he were tired to the point of exhaustion. He'd fallen into another of the traps she enjoyed setting for him.

He said, 'The last I heard, *you* were complaining about flibberty hopping after her. You complained over dancing attendance to her every whim. But now it's *my* manners.'

'Or the lack thereof,' Peace told him.

He would not bother retaliating. He said, 'Look, if you want me, then you'll know where to find me. I'll be out in the barn.'

She was not privy to their conversation, but as Sherbrook spoke, Lilith saw the shining orb dim and decrease in size, and she heard Sherbrook asking, 'Skip?'

'Yes?'

'Move me, Buckaroo!'

Skip asked, 'Aren't you forgetting something?'

'What?'

'It's just a little word...' Skip told him.

'Oh no—not you, too!' Sherbrook exclaimed. 'Please!'

And Skip laughed, telling him, 'Just joshing!'

As she watched, Lilith saw the sphere pulse several times. It flickered and then—there they were again as individuals, all but the one of their number who'd gone off to the barn. They stood together at an opposite side of the room. 'You are quite something, aren't you?' she said, smiling, 'If I hadn't seen it myself, I could not have believed it.'

'We've always believed your kind "...quite something" too.' Peace admitted.

And, Piedmont, not wishing to seem provocative, but as he saw the matter, expressing an honest opinion, said, 'For most part, as something quite errant and unreliable.' Smiling, he offered, 'No offence intended of course,' and he glanced away, in case Peace, misconstruing his motive, admonished him, as she had Sherbrook.

'Errant?' Lilith asked. She was thoughtful, 'Why would you believe...'

Before she might complete the sentence, Piedmont, shaking his head from side to side, hastened, 'I meant nothing—in truth—I did not. Pay me no heed—no mind at all.'

But, Lilith would persist. She said, 'It seems very obvious that there are many things we need to discuss. Before we do though, I want you to show me what you've done with my brother. I want you to take me to him.

* * *

Standing gathered at the graveside, she asked, 'You interred him ... in the cryo-unit, you said?'

'The ice-tomb—yes,' Skip replied.

'But, *why* would you do such a thing?'

'Ah... Now that you ask, I'm not certain as to why.' Skip confessed, 'At the time of discussing what to do, I recall that we decided it best to not cause him unnecessary disturbance.'

Both, Skip and the bard had moved back away from the graveside, away from Lilith and the others. Voice soft, so as to avoid being overheard, Skip told Piedmont, 'Now she weeps, and yet before we came outside all was fine. She knew gazuzzlement was his, and had accepted the news of his passing, but look now.' He said, 'We should have stayed at the cottage and not brought her out here, because she sees the grave and now mourns anew.'

'She has not taken news of you burying him in the ice-tomb at all well,' Piedmont said. 'I have no idea at all as to why it should be so. Strange, peculiar creatures, aren't they? They're reliable in that a common-sense reaction to anything we do should not be expected.'

'Mm? Oh yes!' Skip agreed, 'They're erratic beyond belief.' Glancing towards the barn, he saw Sherbrook standing near the building's big red open doors. As it happened, he was looking their way. Sherbrook waved to him and Skip waved back. Hearing Lilith sobbing was not pleasant. Skip wished, that along with Sherbrook, he'd thought earlier of leaving the group. Returning his attention to Piedmont, he whispered, 'I don't know how Fixer can bear being over there with them. I'd have thought he'd prefer staying back here with us.'

'And for that matter, Simple Rudy,' Piedmont said.

'They hope to console her, I suppose,' Skip said. 'But look now. Sherbrook comes our way.'

Turning, Piedmont said, 'He's thick isn't he,' which was intended to pass as humour, but Skip, seeing Sherbrook flibberty hopping their way, nodded agreement. 'Out of the way—wasn't he?' Piedmont declared, 'But now going against all sense, he thinks to join us.' Sherbrook would be with them in moments.

Skip told Piedmont, 'I hope he says nothing to make matters worse.'

Drawing up next to them, Sherbrook declared, 'Buckaroos!' but got no farther.

'Shh!' they admonished. 'Our Tall One mourns the loss of her loved one. She is most pitiful in her distress.' Even as Piedmont spoke, four faces turned back from the graveside to face them.

'Forgive me. I *do* apologize,' Sherbrook called, feeling abashed after displaying insensitivity and causing disturbance, but then, thinking better of making further apology, he called, 'Tall One, Lilith, don't cry!' and he went flibberty hopping to join her at the graveside. There lay Mydor. Tender green shoots pushed their way to the surface of the mound covering the burial. Noticing them, Sherbrook commented, 'Grass will not grow upon the graves of those who were sustained in life by feeding upon new greens. That's correct, isn't it, Nancy?'

'That's as my mother told me,' Nancy agreed.

But then Sherbrook, going off at a tangent, and smiling, asked, 'The beautiful blue beast in yon' barn was *his*—wasn't it?' Gesturing to the place of rest, he suggested, 'If he was here, then I would ask him to teach me its ways. I would ask for instruction in its operation.' Lilith stared down at him, tears stained her cheeks, but her weeping stilled. Sherbrook questioned, 'If he were here *now*, and I asked it of him, do you think he might grant such a wish?'

Lilith, returned his gaze.

Tump is One, she thought.

By means well-nigh miraculous, a means unknown to her, but without benefit of machinery or technology, they'd succeeded in raising the frequency of energy high enough to achieve that which her father, her brother, Mydor and she—not to mention, James Millthorpe and Jeremy Crenshaw and the rest of them, could not even dream. And now this one—Sherbrook—wanted driving lessons... The thing he most wanted was to drive a pick-up.

Unable to prevent doing so, she burst into short, merry laughter. She wiped at tear-stained cheeks, and next, bending to meet his bright, unflinching gaze, she told him, 'You know what? I just bet he would! In fact, I know it. He'd be happy to grant your wish.' She reached out to him to ruffle the fur of his head. Sherbrook did not flinch. He did not enjoy having his head played with, but he was thrilled at her agreeing to teach him, and was glad seeing her smile.

'Well,' Sherbrook said, 'I'm *thrilled* by such an opportunity!' And he meant it.

Beast

PICK-UP

'I must teach you my language,' Lilith said, 'language of Tall Ones.' She chatted as she worked. She said, 'We won't have to depend so much, then, on the translator. A is for apple,' she told herself, 'and B is for beets,' she smiled. 'C, of course, is for carrots.' She chortled, deciding, 'Those examples will appeal to them.'

Hearing her, Piedmont, in an aside to Peace, questioned, 'Does she believe our stomachs are all we think of?'

Peace, shaking her head, replied, 'Mm, *she* certainly enjoys preoccupation with food-stuffs.'

Wiping at her brow with the back of a hand, Lilith told Sherbrook, 'You can stash these tools in back. We might need them again. I hope not, but you never know. That's right. Just toss 'em back there.' She said, 'Thank you Sherbrook.' And then, 'I can't get over the number of them! I've never seen so many spiders!' Earlier, when she opened the hood, evidence of web spinners was everywhere. 'Spiders!' she'd exclaimed, 'I've never liked them!' She'd brushed grey strands of clinging web from a sleeve of her jacket.

Peace had agreed, commenting, 'The heart of the beast is infested with them!'

Stowing tools into the back of the pick-up, Sherbrook discovered an item of interest, a rather worn copy of a magazine.

Seeing him with it, Lilith told him, 'It's something my brother subscribed to. He loved it. It's called *A User's Guide to Success in Living off the Land*.' She added, 'They published all kinds of interesting articles.'

Sherbrook leafed through pages and was curious; there were photographs and illustrations depicting so many unusual, fascinating things. He said, 'Bard, this will appeal to you. It's a marvellous example of scratching.' He gave the magazine over to Piedmont, who at the mention of his area of expertise, had moved closer.

Considerable time was spent lavishing attention on the pick-up. Apart from much else, Lilith had inflated the tires by using a hand-pump. The laborious task had taken ages and she was pleased when it was finished. She'd gone on to top up the engine oil from a drum found in the locker near the carpentry-bench; she'd checked the battery, which surprised her by being fine enough, even after the passing of so much time. She had fussed over the rest of the vehicle, with folk hovering close by. They had gathered as a group, and all but Piedmont observed progress made with the vehicle's resurrection. The bard, in leafing through *The Users Guide* was astonished by the quality of the publication. He did not understand Lilith's easy dismissing it.

'It's just a magazine,' she told him.

But, turning pages, he muttered and then every so often, voiced exclamation, such as, 'This is *wondrous* clarity of mark! Look at this! They have images of *actual* territory depicted here! Repeated, curious stabbing motions were made and he brushed a paw against pages in disbelief.

At one point, Lilith told him in off-paw manner, 'I'll have to teach you to read, Piedmont.'

He responded, 'Oh yes, would you? I would very much appreciate learning to better understand this!'

Sherbrook had stayed close to her. She gave him small tasks so that he was involved, so that he felt useful. 'Pass me the lug-wrench now please Sherbrook. Thank you. Have everyone stand back now. We don't want anyone hurt do we?' He'd stayed back, watching her use the jack. Lilith replaced one rear wheel with a spare, and after the tires were inflated she declared the task completed; the old workhorse was ready for testing.

When she seated herself behind the wheel and invited them to accompany her in the cab, Sherbrook released a joyous whoop, telling the others, 'Quick now—get in! Get in! This is it!' And then, seeing both Piedmont and Peace Darkling reluctant to do so, he yelled, 'Come on, for deeks' sake! Don't spoil it. Let's go!'

Knowing he'd waited long, and the opportunity meant so very much to him, they pushed themselves to show willingness, but all the same, Peace told him, 'Sherbrook, although I wish I could, I don't think I'm able to hop so high.' Piedmont, seeing a way out of getting aboard the beast, nodded in agreement, 'Yes, it's far and away too high for me too!' Looking to Lilith,

Sherbrook insisted, 'After all the work we've done, they *should* come!' He told Skip, 'Just, move them, Buckaroo, or we'll never get going!' No sooner was his request uttered, than they found themselves in the back where they would ride, along with Simple Rudy and Clever Fixer. Unlike the other two, Fixer expected to enjoy the experience as much as Sherbrook would. Nancy and Skip rode up front with Lilith, but Sherbrook sat closest with her. He was most conscientious in noting all that she did.

Before climbing aboard, Lilith took down a small metallic object from where it hung on a nail, which long ago was driven into one of the barn's supporting posts. Now seated behind the wheel, she held out a hand, palm upward for Sherbrook's attention. She told him, 'This is the ignition key. It's used to start the truck. Watch now.' Sherbrook needed no urging. In following her every move, his attention was unwavering. Fitting key to ignition and sounding nervous, she said, 'I hope I haven't forgotten anything, but here goes nothing, I guess.'

She turned the key. The blue pick-up roared into life! Lilith, grinning, exclaimed, 'Oh, wow! How about that after so much time!'

Next to her, Sherbrook was beside himself with excitement. He'd expected the extraordinary, but the sound of the motor in the confining space of the barn was a lot louder than he'd imagined. It sounded most ferocious!

The rear-view mirror did not provide adequate view of those in back. Twisting in her seat, Lilith glanced beyond the rear window. She said, 'They all seem suitably terrified back there.' She instructed Sherbrook, 'Tell them to hang on tight, we don't want anyone flying out.' Sherbrook shouted instruction, and then turned back as Lilith gunned the engine several times and the beast snarled fit to bust! Then when it calmed, she told him, 'Now watch me. See what I do.' She said, 'Clutch in. Then, shift into reverse—and now—easing back—back we go.' Within a moment they were out in the yard. Lilith asked, 'How are they, Sherbrook? Still with us?' She said, 'Tell them we'll be going a little faster now.'

Sherbrook was all but overwhelmed by excitement and without troubling to look behind, called, 'Hang on everyone! We are ready to helter!'

'Clutch in,' Lilith said. 'Shift into first gear.' She moved the stick shift and then said, 'Easing back on the clutch, and—we're off! Do you see?' She told him, 'It's as easy as pie, when you know how.'

'Easy as pie,' he echoed.

Glancing to them, she explained, 'Pie, of course, has nothing to do with it. I'll acquaint you with *that*, at some other time.'

Skip, looking to Nancy, who sat close by him, commented, 'They *are* cunning, aren't they? Who could guess that something of this sort could be so enjoyable?' Nancy replied, 'Oh yes, Tall Ones are amazing, but we're accomplished too.'

Lilith was telling Sherbrook, 'Now, clutch in—and shift into second gear. She told him, 'The realm is spacious, Sherbrook, but to have real fun, travelling an open road is the thing! We could go a lot faster then and you'd see what I mean.'

'Open road!' Sherbrook exclaimed.

'Yes. A great long ribbon of highway,' she said, 'Stretched out before us for miles and miles.'

Lilith took them along the dirt track leading from the barn and around behind the orchard. She said, 'These trees will soon be blossoming.' Espying a tree in particular, she said, 'I just adore peaches!' She said, 'We'll drive around for a while, but when we get back to the house, I'm going to show you my most beautiful warren. You'll love it, I know you will.'

'*You* have a warren, Lilith?' Nancy asked. 'Perhaps, you tease?'

'I would never do that,' Lilith said. 'Never. Just wait and you shall see what I mean.' Next, after halting the pick-up, she opened her door, got out and told Sherbrook, 'Okay, buddy. It's your turn now. Slide over.' Leaning against the cab, she asked, 'How are you guys in back? Have you enjoyed the ride?'

Piedmont replied, 'At first I confess, I was sick to my stomach with dread and fear of it, but then—yes, it's not so terrible is it?'

Both Peace and Simple Rudy nodded agreement. Simple Rudy offering, 'It's something I believe I could get used to.' He hastened adding, 'Although it is noisy.'

Peace smiled, saying, 'I like the feeling of the breeze blowing against my fur as we travel.' She said, 'When Tump travels it is instantaneous. There is not the same quality of relaxed enjoyment.' But then seeing Sherbrook moving behind the wheel, she lowered her voice to make a discreet enquiry. 'Would you very much mind, Lilith, if I flibberty hopped my way home, because the idea of allowing Sherbrook control, I confess, is cause for uncertainty.'

Lilith laughed, 'There's no harm in him learning. I'll be beside him, and if help's required, I'll take over. But if you want to go on foot, that's fine.'

Then from the vehicle's cab came deplorable cussing, as Sherbrook, now in the driver's seat, discovered that his feet did not reach the pedals. He was not capable of seeing anything beyond the windscreen, as, stretching and contorting he attempted peering past the steering wheel and over the vehicle's dashboard. 'Deeks! Oh, deeks! My kadoodling legs are *way* too short and so is the rest of me! What will I *do?*' He had an idea! He turned to Skip, imploring, 'I know, we'll become One! I shall take a Tall One form, then I *will* drive the truck!' Beseeching, Sherbrook cried, 'How about it? What do you say?' The others would have to agree, but Peace and the bard already proceeded back along the dusty track from orchard to cottage.

Lilith leaned into the cab, telling him, 'Slide over, Sherbrook. We'll soon get back to the barn and I'll attend to solving the problem.' She would use fencing-wire in affixing wooden blocks of suitable sizes to the vehicle's pedals in order that his feet reached them. He might also sit, raised higher on a firm cushion borrowed from the parlour. For the mean time, seeing his expression of misery, she told him, 'I'm very sorry, Sherbrook.'

He said, 'It's not your fault. I'm *short!*'

But she insisted, 'No. You're not short. The pick-up's a little on the large size, that's all.'

'Don't mind, Sherbrook,' Nancy said. 'You'll be driving soon enough.'

Skip told him, 'I don't know what all the fuss is about. If it were me, I'd move and be done with it.' Glancing about the truck's dusty interior, he said, 'It's all very fine and I do understand your infatuation with it. It's loud and impressive, but it's nothing by comparison with our way of getting about.'

'Yes, Buckaroo, but...' Sherbrook wanted to explain, but was cut short by Lilith's enquiring, 'Skip? You're in charge of moving?'

'Yes,' he told her, 'I move Tump.' Lilith had started the motor. She let it idle.

'I have several questions for you. You're the seer?' she asked, 'What does that entail?'

'Seeing future events and outcomes,' he told her.

'Yes. He sees events before they unfold. But, true to say, as I see it,' Sherbrook said, interrupting and sounding self-important, 'over recent time he's not been so accurate as once was, and there are many occasions when he sees not much at all of real worth.' Noting the way Skip glared, Sherbrook hastened to amend, 'It's not his fault. He's not to *blame*. It's just that as we attempt more and more difficult tasks, his talent's a little hard-pressed.'

Clever Fixer and Simple Rudy, having forsaken the bed of the pick-up, had come to stand near Lilith's open door.

Fixer elaborated. 'Both, Skip and Simple, each in his way, see for us. They are eyes for Tump. Even since Nancy joined us, though—making for far greater accuracy in undertakings—there are areas of mystery remaining, which still beset our efforts. We do not fail in any endeavour, but we lack complete enough understanding; we fall short and would prefer it were otherwise.'

It's, the map, Lilith thought. Her father, too, had considerable difficulty in dealing with its complexity. She sighed, and then asked, 'Will you explain your parts in Tump? Explain your roles? Each has his or her talent. I see that but tell me if you can—how does it work? How has it come about? What exactly *is* Tump?'

Skip began. Then as they began speaking at once, confusion was Lilith's lot until Skip commanded, 'Hush now! I shall tell it.' And so he did—with just occasional interruption from the rest. As the last to join with Tump, Nancy had the least to offer by way of explanation and so she remained quieter than the others. The tale they told was astounding. Folk of Fur were simple folk of meadowland and yet, through dint of self-belief and faith in questing, realization was theirs. A form of enlightenment was achieved, a state allowing them awe-inspiring ability. Lilith wondered, was such a state of realization possible only for their kind?

The tale Skip related involved visits to other realms. He spoke of inter-dimensional travel, of Tump journeying without advantage of technology. He claimed a visitation by Elder Tump—Tump returned to them from future time. The miraculous was theirs, and had resulted from practical application of ability. Lilith wished it were possible to introduce them to her father, Terrence.

She was perhaps most curious when learning of Nancy's talent. Request might meet with refusal but she enquired, 'Nancy—will you allow me to look into you?' She said, 'I cannot describe your story's effect upon me. I have difficulty getting my head around it. And that's to say, I believe all of it and yet I *can't* believe it!'

Fixer responded, 'Well, for our part, we believe achievement of your kind is without equal. You have created a wonder of your own, a realm unto itself—the *Dove!*'

Again they spoke at once. But then a voice rising above the others, offered, 'Look into me now, Lilith, and you shall meet yourself. When I have stepped aside, you may learn of much good to come.'

Lilith moved close to Nancy, and looking into her, could at first see nothing at all. Then, though, it was as if a peculiar fact were realized, and realized not by her, but by another on her behalf. Observation followed, and that realized was commented upon. 'These eyes are the brightest, the clearest ever seen. It is not just their shining which entrances, but far more. Glimmering rises up from great depth to shine forth as if pretence of comforting embrace is intended, but now—too late—I am not with fairness met, but am drawn down to go beyond the source of brightness to a still place of stygian gloom and silence. And now who am *I*? What will become of me?'

Then, an immense and all encompassing bright sky replaced darkness! A terrible sound of great shredding was heard and an opening was offered, an opening to an endless white space. As if pushed through an open doorway to then be caught up by rushing winds, she felt herself borne, rushing aloft, aloft to a far off place where mind was no longer encumbered by belief in any notion of linear thought. All was "known" as occurring at once. All was One.

ONE.

Nancy blinked.

And for a second time after the passing of an age, Lilith awoke.

'Friends, I now understand what's happened. I've seen it all and there is much to do. Almost as afterthought, Lilith added, I'm astonished that having achieved immortality, none of you is impressed enough to have mentioned it!'

'Immortality?' Fixer asked, grinning.

Lilith said, 'Yes. The Frequency of energy—spirit within, or life force—call it what you will—is raised high, high enough to mean that an on-going process of rejuvenation resulting in great longevity is yours. It may be true that death will not take you.' Seeing their expressions, she asked, 'You mean you didn't know?'

'Gazuzzlement is defeated then—in your opinion?' Fixer asked.

Receiving her nod of agreement, Clever Fixer, with long held dream realized, fainted clean away.

Most Beautiful Warren

'Power broadcast from the transmitter in the basement failed to reach the "collector" at my brother's section of the cryo-unit,' She told them. 'It's too late to benefit Mydor, but we need the power back on. We need it working up here in the cottage and I can't figure the problem with the transmitter unless you move me,' Lilith said. 'The transmitter is down there.' They were gathered in the parlour, and stabbing with a finger she pointed to the floor, explaining, 'When I was a child, just after Father developed a means of teleporting, or moving, as you have it, he removed the staircase and sealed the work-shop against intrusion. Other than teleporting, there's no way into the basement.' Gesturing to the floor, she said, 'I don't have a jackhammer handy right now, so, Skip move me down there because I must see to solving the problem.'

'We will all come with you, Lilith,' Peace said. 'I want to see your chambers.' She smiled, asking, 'And when you've fixed the electrical problem, you will show us television?'

'Television? Yes, I will show you it,' Lilith said. 'What you will see is anything but pleasant—in fact it's a most gruesome spectacle—but yes, I will share with you all I know. You will see all that happened long ago when I first came here.' She explained, 'With some of the systems working, it can be a lot more comfortable here.' She stood close to the wall bearing the large flat-screen and placed a hand against it. 'As I've said, this is a television screen but before it will work it needs power.' She said, 'Water is still pumped from the stream to the holding tank, supplying the kitchen and bathroom, and so the pump is still powered but the cottage lights don't work and neither do the stove or refrigerator in the kitchen.' Mindful of the power failing, she said, 'I'm lucky to be alive.' She sighed. 'But now we *do* need the T. V. working.'

She saw Sherbrook, Piedmont and Fixer cast each other meaningful glances. Seeing she noticed them, Sherbrook explained, 'We've long wondered over the wonderful smoothness of the large wall.' She smiled, 'It's a flat screen,' she told him, 'a very large one.' And then, returning her attention to Skip, she enquired, 'What *is* the matter, Skip? I'm more than ready.'

He said, 'Yes, but what if something goes awry?'

'I trust you,' she said. 'If anything goes wrong, I won't sue you. I promise!' She laughed. 'Come on maestro! Without delay!'

'All right then,' he said, 'but first, there is something which has long puzzled me and, if you are able, I would like you to explain it for me.' He went on, 'When our elders travel between realms—which we, young Tump, thus far have not attempted—light flashes and there is a scent of hot cinnamon buns, and an enormous kazooning sound. It's always puzzled me that when we move to and from the realm of the *Dove*, there is no accompanying sound.' Appearing most conscientious and sounding very serious, he explained, 'In thinking of moving you Lilith, I don't much like the thought of inviting disaster. When I moved you that first time, I did not know you at all, and then I believed you close to gazuzzlement, and so, I saw little chance of harm in it, but now there may be risk to your safety.'

'It's true. Things *have* gone astray in the past, with Skip's moving,' Fixer volunteered.

Peace, directing the fixer a most critical look, muttered, 'Things, Fixer? I do not consider myself a *thing!*'

Lilith questioned, 'Hot cinnamon buns? Buns?'

'Yes,' Skip responded, 'but the aroma of buns is of little importance. The question is more why, when we move to and from your realm, no great kazooning results?'

Lilith smiled. She said, 'The *Dove* is no realm as others are. She is not at all natural. *Dove* is an artificial construct, a product of invention, and whilst it can be seen as mimicking natural-occurring phenomena, it's not going to behave, when its confines are breached, in the same way as those realms with which your elders are familiar.' Holding her hands before her, she said, 'Whilst naturally occurring realms possess great individuality and are separated by a membranous, buffering energy, I will describe the *Dove* as *very* different. *Dove* is … as two hands touching.' She put her hands before her, the palms pressed close together. She said, 'Two hands as one.' She said, 'There is Tump—seven of you—and then Tump is

One. That's as it is? But then,' she said, 'It's not a good example of what I mean...' She thought before continuing, then said, 'If two hands are separated, one from the other, they are separate and yet strong similarity is shared. As left and right hands they are not one and same thing.' She said, 'Attempting to give an adequate explanation is difficult but there is not one *Dove*. There are two! Two *Doves* are extant at once and occupy very different locations.' Lilith sighed and then said, 'Where I come from, back home, the *Dove* did not wreak havoc when departure was effected. The Thiery farm, the cottage, the stream and meadow still remain there. The place is the same as ever was, and as for my father, he is there...' Holding arms wide out at both her sides, she said again, 'Two hands ... you see?' Bringing the hands together again, she sighed, 'How I wish—how I long for a reunion of hands.' None spoke, but they looked to her and waited. Lilith admonished herself for not having given a clear enough explanation. They'd still no idea at all, she thought, of what she'd meant. She admitted, 'I ramble,' but then she insisted, 'Skip, there is no danger at all, and you *must* move us.'

Pointing to the floor at his feet, Skip asked, 'Then, the warren which you describe as lying beneath us, is no realm within realm? It does not constitute another realm, as does *Dove*, in its sojourning here, as a small realm transposed within our own? There is no complication so far as you're aware, which could cause a dire outcome?'

'No,' she told him, and her expression revealed something of surprise. 'The laboratory is a part of *Dove*. They are one and the same realm.'

Seeing no likelihood of an untoward occurrence, Skip agreed and declared, 'We are there! And in the very same instant, they were!'

In the basement, where all about them lay in deep darkness, Lilith could see nothing of her surroundings. She rubbed at her eyes, willing them to adjust to the dark. Possessing excellent night-vision, Folk of Fur had recognized the extensive size of the warren. They made out forms and the shapes of those things known to them. There were table-like workbenches, walls, doors and many other things they could name, but as well, much of it was strange.

Peace exclaimed, 'This place is large enough for a great gathering of folk!'

Piedmont, said, 'Again—we find ourselves outdone by Tall Ones!'

Hearing him, and realizing he was close by, Lilith responded, 'Venerable one, if you will lend me your paw, then you can show me the way to a light switch. We Tall Ones may outdo you in many areas, but I cannot see as you do.' She hoped against hope that the lights down here were still in working order. Again she asked, 'Piedmont? Where are you?'

She felt his paw touch her hand, and he questioned, 'Just what is it you seek? Where would you have me lead you?'

'To the wall,' she said, taking a hold of his paw, 'There is a doorway with a cupboard standing near it. There's a switch on the wall nearby, for the lights.'

Skip called, 'It's this way, Piedmont!' Reaching up, not knowing what he should do, he happened to push against it, and of a sudden, the place was flooded with light.

'Ahh!' they exclaimed as one.

Lilith, letting go of Piedmont, then declared, 'Let there be light! Oh thank you Skip!' She crossed the wide, white expanse of the laboratory, weaving her way past workbenches supporting so much of her father's work, past apparatus of every variety: computers, tools and electronic components. The endless array of things familiar to her, all proved that apart from all else, Terrence Thiery was not the tidiest of individuals. She went to a large machine, which—occupying an area of its own—was surrounded by high, enclosing barriers of metal-mesh construction. She moved first to unlatch and open a gate, and then stepping inside, she stood before the collector.

She informed, 'This device borrows energy, electrical energy from the realm. Nothing is wasted, because nothing is consumed. In all realms there is a natural movement of energy—as of atmosphere, of waters, of river or ocean—and by means of certain trickery—in use of this device—we tap into a powerful force. After being side-tracked, or diverted by the collector, for our use, power is returned back to the energy-body of the realm.

'I declare it as work of Great Grandfather's paw!' Piedmont said, and would not go close to it.

'It is a work of the great Terrence Thiery,' declared Clever Fixer, both awed and delighted by such marvel.

Sherbrook exclaimed, 'First the truck, and now this!'

Peace said, 'Yes, but it does nothing.' She said, 'It's *bruk,*' and she heard Piedmont chortle. She asked, 'Is it cause for concern?'

'It is,' Lilith said, 'but now, I think I see the problem.'

Lilith sounded sad, and Nancy asked, 'What is it?' Following Lilith's gaze, Nancy thought she noticed something there, something not quite belonging with the rest of the collector. Pointing, she enquired, 'Can *that* be the problem?'

'Yes. It's Pedro and his cage.' Lilith said, 'His cage is welded fast to the transmitter and has disabled it.' Resting there, trapped amongst a tangle of bent and twisted wires—the remains of a cage—was the corpse of a tiny creature. The corpse was dried and shrunken in appearance. 'He was a mouse,' Lilith said. 'Just a mouse.'

When Pedro was sent forth upon the second of his voyages, he'd gone who knew where? He may have journeyed to future time, or perhaps before that, he'd gone elsewhere and else-when, to a place and time uncharted— uncharted, and not at the time of his setting out, revealed by the map? Answers might be sought for many questions. There was one thing, though, which was all too clear and that was, Pedro had returned to more or less the correct location, but with disastrous timing. Had he returned to the laboratory during the earlier time, when the Thierys had anticipated his arrival, then the problem, caused by the wire cage melding with the collector's transmitting component, receiving immediate attention, may have been resolved. As it was though, his returning to the *Dove,* only after the siblings had entered the cryo-unit, meant that Mydor could not survive.

Lilith told them, 'We will organize an alternative light source and then carry out repairs. And then we'll move back to the parlour.' Wasting no time, she instructed, 'Fixer, I'll get the tools and you will assist me.'

But, thought Lilith, when power is restored and you learn of your beginning, will you thank me then? Will you still be inclined to friendship with me? So far as Piedmont the Bard was concerned, she doubted that he would want to know her.

It was not long later that they were seated together as a tight-knit group in the parlour. Looking to them in turn, Lilith said, 'Folk of Fur are not long lived, not in comparison with Tall Ones.' She reiterated, 'Your generations are of short duration and humans live far longer lives, but now, in your case, there is a difference. *Your* energy sings! It is raised high and so Tump may well carry forward for time without end.

'Death will be mine, but for Tump it may not be anything the same. Tump has outwitted gazuzzlement. Tump is One and you are the proof of it.

'Now all of that, which I'll show you—everything you will see— took place not so far back in time, not as Tall Ones know it. There is no tactful way of imparting the truth. I wish there were, but there isn't.' Looking to Piedmont, she said, 'I believe, venerable one, that you are in for something of a shock. I would spare you disappointment, but if truth be served, I can't.' She said, 'Those decorated shields, so treasured in your quarters, out there in the laundry, are not relics of any bygone, glorious battle won, not at all. They are lids of trashcans, and neither of them was carried into battle by anyone known as Great Mydor. There was *no* Great Mydor. The one known as Mydor, was brother to me.' She said, 'He who owned the shield bearing the emblem of Brother Eagle's claw *was* Folk of Fur. That much is true. He called himself Zechariah the Great, but despite his vain enjoyment of others thinking him grand, he was no great hero at all, although,' she added, 'for the short time of their acquaintance, my brother and he liked each other well enough.' She said, 'Mydor was fond of them all, even the most ferocious of them, including those known by you as changed ones.'

She saw, Piedmont was not distressed, not the least upset, as she had imagined him. In learning that the detail of the history of folk might be disputed, she had believed he might be undermined and shattered, but such was not the case. As she spoke, he'd permitted himself a distracting gesture. He stroked at his whiskers, which she interpreted as indicating nervousness, but now that she'd finished speaking the gesture was disallowed, and Piedmont cleared his throat before making pronouncement of his own. Seeing him confident, was cause for relief and when he spoke, she was more than a little surprised.

'I have long known the records were false.' He said, 'In making a record of an event, truth ever falls victim. Facts are malleable. A scholar must always maintain something of a philosophical approach.

'The greatest spoil of war is perhaps, a victor's assumed right to record *their* version of the event, and then ... time has the power to alter.' He said, 'Folk have always known, that long ago Tall Ones were victorious.' He said, 'All of that recorded by means of scratching and verse and passed down through generations of folk, though there may be little truth to any of it, has sustained us.' He offered, 'Do not concern yourself on my account. I look forward to seeing the event played out.' He said, 'Activate your television, and do not worry over my reaction. As bard to Folk of Fur, I am ever grateful for the opportunity to better acquaint myself with truth.'

'Bard,' she said, 'you stand tall in my estimation.'

'Thank you,' Piedmont told her, and it seemed that they saw each other for the first time.

Always present in the room was a small, black, box-like object, but they'd not guessed its use. Lilith slipped a small bright-shining disc into a thin slot, and told them, 'Before I show you this, it should be understood that trouble for us, Mydor and myself included, began when an individual known as Millthorpe, gained knowledge of my father's work.' She said, 'Even consulting the tree, we did not discover the occasion or means of Millthorpe's theft. I have always known though, that I am to blame. I made a foolish mistake—an omission. Later, Millthorpe and his friend went on to emulate the results achieved by my father, and...' She said, 'I shall never forgive myself.'

'When my brother and I arrived in your realm, James Millthorpe's so named *Mission: Blue House* was already present. You see,' she explained, 'Mydor and I believed that in our realm of Earth, *Dove* was constructed first. She was built way *before* any other inter-dimensional vessel. But, upon our arrival in the realm of Folk of Fur, Mydor and I were confronted with the fact that *Blue House* had arrived here *before* us.' She said, 'Had we arrived first, then so much might have been prevented.'

'You were gollystomped!' Sherbrook exclaimed.

Lilith said, 'Yes, I suppose that might be it. We were gollystomped.' Smiling, she said, 'Don't sit too close now, and do try to remain calm.'

They saw the parlour wall *come to life!* Great kazooning erupted from concealed speakers and thundering filled the cottage! The entire wall moved as a scene of awesome, ferocious battle played out! So real was it that they leapt back, hiding their faces with paws! Sherbrook was no slouch when it came to facing danger but, leaping from the sofa, he rolled across the floor to crouch in a corner. He readied himself for what might follow! Clever Fixer just could not move! Shrieks came from the gals. They clutched at each other in panic! Skip and Simple Rudy remained calm.

Simple commented, 'The map sometimes shows frightening spectacles as this.' Skip smiled. He was subjected to far worse, he thought, in company of elder Skip, in the Tall Ones' realm.

Dove was transposed upon the fabric of the sky of a new world, and it floated, drifting. The new world spread out so far below, they were sure they would fall into and beyond the smooth surface of the enormous flatscreen. This was Brother Eagle's view of the world.

Down there upon the distant, wide brown plain, battle raged between opposing forces. At first, wisps of scudding cloud lying between *Dove* and the plain below obscured the scene, but then *Dove* descended lower, and the voices of Lilith and another were heard speaking. They spoke at noisome volume and, Tump was confused. Lilith was here with them in the parlour, and she spoke not at all.

Another voice, one they were not familiar with, commanded, 'System alert. Sweep the territory. Display the field down there! Bring up sound. Let's hear it!'

It was the voice of her brother, Mydor. Sound within the parlour all but deafened until Lilith made an adjustment to the device she held. Still though, coming to them were shrieks, groans and moans of those sustaining injury, and worse—meeting gazuzzlement! There was cruel mayhem: sounds of strange weaponry, roaring and kazooning, zinging and bellowing and blue light! Folk of Fur dealt the cold blue light of Hargolin, flaring against the orange-red fire of Tall One weaponry! All raged before them, and all of it was so *real!* Over such loudness was heard much confused, panicked babbling, as voices of Tall Ones threw out urgent questions, and their fellows made response.

'I read, Crenshaw—read you! What are they!'

Through the sizzling sound of breaking static came, 'Copy, sir—do you copy? They're armed and aggressive! No, they're not rabbits!'

Following another break in clear transmission they heard, 'No—*not rabbits!* And, 'Rabbit-*ish!*

'Fine, sir! Have it your way!'

A voice shrieked, 'Standish is down! *Blue House* is down Sir! We're hit!

Sherbrook enquired of the fixer, 'For deeks' sake, what *are* they jabbering about?'

'They refer to folk as creatures recognized and known by them as *rabbits!*' Fixer clutched at the edge of the sofa. He clutched so hard, his claws pierced the plaid-patterned fabric covering.

'*How dare they!*' Peace Darkling declared. 'They have no idea of us, not the least! Yet, even as imposing their presence in our world, they have gall enough to assume to *name* us!'

Nancy was heard agreeing.

Then, in scanning the field of battle, other voices came to them, voices possessing the familiar ring of Folk of Fur!

The voice of someone commanding the defending force, the voice of a leader, was heard ordering, 'Push forward now, Keeper! Seize the moment! Crush the Tall Ones. Show no mercy! Take no prisoners!'

There was the loud, voluminous sizzling of Hargolin! Nancy, recognizing the voice of Zechariah the Great, cried, 'It's him! It's Zechariah the Great. How *can* any of this be!'

'It is both a visual and auditory record of a past event,' Piedmont said as if knowing more than he did.

As darkening smears, set against the colour of a summer-dry field, copious blood flowed free—the life-blood of invader and defender both.

There was a moment in which Peace cried, much as Nancy had before her, voice querulous and puzzled, 'It is myself I hear! But *how can it be?*'

Lilith reassured, insisting, 'No! It's Francis you hear!'

Then Peace knew it was so.

Francis, engaged in close battling the foe, cried, 'You will never find your maker, Tall One! Flee to darkness beyond gazuzzlement!' In the parlour they heard the aggressor utter a shocking exclamation. They were sky-borne witness as yet another Tall One was cut down. With his torso sheared away from dark, armour-clad supporting appendages, the Tall One fell to the ground. The muscular body rolled twitching, into a low, confining ditch. The Tall One's mouth hung wide, forever silenced.

Thoughts of one such as Lemrik, a changed one, struck down in the heat of battle could never be imagined.

Brought down to sound of a barrage of explosions, Lemrik lay where he fell, recalling the tune of a song heard whilst young. Memory did not allow for complete recall of lyric or melody but, whilst awaiting gazuzzle-ment's embrace, he was comforted by scant recollection. As blood spilled to ground, and despite vision blurring, he noted, close by him, an unrec-ognized variety of plant. Seeing the plant gone to seed, he did not possess strength to reach for it. If Mother were present, or friend Mavis perhaps, they would pluck it away for him. He was far from home, from either New Warren Central or Borderland. He clutched at the seed-pouch, the product of nimble paws; love's gift. And then, gazuzzlement personified, and witnessed as a bright-shining presence, came flibberty hopping, long arms extended, offering kind comfort. He was invited to journey in true company to a place other than this.

Gazuzzlement bent low, 'Leave yourself here, good Lemrik, 'pon soil of battle-ground.' It said, 'Come with me. Come, journey to a better place.'

Scanning and recording continued in accordance with the dictate of the *Dove's* computers. Sensor drones, recording those parts of the battle car-ried out for most part at distance from the Millthorpe vessel, now moved closer in, to record detail of the vessel itself. Sweeping overhead, the ship was seen as resembling nothing more than an enormous web spinner; a machine, which, advancing upon its many long, dark appendages was apparently unstoppable. At intervals along its sides there were points of entry and exit, and many warring, bright-striped changed ones targeted these. Veritable storms of blue fire erupted at those points and dreadful clamouring was heard. Unceasing transmission of messages issued from the vehicle, and those transmissions intercepted, did not possess quite the same confident note as those heard earlier.

But those Tall Ones aboard the vessel, in disregard of its faltering, vowed nothing but, *'Fight on!'*

'Intruder detected! Sir, it's the Thiery bird! I have coordinates, sir!'

'Lock on, Mazengarb! *Fire at will!'*

From Lilith, came, *'Mydor! We're hit!'*

'We'll drift,' he said. 'Millthorpe will not win this. We'll put an end to their plan.' Mydor was calm and addressing the computer, commanded, 'Drones return. Set a drifting course and bring *Dove* to the far edge of the plain below—to this point.' He stabbed at a holographic screen and a dis-embodied voice responded, 'Location confirmed.' He might not hear that voice—his father's—communicating as the computer again. Following a drifting course, they were going down fast! They would not save themselves *and* ensure defeat of Millthorpe's Mission. Resolve firming, Mydor commanded, 'Maximize power to the shield! Set the *Dove* deep within the field below, beneath the hill, below that great standing stone!'

'But, Mydor, if we power up—'

'Quiet now, Lilith. Raise output as commanded!' Twisting to face her, he told her, 'The resulting wave will emanate out across the field!' He said, 'We are a pebble tossed into a pond! A rippling will occur and *Blue House* will never survive the effect of it! *Dove* is struck and will go down, but Millthorpe's mission will pass with us!' He commanded, 'Shift frequency—shift the *Dove* out of phase with the realm!' And, 'Hold on, Sis'!'

Even as warning was given, the great vessel dipped lower and conforming to instruction, her computers saw her transposed upon the substance of the realm. The *Dove* came to rest as Mydor wished, out of phase with the energy of the realm. The ground with which she shared space was all but undisturbed and yet, not all about remained as was, for, as Mydor predicted, a "rippling" of energy occurred, and increased then in intensity as it traversed to far reaches of the plain. At the highest point upon the hill, above the Dove's resting place, resonating beset the great jutting stone. Resonating, which continued until the stone was split asunder from top to low-most point.

At an end of the high stone-clad tunnels recently excavated, in line with the plan laid out by Zechariah the Great, was a warren similar in layout and design to that of the old Borderland. Zechariah's great meeting place, consisting of a large chamber, excavated by means of many hard toiling changed ones, was rendered unstable by dint of a partial cave-in of its high, vaulted ceiling. Damage sustained would not much matter, for following the Great War there were few survivors. All that remained to occupy the damaged chamber was Great Zechariah's throne, a rough assemblage of large and smooth-worked stones. These stones had caused a very small rent, a tearing to the outer edge of the *Dove,* which after eons passing would be discovered and provide access to the realm of *Dove* for one known as Bunty—Bunty of Ground Spring Warren—whose new friend, Skip, when hazarding opinion of the assemblage of stones and the purpose thereof, would propose that some sort of table was meant; but then, he was guessing. Of another matter he was more definite. There was not the slightest possibility of his fitting himself through such a small hole to enter from the cavern to a place of mystery.

Tump watched as Mydor ordered, 'Transporter—gather them in!'

A small band of survivors were taken from the field. Teleported away from a bloodied field to arrive in the *Dove*. Finding themselves captive, as they believed, of Tall Ones, after all they'd endured, several changed ones amongst them, threw themselves face-down upon the cottage lawn as a sign of defeat and surrender, but Zechariah the Great and Bernard wasted no time at all before marching, shields raised before them, to confront Mydor.

They enquired then, as if knowing it as foregone conclusion, 'We are for gazuzzlement then?'

Mydor smiled and said nothing at all.

Francis Darkling, who'd stayed back at the lawn's far edge and close to the meadow, called, 'These are not warriors. They are very different!' Coming out onto the cottage veranda was a dark-haired doe, and Francis recognized, by means she little understood, that these Tall Ones would not attempt harming them.

Piedmont was perhaps the more avid viewer now that the terrifying scenes of battle were over. He asked, 'Do any of you see what I see?' He pointed towards the screen, 'Look! Right there on the grass! It's the thing long ago decided as a receptacle for droppings! It's one and same!'

Lilith laughed, telling him, 'It's my birdbath venerable one! That's what it is!'

'A place provided for feathered brothers and sisters to bathe...' he said, sounding nonplussed. 'Why is *it* no longer here in the realm, but outside?' He explained, 'It was part of the furnished quarters provided us by Leader Crenshaw.'

'A simple mistake on my part,' Lilith admitted, 'I sent it out by accident, out from the *Dove,* with Folk of Fur.' She then enquired, 'Crenshaw. You mentioned the name, Crenshaw?'

'Yes—Crenshaw.' Piedmont paused then offered, 'Names were confused weren't they—along with so much else? Over time, many, many names must have been appropriated by Folk of Fur.'

'Yes, Bard. I believe you're correct.'

'I'm not sure whether to be saddened,' he said, 'or, to laugh outright.'

She offered, 'Perhaps a little of each is appropriate response.'

He asked, Then, 'Lilith, which of them began it all? Which of them began our world? Will you say?'

'Their names were Bernard and Francis.' Thinking back, she said, 'They were the two, sent forth. And of course, there was the small matter of my birdbath, and following upon that was my dear friend, Bessie. Bessie the dove was sent off, carrying the seed.' She added, 'Without my brother and I to care for it, knowing its fate, the tree had produced the seed.'

'Whatever became of Zechariah?' Nancy asked.

'Out there...' Lilith gestured. 'He occupies a place over near the orchard.'

'Oh,' said Nancy, and no more.

Skip asked, 'Why were you and Mydor in the kitchen, imprisoned in the tomb of ice?'

'We took our chances,' she said. 'We took our chance at survival by extreme means and hoped we might be found at a far off time. In the kitchen—is that your meaning? In the kitchen rather than a place such as the laboratory?' She said, 'Because my wonderful brother, Great Mydor, wished to see a favourite place. He thought the orchard was best seen from the kitchen window of a morning. Upon waking from cold sleep, it's what he wanted as the first sight greeting him. That's why we were there.'

She depressed a button of the device in her hand and the screen went black.

Skip said, 'Hush. No one speak now.' He asked, 'Is it Bunty I hear?'

Going to the cottage doorway, Sherbrook announced, 'Yep, you're right. It's him, the twerp!'

Coming across the lawn out front, Bunty cried, 'Catastrophe befalls us! An army is topside! Ground Spring is surrounded. You must come quickly! Oh help!'

Skip told him, 'Old news, Bunty! Fear not. We're on our way!'

ARISE!

Zechariah waited for a leader or even someone acting as messenger, to come forward and speak with him. In an aside to Francis Darkling, he said, 'Can you imagine their feeling of trepidation? I can! Just look at them. Fear shows upon every face! The air is thick with the scent of dread!' He decided, 'We shall wait awhile longer, Francis. The troops are positioned and now they can stand easy. We'll draw this out. I will enjoy whatever it is they decide as their first move.' He then asked, 'Do you see the creature, Tump, hiding anywhere in yon' sorry gathering?' Francis said nothing, and so, he questioned, 'Why, so quiet, Francis? Have you second thoughts?' Expression sour, and before she could respond, he asked, 'Francis—after having your way in insisting we drag ourselves here, you don't doubt the rightness of that decision, do you?' Still, she did not speak, and he said, 'Bernard informed on you Francis. As loyal servant to me, he had no choice. He informed of your coercing me into setting us upon the present course. In truth, Francis, you underestimate me.' He turned away from her.

She'd not responded to direct questioning, but now Francis admitted, 'Leader, I don't like any of this. I'm feeling most uneasy.'

'Uneasy?' Zechariah asked, sounding preoccupied and vague. He asked, 'Where *is* the Keeper? He should be at my side.' Searching about, there was no sign at all of Bernard. Then he said, 'There's no cause for uneasiness, Francis. This insignificant warren with its poor pathetic creatures can be dispatched in a blink.' After a momentary silence, he offered, 'Mention of your treachery has upset your natural equilibrium, that's what it is, but fear not, Francis, your unfortunate lapse is behind us. You see I'm nothing if not forgiving. I am, by very nature, forgiving.' He cautioned, 'Of course, never assume largesse too forthcoming. We all have natural limits.' Casting a severe look, he told her, 'Even dream again, Francis, of employing Hargolin against me and you will own a most terrible fate.' Then smiling, he enquired, 'Lemrik, isn't it? He's the one lugging the ancient doe? In any case, whoever he is, it's time to get him over here, with her. Attend to it, Francis. I'll need her here before negotiations begin.'

Exiting Ground Spring Warren and confronting so horrifying a spectacle, Leader Crenshaw's feeling was one of abject helplessness. He must feign calm in facing imminent annihilation. He would steel himself and await word from whomsoever commanded such an awesome number of warriors—warriors of such dreadful, unnatural appearance—of so obvious, gazuzzling intent. He wondered, apart from annihilation of his territory and its inhabitants, what was it they wanted? What *could* they seek of the good folk of Ground Spring? Whatever it was, Crenshaw knew it was nothing within his power to give. Even granting the right to drink from the spring would present impossibility. Permitting even so little, to each of so large a number of individuals, would risk total depletion of the resource. Wouldn't the agonized ground, sucked dry by the oppressing hoard, cry out? There were other questions. From *whence* had they come? Were even greater number of them farther afield, or was this all that they—local folk—should expect? They were nothing any sane individual would wish to meet, and for the first time as leader of Ground Spring, Crenshaw would rather he were not leader at all. He was unable to get past the evidence of his eyes. It was too mad! An actual *army* had come visiting.

His poor mind cringed in attempting to deal with the unlikelihood of such a reality and, recognizing defeat, it might give up on him. Then, Crenshaw, mind still awhirl and flying off in various directions at once, knew that if they wanted to drink, which was all Ground Spring could offer any passers-by, they might just as well go right ahead and help themselves. Although he was entrusted with the management of things hereabout, there was nothing he could do to prevent this lot doing just as they pleased. By now, others had arrived, and so he stood in company of relatives and friends, feeling very alone.

When the bard arrived to stand at his side, the leader was very glad to see him. For Crenshaw, the bard was a reminder of sane conservatism and normalcy. His presence now was a welcome distraction.

The bard stood then, surveying the hoard. He did not speak. For his part, Crenshaw greeted the bard, by observing, 'We haven't seen you for some considerable time, friend.'

To which, Piedmont then responded, 'Yes, it's as you say, Leader.' He offered, 'Our little group has been rather busy of late. We go about our business, moving to and fro, hither and yon'. How about you, friend Crenshaw? How have you been keeping?' As respectful acknowledgement, he nodded to several of those gathered. 'How are the family?' he asked. 'All are well, I trust.'

'Oh yes, well enough,' Crenshaw allowed. He gestured, as if dismissing the assurance given, before amending, 'That was true until this morning.'

With the barest of smiles, and keeping his voice low, Piedmont, looking to the insurgents occupying the field before them, acknowledged, 'Yes, they make for a most impressive sight don't they?' He hastened, adding, 'That is of course, as they see themselves, whereas we cannot take such a blatant example of exhibitionism with seriousness.' He observed, 'Yon' diminutive and rather comical leader aims to rattle us. By neither acting, or troubling to declare his intention, he ensures suspense builds amongst the good, hospitable folk of Ground Spring.' Gazing about, he confirmed, 'Suspense is palpable...' And then looking more to Crenshaw, 'Challenged by such a pathetic ruse, we know better than allow ourselves to be overtaken by panic, don't we friend Crenshaw?' The bard shrugged and his smile increased. Solicitous, he advised, 'In remaining calm, an impression of authority can be maintained.' He said then, 'Ah now, I see good company approaches.'

After moving from the *Dove,* the others had exited Ground Spring by way of one of the warren's narrow, escape burrows. Now, they flibberty hopped, weaving their way through the crowd to join Piedmont and Crenshaw. Piedmont was the first to have left the *Dove.* He'd taken leave of them, hurrying off after first studying the map, which showed him doing so. And now, they were here.

Sherbrook, the first of them to speak, greeted Crenshaw, 'Hello there, Leader.' And in considering the leader's dilemma, said, 'I imagine that you're not inclined to offer this lot hospitality, not as you showed us?' He smiled in a supportive manner and then looking across a short dip in the landscape to the great gathering of legions, remarked, 'They're rabble aren't they.' To Piedmont, he observed, 'In the flesh, they're very different from what we've seen. They're rabble, but it must be admitted that they present an awesome sight.' Spotting the brothers, Dimster and Dempster, as they waved from the crowd, he returned the courtesy.

He heard Nancy exclaiming, 'Why look! Riding there, astride yon' great beast! *It's Mother!'*

Peace, knowing that in an instant Nancy might helter away, rested a firm paw upon the gal's shoulder. She insisted, 'Tump will wait.'

After arriving to stand upon the grassy knoll in the company of Leader Crenshaw and the others, Peace was quick in assessing the situation. Troops surrounded Ground Spring Warren. Their ranks stretched wide. They covered the plain and the small hill at every side. There was a detachment of changed ones, gaudy-striped beasts, stationed there on the hilltop near the great split-stone. From the highest vantage point they surveyed the plain below and their gaze encompassed every entry and exit point of Ground Spring Warren.

Up there, a changed one, gesturing to the entryway of the spiral excavation carried out during an earlier time by Skip, observed, 'This opening resembles *our* work and not the work of normals. He kicked several boulder-sized stones away from the entryway, and going close, commented, 'It's not as large as tunnels made by us, but the work to the walls was well executed. The stones are smoothed. It's good work.' Lolling close by, several others glanced across to him and nodded, agreeing with his estimation.

Tump and others stood on the low knoll. At a short distance from them, beyond a place where the terrain dipped before rising again and then levelling out, but not so far away as to make for difficulty in discerning expressions upon countenances of those stationed at the front of the multitude, disagreement was seen to break out. Argument was caused by changed one, Lemrik, after he was ordered to take Mavis Noy-Breen forward to those of leadership. Lemrik obeyed, but upon arriving at the front of the ranks and hearing Zechariah the Great command, 'Drop the hag right there, Lemrik; there's a good lad. We'll get right down to the business of dealing with the locals,' Lemrik would not agree to do so.

Hearing the leader instruct him so, and taking the command in a literal sense, Lemrik, bone-weary after journeying so far, was quick to take offence and, was offended enough to voice a most ill-conceived, defiant outburst, 'No. We have travelled far together. I will *not* now *drop her!*'

Whereupon, hearing himself addressed thus, and by a changed one, Zechariah was outraged. He ordered, 'Francis, *dispatch the insolent one!*' He commanded, 'Take good care not to damage the baggage—but make an example of him! I've tolerated quite sufficient disobedience of late, and will have no more of it!' So saying, he executed a cutting motion with a paw held high to his own throat. Mavis Noy-Breen was furious and attempting to stay harm from her newfound friend, cried, 'Leave the poor youngster be! Lemrik's committed no wrong!' She accused, '*Monster! Pathetic Zechariah!* You are, and ever were, nothing but trouble for Folk of New Warren! You're as thick as *cabbage!*'

Following such judgment, low murmuring was heard issuing from most forward ranks. 'Zechariah the Great was named *thick! Thick as cabbage! And, by the geriatric doe!*' Word passed back, passed from one to other and, it was not long before the sound of hubbub rising from ranks far distant, reached those of the leadership to fuel great uncertainty.

Bernard had come to stand with Zechariah and Francis, but seeing the leader lose his temper, the keeper rued his sense of timing. He wished he'd remained where he was, back there amongst those of distant ranks, chit-chatting and quite enjoying the pleasant morning. Thus far today there was nary a cloud in the sky and all he'd spoken with were glad to have arrived here at this place. There was widespread, unanimous expression of relief. They'd marched far and at last had arrived. Where they'd arrived and the real purpose for their presence here did not seem to matter much. It was the middle of nowhere. But after taking their positions in accordance with orders, they were allowed to rest easy and that was appreciated.

But now, Francis was ordered to dispatch Lemrik, and that did not seem at all fair, not as the keeper viewed the matter. The leader was tired, of course, as indeed were all. The leader's state of near-exhaustion was etched upon his countenance, making it plain that leadership presented a weighty responsibility, and not for the first time during the long march did Bernard sympathize with Zechariah. Commanding Francis to deliver gazuzzlement to the changed one, though, was a mistake.

Bernard, in attempting to forestall an undue, hasty action, offered, 'Good morning to you Missus Noy-Breen.' Smiling then, from one to other of those present, and appearing very relaxed, 'Leader? I've taken the liberty of allowing those changed ones farthest back in ranks to sit. They may make a picnic of it whilst our next move is decided.' Explaining, he said, 'There's grass back there and whilst it is true that it's somewhat parched and dry, the lads were feeling a little peckish, and so I thought they might go ahead and tuck in.'

'Picnic? Tuck in?' The leader was anything but pleased, but thought to ask, 'Keeper, what do you suppose is our *purpose* in being here?'

Bernard drew-up to attention. 'As I understand it, we're here to attempt making something of a swap. We intend exchanging Missus Noy-Breen for some sort of mystery power, residing in the paws of a *thing*—a mysterious thing—calling itself Tump.' Having paused, Bernard went on to address several troops standing close by, instructing them, 'Order silence in the ranks, will you? I'm speaking, and would appreciate the leader hearing me.' Facing Zechariah again, he apologized, 'Sorry about that.' He said, 'I was saying... My understanding is that we're here to find a creature. As to the detail, I'm a little hazy, but I believe we're to intimidate and frighten this lot.' Gesturing towards the residents of Ground Spring Warren, he went further. 'We're to frighten them into submission and so far as that's concerned, there may be serious intimidation involved, bullying to the point of gazuzzlement, for sure! With that in mind, I must say that as *I* see them, the local inhabitants seem petrified as it is. You have just to look at them. If it were up to me, I believe I'd ask them outright to give over the creature, and then I'd move in and settle for a while in the shade beneath yon' trees.' He waved a paw in the direction of a dense-growing copse of trees situated above Ground Spring Warren, up there where the grass looked soft and lush-green and not yellowed as that of the plain. When the leader said nothing, but stared back at him, Bernard persisted, 'I believe we could all benefit from a good rest. I know I could. My poor legs are numb and at one and the same time are paining something *dreadful!* And then, although it is *such* a nice morning, my head's not feeling the best.' He added, 'I believe it's due to glare. The sun's a little *too* bright for my liking.'

Before Zechariah the Great had the opportunity to respond, hubbub renewed. On this occasion the sound of it was nothing like that heard before. This was the sound of awestruck voices, not of voices delighting in merriment or mischief at thought of the leader's embarrassment. Turning to ascertain the cause of such commotion, Zechariah, Francis Darkling, Bernard and those close with them saw many, many paws pointed to the sky. Following the direction those paws gave, and looking high overhead, a most uncommon sight was realized.

A translucent, rainbow-hued and slippery-wet looking orb floated on high. It was overhead and huge against the blue sky. As all necks craned in looking up, a second, identical orb sloped into view in a wondrous fashion, coming from direction of the great split stone. After slowing, it drew close and hovered nearby the first of them. Other orbs soon entered the sky and now they came from every direction. Within a very short time, a multitude was present, hovering above. They did not touch against one another but remained apart from their fellows. Seeing such number of them, Zechariah wondered at their equalling or even outnumbering those troops comprising his army's awe-inspiring legions.

Every resident of Ground Spring Warren, Zechariah and his army of followers and young Tump stared upwards.

Then came a voice, a voice sounding thin and clear on the warm air. The sound of it touched light to ear, as the softest breeze, and there was a quality of lilting merriment to it. That spoken could not be misunderstood by any of those attending.

'Know, that we are Tump! Tump is One, One in the All. The All of, Great Grandfather.

'None should fear.

'When all is done with, then none is left behind.'

The voice declared, 'But for now, Zechariah the Great, you and those of your company—save for one, named by you as geriatric baggage and hag—must depart this place to make both END *and* BEGINNING!

Zechariah smiled. His name had been pronounced by something of a deity and he could not help but be flattered. He'd not given much thought to the rest of the announcement. Then, though, he was less certain of himself, for coming from far afield a disturbing sound of murmuring reached him. The sound grew and grew until the loudness of it was undeniable. Now it was no murmuring, but a plaintive sound of crying! Next, filling his ears was fearful howling and shrieking, and so terrible was it, that it could not be taken to mean anything other than gazuzzlement threatened those of the ranks! With each passing instant the cries grew louder until, Zechariah knew fear.

Once more the lilting voice addressed him and those who'd come so far in his company.

'You will go back now, Great Zechariah, back to the time when the realm has need of you.'

As those of Ground Spring looked on, and as well, young Tump, Zechariah and so many others *vanished!*

Of the multitude assembled upon the plain, just one remained. She was Mavis Noy-Breen.

None of Zechariah's army remained. Mavis, in searching about saw that her friend, Lemrik, was gone with the rest of them! A short distance from where she stood, the folk of Ground Spring Warren appeared dazed and starry-eyed.

Looking about in awed amazement, Nancy chanced to catch sight of Sara. It was the first time since Sara's departure from New Warren Central that Nancy had seen her friend, and now she knew that Sara and her family had succeeded in making themselves safe at Ground Spring Warren. As she looked on, she saw Sara heltered, rushing away from the gathered throng to aid Mavis, who, standing alone on the wide, now empty field, shook from top to toe with dread uncertainty.

A voice, sounding ominous and thundering, reaching from all directions at once, declared, 'THE REALM BEGINS!'

With those words spoken, Zechariah and his company had arrived. They had arrived at a long ago point in time, a time occurring before the excavation of the realm's very first burrow. They'd arrived to find themselves in a virgin world, a place uninhabited by least of Folk of Fur, and delivered to such a time and place it was clear to Zechariah the Great that much was the need for his expert attention.

With Zechariah dispatched, the voice from above sounded again, 'Young Tump—you seven! You there with the good folk of Ground Spring! Bid farewell now to friends and with us—you must arise!'

Looking one to other, they chorused, 'Tump is One!'

'Arise! You are invited to enter the higher realms of the All! Join with folk of many realms, of realms without end. Join with folk of every form, of every imaginable aspect and quality, with folk so unlike Folk of Fur that strangeness defies belief.'

The elders explained, 'In rising, we will take you lofting even so high as to that realm favoured over all others by Great Grandfather. You may ask anything of Him. He holds nothing back from us. He keeps no secret. There are those things imagined as withheld—imagined by those of us whom He, in the first place, dreamed into the creation.'

Young Tump assumed the form of a bright-glowing orb, and then guided by unerring elders, they floated upwards, going higher and higher still, in company of a great multitude of others so that it was not long and Ground Spring Warren was left far behind. They arrived at a vast place of immutable darkness and stillness, where soft-glowing light, emanating from so many of their kind, joined with starlight to punctuate the otherwise blackest of nights. But then an elder insisted that this was just the beginning. They'd still to travel *much* farther!

And then that same clear voice, which earlier was heard ringing throughout the sky over the wide field, nearby Ground Spring Warren, sounded again. Piercing impenetrable seeming silence. 'We await formation of the great burrow. We wish to draw close with you!'

Suspense filled, long moments followed and then of a sudden, an end came to the silence and the heavens split asunder. Darkness opened, and it was as if a way were made between starry constellations. A great immensity of a burrow, a tunnel of awesome and mind-staggering size, was forming in the heavens over and before them! The immense tunnel began rotating, slow turning, and as it turned, light defined its circumference and walls. At the furthest most visible end of the tunnel white light, showing as not much more than a bright needle's point, beckoned. A voice cried out, 'And now we journey on!'

Young Tump exclaimed, 'We can never climb so far!'

The elder responded, 'Yes, you can! We *will!*' And even as that voice insisted, young Tump was drawn upward by an embracing and mysterious, comforting force. They went faster and still faster upward, so that soon the walls of the great tunnel appeared as nothing but bright-blurring light, and up, until they came to a new place—a place known to the elders as a world existing between realities—between the reality of wakefulness and the realm of dreaming. Here, in this place, questioning might receive answer. Knowledge of all things would be known and yet, even so, this place was not so high as the highest, where light is most clear and where, despite it seeming strange, darkness too, is acknowledged as integral to All.

A legion of orbs, spheres of light ranging from great to small and having origins in many locations of time and space, now converged. They gathered, swarming. They began coalescing and merging. For Tump, perception now underwent new altering. The realm they found themselves in was one where beginning and ending have no place.

Friend Emily was glimpsed. She was very far off at first and she played at rolling a hoop. Then seeing Emily, of a sudden closer, Nancy realized that it was no hoop that Emily pushed but a living creature, a creature gripping its tail in its mouth so that its long body had formed something of a hoop. And there was Zechariah. He was not now quite so great, or perhaps it was that he did not see himself as such. He seemed to Nancy a lot happier, if compared with the Zechariah she was until now best acquainted with, and seeing him anew, it was noted that amongst his other changes, his betterment could be attributed to his having become a good deal less demanding of others. He was in company of Bernard, and they waved to her from across a flower-filled meadow.

Skip, Sherbrook and Simple Rudy waved, seeing good old Uncle Bucky. There he was, and seeing him was a reward of very special kind, after missing him for so long. Bucky seemed content enough, as he carried on conversation with at least a dozen attentive versions of himself. There were, close by, many versions of Lillian, resting in each other's company in lush green grass by the side of a babbling brook, where, one and all delighted in taking the sun. There were changed ones: Chance, Lemrik and Thorny engaged in happy conversation with a creature resembling an over-sized, winged minnow. Great Grandfather's garden held so many wonders and replete in its glory, it stretched all the way to infinity and who could say, but perhaps even farther.

Besides all else they saw themselves, and not just once, twice, or several times over, but indeed, countless times over. There was Sherbrook and there too was Weed. There were the lost orphans of Brickfield realm, lost no more. There were Mavis and Sara, along with fine husband, Finius, and the children, Dandelion, Violet and Abernathy. There was, of course,

Charlie, and then as well, the good Doctor Stone and all of the rest of them. Here was every one of those known to them and a great many folk they knew not. Such number was present but not the least impression of crowding prevailed.

In the midst of sound of very many goings on, Clever Fixer believed he heard a familiar voice questioning, 'How about it? Would you like it, do you think, if I were back with you?' There was Skibeau, as if appeared from nowhere at all, and he declared, 'I know now what comes of this! Far more comes of separation than ever I dreamed possible, and so I'm now of the opinion that we must unite forces. We're best off together. And so how say you, Clever?' The fixer was of no mind to argue or disagree. He watched as a flock of white doves circled overhead, and as he stood there taking in the detail of a most picturesque landscape and the bluest sky of all, he questioned whether he just might make out the presence of an old friend, soaring aloft amongst those others of her kind. All was most pleasant here and urged by so much wonder, to allowing the most gener-ous aspect of his nature its way, Fixer could not other than respond, 'Sure, Skibeau. You're a kadoodler for sure but why not!'

In recognizing fact of there being just too many bards assembled at the meadow's edge, Piedmont wondered whether or not so many of them could be of high renown. He thought, it could not be so! If so many of them were of *his* conscientious and hard working nature, then it would not be long and they'd fill all of creation with an absolute mountain of scratchings, which at some point must make for impossible confu-sion. Whilst imagining several other consequences resultant of there being so many versions of him, he happened to glance upwards and in so doing, caught sight of Crenshaw. There he was, friend Crenshaw engaged in conversation with a Tall One! This was not of itself very surprising, but seeing them standing together in a great field of veg', awareness dawned in Piedmont. He realized that the Tall One, with whom his friend got on so well, was also named Crenshaw, and as if despite himself the bard experienced some difficulty in accepting the definite fact of it.

Then, Skip was heard, 'This is all well and good ... but what happens after seeing so *much*, after learning so much? Our quest will be over! It will be *over* and almost before we've begun!'

An elder chortled, 'No, no, that's just not the way of it!' Then, becoming more serious, the wise one said, 'Very soon now, Great Grandfather is going to question you. He will question all seven of you, regarding your truest feeling for the Tall One, Lilith.'

'And we will respond by admitting to holding her in certain fond regard,' Skip said.

'Yes, that's correct. And then, next, He will enquire as to whether or not—to even the slightest degree—you may feel you've forsaken her. He'll wonder if you fancy you've left her behind ... as good as abandoned her to the *Dove* and the nastiest of helpless plights.'

'Yes, I see,' Skip said, and then was silent for several moments.

Speaking on behalf of all seven of them, he could not but agree, 'Yes. I understand. At least, that is, I'm beginning to grasp the gist of it.' He ventured, 'Great Grandfather may next ask something along the lines of, 'Will you decide to abide with me for all of eternity?'

The elder responded, 'There's always the possibility of Him asking that. But then of course, you being you, your answer will always be, 'Thank you, but with all due respect and no offence intended, our answer must be no. We ask, rather that you allow us return and assist the Tall One. She is of good heart and we, as Tump, would learn all we can of love.'

'Which is much as I thought,' Skip said. 'And by the way, knowing that I knew so much, tells me that I see again. I'm relieved, because I've lately wondered if the ability has as good as decided to forever desert me.'

'You have nothing at all to worry over. Don't trouble so. You've only just begun.'

And as Tump proceeded in journeying farther—rising ever higher—infinity opened before them and entities, manifest as orbs of light in their absolute gazillions, were everywhere moving about.

Skip, displaying great temerity, enquired, *'Is all of it real*—all of this we are shown? Or—and tell the truth now—is kadoodling involved?'

Elder Skip told him, 'All of it—each thought—all seen—all felt—every idea entertained—all those met with—without exception—all of it is real.'

'And Tump goes back?'

'Indeed it does.'

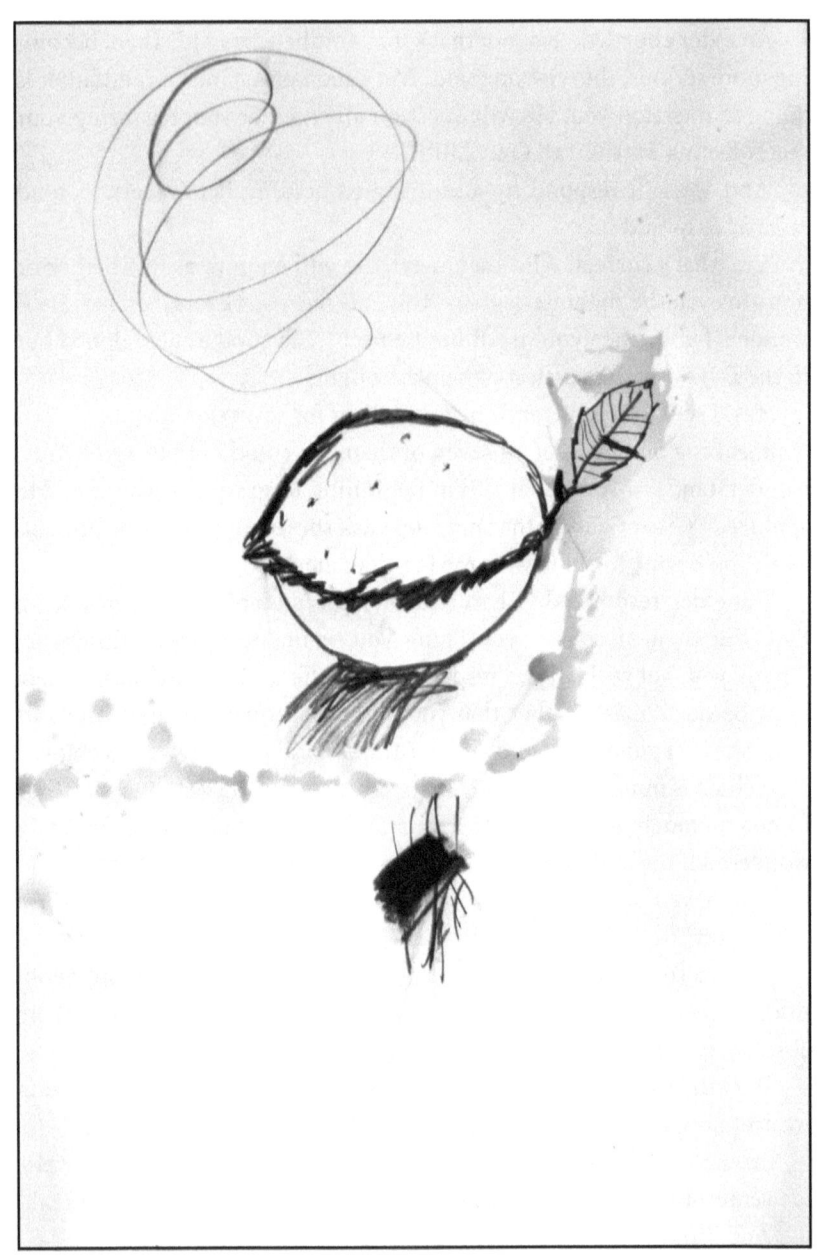

Seed

FOR LILITH

'Are you certain that it can be done?' Lilith asked.

'Yes!' they exclaimed. 'With all we have learned, we can now move between realms, not just to and from the *Dove*. We can go anywhere and anywhen!'

They all spoke at once, but she heard Skip, 'We can take you home, Lilith!'

After hushing the others, Peace said, 'If you will trust us, Lilith, we would like to surprise you.'

Lilith, was not fond of surprises. What did they intend, she wondered. Then, after several moments of puzzling, she thought she knew, and asked, 'You will return me to my realm—to a time *before* Mydor and I set forth in the *Dove*. Is that it?'

They chorused, 'Yes!' They were not disappointed but pleased by her correctly guessing their intention.

'There will be two of me then. There will be Mydor and my father. Mydor will live, but there will be *two* of me! I can't help but wonder how she—my other self—will take to the idea.' After a moment, she said, 'I did not meet myself before coming here to your realm and so perhaps it is not at all possible. Perhaps it does not eventuate.'

'If we take you back to meet yourself, Skip said, then a new line is born, a time line where you may live as twin to your other self and she, to you, but that is *not* what we propose.'

'It's not?'

'No. We will return you to a time occurring before your birth, Lilith and in doing so will spare your parent gazuzzlement. There will then be two Liliths, with you, the elder—as we coexist with our elders, so shall you, with your younger version.'

'Fear not,' Simple assured, 'I have consulted the tree and the new line is present. It's there in the map. We have chosen, and it comes to pass as Skip describes.'

'If you are agreeable, Lilith,' Clever Fixer asked, 'May Sherbrook and I take the shirts we're wearing?' He explained, 'They are our favourites, and Mydor is not grown. He's still not much more than a sprout. He can't mind.'

Looking from Fixer to Sherbrook and smiling, she told them, 'If it pleases you, you may take the entire wardrobe with you.'

Piedmont hurried to insist, 'I *must* take the scratchings!' He asked, 'I hope none of you will mind too much? I do realize they take up considerable space and it may seem ridiculous of me needing them, after finding that the lives of so many—as recorded in the scratchings—amount to not much more than fiction, but still, I cannot bear the thought of leaving them!' He pleaded, 'They are precious to me. It's force of habit, I suppose.'

Sherbrook told him, 'It's fine, Bard. We do understand.'

Skip informed, 'I've already made allowance, Piedmont. I knew you'd insist upon taking them. Console yourself, knowing that our historical records are no more untrue than those of others.'

Sherbrook was somewhat circumspect in broaching a matter dear to him. He ventured, 'When we arrive at our destination, we won't want to flibberty everywhere, will we?' He said, 'I should just say it. I believe we should take the pick-up with us when we go. When we're there, it will, for one thing, make transporting the scratchings a whole lot simpler.' Looking from one to other, he enquired, 'How about it? What do you say?'

Lilith told them, 'Sherbrook makes a good point. It's not easy getting about in my realm without suitable transport. You won't want to move each and every time you find you have to be somewhere.' She said, 'As an example, we cannot lug the tree about with us. We'd make a ridiculous spectacle of ourselves. But, Skip, can you do it? Can you move the pick-up?'

'Oh yes.' He sounded self-assured, which gave Lilith cause to wonder whether or not he might be a little overconfident. She would just have to trust him, she thought.

Changing the topic of conversation, she said, 'If Bunty is agreeable, then before we leave I will open wider the tear in the *Dove's* shield at the place where he comes and goes. Then, folk of Ground Spring may prosper. They will enjoy the luxury of a real stream and a meadow all their own.' She saw that Sherbrook was pleased by the idea, but he was impatient over hearing too vague agreement regarding the truck.

Nancy exclaimed, 'Oh yes, Lilith! That will be wonderful for folk of Ground Spring! Bunty will feel important all over again.' She said, 'I must farewell Mother. And there's Sara and the others. I must say goodbye to the children.'

'I will want to see friend Crenshaw for a last time,' Piedmont said.

It was agreed then, each of them must attend to their last remaining duties, fulfil obligations before final leave-taking. They would meet then, back at the cottage, before departing from the *Dove*.

It was not Lilith, but Peace, who returned to the subject of them taking the pick-up to Lilith's world. She admitted, 'I'm not fond of the truck, but I suppose if there's a good, useful purpose for having it, then we *should* take it with us.' She saw Sherbrook smiled; he was mighty satisfied, and the matter was settled.

Peace would request, 'Come, stand close by me Lilith.' She would ask, 'Are we ready?' When all were prepared to move she would announce, 'Hear me then…

'Tump is One!'

She would order, 'Stand ready, Bard!'

And, 'Rudy! Plot our course!'

She would command, 'Sherbrook, Ground us!'

And, 'Nancy—stand ready!'

Then, 'Clever Fixer! Engage the gate!'

And, 'Skip! *Move us!*'

For the very first time, of its own volition, with *almighty terrible kazooning*, young Tump would depart not just the realm of the *Dove*, but their home realm, the realm of Folk of Fur.

Arriving at a considered location, the first thing Clever Fixer declared, as he looked about the place, was, 'It was very remiss of me not fare welling the old place—the cottage, the meadow and stream. Pleasant times were had there.' He was sad sounding, when complaining, 'I said my goodbyes to all and sundry, but then forgot the place itself.'

'The *place* will not at all mind, Fixer.' Peace told him, doing her best to seem strong. 'Places do not mind.'

'I'm not so certain of that,' Fixer said, 'There are places I could name, where, if one does not go with care enough, then all sorts of things can begin going awry. It's as if those places do possess minds of their own.' After pausing, he said, 'I think that I shall alter my form, as learned during our rising high. And judging by my feeling, a feeling gained from *this* realm, you should all be wise and follow my example. Looking to Lilith he said, 'I mean no offence, Lilith. It is my impression of the place. I feel a need for wariness and caution, now that we're arrived in your home realm.'

He asked, 'Allow me out of the truck please, Skip, if you will.'

Skip pushed back, making himself small against the pick-up's bench-seat, and Fixer squeezed past him. Once outside, Clever hopped for a short distance along the sidewalk. He halted then, and stood at a place where a street lamp cast a pool of yellow light upon the pavement. He waited for a moment, and then—in a trice—assumed the form of a most debonair Tall One. The light from the lamp was not bright, but still his new black shoes gleamed! He wore his great coat, which had grown at least several sizes larger than it previously was, and as well, he wore black stovepipe trousers. He wore the same fine, colourful shirt of Mydor's, which tended to clash somewhat with his new, deep crimson waistcoat, and then there was his feathered hat. He could not give it up. He was very dapper and his eyes sparkled, showing he knew there could be no doubting it.

Clever Fixer was at last arrived in America!

The street was not busy and that suited them. Lilith knew relief; in experiencing excitement over returning home, she'd not so much as thought to warn them of the many dangers they might encounter. They might have materialized at a location where harm could befall them. She was neglectful, and regretted her thoughtlessness.

Sitting beside her, Skip turned away from Clever Fixer, who still paraded his vanity, to see Lilith, and said, 'Your light dims, Lilith. You should not be concerned. We know well what we do. Tump is most skilful. Before moving we decided this location safe enough.'

'You know my thoughts?' Lilith asked.

'Some,' Skip told her, 'but I would never pry.' Returning to the subject of their present location, he gave extra assurance, 'No one comes this way, not for some time yet. This street is no main thoroughfare, but the location is convenient in that it's not too far from the home of a very skilled and kind Tall One, known as Doctor Robertson.' He said, 'We must visit with him. We will arrange a rendezvous with your parents and the young Mydor. They will meet with him tomorrow morning, when they rush, heltering along a country road, on their way to the hospital located at the far distant township of Wycombe Falls. The vehicle driven by your father, Terrence, will break down when they're part way there. The map shows the route taken by the Thiery family, and so on this occasion, after we see to it, when your father's vehicle fails, then, Doctor Robertson is present there. He is there when his skills are most needed.' Returning her smile, he said, 'And so you see … your mother lives, and you are happier.'

'She who is happiest,' Lilith said, 'will not be me.'

'No. That's true,' agreed Skip, 'but as outcomes go…'

'Yes, as outcomes go it's wonderful! It's marvellous!' she exclaimed, 'Oh, thank you, Skip! Thank you, Tump!' So saying, she hugged him close to her, and that, he felt, was taking things to extreme but he was reminded that he'd seen all of it, and long before this. He'd seen her hugging him half way to gazuzzlement.

Serious now, Lilith, asked, 'But, Skip, this Doctor Robertson. You say, we must visit him, but does he act upon such an odd request? Will he abandon all to head out into the countryside on trust? Does he get there in time? How can he believe his service is needed?'

'Of course, he doesn't *know* the actual truth of it,' Skip said. 'At first he wonders over pranksters making a dupe of him. His light reveals his doubt, but then he is curious. Besides which, Doctor Robertson is a true healer and will not leave to chance any possibility of harm befalling another. He *will* be there, Lilith, don't doubt it. Even now, as I see it, the good doctor attends your mother. And then, after ensuring your safe delivery, he drives the Thiery family to the small hospital at Wycombe Falls. He returns after that to his home, where he goes straight to his plantings.' Seeing her curiosity, he explained, 'Doctor Robertson loves orchids and lilies. Yes—lilies.' He said, 'There's just one other thing… It's a detail and nothing to concern yourself with, because Tump will follow up on it.'

'What is this other thing, this detail?' Lilith asked, knowing small apprehension.

Skip said, 'Payment always falls due, doesn't it?' He added, 'And that seems more true in this realm than others.'

'Skip?'

Sighing, he said, 'The fact is that he's so grateful for Doctor Robertson's assisting in time of such need, that Terrence gives, Doc'—as he refers to him—his most treasured possession, which we all know is…'

'The seed!' she exclaimed. 'You can't mean the seed! Oh, mercy me! The foolish man!' Covering her mouth with a hand, she muttered, 'I'm sorry. I didn't mean that. I should not have said it, but…'

'Tump will follow Doctor Robertson,' Skip assured. 'Of that you can be certain.' He smiled, adding, 'When Tump rose high and met with Great Grandfather, we learned to trust His outcomes.'

Lilith was not so certain.

During the morning of the following day, at the approximate time of Doctor Robertson's setting out to aid the Thierys, Tump and Lilith, with the tree of Great Grandfather covered by a dark tarpaulin, transported in the rear of the pick-up, took the road to the small township of Battle-Seed. Riding in back with the tree, Peace, lifting a corner of the canvas covering, offered the tree such comment and comfort as, 'Fret not, dear friend. You are safe enough here, although I do declare the road *is* a rocky one!'

The long, dusty road, leading from Wycombe Falls to Battle-Seed, was indeed dusty. It was pot-holed and corrugated, but Sherbrook drove for a good part of the way at full-throttle. He drove like the wind, making skimming flight over such rough terrain, and it was not long before they were there. After pulling in and parking out front of *Millthorpe's General Store*, Sherbrook, in the guise of a nattily attired Tall One, left the rest of them waiting outside in the pick-up, whilst he partook for very first time, of an activity known as shopping.

Strolling into the place, he was addressed by a man standing behind a counter.

'Howdy stranger… Fine morning.'

To which Sherbrook responded, 'Sure is, bud!' Glancing about the place and seeing so many items of interest, Sherbrook asked, 'You wouldn't happen to carry A *User's Guide to Success in Living off the Land*?'

The assistant was, himself, an avid fan of the publication and he responded, 'Sure do pardner. Excellent read, ain't it though?' He directed Sherbrook to a metal rack, telling him, 'You'll find the latest issue right there, friend.' Sherbrook took up a copy and took it across to the counter. The man declared, 'You know the *User's* is about the last in a line of such publications. It's like so much else. Don't make 'em like they used to!'

'I know just what you mean,' agreed Sherbrook. He enquired, 'Would you have the time?' He tossed several coins rattling onto the counter-top. Gathering up Sherbrook's payment, the clerk lowered his head before consulting his watch, and having noted the correct time, he looked up and realized that his customer was no longer present.

The clerk, Stanley by name, declared, '...darndest thing!' He shrugged and set to counting coins. He tipped them one by one into the change-drawer and in doing so, noted that one amongst them was not as should be. It was a foreign thing, no *real* coin at all. He exclaimed, 'Zoiks! Never trust a stranger!' Studying it, he noted an inscribed image. Then, on the reverse side was what looked like the claw of an eagle—an eagle's claw—grasping at something he could not quite make out. And too, there was an inscription—words, or such. He could not know that those marks might be translated to convey: *Brickfield Bunny Club—Token—Admit one.*

Min came in from out back. He said, 'Here, Min—catch!' And, 'It's play money sweetheart!'

Seeing the face of a big old rabbit depicted, Min exclaimed, 'Thanks, Grandpa!'

He told her, 'You're welcome kiddo!'

'You're welcome too, Grandpa!'

Together they chorused, 'Any ol' time, kiddo! Any ol' time!'

Three days later was a day of bright sunshine and warming breeze; one of those summery days when small dust devils whirled across the surface of the road. She watched from the stores front stoop and saw devils die; they died, almost before they'd formed. It was the day they planned upon visiting Min's favourite cousin, Jeremy, and his parents. Jeremy had injured himself while climbing a tree, Grandpa said, and so the boy could do with some cheering up. It was a Saturday, which meant they would shut-up shop at noon, and then they'd go the short distance to the big house.

Compared with the store, the house was a palace, an absolute mansion, Min thought, and she'd always loved visiting there. She was fond of her cousin, Jeremy, and so of course, it was not just the old house she looked forward to seeing. It was the afternoon during which her cousin insisted she swear a most secret oath.

Arriving at the top of the stairs, Min crossed the wide, carpeted landing, and not wishing to disturb him in case he was sleeping, she knocked softly at the door of his room. She wondered if the sound could be heard by any other than she. Jeremy did not sleep but rested in bed, and at first he did not answer. But after a moment, he called, 'Come on Cous'. Enter if you dare!' He'd been expecting her visit and his sense of humour was undiminished.

Sitting at the patient's bedside, Min was nervous. She was unaccustomed to visiting the sick and was perhaps too forthright, enquiring, 'Are you in terrible pain, Jeremy?' His smiling showed he did not suffer much, and so she admonished, 'You should never climb trees again, Jeremy. Not ever!'

He laughed, telling her, 'It's just a sprain, Min. It hurt, but only at first. I'm not dying or anything.' He explained, 'It's my mother—she nags and fusses a lot. The worse part is staying in bed the whole time. I'm bored.'

She told him, 'I've brought something interesting to show you.' She slipped the treasure from her pinafore pocket. Holding it out for Jeremy's approval she said, 'It's no ordinary coin. It's very rare, I think.'

Jeremy took the coin from her to better examine it, but after studying it for just a moment, he commented, 'Mm ... a rabbit coin. I guess I see what you mean. But, if you go over there to my bureau, and look in the top drawer ...' He changed his mind then, and rather than have her do it for him, he flung his covers aside and lowered himself to the floor. He returned her coin, explaining, 'It's great Min, but wait 'til you see what I've got.' Seeing him hobble, Min winced. She would offer assistance, but knowing Jeremy, he would refuse help. His bandaged leg was impressive, but he was right, a sprain was not something too serious; it was not in the same league, for instance, as a broken leg.

He came back to the bedside and held out his hand. He held the hand closed while entertaining second thoughts. Perhaps he would not reveal what he held. He drew the hand back from her and put it close to his chest and told her, 'Before I show you this, you're going to have to swear never to tell.'

'Oh, I never would, Jeremy.' Thought of his not trusting her was distressing; she had trusted him with the knowledge of her own treasure. But when he told her that he'd taken it from the desk in Doctor Robertson's consulting room, understanding dawned. Jeremy had dared steal and, from someone as important as Doctor Robertson!

Watching her, Jeremy insisted, 'Now, repeat after me... I swear that I will *never* rat on my cousin and best friend Jeremy Crenshaw. If I break my vow I will end up burning in hell or some place even worse. This is an oath and I will *never* tell!'

She'd not recited half of that when he opened his hand. Resting on his palm was a most beautiful thing. She thought at first it was small stone of an attractive blue colour, but as she moved closer to better examine it, Jeremy exclaimed, 'It's a seed. It speaks!'

Acknowledgements

With special thanks to Susan Proud for whose support, help and encouragement through the writing of this story I am grateful. Thanks to Dianne Farrow and Janet Munton. Thanks also to Fauve Masters, Henry, Joseph and William Proud.

J. B.

About the author

The author and his family reside at the bottom of the world, in Tasmania. Their home is shared with a rescued cat named Cat, and they enjoy a glorious view of the mighty Huon River.

The island is home to many peculiar folk of fur and as yet, new greens are not a problem.